CHINA BRIDE

The second sweeping novel
in the best-selling series
about a great family

THE RAKEHELL DYNASTY

From the producer of
The Kent Family Chronicles,
The Australians, and the
Wagons West series.

D0042725

CHINA BOUND!

The future of the Rakehells
is tied to the Orient.

Jonathan Rakehell whose vision set the family to building the clipper ship that has transformed the East-West relationship—is returning to China to wed the love of his life. Mobs enraged by the opium trade attack him as he journeys to the side of

Lai-tse lu the beautiful daughter of a Chinese merchant who has pledged to wait for Jonathan and who is now being sought by the emperor himself as a bride for one of his family.

Charles Boynton Jonathan's English cousin who has been his ally must now contend with his father's prejudices and the fact that England supports the opium trade.

Bradford Walker Jonathan's jealous brother-in-law, whose villainy is soon to be uncovered totally, joins forces with an implacable enemy.

Soong Chao Lai-tse lu's wise and wealthy father must choose between his daughter's happiness or the ancient traditions of his country.

The Marquês de Braga the sadistic governor-general of a Portuguese colony, whose desire for revenge is matched only by his insatiable carnal appetites.

Owen Bruce the Scottish commissions merchant, Jonathan Rakehell's sworn enemy, deals in drugs—and death.

Elizabeth Boynton Charles's sister, a spoiled heiress, learns that the love of her life belongs to another woman.

Also by Michael William Scott

The Rakehell Dynasty—Volume I
The Book of Jonathan Rakehell

Published by
WARNER BOOKS

The Rakehell Dynasty
Volume II

CHINA BRIDE

Michael William Scott

WARNER BOOKS

A Warner Communications Company

WARNER BOOKS EDITION

Produced by Lyle Kenyon Engel

Cover art by Tom Hall

Warner Books, Inc., 75 Rockefeller Plaza, New York, N.Y. 10019

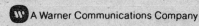 A Warner Communications Company

Printed in the United States of America

First Printing: May, 1981

10 9 8 7 6 5 4 3 2 1

For My Wife

An Author's Note

I am deeply in the debt of my distinguished English colleague, Vivian Stuart, a member of three prominent British organizations: the Society for Nautical Research, the Navy Records Society, and the Military Historical Society. She has advised me, with painstaking care, on every aspect of the operations and building of the great nineteenth-century clipper ships in order to ensure that everything regarding them that appears in the pages of the Rakehell Dynasty Series is authentic. I am eternally grateful to her.

The Opium War, which forms the background of this story, was complicated, dragging on for two years. The battle at the Bogue mouth (November 1839) which initiated the hostilities between the British and the Chinese occurs in CHINA BRIDE shortly after Jonathan Rakehell's first visit to Canton. This skirmish is followed by a British excursion to the north, where Charles Elliot's negotiations with the Chinese soon break down. At the time of Jonathan's second visit to Canton, Elliot and the British fleet have returned to the Pearl River Delta and are threatening to attack Canton itself. After the assault on Canton (1841), during which time Jonathan is cut off from his ship, the British head north again to attack or capture Amoy, Tinghai (on Chusan Island), Chinhai, Ningpo, Shanghai, and Chinkiang. For the purpose of clarifying the story for the reader, I have telescoped some of these actions in the north, setting them in a city I have elected to call Kuan-choy. In all other respects, the background and settings in the East are accurately portrayed.

—M.W.S

CHINA BRIDE

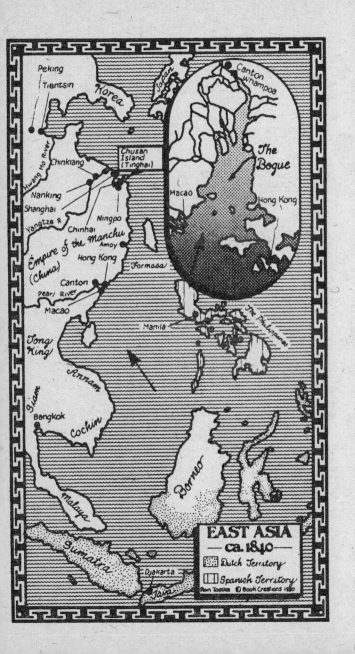

Book
I

I

In 1839, the port compound outside Canton, the crowded, teeming capital of the southern Chinese province of Kwangtung, was a cramped, isolated community. By imperial decree it was the only place in which foreigners were permitted to live and trade with China, other than the small Portuguese colony of Macao on the South China Sea. At the port complex, less than seventy-five miles from the sea on the Pearl River Delta, merchants from Great Britain and the United States, France, Spain, Denmark, the Netherlands, and Sweden anchored their vessels and unloaded their cargoes, filling the holds again with the precious tea, silks, and porcelain which the West demanded. This toehold on the Orient was precarious: the anchorage at Whampoa was confining and overcrowded, and the enclave of factories—warehouses and residences—just outside the walled city of Canton, occupied no more than fifteen acres of Chinese soil.

Foreigners labored under great difficulties. Wives were not permitted to enter the compound at Canton and were forced to reside at Macao while their husbands conducted their business. The movements of these men were severely restricted, and few, other than Rear Admiral Sir William Alexander, commander of the Royal Navy squadron stationed in the delta for the protection of British commercial shipping, were permitted to pass the heavily guarded gates of the compound and enter Canton itself. And the foreigners were forced to compete with a prominent Chinese, Soong Chao, a wealthy mandarin, third class, who owned three warehouses and was the head of the co-hong, a small group licensed by the Tao Kuang Emperor to deal with outsiders.

The long-time residents of the compound outside Canton had no complaint about Soong Chao, however. In his dealings with them he was honorable and honest, a man of integrity. What was more, his daughter, Soong Lai-tse lu, was, in their estimation, the most beautiful girl they had ever seen. This view was enthusiastically corroborated by ship captains and other new arrivals fortunate enough to catch a glimpse of her when she paid an occasional visit to the warehouse offices of her father, always accompanied by the family majordomo, Kai. Everyone from the oldest factor, or foreign concession director, to the youngest able seaman agreed that Lai-tse lu was exquisite by the standards of any nation.

Far taller than most Cantonese because her family had come from the north of China, Lai-tse lu had a slender, perfect figure, with high, firm breasts, a tiny waist, and a long, smooth line of legs and thighs. She invariably wore a high-necked, snug-fitting cheongsam, a dress favored by the Chinese upper classes, usually of silk embroidered with designs in gold or silver, and always with a skirt slit high on both sides. Her straight hair, so shiny it looked blue-black, cascaded down her back. Her cheekbones were high, the shape of her chiseled face flawless, and her lips, which she colored delicately with a pale rouge, were full enough to be provocative yet always demure. Her most arresting feature was her eyes: fringed with thick lashes and luminous, they looked as though they were a deep violet in the sunlight. The few who had felt the impact of her direct gaze were stunned by it.

Except for Sir William, who was a friend of the family, no one arriving in Whampoa and doing business at the warehouses and factories ever came near her. In addition to the ever-present Kai, she was usually shepherded by Sarah Applegate, a crusty widow from New England who had acted as Lai-tse lu's governess during the better part of the girl's twenty-four years. The outsiders knew nothing about Missy Sarah, so they had no idea that Lai-tse lu spoke a fluent, almost accentless English, just as she was also at home in French, German, and Spanish.

Rumors about the girl abounded. There were some who swore she was Soong Chao's concubine rather than his daughter. Others were convinced she was the mistress of Lin Tse-hsü, the new imperial viceroy for Kwangtung, who was determined to stamp out the opium trade. Only one person in Canton suspected the truth. Owen Bruce, a Scottish factor who was making a fortune illegally importing opium, had reason to believe the girl was betrothed to an American—Jonathan Rakehell, sea captain, builder of the remarkable, swift clipper ships that were revolutionizing world trade, spent a year in Canton and was closely associated with Soong Chao. On one occasion Bruce had seen Lai-tse lu with young Rakehell, his sworn enemy, and the way they had looked at each other had told him they were intimate.

The Scotsman had no way of knowing that he had guessed the truth. Jonathan and Lai-tse lu had exchanged promises, she wore a gold ring that he had made for her, and she had given him a precious medallion of jade. Two years had passed since Jonathan had left Canton for his home in New London, Connecticut, where his family had been building ships for five generations, and Soong Chao's patience was wearing thin.

"Two years is a long time," he said to his daughter one day as they ate in their dining pavilion, one of the many buildings in the palatial Soong compound, surrounded by stone walls, that stood high on a hill at the far side of Canton. "I agreed to your marriage with Jonathan, provided he return to you within a reasonable time. Two years is not reasonable."

"He loves me as much as I love him," the girl replied quietly. "He will come for me."

"I hope so." Plucking chunks of lobster and crabmeat from his porcelain bowl with a pair of chopsticks, Chao sounded unconvinced, and his eyes behind his heavy-rimmed glasses were unfathomable.

Lai-tse lu appealed to Missy Sarah. "Do you remember that when Jonathan's cousin, Charles Boynton, last came here from his home in London, he told us that Jonathan thinks only of me?"

"I recall it well," Sarah Applegate said crisply. "But that was many months ago. I don't for a moment doubt that Jonathan was sincere in his intentions when he last saw you. But his father is rich, his clipper—*Flying Dragon*—made him wealthy in his own right, and a young man in his late twenties has many different interests. I'm not accusing Jonathan of being fickle, mind you, because I honestly don't think he's that kind. But with all the right, honorable intentions in the world, he may have been attracted to someone close to home. He wouldn't be the first."

"Never!" Lai-tse lu said fiercely, her long, lacquered nails digging into the palms of her hands. She had been eating bamboo shoots with seafood and herbs, one of her favorite dishes, but all at once she had no appetite. Composing herself with difficulty, she asked to be excused.

Missy Sarah felt desperately sorry for the lovesick girl and nodded.

Lai-tse lu left the table and started off toward her own small, pagodalike house, making her way along the tiled walk past banks of massed flowers in contrasting colors, tiny ponds filled with lily pads, and toy islands connected by miniature bridges.

"Chao," Missy Sarah said accusingly, "you know she always becomes upset when you mention even the possibility that Jonathan might not return."

"Then why isn't he here?" Chao replied stubbornly. "I didn't want to tell her this, but a Rakehell and Boynton clipper put into Whampoa just this morning from the Dutch East Indies. Jonathan wasn't on board. I inquired about him from the ship's master, who's been sailing on various missions for the Fat Dutchman out of Djakarta for months, and has had no news from home. A feeble excuse, in my opinion. And I've even written the Fat Dutchman, with whom I do as much business as with anyone, and he could tell me nothing about Jonathan except that the ships he builds are exceptional. I already know that."

"Oh, dear." The gray-haired woman's midday meal consisted exclusively of vegetables, which she relished, but today her chopsticks moved in slow motion. "It's true I've known few of my fellow Americans in the many years I've lived here. But I still think of myself as a competent judge of character. And I would have sworn that Jonathan is both reliable and constant in his affections."

"I'm fond of him myself," Chao said, studying the dragon of tiny, inlaid tiles of gold and silver that decorated the far wall. "As a ship designer he is a genius. As a sea captain he's very competent. And he is a shrewd man of business. But none of those qualities necessarily mean he will be faithful to a woman. Any woman.''

"I hope time will prove you wrong," Sarah said.

He removed his glasses and slowly cleaned them with a square of unbleached linen. "We may not have all that much time at our disposal.''

"Oh?" Something in his tone made Sarah's blood run cold.

"This afternoon," he said, "I am meeting in my office with Dom Manuel Sebastian, the Marquês de Braga.''

"The Portuguese governor-general of Macao." It was plain she disapproved of the man. "From all I've heard about him, I'm glad you haven't brought him here.''

Chao chuckled mildly. "He's furious because he hasn't been granted a permit by the viceroy to enter Canton. Not only because he's very wealthy and a high-ranking nobleman, but because of his position at Macao, he thinks of himself as the highest-ranking European in the Orient. I could obtain a visitor's permit for him, of course, but so far I've seen no need to apply for one.''

"What does your business with Dom Manuel have to do with Jonathan Rakehell?" Sarah demanded.

The merchant prince sighed. "His note requesting the meeting made it plain he wishes to consult with me on a personal matter, not business.''

The woman was silent for a moment. Then she spoke with great force. "Don't tell me he has an interest in Lai-tse lu!''

"You may recall the reception that Sir William held on board his flagship on the occasion of Queen Victoria's birthday. The Marquês de Braga sailed to Whampoa from Macao on a Portuguese frigate—the only ship of that size Portugal maintains in the East, as I understand it. We remarked at the time that he couldn't take his eyes off Lai-tse lu.''

"He's forty-five if he's a day, almost twice her age," Sarah said. "He's arrogant and fat, with the table manners of a hog. What's more, I've heard tales—as I'm sure you have—of his harshness and cruelty in his administration of the Macao government.''

"I rarely pay attention to rumors," he replied unhappily. "What I know as facts are that Dom Manuel is one of the leading nobles of Portugal, and through his sister is related to

19

royalty. He owns at least a half-dozen huge castles and palaces and is enormously wealthy. Also, he is a bachelor.''

''With a half-dozen Cantonese concubines in his Macao palace, you may be sure,'' she said with a sniff. ''Even if we received word this very day that Jonathan Rakehell has died, surely you can find a more suitable husband for Lai-tse lu than the Marquês de Braga!''

''Thanks in part to her heritage and partly to the way you and I have reared her, Sarah, it isn't that easy. She's a mandarin of the third class, through me and through her late mother. Only the imperial family and the scholars who devote themselves to the academic world and remain celibate comprise the higher classes. I know of no one in the third class who is eligible, and I would lose face if she married someone of a lower mandarin class. That is one reason I did not protest overly much when she and Jonathan wanted to marry. Also, you and I—for better or worse—have exposed her to many Western ways. She is too intelligent and too highly educated to be content with a life little better than that of a concubine in a marriage to some dolt of a provincial official.''

''I defy you to tell me she would be better off with the Portuguese! Or, taking the way she feels into account, that she could be happy with anyone except Jonathan Rakehell.''

Chao knew she was right and therefore retreated into a dignified shell. ''For thousands of years,'' he said, ''Chinese daughters have been given in marriage to husbands chosen for them by their fathers. Their happiness is of far less importance than their status, and most have not even met their husbands until they have been betrothed. It is my responsibility to determine what is best for Lai-tse lu.''

Just when Sarah Applegate thought she understood Soong Chao, the differences in their backgrounds rose like a thick wall between them, making communication impossible.

Chao washed his hands and mouth in a bowl of scented water in which chrysanthemum petals were floating. Then, ringing a silver bell in the shape of a frog, with a carved ivory handle, he stood.

Within moments eight bearers in the purple uniforms of the house of Soong appeared with his sedan chair. Behind them walked the broad-shouldered, tall Kai, majordomo of the household, who was dressed in black and carried a curved, double-edged sword hanging from his belt. It was narrow near the hilt, then became broader toward the tip, and the hilt itself was decorated with seemingly meaningless symbols. Only a select few knew that the archaic animals carved in the hard wood signified that Kai was a member of the secret Society of Oxen. A powerful, patriotic organization, the Society was devoted to the well-being of the Middle Kingdom, and it used any means, including those that were illegal, to achieve its ends.

Sarah Applegate had no opportunity to speak privately with Kai, but she looked at him intently.

Kai understood at once. Trouble of some sort was brewing and probably involved Lai-tse lu, to whom both were devoted. He nodded almost imperceptibly.

Chao had a final word for the governess. "I forbid you to repeat even a hint of our conversation to my daughter," he said as he climbed into the sedan chair.

Like the others who lived on the hill and kept handsome estates, Soong Chao believed it would have been demeaning for a man of his prominence and wealth to walk through the city to his office on the waterfront. When the bearers reached the base of the hill they had to push their way through masses of people. The streets were narrow, most of them lined with tiny houses of clay, stone, and concrete. These dwellings were crowded close together, with entire families living in single rooms, and many had no amenities. A hole cut in a roof usually served in place of a chimney, and gutters that ran behind each small building were used to dispose of garbage and human waste. The women made great efforts to keep their families clean, but clothes that had been washed had to be spread on the slanting, tiled roofs to dry. Children had no place to play except the streets, dogs wandered in packs, and most householders kept cats as pets to reduce the population of mice and rats. More often than not, children were either naked or wore only ragged loincloths.

The public squares where the great temples and various government buildings were located were enormous, and most were lined with li-chi trees, which the superstitious regarded as sacred. Even here, however, people were everywhere. Dancers, jugglers, and singers entertained in the open, hoping to obtain a few coins, while vendors offered roasted nuts, bits

21

of meat on tiny skewers, or chunks of bread soaked in water buffalo milk and then fried. Milling throngs overflowed the open-air market district, and the streets where the fortune tellers and soothsayers worked and lived were so clogged that passage through them was impossible.

Imperial soldiers in dusty yellow uniforms, carrying ancient muzzle-loading matchlocks, wandered around in groups of three and four. The crowds parted for them. And Kai, walking ahead of the sedan chair, cleared a path by the simple expedient of twirling his huge sword expertly over his head, keeping it in constant motion.

Unlike most aristocrats, Soong Chao did not hold a perfumed handkerchief to his nostrils. He knew the people, and in spite of the difference in their financial stations, he felt he was one of them. The odors of humanity, the sweat, the roasting chestnuts, the garlic and onions and herbs that flavored the meals being cooked on tiny wood stoves, some of them in the open streets in front of the cramped houses, were the essence of the Middle Kingdom itself. Devoted to the emperor and his subjects, Soong Chao loathed those foreigners who tried to take advantage of an illiterate, hardworking, patient people who lived on hope for the future. His hatred was greatest for those who obtained opium in India and those traitorous Chinese who bought it with silver. The use of the habit-forming drug which sapped the lives of addicts was a menace to the civilization he held dear, and he was in total agreement with the new imperial viceroy, his friend, that the practice had to be ended.

They differed on the means, to be sure. The viceroy wanted to penalize the suppliers, but Chao demurred. They were foreigners, men whose warships and cannon were far superior to China's arms, so he preferred to concentrate on the Chinese smugglers and those who sold the drug to the poor who could ill afford to buy it. Ah, well. Soon the problem would be resolved—unless Lin Tse-hsü went too far and began putting Englishmen and Frenchmen on trial, then executing them. If that should happen—and the foreign devils were very sensitive when their citizens were killed or abused—there was no way of telling what might happen. He needed to confer again with the viceroy and urge him, even more vehemently than he had done previously, not to arouse the European governments.

Sitting back in his sedan chair, Soong Chao considered what would happen if he did walk to his office. In no time he would lose his purse, the silver buttons from his coat, and perhaps a portion of the rich silk itself. To be sure, the people of Canton were not vicious, but the gap that separated the rich and poor was so great that those who were poverty-stricken and hungry would not be able to resist temptation.

The bearers reached the Petition Gate, a pagodalike arch of stone, decorated with imperial dragons and stylized chrysanthemums, which had been the imperial flower for the two hundred years the Manchu conquerors of the Middle Kingdom had been in power. The Leader of One Hundred in charge of the sentry detail drew his sword and stood stiffly at attention, and his men presented arms with their matchlocks.

Soong Chao nodded pleasantly, then dismounted from his sedan chair and, grateful for the opportunity to stretch his legs, walked through the foreign concession to his office. No stranger seeing this middle-aged man in the black silk robe, matching small, brimless hat, and embroidered slippers would have realized that he was one of the most influential of the Tao Kuang Emperor's subjects.

His office, located on the second floor of the largest of his three warehouses, was an almost exact replica of the quarters he used for transacting business at home. A thick rug decorated with *Yin* and *Yang* symbols covered the floor, and exotic plants were hanging between the windows, but the walls were otherwise bare because he wanted nothing to distract his attention from his work. The only furniture consisted of four very large hassocks, each with silk cushions piled on it, and on either side of the hassock that Chao used were two large tables, each with legs of carved figures from mythology. Documents of parchment and wax tablets bearing various inscriptions were piled on both.

Cleaning his glasses again, he picked up the daily list of items sold to foreigners and those purchased from them. As he had anticipated, the largest volume of current business was being done with the Rakehell and Boynton clipper currently tied up at the American wharf.

Chao frowned and gazed out the window at the graceful vessel. He already knew it had been designed and built by Jonathan Rakehell, and he was troubled. He felt truly close to

Jonathan, whom he had learned to trust implicitly and had welcomed, after initial hesitation, as his future son-in-law. Lai-tse lu was his only child, and although she would never have financial worries, her future was his principal concern.

Certainly he could not wait indefinitely for Jonathan to return to China. He was prepared to give the young American an additional grace period of six months, but thereafter, if he still did not come back to claim his bride, it would be necessary to arrange another marriage for her.

A member of his staff came to him with word that the Marquês de Braga had arrived, and Chao stood to greet his guest.

Dom Manuel Sebastian, following the Portuguese custom, was wearing clothes that had been stylish elsewhere in western Europe a half-century earlier. His corpulent body was encased in snug silk kneebreeches that emphasized his fat; his embroidered, swallow-tailed coat and matching waistcoat sported gold buttons; and there were gold buckles on his shoes. Evidently he was fond of gold, wearing a huge signet ring on one hand and two rings, each with a precious stone set in it, on the other. His heavy jowls and the hollows beneath his eyes indicated his fondness for food and drink, and his receding hairline also made him look older than his forty-five years. But his eyes were sharp, missing nothing, and it was plain that the governor-general of Macao was no fool.

The two men exchanged bows, and Chao was sufficiently conversant with Western customs to extend his hand before he waved his visitor to a hassock. They exchanged amenities while a manservant brought in a pot of tea. This was no ordinary beverage and was available only to those of great wealth. It was virtually colorless and, when poured into cups of wafer-thin, semitransparent porcelain, looked like hot water. But its taste and scent were extraordinary, and half of the entire crop was reserved for the exclusive use of the imperial family in Peking. Chao served it only to his most important guests.

At last Dom Manuel broached the subject of his visit, speaking in strongly accented Mandarin. "It is my hope," he said, "that I will be granted a visa to enter Canton soon because I am eager to pay a call at your home."

"Ah," Soong Chao said noncommittally.

"It was my good fortune to be presented to your daughter

24

on the occasion of Queen Victoria's birthday,'' the Portuguese declared, moistening his thick lips. ''As I am sure you know, her beauty is incomparable.''

''So I have been told by many of her admirers.'' Chao folded his hands across his stomach and, sitting cross-legged, resembled a stone Buddha.

''It is strange that she is still unmarried. One would think that many suitors clamor for her hand.''

''There have been many,'' Chao admitted, then added with a thin smile, ''but I have indulged her whim to remain single. Besides, as Your Excellency undoubtedly realizes, it is no easy matter to find a suitable match for her. I would not tolerate her union with a fortune hunter, and it is not easy to find a husband of her high-born class.''

''Is it possible,'' the governor-general asked, ''that you would permit her to marry a member of another race?''

Soong Chao saw no reason to dissemble. ''That would depend entirely on the man,'' he said honestly, and thought of Jonathan Rakehell.

''Then let me present myself as a suitor.'' The relieved Dom Manuel become bolder. ''My ancestors have held a high place in the nobility of my country for eight hundred years, which I realize is a short time by your standards. I know you are a man of substance, but I do not boast when I say that I am far wealthier. There can be no more than a dozen men in all of Europe whose fortunes equal mine.''

The Chinese nodded impatiently; he already knew the nobleman's position.

''As my wife, your daughter would rank second only to members of our royal family. I would grant her the privilege of redecorating my many homes as she wishes. I am also willing to promise that, when I relinquish my present position and return to Portugal, I would bring her regularly to Canton to visit you. And naturally, my dear Soong, you would always be welcome at our homes. Furthermore, she would have clothes and jewels suitable to her high station, with an even larger staff of servants to attend to her needs than now wait on her.''

''You are generous,'' Chao conceded. ''What are your thoughts regarding her dowry?''

Dom Manuel's smile was bland. He had planned his campaign with great cunning, and now he had the opportunity to

25

play his strongest card. "I ask for no dowry," he said blandly. "I have no need for greater wealth than I already possess. The hand of your daughter would be treasure enough."

The gesture was so generous that Chao was impressed. As he well knew from his dealings with Europeans, the customs of East and West were far different, and only rarely did they coincide, but it happened that the principle of paying a dowry when marrying off one's daughter was common to both worlds. Lai-tse lu's happiness was a paramount consideration, to be sure, but no man of business could overlook the fact that he would save many thousands of silver yuan in the agreement that the Portuguese nobleman was suggesting. Certainly it made the offer more attractive.

"You would waive such a payment?" Chao wanted to be sure he understood the unusual terms.

Aware that he had scored, the governor-general of Macao smiled. "Gladly," he replied.

Even though Lai-tse lu regarded herself as deeply in love with Jonathan Rakehell, this had to be weighed seriously. "I will be frank with you," Chao said. "My daughter has an attachment to someone else, although she has not seen him in a long time. She will do as I direct her to do, naturally, but I would prefer that she enter into a marriage with you of her own free will."

"I share that wish, of course." Dom Manuel took full advantage of the situation. "Bring the lady to Macao for a visit. You will be my guests, and I trust she will become amenable to our union after she has had an opportunity to become acquainted with me."

He appeared to be wise as well as wealthy and powerful, and Chao thought still more highly of him. "I accept with great pleasure," he said.

Convinced that the girl was already his, Dom Manuel allowed himself to smile broadly.

Soong Chao knew his daughter, however, and did not share the other man's optimism. A long, difficult struggle lay ahead before she would agree to give up Jonathan Rakehell for a man she did not know.

Macao was unlike any place Lai-tse lu had ever seen. Her father had elected to travel overland by easy stages, and his

26

entourage, which included Sarah Applegate, Kai, and twenty heavily armed guards, made the journey in two days. They were transported into another world when they reached the tiny Portuguese colony on the coast of the South China Sea.

Strictly speaking, they were still in the Middle Kingdom because the Portuguese paid an annual rental fee for use of the territory to the Imperial Chinese Treasury, and trading ships from Europe were required to pay duties to an imperial customs house at the harbor. But the Portuguese had lived in Macao for three hundred years, and that occupation had created an atmosphere that was unique. Here East and West truly met and mingled.

A large church, with a cross at the top of its high spire, stood directly across the street from an even larger pagoda where the Chinese who lived in Macao worshiped. Slate-roofed houses with ornately carved balconies, built in the style that had been standard in the Middle Kingdom for thousands of years, stood adjacent to European dwellings with far smaller windows, boxlike structures that lacked the graceful lines which the Chinese regarded as essential. Only the colors of the European houses, all of them in pastels of blue and green, yellow and orange, made them attractive. The roads were cobbled, as was a promenade that extended for a mile and a half along the waterfront.

The people strolling on the promenade, particularly the women, fascinated Lai-tse lu, who had never seen any Western woman other than Missy Sarah. The heat and humidity of Macao were stifling, and the ladies dressed accordingly in loose-fitting, ankle-length gowns of light silk or cotton. Most wore huge hats with floppy brims, their headgear always matching their dresses, and without exception they carried parasols to protect their pale skins from the subtropical sun.

Lai-tse lu studied the ladies carefully, knowing they resembled the people she would meet after she married Jonathan and moved with him to the far-distant United States. Very few, she thought, looked attractive; she would continue to wear Chinese attire when she went to America.

On the roads were Western-style carriages, some pulled by teams of two or four horses, and the girl had to admit to herself that these vehicles looked more comfortable than the sedan chair in which she was obliged to ride. Every Western

27

man, regardless of his nationality—and many countries were represented here—carried a sword. It was astonishing, too, to see expensively dressed European women of her own age walking with their companions, unprotected by armed guards.

Many of the European houses were large, but their gardens were small and the flowers in them grew in careless disarray. Obviously the foreigners lacked the sense of order, balance, and shadings of color that contributed to the beauty of every Chinese garden.

At the far end of the promenade stood an ugly stone fort, bristling with cannons far larger than any in the possession of the Imperial Chinese Army and Navy. Behind this structure was a huge, formless building of stone and wood, painted a garish white, and the presence of Portuguese troops, sweltering in uniforms of heavy wool and carrying modern muskets, told the girl that this had to be the palace of the governor-general. She thought of the many handsome buildings in Peking's Forbidden City, where the Tao Kuang Emperor and his family lived, and she shook her head. Europeans had no concept of beauty.

She was not sorry she had come to Macao, however, because this visit would help to prepare her for the life she would live with Jonathan in America. To be sure, when her father had told her they would pay a visit to the governor-general, she had been in no position to protest. After a lifetime of obedience, she would have been rudely disrespectful had she done anything but bow her head in submission to his wishes.

But a visit to Macao did not mean she would marry the Marquês de Braga. How she would be able to refuse if her father insisted was a problem she had not yet solved.

The soldiers saluted, the ugly palace gates were opened, and a number of European ladies strolling on a path that led to the front door of the building gaped openly at the Soong party, especially the young woman who rode in a sedan chair behind that of her father. No well-bred Chinese would have stared so indelicately, and again Lai-tse lu was surprised.

Chinese servants who looked ridiculous in Western uniforms that included swallow-tailed coats, kneebreeches, white stockings, and buckled shoes, opened the doors, and Dom Manuel Sebastian came onto the portico to greet his guests. He was perspiring heavily and mopped his florid face with a huge silk handkechief.

After exchanging greetings with Soong Chao, the governor-general insisted on helping Lai-tse lu dismount from her sedan chair. His touch was clammy, and only rigidly exercised self-discipline made it possible for the girl to conceal her indignation when he bent over her hand and kissed it.

"Welcome to my home," he said.

From what she could see as they walked inside, the place was airless, dark, and crammed with far too much ugly, Western furniture. Never could she live in such a house.

Relieved when she and Missy Sarah could escape to their own suite to bathe and change their clothes, Lai-tse lu felt a trifle more at ease when the maidservants who filled a tub with hot water proved to be Chinese.

Both spoke the Cantonese dialect, and one said shyly, "You are the first Chinese lady who has ever been entertained here."

Lai-tse lu's feeling of insecurity became greater, but she managed to curb her anxiety somewhat as she dressed in a figure-hugging cheongsam of silver, then dabbed delicate hints of silver on her eyelids before donning slender earrings of silver that descended almost to her shoulders.

Sarah Applegate entered her charge's bedchamber, and even Lai-tse lu realized that her high-necked, long-sleeved dress of black taffeta was old-fashioned and stiff

Missy Sarah, as always, was not concerned about her own appearance. "You look beautiful, naturally," she said, "but don't use that as an excuse for bad manners "

Lai-tse lu couldn't help giggling.

"I mean it, my dear." Although they often conversed in English, the chaperone addressed her in Mandarin, which was her custom when delivering a lecture. "You will be meeting the wives and daughters of Portuguese, English, and French gentlemen this evening. They'll notice everything you say and do."

"Will we be using knives, forks, and spoons at dinner rather than chopsticks?" The girl's eyes and tone of voice were guileless.

"We shall. I've already found out that much from the maids."

"Well, you taught me how to use them years ago, and I've often practiced since that time. So my Western table manners will be perfect."

"That isn't what I mean, and well you know it," Missy Sarah said, her voice suddenly grating. "I thought you were going to slap the governor-general's face when he kissed your hand. Or, at the least, wipe the back of your hand on your dress. That's inexcusable!"

"He looks like a toad," Lai-tse lu replied, her air still innocent. "And," she added, "his touch is like that of a toad, too."

"It was many years ago that I found you playing with a toad in the garden and felt obliged to spank you." Missy Sarah softened when she felt a wave of sympathy for the girl. "I don't approve of the Marquês de Braga, either, you know. But there are dozens of unmarried noblewomen in every nation of Europe who would be delighted to become his wife."

"I freely give him to them." Lai-tse lu's eyes hardened.

"I beg you not to be difficult. I've spoken to your father many times. He says the best he could do for you at home would be to arrange a marriage for you with Shaong Wei, the young cousin of the Tao Kuang Emperor."

The girl was incredulous. "Shaong Wei has the 'Western disease,' and everyone knows it. The emperor and his sister have tried for years to find someone reputable who will marry him, but they can't!"

"It's true that Shaong Wei drinks too much," Sarah replied. "Ordinarily someone of royal blood would be obliged to marry a princess. But that is the whole point of what I'm trying to tell you. The emperor and his sister are desperate. For whatever their reasons, they believe Shaong Wei is susceptible to beauty and intelligence, and they would be delighted to have him marry you in the hope that you would reform him."

"I'd kill myself rather than marry him!"

"Your father has no intention of offering you to the emperor for the purpose, so there's no need to be so dramatic. He has reminded me, however, that the Marquês de Braga holds a high rank in the nobility of his country and is therefore a suitable match for a mandarin of the third class. He is also a man of very great wealth."

Lai-tse lu switched to English. "My father knows—and

so do you, Missy Sarah—that I've promised to marry Jonathan. My father agreed."

"Two years is a long time to wait. Not only has Jonathan failed to return, but you've had no letters from him. That is inexcusable, don't you agree?"

"Whatever his reasons, I trust him!"

"I know you still love him, and I wish with all my heart that he would come for you. But I warn you, your father's patience is exhausted, and he won't wait much longer."

The girl raised her head defiantly, her violet eyes blazing, but she knew better than to comment.

"We must not keep our host waiting," Missy Sarah said as she led her charge out of the room and walked with her to the broad marble staircase that led to the drawing room below. She had done her duty in accordance with Chao's wishes, but she still felt great pity for the girl who would be heartbroken when she finally realized that Jonathan was not returning to China to claim her as his bride.

Ravishing yet regal, Lai-tse lu created a sensation when she descended the stairs. A proud Dom Manuel led her around the room and presented her to his large company of guests— Portuguese, British, and French nobles, military officers, and wealthy merchants, who were present with their wives. The cream of Macao society was assembled, although the girl did not realize it.

All she knew was that, although the men were friendly and eager to chat with her, the ladies maintained a reserve, holding her at arm's length. She assumed correctly that they were jealous of her beauty, but not until she heard them speaking only in English or French did it dawn on her that she was being snubbed because they considered her a member of an inferior race. Like most Westerners, these ladies made no attempt to learn the language of the people in whose country they were guests.

She bided her time, speaking only in Mandarin until the governor-general escorted her to the dinner table and seated her at his right. Then she smiled across the table at the gray-haired wife of a major general in the British Army. The woman had a pinched face and obviously disapproved of her. "Lady Williamson," she said in her American-accented English, "I hope you're enjoying your stay in my country."

There was a moment of shocked silence as those within earshot realized she could speak English.

Giving the general's wife no time to reply, she repeated the statement, in French, to the wife of a diplomat from Paris.

Dom Manuel was delighted and beamed at the girl.

By now Lady Williamson found her voice. "I regret that I'm not permitted to visit your country. As you must know, your emperor admits no foreigners to China."

"Ah, but Macao is part of the Middle Kingdom," Lai-tse lu said sweetly. "Surely you've noticed that the flag of the Middle Kingdom flies beside that of Portugal. And I understand that of the fifty thousand people in Macao, fewer than five thousand are European."

Dom Manuel laughed happily. "Quite true, Miss Soong, and very clever you are in your powers of observation."

The atmosphere eased somewhat, and although the ladies were not cordial, courtesy required them to include the exquisite daughter of Soong Chao in their conversation. After dinner, when the women withdrew while the men remained at the table to drink port, the atmosphere became sticky again. But Lai-tse lu persisted, speaking first with one, then with another, and some of the ladies, admiring her courage and wit, warmed toward her.

She was deep in conversation with the wife of a British commodore on the subject of art during the Ming dynasty when the men joined them. Dom Manuel immediately offered to show Lai-tse lu his garden. There was no way she could refuse, and she curbed an almost instinctive desire to shrink from him when he took her arm.

"Gardening is one of my hobbies," he said as they walked through a pair of open French doors. "I grew those roses myself."

Lai-tse lu looked at several undernourished bushes, and could think only of her own gardens at home, ablaze with color. "Very pretty," she murmured.

He told her at length about the chrysanthemums he had planted. For some reason unknown to him they had withered and died.

She could have told him that only members of the imperial family and those to whom the emperor granted permission were allowed to grow chrysanthemums, which were the imperial flower. The goddess of the harvest, according to an ancient legend, not only killed the flowers planted by outsiders who defied custom, but inflicted punishment on them. It was far easier, however, merely to nod and murmur an occasional platitude.

Not only was Lai-tse lu bored, but she was suffering from a headache which she attributed to the stuffiness of the dining room and the gargantuan Western meal that had been served. They had started the meal with small fish over which oil had been poured, then gone on to a hearty meat and vegetable soup, a fish course, a fowl course, a roast, numerous overcooked vegetables, an overpowering sweet, and finally a variety of cheeses. The girl had taken token portions, barely nibbling, but even so she felt she had eaten too much. The very thought of being served such meals every day of her life made her want to scream.

Unaware of her distress, Dom Manuel chatted at length and seemed pleased with himself when they returned to the drawing room.

Some of the guests were drinking considerable quantities of liquor, which the girl had never seen happen in a gathering of her father's friends. Several wives decided the time had come for them to take their husbands home, and Lai-tse lu used their departure as her excuse to retire to her suite.

She had already changed into a dressing gown of peach-colored silk with a wide sash around the waist when Sarah Applegate joined her.

"You handled yourself well tonight," she said. "You've made your father proud."

"Thanks to both of you, I have good manners. It would have given me great pleasure to administer the Torture of One Thousand Delicacies on some of those women." Lai-tse lu shuddered. "Can you imagine how awful it would be to become the Marquêsa de Braga and see those people regularly? It would be a nightmare."

Missy Sarah knew precisely what she meant and privately agreed. But she felt compelled to say, "I'm sure you'd be free to choose your own friends."

"The wife of the Royal Navy commodore—I can't recall her name—has studied the art of the Ming dynasty, so I had something in common with her. None of the others knew anything about the Middle Kingdom or her people, and had no interest in them, either. They're here because their husbands are earning huge sums of money at the expense of our poor, hardworking people. I could never be friendly with any women like that!'' Lai-tse lu spoke quietly but firmly.

''The purpose of this visit is to make it possible for you to become acquainted with the Marquês de Braga,'' Missy Sarah said bluntly.

''I already know him well enough, thank you. He's not only homely, he's also a dreadful bore.''

''By the end of our stay, I'm certain he will present a formal petition for your hand in marriage.''

''My father will not force me to marry him.''

The governess who had known and loved Lai-tse lu since infancy came to her and put a hand on her shoulder. ''Chao has often indulged you, child,'' she said. ''From time to time I've accused him of spoiling you, and he freely admits it. But don't make the mistake of thinking you'll have your way in this. You should be married, and there are few men in China who are eligible.''

''Jonathan is more than eligible. Jonathan—''

''—is many thousands of miles away, halfway around the world!'' the older woman interrupted forcibly. ''He should have returned a year ago, but he hasn't even had the courtesy to write you an explanation of the delay. All we know is that Charles Boynton told us he thinks of you constantly and will come to you as soon as he can. That's not good enough.''

''It is for me.'' Lai-tse lu spoke with deep conviction.

''Well, it isn't for your father. He's been patient, but he feels he can't afford to wait any longer!''

On the last day of the visit to Macao, Dom Manuel fulfilled Sarah Applegate's prophecy by making a formal request of Soong Chao for the hand of his daughter.

The Chinese merchant realized she would resist and that he might need time to convince her that he knew what was best for her. ''I shall speak to her as soon as I return home,'' he said, ''and then I shall write to you without delay.''

The nobleman stared hard at him.

Chao knew that behind the man's amiable façade there lurked a potentially dangerous enemy. The Marquês de Braga was accustomed to getting what he wanted. Although he had originally been prepared to give Jonathan Rakehell a six-month grace period, Chao now saw the advantage in acting expeditiously. "Rest assured that I shall present your cause favorably and fervently, Dom Manuel."

A quick smile again creased the face of the Portuguese nobleman. "Then I am in your debt for the rest of our lives, sir."

Obviously he thought he had won his bride, but Chao did not share that conviction. He made no mention of the formal proposal to Lai-tse lu or Missy Sarah.

His daughter, he noted, sighed in relief when they crossed the Macao border.

Deeply troubled, Chao wondered how he might best raise the subject. More often than not, he and Lai-tse lu dealt subtly with each other, but in this instance, he finally decided, he would need to speak bluntly.

He waited until they returned home and ate a light meal, a soup of chicken broth, scallions, and thin mung bean noodles, followed by shrimp with sliced water chestnuts and peapods. Then, with a quick glance at Sarah, he said, "Daughter, Dom Manuel Sebastian has requested that you marry him."

Lai-tse lu made no reply, and her face revealed that she was not surprised.

Missy Sarah observed that the girl's backbone stiffened.

"I have informed him that I would speak with you and would write to him immediately."

Still Lai-tse lu remained silent.

"I shall apply to the imperial viceroy for permission to marry a foreigner," Chao continued. "He will grant it, I am certain."

A faint smile appeared at the corners of the girl's full mouth. "The Princess An Mien, sister of the Tao Kuang Emperor, is my good friend," she said, speaking at last. "If I write and explain my circumstances to her, I know she will have the permit rescinded."

So that was her game, Chao thought, and he glowered, even though he admired her cleverness. An Mien, who was a close confidante of her all-powerful brother, was dedicating her life to the improvement of the lot of women in the Middle Kingdom. She was fond of Lai-tse lu, and there was no doubt she would be sympathetic to any plea the girl made to her. So, Chao concluded, the time had come for him to be very firm.

"You were reared in the traditions of our people," he said. "Just as I obeyed the will of my father, even when I thought my ways were superior to his, so shall you obey my will. It is my desire that you marry the Marquês de Braga. You will do as you are told."

Without a word, Lai-tse lu rose and went off down the path to her own small house.

Chao looked at Sarah. "Well?" he demanded.

"You have presented her with your ultimatum," she said, "but her will is strong, and I have known her to outwit many people. Including you, Chao. I cannot predict whether or not she will obey you. All I do know is that neither Dom Manuel's title nor his wealth have made the slightest impression on her. She doesn't think much of him."

Chao indulged in the rare gesture of clenching his fists. "She will do as I have commanded her," he said loudly.

Lai-tse lu heard him as she opened her door, went into her sitting room, and collapsed on a hassock. Staring at the gold band Jonathan had given her, she twisted it on her finger. Since the day he had placed it on her right hand she had worn it there, and she knew that, when she married him, she would transfer it to the fourth finger of her left hand in accordance with the custom of the West.

In a sudden gesture of defiance, she removed the ring and slipped it onto her left hand. All at once her finger tingled, and the sensation spread quickly, spreading past her elbow into her upper arm and shoulder. Not even members of the highest classes were immune from the superstitions in which the people of China believed, and the first thought that came into her mind was that Jonathan was communicating with her, telling her that all was well and that he would come for her.

Then she shook her hand and arm, and the feeling vanished. The sensation had lasted no more than a second or two, and she was unsure that anything out of the ordinary had taken place.

Deeply troubled, she undressed and went to bed. She remained wide awake for a long time, but common sense told her she could not solve her problem alone. In the morning she would seek advice from Missy Sarah, and if necessary she would go to her father, humble herself, and beg him not to force her to marry the Marquês de Braga. At last she became drowsy and drifted off.

She had been thinking so much of Jonathan that it was only natural, perhaps, that she dreamed about him. All at once he stood before her, ruggedly handsome and bronzed, and she could hear his deep resonant voice clearly as he said, "Wait for me, my dearest. I am preparing for my voyage now, and when I join you I'll explain the reasons for my delay, which couldn't be avoided. Wait for me!" Gradually he faded from sight, blending into the darkness.

Lai-tse lu awakened in a cold sweat, and did not sleep again for the rest of the night. Now she knew what had to be done.

Her father and Missy Sarah were already at the table, eating their usual simple breakfast of broiled fish and rice, when she joined them.

They listened to her account of her dream, neither of them interrupting. Soong Chao had not rid himself of superstitions, although he was reluctant to admit it, and Sarah Applegate had lived in China long enough to have accepted many of the nation's beliefs.

As the girl picked up her chopsticks and porcelain bowl, she saw the gold ring, still on the fourth finger of her left hand, so she told her father and governess about the strange, tingling sensation she had felt when she had transferred the band from her right hand.

Chao removed his glasses and polished them, a sure sign that he was disturbed.

"My dream will come true," Lai-tse lu said. "Jonathan will come to me."

Her father pondered for a time, his expression giving no clue as to what was passing through his mind. "Very well," he said at last. "I will inform Dom Manuel that I can give him no reply for six months. I will wait until six months from today for Jonathan to return. If he has not come by that time, you will become the Marquêsa de Braga. That is my final word."

II

A chilly wind blew across the Rakehell and Boynton ship-yard in New London, Connecticut, but Jonathan Rakehell did not feel the cold. He stood on the deck of his magnificent new clipper ship, the *Lai-tse lu,* exulting as he watched workmen putting the finishing touches on the vessel. Within two weeks she would be ready to sail on her maiden voyage. A ship of almost two thousand tons, she was larger by far than any of the other clippers he had built, ships so swift they were revolutionizing world trade.

Her hull design was long and low, with a draught deeper aft than forward. She had a very sharp-raked stem, and an inclined, overhanging counterstern, thus reducing the area of hull in contact with the water. She had frames of live oak, copper-fastened throughout; her stern was sheathed with expensive, imported red copper, and her flush deck was fitted with hatch coamings of Honduras mahogany. Her rails, companions, and skylights were made of the same wood, and because of the need to protect herself from the pirates who attacked merchantmen in the Orient, she mounted sixteen brass cannon. Unlike the windjammers that would thrust through waves, she would clip through them, enabling her to sustain a steady speed of at least twenty knots when the winds were favorable.

How Jonathan awaited the day she would sail! When he had returned from his sojourn in the Orient, intending to go back for Lai-tse lu, he had been shocked to discover that a single indiscretion had forced him to pay a frightful penalty. Louise Graves, his family's neighbor, had given birth to his son during his long absence, naming the boy Julian. Honor had forced him to enter into a loveless marriage with Louise.

Now she was gone, plunging to her death from a scaffolding beside the new clipper ship. He had no idea whether her death had been an accident or a suicide, and he probably would never know. What he had no way of learning was that his overly ambitious brother-in-law, Bradford Walker, the husband of his sister, Judith, had been responsible. Jealous because the head of the company, Jeremiah Rakehell, had just made his son a full partner and had given him the freedom to build clipper ships at will, Brad had gone to Louise in secret and had told her of Jonathan's abiding love for the Chinese girl.

Certainly that love was foremost in the mind of the young shipbuilder and sea captain. His cargo would arrive in the next few days, he was hiring the last members of his new crew, and then he would sail to Canton, where he would marry Lai-tse lu. The prospect of their reunion filled him with joy, and he fingered the medallion of jade she had given him. He wore it on a chain suspended from his neck, and anticipating the day he would see his love, he thrilled at the touch of the smooth jade. On it was a symbol of the Tree of Life, its three branches standing for health, wisdom, and honor. He who possessed all three had no need for anything else on earth.

This was no time to daydream; there was too much to be done, and Jonathan summoned his new first mate with a shout. "Mr. Ellison!"

Prematurely gray-haired in his late thirties, Homer Ellison made his way forward. Although he held master's papers of his own, he had been delighted to sign on as mate after spending too many years on land. He had been crippled by a drinking problem, but hadn't touched whiskey for a year, and he was grateful to Jonathan for giving him the chance to return to the profession he loved. "Sir?" he asked.

"Keep an eye on the workmen who are finishing the fittings in the passenger cabins, if you will." This unusual clipper boasted several cabins for passengers because Jonathan was convinced that many travelers would want to take advantage of a clipper's speed. "I've got to go ashore."

"Will you be coming back today?"

"I'm afraid not. There aren't enough hours in a day."

Ellison grinned. "Don't give it a thought, sir. I have nothing better to do, so I'll hang around as long as the workmen stay."

"I appreciate that, Homer." Jonathan stepped onto the dock to which the ship was tied, walked a short distance, and then paused again. The clipper's suit of sail, more than thirty thousand square feet of canvas, had just been delivered that morning, and was being carefully inspected. Three men were bending over a sail spread on the dock. Elijah Wilbor, the second mate, was a young daredevil with red hair and freckles and would be sailing with the vessel's master for the first time. Jonathan had selected him because he had the instinct for handling a rakish ship that could maintain remarkably high speeds for long periods when the wind was right.

Oliver, the boatswain, was one of the few black men in the Rakehell and Boynton fleet to hold a petty officer's post. A onetime slave whose return to South Carolina Jonathan had blocked, he had returned the compliment by saving the master's life on their previous voyage to the East. They understood each other well, and Oliver's nod was an assurance that no flaws had been found in any of the sails. The third member of the trio was a veteran sailmaker who had been in the company's employ for twenty years, and he, too, appeared satisfied.

"All's well, Captain," Elijah Wilbor said. "Just seeing all this canvas gives me the itch to be under way."

"We can't sail too soon for my taste," Jonathan replied. He walked rapidly across the busy yard to the modest, white clapboard administration building. Mounting the stairs to the second floor two at a time, he did not pause in his own cramped quarters, but went instead to the corner office of his father.

Portraits of Jeremiah Rakehell, his father, grandfather, and great-grandfather looked down at him from one wall of the spacious room, and with his hair graying at the temples, his ruddy complexion and lined face, Jeremiah Rakehell bore a strong resemblance to his forebears.

Jonathan knew he looked like them, too, just as he was a younger version of his own father. It would be interesting to see, when little Julian grew older, if he was cast in the same image. The women of the family differed, but the men invariably were tall and rangy, with brown hair and pale, penetrating eyes.

Jeremiah looked up from the statistics on European trade

that he had just received from his brother-in-law and partner in London, Sir Alan Boynton. "Time to go already?" Father and son almost always walked to and from work together.

"No, I'm leaving a bit early today. But I want to discuss a problem with you, Papa."

The older man waved him to a chair.

"I've been concerned about Julian while I'm away."

Jeremiah chuckled. "The household staff and I will manage," he said.

"I'm sure you can, but that isn't fair to you. Or to Julian, who needs a lot of attention at two and a half."

Knowing his son, Jeremiah realized he already had a well-defined plan in mind.

"As you well know, Papa, Charles Boynton has left little David with Ruth Barker." Jonathan's cousin, closest friend, and now a junior partner in the company, had sired a son by a girl in China; Alice Wong had given her life for him, and he had brought David to New London, leaving him there in the care of a young widow until he summoned the courage to tell his parents in England that he was the father and custodian of a part-Chinese child.

"You're not thinking of leaving Julian with Ruth, Jonnie?"

"Not exactly. If she's willing, I'd like her to move with David and his nursemaid, Wu-ling, into our house. I'd pay her, naturally, and I know she can use the money. She'd also save on food bills. We have more than enough room, and they wouldn't be in your way or annoy you. Most of all, Ruth would relieve you and the household staff of the day-to-day responsibility for Julian."

"That's thoughtful of you." Jeremiah weighed the proposal.

"There are other aspects that I like," Jonathan said. "Julian and David will benefit from spending a portion of their childhood together. Also, Wu-ling is just learning English, so she speaks to David in Chinese. Julian would start to learn the language from her, too." Charles had hired Wu-ling to look after his son because she was the younger sister of the late Alice Wong.

Jeremiah leaned back in his chair, studied his son, and asked almost too casually, "Why should it be an advantage for Julian to become familiar with Chinese? I'll grant you our trade in the Far East is increasing rapidly, thanks to your efforts, but by the time Julian takes charge of the company he'll be able to hire many assistants who know both Chinese and English.''

Jonathan thought instantly that his father had guessed his real reason for returning to China himself. It was best to reveal the truth now, all of it, rather than wait until the eve of his sailing, as he had intended. ''You know from my ledgers that one of the principal reasons my stay in the Orient was so financially successful is because I spent a year in the employ of Soong Chao. His daughter, Lai-tse lu, and I fell in love.''

''You've named the new clipper after her.''

''Yes. When I came home and discovered Louise had given birth to Julian, it was only right that we get married. But the clipper was for Lai-tse lu. I was going to make a gift of the ship to her, since, as you know, I built this clipper with my own funds. Now, if Lai-tse lu will still have me, I want to give her the clipper as a wedding gift.''

''You think she's waited all this time for you?''

''All I can do is hope and pray.''

''Does her father approve of her marriage to a Westerner?''

Jonathan had to be honest. ''He didn't at first, but he came to understand that we were sincere, and eventually he gave his approval. I hope you'll feel as he does.''

''And if I don't?''

''In that case,'' Jonathan replied firmly, ''I'd give my share of Rakehell and Boynton to Julian in trust, and I'd start a new company of my own.''

''If you failed to do less, I'd be disgusted with you,'' Jeremiah replied, smiling broadly. ''I've learned to put great faith in your judgment. I'm sure that you and the young lady realize that both of you will have problems when you bring a Chinese wife to a provincial town like this.''

''I've thought a good deal about it, Papa. Lai-tse lu speaks a perfect English, thanks to her American governess, and she'll charm everyone in New London.'' He realized that the parents of his late wife might not approve, but he refused to worry about their attitude. ''By the way,'' Jonathan continued, ''I think you know her governess—Sarah Applegate. When I was in Canton, she told me she knew our family.''

''Sarah Applegate!'' Jeremiah became lost in thought.

"Yes, I knew her. So that's what's become of Sarah Applegate—a governess in China."

"Yes, and you probably know then that she's a wonderful woman. She's devoted to Lai-tse lu, like a mother to her. They're going to have a difficult time parting when Lai-tse lu comes home with me."

"I'm sure you'll do what's best for this girl and for Julian," Jeremiah said.

"I've never loved anyone else, and neither has she. So I know this is right."

"I'll make her welcome here, as you must know." Jeremiah stood and formally shook his son's hand. "Meantime, make your arrangement with Ruth, if she's agreeable. Bring her and David to the house for supper tonight. Wu-ling, too. Julian isn't the only one in the family who'll find Chinese useful."

As Jonathan left the yard, walking with a rolling seaman's gait as he made his way to the nearby house of Ruth Barker, he reflected that he was fortunate to have Jeremiah Rakehell for a father. He hadn't admonished or criticized Jonathan for his indiscretion with Louise before going to the East and falling in love with Lai-tse lu, and he was willing to accept the Chinese girl as his new daughter-in-law. Papa was truly a good and generous man.

Although the day was chilly, David and Wu-ling were in the yard of the modest Barker house, where the teenage girl was pushing the little boy in a swing suspended from the stout branch of an elm. Wu-ling greeted Jonathan in her native Cantonese.

He replied in her own tongue, chatting with her briefly, as he always did in an effort to improve his command of Chinese. She had been a scrawny child when Charles had brought her to New London, but now she was filling out, and she began to remind him of Alice, whom he had known through Charles. If he guessed correctly, it wouldn't be long before she was a beauty in her own right.

Wu-ling helped David to the ground, and the child hurled himself at Jonathan, delighted to see him.

Able to understand only a word or two of the babble of a boy not yet two years old, Jonathan picked him up and hugged him. "I'll push you on the swing myself before I leave," he promised.

43

Then he steeled himself for his meeting with Ruth. Her father, now retired and living in the South with his son, had been the chief carpenter at the Rakehell yard for many years, so Jonathan had known her all of her life and had no idea why he felt a trifle uncomfortable when he was with her. Perhaps it was because she had been Louise's only close friend and confidante. Perhaps it was because Edmund Barker, his second mate and Yale College classmate, had been washed overboard in a storm and had drowned while in the Rakehell service. Possibly it was because Ruth always seemed tense in his presence, but he guessed that was his imagination playing tricks on him.

Ruth had seen him from a parlor window, and after dabbing her lips with a faint touch of rouge, she hurried to the door, a fixed smile of greeting on her face.

Jonathan removed his high-crowned, broad-brimmed beaver hat and kissed her lightly on the cheek.

Ruth hoped he hadn't noticed she had held her breath for that instant, and she continued to smile as she led him to the parlor. "You left the yard early today," she said.

Her powers of observation were acute, he reflected. "That's because I have something important to discuss with you."

Again she caught her breath, then found the excuse of going to the kitchen for a pot of tea, which gave her the chance to compose herself. No one on earth knew she had been madly in love with Jonathan since adolescence, or that she had married Edmund—bless his memory—only because Jonathan no longer had been available. It was too much to hope, now he was a widower, that he intended to propose marriage to her.

Jonathan sipped his steaming tea and explained his plan to her in detail. "You'd have no living expenses," he concluded, "and I'll gladly pay you fifty dollars per month. What's more, the business at the yard is expanding so rapidly that we're bringing in shipwrights and carpenters from Massachusetts and Rhode Island. So you'll have no trouble renting this place for at least twenty-five dollars per month. What with the money you get from Charles to look after David, plus your Rakehell widow's pension, you'd save a tidy sum each month."

Ruth was overwhelmed. By living in Jonathan's house and taking care of his son she would be drawing closer to him,

44

and perhaps he would see her in a new and different light by the time he returned from the Orient. "Would I be disturbing your father?"

"Not at all. He's a man of fixed habits. He reads the newspapers at breakfast, and then goes off to the yard. When he comes home at night, he plays with Julian for a half-hour, then after supper he goes off to his library, where he reads until bedtime."

"I truly wouldn't be in the way? And Wu-ling would be welcome, too?"

"Between you and me, the household staff is fairly efficient, but Miss Nan is going to retire this month. Papa will need another housekeeper to take charge, and that's what you'd be. As for Wu-ling, he'll be delighted to have her there. Just today," he added with a chuckle, "he told me he wants to learn Chinese."

"Then I accept with great pleasure," Ruth said with dignity.

"You may change your mind when Julian is in a contrary mood and influences David, too."

"I'll manage to handle them."

"I'm quite sure you will, which is why I'll have peace of mind while I'm away. Come along to supper, and we'll bring Wu-ling and David with us. I'll show you through those parts of the house you don't know, and later, at supper, Papa and I can answer any questions you might have."

"How soon will you want me to move in?"

"By next week, if that's convenient. I hope to sail by the week after next, and you'll want to settle into your routines before I leave."

They walked together to the Rakehell mansion on Pequot Avenue, with Jonathan carrying David and insisting that Wu-ling stay beside them instead of dropping behind. He took care to include the girl in their conversation, explaining in her own language what she failed to understand in English.

Wu-ling marveled at this wealthy, powerful man who, like his cousin, Charles Boynton, refused to make class distinctions and treated her as an equal. She knew by now that the stories she had heard in Canton about the *Fan Kuei*—foreign devils—were wildly exaggerated. Jonathan and Charles would

45

be mandarins of a high class if they were Chinese, but they refused to allow her to kowtow to them. She loved living in America, and she hoped that when Charles took David to London, bringing her, too, she would find England as much to her liking.

The Rakehell house thrilled Ruth Barker, as it always had, even though she often brought David here to play with Julian. The furnishings were plain, with the emphasis on practicality rather than style. Most tables and chairs were made of polished New England maple, the rugs that covered the hardwood floors had been manufactured in Massachusetts, and even the drapes were of wool rather than silk. No stranger visiting here would dream that the Rakehells had been among Connecticut's wealthiest, most influential families for generations.

One oddity was that the main parlor stood at the rear of the house, as did the principal bedrooms on the second and third floors, rather than at the front, facing Pequot Avenue. The reasons were self-evident the moment one entered the parlor. Its oversized windows looked out on the estuary of the Thames River, which flowed into Long Island Sound, and on a very clear day, with the aid of a mariner's glass, one could see past Fisher's Island and actually make out Montauk Point, at the tip of Long Island. For generations the Rakehells had watched from their own house as their ships sailed into the open Atlantic to and from the British Isles, Europe, North Africa, and, in recent years, the Far East.

The mere thought of becoming Jonathan's wife and someday becoming the mistress of this mansion made Ruth dizzy. On occasion she wondered if she could have cared as much for Jonathan had he been anyone other than a Rakehell. But she always banished the thought from her mind, reminding herself that she was posing an unfair question. She appreciated the value of money, to be sure, never having known luxury, yet at the same time she could not separate Jonathan from his heritage.

Sitting between him and his father at the supper table, eating the simple but full fare of corn chowder, fried clams, roasted beef with vegetables, and apple pie, she could not help daydreaming. For the first time there appeared to be at least the possibility that her lifelong wish might come true.

46

*   *   *

Bradford Walker paced his office at the Rakehell and Boynton yard, cursing his bad luck. No matter what he did, he was always a step behind the Rakehells. He was tall, but not quite as tall as his father-in-law, and that damned Jonathan towered above him. They stayed thin, even though they were big eaters, while he, at the age of forty, was gaining a paunch. His hair was thinning, but the Rakehells, for generation after generation, had never known baldness.

In a sense, to be sure, he knew he shouldn't complain. Through Judy's inherited interest in the company he controlled ten percent of the Rakehell and Boynton stock. He also had five percent in his own name, and he held a seat on the board of directors. He was in charge of the old division at the yard, building the brigs and other standard vessels that would still be in demand when the fad for Jonathan's clipper ships died away.

Yet he could not deny the fact that Jonathan had moved ahead of him in the hierarchy and had been made a full partner. He and Charles Boynton were in the direct line of descent, and it was inevitable that they would succeed their fathers as the managing partners of the American and English branches of the company. Consequently, Brad could rise no higher than his present place, no matter how long he worked.

His efforts to sabotage Jonathan's first clipper, *Flying Dragon,* had not only failed miserably, but Jeremiah Rakehell had learned of his activities and had warned him that even his family ties would not save him if he meddled again.

He thought his luck had changed when Judy repeated to him what she had learned in confidence from her brother, that he was in love with a Chinese girl. Naturally he had repeated the information to Louise, after swearing her to secrecy, and he had been certain she would create a scandal that would destroy Jonathan. The Rakehells behaved as though they were shock-proof, but there was a strong streak of the Puritan in the family, and Jonathan most likely would have been dismissed if his father and Sir Alan Boynton had learned the truth about his affair with an Oriental.

But the moody, undependable Louise had told the secret to no one and instead had jumped to her death. There was no doubt in Brad's mind that her fall had been deliberate. But he refused to blame himself. He had tried to help her, and it wasn't his fault if she had been too weak to withstand the impact of the true story of her husband's indiscretion.

It served no useful purpose to look back over his shoulder, Brad decided. His chances of ruining Jonathan had narrowed, but one card remained, and he intended to play it. Smoothing his hair and straightening his cravat, he donned his beaver hat and lightweight silk cloak, then left the office and wandered past the row of docks extending into the Thames River until he came to the berth of the new *Lai-tse lu*. A hideous name for a ship.

Dusk had come, and with the sky turning dark the workmen preparing the ship for the China run were coming ashore, struggling into their coats and carrying their lunch pails. Brad stood at the far side of the dock, where they wouldn't particularly notice him, and waited. At last his patience was rewarded.

First mate Homer Ellison turned the ship over to the night watchmen, donned his pea jacket and bicorne, then stepped ashore.

Brad hailed him at once. "Homer! Just the fellow I want to see!"

In earlier years Homer had sailed several of the ships Brad had built and was pleased to see him now. "How are you, Brad?"

"Fine, thanks, and delighted to learn you're on the company payroll again and going back to sea."

"It's been a long time," Homer replied. "And my own damn fault that I was on the beach for so long."

Brad ignored the self-deprecating comment. "Which way are you headed?"

"I'm staying at a little boardinghouse on Bank Street." Homer preferred not to mention that his wife had left him when his drinking had become unbearable and had managed to obtain a rare legal annulment of their marriage.

"I'm going in the same direction. When do you sail?"

"The ship is almost ready, and we began stowing her cargo today."

"More of Jonathan's cotton-spinning looms from Massachusetts, I'm sure."

"Yes, I'm told they earned a heap of money when the Chinese found them superior to their old-fashioned looms. We're also carrying a cargo of medicinal powders and elixirs.

They take up very little space, and there should be a great demand for them in China, where no Western medicines are available."

Brad was forced to admit to himself, grudgingly, that Jonathan was a shrewd businessman. He said nothing, however, until they reached Bank Street, which stood on the waterfront. Here were most of the taverns and bordellos frequented by visiting seamen, and he pulled the brim of his hat lower as they approached a small establishment where, he knew, he would be given a private booth at the rear. "Let me treat you to a minor celebration of your good fortune," he said, and stopped at the tavern entrance.

Homer Ellison hesitated, not wanting to offend Jeremiah Rakehell's son-in-law. The offer surprised him because Walker was known as a penny-pincher and rarely extended hospitality to anyone.

"Come on," Brad insisted, and took his arm.

The proprietor immediately recognized the expensively attired patron, but did not address him by name as he conducted the man and his companion to the secluded booth where they could not be seen by customers sitting at the bar.

"I believe I'll have a glass of West Indies rum," Brad said, "with a glass of water on the side. What about you?"

Homer smiled and looked up at the proprietor. "I'll have either tea or coffee, whichever is available," he declared.

"Have a real drink with me," Brad said.

The veteran seaman shook his head. "I haven't touched whiskey, gin, or rum in a year. I won't even drink wine or a glass of ale anymore."

"One small rum won't hurt you," Brad said.

Homer's smile was tight. "It would be the finish of me. When I take one taste, I don't know when to stop. I spent far too long in the gutter, and I don't rightly aim to fall into it again."

Brad winked at the proprietor. "Bring him a glass of rum as well as the coffee he wants. If I can't persuade him to drink it, I'll have it myself."

"No offense meant," Homer said after the proprietor went off for the order. "But there's one lesson I've learned. Anyway, I'm grateful for the offer."

Their conversation became desultory until their order arrived. Homer carefully spooned sugar into his black coffee as Brad raised his glass. "Happy sailing!" He sipped his drink, then added, "I wish you'd join me."

Homer stared at him, aware for the first time that he was being strangely insistent. "I've told you I can't drink," he said sharply.

Brad remained genial, seemingly unaware of his guest's irritation. "Well, I'll leave your glass here in case you change your mind," he said, and pushed the drink of rum closer to the other man.

Homer didn't want to protest yet again, so he said nothing, but his eyes became hooded. Why should Jeremiah Rakehell's son-in-law try to harm him? He had no idea.

Leaving the rum untouched, Homer drank a second cup of coffee, and soon thereafter they went their separate ways. The mate stopped at a small inn for a plate of beef stew on his way back to his boardinghouse and continued to think about the strange encounter. Suddenly a possible solution to the riddle occurred to him.

Perhaps Bradford Walker was using him as an instrument to cause problems for Jonathan Rakehell. A first mate on a ship, who drank in secret, could create irreparable damage on a long voyage. The notion was so unreasonable that Homer tried to dismiss it from his mind, but the thought nevertheless lingered.

He might never find out Walker's motives, but he was certain of one thing: never again would he trust the man.

Ruth Barker quickly settled into the Rakehell mansion, and her hope of marrying Jonathan soared. She saw him at breakfast, dinner, and supper, and whenever he devoted time to Julian and David, which he did for at least an hour each day, she was also present. He was invariably amused and touched when David called her "Mama," and she realized it wouldn't be long before Julian began to address her in the same way. Perhaps the child would plant the idea in his father's mind.

Then one week before Jonathan was scheduled to sail, the Rakehell and Boynton clipper that had been in the Orient returned, making the voyage from Canton to New London in one hundred and two days, only forty-eight hours longer than the record-breaking voyage that Jonathan had made in *Flying Dragon*. The ship's master, Captain Samuel Green, was invited to the

Rakehell house for supper, as Jonathan was eager to learn the latest news from China.

The grizzled Captain Green arrived just as Jonathan was ending his customary romp with the two little boys. The children had already eaten, and Ruth began to round them up and take them off to bed.

"No, Mama," David said, and for once he spoke clearly.

Julian, who was a year older than his cousin, had a far better command of English. "We play more, Mama."

A chill shot up Ruth's spine. At last Julian had referred to her as "Mama" in his father's hearing.

Jonathan grinned but made no attempt to correct the child, which raised Ruth's hopes still higher. "Do what you're told when you're told to do it," he said. Picking them up and hugging them, he handed them to Ruth. "Can you manage two little squirmers together?" he asked.

Flushed and excited, she could only reply, "Of course." And as she started toward the stairs she gently bounced the children in her arms and said, "You are my good little boys, such good little gentlemen."

Jonathan's approving chuckle followed her up the stairs. Her campaign seemed to be succeeding even better than she had dared to hope.

By the time she returned to the parlor, stopping off first in the kitchen to see what progress the cook was making, Samuel Green and Jeremiah Rakehell were drinking glasses of whiskey cut with water, while Jonathan, as always, confined himself to a small glass of sack.

Ruth was flattered when he rose, poured sack for her, and handed her the glass. He was already treating her as he would a wife!

"I spent only a week in Whampoa, unloading the cargo of spices from the Fat Duchman in Djakarta and picking up the cargo that Soong Chao had waiting for me," Samuel Green said. "I didn't have too much opportunity to learn about local conditions. I left the cargo manifest in your office this afternoon."

"I've already glanced through it," Jonathan replied. "Tea, silks, and porcelain. I'll go over it in detail with you tomorrow." His voice became almost too casual. "How did you find Soong Chao, Samuel?"

"Our association with him is valuable, I can tell you! Rakehell and Boynton are his favorite trading partners. A couple of the American companies—and most of the British and French—smuggle opium on the side, and Soong will have nothing whatever to do with them. He's blame near as adamant as the new imperial viceroy for Kwangtung, Lin Tse-hsü."

Jonathan well knew Chao's attitude toward opium. "How is his health?"

"This was the first time I ever met him, but he seemed fine to me. He's worried, of course, as everyone else is. Everyone in the compound is certain that the new viceroy is pushing too hard and too fast to end the traffic in opium. Some of the factors—Owen Bruce in particular—are outraged."

"Bruce is one of the worst offenders, so it's only natural that he's upset."

"He's still a subject of Queen Victoria, and so are a dozen others who import opium from India."

Ruth couldn't help interrupting. "How is this smuggling accomplished?"

"Canton is seventy-five miles from the open sea," Jonathan explained. "Foreign ships sail up the Pearl River Delta, and there are many islands as well as innumerable little coves and harbors on both shores of the mainland. Perfect hiding places for local smugglers."

"They're Chinese?"

"Almost without exception. A foreign merchantman drops anchor for as short a time as an hour or two. The smugglers come to him in their rather large junks, or sometimes in a whole fleet of tiny sampans. They remove the opium, which is concealed in tea chests. Silver changes hands, and that's the end of the transaction."

"The viceroy," Samuel added, "is determined to put every Chinese smuggler to death. Now he's beginning to crack down on the foreigners, too, especially those who actually dare to use their warehouses as hiding places for opium. And that's where the danger lies. Admiral Alexander has a powerful Royal Navy squadron stationed in the delta, off Whampoa, and if Lin Tse-hsü begins to arrest and punish British subjects, there will be hell to pay, if you'll pardon the expression, ma'am."

Jonathan considered what the captain had said. "The British government is under great pressure from merchants who are earning huge fortunes in the opium trade. Not that the British are the only ones with a flourishing trade there."

"Indeed they aren't," Jeremiah said with a sigh. "I know of several companies in Massachusetts and Rhode Island that have been urging President Van Buren to send some warships to Canton to protect their interests in the opium trade. The French and the Dutch and the Danes—and all the rest—are doing the same with their governments."

"The heart of the problem," Jonathan said, "lies in the fact that China is almost totally cut off from the outside world. The emperor and his advisors don't understand Western ways and don't care to learn, and at the same time, we in the West have a great deal to learn about the Chinese. Aside from Whampoa and Macao, China is still closed to foreigners. A few of us have been granted the right to go into Canton from time to time, and if the rumors are true, a number of missionaries have sneaked into the country and are there illegally. But, in effect, China is a closed society, and the Chinese refuse to buy Western goods. Is it any wonder, then, that Western merchants have turned to the lucrative opium trade?"

"What will happen in China?" the wide-eyed Ruth asked.

"Only the Almighty can answer that question," Jonathan said. "Sir William Alexander is a splendid gentleman. Uncle Alan knows him far better than Charles and I do, but just on the basis of my own association with him, I can tell you flatly that he's civilized and compassionate. All the same, he's under orders. If British subjects are harassed, attacked, and either injured or killed, he's obliged to retaliate." He turned to Samuel as their clam chowder was removed and they were served large platters of swordfish, which would precede the roast. "What's new in Macao?"

"Very little. The Portuguese are careful not to offend the Chinese, and vice versa." Samuel smiled. "I did hear some gossip, but I can't substantiate it, so perhaps I shouldn't repeat it."

"Even gossip can be important in our business," Jeremiah said.

His son nodded emphatically.

"Well," the sea captain declared, "Soong Chao has a daughter who is a real beauty."

Jonathan felt a rush of excitement at the reference to

53

Lai-tse lu. He hoped his voice didn't betray his deep feelings as he said, "I've heard of her."

Something in his expression caused Ruth to study him surreptitiously for a moment, but his face was inscrutable.

"I just saw her once, and she's so beautiful she almost bowled me over. As I was leaving her father's office one day she was just arriving there, guarded by the tallest, huskiest Chinese I've ever seen. He was carrying a sword, shaped a bit like an Ottoman scimitar, that looked too heavy for anyone else to lift, much less handle."

Jonathan grinned in relief. If Lai-tse lu was still being guarded by Kai, there was no need to be concerned for her welfare. Kai was a master in the ancient martial arts of China and had taught Jonathan many of the techniques.

"Did you ever meet the Marquês de Braga, the Portuguese governor-general of Macao, Jonathan?" Samuel asked.

"No, but I heard all sorts of stories about him. He's enormously wealthy, and supposedly has kept a whole stable of European and Chinese concubines. And he's very dictatorial, inflicting harsh punishment on anyone in Macao who disobeys or even questions his edicts."

"That's the fellow," Samuel said. "According to a rumor I heard just before I sailed—and most of the Americans and British in Whampoa accept it as a fact—this Dom Sebastian wants to marry Soong Chao's daughter."

Jonathan grew pale beneath his perennial tan. "That's not possible," he muttered.

Unaware that he was treading on sensitive ground, Samuel Green grinned. "According to another rumor, the emperor and his family are considering her as a wife for a fellow named Shaong Wei, a young cousin of the emperor. He supposedly drinks too much, which is rare in China, as I understand it. For the girl's sake I hope it doesn't work out that she's forced to marry him. As you know, the slightest wish expressed by the emperor is a command, and no Chinese would be able to turn down such a suggestion."

Ordinarily Jonathan was able to control and conceal his feelings, but his hands began to tremble and he stopped eating.

The sea captain continued to chatter, enjoying the gossip he had heard. "The permanent residents of the compound at Canton are placing their wagers on the Portuguese. What complicates the issue is that Soong's daughter supposedly is in love with someone else. Nobody seems to know whether he's Chinese or a foreigner, but everyone agrees that—for whatever the reason—he isn't in Canton. Anyway—and all this happened over three months ago, before I left—her father is said to have given her six months to marry this man. If she hasn't gone through with the ceremony by the end of the half-year, and if the emperor hasn't intervened, her father will give her to the Marquês de Braga."

Jeremiah understood the reason for his son's consternation and silently sympathized with him. All Ruth knew was that Jonathan was visibly upset.

Samuel shrugged. "Whatever happens, it shouldn't have any effect on our trade relations with Soong Chao."

"Can you be more specific?" Jonathan asked hoarsely. "I'd like to know the source of all this gossip."

Samuel was surprised by his intensity. "I can't cite any one person," he said. "The American and British factors, their assistants, and some of the captains in the Oriental trade who make their permanent headquarters at the compound all seem to know about it. While I was there, it was the principal topic of talk and speculation. Maybe because the girl herself is so pretty."

A thin white line formed around Jonathan's mouth.

Samuel turned to Ruth with a further explanation. "Foreigners who come to Canton don't really know Soong's daughter. Her huge bodyguard would lop off the head of anyone who tried to pass the time of day with her. But she's so beautiful that men fall in love with her at sight, even from a distance."

Suddenly Ruth understood why Jonathan had been so uneasy. He obviously was in love with the beautiful Chinese girl.

They went to the parlor for their coffee, and Jonathan was uncommunicative, apparently lost in thought. When Samuel Green departed, he accompanied the guest to the door, then returned and addressed his father.

"I won't have breakfast with you in the morning, Papa," he said. "I'm going to the yard at daybreak."

"So I suspected." Jeremiah rose from his chair, said good night to Ruth, and then paused for a moment at the threshold. "Call on me for any help I can give you in speeding your sailing, Jonnie," he said.

Jonathan began to pace, as he often did when he was deeply disturbed.

Common sense told Ruth Barker that she should retire, too, but she felt compelled to learn more. Perhaps she had been wrong to nurture the lifelong dream that the time would come when Jonathan would marry her, but now, when it appeared he might slip away from her again, she was prepared to fight for her own future happiness. Although she was not bold by nature, she told herself she had to let him know she cared for him.

Jonathan stopped pacing and stood in front of her. "I had hoped to stay at home long enough to help you become adjusted to routines here. I hope it won't impose a hardship on you if I sail for the East sooner than I had planned."

"I'm sure I can cope with any problems that might come up, and there's no need for you to worry about Julian." She paused, drew in her breath, and then blurted, "But I'm going to miss you, Jonnie."

Her tone caused him to peer at her more sharply, and the expression in her eyes told him what she was incapable of putting into words. The unexpected complication startled him, and as she was the last person on earth he wanted to hurt, he sat opposite her. "Let's have another cup of coffee, shall we?"

"The pot is cold. I'll get some hot coffee from the kitchen." Her heart hammering, Ruth quickly left the room.

By the time she returned and found Jonathan hastily scribbling notes on a sheet of foolscap, she had managed to regain her surface composure.

He put aside his notes, thanked her for the coffee, and said gently, "You and I have known each other for a long time."

"A very long time," Ruth agreed. How vividly she remembered taking her father's midday meal to him at the shipyard on Saturdays, when she had been in her early adolescence, in the hope of seeing Jonathan and exchanging a few words with him.

"You were Louise's friend. Her only friend," he said. "Just as Edmund and I were like brothers. And his loss had drawn me even closer to you." Although his mind was seething with the specifics of expediting his departure, he realized he needed to concentrate on this delicate confrontation. "Under ordinary circumstances, I reckon it might have been possible that you and I might have married one day in the future.''

She returned his gaze courageously and somehow summoned the nerve to say, ''But circumstances aren't ordinary.''

''You heard the talk that Samuel Green was repeating at the supper table,'' he said, ''so perhaps you've guessed the rest.''

Unable to trust her voice, she could only nod.

''I fell in love with Soong Lai-tse lu during the time I spent in the East, working for her father. And she fell in love with me. If you hadn't heard from Louise what I'm about to say, I'll tell you something in confidence right now. Louise and I were—indiscreet. Before I went off to China. Julian was born while I was away and Louise and I were married in private on the very day I came home. But for her sake—and Julian's—the families put up a front by letting it be known we had been married before I sailed.''

''I knew,'' Ruth said flatly.

''I never wrote Lai-tse lu because I didn't know how to tell her what happened. But now I've got to reach Canton in three months—assuming that Samuel's story about her father setting a deadline is correct, as I'm afraid it is.''

Ruth clung to a thin thread of hope. ''What will happen if you miss the deadline and find her already married?''

''I can't allow that to happen,'' he replied grimly. ''My new clipper is the fastest ship ever built, and somehow I've got to race her to Canton in time. You see, I'm positive, in spite of our long separation, that Lai-tse lu still loves me the way I love her.''

Jonathan stood abruptly, went to her, and gripped her shoulder. ''You're a wonderful woman, Ruth, and I wish you the happiness that I can only pray I'll find for myself.'' He stalked out of the room quickly.

She sat for a long time, then placed the empty coffee cups and pot on a tray, which she took to the kitchen. Realizing she would not be able to get to sleep, she stayed up a long time carefully washing and drying the cups, saucers, and pot. Finally, faced with the knowledge that she could not linger indefinitely, she picked up her oil lamp and slowly mounted the stairs.

When she reached her own chamber, she was still reluctant to retire, so she sat at the window, staring out at the night-black sea that had taken one husband from her and was denying her the man she loved.

A tap sounded at the door, and Wu-ling came into the room, concern and sympathy in her dark eyes. "Missy Ruth sad," she said, deliberately speaking in English, which Ruth was taking so much time and effort to teach her.

Inclining her head, Ruth made no reply.

The young girl came to her, knelt beside her, and hugged her. "The man Missy Ruth wants loves another," Wu-ling said.

It was astonishing that someone in her early teens could be so observant, and Ruth wondered if the Chinese girl was endowed with preternatural wisdom. "Have I been all that obvious?"

Wu-ling shook her head. "Nobody else see. But I see. Missy Ruth has been so good and kind to me, and I see. I see how she love Mister Jonathan. But Mister Jonathan love someone else."

Looking into the girl's intent eyes, Ruth embraced her, then laughed harshly. "No one has ever died of a broken heart. The ailment is uncomfortable, but it isn't fatal."

Wu-ling rose effortlessly from the floor, moved the oil lamp closer, and placed a small table in front of her benefactress and tutor.

Ruth sensed a feeling of excitement in the girl and looked at her curiously.

Reaching into the pocket of her new, Western-style bathrobe, Wu-ling giggled as she removed a bundle of smooth sticks, tied together with a tasseled cord of silk.

Taking the bundle from her, Ruth saw that the sticks, all of them approximately four inches long, were dyed every color of the rainbow.

Wu-ling giggled, then regained her composure. "My grandmother, great-grandmother of David, taught me ancient art of telling future with sticks. I brought sticks with me from Middle Kingdom."

Ruth was in no mood for a game of fortune telling and firmly placed the bundle on the small table. But the Chinese girl refused to be put off. She carefully removed the cord and, extending the bundle, directed, "Missy Ruth close eyes and pick out one stick."

Trying to humor her, Ruth did as she was bidden, and when she opened her eyes she saw she had taken a stick of a pale pink color.

"Put on table and do again," Wu-ling commanded.

Ruth ultimately took six sticks from the bundle, the darkest plum-colored, the lightest an off-white. Only now did it occur to her that they were made of ivory and obviously had been prized in a family as poor as Wu-ling's.

The young Chinese girl bent over the table, her eyes serious and her manner intense as she arranged the half-dozen sticks in a variety of patterns, each time studying the results and then shuffling them again.

Bemused in spite of her heartache, Ruth watched her, guessing that she was seeking the most harmonious color combinations.

At last Wu-ling raised her head, and now her eyes were shining. "Soon the grief in Missy Ruth's heart will become dry, just as kernels of rice dry in the strong sun of summer."

Ruth would have sworn she was not superstitious, but the solemn pronouncement intrigued her. "Why is that?"

"Soon there will be new love in Missy Ruth's life," the Chinese girl announced.

Not wanting to hurt her feelings, Ruth refrained from smiling, but a note of incredulity crept into her voice as she said, "Really, Wu-ling! Do you mean to tell me that I'm going to fall in love with someone else?"

The girl gathered the ivory sticks, put them into the bundle, and carefully retied the silk cord. She replied in her native Cantonese dialect, then struggled to translate what she had just said into English. "Love have many faces," she declared cryptically, and swept out of the room before she could be questioned again.

Jonathan and his two mates worked feverishly to prepare the *Lai-tse lu* for her long voyage to the East. The cargo of lightweight New England looms, in such great demand in China, was carefully loaded in the hold. Supplies of salt fish and jerked meat, flour and bacon and hardtack were taken on board, and the markets of New London and its environs were scoured for the lemons and limes that would ward off scurvy, which seamen dreaded. The sailmaker supervised the storage of a spare suit of sail, medicines were placed in a locked cupboard in the master's spacious cabin, and livestock to be slaughtered and consumed on the voyage were taken to a special pen on the deck.

First mate Homer Ellison and second mate Elijah Wilbor, both of them bachelors, went on board the night prior to the sailing, as did Oliver, the boatswain, and the unmarried members of the crew. Additional seamen had been given bonuses to enlist at the last moment so that two sailing crews would be on board, and the clipper would sail with a complement of three officers and fifty men. Never before had this new type of vessel, which Jonathan had been so influential in developing and designing, carried so many seamen, the master being determined to reach Canton in the shortest possible time.

It was still dark when married members of the company arrived and bade farewell to the wives and children who had accompanied them to the Rakehell and Boynton wharf that jutted out into the water of the Thames. Members of the Rakehell family arrived in two carriages a short time before daybreak, and Jonathan's sea chest was taken to his cabin, along with a case of books and several cartons of jellies, preserved fruits, and other delicacies intended for his own consumption.

Jeremiah Rakehell followed his son out of the first carriage, and little Julian jumped to the ground unaided. David tried to follow his cousin's example, but the distance was so great that he hesitated, and Ruth Barker, the last to emerge, picked him up and carried him. In the second carriage were Jonathan's sister, Judith Rakehell Walker, her two children, and Wu-ling. Bradford Walker was nowhere to be seen, and the embarrassed Judith could offer no explanation for her husband's absence.

Jonathan was relieved that his brother-in-law had not seen fit to be present. Brad's hostility toward him was so apparent that his presence would have made everyone in the small party uncomfortable.

Under routine circumstances the sailing of a major Rakehell and Boynton ship to a destination halfway around the world would have been a gala occasion. Dock workers, office staff, and the carpenters and shipwrights who had built the clipper would have been on hand to wish her godspeed. A volunteer band would have been present to play lively airs, and hundreds of New London's residents would have come to the wharf for the festivities.

But this was no ordinary departure. The *Lai-tse lu* would sail on the early tide, and most people in town were not yet awake. Aware of the rapid passage of time, Jonathan dispensed with ceremonies. He took the letter Wu-ling had written to her grandmother in Canton, her only living relative, and he promised faithfully not only to deliver it but to read it to her.

After hugging his niece and nephew, he turned to kiss his sister. "Fair weather and godspeed, Jonnie," she said. "May you reach Canton in time."

"I will, Judy, God willing," he replied, then scooped up his son and David, kissing each of them.

Ruth stepped forward self-consciously. "Give this to Lai-tse lu for me, please," she said, and opening a small book, showed him a dried rose that had been pressed between its pages.

He took the book from her and kissed her lightly on the cheek. "This means more to me than you know," he told her, "and Lai-tse lu will treasure it, too."

Jeremiah Rakehell's farewell to his son was brief, almost brusque. There was so much they could have said, but they knew each other so well that words were unnecessary. "You sail on a fair wind, Jonnie," the older man said as they gripped hands.

"I do, sir." Jonathan grinned at him for an instant, settled his tricorne firmly on his head, and carrying the book with the pressed rose in it under one arm, walked with long strides down the wharf.

Oliver's silver whistle piped the captain aboard, the shrill notes rising and falling.

As Jonathan made his way to the quarterdeck, where the officers awaited him, Homer Ellison lost no time and ordered the topsails and jibs set. Then he and Elijah exchanged salutes with the master.

"I'll take the first watch, gentlemen," Jonathan told them, and directed Oliver to cast off.

There were no other ships in the estuary as the clipper began to move downstream, and Jonathan had elected to sail

61

without the assistance of one of the steam-propelled tugs which were now in use on the waterway. Day was breaking, the ship was before the wind, and sailing conditions were ideal.

"Loose and make all plain sail!" Jonathan said. "Haul aft the sheets!"

The entire crew, at sailing stations, went to work.

The orders came more rapidly now. "Away aloft! Man tops'l sheets! Haul taut! Let fall tops'ls and courses! Sheet home!"

Flapping in the wind until they began to fill, the great sails began to spread about the graceful clipper's decks.

The yards were braced up to an angle of about twenty degrees, and the *Lai-tse lu* gathered speed as she headed into Long Island Sound. She would sail past Montauk Point at the eastern end of Long Island into the open Atlantic, then head south, following the coastline of the United States into the Caribbean on the first leg of the long voyage.

The clipper began to pitch and roll slightly in the "corkscrew" motion familiar to every seagoing man. Green water frothed in her wake, masses of billowing, white canvas soared above the deck, and Jonathan, inhaling the scent of salt air that he loved so well, knew he was on his way.

I'm coming, Lai-tse lu, he said silently. Wait for me, my one and only love.

III

Charles Boynton stood at the windows of his office in the London shipyard of Rakehell and Boynton, on the Southwark shore of the great River Thames, and looked at the crowded buildings on the opposite bank. Before the day ended he would create a sensation in the financial district, called the City, and he thoroughly enjoyed his feeling of triumph.

A year younger than his cousin Jonathan, almost as tall and his build equally trim, Charles was one of the most handsome, dashing young men in England. And, according to the young ladies whose charms failed to impress him, he was only too well aware of his magnetism. He was willing to concede that he had a high opinion of himself, but today that view was well deserved.

Lying at her berth was one of the newer Rakehell and Boynton clippers, the *Elizabeth,* named for Charles's sister by adoption. It was too bad that Elizabeth Boynton herself was off at school in France; he knew she would share his feeling of pure, fierce joy.

In brief, he had accomplished the impossible, thanks to his and Jonathan's close friendship with the Fat Dutchman, the shrewdest of international traders, who made his headquarters in Djakarta, capital of the Netherlands East Indies on the island of Java. Before sundown every banker and merchant in London would be hailing his accomplishment as a stroke of genius.

Charles adjusted the cuffs of his fine lawn shirt, slipped into his sharply tailored coat of worsted, and checked his hand-sewn boots to make certain they carried their customary sheen. Wherever he went today, he would be the center of all eyes.

A tap sounded at his door, and his father's private clerk stood in the entrance. "If you please, Mr. Charles," he said, "Sir Alan wants to see you at your earliest convenience."

"I find it convenient right now, thanks," Charles said with a grin, and hurried off down the corridor to accept his father's congratulations.

Some of Sir Alan Boynton's competitors, obviously jealous of his great success, called him the Buddha. The nickname was unfair, although it was true he was rotund, had a receding hairline, sleepy eyes, and a habit of folding his hands over his considerable paunch. But there was nothing of a Buddha's gentleness in Sir Alan's aggressive, abrasive nature.

Glancing up as his son entered his spacious corner office, in which models of a dozen London-based Rakehell and Boynton ships stood on a corner table, Sir Alan gestured toward a chair. "Sit down."

Noting that he was not smiling, Charles sat.

"I hope you're free to have luncheon with me at the club," Sir Alan said.

Charles had planned to celebrate his triumph by paying a noon visit to an amenable brunette for whom he had a passing fancy, but a rare invitation from his father was the equivalent of a command, and the brunette would have to wait. "I'll be delighted, sir," he said.

Sir Alan grunted. "You look rather pleased with yourself today."

Charles bridled. He had expected praise, and the lack of it galled him. "I have good reason to be pleased. In case you haven't heard, Father, the *Elizabeth* arrived from Djakarta early this morning with her hold crammed with black pepper! Black pepper, sir! More precious than gold—or the accursed opium our competitors take to China. All of Great Britain, Europe, and the United States crave black pepper. It comes only from the Dutch East Indies, every last peppercorn of it, and for the first time in more than two hundred years the monopoly of the Dutch has been broken. The first time, but far from the last."

The older man's eyelids drooped, a sure sign that he was annoyed.

His son's anger flared still higher. "Even by selling it at

fifteen percent less than the Dutch charge our wholesale dealers, we're going to clear a bloody fortune on that cargo.''

"I'm well aware of our situation," Sir Alan said dryly. "I've just had a visit from Lord Trumbull, of the Foreign Office. The Netherlands Minister was waiting for him when he arrived at work this morning and has already delivered a violent protest.''

Charles laughed aloud and rubbed his hands together.

"Her Majesty's Government," his father said severely, "are asking us—formally—to reveal how and where we acquired that cargo.''

"Her Majesty's Government may go to the devil," Charles said. "Neither the master of the *Elizabeth* nor I—the only two men in London who know where we got our hands on that pepper—will reveal any information to the Foreign Office or anyone else. We fully expected the Dutch to buzz like angry hornets.''

"Lord Trumbull expects you to call on him this afternoon," Sir Alan said.

"With pleasure, sir. But I shall tell him nothing. We've broken no laws.''

"Granted, Charles, but the Foreign Office is embarrassed.''

"Queen Victoria pays her officials fair wages to compensate them for the delicacy of their personal feelings, Father. I assure you I shall take a firm stand. I might even be impelled to remind Lord Trumbull that the companies picking up opium in India and smuggling it into China are breaking Chinese law. But the emperor has no envoy stationed in London, so the Foreign Office closes its eyes to the nastiness of the opium smugglers. The Royal Navy has a squadron on station off Whampoa, and one of these days we'll become involved in a war with China over the opium question!''

"I prefer to let that subject wait until we're at lunch," his father said. "Are you sure you'll reveal nothing about your source of pepper to the Foreign Office?''

"Only fools are positive, sir, but I'm quite sure.''

A reluctant laugh rumbled upward from the deeper regions of Sir Alan's belly. "I must say, Charles, you've become as cool and contained as anyone I've ever known in business.''

Charles knew the faint compliment was the only accolade his father would give him, but it was enough. "They're saying I take after you, sir."

Sir Alan chuckled again. "I must admit I was rather pleased by a remark that was repeated to me at the club the other day. 'The old one is a pirate, and the young one is a cutthroat.' How does that strike you?"

"I'm flattered," Charles said, and stood.

"Join me here in an hour," his father said, "and meantime you might want to warn the master of the *Elizabeth* that attempts will be made to persuade him to talk out of turn."

"I've already taken that precaution, and you may rest assured he'll keep mum. I've reminded him that his share of the cargo—and of future pepper cargoes—is one-eighth of our total profits. After a few more voyages he'll be in a position to retire for life." Charles strolled back to his own office.

Sir Alan shook his head. Charles had matured so much since he and Jonathan had gone off on their first voyage to the Orient together that it was unfair to think of him as a boy. He had become a responsible businessman as well as an exceptionally competent ship's master when he elected to go to sea himself. So he deserved to be treated with the respect he had earned, even though he continued to lead a wild and unorthodox social life, sleeping with the town's more expensive strumpets and, on occasion, drinking more than was good for him. Ah, well, perhaps they could reach an understanding at luncheon, which was the reason Sir Alan had issued the invitation.

At noon they descended to Sir Alan's new carriage, with his baronet's crest on the door, and the coachman, negotiating in traffic with skill, drove them across London Bridge, then took them to the club by way of Fleet Street and the Strand.

The gentlemen's club, a rabbit warren of small, cramped rooms, was one of the oldest establishments of its kind in London, and as father and son made their way to the cavernous dining hall, the largest chamber in the five-story building not far from St. James's Palace, men engaged in conversation stopped speaking and stared at them. Others, seated in overstuffed chairs as they enjoyed a premeal drink, peered at them over the tops of their newspapers.

"I see the news of your exploit has made the rounds," Sir Alan murmured.

Charles nodded and held his head high. This was a moment to be savored.

His father led him to a small table for two in a corner, a signal to fellow members that they intended to hold a private talk and did not want to be disturbed.

Sir Alan indicated that he was not lacking a sense of humor. "It might be appropriate to start the meal with two small glasses of Dutch gin," he said.

As they sipped their drinks, they discussed family matters.

"I had a message from your mother just before we left the office," Sir Alan said. "Elizabeth arrived home from France this morning."

Charles knew his sister had not been expected until later in the week. "Nothing has gone wrong, I hope."

"On the contrary, she took the lead in persuading the headmistress to dismiss the English girls for their holiday several days early." Shaking his head and chuckling, the older man added, "You'd think the girl had been born a Boynton. She has my tough hide and Jessica's Rakehell drive. She's every bit as incorrigible as you, Charles, and may the Lord pity the man she marries."

"He'll need to be quite a man."

"The message also said a family letter had arrived from Uncle Jeremiah. Jonathan has sailed for Cathay in his new clipper."

Charles felt as though an electric current had shot through his body. Of all members of the English branch of the family, only he knew of Jonathan's romance with Soong Lai-tse lu, and he was elated for his cousin's sake. But, knowing of his father's bigoted attitude toward people of other races, he preferred to let Uncle Jeremiah break that aspect of the news to his parents.

Sir Alan ordered briskly for both of them, and soon they were served their first course, two platters of raw oysters. Seemingly concentrating on his food, the older man spoke quietly but earnestly. "There's something I want to discuss with you. I daresay you know that the mothers of eligible

67

daughters regard you as the catch of London. Their interest in you will be doubled when they learn of your pepper coup.''

Charles instantly became wary. No young lady in London would want him as a husband when she learned he had a son who was one-fourth Chinese. And he had no interest in the eligible young ladies, either, because he fully intended to bring David to London at the first opportunity and rear him openly as a son and heir. The eligible ladies of London were as nearsightedly prejudiced as his father.

''In addition to what you'll inherit as my principal heir,'' his father said, ''you've scored some brilliant successes in your own right. That's why Uncle Jeremiah and I were pleased to admit you to the company as junior partner. Do you have any notion of your overall financial worth?''

''I haven't taken the trouble to figure it out,'' the younger man replied. ''I've been too busy expanding my end of the business.''

''Well, you aren't yet a millionaire, but you're not far from it. All of which makes you a very attractive target. Only the other day Lady Rachel Hubert's father hinted to me rather broadly that he wouldn't be opposed to a marriage.''

Charles made a wry face. Lady Rachel was pretty and vivacious, but she was a snob whose interests in life were limited to the activities of her own, small social set.

''You needn't turn up your nose at her,'' Sir Alan said, becoming slightly belligerent in spite of his determination to remain calm. ''Her father is an earl, you know.''

''For all I care he could be a duke. No, thank you.''

''Well, then.'' His father tried again. ''I believe you're fairly well acquainted with Sir Robert Spencer's daughter, Margaret. Sir Robert owns some of the largest storage warehouses in London, you know, so—strictly from a business point of view—it would be a natural union.''

''Business isn't that important.'' Margaret Spencer, as Charles had ample personal reason to know, plunged enthusiastically into affairs with men who attracted her.

His father was not yet ready to give up, and a harsh note crept into his voice as he said, ''You could do worse than to consider Diane Lewis. She's quite handsome, is she not?''

Charles's nod lacked enthusiasm.

But Sir Alan persisted. ''Her mother is one of your mother's closest friends. The social standing of the family is impeccable. And Philip Lewis's woolen mills earn an income on the same level as mine. The union would be very solid."

Charles would never forget a long, bitter discussion he had held with Diane years earlier, when she had argued vigorously in favor of the retention of slavery in Great Britain's West Indian colonies and the United States. He could imagine how she would react to the prospect of rearing a Eurasian stepson. "Diane and I have known each other most of our lives, it's true," he said, "but we have little in common."

His father's frustration was momentarily relieved when the serving of their main course afforded him a temporary respite. He stared at the steak and kidney pudding. "Dear me. I seem to remember your mother saying at breakfast that we're having this very dish for dinner this evening."

The son thought hard. "I can't recall for certain, but I believe she did."

"Oh, well. No matter."

For once Charles was in complete agreement with his father, as his indifferent shrug indicated. The men of the family regarded so many things as more important than the food they ate—as long as they ate well.

Sir Alan began to eat, then paused to sip his claret. "I'm not trying to drive you into a corner or dictate to you, my boy. You're old enough and responsible enough to lead your own life in any manner you choose. But that's my whole point. Your mother and I believe the time has come for you to settle down and have children. You'll need a son or two to carry on after you. The way our business is expanding demands it."

Charles was strongly tempted to tell him that he already had a son, and that Ruth Barker's letters indicated the boy was exceptionally bright. But he would be courting catastrophe if he revealed too much too soon. His father needed to be prepared for the announcement, which meant he would be obliged to confide in his mother and seek her help, even though he was afraid his news might upset her badly.

"Let me think about your advice, sir," he said, evading the inevitable showdown and berating himself for a lack of courage. "What you suggest is sensible and requires a great deal of thought."

Sir Alan was pleased. He had been afraid that his son

would reject the idea of marriage, and he had deliberately chosen the club as the place to hold their talk because he had known that Charles would control his temper here. Jessica would be happy, too, that he would at least give consideration to the possibility of taking a wife. His optimism soaring, he ordered a savory instead of a sweet for a final course, broiled herring roe on toast, which both of them liked.

There was nothing to be lost by launching into another touchy subject, and Sir Alan took the plunge. "There's something else I want to discuss with you. A number of our directors, including Lord Bates and Mr. Simpson, are becoming restless. They see the huge profits our competitors are earning in the opium trade, and they're pressing me to follow their example. I'm thinking of taking the matter up with Jeremiah to see if he'd now be willing to enter the opium trade."

Charles stiffened. "You know Uncle Jeremiah said he'd have no part in the filthy traffic, and neither will I or Jonathan. I've seen what opium does to the poor devils who become addicted to it. I can assure you that if opium were introduced into this country there would be a public outcry that would soon make its sale as illegal here as it is in China."

Sir Alan smiled indulgently. "The very nature of the British character would prevent our people from using the stuff. The Chinese are weaker and consequently lack the moral fiber to resist it."

His son knew he actually believed what he was saying. "Permit me to contradict you, sir. What you say is rubbish. Opium is an exceptionally powerful drug, and national character is irrelevant. There are Englishmen in Macao who are addicted to it and have become human wrecks as pitiful as the poor Chinese who use it as a way of finding escape from grinding poverty."

"You've made two long visits to the East, and I've never been there. So I am not in a position to deny your observations." His father took refuge in pomposity. "I'm merely trying to retain a perspective as a businessman. The position you've taken is denying Rakehell and Boynton huge profits, and our stockholders are quite right to demand that we engage in a very lucrative trade."

"Our profits on the pepper cargo that arrived this morning should silence them."

"For the moment, perhaps, but they'll soon be hammering at my door again."

"Let them hammer! I'm not threatening you, Father. I merely state as a flat fact that the day Rakehell and Boynton enter the opium trade, Jonathan and I will leave the company and form one of our own. That's how strongly we feel about dealing in opium!"

That afternoon Charles stayed late at the shipyard because he wanted to supervise the unloading and storage of the valuable black pepper himself. His father had departed much earlier, and night had fallen by the time he drove in a company carriage to the Boynton town house in fashionable Belgravia. All of the homes here were similar, each of three or four stories, painted white, with handsome Greek columns decorating the entrances.

"Sir Alan and Lady Boynton are in the second floor sitting room, Mr. Charles," the butler told him.

Realizing that his parents would be finishing their predinner sack, Charles mounted the marble stairs to the second floor two at a time.

As he entered the sitting room, a tall girl with long, blond hair and blue eyes of startling intensity rose to greet him. "I was beginning to wonder if you were staying away because you knew I had come home," Elizabeth Boynton said.

Charles greeted his sister with a kiss, then held her at arm's length as he inspected her. "Oh, we are growing up, aren't we? Very modishly dressed in the latest French fashions. Much more than the beginnings of what could become a perfect figure if one curbed one's appetite for chocolates. And I do believe I detect signs of lip rogue and that black substance, whatever it is called, on the lashes."

"Don't tease her, Charles," Jessica Boynton said.

"Let him natter, Mama," Elizabeth said, demonstrating her newly acquired aplomb. "I'd be disappointed if he didn't try to tease me, you know."

"Touché," Charles replied, and poured himself a glass of sack from a crystal decanter.

Jessica Rakehell Boynton looked at her children in turn and obviously was proud of both, the adopted daughter as much as the son she had given birth to. Jessica herself had the sharp Rakehell planes in her face and the angular figure that was a common family trait, but she was not lacking in femininity. In spite of her direct, often blunt approach, she could be soft and gentle on occasion, and she took obvious pleasure in her children. "Don't tarry over your drink, Charles. Your father is attending a meeting this evening, so we'll be dining in a few moments."

"Don't hold off on my account, Mother," he replied. "I'll bring my glass to the table." He turned to his sister. "You've truly blossomed in France, child."

"I was going to congratulate you on the pepper cargo that Papa told us arrived today," Elizabeth replied. "But if you insist on patting my head, I may choose to ignore you. Permanently."

"Bravo," Sir Alan said. "The only women who can handle Charles are those who put him properly in his place."

The butler announced that dinner was served, and the family adjourned to the dining room.

Charles noted that Elizabeth took only a token portion of her mutton and barley soup, and he did not tease her again. It was heartening to see that she was truly becoming more adult and had the sense to avoid fattening food. "I understand you had a letter from Uncle Jeremiah today, and that Jonathan has sailed for China in the *Lai-tse lu*. What other news is there?" Charles asked his mother.

"Jeremiah tells us that Ruth Barker, the widow of your former shipmate, has moved into the Rakehell house to look after Julian while his father is away," Jessica said.

That meant David had moved in with the Rakehells, too, and Charles was pleased. He knew he would soon receive a letter from Ruth on the matter.

"Oh, dear," Elizabeth said

Her parents and brother looked at her.

"I don't remember Ruth Barker. Is she pretty, Charles? Is she charming and personable? I hope not!"

"She's all those things," Charles said. "Why should it matter, child?"

"I am no longer a child," Elizabeth said with severity. "And you're quite dense. Jonathan is a widower now, which makes him vulnerable, especially if there's an attractive widow living in his house."

Sir Alan and Jessica exchanged a quick glance. "By now," the latter said, "I would have hoped you'd outgrown your fascination with Jonathan."

"Never, Mama," the girl said quickly. "I was either seven or eight when I made up my mind to marry him someday, and nothing has ever happened to change my mind. Remember he's not my blood relative. I was in despair when he married Louise, and if he should marry this Barker woman—or anyone else—before I'm old enough, I shall put poison into her soup!"

Sir Alan laughed indulgently. Jessica was not amused, however. It was time that the girl began to develop an interest in boys who were members of her own generation.

Charles, who knew the purpose of his cousin's voyage, did not look at Elizabeth but concentrated on his soup.

The girl was shrewd enough to guess there might be a reason behind his silence. "*Lai-tse lu* is an odd name for a clipper ship," she said. "Obviously it's a Chinese saying or name. What does it mean?"

Charles worded his reply carefully. "I'm sure Jonathan will give a full explanation at the appropriate time," he said.

They were interrupted by the serving maids, who brought them steak and kidney pudding, and father and son exchanged quick, guilty grins.

"You're impossible, both of you. Is this what you had for lunch at the club today?"

"I can't remember, Mother," Charles said. "We were discussing such important matters that we ate without paying much attention to our meal."

"Quite true," his father added. "Among other things, my dear, we were talking about the hope you and I share that Charles will marry soon."

"Ha!" Elizabeth said. "What girl in her right mind would have him?"

"My greatest regret," Charles told her, "is that I named my new clipper after you. It's an honor you don't deserve."

Sir Alan frowned. Mindful of his son's promise to think about the possibility of marriage, he didn't want a prolonged discussion that would cause Charles to change his mind. So he quickly changed the subject. "We also discussed my serious problem of the demands by the company directors that we enter the opium trade, and I told Charles I intend to take the matter up with Jeremiah.''

Everyone at the table gave him total attention.

"I made it clear,'' Charles said, his smile fading, "that Jonnie and I would leave Rakehell and Boynton to form our own company rather than carry opium in any of our clippers. Or if any of the older ships in the fleet took opium to China.''

Elizabeth looked at her brother with genuine admiration. "Good for you, Charles. Anyone who would smuggle opium into China is loathesome.''

"There will be no need for you and Jonathan to make such a sacrifice, Charles,'' Jessica said with quiet intensity. "If necessary, I shall spend every thruppeny bit of my own to buy the stock of any director who tries to force Rakehell and Boynton to engage in the disgusting opium business!'' Her opinions on the subject had changed of late, and she no longer thought her son's attitude unrealistic. The opium trade was immoral, and she was certain her brother, Jeremiah, continued to feel that way, too.

Sir Alan knew precisely where his whole family stood. Jessica's Rakehell conscience had influenced her thinking on the matter; she was as idealistic as Jeremiah and Jonathan. It would probably be useless to reason with his brother-in-law, and he could only hope the passage of time would cause the family to change their minds. In the meantime, additional cargoes of pepper from the Dutch East Indies might persuade the board of directors to mute their protests.

A deep-dish plum pie ended the meal, and Sir Alan did not linger over his customary port and a West Indian cigar, but hurried off to his meeting. Jessica returned to the sitting room with her children, Charles carrying his own glass of port, and after obtaining his mother's permission to smoke, he lit one of the small cheroots that he favored.

"Don't tell me you're actually intending to spend an entire evening at home,'' Elizabeth said to her brother.

"Oddly enough, I am,'' he replied. "In honor of your homecoming.''

"Thank you,'' she said with sincerity. "But don't stay on my account. I shall be on my way to bed in a few minutes.''

"Really? Don't tell me that life in a French boarding school has given you an intelligent habit.''

"In the dormitory," she said, "we whisper half the night, solving the problems of the universe. Especially anything to do with males. But the Channel crossing last night was miserable. The sea was choppy, and I'm the member of this family of sailors who becomes violently seasick. So I didn't sleep a wink."

"Even experienced seamen sometimes become ill," Charles told her. "Occasionally it happens to Jonathan and to me."

"Never Jonathan!" Elizabeth said.

He ignored the interruption. "The commander of our China squadron, Admiral Sir William Alexander, told me on my last visit to Whampoa that he sometimes becomes ill when he first puts to sea after spending a long period on land."

"In that case I'm in distinguished company and refuse to feel ashamed of myself." The girl went to her mother and kissed her. "Forgive me if I collapse. Good night, Mama, and the same to you, dear Brother."

Charles grinned after she left the room. "It's astonishing, you know, but she really is growing up. She'll be a heartbreaker once she outgrows her nonsense about Jonnie."

"Oh, she'll forget him fast enough," Jessica said cheerfully, "as soon as she finds some boy who sparks her interest. Now, as for you, Charles, there's no need to keep me company. If you had previous plans for the evening, keep them. I'm reading Henry Longfellow's new book, *Hyperion,* the first romance in prose he's written, and I'm fascinated by it."

"I hate to interrupt your reading, Mother, but I need your help and advice."

She hadn't had such a request from him since he had been in his mid-teens, more than a decade earlier. So she raised an eyebrow, then said quietly, "Let me get my needlepoint, and we'll have a chat."

When she returned to the sitting room a few moments later with her frame, yarn, and needles, she noted that he had refilled his port glass.

Charles was somewhat nervous. "I'm sure Father has already told you about our chat at luncheon," he said. "Just as I'm sure you and he have discussed possible wives for me. Diane, Margaret, and so on."

Jessica nodded. Apparently what Alan had told her was

true: Charles was taking the suggestion seriously. "I gather you found none of the girls he suggested suitable."

He cleared his throat. "That's beside the point, in a manner of speaking. I want to tell you a little story, Mother. A true story. When Jonnie and I first went to China, I had an affair with the—the most expensive courtesan there. Her father was an English seaman and her mother was Chinese. Her name was Alice Wong."

His mother tried to speak calmly. "I know that you must have had your dalliances, but they have nothing to do with marriage."

"I'd give the idea damned serious thought if she were still alive, but she's dead, unfortunately. She gave her life to save mine on my second visit there."

"I see." She listened carefully, aware that he was under a great strain.

"Shortly after her death, I discovered—on that same visit—that Alice had given birth to a son. My son."

His mother gasped, then managed to regain her composure.

"She named him David because she had been studying the Psalms. He was living in a typical Cantonese hovel with his grandmother and Alice's young half-sister, Wu-ling. I brought David to New London, with Wu-ling as his nursemaid. Ruth Barker took them in, and I've been paying her to take care of them. I'm sure they moved into Uncle Jeremiah's house when Ruth went there to look after Julian during Jonnie's absence."

"Just imagine," was all she could say. Then she thought to add, "Jeremiah didn't mention a word of all this to me. You'd think he'd be candid with his only sister!"

"Uncle Jeremiah has been discreet. But that's neither here nor there. David is my son, Mother; I've adopted him formally and had him baptized in New London, and now I want to bring him up myself. I want him recognized by you and Father as my son. I'm proud of him, just as I was proud of my relations with his mother."

Jessica pondered for a time. "Even if it would accomplish something positive to scold you, Charles, I wouldn't. What's done is done. I didn't know the girl, so I must rely on your judgment of her, and if you say she was a person of character,

76

that's quite good enough for me. As for your son, of course you want him with you!''

"You do realize he's one-quarter Chinese, Mother.''

Jessica glowered at him. "If you think that matters, you don't know me very well, Charles. You're speaking of my grandson!''

He grinned at her.

She smiled in return, and the rapport they had known throughout the better part of his life was reconfirmed.

"I don't believe Father will be as broad-minded,'' he said.

Her smile faded. "Quite so.''

"I've been tortured by this separation from my son, Mother. Unnecessarily tortured. The *Elizabeth* is scheduled to sail to New London on a regular cargo run next week, after her hull has been scraped and repainted. I intend to be on board. I'm going to bring David and Wu-ling back to London with me.''

"I would be happy to welcome them to this house,'' she said.

"Would Father?''

"I—I don't know.''

"Father and I quarrel about anything and everything, as you know only too well. The old lion and young lion resenting each other. So I don't dare mention David's existence to him. He'd explode, I'd lash back at him, and before we were done we'd create a permanent rift between us.''

"So you want me to tell him about David?''

"I hate to impose on you, Mother.''

"It's hardly an imposition. Of course I'll do it. I'm the only person alive who can manage your father. And that only on occasion. But I can't guarantee I can win his acceptance.''

"If I must,'' Charles said, "I'm willing and able to buy a house of my own and live there with my son.''

"Who would look after him?''

"Wu-ling, of course.''

Jessica shook her head. "An adolescent Chinese girl making her first trip to England? You're not being realistic, Charles.''

"Then I'll hire a governess, a housekeeper, and a cook. I'm sure you realize I'm well able to afford the establishment of my own household.''

77

"To be sure, but it would be wrong when there are so many empty rooms here. What's more," she added wistfully, "you'd be depriving me of the daily company of my grandson."

"I'd be far happier to bring David and Wu-ling here, Mother. Provided Father will accept the situation."

Jessica sighed, and for a time she was silent. "Let me be as honest with you as you've been with me. Your father would swallow your position far more easily, and so would everyone we know here, if you had a wife, Charles. Someone who could be a mother to your son and a counselor to the Chinese girl. I gather she's approximately your sister's age."

"More or less the same."

"The boarding school in France is helping Elizabeth to mature, but I can't imagine giving her any real responsibility. I doubt if your Wu-ling would be able to discharge a heavy load, either. She needs someone who will guide and help her. I'll gladly do what I can, naturally, but I'm too old. The job needs a far younger woman."

"I'm forced to agree with you, Mother. But the problem seems insurmountable. Father rattled off a list of young ladies you and he think eligible. Not one of them would willingly accept a stepson who is one-quarter Chinese, and you know it. The upper classes in this country are so insulated from the outside world that they're the worst snobs on earth. I couldn't tolerate it if my wife secretly felt contempt for my son and patronized him!"

"You're right, I'm afraid, and I'll admit the problem is difficult. But the fact remains that you'll have far smoother sailing if David has a mother and Wu-ling a big sister."

Charles's smile was painful. "I've never yet performed any miracles, but I'll do what I can, Mother."

"That's all I can ask. And after you're well on your way to America, I'll break the news to your father. May the Almighty defend all of us!"

Charles could have taken command of the *Elizabeth* himself, but he preferred to leave the master who had sailed the clipper to Djakarta and back in charge. The voyage of no more than three weeks' duration would give him uninterrupted time

78

to attend to huge quantities of paper work that he found the least appealing of his duties. Consequently, he sailed as a passenger.

The lure of the sea was almost too much for him, and at first he spent several hours each day on the quarterdeck, always going there when the weather was foul. That was his privilege as one of the clipper's owners, but he realized he was being unfair to the captain, who had the sole responsibility for sailing the ship. So he curbed his natural impulses, spent the better part of his time working in his cabin, and when he went on deck, confined himself to harmless pacing. By avoiding the quarterdeck, he was neither making a nuisance of himself nor placing the master's authority in jeopardy.

On the twentieth day of the voyage the clipper, as sound as the others that Jonathan had built, rounded Montauk Point, entered Long Island Sound, and soon thereafter reached the Rakehell and Boynton docks. Minutes later Charles arrived at the headquarters building and went straight to his uncle's office.

Jeremiah Rakehell jumped to his feet when he saw his lean, tanned nephew standing on the threshold. "Good Lord, Charles!" he exclaimed. "I knew the *Elizabeth* was due, but I had no idea you'd be on board!"

"I decided to come when she returned from Djakarta, so there was no time to notify you, Uncle Jeremiah." They shook hands vigorously, and Charles reached into his pocket for separate letters from his parents. "I've come to discuss ways we can make more clippers available for the pepper and spice trade with the Fat Dutchman. And most of all, I've come because of David. How is he?"

"Thriving. Ruth does wonders for him, and Wu-ling is a great help." Jeremiah waved his nephew to a chair. "Have you told Jessica and Alan about David?"

"My mother knows. And will accept him."

"Of course. What about your father?"

"Mother is telling him while I'm here."

Jeremiah nodded but made no comment, and then glanced at the ship's clock that stood on the mantel above his office fireplace. "David and Julian should be awake after their naps now. Go straight to the house, why don't you, and you and I

79

will have a great deal of time to talk about family and business matters later. I'll have your sea chest and other gear sent along when they're brought ashore."

Grateful for his understanding, Charles took his leave, walking to the Rakehell house along the familiar waterfront.

The housemaid who answered his knock was surprised to see him, but he put a finger to his lips, and she joined in the conspiracy, grinning as she pointed up the stairs.

Mounting the steps two at a time to the second floor, he followed the sound of Ruth Barker's voice emanating from the nursery playroom, then paused at the open door to take in the scene.

Ruth was seated in a rocking chair, looking very attractive with her dark hair falling in waves below her shoulders. He did not notice that she was wearing an old dress. Her arms encircled David and Julian, who were sitting on her lap, listening intently to a story she was reading to them. Both of the children had grown in the time since he had last seen them, and his heart pounded as he stared at his son. Wu-ling was seated at a small table across the room, practicing writing English in a composition book.

Making no move and no sound, Charles continued to stand in the entrance.

At last David became aware of the stare, looked up, and saw his father, whom he recognized instantly. "Papa! Papa!" he said, pointing to Charles, and sliding to the floor, the baby ran as fast as his short legs could carry him.

Charles scooped him up and enveloped him in a bear hug.

There was pandemonium in the playroom. Julian began to shout, and at the same time a delighted but shy Wu-ling began to babble, mixing Cantonese and English unintelligibly. Some moments passed before Ruth, who had risen, too, could extend her hand and say with a broad smile, "Welcome to America, Charles."

He took her hand and kissed her lightly on the cheek. "I'm happier to be here than you'll ever know."

"Mama!" David said after his father released Ruth's hand.

So his son was calling her Mama.

"Mama," Julian repeated, walking to her and taking her hand.

He, too, referred to her as Mama. That might cause complications if Jonathan's quest for Lai-tse lu was successful. "I seem to have interrupted at a critical time," Charles said.

Ruth tried in vain to draw her hair into greater order behind her ears. "Indeed you haven't," she said, adding firmly, "No more stories until bedtime, boys. Your papa has come a long, long way to see you, David."

The stocky child, still held in his father's arm, looked at him delightedly. "Boat! Boat!"

"Yes, boat. Papa come on boat—clipper. Say 'clipper,' Davie. 'Clipper.' "

The boy, looking at him solemnly, repeated the word, and Charles laughed out loud. So David was already learning about clippers!

"My papa went on clipper," Julian said, old enough now to begin forming sentences. "Clipper—tops'l—sheet," he went on, showing off his growing vocabulary.

Even the little boy's nautical terminology was accurate, Charles noticed. He reached down and hefted Julian with his free arm. "You boys are going to build the fastest ships in the world, maybe even faster than the ones we sail now."

"I hope you don't disapprove of my move here," Ruth said anxiously, "but it seemed so right for the children that I accepted at once when Jonathan suggested it."

"I couldn't think of a better arrangement," Charles told her. Wu-ling was eager to gain his attention, too, so he turned to her and said in Cantonese, "You looked like a child when I last saw you. Now you look more like a woman." He noted that she bore an increasing resemblance to Alice Wong.

The girl elected to reply in English and said with great dignity, "I grow older and soon shall be a woman."

"Just listen to you! Ruth, you're responsible for her command of English."

"No, I've helped, but Wu-ling herself is responsible. She's a diligent student."

"Mama read us the book," Julian said. "Mama teach us to read."

Ruth smiled as she said, "I've been reading to them about—just as you would expect—boats."

David's huge, dark eyes continued to focus on his father as he echoed his cousin, "Mama read, Mama read."

Charles's roars of laughter mingled with the delighted squeals, giggles, and shouts of the two boys.

Ruth took advantage of their preoccupation to hurry off to her own room, where she rearranged her hair, changed into a somewhat more attractive dress of bombazine, and added a touch of rouge to her lips. There was no reason Charles should see her at her frumpiest.

A messenger soon arrived from the shipyard, carrying a note to Ruth from Jeremiah. If she found it convenient, he said, perhaps she would invite the Walkers to supper. She conferred with the cook, then scribbled a hasty word to Judith, extending the invitation to the Walker family and explaining that Charles had just arrived.

Preparations for the small dinner party on such short notice kept her busy, and she did not see Charles and the children again until it was time for the boys' supper. "Wu-ling will give you your baths now," she said. "No more games for now."

David and Julian, who had been sailing a clipper ship that existed only in their imaginations, quietly went off with Wu-ling.

Charles was astonished by the control Ruth exercised over them without raising her voice.

"You can watch them when they eat," Ruth told him, "but there's time for you to have a drink first, if you wish."

"I do wish, but only if you'll join me."

She hesitated, uncertain how to react to the invitation.

Charles took her arm, insisting she accompany him, and they went down to Jeremiah's comfortable study. There he poured her a small glass of sack, then mixed himself a mild Scotch whiskey and water. "You've done marvels with David," he said, raising his glass to her. "I salute you, Ruth."

"I deserve no credit," she replied. "He's so adorable that I can't help loving him. And he has such a quick, facile mind! He's as intelligent as Julian, which is the highest compliment I can pay him."

Charles eyed her narrowly, his mind churning. For years he had thought of her as the friend of Louise, then as the wife of Edmund, but he had always been aware that Ruth was a most attractive woman. "You're being too modest," he said.

She was embarrassed and changed the subject. "How long will you be here?"

"That depends," he replied cryptically. "We'll talk about it tomorrow, after the excitement of my arrival has worn off."

Wu-ling summoned them when the children were bathed and ready for their supper in the playroom. Charles and Ruth joined them, and the former was delighted to see his son using a spoon to feed himself, his appetite prodigious. "He eats almost as much as I do," he said.

Ruth laughed. "He likes breakfast, dinner, supper, and as much food as he can cadge between meals. I believe in allowing a growing boy to eat as much as he can hold comfortably."

Charles was impressed by her self-assurance. She was a natural mother, he thought, and it was unfortunate that she had brought no children of her own into the world before Edmund's untimely death at sea.

The two little boys were put to bed after they had eaten, and at Charles's insistence, Wu-ling accompanied him and Ruth to the parlor. Moments later Judith Walker arrived with her two children, young Judy and Brad, and soon after, Jeremiah Rakehell came home from the shipyard.

Only Bradford Walker was missing, and he arrived just moments before the party adjourned to the dining room. His eyes were bloodshot, the odor of whiskey was heavy on his breath, and he was barely civil as he went through the motions of greeting the young Englishman.

His presence changed the atmosphere. Judith, who looked strained in Charles's opinion, promptly withdrew into a shell, falling silent and speaking only when directly addressed. Her children became inhibited in their father's presence, too, and although they ate hungrily, showing the appetites of rapidly growing youngsters, they shut out the adult conversation that swirled around them. Even Wu-ling, always effervescent in spite of her shyness, sat solemnly, conscious of Walker's disdain for her because she was a member of another race.

Jeremiah and Charles carried the brunt of the conversation as they were served a typical New England dinner of steamer clams, clam chowder, boiled lobster, corn on the cob, and young potatoes boiled in their jackets. They talked at length about the impact of the new clipper ships on world trade. The speed of these remarkable vessels was transforming and increasing the trade between nations, and Jeremiah agreed heartily when Charles said, "The clipper is making the world smaller and binding people of many nations more closely together. It gives me a feeling of great satisfaction to know that I'm helping to make the countries of the West more familiar with the products of China, India, and the East Indies, just as we're helping them by making our manufactured goods available to them. There's far more than profit involved."

Bradford Walker glowered at him, looking contemptuous. "I'm tired of hearing about the wonders of clippers. The brigs and schooners that have been the backbone of the merchant fleets of the Western world for generations still carry most goods in international trade. And they will for generations to come. They're the heart and soul of our company, and of every other company in the United States, Britain, France, the Netherlands—every country that engages in trade on a large scale."

Before either Jeremiah or Charles could reply, Ruth joined in the talk. "You're wrong, Mr. Walker," she said quietly.

Her unexpected intervention jarred Charles, who looked at her in admiration.

Walker demanded of the young widow, "What do you know about it?"

"My father was the chief carpenter for the Rakehell and Boynton shipbuilding program in America for forty years," she said, speaking quietly but firmly. "He supervised the construction of most of your fleet's schooners and brigs. At one time he wanted to have nothing to do with the building of clippers, but on his last visit here some months ago—he lives in retirement with my sister in South Carolina now—he inspected the *Lai-tse lu* and some of Jonathan's other clippers, and he wished that he were twenty-five years younger. He now believes the clipper is the ship of the present and the future, and so do I."

Walker's laugh was sneering. "I don't need an old carpenter to tell me my business."

His insult was unnecessary, and Charles became annoyed on Ruth's behalf, but the young widow was well able to defend herself. "I don't take his word, either. But I'm in total agreement with Charles and Jonathan. And I've lived in this house

84

long enough to have heard various statistics, so I know the clippers are now providing Rakehell and Boynton with the better part of the company's profit."

She was right, Charles thought, and silently cheered her.

Judith threw her husband a warning glance, hoping to persuade him to drop the matter.

Walker was thoroughly incensed, however. The division he managed was of shrinking importance, he was being outdistanced by Jonathan and Charles, and he knew only too well that, in the years ahead, they would succeed their fathers as the heads of the company while he would rise no higher. "Clippers are a fad of the moment because of their speed," he said. "Their holds are so small they can carry only specialized merchandise."

Ruth, who was aroused, smiled sweetly. "The *Lai-tse lu* carries as many tons of cargo as any of your brigs and schooners."

"So she does," Charles said. Here, to his amazement, was a young woman who not only understood shipping but was not afraid to express herself. He viewed her with increasing respect.

Jeremiah Rakehell decided the argument had lasted long enough, and to Judith's relief, he changed the subject before Walker became even nastier.

They finished the meal with a cake of rich, moist chocolate, and Charles, aware that Ruth was also in charge of the domestic affairs in the Rakehell household, said to her, "The cocoa for this chocolate doesn't come from the Caribbean. It's too dark."

"You're right," she replied with a quick smile. "The cocoa came here from Djakarta, part of a shipment from your friend, whom you and Jonathan call the Fat Dutchman. It's so superior that I instruct the cook to use no other kind."

"It's unique," he said. "The market for it is insatiable."

Walker was so nettled that he insisted on taking his family home soon after they left the dinner table and retired to the parlor for coffee.

"Make some time for us to have a real chat tomorrow," Judith said to her cousin as they left.

Charles tried to think in terms of the next day's schedule. "Indeed I will. It can't be during the morning, because I've got to spend several hours at the yard with Uncle Jeremiah.''

"Join us at our noon meal, Judy,'' Ruth said thoughtfully. ''Your children will be in school, David and Julian will be finished with their own meal and taking naps, and they usually sleep for a couple of hours. So you and Charles can have time for a real visit.''

She managed such problems with consummate ease, Charles reflected.

Jeremiah stayed up beyond his usual bedtime to hear about the doings of the Boynton family, but ultimately he yawned repeatedly. Wu-ling was the first to go off, and soon thereafter Jeremiah went to his own room, leaving Ruth and Charles in the parlor.

"If you're sleepy, too, we'll make the time tomorrow for a chat,'' the young widow said. ''I do want to tell you everything I can about David's development.''

"Tell me now,'' he replied, and, helping himself to a splash of brandywine, offered her a drink, too.

She shook her head, then launched into a full account of his son's progress, discussing everything from his physical state to his rapid mental development.

Her ability to organize the material and explain it lucidly impressed him as much as the facts she related. Edmund Barker had been a very fortunate man, and Charles couldn't help speculating that, with the right clothes and cosmetics, she would be a genuine beauty. Something else was missing, and he finally decided that Edmund, who had been modest and retiring, probably had never managed to awaken her. Although she had been married for more than a year, he thought it unlikely that she had ever known passion. Married to the right man, she would bloom.

Later that night, after they finished their conversation and went their separate ways, Charles could not sleep. He had taken to heart his mother's advice that he would win far greater acceptance for David if he was a married man, and he found himself thinking about Ruth. She was the daughter of a humble carpenter—but she was a woman of spirit and courage.

Little David clung to her, obviously worshiping her, and would be far happier if she continued to rear him.

He himself was attracted to her physically and admired

her sound knowledge of the shipping business, a quality he had always respected in his mother. The young ladies he knew in London were indifferent to the careers of the men they knew. Only social position mattered to them, but Ruth would be a true partner, like his mother.

Aware that he sometimes acted impulsively, causing problems for himself and others, he warned himself not to leap too quickly. He would be wise to remain in America longer than the week to ten days he had planned to stay. With the advent of warmer weather a Rakehell and Boynton clipper would be sailing to England every other week, so he could release the *Elizabeth*, allowing her to remain on her regular schedule, and he could arrange to return home later.

In the meantime he would pay court to Ruth Barker. Subtly, delicately, because he didn't want to hurt her in the event that he finally concluded a marriage would not be suitable.

He had to admit he did not love her, and did not know if he ever would, but he had never truly loved any woman. Perhaps he was too self-centered ever to give himself completely and unstintingly. On the other hand, Ruth had so many virtues, so many good qualities that he hoped he would learn to love her. He was confident, to be sure, of his own ability to dazzle her and sweep her off her feet.

Her devotion to David was real and deep. He had no doubt that she and his mother would establish a rapport because they were alike in so many ways. As for his father's reaction to her, he could make no predictions, just as he had no idea whether David would be accepted by his grandfather.

Charles remained awake for the better part of the night, and when he finally went to bed for a few hours, he dropped off without delay. In the days ahead he would explore and weigh every aspect of a possible permanent relationship with Ruth.

For the next few weeks Charles spent as much time with his son as he could without neglecting his conferences and other duties at the shipyard. Gradually he and his uncle hammered out a new schedule of sailings on a worldwide scale for the fleet's clippers, which included two new vessels that were nearing completion. During the hours he spent with David, he saw to it that Ruth was present, and he made certain that she was nearby after supper every evening.

Wu-ling, who was far more worldly than Ruth in spite of her youth, was the first to sense that there were undercurrents beyond those of an employer and a rather special governess. "My ivory sticks spoke the truth," she said with a giggle.

Ruth had been conscious of Charles's attentiveness but had refused to give it any significance. "I don't know what you mean," she said, the reddening of her cheeks belying her words.

"Soon Mr. Charles will ask you to marry him," the Chinese girl said, becoming solemn.

"I think not." Ruth regarded it as highly unlikely that he had fallen in love with her.

"You will see," Wu-ling replied confidently. "Do not be surprised when he speaks to you. And please, Missy Ruth, if you go to England with him, take me, too."

"Wherever I go, you will go." Ruth was touched by the adolescent's need for her.

That night, after a long and particularly lively conversation with Charles in the Rakehell parlor, Ruth made a sustained effort to analyze the situation. Undressing slowly, she reflected that she had no idea what Charles felt toward her. At the moment her own feelings were of paramount importance.

First and foremost, she was not in love with him, and she doubted that she would ever love any man other than Jonathan, whom she had lost. On the other hand, Charles was handsome, dashing, and personable, and she knew she was drawn to him. Whether the magnetism responsible was caused by his family similarity to Jonathan in both appearance and character was something she found herself incapable of determining. She could not probe that far beneath the surface, and it was enough that she enjoyed every moment they spent together. In fact, she couldn't even blame herself for flirting with him occasionally.

His interest in her was flattering, and she was realistic enough to know that a marriage to him would be advantageous in many ways. She was poor, and until she had moved into the Rakehell house, it had been a struggle to live on the small pension the company paid her as Edmund's widow and on her fee for acting as David's governess. Charles was enormously wealthy, growing richer each month, and if she became his wife, her financial worries would be ended for all time. One day he would inherit his father's baronetcy, too, and although her social ambitions had been limited, she had to admit she would like being known as Lady Boynton.

She had met his parents on their many visits to New London, and she felt reasonably certain she would be able to get along with his mother. Jessica was a Rakehell, after all, so she put on no airs and had a realistic, no-nonsense approach to life. Sir Alan, on the other hand, was something of an enigma to her, and never knowing what he might say next, she had found it difficult to converse with him.

Certainly she could live up to her domestic obligations as Charles's wife. Whether his aristocratic English friends would accept her as an equal, however, she had no way of determining. She knew nothing about the upper-class English, and her pragmatic streak forced her to put the question aside. It was best not to dwell on matters about which she could not form a definite judgment.

Perhaps the single most important factor in propelling her in the direction of accepting a proposal of marriage was her relationship with David, which would be solidified and made permanent. She loved the little boy who called her "Mama" and who depended on her for so much, and the mere contemplation of being separated from him was unbearable. David, she told herself, was the deciding factor.

Probably it was a mistake to give too much credence to Wu-ling's opinion. Common sense told her to stop speculating, to accept each day she spent with Charles for its own sake and not try to peer into the future.

One day, about three weeks after his arrival in New England, Charles surprised her by asking her to dine with him that night the Waterfront Inn, the only public house in New London frequented by people of substance. "We'll wait, of course, until David and Julian have gone to bed," he assured her.

Her intuition told her that Charles was going to propose that night; and suddenly thinking of Jonathan and growing hesitant, she found a reason to object. "It wouldn't be right to let Mr. Rakehell eat alone."

Charles grinned at her. "You're wrong. Uncle Jeremiah is busy preparing his annual report to the company's American stockholders, and he welcomes the opportunity to spend an evening by himself. I've already had words with him, and he said the outing will be good for both of us."

"Oh." She had been robbed of a legitimate protest, and now it would be ungracious to refuse.

That evening she dressed in a gown of dark taffeta with a modest neckline and full skirt, which she had not worn since the night Edmund had last come home from the sea. And Wu-ling prodded her, demanding that she wear lip rouge. Then the young girl took charge and placed a soft circle of black kohl around her eyes, which enhanced them and made them look far larger.

Even David noticed the difference in her appearance as he and Julian were eating their supper. "Mama pretty," he said.

Charles nodded emphatically. "You're right, son, and you're observant. She's very pretty."

Ruth felt her face growing warm beneath a thin coating of rice powder.

Charles took her to the inn in a Rakehell carriage he borrowed for the occasion. Only once in her life had she visited the Waterfront, and in spite of her determination to note every detail, she paid scant attention to the comfortable decor; and the food, supposedly the best of any public eating place between New Haven and Providence, was tasteless to her.

Charles exerted his utmost charm, regaling her with anecdotes about the Fat Dutchman and other unusual persons he had met in his travels. Not until they were about to leave the table did he say quietly, "I'm planning to go back to England in the near future."

Ruth began to wonder if her intuition about a marriage proposal had been right. Perhaps the unexpected supper party was Charles's way of thanking her for all she had done for David.

She was silent as they returned to the Rakehell house in the carriage, and merely nodded when Charles suggested they stroll on the beach that faced the estuary of the Thames. The evening was so warm that she shed her drab cloak of dark wool, and Charles gallantly carried it for her. When they reached a huge, flat boulder he lifted her to a sitting position on it and took his place beside her. A three-quarter moon formed a soft glow in the star-filled sky, casting a silvery reflection on the water and creating a romantic atmosphere, but Ruth hated herself for remembering that Jonathan had been with Louise Graves on this very beach on the night that had led to the unexpected birth of Julian.

Speaking without preamble, Charles told her in detail about his affair with Alice Wong, her sacrifice of her own life in order to save him when he had been attacked by unknown enemies, and the subsequent discovery that their son lived with Alice's grandmother and young half-sister in a tiny, impoverished Canton dwelling. "I brought David and Wu-ling here with me, and you know the rest," he told her.

Deeply affected by his account, Ruth could only ask, "Why have you told me all this?"

"Because I wanted you to know," he said quietly. "Now I'll bring you up to date. I intend to take David and Wu-ling back to London with me."

Ruth could not conceal her anguish, and Charles gently grasped her hand. She wanted to withdraw, but a powerful instinct impelled her to make no move.

"I very much want you to come with us," he said.

"I'm sure there are many competent governesses in England," she said. "Besides, Jonathan left Julian in my care."

"We can take Julian with us for a visit. It will be at least a half-year before Jonnie returns, and with any luck he'll bring his bride, Lai-tse lu, with him."

She felt a stab of pain.

"I've already spoken to Uncle Jeremiah, and he's willing. As for your coming as a governess, that isn't the role I have in mind for you."

Ruth sat unmoving.

"I've admired you for years, long before you married poor Edmund. I rejoiced for him when you became his wife, but at the same time I envied him." Charles spoke fluently and forcefully. "I stood beside him when he was washed overboard by a tidal wave and drowned, and that was one reason I took a measure of responsibility for you. But it wasn't the principal reason. Not until I went back to England did I realize the extent of my interest in you, Ruth. I came here on this trip not only to see my son, but to make certain my interest was

91

genuine and abiding." He knew he was shading the truth, but a woman had a right to expect romantic trappings when a man proposed to her.

Ruth realized his grip on her hand had tightened.

"I'll admit I've known many women, probably too many," Charles said. "But I've never before asked anyone to marry me, so forgive me if I'm a trifle gauche. I can only add that I've come to love you. So—will you be my wife?"

Wu-ling's prophecy had come true! Ruth hesitated, then blurted, "I—I don't know what to say. I—I admire you greatly. But I'm not sure—that—I love you." As she spoke, she couldn't help remembering her feeling toward Jonathan.

"I'm certain I'll awaken your love," he replied. "It's a risk I'll gladly take."

Again she hesitated, and suddenly she took the plunge. "I'm willing to take risks, too. I accept, Charles."

Without a moment's delay he took her in his arms, and his kiss was as passionate as it was practiced.

Never had Ruth experienced such a kiss, and she fought hard for self control. When he finally released her she gasped, then managed to say, "I'll try to be a good wife, Charles, and a good mother to David."

"You're all I want," he replied. Noting that she was finding it difficult to regain her breath, he knew he had achieved another victory, perhaps his greatest.

They broke the news to Jeremiah Rakehell that same evening, and he was overjoyed. "You deserve each other," he said, and kissed Ruth. "Welcome to the family. I assume you'll hold the ceremony in England."

"I prefer to be married here," Ruth said, "so my father, my sister, and her family can come up from South Carolina for the wedding."

Charles did not say that he had influenced her decision, wanting to confront his own family with an accomplished fact. "We're sending a messenger off to South Carolina on one of the smaller clippers tonight, with orders to bring Ruth's relatives back. So she should be able to schedule the ceremony within two weeks, and we'll sail that same day on our clipper, the *Green Frog*."

The next fortnight was the busiest Ruth had ever known.

Charles purchased a large diamond ring for her, the first piece of valuable jewelry she had ever owned, and insisted on paying for a new wardrobe for her. He accompanied her when she purchased the fabrics, making certain she obtained the finest silks and satins, and he gave a steady stream of instructions to the seamstress, whose modest tastes were too similar to Ruth's. "In London," he told his bride-to-be, "you'll find that no young woman we'll see socially wears gowns with sleeves, high necklines, or gaudy skirts in the evening. But this wardrobe is just the start. We'll visit a dressmaker I know in London, and one day soon we'll go to Paris for the finishing touches."

Ruth was dazzled but managed to keep her sense of balance. Her wish that they be married in an intimate ceremony at St. James's Church in New London, in the presence of no one but family and a few close friends, as befitted a widow, was honored. She decided to wear an unadorned skirt of peach-colored silk, set off by a dark, tailored jacket, which she would wear on board ship. As a concession to Charles, she wore a poke bonnet.

Among the few who were invited to the ceremony were the parents of the late Louise Graves Rakehell, but their relations with Jeremiah had cooled since their daughter's tragic death, for which they held Jonathan responsible. They seldom saw Julian, their grandson, even though their house was located directly across Pequot Avenue from the Rakehell home, and brief, prim note announced that Dr. and Mrs. Graves would be unable to attend.

Ruth's father, still robust in spite of his advanced years, and her sister and brother-in-law arrived a few days before the wedding. They scrutinized Charles with care, and he went out of his way to charm them, so they gave the match their complete approval.

The standard Anglican ceremony was performed. One of Ruth's former classmates acted as her matron of honor, and Jeremiah proudly stood up with his nephew. Wu-ling, weeping with joy, attempted to keep David and Julian under control, but the task was too great for any one person, so Judith Walker assisted her, and between them they prevented the two little boys from interrupting the proceedings.

A reception was held on the lawn of the Rakehell house

Bradford Walker drank to excess, then hurried off to his own house, to the mortification of his wife, but no other untoward incident marred the celebration.

The belongings of the departing newlyweds had already been stored on board the clipper, and an hour before the *Green Frog* was scheduled to sail on the afternoon tide, the entire wedding party went to the Rakehell and Boynton yard. Everyone kissed the bride and the two little boys good-bye, and Jeremiah handed Charles letters to his parents and several bulky pieces of business correspondence for his father.

Then he gripped Ruth by the shoulders. "I couldn't wish you greater happiness if you were my own daughter-in-law," he told her.

She thanked him, trying to squelch the thought that she still wished she had become Jonathan's wife. "We'll bring Julian home as soon as we learn that Jonathan has arrived," she promised.

Charles picked up the excited David and Julian, placed them on his shoulders, and followed his wife onto the ship. The quarters were more than adequate but far from ideal. The bridal couple would share the only passenger cabin on the nine hundred ton vessel, which was almost as spacious as that occupied by the clipper's master. The two mates had evacuated their cabin for Wu-ling and the two small boys, who would share the second berth.

The little group stood on deck as the *Green Frog*, assisted by a steam-propelled tug, edged slowly away from the pier, gathering speed as her yards were braced round and her sails filled. Ruth and Charles kept a tight hold on the hands of Julian and David, and Charles carefully explained each step of the nautical procedures to the boys, who listened intently, understanding what they could. Julian, who had already sailed with Jonathan on a number of occasions, seemed to understand a great deal, and Charles vowed that his own son would develop a love for the sea, too.

As the clipper moved into the waters of the open Atlantic, where the sea was choppy and the swells strong, she began to "corkscrew," and a sudden thought came to Charles that had not occurred to him earlier. "I hope you're a good sailor," he said, afraid that seasickness might spoil his bride's honeymoon.

Ruth laughed. "Never fear. This is my first voyage on a

clipper, which I love already. But I'm the daughter of a ship's carpenter, and I've gone to sea more often than I can remember. No matter how rough the weather, I'll enjoy every minute of it.''

Charles embraced her, ignoring the proximity of several crew members. He had chosen the right woman for a wife.

Wu-ling was introduced to the mysteries of the small galley by the cook, and caught on so quickly that she prepared the early supper herself for Julian and David. Occasionally she eyed the buckets of sand that stood nearby, ready for use if the stove or some of the food should catch fire, but in the main she showed her customary ability to adjust to her surroundings with ease.

Ruth told the children the bedtime story they expected from her, and they dropped off to sleep, lulled by the gentle rocking and creaking of the ship, the sound of waves slapping against the hull, and the whistling of the breeze through the rigging. Then the bride, groom, and Wu-ling adjourned to the crowded officers' cabin for supper with the captain and the second mate, the first mate having taken the watch.

The master produced a bottle of wine for the occasion. The young second mate eyed Wu-ling repeatedly but said little, and the girl, aware of his interest, fell into a shy silence. Ruth called on her inner reserves and managed to chat with Charles and the captain as though she had been the wife of a ship's owner for many years.

Wu-ling retired soon after the meal, and Charles strolled to the fantail with Ruth. His arm encircling her, they watched the clipper's wake, looked up at the clouds drifting across an almost clear sky, and studied the reflection of an almost full but fading moon on the water.

"Listen," Charles said happily. "Do you hear it?"

Ruth strained, but the silence seemed all-pervading. "I don't hear a thing," she replied.

He laughed. "The singing of the wind through the shrouds. The slapping of the water against the hull. The changing patterns of the creaking noises made by the ship's timbers. They're what Jonnie and I have always called the music of the sea. No matter how long I live or how wealthy I'll become, I can't follow my father's example and gradually spend more and more time ashore until I'm chained to my desk. Something

95

inside me demands that I go to sea from time to time in order to restore my soul.''

She knew Jonathan felt the same way, and reflected that he and his cousin were even more alike than she had realized. Damn Jonathan! This was no time to think of him.

"Come along," Charles said abruptly, and led her toward their cabin.

Ruth knew what awaited her and felt strangely apprehensive, which was ridiculous. She was no innocent virgin but a previously married woman who had gone to bed with her first husband nearly every night they had spent on shore together!

Deep down, however, she knew what was troubling her. Whenever Edmund had made love to her, she had pretended to herself that he had been Jonathan. And she was afraid she would succumb to the same delusion again. But she couldn't permit that to happen, for the sake of her own sanity and the health of her marriage.

Charles lighted two expensive, smokeless French tapers, their glow muted by opaque shades, then closed and bolted the door. Turning to his bride, he began to undress her, the process slowed by his expert caresses.

Ruth shivered slightly, but submitted to his ministrations, praying that no image of Jonathan would appear before her.

When she was nude Charles quickly removed his own clothes, then kissed her with abandon, and bore her down onto the wide berth. Knowing precisely what he was doing, his stroking became more insistent, more demanding.

Squirming involuntarily beneath his touch, Ruth knew only that she was being aroused to a pitch of desire she had never before experienced. She wanted him very much. But her bridegroom was in no hurry, his hands continuing to roam freely as he acquainted himself with every part of her body. Her desire soared still higher, becoming intolerable.

Charles sensed when she could tolerate no more, and then he took her, tenderly yet passionately. Never had she known such ecstasy, her yearning all the greater because she knew he was Charles, not Jonathan. He was giving her no chance to indulge in fantasies.

His thrusts became more violent, and all at once she found release, something she had never achieved with Edmund. Charles quickly joined her, and for a seeming eternity they moved in unison until, still embracing, they became still and drifted into a light sleep.

Ruth had no idea of the passage of time. Suddenly she was wide awake, however, and knew only that she wanted more of Charles's lovemaking. He was breathing evenly, his eyes closed, so this time she took the initiative, shamelessly and without guilt. Soon he awakened, instantly took charge, and returned her passion with equal vigor. To Ruth's astonishment she found release again, enjoying the second experience even more than she had the first.

Charles stood long enough to extinguish the tapers, then returned to the berth, falling into a deep sleep almost as soon as he folded her in his arms.

Snuggling close to him, her body pressed against his, she found herself hoping that David and Julian would sleep late enough in the morning so she and Charles could make love again before they arose. Smiling and suppressing a giggle, she told herself: I'm a wanton with an endless craving for sex, but I never knew it. Then she sighed silently, reflecting that although her husband was still a stranger to her in many ways, he was the perfect lover. Satiated and contented, she wanted to shout aloud that Charles had cured her of her obsessive yearning for Jonathan. She hoped.

Book
II

I

Lin Tse-hsü, imperial viceroy for Kwangtung Province, looked like a mild-mannered ascetic. He was short and slender, wore ankle-length silk gowns of chrysanthemum yellow, as befitted his high rank, and never raised his voice. He padded quietly through the huge palace that was his headquarters, dropping in unexpectedly at the offices of his staff members, whom he treated with casual informality, and his principal cook was the authority for the statement that he ate little except boiled chicken or fish, raw vegetables, and unsalted, boiled rice. He was a bachelor, he kept no concubines, and one of his first acts after arriving in Canton had been to dismiss the score or more fortune tellers and soothsayers who had been retained by his predecessor. But the surface manifestations of his character were deceptive.

The burly Lo Fang, for two decades the palace majordomo, revealed the truth to his close friend and fellow member of the secret, patriotic Society of Oxen, Kai, who served in a similar capacity in the household of Soong Chao. "Lin," he said, "is a fanatic. He leaves matters of taxation, administration, and justice to members of his staff. His one obsession in life is the total elimination of the opium trade. I'm convinced that is the reason the emperor appointed him as viceroy. He will do anything, no matter what the consequences, to stamp out the drug traffic. We are entering a very dangerous period, and no man can predict what will happen."

When Lin first came to Canton, he announced his intentions of dealing severely with all who bought or sold opium, but he took no action to match his words. So the foreigners who brought opium to China, particularly the British merchants, and the Chinese who purchased cases of the drug illegally soon reverted to their old ways.

Then, suddenly, Lin struck. First his troops raided a supposedly uninhabited island in the delta of the Pearl River, where many tons of opium had been concealed. Eight of the emperor's subjects were captured in the raid, and three of them, who were underlings, were promptly beheaded in a public ceremony. The others were placed in bamboo cages, so cramped they could neither sit nor stretch out, and these cells were suspended in the great square in front of Canton's Temple of Heaven. People were encouraged to throw garbage at the prisoners, prod them with pointed sticks, and otherwise torment them. Given nothing to eat or drink, the smugglers grew weaker, but before they could die they were hauled from their cages and slowly tortured to death in the square, with tens of thousands of the emperor's subjects watching the spectacle in uneasy silence.

Less than a week after the last of the criminals had been executed, Lin again demonstrated that he meant business. Early one morning, just as the foreigners who supervised the operations of the factories and warehouses were arriving at their desks, hundreds of yellow-clad imperial troops marched through the Petition Gate. All of them carried ancient matchlocks, muskets that were so rusty they would have exploded had they been fired, but bayonets were attached to the weapons, and the officers in charge tolerated no nonsense as they sent their troops through each of the warehouses in a search for opium.

Soong Chao, who had nothing to fear, opened his doors to the soldiers and, cooperating with the officers, personally conducted them through his buildings. The Swedes and the Danes, who had no opium concealed in their factories, were equally cooperative. The Americans, after hesitating, also allowed the troops free access to their warehouses, but the factor in charge nevertheless felt compelled to protest to Lo Fang, who was in command of the search. "As a matter of principle," the Yankee declared, "I object on the grounds that no one has the right to enter our property."

Lo Fang politely recorded the protest, and the troops made their search.

Several of the British factories were the main targets of

he searchers, and the most intensive hunt was conducted in the complex managed by Owen Bruce, in whose factory opium had been found during a raid conducted a few years earlier. The florid-faced Scotsman stationed himself at the entrance to his largest warehouse and, spreading his arms, refused the troops permission to enter.

The high-ranking officer in command of the unit immediately summoned Lo Fang.

The imperial viceroy's majordomo took in the situation at a glance, then addressed Bruce in Mandarin. "If you do not stand aside," he said, "I will be obliged to use force. You may look at the muskets of our soldiers with contempt, but the metal of their bayonets is very sharp."

Bruce pretended he didn't understand.

Lo Fang spoke quietly, a hint of a smile appearing at the corners of his mouth as he removed his skull cap, revealing a totally bald head. "It is known that you speak Mandarin," he said. "Do not tempt me to take actions you will regret."

The Scotsman's bluff had been called, but he still had no intention of yielding. "This factory is under the protection of Queen Victoria," he said.

"My troops recognize only the authority of the Tao Kuang Emperor," Lo Fang replied. Taking a single step forward, he picked up Bruce as though he were almost weightless, and set him down again some feet from the entrance.

Humiliated and furious, the Scotsman watched in impotent rage as the imperial troops marched into his warehouse and quickly spread out under the direction of officers who had been trained to search for opium.

The hunt proved successful. More than two hundred caskets marked "Tea," each of them weighing fifty pounds, were found to contain a hard-caked, gummy substance that in no way resembled tea. Lo Fang ordered the cases piled high on the waterfront.

Even though Bruce had been caught red-handed, he persisted in his attempt to regain possession of the opium. "You have no right to confiscate property from my factory!" he shouted in English, then repeated the protest in Mandarin.

Paying no attention to him, Lo Fang had the cases of opium surrounded by troops. Then oil was poured on the cartons, and the imperial viceroy's majordomo applied a flaming torch to the puddle that formed at the base of the pyramid. Soon clouds of black smoke, its odor the unmistakable, sickly-sweet smell of burning opium, rolled across the harbor. Drugs worth millions of the solid silver yuan that was the basic currency of the Middle Kingdom were being destroyed.

The troops stood impassively, their bayonets forming a fence through which no man could pass. Owen Bruce grew pale as he watched a huge fortune in contraband drugs being consumed by the flames.

Lo Fang was not yet finished with him. "I bring you the solemn warning of the viceroy of the Tao Kuang Emperor," he said. "On this occasion you are being punished enough by seeing your illegal opium going to waste. If you smuggle more opium into your warehouses in the future, you will pay with your life!"

The incident created a sensation in the foreign community, and there was a brief flurry of excitement in Canton itself, where the Fan Kuei were despised. Only one person, far beyond all others, was aware of the possible long-term consequences of the raid.

The Princess An Mien, younger sister of the Tao Kuang Emperor, was paying an informal visit to Canton, supposedly traveling incognito. She had been accompanied from Peking by an entourage of sixty persons as well as one thousand guards of the imperial legion, and an entire wing of the viceroy's palace had been set aside for her use, but the fiction that she had not come to Canton was politely maintained. The imperial ensign, always raised when the emperor or one of his close relatives was in residence, was nowhere to be seen, and the princess granted no formal audiences.

A slightly overweight woman with an erect posture, An Mien was now in her early thirties. As always, she wore an unadorned, ankle-length cheongsam of pure silk, with a huge jade ring, on which an imperial dragon was carved, as her only jewelry. She sat now on a low, padded stool and smiled at her visitor as they sipped tea from exquisite, semitransparent cups, which the princess had brought with her. It would have been beneath the dignity of the emperor's sister to use any porcelain other than her own.

"I'm grateful to you for coming to me so quickly after I

sent word to you that I arrived here," she said. "Perhaps you can see the advantage of making an incognito visit."

"Of course, Your Imperial Highness," Soong Lai-tse lu replied, seemingly unruffled, although she had hurriedly changed into a peach-colored cheongsam, with which she wore pink jade earrings and pink slippers. "By making your visit unofficial, you need to see only those whom you wish to visit you."

"And to visit you in return, my dear," An Mien declared. "In fact, I hope I'll be invited to your house to dine tonight. I simply cannot abide the food served by Lin Tse-hsü."

"I will be honored, and so will my father."

"And I'll be assured of a palatable meal." The princess giggled. "Lin should have been a Taoist monk, you know."

"So I've heard."

"I never give advice to my brother unless he seeks it, but I wish I hadn't remained silent when he made Lin his viceroy for Kwangtung."

Lai-tse lu nodded gravely. As a friend and protégée of the woman who was doing so much to improve the lot of her sex in a nation completely controlled and dominated by men, she spoke her mind freely. "I've been told on good authority by Kai, our majordomo, that the viceroy is a fanatic."

"That's too mild a term. He could have executed the drug smugglers quickly in a public ceremony, but instead he had them tortured for days. How disgusting. I suppose you saw the spectacle."

"I did not, Your Imperial Highness! I avoided the area around the Temple of Heaven while the prisoners were on display there."

"I would have done the same," the princess declared. "I just hope Lin didn't go too far today in his raid on the warehouses."

"The raid should be ended by now," Lai-tse lu said, accepting another cup of tea.

"I hope you're right. I instructed Lo Fang to come to me before giving the viceroy his official report. I'm worried."

"So am I. The viceroy is like so many high officials I've known. They have no understanding of the outside world, and they insist on believing that other nations should pay homage to the emperor."

105

"Their attitude flatters my brother." An Mien's voice became confidential. "But I don't mind admitting to you that my blood ran cold when I saw the hundreds of modern cannon on board the British warships in the Whampoa roads. Our puny war junks, armed with ancient cannon that haven't been fired in centuries, would be blown out of the water if real unpleasantness should develop. I tried to urge Lin to be cautious when I arrived last night, and he told me in confidence about today's raid. But he is convinced the Middle Kingdom is invincible."

"Our generals and admirals feel the same way. I hear them boasting when they dine with us, and their arguments are all alike. The Middle Kingdom is so huge and has so many people that we have absorbed all of our would-be conquerors for more than four thousand years."

"You've seen more of the English and Americans than most," An Mien said. "What is your honest opinion?"

"I know nothing about waging war, Your Imperial Highness. But I've seen the guns of the British squadron at close range, and I've inspected the small cannon on board the clipper ship of the American I intend to marry. Those cannon are strictly defensive weapons, but I'm certain they could destroy an entire fleet of our war junks."

"So you would advise Lin not to go out of his way to insult the British and French and other foreigners who keep naval squadrons off our coast."

"His Excellency, the viceroy, does not seek advice from me, ma'am," Lai-tse lu said politely.

"I want the truth, girl! You have served the Celestial Emperor well in the past by speaking candidly. I expect no less now!"

"Very well, Your Imperial Highness," Lai-tse lu said with a sigh. "I believe we would suffer a humiliating, catastrophic defeat in a war with the Fan Kuei. We may have invented gunpowder and weapons of metal, but our weapons are primitive by today's standards."

"How I wish I could persuade my brother to listen to you. Unfortunately, his generals and admirals tell him what he wants to hear, so—being a man—he closes his ears to anything that might be unpleasant or disturbing."

Lai-tse lu could only nod. By agreeing aloud with the

princess, she would be guilty of criticizing the emperor, a luxury enjoyed only by his outspoken sister.

An Mien changed the subject abruptly. "Have you heard from your American as yet?"

"No, Your Imperial Highness, although I'm certain he'll soon arrive." The girl revealed her vivid dream in which Jonathan had asked her to wait for him. She said nothing about the gold ring which Jonathan had given her and which she still wore on her left hand.

"In a few weeks the half-year deadline set by your father will be at hand. I would intervene with him if I could, but not even a woman in my position has the right to question the authority of a father in his own household."

Lai-tse lu raised her head high, and although she spoke softly, there was a metallic ring in her voice. "I cannot and shall not be forced against my will to marry Dom Manuel Sebastian! Even if I were to learn that Jonathan Rakehell is dead, I wouldn't marry the marquês."

The princess admired her spirit but was concerned for her. "You realize, my dear, that your father would have the right to send you off to his country estate and keep you there?"

"Let him! I prefer to rot there for the rest of my days rather than become the Marquêsa de Braga."

"I can't say I blame you. He's one of the few foreigners ever granted an audience with my brother, and I must agree that he's loathsome." An Mien became lost in thought. "I can offer you an alternative that's none too attractive. As you may have heard, my brother is worried about our young cousin, Shaong Wei. He drinks huge quantities of European brandywine when he can arrange to have it smuggled to him. And when he can't get it, he drinks himself unconscious on our own mao tai. All I need to do is to speak a word to my brother, and your father will receive an imperial decree, ordering him to give you to Shaong Wei as his bride."

Again Lai-tse lu had to speak carefully. "You make him appear less than appealing, Your Imperial Highness."

An Mien appreciated her diplomacy. "You're wrong. Shaong Wei has great charm, and under the influence of a wife who is strong and intelligent as well as beautiful—someone with your qualifications, my dear—he might reform."

"Perhaps there are other ways I can serve the Celestial Emperor," the girl replied.

They were interrupted by a serving maid, who announced that Lo Fang had returned from the waterfront and craved an audience.

"Show him in," An Mien said anxiously.

The viceroy's majordomo came into the chamber, lowering himself to the floor in a kowtow so deep that his nose touched the rich rug.

"Never mind the formalities," the princess said. "And you may speak freely in the presence of Soong Chao's daughter."

Lo Fang told them in detail about the raid.

Lai-tse lu long had known that Owen Bruce was a sworn enemy of Jonathan Rakehell, and it pleased her that such a man had lost a fortune trying to smuggle opium into the country.

"But the raid was just the beginning, Your Imperial Highness," Lo Fang said. "Now the commander of the British naval squadron is demanding an interview with the viceroy. And if I know Lin, he will refuse."

"Then I shall be obliged to use my influence and persuade the viceroy to grant the interview. In fact, I shall be present behind a screen. Whom do you recommend as a translator?"

Lo Fang glanced at Lai-tse lu. "Only one man in Canton has a command of both Mandarin and English. Soong Chao."

A sudden thought came to Lai-tse lu. "My English is better than my father's. I will gladly volunteer my services as a translator."

An Mien brightened but made no immediate reply. "Go to Lin with the request for the interview," she told the majordomo. "And say that I will join him in a moment to deliberate with him."

Kowtowing again, Lo Fang withdrew.

"Did I sense something out of the ordinary in your offer, my dear?" the princess asked.

Lai-tse lu nodded modestly. "You have taught me that a woman who uses her wisdom with subtlety is capable of exerting great influence in the world of men. My father could translate literally as well as I can do, but perhaps I can inject some words of moderation into the meeting. Otherwise, the viceroy will bluster. The British admiral, who has been a guest in my father's house on many occasions, will shake his fist in return. And the situation would become far worse than it would have been had no interview been granted."

An Mien approved at once. "You shall translate," she said, "and by preventing the outbreak of war, at least for a time, you will be performing a service of great value to the Celestial Emperor and all of his subjects."

The firm intercession of the Princess An Mien caused the imperial viceroy to change his mind, and a messenger brought word to Rear Admiral Sir William Alexander on board his flagship, H.M.S. *Invincible*, that he would be received that same afternoon. Now it was the admiral's turn to create difficulties, and he announced that he wished to use an escort of his own Royal Marines to conduct him through Canton to the palace.

His unexpected, stubborn attitude made it necessary for Soong Chao to intervene. "An escort of armed Fan Kuei in uniform could not protect you, Sir William," he said. "In fact, their presence would so inflame the people of the city that blood would be sure to flow. Some of your marines would die, and so would many of the Canton poor. And your own life would be in great danger."

"Thank you, Mr. Soong, and I'm sure you mean well. But what you don't understand, old friend, is that I intend to make a stiff protest to the viceroy. So I'm damned if I'll put myself in an untenable position by allowing imperial troops to escort me!"

"There will be no need for you to depend on the kindness of Lin," Soong declared. "My own majordomo and members of my household staff will provide you with an unobtrusive, secure escort."

The admiral accepted, and not until he came ashore in mid-afternoon, clad in his glittering blue and gold full dress uniform, did it occur to him that he had been outsmarted in a manner to which he could not object. A curtained sedan chair had been provided for him, and neither his uniform nor the color of his skin could be seen behind the screen of beaded bamboo.

Only twelve guards, not including Kai or the four chair bearers, were required to see him through the Petition Gate and

109

across the teeming city to the huge, walled palace that stood on Canton's highest hill just inside the gates of the ancient metropolis. The admiral emerged from his cramped quarters with his dignity intact.

Lo Fang led him to the audience chamber, where Lin Tse-hsü was seated on a throne with carved dragons for arms and which rested on a base of four lions, carved out of ivory. A screen of silk stood nearby, obviously concealing someone, and Sir William was further surprised when he saw Soong Lai-tse lu, whose peach-colored cheongsam and jade jewelry made her appear as though she were on her way to a garden party.

"Good afternoon, Sir William," she said as the admiral entered the high-ceilinged chamber. "I have been engaged as the translator for this meeting."

"In that case," he replied gallantly, "I shall enjoy the occasion far more than I had anticipated." Turning to the impassive viceroy he saluted stiffly.

"Why does the Fan Kuei sailor not kowtow before me?" the viceroy demanded, a petulant note in his voice.

"His Excellency," Lai-tse lu said in English, lying baldly, "understands that Westerners do not kowtow, so he freely dispenses with the obligatory form of greeting."

Sir William was pleasantly surprised. "Thank His Excellency, and tell him I bring him the personal greetings of Her Majesty, Queen Victoria."

"The Royal Navy forbids him to kowtow to anyone but his queen," Lai-tse lu said glibly in Mandarin, "but he is certain that if she were to come here, she would gladly kowtow before the viceroy."

Lin leaned back against his throne and smiled faintly

The Princess An Mien, seated behind the screen, had understood every word in both languages and found it difficult to curb a desire to giggle.

"I have come here," Sir William said, "to protest on behalf of Her Majesty's Government for the invasion of British property by Imperial Chinese troops and the illegal seizure of what a British factor, Mr. Owen Bruce, informs me were two hundred boxes of harmless tea."

"The admiral is upset," the girl told Lin, "because our troops found opium in a British warehouse."

"I also am badly upset," Lin declared. "No man has the right to bring opium into China!"

"His Excellency says opium was confiscated, not tea." Lai-tse lu glanced at Lo Fang, who raised a finger to his nose. "The smell of burning opium on the waterfront was very strong."

Sir William well realized that a portion of his protest was tenuous. He had not believed that the cases the troops had destroyed had contained tea and knew Bruce well enough to doubt the man's word. "No one," he said, "hates the opium trade more than I. If I had the final word of authority, I would cheerfully hang every last opium smuggler!"

"The admiral," Lai-tse lu said, "is ashamed because one of his countrymen was smuggling opium. He would like to hang the man."

Lin Tse-hsü smiled broadly. "The day will come when he will hang. Rest assured of that!"

Lai-tse lu thought it wise to leave that comment untranslated.

"Nevertheless," Sir William said, "there is a principle at stake. Her Majesty's Government will not tolerate the invasion of British property and the seizure of British goods."

This was the heart of the dispute, and Lai-tse lu realized she would be doing a disservice to everyone concerned if she colored the statement, so she made a direct, blunt translation.

The viceroy promptly replied in kind. "The Fan Kuei are the guests of the Celestial Emperor. Their presence here does not grant them the right to ignore imperial decrees. All aspects of the smuggling of opium into the Middle Kingdom are prohibited, and any man who breaks our laws is committing crimes punishable by death."

Again Lai-tse lu translated literally.

"I am compelled to remind His Excellency that the purpose of the Royal Navy's presence in the delta of the Pearl River is the protection of British lives and property."

The girl translated accurately, then added, "But there is no dispute between us other than the issue of opium traffic in which we hold the same position."

Lin's expression remained unchanged, but there was a hint of incredulity in his voice as he asked, "Does the Fan Kuei sailor actually offer to help me in my campaign to rid the Middle Kingdom of the vice of opium smuggling?"

Here was Lai-tse lu's chance! "His Excellency," she

said, "states there are no differences of consequence between you, and he suggests that you work together to prevent the introduction of opium into the Middle Kingdom."

Sir William lived according to a strict code of personal morality, and although no British law prevented the carrying of opium to China and its sale to greedy middlemen, he could not resist such an appeal. "Tell His Excellency I have done everything in my power to prevent smuggling by British merchantmen."

Lai-tse lu knew from his talks at her father's house that he was speaking the truth, so she translated correctly.

"Tell him further," the admiral went on, "that I shall write to their Lordships of the Admiralty in the immediate future and ask them to grant me greater authority to intervene." He fully intended to write such a letter but thought cynically that such a request would do little except perhaps speed his own retirement. He knew, realistically, that too many men in high places in London were making fortunes in the opium trade and that the suggestion of a mere rear admiral in the Royal Navy would have no practical effect on the situation.

But Lin was elated when he heard the translation. His obsessive desire to end the traffic in drugs was so great that he regarded anyone who did not agree with him as an enemy, while those who felt as he did were staunch allies. The British officer's obvious sincerity warmed him, and he stood impulsively, then bowed, an honor that one in his position rarely accorded anyone other than members of the Celestial Emperor's family.

Sir William had been stationed in the East long enough to realize he had been given a highly unusual salute, so he returned the compliment by bowing from the waist.

There was a sudden thaw in the atmosphere, and the smiles of the two antagonists were cordial.

Lai-tse lu decided the moment had come to insert a thought of her own into the talk, so she spoke firmly, first in Mandarin and then in English. "According to an old saying, brothers who deal honestly with each other move mountains when they stand shoulder to shoulder."

The viceroy nodded, as did Sir William. It did not occur to either of them that the girl had initiated the comment, that neither of them had made the observation.

The meeting soon came to an end, with the admiral sending the best wishes of Queen Victoria for the health and prosperity of the emperor; and the viceroy, not to be outdone, expressing the devout hope of the Tao Kuang Emperor that the young British queen live in peace until the age of one hundred years. As a final gesture, Lin Tse-hsü unbent sufficiently to walk with the visitor to the courtyard, where Kai and the other members of the unobtrusive escort awaited the admiral.

Never before had representatives of the Middle Kingdom and Great Britain come so close to achieving a true meeting of the minds.

The Princess An Mien was delighted, but she remained cautious a short time later when she went with Lai-tse lu to the luxurious home of her father and explained the girl's exploit to Soong Chao. "It was wonderful to see two natural enemies in agreement with each other," she said. "But soon they will be in conflict again, I fear, because Lai-tse lu will not always be on hand to smooth the waters. At least we can be grateful that today's incident did not start a war."

Chao was proud of his daughter's accomplishment, but his basic concern was not alleviated. "I regard a war with one of the Fan Kuei nations as inevitable," he said. "Probably Great Britain, because her trade with us is so much greater than that of other countries, and because her merchants have huge profits at stake in the opium trade."

"Why do they defy our laws?" An Mien asked as, accompanied by Lai-tse lu and Sarah Applegate, they adjourned to the dining pavilion for what the girl had promised would be a "simple" meal.

"As I judge the people of the West from my own business dealings with them," Chao replied, "they do not regard the Middle Kingdom as a true nation. They see a vast, sprawling land, most of it closed to all foreigners and populated by so many millions of people that they believe we are ungovernable."

"What they fail to realize," Lai-tse lu added, "is that ancient traditions hold us together as one people. Our government is weak because only the Celestial Emperor exercises real power and cannot delegate his authority easily to those he appoints as his provincial leaders. They see our hopelessly old-fashioned defenses, so they feel contempt for us. They can't realize that our strength lies in the respect we show for our ancestors and our obedience to their ways.''

"If you are right," the princess said, "and I have no way of knowing myself because I have never met any Fan Kuei and am forbidden to deal with them, our future is hopeless."

"No, never that," Chao said vigorously. "It may be that we will be defeated and humiliated in battle, but our people have resilience greater than that of others."

"That is true," An Mien conceded. "My Manchu ancestors came to the Middle Kingdom as conquerors, but over the centuries we have become more Chinese than those whom we rule. They have absorbed us so completely that we have accepted their institutions and customs and have abandoned our own."

Sarah Applegate took almost no active part in the conversation because she was too busy supervising the serving of the elaborate dinner the kitchen staff had prepared. An Mien, living as she pleased, constantly defied tradition, and never before had a member of the imperial family eaten a meal at the home of a private citizen, even one who was a member of the third mandarin class and enormously wealthy in his own right.

So the dishes being offered to the honored guest were among the most sophisticated in the almost limitless Chinese menu. One was a Cantonese delicacy known as steak kew, in which one-inch cubes of beef and diced onions had been combined with oyster sauce, soy sauce, pepper, and cornstarch, to which minced garlic and slivers of ginger had been added. While this mixture soaked, various vegetables, among them snow peas, broccoli, and asparagus had been blanched and set aside with wedges of tomatoes, a fruit still regarded as poisonous and inedible in the West. The beef mixture was cooked for no more than a minute or two in very hot peanut oil, seasoned with sesame oil. When the meat became crisp on the outside but remained pink inside, the entire mixture was poured over the blanched vegetables and served.

The timing had to be precise, with the oil still sizzling when the dish was served. Only the most accomplished of cooks could prepare such a dish, and An Mien paid her host the compliment of asking for a second helping.

Other exquisite dishes followed, among them shredded lamb with deep-fried bean-thread noodles, bamboo shoots, snow peas, water chestnuts, and dried forest mushrooms. Yet another was a clam dish that was a Peking favorite and that Lai-tse lu well remembered from her visit to the princess in the Forbidden City. Steamed clams and mussels, still in their opened shells, had been marinated for hours in soy sauce and rice wine, to which crushed, dried chili peppers, minced garlic, and rice vinegar had been added. This dish was served cold, and the diners picked the clams and mussels from their shells with their chopsticks, dipped them in the sauce, and ate them one by one.

The meal ended with the serving of a seaweed soup whose preparation required such deftness that only the most talented cooks dared to make it. Ground pork butt and a small quantity of dried shrimp were added gradually to a basic chicken stock, in which dried seaweed then simmered, and shortly before serving, various other ingredients were added, among them chopped green onions, a small quantity of sesame oil, and fresh bean-curd cakes, cut into small cubes.

An Mien belched politely to show her appreciation of the meal, and as they sat over tiny cups of a fragrant, perfumed tea so pale in color that it looked like hot water, she decided the time had become appropriate for her to offer what help she could to Lai-tse lu. "Is it true," she asked Soong Chao, "that we will soon lose your daughter to a Fan Kuei nobleman?"

There was more than a hint of disapproval in her manner, and the girl's father became uncomfortable. "The Marquês de Braga has asked for her hand, but no formal betrothal has taken place as yet."

"There will be no betrothal for another few weeks," Sarah Applegate added.

Lai-tse lu was grateful to her governess for her support.

"I have heard many tales about Dom Manuel Sebastian," An Mien said lightly, "but they cannot be true. It is said he rules in Macao with the pomp and ceremony of the Celestial Emperor. It is also said that he keeps at least fifty concubines of many nationalities, and that in spite of his wealth he is niggardly, paying his servants low wages."

Chao removed his glasses and polished them. "I cannot verify any of these tales," he said. "All I know is that the marquês is one of Europe's greatest nobles and that his wealth is greater than that of many kings."

The princess cut to the heart of the matter. "I have offered Lai-tse lu a marriage to our cousin, Shaong Wei, if she wishes it."

As Chao well knew, an offer from the emperor's sister took precedence over any other plans he might make for his daughter. Glancing first at An Mien, then at the girl, he realized he had been placed in an untenable position.

Lai-tse lu allowed herself the luxury of a tiny smile. An Mien's gesture had returned control of her destiny into her own hands. Now, if Jonathan did not appear by the time her father's deadline expired, she could stall—at least for a time—by claiming she was weighing the question of whether she wanted to marry Shaong Wei. She would not be able to procrastinate indefinitely, however, because sooner or later her father would be compelled to call her bluff. Until then, the princess had granted her the boon of more time. Still clinging to her dream, she knew in her heart that Jonathan would return to her, and only concrete proof of his death would destroy her hope.

The *Lai-tse lu* sailed steadily southward through the North Atlantic and the Caribbean Sea. The weather remained favorable, with headwinds encountered only occasionally, and Jonathan Rakehell took full advantage of his good fortune, driving himself even harder than he drove his men. Frequently he spent long hours on the deck in order to coax more and yet more speed from his huge sails, and the clipper lived up to the best of her breed, slashing through the green-blue water at a remarkable, sustained speed of twenty knots.

Even when the ship approached the equator and came to the dreaded Doldrums, Jonathan's luck continued to hold. When the breeze died away, a ship could be forced to sit motionless in a glazed sea for day after helpless day, but he told himself repeatedly that the forces of nature were on his side. The winds became gentler when the clipper came to the Doldrums, it was true, but they continued to blow steadily, and they became brisk again as he moved into the South Atlantic.

Anxious to lose no time, he restricted his visit to Rio de Janeiro when he arrived there for water, fresh meat, vegetables, and fruit. Refusing to grant his crew shore leave for as much as a single day, he bought the supplies he needed from the service boats that quickly surrounded him. And, because no one went ashore, he was spared the time-consuming need to negotiate with the local authorities for the passports required for that purpose.

Putting out to sea again after spending less than a full day at anchor, he rejoiced that the weather remained favorable. Occasional squalls were no handicap as he sailed into the temperate zone, and one night, during a gale, he took over command, spending the entire night on deck. He was tired but exhilarated, and with each passing day he became increasingly certain that he would reach Canton in time to prevent Lai-tse lu's marriage to someone else.

Then, as he drew nearer to Cape Horn at the lower tip of South America, there were signs that his fortune was changing. The skies became leaden, the sparkling sea turned a dirty, angry gray, and the winds grew erratic, forcing the officer on watch to tack more frequently. Rain fell, drenching the men working in the open and soaking the sails, and each day the cold, clammy fog in which the clipper was enveloped became thicker.

One afternoon, after being relieved by Elijah Wilbor, Jonathan went wearily to the officers' cabin—or cuddy—for a mug of black coffee. Peeling off his oilskins, he lowered himself into a chair and stared gloomily through a porthole whose glass was streaked with salt spray that a steady, cold rain was washing away. There were periods at sea when a man never felt dry. His clothes were wet, his bedding was damp, and a seaman would give his soul for a day on shore beneath a warming sun.

Holding his mug in both hands, Jonathan told himself gloomily that nature was repaying him in full for his overconfidence. It was virtually impossible to sail halfway around the world without encountering foul weather, and he was now earning his full share. But he had no right to complain. Until now, at least, he had been forced to reduce sail only infrequently, and he still had a good chance of setting a new record for the New London to Canton run, although a record for its own sake meant nothing to him on this particular voyage. He had far more at stake.

Homer Ellison came into the cuddy, blinking sleep from

his eyes, and helped himself to coffee from a pot that the cook always replenished. He walked to a porthole and looked out for a time, saying nothing.

Jonathan knew what was going through his mind and refused to subscribe to the superstition of seamen that trouble was certain to strike if potential problems were mentioned aloud. "I reckon we may be in for some headaches if the weather doesn't ease by the time we reach the Straits of Magellan."

Homer scratched his chin, sipped his coffee, and murmured, "Aye."

There was no need to elaborate. Under the best of conditions, the Straits of Magellan, the water passage separating the South American mainland from the group of islands known collectively as Tierra del Fuego, was exceptionally difficult to navigate. There was one large island, five of medium size, and small islets too numerous to be counted. Rocks on which even a large ship like the *Lai-tse lu* could founder jutted up out of the water in unexpected places and, depending on the tides, others were submerged. High mountains soared on the mainland, creating strong winds, and Tierra del Fuego, about twenty-seven thousand square miles in area, was inhabited only by sheepherders. The entire area was bleak, its desolation striking fear in the hearts of all but the most redoubtable seamen.

The one advantage offered by the Straits of Magellan was that it enabled a ship's captain to sail within hours from the Atlantic to the Pacific. Jonathan had negotiated it twice on voyages to and from China, so it had no terrors for him, but he knew he had to treat the waterway with great respect. Ever since childhood he had heard of ships that had foundered on the rocks after following false inlets that led nowhere, and in the past decade he had known of two Rakehell and Boynton merchantmen that had been forced to turn back when consistently foul weather had made it impossible for them to sail through the Straits.

"We'll manage, Homer," he said.

"That we will," his first mate replied.

Both men knew they had their work cut out for them. As the clipper continued to sail southward, buffeted by heavy winds and towering waves, they and the crew caught occasional glimpses of the mainland when the fog lifted. This portion of

Argentina, known as Patagonia, was a vast wilderness, a land where the mountains reached toward the sky and the sea battered against high cliffs along the shore. The seamen muttered to each other whenever they looked in the direction of the inhospitable coast.

Jonathan hoped to enter the Straits soon after daybreak, when he would be able to see the rocks that created such dangers to shipping. As he necessarily edged closer to the land, the wind increased, blowing in such violent gusts that he had to reduce sail.

Homer Ellison joined him, Oliver, and the helmsman on the quarterdeck, although he was off duty. He studied the American flag flying from the masthead, then observed the effect of the wind on the sails. "Not much room to tack going into the channel, it appears, Captain," he said.

Jonathan gauged the entrance as best he could, knowing the wind would reach a gale velocity once he actually sailed into the Straits. "I'm trying," he said, "but I'm not sure we can make it this morning."

Even as he spoke the sky turned darker again, and a drenching rain, propelled by the wind, blew into the men's faces.

The upper yards were sent down, and the storm-staysails were set to keep the ship's head to wind. Jonathan continued to move forward, but the headwinds were so powerful that he made little progress. No matter how great his personal desire to reach Canton as quickly as possible, he knew he had no right to endanger the lives of his men and place his ship in jeopardy.

He sighed, looked in silence at his charts for a time, and then said, "There's a sheltered cove about a mile to the north of us. We'll put in there until the weather improves."

The *Lai-tse lu* beat her way back up the Atlantic coast, entering the cove with difficulty. Even here, with cliffs rising hundreds of feet on three sides, the wind remained strong and erratic, and the surface of the water was ruffled by whitecaps.

Jonathan ordered the best bower lowered and put out a stern anchor, then the remaining sails were lowered. "We have no choice," he said. "We'll have to ride out the storm here." The wind mocked him by howling around the bare masts.

The crew settled down for a wait of undeterminable length.

119

But Jonathan knew that the weather could change very suddenly in this desolate area, so full watches were maintained around the clock. And both of his mates well knew, whenever he went off to his cabin to snatch a few hours of sleep, that he was to be awakened immediately in the event that the weather improved.

Tensions ran high on board the clipper. The cook did his best to alleviate them, preparing stewlike soups and baking fresh bread, delicacies he found it difficult to make when the ship was under way. But the spirits of the crew did not improve, the men absorbing the mood of the ship's master.

Jonathan prowled the deck by the hour, oblivious to the incessant, driving rain. Repeatedly he halted, searched in vain for a break in the solid clouds of dark, ominous gray that scudded overhead, and then resumed his pacing.

A full week passed, then the gale abated somewhat, and Jonathan decided to weigh anchor and make a run for it. To his dismay, the winds picked up again and created many new problems.

Jonathan's log reflected his frustrations:

Straits of Magellan
Course s 64 E. Lat. 48.28 S. 57.29 Wind Westerly Force Gale.
Tuesday. Weighed to run between Elizabeth and Magdelåne Islands. Got through but before we could get into Royal roads to anchor, the flood tide set us back. Brought up in 8 fathoms off NE and of Elizabeth Is. NE wind, freshened to gale force. Heavy swell.
Wednesday. Weighed and worked to windward. Head swell continuing. Carried away main topsail and a lower spanker before it could be furled and fore topmast staysail. Stove in quarter galleries. Brought to in Laredo Bay to repair damage. Every appearance of another gale from NNW Anchored in 7 fathoms.
Thursday. Thick, hazy weather, but gale abating.
Friday. Fresh water supply running low. Repairs completed. Weighed. Light northerly breeze but weather still dark and dirty. Rounded Cape Froward. Light, baffling wind; thick haze. Trimmed and set studding sails. Mate suggested putting back to Port Famine,

small Chilean settlement there. Refused; decided to make for Fortescue Bay and get our water there.

Saturday. Worked into Fortescue Bay, tacking twice, and came to in 7 fathoms. Found an American brig in the Bay, and the English brig *Caspar*, the latter dismasted. Supplied master with spare jibboom. Landing party replenished water casks. Gale force wind from NNE.

Sunday. Thick haze, but wind abating, veering northerly. Weighed at 1 p.m. Passed Port Parda, came to in 20 fathoms Mercy Harbor.

Monday. Weighed under reefed topsails. Passed Cape Pillar. Haze very thick. Observed rocks SSW about five miles, which proved to be the Evangelists. Break in mist showed land ahead. Shortened sail. Breeze freshened, heavy swell, wind light and westerly by evening. Set course for Valparaiso.

The worst was over. After navigating the Straits of Magellan the great clipper only encountered fair winds, and the voyage to Valparaiso was uneventful. But Jonathan was near despair He was hopelessly behind his schedule, and with no way to make up for lost time, he would arrive in Canton long after the deadline set by Soong Chao for the betrothal of his daughter to the Marquês de Braga.

Still more time would be lost in Valparaiso, as he well realized. He would need supplies, and more permanent repairs to his ship would be required than he had been able to make after the storm. And common sense told him to grant the ship's company twenty-four hours of shore leave They desperately needed that break.

Crowding on full sail, he could only pray that he would reach Canton before Lai-tse lu was compelled to marry another man.

Soong Chao sat in the pavilion he used as his office at home, immersed in the shipping reports recorded on wax tablets that were piled high on the table beside his padded, three-legged stool. But he was always aware of his surroundings and looked up when he heard the sound of his daughter's high wedged heels on the gravel walk.

Lai-tse lu had never looked lovelier. Her slender body was sheathed in a cheongsam of violet silk, and with it she wore matching jade earrings, a bracelet, and a huge ring. There was a hint of violet on her eyelids, too, but the smudges beneath her eyes could not be erased, and her expression was apprehensive. "Missy Sarah told me you wish to see me, my Father," she said.

Chao nodded and waved her to a padded stool.

She shook her head. "If you don't mind, I prefer to stand."

"As you wish." He removed his glasses, polished them vigorously, and then cleared his throat. "In three days I am obligated to send a message to the Marquês de Braga," he said. "I gave him my solemn word that I would inform him whether you will marry him."

"I can't yet decide," the girl replied promptly. "I am still considering the offer of the Princess An Mien to marry her cousin, Shaong Wei."

Soong Chao's expression did not change. "I am reminded," he said, "of the fable of the nightingale that imagined she had become an owl. She was convinced she was emitting the deep hoots made only by the owl, but in truth she continued to sing like the nightingale she had remained."

Lai-tse lu looked down at the tips of her sandals. "I have no right to fool you, my father," she murmured. "It is true that I have given no thought to a marriage with Shaong Wei, any more than I have seriously considered marriage to the Marquês de Braga."

Her father sighed.

She looked at him, her eyes enormous. "I have given my heart and my soul—yes, and my body—to one man. Never will I love anyone else, and never will I marry anyone else."

"You make this difficult for both of us," he said.

Tears came to her eyes, and she blinked them away. "I have honored you and respected you all the days of my life. Never have I failed to follow the precepts of our ancestors. My love and respect for you are as great as they have ever been, and much as I hate myself for defying you, I cannot obey you in this one matter, my Father."

"You are my only child," Chao said, "and with the help of Missy Sarah I have reared you since the tragic death of your

122

mother. I, too, have followed the precepts of our ancestors. Even more, I have taken the fortune I inherited, and have multiplied it many times. It is true that I enjoy living in comfort, but I have no need for the great fortune I have amassed. I have earned it to provide for your future and that of my yet unborn grandchildren. What good will my gold and silver, my precious jade and ivory do if I cause you lifelong unhappiness?''

"Send me to our estate in the hills and let me live there as a prisoner for the rest of my days, if that is your will. Subject me to a public lashing with a whip of leather in the great square that stands before the Temple of Heaven, if you wish to inflict such punishment on me. I shall not complain. Neither shall I marry the Marquês de Braga. Nor anyone other than Jonathan.''

"When Jonathan asked for your hand," Chao said, "I gave my consent in good faith. Of all the young bachelors I have ever known, I have admired none more than I admired Jonathan Rakehell. For many months after he returned to America, I was comforted and relieved by the thought that he would take you far from the Middle Kingdom, where a terrible war with the Fan Kuei surely will start at any time. But Jonathan has not been true to our trust in him. Almost two years have passed since he sailed away, and in all that time there has been no word from him.''

"I admit that Jonathan's silence has confused and hurt me, too," Lai-tse lu said. "When Charles returned here, I fully expected him to be carrying a letter from Jonathan, but he carried none. Each time a Rakehell and Boynton ship comes to Whampoa, I am always certain her captain brings me a letter, but there has been no letter. All I can say is that when Jonathan comes, he will explain.''

Her father spoke gently. "He may not come. You have been sheltered from many of the world's realities, so you don't realize how faithless—and how forgetful—men can be.''

"I have learned more than you know, thanks to the teachings of Missy Sarah and Kai. It may be that I am still naive, but I swear that Jonathan will come for me. So I beg you, my Father, put off the Marquês de Braga. Tell him that I am ill, or that political conditions are too unsettled. Give him whatever word you wish to put him off for a time.''

"How much longer do you want?" Chao was deeply pained.

"Each morning when I awaken I know that Jonathan will return to me. It is not a wish or a hope. It is a fact. If I should awaken some day without that certainty in my heart, then I will know I have waited in vain. And no matter what may become of me, I will do whatever you wish. I will even marry the Marquês de Braga, if that is your will."

She was so dear to him that he could withstand her pleas no longer. "Very well," he said. "I shall wait. But only for a short time. I will hold off the marquês as long as I can, but he is a man of great power, and if Jonathan does not appear soon, I will no longer have a choice."

Her father was being more generous than she had dared to hope, and bowing her head in submission, Lai-tse lu walked back to her own quarters, not even noticing the flowers blooming in the formal beds that lined both sides of the gravel path.

II

The Fat Dutchman sat in his peacock throne chair in the middle of the lush, tropical garden of his house on the outskirts of Djakarta, the capital of the Netherlands East Indies, and was at peace with the world. Smoking a long, dark cheroot of Javanese tobacco and sipping a tall glass of passion fruit juice, he was thoroughly enjoying his favorite time of day, the hour before dinner when he contemplated, in loving anticipation, the meal he would consume. His shirt was open at the throat, his sleeves were rolled up, and when beads of sweat appeared on the crown of his completely bald head, one of his nubile serving maids, barefooted and clad only in an ankle-length, multicolored skirt of batik, wiped his head with a cloth of perfumed cotton. Two other girls, in a similar state of undress, fanned him with palm fronds, and a half-dozen others lolled on the thick, green grass, awaiting his command to bring him another cheroot or a fresh glass of fruit juice.

There was no sound but the murmured conversations of the girls, some of them Malaysians, some native Javanese, and some Chinese. In the background, as always, were the raucous squawks of the many parrots resting on perches.

Contemplating the scene at this peaceful retreat, the Fat Dutchman knew he had good reason to be content. He was the wealthiest merchant in the East, even more powerful than his friendly trading partner in Canton, Soong Chao. He had achieved such a stranglehold on the trade of the Indies that the Dutch officials in Djakarta looked the other way when he elected to send shiploads of such goods as pepper and spices to his young associate in London, Charles Boynton. The Fat Dutchman was very fond of Charles and his American cousin, Jonathan Rakehell. Never would he forget that Jonathan had kept his promise and had built a clipper ship for him immediately after his return to America from the Orient. And since that time, in spite of the clamor everywhere for such vessels, Jonathan and Charles had provided him with another. The Fat Dutchman was eternally grateful to those who served him faithfully.

That gratitude was extended to the girls of his entourage. Only he and they knew that, because of his impotence, they provided him with no more than attractive window dressing that enhanced his image. From time to time, as a favor to important visitors and to the girls, he gave one of them to a guest for a night. And those who served well for five years were certain of winning an ample reward. Within the past year he had arranged the marriage of one to a powerful Javanese chieftain, had seen to it that another had become the sole mistress of his trading partner in Bangkok, and had negotiated a deal whereby a third had become the principal concubine in the household of the Muslim caliph of Luzon. Truly, the rewards were great, and while they were with him the girls had little to occupy them other than to primp and enjoy the many gifts he gave them.

The Fat Dutchman's sunken eyes, half-concealed by his fleshy lids, lighted when he saw his favorite emerge from the house and sweep past the ever-present security guards on duty at the entrance to the garden. It was apparent at a glance that Molinda was set apart from the other girls, and not only because she wore a breastband of tissue-thin silk. Her skin was as pale as that of a Caucasian, thanks to her Balinese mother and her French father, a physician who had died when she was a baby.

Educated by missionaries in Bali, Molinda had learned to speak Dutch, French, and English as fluently as she could converse in several Chinese and Javanese dialects. She could read and write with facility, and she was so adept that she had gradually taken over many aspects of the management of the Fat Dutchman's business activities. Certainly he trusted her far more than he did the Dutch and Javanese who worked in his Djakarta office.

What delighted him most about Molinda was her physical beauty. Her features, from her violet eyes and high forehead to her full lips and delicate chin, were perfect, and her slender yet completely feminine body, which she carried with a grace that only the women of Bali could achieve, was dazzling. The security guards gaped at her, as they always did, but she was so accustomed to admiration that she did not even notice the attention they paid her.

She wore a pale orchid in her hair, which was a glossy black, and the kohl that rimmed her eyes had been applied with a sure touch, as had the glossy red stain that emphasized her sensuous mouth. The Fat Dutchman had made a great bargain when he purchased her from the pirates who had stolen her from the missionary school in Bali. She was a remarkably beautiful woman.

At the moment she was also irritated, which he noted as she came toward him, frowning slightly, her manner aggressive.

He immediately offered her a wicker chair beside his and waved the other girls out of earshot. "It is too hot today for unpleasant talk," he said, and emitted the mirthless laugh that often punctuated his speech. "Besides, I don't want my appetite for dinner spoiled."

"I've never known anything to spoil your appetite," Molinda said, and thrust a document at him, removing it from the sheaf she was carrying.

"What's this?"

"I've been checking your correspondence with Meinheer van der Greif in Amsterdam, and you've been negligent," she said angrily. "You've sent him six shiploads of spices from Sumatra in the past year and a half, but he complains bitterly in this letter that you've withheld two shiploads of coconut oil from Borneo."

"I commend your diligence, dear Molinda. Heh-heh." The Fat Dutchman patted her head. "If you had checked the ledgers, however, you would have discovered that I withheld the coconut oil because—"

"I know," the girl said, interrupting him rudely. "He hasn't yet paid you for the last shipload of spices. What you haven't taken into account are the facts I've put together from the office staff in Djakarta. Van der Greif operates on a very thin margin. He won't be able to pay for the spices until he earns a profit on the oil.''

He raised a wispy eyebrow. "Would you have him remain in permanent debt to me?''

"Hardly." Molinda was as forceful as she was lovely. "Send him the oil, but increase the price by half. Then send him nothing more until he pays in full for the oil. In that way you cover yourself and take no financial risks.''

"Heh-heh. Attend to it, dear Molinda. You display a genius for business almost equal to my own.''

The girl plucked another document from the sheaf. "Here is a letter just received from Charles Boynton in London.''

"Aha!''

Molinda knew he was teasing her by referring indirectly to her affair with Charles on his last visit to Djakarta. The Fat Dutchman had given her to him during his stay, and to her own astonishment the relationship had become very significant to her. "He encloses a draft on a bank in Rotterdam for two thousand pounds sterling more than the purchase price of the load of pepper you sent him. He explains he's grateful to you.''

"Do you disapprove?''

"If you want my opinion, return the two thousand pounds sterling to him.''

"Heh-heh." The Fat Dutchman stared at her, his cold, deep-set eyes unblinking. "I do believe you're so enamored of Charles that you've allowed your feelings to color your business judgment.''

"Not at all,''Molinda said crisply. "Rakehell and Boynton need you, but you also need them as you expand in the English and American markets. They could have charged you outrageous sums for the clippers you wanted so badly, but they were fair, scrupulously honest. Return the compliment by sending the extra money back to Charles at once, and if I understand the Anglo-Saxon temperament, which I believe I do, you'll bind Rakehell and Boynton to you for all time.''

"Heh-heh," he murmured softly. "Dear Molinda, your acumen never fails to astonish me. I hope you're giving serious thought to my offer to make you a junior partner in my enterprises.''

"Oh, I still think about it now and then," she replied with deliberate indifference. She couldn't tell him the truth because

128

he would not understand. She was ambitious and, although only twenty-two, was so confident of her own talents that she felt certain she could achieve great success in the world. But that would be impossible here in association with the Fat Dutchman. Her real status would not change if she accepted his offer. She already held a unique place in his household, but even as a "junior partner" she would remain a slave girl. The Fat Dutchman probably would give her a bank account of her own, but she would not be able to control it, any more than he would allow her to trade, buy, or sell merchandise without his authorization. She already had acquired more gaudy jewelry than she cared to wear.

Above all, she yearned for freedom—the right to live as she wished, do what she pleased, and work for herself. That desire was the great gift Charles Boynton had given her in the long talks they had held after making love. Only in Great Britain and America, she had gleaned, were women in charge of their own destinies, and even in those advanced lands few women ever acquired true liberty. That was what she wanted for herself, even though the goal seemed impossible to obtain.

The Fat Dutchman's eyes bored into her. "What you're telling me is that you want a more active sex life than I can offer you."

"Well, yes," Molinda said, knowing his views of women were so limited that he was incapable of grasping her real yearnings.

"That's natural enough, heh-heh. The young who haven't yet been ruined by dissipation have such urges." His hamlike hand descended to her thigh and stroked it absently, and he enjoyed the feeling of her warm, firm flesh beneath the thin coating of batik.

The gesture was as distasteful as it was pathetic, but Molinda was in no position to protest or draw away. Even if he made her a "junior partner," she would continue to be subjected to these meaningless advances, and her determination to take herself elsewhere and start life anew was hardened.

"I suppose," the Fat Dutchman said genially, "that you think of yourself as being in love with Charles Boynton."

"I know nothing about the meaning of love," the girl replied truthfully.

"But you'd like to spend your days with him. And your nights, heh-heh."

She could see where the conversation was leading, and her hope flared. Charles would not hold her in bondage, which was repugnant to him, and would be certain to set her free after they spent enough time together to satisfy his lust. "Yes," she said carefully. "It has even occurred to me that there is a way you can win his gratitude for all time. Present me to him as a permanent gift."

The idea intrigued him, and he leaned back in his peacock chair, puffing on the stub of his cheroot as he considered it.

"I will continue to serve you faithfully," Molinda said, "and not only for the present. Think of how helpful it would be if you had a private representative at the headquarters of Rakehell and Boynton who could keep you informed of all their commercial activities."

He leaned toward her and pawed her bare shoulder. "Dear Molinda, you are clever beyond compare! You're useful to me here, but the services you could perform by acting as my eyes and ears at the heart of one of Britain's most prominent trading companies would be priceless!"

He had taken the bait, and her heart pounded, although she remained outwardly serene.

"When will Charles pay his next visit here?" he demanded.

He was unable to read without his glasses, which he hated to wear because they steamed, so she took the letter from him. "He promises to return to Djakarta within a year. He's eager to make a long-term agreement with you on pepper, in return for any British or American products that you want."

"Weapons are our greatest need. Small, modern firearms. Write him accordingly, and I'll sign the letter." The Fat Dutchman looked at her solemnly. "I trust a year isn't too long for you to wait for him, heh-heh."

"It will pass quickly," Molinda said, and, gathering her documents, returned to the house. Her expression was demure, but there was a new spring in her barefooted step and her hips swayed provocatively in the Balinese manner. True freedom at last beckoned, and although Charles Boynton didn't yet know it, he was the instrument through which she would achieve it.

*   *   *

The *Green Frog* made her way slowly up the Thames to London, the great river somewhat less crowded than usual because the day was Sunday. Only a skeleton force was on duty at the Southwark yards of Rakehell and Boynton, but the ship was docked without difficulty under the direction of a pilot, and Charles said the unloading of the clipper could wait until the following morning.

A carriage and team of horses were brought to the waterfront from the company stable; and after the baggage was tied to the roof, Charles took the reins himself, with Ruth seated beside him on the box, while Wu-ling and the two little boys rode in the interior of the coach.

Ruth was awed by the skyline across the river as Charles identified the Houses of Parliament, Westminster Abbey, and the solid structures of the Whitehall complex, including the palace of Queen Victoria and the major government buildings. They crossed the river, riding past St. Paul's Cathedral, the great banks, and mercantile houses, and Ruth sat in stunned silence.

She had never visited any city larger than Boston, which was one-tenth the size of London, and she felt like a gawky provincial, uncertain that she could live up to her responsibilities as the wife of a prominent shipping magnate and the daughter-in-law of one of Great Britain's prominent men of commerce.

Charles read her mind and took her hand. "Never fear," he said. "You'll take this town by storm."

"I'd rather be accepted quietly, without any fuss," she replied.

"You shall set your own pace," he promised her. "But I must warn you that my mother will plan a gala assembly in your honor. Our ballroom isn't used very often, and Mother won't miss this opportunity to fill it with two hundred guests."

"I daresay I'll survive," she murmured with a faint sigh of resignation.

"You'll charm everyone you meet," he told her with a chuckle. "The only possible exceptions are several girls who had marriage in their eyes whenever they looked at me."

"I respectfully urge them to keep their distance from you," Ruth said, "because I'm prepared to scratch their eyes out if they dare to come near you."

He laughed loudly.

"Seriously," she said, "the only person who worries me is your father. I've known both your parents for years, of course, and I know Lady Boynton will be polite, no matter what she might feel. But just the thought of Sir Alan's reaction sends shivers up my spine."

Charles sobered, too. "Don't worry," he said. "Father has been so eager to see me married that he'll be the tamest lion you ever saw." He hesitated, then told her his own concern. "What worries me is how he'll react to David. I told Mother that I have a Eurasian son, but Father knows nothing. Unless Mother has had the courage to break the news to him. Of all of London's two million insular, closed-minded people, there's no one more bigoted than my father."

She squeezed his hands. "Both of us will survive nicely, and so will David."

"Thank you. I just wanted you to be prepared. Because I'm ready to buy or rent us a house of our own, if it should be necessary."

"You actually think it may be that bad?"

"I'm prepared for anything," he said.

A short time later they drove up to the front door of the imposing house in Belgravia, and Ruth swallowed hard. Just the prospect that this handsome establishment might become her home increased her apprehension.

A groom appeared to take the horses and carriage, the butler supervised the unloading of the luggage, and one of the serving maids hurried upstairs to inform Sir Alan and Lady Boynton that Mr. Charles had come home from America.

Charles led the way into the house. Ruth followed, holding the hands of the children, with a nervous Wu-ling, overwhelmed by the grandeur of the mansion, bringing up the rear.

Sir Alan and Lady Boynton came down the stairs to the huge, tile-floored entrance hall, then stopped short when they saw the group entering the house.

Charles wasted no words. "Ruth and I were married just before we sailed from New London," he said.

Jessica Rakehell Boynton blinked in surprise, and then a slow smile spread across her face. "Oh, my dear," she said,

132

instantly embracing her new daughter-in-law. "How wonderful. I'm so happy for both of you. For all of us."

Ruth was so relieved she was afraid she would weep.

Sir Alan was surprised, and he was incoherent. "Well," he said. "Well." Then he stepped forward, too, to kiss the girl his son had so unexpectedly married.

No longer concerned about her own reception, Ruth nevertheless held her breath as she awaited the Boyntons' reaction to the rest of Charles's news.

"You already know Julian," he said. "He's come for a visit with us."

Lady Boynton stooped to kiss her grandnephew. "Even though I haven't seen him since he was a baby," she said, "I'd have known him anywhere." Then she said to the little boy, "You look exactly like your papa and grandpa. And like me. All Rakehells have such a strong family resemblance."

Ruth's fingernails dug into the palms of her hands as she watched Sir Alan stiffly shaking the little boy's hand.

Charles cleared his throat. "This is Wu-ling, who has come from Canton," he said. "She is the sister of the late Alice Wong."

The ill-at-ease Chinese girl wasn't sure what to do, so she curtsied.

Lady Boynton tried to make her comfortable. "Welcome to London and to our house, Wu-ling," she said. The girl smiled, and Sir Alan nodded to her but obviously had no idea why she was a member of the party.

Charles bent down and picked up the smaller boy. "And this," he said, his voice firm and a trifle too loud, "is Alice Wong's son. David. My son—David Boynton."

Sir Alan glanced at the boy and his face grew pale. Then he looked at Charles. "Please excuse me," he said, then turned on his heel and made his way slowly up the stairs.

Jessica exchanged a quick look with Charles, then took her grandson from him, hugged the boy, and smothered him with kisses. Her reaction was so natural, so spontaneous that tears finally came to Ruth's eyes.

Charles, to be sure, was defensive. "I might have known he'd behave that way," he said.

His mother was resolute. "I'm afraid I failed you, Charles.

133

I tried to prepare him, but he refused to listen to me. But never fear," she added, including her new daughter-in-law as she continued, "Alan will come round. In his own good time."

She was continuing to hold and hug David, who was thoroughly enjoying the attention. Charles grinned, then sobered. "I don't want to embarrass you, Mother," he said, "but Ruth and I are prepared to take temporary quarters in a hotel until we can find a house of our own."

Jessica was shocked. "You'll do no such thing!" she said indignantly. "You were born here. This is your home. Your wife's home and your son's home. I won't permit you to live anywhere else, not for a single night! And I think we've been standing in this drafty hall long enough. You must be hungry and tired. Come along, Ruth. I'll show you the suite I've kept ready for Charles and his wife for years. And Wu-ling, of course, will be in the governess's room, on the nursery floor. After you are all settled, we'll have something to eat. Boys, as it happens, the cook baked a huge chocolate cake today, so just be patient for a few minutes longer, and then you can eat to your hearts' content."

She led the way up the stairs, still carrying David. Julian scampered after them. Charles followed more slowly, one arm around Ruth, the other sheltering Wu-ling.

But as she mounted the stairs, it was obvious to Ruth that, in spite of her new mother-in-law's genuine, generous hospitality, serious problems lay ahead.

The young family quickly settled into the routines of their new life. Ruth was delighted with her sitting room and bedchamber, as well as the separate dressing rooms for her and for Charles. The children had adjoining rooms, one a bedchamber and the other a playroom, similar to what they had enjoyed at the Rakehell house in New London. And Wu-ling was overwhelmed by her own bedroom, which was larger than the entire house in which she had lived with her grandmother in Canton.

Ruth established a regimen for David and Julian almost identical to what they had known in New London. The only difference was that Lady Rakehell joined her and Wu-ling when she supervised the children's meals. The older woman also insisted on replacing Ruth as the bedtime storyteller several evenings each week.

At Jessica's suggestion a tutor was hired for Wu-ling, and a dressmaker, a cobbler, and a milliner were summoned to the house to prepare new wardrobes for Charles's wife and the Chinese girl. Jessica also insisted that Wu-ling join the family at meals, and from the outset she made it emphatically clear that the girl was to be treated as a member of the family, not as a servant.

Sir Alan made a great effort to insure that his daughter-in-law felt at home. He told her news of the United States, subscribed to New York and Boston newspapers for her, and made certain to include her in every conversation. He exerted himself to be polite to Wu-ling, and although it was difficult for him to unbend with her, he never allowed himself to forget that she was a guest under his roof.

But he could bring himself to go no farther. He discussed business freely and at length with Charles but never mentioned personal matters. Above all, he totally ignored David, acting as though the child did not exist. At no time did he visit the third-floor nursery and playroom, and when the children came downstairs, he chatted briefly with Julian, never as much as glancing in his grandson's direction.

Jessica did her best to smooth the situation. "Unfortunately," she told Charles in Ruth's presence, "your father always felt ill at ease with small children. I don't recall his paying the slightest attention to you before you could walk and talk. Luckily for Elizabeth, she was old enough to converse fairly fluently at the time we adopted her."

The strains of living under the Boynton roof were relieved somewhat for the newlyweds because they led such an active social life. Charles's many friends, including classmates from Eton and Oxford, friends of his parents, and business associates, invited him and Ruth to so many dinner parties that they were absent from the house three or four evenings each week. And on Sundays, after church, when there were few social activities, Charles took Ruth, the children, and Wu-ling on sightseeing trips around London, thus making it unnecessary for David to sit at his grandfather's Sunday dinner table without being recognized.

The tensions were further alleviated when Elizabeth returned from her year of attendance at a French boarding school. Her brother's marriage delighted her, and she made no secret of her reasons.

"When I heard you had moved into the Rakehell house," she told Ruth, "I was dreadfully afraid you had designs on Jonathan."

Charles laughed. "Now that you're a member of the family," he said to his wife, "you'll need to know our biggest secret. At the age of six—or thereabouts—Elizabeth decided she was in love with Jonathan, and ever since that time she's been setting her cap for him."

Ruth smiled, thinking it ironic that she, like her adolescent sister-in-law, had long imagined herself in love with Jonathan. Absorbed in her present, busy life, she could only hope she had rid herself of yearnings that now, more than ever, could not be fulfilled.

Elizabeth did not regard the revelation as amusing. "Charles may laugh at me all he pleases, but in a few years I'll be old enough for marriage. And when I am, I fully intend to become Jonathan's wife. You'll see."

Charles's quick, warning glance told Ruth not to mention Jonathan's reason for returning to the Orient. Later the young woman confirmed that her guess had been correct. Elizabeth knew nothing of Lai-tse lu's existence, and Jessica had decided it was best to say nothing in the hope that the shock of his remarriage would cure the girl of her childish obsession.

Somewhat to the surprise of everyone in the family, Elizabeth and Wu-ling quickly discovered that, in spite of the disparity of their backgrounds, they were kindred spirits. Soon they became inseparable, sharing secrets, whispering in corners, and, in the presence of others, speaking in a cryptic Sino-English that no one else could understand. Elizabeth's friends took to Wu-ling, too, regarding her as exotic, and girls and boys alike sought her friendship. What was more, the lovely young Chinese girl was becoming totally familiar not only with the English language, but with English manners and customs, as well.

Elizabeth begged to remain at home and complete her education with a tutor. To Jessica's surprise, her husband readily agreed.

"It does her a great deal of good," he said in the privacy of their bedchamber, "to be exposed to someone from a far different world. An association with Wu-ling is better for her than spending another year in France."

Jessica agreed, but couldn't help asking, "Alan, how can you be so broad-minded on one hand when on the other you refuse to recognize David's existence?"

"We're discussing two different matters," he replied curtly. "One isn't relevant to the other."

She knew from the way he clamped his jaws as he extinguished his bedside oil lamp that the discussion was ended.

Subsequently Jessica tried a different tack. Frequently she gave luncheons and teas in order to introduce her new daughter-in-law to her friends, and these occasions almost invariably included brief appearances by Julian and David, who was openly presented as Charles's son. It was inevitable that eyebrows should be raised in private, but David was his own best propagandist, and distinguished members of some of England's greatest families soon came to accept him because of the warmth, charm, and intelligence the child displayed even at his young age.

"If the Cecils can accept David," Jessica demanded of her husband, "why can't you?"

"They aren't related to him. I am," he replied.

The newspapers of London were filled with articles regarding the increasing complications in the relations of Great Britain and China, with the emphasis placed on the refusal of the Chinese to engage in normal trade with British merchants. The press dealt lightly with the opium smuggling problem, which, as many editors privately admitted, could not be defended.

The younger aristocrats of London came to know China through Wu-ling. She and Elizabeth created something of a sensation at a party given by the Marquess of Belmont for his daughter, Lady Pamela, who was the same age as Elizabeth and Wu-ling. Wu-ling attended the affair in a pretty English party frock, while Elizabeth, using subtly applied cosmetics to give her a Chinese look, appeared in a cheongsam. The two girls became the talk of fashionable London, which pleased them enormously.

Word of the incident reached Windsor Castle, and soon thereafter the twenty-year-old Queen Victoria invited her old friend, Charles Boynton, to tea. In a note written in her own hand she urged him to bring the two young girls as well as his wife.

Lady Boynton firmly vetoed the plan of the two girls to wear cheongsams. "You will dress appropriately," she said.

Consequently both wore party dresses of identical ivory-colored silk. Unknown to Elizabeth's mother, however, they had found a pair of large, green jade rings in a curio shop, and after leaving the house they slipped them onto their fingers.

On the hour-long carriage ride to Windsor, Charles issued specific instructions on how people were expected to behave in the presence of royalty.

Queen Victoria received her guests in her modestly furnished private apartment in the magnificent, eight-hundred-year-old castle. Slender, vivacious, and quietly dressed, she looked as ingenuous as Elizabeth and Wu-ling. Like them, she wore her long hair loose, and it fell freely down her back.

Charles bowed low, Ruth curtsied to the floor, and the two young girls followed her example, both of them privately disappointed because the tiny queen resembled scores of girls they knew.

A cart filled with small, crustless sandwiches of cucumber, of beef, and of watercress was wheeled into the room, and the servants withdrew. Victoria poured the tea herself, and after chatting briefly with Charles about mutual acquaintances, she announced, "I'm fascinated by China!"

"Is there anything in particular you'd like to know, Your Majesty?" Charles asked.

"Indeed!" The queen turned to Wu-ling. "Do you speak English?"

"As best I can, Your Majesty," the girl replied.

"I'm so glad," Victoria said. "I believe you're the first Chinese ever to take up residence here, and I must ask you How does it feel to come to a civilized land?"

Charles cleared his throat, then saw Wu-ling's face and decided it would be discreet to let the girl provide her own answer.

"The civilization of China was very old," Wu-ling said solemnly, "when the people of these islands lived naked in caves. I have visited many museums here and have been the guest in the homes of many prominent people, but nowhere have I seen sculptures and paintings that can compare with those of the Middle Kingdom. People here are proud of their gardens, but even those of the wealthy—and those of Your Majesty yourself, which we saw as we drove through the Windsor grounds—are only as lovely as those of our poorest peasants.''

Ruth hoped the girl wasn't going too far, and Charles bit back a grin, but the young queen nodded eagerly. ''Tell me more, please. I wasn't being impertinent, you know. My tutors crammed me with information on Britain and Europe, but China was never mentioned. I want to learn all I can.''

''I'll see to it that Your Majesty receives several books on Chinese art that I brought home with me from Canton,'' Charles said.

Before Victoria could thank him, the eager Wu-ling resumed her recital. ''Gunpowder was invented in the Middle Kingdom, but our Celestial Emperors and their subjects use it only for purposes of defense. Never have our armies invaded the homelands of weaker nations. We invented paper, and we invented printing. Without these tools, the whole world would still be made up of barbarians.''

''How marvelous!'' Victoria clapped her hands together. ''I hope that someday I'll have the opportunity to meet the—ah—Celestial Emperor.''

Wu-ling shook her head, ignoring a warning look from Charles. ''That will not happen, I believe. The Celestial Emperor rules the Middle Kingdom, the land that lies between heaven and the lower regions. So all other kings and queens are inferior to him. The English are very proud, and I have heard it said that the ruler of the English would not kowtow to him.''

''Kowtow?'' Victoria was puzzled.

''You would be required to prostrate yourself on the floor before his throne,'' Charles said with a broad grin, ''and as I understand it, the ceremony would not be complete until you touched your nose to the rug.''

The queen giggled. ''I can see that might create a bit of difficulty,'' she said.

Suddenly everyone was laughing aloud.

More tea was poured, and Wu-ling became bold enough

to say, "I, too, am curious. Does Your Majesty know why your subjects defy the laws of the Celestial Emperor and smuggle opium into the Middle Kingdom?"

Victoria was puzzled. "I know nothing about opium."

"It is a vicious, insidious drug, ma'am," Charles said. "It produces dreams and a feeling of well-being, but its frequent use causes those who smoke or otherwise ingest it to waste away. It literally destroys the user physically."

"Oh, dear," the queen said. "I must inquire of my prime minister about this. Lord Melbourne has been teaching me many things about matters of state, but he's so busy he rarely has time to answer all of my questions, I'm sorry to say."

Melbourne, Charles thought, would find it embarrassing to speak to her with candor about the opium problem. "Perhaps, when I make my next voyage to China," he said, "the prime minister and the Cabinet would approve should Your Majesty like to send a message to the Celestial Emperor."

"What a nice thought, Charles," she said. "I think I should like to write the Celestial Emperor."

Charles had been keeping an eye on the clock over the hearth, and precisely one hour after he and his party had arrived they took their leave. Elizabeth babbled on the carriage ride back to London, and Ruth was talkative, too. But Wu-ling remained silent for the better part of the journey, and not until they were nearing the Boynton house did she speak.

"England and China are very different," she said. "Here the queen poured tea for me, a nobody, with her own hands. In the Middle Kingdom the lowborn are not allowed to enter the Imperial City, much less the inner portion, the Forbidden City, where the Tao Kuang Emperor lives. But suppose the Celestial Emperor had consented to see me. If I had spoken one sentence of criticism of the Middle Kingdom—as I criticized England to the queen—an executioner would have removed my head with an ax. Yet, for all the good things they do, the British still smuggle opium into China, though no Chinese bring it here."

Elizabeth, who had been wide-eyed, nodded solemnly. "The world is strange," she said.

The Great Wall lay to the northwest of Peking, a monumental feat of engineering and human effort intended to prevent invaders from overrunning the Middle Kingdom. But the rulers of the Manchu Dynasty, whose ancestors had conquered China, made certain that their own persons and those close to them were secure. In the heart of Peking lay a vast, walled area known as the Imperial City, and here the officials of the government, the bureaucrats, and the clerks lived and worked. Deep within the Imperial City lay another compound surrounded by high walls. This area was the Forbidden City, guarded night and day by smartly clad troops of the imperial regiments. Within that compound lived the government ministers and their families, as well as the corps of eunuchs, the Middle Kingdom's real administrators, who kept their ranks filled by inducting the nation's brightest and most promising youths, then educating them for many years before granting them any real power.

In the exact center of the Forbidden City was yet another walled compound, so sacred that it had no name. Here, within the thick stone walls of its many buildings, lived the Celestial Emperor and his relatives, his wives and children, as well as his nine hundred concubines, most of whom had never set eyes on the present mild-mannered occupant of the Chrysanthemum Throne.

The Tao Kuang Emperor, who dressed extravagantly only on state occasions, was tall and slender, having inherited his broad-shouldered physique from his ferocious Manchu ancestors. That was the only resemblance he bore them, and any arrogance he possessed was innate, since he had known from earliest childhood that he would become the absolute monarch of the most populous nation on earth. Ordinarily he wore the simple, black silk robe of a scholar, and his feet were clad in slippers so old that the dragons embroidered on them were faded. His expression was mild, perennially thoughtful, and his absentminded walk was slightly stooped. As several of his wives told him with great tact, he was inclined to shuffle.

The gorgeous pagodas of the Forbidden City were filled with priceless works of art, and even the walls of many of the more ornate structures were carved inside and out. Within these walls were statues of gold and silver, ivory and jade, paintings too numerous to be counted, vases and other porcelain objects, some taller than a man, that were precious beyond compare. Most floors were made of marble, laid in intricate designs, and over some were thrown rugs of rare beauty.

But the Tao Kuang Emperor took his surroundings for

granted, ignoring them, just as he consistently refused the rare and exotic dishes prepared by the corps of more than three hundred cooks. Members of his household were in despair because he preferred to eat plain boiled rice to which bits of chicken or pork occasionally were added, the mung bean noodles that were a staple fare of the poor, and the long, thin wheat noodles that Marco Polo, a visitor from the West generations earlier, had taken back to Venice with him and had called spaghetti.

The Tao Kuang Emperor spent the better part of each business day perched on his stone Dragon throne, which he found so uncomfortable that he heaped silk cushions on it. As he squirmed there, watching his ministers kowtow, he had to listen to their interminable reports because, when they finished making their long speeches, his duty required him to ask intelligent, penetrating questions, then make decisions. No one else in the entire Middle Kingdom had the authority to make these decisions, and as the Celestial Emperor well knew, a simple nod of his head could affect millions of his subjects.

A slave to his duty, as his father before had been and as his oldest son was in training to be, he had no serious vices. At breakfast he drank too much strong tea, which caused him to suspend his morning audiences while he retired to use a chamber pot hidden by a screen behind the Dragon throne. He enjoyed a peasant's seasoning of garlic and a little sesame oil on his noodles, to which his senior wife objected, so he refrained from sleeping with her on the nights he had eaten it. Rice wine upset his delicate digestion, and mao tai, the potent sorghum-based liqueur, caused him to become sick to his stomach.

At the end of each day, when thousands of servants were lighting oil lamps throughout the Forbidden City, the emperor took his only escape from duty, walking down a long corridor, absently returning the salutes of his personal regiment's troops, and entering a small, unadorned pagoda whose walls were bare. The only furniture consisted of several padded, three-legged stools, and no matter what the crisis, no minister of state, no high-ranking eunuch, and no wife was permitted to interrupt him here.

As usual, the only person in the room was the Tao Kuang's younger sister, the Princess An Mien, clad in a smart but simple cheongsam. None of his wives held the rank of empress, and it was generally conceded that, in fact if not in title, An Mien held that position.

An Mien kowtowed before her brother only on state occasions. Now she looked up from the tablet on which she was writing rapidly with a stylus, forming the characters with a bold, flowing hand, and smiled absently at him, then resumed her writing.

The Tao Kuang Emperor sank onto a stool, looked around him, and sighed. The hour of peace he spent here every day was the only respite he knew, and he relished it. He gazed for a time at the charcoal fire burning in a brazier at the far end of the pagoda. Then he hauled himself to his feet, slid open the door, and picked up a large copper container packed in snow. He carried the container to his stool and filled an exquisitely carved jade cup of imperial yellow with chilled, sweetened tea. An Mien prepared it for him herself each day because no one else knew how to mix it to his liking.

Pulling off the close-fitting cap, studded with hundreds of huge pearls, that was a symbol of his exalted rank, the Tao Kuang Emperor sighed and scratched his head.

"You have had a difficult day, my brother," An Mien said, a hint of sympathetic understanding in her voice.

"Two rivers in the middle provinces have flooded, and no one can give me accurate statistics on how much of the rice crop has been destroyed. I had to condemn three murderers to death by the Thousand and One Tortures because the weakling governor of Szechuan lacked the heart to pronounce sentence on them. And there has been another incident in Whampoa with the dragon-accursed English. I've almost made up my mind to close Whampoa to the Fan Kuei and retake possession of Macao from the Portuguese."

"Don't," his sister said succinctly.

"They're not worth the trouble they cause us, and in spite of all that Lin Tse-hsü is doing, the tide of opium being smuggled into the country is becoming a deluge. Our pitiful dribble of trade with outsiders is more trouble than it is worth."

"There will be real trouble if you try to expel the foreigners," An Mien told him.

"Then I shall destroy them." He removed a slipper and scratched the sole of his foot.

"You've been listening to your admirals and generals

143

again. Kuang, you spend your entire life behind these walls. You have no idea of what is happening in the real world, and you're forced to depend on the observations of others. Listen to me, because I see with your eyes! The warships and cannon of the Fan Kuei, especially the British, are mighty. Their soldiers and sailors use powerful firearms that make our matchlocks and the weapons of our ancestors look absurd. The British and French will go to war if you try to expel them. I don't know what the Americans will do, but the Portuguese will join them, and so will the Spaniards. And perhaps the Danes. They'll defeat you, humiliate you, and force you to sign a demeaning peace treaty with them!''

The Tao Kuang Emperor gulped down another cup of the chilled tea. ''You forget the Chrysanthemum Throne is invincible,'' he said.

''*You* forget that the Chrysanthemum Throne is occupied by a man, not a god, as our poor people believe. And at the end of a day's work he is so tired after listening to conflicting advice from men who want only to advance their own interests that his mind no longer functions clearly.''

''Would you have me surrender to the demands of the Fan Kuei?''

''Compromise with them, Kuang. Then, little by little, subvert the rights you grant them. Encroach on those rights. Nibble, as a mouse nibbles through a wall!''

He sighed. ''We'll discuss this more thoroughly another day. You're right, An Mien. My mind is muddled this evening. But I've never tasted better chilled tea. I wish you'd give the recipe to one of my wives. Or that young concubine I fancy. I can't remember her name at the moment.''

''All five of your wives have had the recipe for years. And the young concubine can't even lacquer her own nails.'' She resumed her writing.

For some moments there was no sound in the pagoda but the scratching of her stylus.

''Can't you write some other time of the day?'' the Tao Kuang Emperor demanded irritably.

''Be patient. I'm almost done.'' She wrote a few more characters, then held out her hand. ''Your seal ring, please.''

Slowly he removed the huge ring that contained the seal

144

of his exalted office, a dragon's head surrounded by a border of chrysanthemums.

An Mien went to a cabinet set into the wall, removed a cake of sealing wax, which she heated over the brazier, then affixed the imperial seal to the parchment document. "There, that's done," she said.

"Am I permitted to know the decree I've just confirmed?" He took the ring from her.

"You have just ordered Shaong Wei confined for the next year in the old imperial palace in Nanking, attended by three of the most distinguished senior physicians of the court," she said.

"Oh, no," he moaned, shaking his head.

"I wrote the document for you, because I knew you didn't have the heart to prepare the directive yourself. An immediate halt must be made to Shaong Wei's drinking, and you know it, Kuang. He's intelligent and charming, but the spirits he drinks are destroying him."

"But your remedy is so drastic," he said, and was deeply disturbed.

"There is no other way," his sister told him firmly. "The physicians admit they can't cure him, but they insist that a woman of beauty and strength, with the mind of a mandarin of the first class, might be able to help him. I agree that he desperately needs such a woman, and this directive gives us a year to find her. If we must, we can even extend the period he'll be kept in Nanking."

"You know very well that I'm willing to sign a decree making it possible for Wei to marry a commoner. And w. agreed that Soong Chao's daughter would be the best choice." The Tao Kuang Emperor looked at her resentfully. "You even went to Canton to make the arrangement, but you returned empty-handed."

"I changed my mind," An Mien said flatly, making it plain that she enjoyed that prerogative. "Lai-tse lu is so lovely, so loyal, and so honorable that I couldn't inflict the punishment of a marriage to Shaong Wei on her. Besides, I learned that she loves an American, the builder of those wonderful new ships-that-look-like-birds, and she's waiting for him to come for her. A forced marriage to Wei would ruin her life."

145

"I have half a mind not to sign a permit for her to marry a foreigner," he grumbled, reminding her of his ultimate authority.

An Mien ignored the threat, knowing it was meaningless. In spite of his severity when he dealt with those who opposed his will, he was endowed with an unexpected compassionate streak that his sister encouraged when it suited her purposes. "Never fear," she said, "we'll find the right girl to tame Shaong Wei."

"Where will we find her?" he demanded.

"In a few days, as soon as I prepare the directive, you will order the secret police to send you two hundred and fifty of their best agents for a special assignment. I will prepare a careful list of the qualifications necessary in the woman who will become Shaong Wei's wife. The agents will search every city, every remote corner of the Middle Kingdom countryside for her. They will be told to send the candidates here, and I will interview them myself. You'll be required to see only those whom I regard as suitable possibilities."

The Celestial Emperor brightened. "I should have known you'd find the right way to take care of this problem," he said. "Of all the millions of women who are my subjects, there must be one who is right."

"Don't forget that when I brought the imperial soothsayer to you the other day, he predicted she would be found."

"So he did." Refreshed and encouraged, he pulled on his pearl-studded cap, then took a last swallow of the chilled tea. "He also said I would be surprised by an unlikely candidate. Well, we shall see. I've grown very fond of that soothsayer, and it would make me unhappy if I should be forced to have him executed for incompetence." Nodding brightly, he went to the sliding panel and disappeared down the corridor that would take him to his own quarters.

An Mien smiled as she closed the panel. For someone whom millions regarded as divine, her brother was very human indeed.

Sir Alan Boynton went directly from luncheon at his club to an investment bank of which he was a director, in order to attend a board meeting. He expected the session to last the better part of the afternoon, so he had informed his princ᳕al clerk that he would not return to his office that afternoon. Somewhat to his surprise, only routine matters were discussed, and the meeting was adjourned far earlier than he had expected.

He had already dismissed his driver and carriage, and on sudden impulse he decided he would do no more work that day. Only rarely did he excuse himself, but there were no decisions of importance to be made, and the paper work on his desk could wait until morning. So he decided to return home and enjoy the luxury of spending the rest of the afternoon in his library, which was filled with books he never had time to read.

Walking briskly, he enjoyed the cool, crisp air and sunshine, and he was in a happy frame of mind when he reached Belgravia.

The butler was surprised to see him. "The ladies have gone shopping, Sir Alan," he said. "I'm sure they would have stayed at home if they had known you'd be early today."

"No matter."

"Miss Elizabeth and Miss Wu-ling are at work upstairs with their tutor. Shall I notify them that you've come home?"

"No, please don't interrupt them. I'm capable of looking after myself, thank you." Sir Alan wandered into the library, went to a humidor, and selected a West Indian cigar, which he lighted with care. Walking to shelves that extended from ceiling to floor, he selected a book of essays by Thomas Carlyle, and settled on a leather sofa, where the sunlight streamed over his shoulder.

Savoring the fine tobacco, he leafed through the leatherbound volume, seeking an essay that would interest him. Carlyle was said to possess one of the more incisive literary minds of the era, but Sir Alan was unfamiliar with his work. He rejected an essay about Goethe, never having read anything written by the German poet, and he continued to turn the pages.

Suddenly he was startled by a pounding sound directly behind the sofa, followed by a series of even stranger noises. He leaped to his feet, and saw Julian and David, surrounded by alphabet blocks, trying in vain to suppress their giggles. So the children were using his library as a playroom!

Sir Alan had two obvious choices. Either he could ring for a servant and have the boys removed, or he could take his book to the parlor, his sitting room, or his bedchamber. He elected to follow a third course: he refused to be driven out of his library by Charles's part-Chinese bastard, whom he refused to recognize. So he resumed his seat and doggedly started to read the essay on Goethe.

The pounding noise resumed and the children, not having been chastized, began to laugh aloud.

Sir Alan tolerated the interruption for as long as he could and as best he could. But it was impossible to concentrate on Carlyle's profound and inventive prose, so he abandoned the effort. Returning the book to its shelf, he couldn't help returning his attention to the small boys, who were now energetically building something with the blocks.

Julian, he reflected, was a splendid lad. Tall for his age, with the wide-set Rakehell eyes and firm chin. The image of Jonathan. What a welcome addition he would be when he took the place that would await him at Rakehell and Boynton.

No one else was near to see what he was doing, and Sir Alan, unable to resist the temptation, found himself studying David, really looking hard at him for the first time.

The boy was husky and well-formed, as Charles had been. And it seemed that he had a quick mind. Julian was trying to spell out his name with the blocks, and David, although far too young to spell, was trying to help him.

"L-L," he called out.

The older child was scornful. "That's E."

David was silent for a moment. "E-E," he said, studying the block intently.

Sir Alan grudgingly approved.

Becoming aware of the man's scrutiny, David turned and looked up at him.

A shock that shot through Sir Alan caused him to gasp. The eyes that gazed up at him were Charles's eyes. He would have known them anywhere.

A half-hour later, when Jessica and Ruth returned from their shopping expedition, they were met at the door by a badly upset butler.

"M'lady, Mrs. Boynton, there was nothing I could do to prevent it! I—I'm so dreadfully sorry—"

"Sorry about what, Perkins?" Jessica demanded.

"Sir Alan came home unexpectedly early and went to the library. I—I didn't realize it at the time, but the two little boys were at play there. I—I haven't dared go near the room!"

Jessica and Ruth looked at each other in alarm, then raised their skirts and raced up the stairs to the second floor. As they drew near the library, they could hear Sir Alan's deep voice.

"Find the V, David. It's the middle letter in your name. No, Julian, don't show him. Let him spell his name by himself."

David held up a block in triumph. "V," he shouted.

"Good lad!" Sir Alan became aware of the two women, who stood together at the threshold.

They were gaping at him in astonishment, and it was plain that the last sight on earth they had expected to see was that of Sir Alan on all fours, playing with David!

"Ah, there you are," he said calmly. "Ruth, you and Charles would be very wise to go through the legal process of adopting the lad. Immediately. It's quite painless, and our solicitors can attend to it as a routine matter. In that way his legitimacy can never be questioned."

They continued to stare at him, and then Jessica finally spoke up. "Alan, I tried to explain to you before Charles's arrival that David already has been formally adopted and has been baptized, as well."

"Oh, well, that settles it then, doesn't it?" Sir Alan said, and he turned back to the child. "Now, find the I, David. No, don't do it for him, Julian. The I is so easy to find, David. Remember? Ah, that's it. Good lad!"

The happy shrieks of the children, mingling with Sir Alan's booming chuckle, followed the two women down the corridor. When Jessica and Ruth looked at each other, both were smiling, but there were tears in their eyes, too.

III

Foul weather and strong headwinds delayed the *Lai-tse lu* on her Pacific crossing, and although Jonathan put in to the port of Honolulu, in the Sandwich Islands, no longer than necessary to take on supplies of fruit, meat, and water, he was six weeks behind schedule. By the time he sailed through the South China Sea and entered the delta of the Pearl River, more than four and one-half months had passed since he had left New London.

He tried to accept the delays with the fatalism of the professional seaman, but his disappointment mingled with a sense of apprehension. If he was too late, finding that Lai-tse lu was already married to the governor-general of Macao, he would never forgive himself.

As he slowly made his way up the delta toward Whampoa, he noted a distinct change in the familiar surroundings. When he had sailed for home two years earlier, the scene had been peaceful, but now scores of Chinese war junks lay at anchor. These curious, clumsy vessels, with their high poops, prominent stems, and battened lugsails, were marvelously seaworthy, and as commercial carriers they were the equals of the brigs and schooners of the Western nations. But as warships they were totally, hopelessly inadequate. Sparkling beneath recently applied coats of black lacquer, each had a huge human eye painted at her prow to ward off evil spirits and also to enable the crew to divine the intentions of their enemies. Laundry hanging from the rigging to dry contributed, too, to the junks' lack of a martial appearance.

More than all else, however, the two cannon mounted

fore and aft on each ship demonstrated their inability to fight a battle with ships of a modern Western navy. These guns were so antiquated that Jonathan could recall seeing only one similar to them. It was used as an ornament in a New London park, and he could recall his father telling him as a child that it had been brought to the New World two centuries earlier by immigrants from England, but actually had been made in the early 1500s. Some were covered with such thick coats of rust that they were inoperable, and those that had been cleaned looked, to someone with an experienced eye, as though they might explode when fired.

Homer Ellison laughed, and so did Elijah Wilbor, as they looked at the junks and their armaments.

"They're more dangerous than you realize," Jonathan told his mates. "Their crews are fearless and prefer to go down with their ship rather than admit defeat. What's more, when they're on a wind they are sometimes loaded with powder, set on fire, and then cast adrift in the direction of an enemy vessel. Avoiding one of them at close quarters without being blown out of the water yourself can be quite a feat."

"There must be at least one hundred of them at anchor, Captain," Homer said. "Why is their fleet so large?"

"I don't know," Jonathan replied with a frown. "This is a new development since I was last here, and I don't like it."

When the clipper reached a point less than two miles from the Whampoa anchorage, the British squadron that lay at anchor came into view, and Elijah whistled under his breath "Whew!" he murmured.

The squadron had more than tripled in size since Jonathan had last seen it. The flag of the rear admiral in command flew beneath the Union Jack from the masthead of a seventy-four-gun ship of the line, the *Invincible*, and beyond her lay another huge seventy-four, the *Redoubtable*. Previously the flagship had been buttressed by two frigates, and now there were five. There were more sleek, swift sloops of war than it was possible to count in a short time, and Jonathan also noted the presence of several small but powerful bomb ketches, which could play havoc in an enemy harbor or cause incalculable damage to a fleet at anchor.

It was obvious to Jonathan that relations between China and the nations of the West had deteriorated badly. The Royal

Navy squadron consisted of at least twenty-five ships, and it was plain they were not here for decorative purposes. The Royal Navy meant business.

No law compelled the masters of merchantmen to report their arrival to the commander of the British squadron when they first came to Whampoa, but protocol was followed by the captain of every European and American ship that came here. Some argued, but only in private, that they were acknowledging Britain's right to control the port, and no civilian wanted to question it.

In spite of Jonathan's eagerness to get to Canton he dropped anchor astern of the *Invincible*, put a copy of his cargo manifest in his pocket, and was rowed in his gig to the warship. A young Royal Marine officer saluted politely as he came on board.

"I've come to pay my respects to the admiral. Do I assume correctly that Sir William still has the command?"

"Indeed he does, sir," the marine replied, and led the way to the admiral's "great" cabin with scores of small, square windows at her aft bulkhead.

Sir William Alexander was making notes in the margin of a report with a quill pen when the visitor came into the cabin, and he jumped to his feet, his weatherbeaten face wreathed in a broad smile. "Mr. Rakehell! I'm delighted to see you, although I must deplore your judgment."

"It's good to see you, sir," Jonathan said, sitting in the chair to which the admiral had waved him. "I was wondering whether you were still here."

"I'll be retiring to my rose garden very soon, thank the Lord. Besides, Charles Elliot has been taking care of matters quite effectively." Captain Charles Elliot, senior superintendent of the trade of British subjects in China, was being recognized more and more as the force to reckon with in the China trade.

They chatted briefly, and then Jonathan said, "I gather that relations with the Chinese are rather touchy."

"A barrel of coarse-grained powder is being exposed to showers of sparks, Mr. Rakehell," the admiral replied somberly, "and may explode any moment. If you're wise you'll unload your cargo, take on tea, or whatever you're buying, and get out before you're burned."

152

"I have other plans, sir," Jonathan said, and gestured out of the windows.

The admiral turned and stared at the *Lai-tse lu.* "Another of your remarkable clippers, Mr. Rakehell. I must say, you and Charles Boynton have been revolutionizing the merchant marine." He peered hard at the figurehead mounted on the stem of the clipper. Then he reached for his glasses. "A figurehead of a pretty Chinese girl in a cheongsam, eh?" Peering more closely, he made out the clipper's name. "Soong Chao's daughter?" he asked, raising an eyebrow.

"Yes, sir." Jonathan drew in his breath sharply. "She's—still in Canton?"

"She was last month, when she acted as interpreter at a meeting I held with the viceroy. And to anticipate your next question, the sly minx hasn't changed. I can't prove it, but I suspect she was interjecting her own opinions into her translations."

Jonathan exhaled slowly. "I was very much concerned," he said, "because I heard some rumors before I left New London."

"China is a nation of rumors and is no place for a man whose skin is your color. Not these days." Sir William was blunt. "Soong Chao invited me to dinner last week and then had to rescind the invitation. There was no way I could have reached his house alive. Unless I had provided myself with a full battalion of Royal Marines as an escort."

"Feelings are running that high, sir?"

"Higher. No foreigner dares to pass through the Petition Gate. Just a few days ago the Marquês de Braga, the governor-general of Macao, came here to see Soong, and they had to conduct their business at Soong's factory office."

Jonathan's anxiety mounted again. Perhaps Soong had concluded a contract to give his daughter to the marquês.

"Your relations with the young lady are none of my business, Rakehell. I'll grant that she's one of the prettiest, brightest girls I've ever met. But if you have any romantic leanings toward her, keep them very quiet. You'd be assassinated on your very first night in Canton, and the American factor would be powerless to save you. In fact, if it weren't for my squadron, every Englishman, American, and European in the compound would have fled to Macao long before now."

"I'm grateful for your advice, sir," Jonathan replied politely, but set his jaw He had not traveled halfway around the world to marry Lai-tse lu, only to be thwarted now.

The admiral's experience with generations of young men had made him a keen observer of human nature. "You'll do as you please, naturally. But I beg you, Rakehell, carry a sword and a brace of pistols when you go ashore."

As a courtesy, Jonathan showed Sir William the copy of his manifest before returning to the clipper. At the very least, Lai-tse lu was not yet married, so he continued to hope

As the clipper crept the remaining distance to the Soong wharves, Jonathan had his new distinguishing pennant hoisted. The flag had a white background, and on it, in green, was the symbolic Chinese Tree of Life, its three branches representing health, wisdom, and honor. The seamstress who had made it for him had used the jade medallion Lai-tse lu had given him as a model And after he gave her this clipper as a gift, he intended to fly similar pennants from every ship in the Rakehell and Boynton fleet.

The clipper maneuvered into a familiar dock, and after Jonathan gave orders that his officers and crew were to carry arms when they went ashore and were not to make an attempt to go into Canton, he leaped onto the wharf His pulse racing, he went directly to Soong Chao's office, where he exchanged greetings with the principal clerk, who had handled most of the paper work during the year he had engaged in commerce while employed by Soong. He delivered his current manifest, then asked, "Is your master busy?"

Pleased that the American Fan Kuei spoke a fluent Cantonese now, the man shook his head. "Today he works at his home in the hills."

"Then I will go to him there."

"You cannot! The soldiers will not permit you to pass the Petition Gate, and they will kill you if you try "

It was obvious to Jonathan that, after two years of separation, he would need to be patient a little longer "Then please send a messenger to Soong—and his daughter—without delay. Tell them that I have arrived."

Having nothing better to occupy him while he waited, he returned to his ship, where a small army of Soong's dockhands already swarmed, and he began to supervise the unloading of his cargo.

He failed to notice a broad-shouldered, ruddy-faced Scotsman who caught sight of him, halted for a moment, and then approached him. "You've come back," Owen Bruce said.

When they had last met they had fought almost to the death, and Jonathan had not forgotten the encounter. Not offering to shake hands, he replied curtly, "And you're still here."

"Aye, now and for years to come. There's no way these Chinks will get rid of me, hard though they try." Completely recovered from the thrashing Jonathan had administered and from the fire in which he had suffered severe burns, Bruce had also regained his arrogance.

"I'm sorry to learn there have been problems," Jonathan said politely.

"The real problem hasn't started yet. But I'll tell you plain, Rakehell, when the smoke clears away, the Union Jack will be flying from the viceroy's palace."

Jonathan refused to allow himself to quarrel with this thoroughly unpleasant man.

The Scotsman grinned maliciously. "I see you've named a ship for Soong's daughter. A wedding present, is it?"

"Something like that."

"There's none more jealous than that Portuguese she's marrying," Bruce said slyly. "When he hears what you've done, you'll be refused a landing permit at Macao."

Keeping his temper, Jonathan nevertheless was disconcerted. It was clear that marriage arrangements of some sort were in progress for Lai-tse lu. But he could not allow Bruce to upset him. "I take each day as it comes," he said, and turned to shout an order in Cantonese to the foreman.

The Scotsman ambled off down the waterfront, chuckling quietly.

Jonathan gradually calmed himself, then studied his surroundings. The officials in the Chinese customs house were coldly correct, as they had always been. The flags of various foreign nations flew over the warehouse complexes, the lawns were still immaculate, and the narrow, twisting side streets were still crammed with taverns, brothels, and inexpensive eating houses. Two young Dutchmen were rolling bowling balls in the direction of tenpins in the side yard of the Netherlands compound, and in front of the American factory three young men were engaging in violent calisthenics. At the far end of the area, where the piers ended, cows were munching on the grass in the foreigners' pasture.

Several Chinese harlots, trying to entice the members of the clipper's crew as they came ashore, gave no indication of hard feelings on the part of their compatriots toward the outsiders, and neither did the youths using their few words of English in order to persuade the newcomers to patronize various shops. In some ways the Orient never changed, and Jonathan was willing to wager that Owen Bruce was still active in the opium trade.

Suddenly a huge hand descended onto the young American's shoulder with considerable force, staggering him, and he whirled. Although tall himself, he had to look up toward the face of the husky, grinning Kai, Soong Chao's majordomo.

"I know Mr. Jon come," he said.

It gave Jonathan great pleasure to address him in fluent Cantonese. "And I knew you'd be here, you rascal."

"Where did you learn to speak the tongue of our city so well?" Kai demanded.

"Wu-ling taught me."

"Ah, Wu-ling. She is well?"

"Yes, and she grows more adult every day. We will have much time to talk about her. How is Lai-tse lu?"

For his own reasons, Kai elected to return to his broken English. "Missy fine. Cry many times, but fine."

"She hasn't—married the Portuguese Governor-General of Macao?"

"Missy refuse," Kai said. "Wait for Mr. Jon."

Jonathan wanted to shout for joy. "Take me to her," he said.

Kai hesitated. "Not easy now." Giving up the struggle, he reverted to his own tongue. "Three days ago, in one of the English factories, Bruce whipped a houseboy for stealing food. The boy escaped into Canton with many red welts on his face and body. Now the people of the city want revenge. Any Fan Kuei who ventures into the city takes the risk of being torn apart."

"I can wait no longer to see Lai-tse lu," Jonathan replied.

"Soong Chao told me to warn you. He also prepared a special pass so the soldiers will allow you to move through the Petition Gate, and he sent some men-at-arms to help you. But you must realize you are taking a grave risk."

"I'm ready," Jonathan declared, and indicated with a wave to Homer Ellison, who stood on the deck of the clipper, that he was leaving.

Kai led him to an alleyway behind the Soong complex, where twenty tall, broad-shouldered men wearing the Soong house livery awaited them. Each carried a ku ming, a curious weapon that had originated in the Han Dynasty two thousand years earlier. At first glance it appeared clumsy. At one end of a metal shaft eight feet long was a conventional, pointed spear. At the other end was a curved, razor-sharp blade, with a second, hooked and barbed blade emerging from it about one foot from the tip. Jonathan had seen the ku ming in action and knew that in the hands of experts it was a fearsome weapon.

"No matter what may happen," Kai told him grimly, "do not halt. I hope to control the people we pass, but if we stop—for any reason—a huge mob will gather, and we will be overwhelmed. Soong Chao has instructed that the blood of the people of Canton not be shed, so do not use your pistols. After we have been admitted to the city, draw your sword, but do not use either the point or the edge. If even one Cantonese is injured, all of us surely will die."

Jonathan nodded but made no reply.

Soon they came to a huge stone Petition Gate, which had a pagodalike top. The officer in charge of the yellow-uniformed sentry detail scowled at the American, as did a number of his men, but the document Soong Chao had prepared was in order, and he was waved through.

The men-at-arms surrounded him in a double phalanx, and with Kai in the lead they set off at a rapid pace through the city, the guards holding their ku ming ready for immediate use.

The streets were crowded, as always, but people hastily gave way before the raised, curved blades of the guards. Those who saw the white man in the center of the phalanx cursed him loudly.

"Son of a filthy swine!"

157

"May your sons be blind beggars and may your daughters be whores!"

Trying to retain his sense of humor and his balance, Jonathan reflected that knowledge of a foreign language could be a handicap on occasion

Kai and the men-at-arms in the front rank had the most difficult time. When crowds became thick ahead, threatening to block their passage, the leader went through the motions of thrusting his ku ming at an imaginary foe, then twirling it over his head. The men-at-arms did the same, and the people grew so quiet there was no sound but that of the sharp blades whistling through the air.

Jonathan had never seen such hatred in the faces of any people, and he wondered if he would reach Soong's house alive. There were shorter routes they could have taken, as he well knew from his many previous walks through the city, but gradually the realization dawned on him that Kai was choosing a path that kept them on the broadest streets. If they should find themselves trapped in a narrow alley, they would be lost.

The route led them past the august and beautiful Temple of Heaven, perhaps the most impressive edifice in the heart of Canton. Here the throngs were even thicker, and Kai slowed his pace, then moved momentarily into the center of the phalanx, beside Jonathan. "We have two choices," he said. "We can take refuge in the Temple, and I can send to Lo Fang at the palace for troops who will assist us. But the mobs are sure to become much greater. Or we take our chances and go on. Which do you prefer?"

Jonathan did not hesitate. "We'll go on," Jonathan said.

Kai returned to his place at the head of the column.

Men and boys by the hundred raced into the great square from the side streets, choking it, and the marchers were compelled to slow to a crawl

Admiring the cool courage of his escorts, Jonathan knew that either they would be forced to break their ranks or be compelled to make real use of their ku ming.

Someone dislodged a paving block, picked it up, and threw it, but his aim was poor and the brick fell short of the column.

Within moments, Jonathan realized, others would follow the man's example and an uncontrollable riot would develop

He had the rare Rakehell quality of remaining calm in moments of crisis, but it was his instinct rather than his mind that told him what had to be done.

Quickly sheathing his sword, which would be useless in a battle with so many, he cupped his hands and called loudly in Cantonese, "People of Canton! Why do you hate me? It is true that I have the skin and hair of a Fan Kuei. But the people of Canton are my brothers!"

His listeners were stunned. Everyone in Canton well knew—and resented the fact—that no foreigner ever bothered to learn their language but insisted on speaking to them in their own tongues, then ridiculed and denigrated them when the people failed to understand.

But here was a Fan Kuei who spoke Cantonese like a native! Even his accent was pure, and an astonished murmur ran through the crowd.

Encouraged by the momentary loss of hostility, Jonathan repeated his strange litany again and again, until his throat became dry.

Kai continued to move forward, as did the men-at-arms, and now they did not brandish their ku ming. Those in the front ranks of the throng yielded their places, and those on the outskirts quietly melted away.

The Cantonese, including thousands upon thousands of illiterates, were a logical, reasonable people, and now that they paused briefly to ponder instead of giving in to blind rage, they became puzzled. No Fan Kuei had appeared inside the city's walls for many days, and the men and women who worked in the Western compound came home at night to report that the foreigners were terrified.

Yet this lone Fan Kuei dared to come into the city. Furthermore, he was being protected by private household troops of some great man. Who was he? Those who knew the livery reported that they were in the employ of Soong Chao, who was respected and generous, giving large sums of money to the poor every year. He was a patriot, too, as they had good reason to know, and the dock workers had told many stories about him, relating that no Fan Kuei ever dared to dispute his word.

Men began to wonder why they were taking the risk of having their own heads opened by a ferociously wielded ku ming. Old women and loiterers decided they had better things to do. Little by little the crowds thinned. Kai increased his pace almost imperceptibly

Now only a hard core of young fanatics remained, and it became a relatively easy matter to handle them. Again the ku ming were twirled. But even those who had no use for any foreigner noted that this Fan Kuei did not draw his sword again and made no attempt to use his firearms. Ultimately, even the fanatics lost interest in the sport and began to disperse.

By now the column had moved from the slums into a neighborhood of better homes. Each dwelling was walled, and as the party climbed the second highest hill in the city the homes became larger. People here were too well-bred to threaten a stranger, and the members of their household staffs were too well-disciplined.

Now only a few small boys watched the progress of the phalanx, and they were respectfully silent.

Kai looked back over his shoulder, and he and Jonathan exchanged broad grins. They had won their gamble against great odds, thanks to the American's quick thinking.

Now that the danger had receded, a tension greater than any Jonathan had ever known built swiftly within him. At the top of the hill stood the familiar wall of Soong Chao's compound, and on the far side of the wall was the only woman he had ever loved.

Kai unlocked the great iron gate, then stood aside, and Jonathan walked alone down the gravel path, past formal gardens, ponds with lily pads, ponds that were connected by miniature bridges, ponds in which brilliantly colored fish swam in the clear water. There was no sound but his own footsteps and the tinkling music of a tiny waterfall.

At the far end of the path Lai-tse lu stood alone. There had been ample time for her to change for this momentous occasion, and her body was encased in a cloth-of-silver cheongsam that set off her hair and skin to perfection. Long silver earrings fell to her shoulders, and on her right hand she wore an enormous silver ring. On the left was the wedding band that Jonathan had given her.

He caught his breath, halting when he saw her. She was even lovelier than the image of her that he had conjured up so many countless thousands of times.

Lai-tse lu stared at him, too. He looked as she had always known he would, rugged and tall, in command of himself and his destiny.

All at once they started to run toward each other, unable to tolerate the suspense any longer. Neither could speak, and their kiss was fierce but tender, passionate but gentle, expressing the longings both had felt during the long, cruel years of their separation. This was the moment they had awaited, their anticipation sustaining them through the difficulties they had suffered, and now that it had finally arrived there was a sense of wonder in their embrace.

At last they drew apart slightly and, still clinging, looked deep into each other's eyes. Their expressions, remarkably similar in a man and a woman from such different worlds, washed away the last of their doubts and fears.

Jonathan needed a long moment to recover his breath, and when he spoke he deliberately addressed her in Mandarin, which he practiced so assiduously. "Never, not for one moment, have I stopped loving you," he said huskily.

Lai-tse lu's silver-lidded eyes were luminous. "Never, not for a moment," she replied in English, "have I failed to love you."

They smiled, then grinned, and suddenly they were laughing aloud joyously. Becoming more aware of their surroundings again, they walked hand in hand to a stone bench that faced a flower bed ablaze with colors that ranged in subtle shades from reds through violets to blues, then to yellows.

Mincing no words, Jonathan immediately explained why his return had been delayed for so long. He told about his indiscretion with Louise Graves the night before he had sailed on his initial voyage to China. He described his son, Julian. Then, he explained how he had been forced to marry Louise in a private ceremony but had remained true to his love for Lai-tse lu. "Louise and I didn't sleep together," he said, "other than that one time. The real tragedy of our relationship was that there was never any genuine love between us."

Lai-tse lu listened silently, her eyes solemn. "What has become of the lady?"

"She wanted to see my new clipper, which I named for you. She climbed a scaffolding beside the ship and either jumped or fell to her death on the wharf below. I didn't know at the time, and I still don't know, whether she killed herself or her death was accidental."

Lai-tse lu closed her eyes for a moment, then asked, "Did she know about you and me?"

He shook his head.

"Perhaps she did. It may be that she loved you more than you knew."

"It's possible," Jonathan replied somberly. "That question has tormented me. So has not knowing how you would react when you heard the truth about my delay."

She returned his gaze. "She was a victim of circumstance, and so were you. Nothing you have said could change my love for you."

Jonathan reached for her.

"Wait," Lai-tse lu said. "I have a confession to make, too. My father tried to arrange a marriage for me with Dom Manuel Sebastian, the governor-general of Macao. I—I have consistently refused to marry him. Just as I have refused the suggestion of the Princess An Mien, who offered me a way out through a marriage to her cousin, Shaong Wei, who suffers from the curse of alcohol."

"How have you found the strength?" he asked, and listened wide-eyed when she told him that he had come to her in a dream promising to return. She also mentioned that, in her mind, they were already married, and that was why she wore his ring on her left hand. When she finished her recital, she opened his shirt to show her that he was wearing the jade Tree of Life medallion she had given him. "Now that I'm here," he said forcefully, "we'll marry without delay."

"That is what I want, too, but it will not be easy in a time of trouble. We will seek the advice of my father, who will know what is best for us to do. We must go to him now. He and Missy Sarah are eager to see you. They are waiting for us."

Holding hands again, they walked to her father's pavilion, where Soong Chao exchanged bows with Jonathan in the Chinese manner, then shook his hand.

Sarah Applegate surprised Jonathan by kissing him on the cheek, but her tongue was still tart. "You should be ashamed of yourself for causing me so much worry," she said. "And it's no excuse that you've now restored my faith In you, and in the honor of New England menfolk.''

Jonathan repeated the story of his unfortunate relationship with Louise, then told them in detail about his son.

"I will love him as I would my own child," Lai-tse lu said.

Jonathan beamed as he looked at her. He now felt the greatest happiness he had ever known.

"Later we will talk about your cargo and what you will take back to America," Chao said. "Now, as you have learned crossing Canton, there are many problems."

"While we've waited we've been discussing the matter of your wedding," Sarah Applegate said. "Ordinarily the ceremony would be held in the Temple of Heaven, but that is not possible these days. The mobs would tear both of you apart. You'll have to be married here, in our own little temple on the property, with no other witnesses except ourselves and Kai.''

"That doesn't matter," Jonathan said, as Lai-tse lu quickly nodded in agreement. "Just so we become husband and wife, nothing else is important ''

"Many things are important," Chao said gently. "The Marquês de Braga is a proud, vindictive man and will become your enemy for life. See to it that you do not visit Macao, now or at any time that he is the governor-general I am told his prison is a place of horror. It is also important that I find some way to smuggle both of you—and Missy Sarah—to the ship so you can sail to America.''

"I hope you don't mind, Jonathan," Sarah said, her tone apologetic, "but Chao has decided I must return to the United States with you. I'm no longer able to leave the estate for fear of being killed, and it might be years before I can move freely around the city again.''

"You're more than welcome," Jonathan replied instantly. "Not only on board ship, but at our home in New London I insist you regard it as your own home, and so will my father.''

The prospect of returning to the land of her birth after spending so many years in the East brought unexpected tears to the woman's eyes. Brushing them away angrily, she could only mutter, "Land sakes!''

The first order of business was the wedding, and after

their interminable wait the two principals wanted the ceremony held as soon as possible. Lai-tse lu and Jonathan were elated when the girl's father quietly proposed that the marriage be held that same afternoon.

A Taoist priest was summoned, and he repaired without delay to the tiny temple on the property, a pagoda with an outer wall of stone and an inner wall of inlaid, gleaming mother-of-pearl.

Missy Sarah went off with the bride to help her dress for the occasion, and Jonathan was given the small, two-room pavilion he had occupied during the year he had lived here. A grinning Kai brought him a loose-fitting ankle-length gown, a round, broad-brimmed hat, and a pair of slippers, all in scarlet silk, the traditional color worn by brides and grooms.

Jonathan donned the costume, wearing the gown over his western sea captain's attire, and then he and Kai went to the temple. The air was so thick with incense pouring from two burning pots that the smoke made the American's eyes smart, and he found it difficult to breathe. At first he did not see the priest, who sat in a Buddhalike posture on a raised platform that vaguely resembled an altar. He appeared to be in a trance and took no notice of the pair's arrival.

He was flanked by two figures on ivory pedestals, and at first glance they, too, resembled Buddhas. Kai calmly explained that the bust on the left, carved of an astonishingly white jade, with sapphires for eyes and a collar of diamonds, was a representation of the highest Taoist deity, the Jade Emperor. The figure on the right, carved of black jade, with emeralds for eyes, represented the second deity in the Taoist pantheon, the Emperor of the Eastern Mountain.

The foreigner felt awkward, but Kai promised to prompt him at appropriate times.

Lai-tse lu entered alone, and in spite of the smoke and darkness, she looked dazzling in a crimson cheongsam, with the Jade Emperor embroidered on the front and the Emperor of the Eastern Mountain on the back. Her only jewelry, other than the wedding band Jonathan had given her, consisted of long, dangling ruby earrings and a huge ruby ring, set in gold, that she wore on her right hand. Soong Chao and Missy Sarah followed her, carrying oil lamps that illuminated the temple, and the girl prostrated herself before the priest. Jonathan, following Kai's whispered instructions, did the same.

They remained in the prone position for what felt like a long time, and then the priest, still appearing to be in a trance, began to deliver a homily in Mandarin.

Jonathan was surprised to learn that he and Lai-tse lu were already married. By donning the appropriate clothes and prostrating themselves they had indicated their willingness to be married, and that desire made them man and wife. It was taken for granted, according to what the priest told them, that neither could put the other aside, and that they would be married to each other as long as they lived. In his sermon the priest directed them to revere the memories of their ancestors and to instill the same precepts in their children. Above all, he urged them to follow the teachings of Taoism and lead lives of contemplation.

Again Kai whispered to Jonathan. "Stand and walk backward out of the temple now. Take care not to touch your bride!"

The American did as he was ordered, and was relieved to breathe the clean air of the garden. A moment later a smiling Lai-tse lu joined him. "If the sermon had lasted a minute longer," she said, "my eye makeup would have started to run."

"The ceremony is ended?" Jonathan asked.

She nodded happily.

"When am I allowed to kiss you?"

"It is forbidden for a bride and groom to touch in the temple," she said, "but now that we are married, we may do as we please."

He took her in his arms immediately.

Chao, Missy Sarah, and Kai emerged from the temple to offer their congratulations, and then, accompanied by the priest, they adjourned to the dining pavilion. The traditional wedding meal was remarkably simple, consisting of mung bean noodles in a stock of beef broth, hard-boiled eggs and seaweed cooked together, wheat noodles and minced clams done in a delicate sauce, and small beef cubes served with snow peas, bean curd, and mushrooms. Pots of ever-present tea were constantly replenished, and toasts were offered with tiny cups of heated rice wine. According to Chinese custom, an elaborate meal might accustom newlyweds to a meal they could not afford again in the years immediately ahead, so only basic dishes were prepared, even in wealthy families.

Had the quarrels with the nations of the West not become acute, hundreds of guests would have been invited to the Soong estate for the festivities, but the absence of guests made no difference to Lai-tse lu and Jonathan. All that mattered to them was that they had been united after a long and painful separation.

Jonathan had no home of his own here to which he could take his bride, so his pavilion in the compound had to serve as a symbolic substitute, and when he slid open the door that led to his sitting room, they found that Kai had been busy: the hardwood floor was littered with uncooked rice. Jonathan insisted on observing one Western tradition and, picking up Lai-tse lu, he carried her across the threshold.

Both were laughing, but as he slid the door closed behind them their mood changed. Both had been celibate for two years, and their mutual desire, their yearning for each other was overwhelming. He carried his bride into the bedchamber, where he undressed her, and she insisted on helping him disrobe. Then they stretched out on the bed together and began their lovemaking in earnest.

Not until now had Jonathan realized how much he had missed this woman who meant so much to him. Not until now had it occurred to Lai-tse lu that her need for this man formed the core of her existence. They were like two parched people suddenly finding themselves in the midst of ample, pure water, and they drank endlessly to quench their thirst.

They became one and found gratification together. Their frenzy subsided simultaneously, allowing them to bask in a sweet after-glow. Even now they exchanged few words other than expressions of their love, and ultimately they made love a second time, then a third. Later they drifted into a dreamless sleep.

When they awakened in the morning, they found themselves locked in an embrace, and both had imagined this scene so often that, for a moment, they found it difficult to believe they were not dreaming. Eventually, when they sat opposite each other in the sitting room, eating melons and rice cakes and drinking strong tea, they knew this was the reality that would last as long as they lived.

Later in the day Jonathan conferred with Chao, and they agreed it would be wise for the clipper to return to America with a cargo of silk cloth. Neither could guess when the outbreak of war might make it necessary to suspend trade. Jonathan told Chao in confidence that he had not only named his new ship for his bride, but intended to present it to her as his wedding gift. And when they reached the United States the principal part of the owner's share of the profits the vessel would earn in the future would go into a new, special bank account that he would establish for his wife.

The unloading of the clipper's cargo of looms would take at least another day, and the procurement and loading of the bolts of silk would require several more days. Jonathan wrote a note to Homer Ellison, instructing him to make all the preparations necessary for the return voyage, and to notify him via a messenger from Soong's factory twenty-four hours before the ship was ready for her voyage

In the meantime the newlyweds spent an idyllic week Jonathan presented his wife with the gift from Ruth, and Lai-tse lu was deeply touched to receive the small book with the rose pressed between its pages. The young couple spent nearly every moment together, interrupted only by Lai-tse lu's need to supervise the packing of her wardrobe, bric-a-brac, and other belongings that she would take with her to the United States. Her happiness was marred by only one cloud that hovered overhead.

"I worry about my father," she said. "If there should be a war with Great Britain—and I don't see how it can be avoided much longer—I am afraid of what might happen to him. Do you suppose we could persuade him to come with us, at least for a visit to America?"

He thought it no more likely that Soong Chao, the owner of a large fleet of junks engaged in international trade, would take a long holiday than his own father would agree to absent himself from the Rakehell and Boynton offices for an appreciable period of time. But it was not his place to discourage Lai-tse lu. "Speak to him," he said. "I'll support whatever you wish to say."

She brought up the subject at dinner the same day, and

Sarah Applegate, also concerned about the man who had employed her for more than two decades, beamed and nodded as she spoke.

But Chao shook his head. "I have no partners," he said, "and not even Jonathan knows the details of my Eastern business. I cannot afford to take a year's holiday. My managers could not carry on the business without me. And I will not have it said that I am a coward."

"A coward, my father?"

"If it should happen that the Middle Kingdom becomes engaged in a war, it is my duty to be here, where I can help my country and our people. I will be content, my daughter, knowing that you and Missy Sarah are safe."

"But you won't be safe, my father!"

He grinned at her, then at Sarah. "I have lived more than fifty years, and in that time I have known plagues and floods, devastating attacks on Canton by bands of sea pirates, and attempts of renegade war lords to capture the city. Assassins have thrown their knives at me, and one time, many years ago, I escaped from kidnappers who were holding me for ransom. I have a knack for survival, my daughter. What is more, I have good reason to live. I look forward to the day when you will bring my grandchild to visit me. No, I will not leave Canton. It is better that we find some way to transport Jonathan and Missy Sarah to the ship."

Lai-tse lu knew he would not change his mind and gave up the effort to persuade him to leave.

Jonathan shared his father-in-law's concern for their safe departure. "I'm afraid I know too little about local conditions to make any suggestions. But it makes me uneasy when I think of the way the crowds in the streets would react if they knew that Lai-tse lu has married a Fan Kuei."

"I have asked Kai and Lo Fang to find the right way," Chao said.

Jonathan was relieved. He was well aware of the two majordomos' affiliation with the secret Society of Oxen, and he was content, trusting in their ability to find an answer to a seemingly insoluble problem.

A few days later Homer Ellison sent word that the clipper would be ready to sail in twenty-four hours. Now the problem became urgent.

The boxes containing the belongings of the two women were sent to the waiting ship. The ease with which this feat was accomplished encouraged Kai. "Tonight," he said, "I meet once again with Lo Fang. Together we will find a way."

When Lai-tse lu and Jonathan came out of their honeymoon pavilion after breakfast the next morning, they found Kai and the viceroy's majordomo, both wearing unadorned black, waiting for them. "In one hour," Kai announced, "we will make the march to the waterfront. Until then, come with me."

They accompanied the pair to Kai's quarters, where they found Sarah Applegate and an old woman who carried a large, ungainly sack of coarse cotton.

"You're wearing a cheongsam, Missy Sarah." Lai-tse lu was surprised.

"I do what I'm told," was the terse reply.

The old woman grinned, showing gaps between her yellowed teeth, then ordered Sarah to open her collar and pull up her sleeves.

The others watched in silence as the woman applied a liquid to her face, throat, hands, and lower arms from a bottle that originally had held Dutch gin. The liquid was a stain, and Sarah's skin became several shades darker. Then the old woman daubed several sticks that looked like thin charcoal at the corners of the American woman's eyes. Satisfied with her handiwork, the crone stood back and chortled.

Unless one examined Sarah Applegate closely, she resembled a Chinese.

"You will ride in a sedan chair, as will Soong Chao and Lai-tse lu," Lo Fang said, "and you will see to it that curtains are not closed. People on the street will not study you too hard and long. They may glance at you, but they will think you are Chinese, and they will pay no further attention to you."

Kai motioned Jonathan to the chair.

The old woman promptly went to work on him until he, too, was transformed.

Lo Fang handed him black boots, trousers, and a black, loose-fitting shirt. "You will wear these, along with a black coolie hat," he said, "and you will be one of the bearers of Lai-tse lu's chair. But heed my words of warning. Your eyes now are slanted like our eyes, but their color cannot be disguised, and no Chinese has ever had eyes so pale. So take care not to look directly at anyone we pass as we march.''

Jonathan changed into the black outfit, vaguely realizing that this was the dress of the Society of Oxen when performing a mission.

When he emerged into the open, he saw that Chao had joined the group and that forty black-clad men, many of them armed with ku ming, stood nearby. His own clothes and weapons were concealed in his bride's sedan chair.

Kai handed the American two knives and told him to slide them into his boot tops. Jonathan had learned to throw a knife with deadly accuracy, in the manner of the Javanese, but he hoped he would not need to utilize his skills.

At a quiet command from Lo Fang, the chair bearers came forward, and Jonathan was given the place at the rear left side of his wife's chair. His fellow bearers ignored him, as did the men armed with the ku ming.

Without further ado the entire group left the estate, and Jonathan held the pole on his shoulders with both hands, as the other bearers were doing. Then the escort formed around the three chairs, with Lo Fang and Kai in the lead.

Jonathan could hear his wife's tense laugh of suppressed excitement, but knew better than to address her. They started down the hill, and he discovered it was no easy matter to keep the pole in place. But he managed, and his own tension lessened a trifle when he saw that passersby paid scant attention to the party. Certainly no one bothered to look at him.

When they reached the bottom of the hill, they came to the teeming slums, and Jonathan took great care not to look directly at anyone in the crowded streets. Then, little by little, he realized that something highly unusual was happening: the throngs melted away rapidly, and most people did not look in the direction of the sedan chairs or the escort. At last the significance of this seeming indifference dawned on him.

The people of Canton well knew the uniforms of the Society of Oxen, and these patriots, who did not hesitate to commit murders and other acts of violence when they found it necessary, represented the ultimate authority. They were held in far greater respect and were far more feared than were the troops of the imperial viceroy's garrison. Obviously Lo Fang and Kai had decided the disguises worn by the two Fan Kuei in he party should be augmented by the influence of the dreaded Society of Oxen, who had to be engaging in a vital mission if they were flouting the law which prohibited the very existence of all secret organizations.

Even when the group marched through neighborhoods dominated by gangs of criminals known as tongs, people saw to it that the procession had a clear path. There was no need for the men armed with ku ming to keep people at a distance. It appeared that no untoward incident would take place, and Jonathan was relieved.

His tension soared again, however, as they finally drew near the Petition Gate, where Chinese leaving or entering the foreign concession were required to halt and answer any questions that the officer in charge cared to ask. But the officer in command of the detail clearly had been briefed. He stood with his back to the procession, conferring earnestly with a subordinate, and the troops on duty stood calmly, making no attempt to halt the procession.

The march did not end until they came to the alleyway at the rear of Soong Chao's principal warehouse. The sedan chairs were lowered to the ground, and Jonathan hugged Lai-tse lu after he helped her emerge into the open.

The men of the Society of Oxen dispersed, none of them acknowledging the presence of the two Fan Kuei.

"I am in your debt," Jonathan told Lo Fang.

"We will meet again," the tall Chinese replied, and turned away.

Sarah and Jonathan washed the stain from their skins in Soong Chao's office, and the American changed into his own attire. Then, with Kai bringing up the rear, he escorted his wife, her father, and Sarah to his domain, the clipper. Water kegs were being rolled into place, the last cargo was being stored in the hold, and members of the sailing crew were already on deck, awaiting their departure.

As they drew near the clipper Lai-tse lu saw her name in gold lettering on the prow, was stunned by the carved figurehead of a Chinese girl, and looked at her husband.

"This is your ship," he told her. "I built it for you."

Tears came to her eyes when he explained that, although Rakehell and Boynton would operate the vessel, the owner's share of the profits would be banked for her. She could not

171

begin to guess how many months he had spent planning, designing, and building this graceful clipper in her honor; she was so overcome she was unable to speak and could only squeeze his arm.

Oliver piped the master aboard, and Jonathan presented his officers and the boatswain to his wife, her father, and Sarah, who stunned the crew by announcing, "Oh, she's trim, and I like her lines. I do believe her courses are the biggest sails I've ever seen."

Jonathan conducted a tour of the ship, and Sarah was quick to note that the clothing boxes she would need on the voyage were already lashed to a bulkhead in the cabin she would occupy, just as Lai-tse lu's necessary clothing boxes were standing in a corner of the great cabin she would occupy with her husband.

The time of farewells had arrived so the ship could sail on the noon tide. Kai went first to Lai-tse lu and bowed to the girl whom he had protected since she had been a small child. "My memories of you will grace the rest of my days," he said.

Sarah Applegate deliberately drained away some of the occasion's sentiment. "Behave yourself, Kai!" she told the majordomo sharply in Cantonese. "Stay out of fights, don't gamble, and stop squandering all your money on stupid fortune-tellers."

Kai grinned for a moment, then asked Jonathan something that had been puzzling him. "What will you do if your country joins the British in a war against the Middle Kingdom?"

"The United States will not wage a war against China. And I will never raise a hand against my brothers. My wife's people are my people now, and I would gladly take up arms beside them." He and the majordomo took each other's measure for a moment, and then Kai abruptly went ashore.

Now it was Soong Chao's turn, and Sarah spoke briskly—a trifle too briskly—in order to hide her feelings. "I've told the cook not to give you too many fried dishes," she said. "And I've spent so many years learning to write Chinese characters that I hope you'll answer my letters."

"All of them, always," he replied gravely. "My heart is

172

light in this moment of parting because my most precious possession is still in your care.''

Jonathan shook his father-in-law's hand. "We'll correspond even more regularly in the future," he said. "And I swear to you that I will do for Lai-tse lu all that you have done in the past.''

"That is why I gave her to you freely and of my own will.''

The time had come for father and daughter to part. Custom prevented members of their class from displaying their emotions in public, but even now the young woman was still a rebel, and she hurled herself into her father's arms. They kissed, then drew apart without the exchange of a word, and both kept their feelings under firm control, remaining dry-eyed as Soong Chao went ashore.

The jibs and topsails were set, the clipper cast off, and as she began to move through the crowded harbor, Lai-tse lu turned to raise her hand for the last time in farewell to her father and Kai. Sarah sniffed loudly.

Jonathan knew a diversion was needed, and as soon as the Stars and Stripes rose to the yardarm, it was followed by his distinguishing pennant, the flag on which the Tree of Life was embroidered.

Lai-tse lu stared at it, then at her husband. "You think of everything," she said softly.

He grinned at her. "Many more are being made during my absence," he said. "As soon as the pennants are ready, I'm giving an order for every ship in the Rakehell and Boynton fleet to fly one. Soon it will be known and recognized in major ports everywhere.''

The sheen in her eyes told him all he needed to know. Though she was saddened by her leave-taking from her father and her homeland, she clearly wanted to be nowhere else but by the side of her husband.

The ladies remained on deck for two hours, and after they went to their cabins to unpack, Jonathan gave the watch to Elijah Wilbor, then asked Homer Ellison to join the dinner party in the officers' cabin.

The first thing Lai-tse lu noticed on the table was a bowl of a sauce long used by the Chinese to preserve meats that was

173

made of strained tomatoes, their pulp, and tomato paste. "Now you brought *ke-tsu-up* just for me!" she cried happily.

Jonathan laughed, shaking his head, and left it to Homer to explain.

"Every American and British ship that comes to the Orient leaves China with a few barrels of *ke-tsu-up*, Mrs. Rakehell," he said. "Most folks at home won't touch tomatoes, which are called love apples and are regarded as poisonous. But any seaman who comes to the East acquires a craving for it, and any cook who failed to take on a supply would be thrown overboard."

"Do the tomato plants grow in America?" Lai-tse lu asked, her eyes wide.

"They grew wild every summer when I was still there," Sarah replied.

"They still do, ma'am," Homer assured her.

"In that case, we'll have *ke-tsu-up* as long as you want it, child," she told the girl. "The recipe is just one of many that I've brought with me for use when you grow tired of American meals."

"But this food is wonderful!" Lai-tse lu was relishing her beefsteak, green beans, and freshly baked bread.

"We'll see if you have the same opinion," her husband said with a grin, "after we've been at sea for a spell and run out of fresh food. Sea fare is an acquired taste. Acquired by necessity."

That evening Jonathan and his bride stood on deck together looking at the lights of Macao as the clipper moved out the delta into the South China Sea. Lai-tse lu shuddered.

"If you hadn't arrived when you did," she said, "I couldn't have held out much longer. I would soon be living there as the Marquêsa de Braga."

As Jonathan put a protective arm around her shoulders, he thought of the warning that the governor-general was a vindictive man As soon as he arrived home, he would issue a directive forbidding all Rakehell and Boynton ships from entering the Macao harbor for any reason. His wife was safe, but his business interests could be jeopardized and innocent seamen in his employ could be made to suffer.

Under the unwritten Portuguese constitution, the royal judiciary was an independent, separate branch of government, responsible only to the crown. In Macao, however, Dom Manuel Sebastian had dispensed with the courts. He alone was the ultimate authority, so he acted as his own dispenser of justice, setting aside a portion of each morning to adjudicate disputes, pass sentences, and make binding judgments. The attorneys who appeared before him knew all too well that it was a waste of time to cite legal precedents. The determination of any issue depended on the governor-general's mood of the moment.

The defendants and the lawyers who represented some of them were relieved when he walked into the high-ceilinged audience hall one morning with a broad, contented smile on his face. He nodded jovially to the captain of the guard who stood at attention beside the high-backed chair that looked suspiciously like a throne, and as he seated himself, adjusting the broad sash of watered silk over the gaudy uniform he had designed for himself, he could be heard humming under his breath. An inaudible sigh of relief passed through the ranks of the prisoners guarded by royal troops in their uniforms of blue and red.

Dom Manuel had good reason to feel pleased. Only moments earlier, after dismissing the concubine who had spent the night with him, he had stood at a window in his private apartment and had seen a junk flying the ensign of Soong Chao dropping anchor in the harbor. Within a short time, he was convinced, he would receive official confirmation of his certain belief that Lai-tse lu would be given to him in marriage. His last letter to her father, demanding an immediate response to his proposal, had been very firm.

His mind elsewhere, he quickly disposed of the first three cases, in each of them ruling in favor of the defendants. Then, as a Chinese member of his household staff came into the hall, he suspended his operations and took a sealed envelope from the man.

The brief letter was courteously worded. Soong Chao deeply regretted his inability to arrange a marriage between his daughter and His Excellency because the man she had long loved had returned to Canton, married her, and taken her with him to her new home.

His face showing no change of expression, Dom Manuel folded the letter carefully, dropped it into a pocket, and nodded to the royal prosecutor.

The official stepped forward. "Your Excellency, two

Swedish seamen engaged in a fight last night at a waterfront tavern. Claiming they had been cheated, they smashed furniture and threatened the proprietor. Let the defendants stand forward.''

Two brawny, tanned soldiers moved toward the governor-general, their eyes bloodshot and their steps uncertain after a night of carousing. One of them started to speak in broken English, a language he had been told the governor-general understood.

The Marquês de Braga silenced him with an imperious wave. "I will not tolerate the disruption of peace by foreigners who think they are above our laws. Let each of these culprits receive fifty lashes with the long whip.''

The two seamen gasped, and even the royal prosecutor was startled, as was the captain of the guard. The attorneys in the hall glanced at one another obliquely, equally shocked. The governor-general was renowned for his harsh punishments, but fifty lashes would leave the two Swedes scarred for life, and their sentence was certain to cause the government in Stockholm to send a stiff protest to Lisbon.

Dom Manuel was impervious to possible complications. He governed his realm as he saw fit, and he well knew that no official in Lisbon—or in Canton—dared to reprimand him. He called for the next case.

A young Chinese woman, the mother of two small children, was accused of stealing a small bag of rice from the kitchen of a local merchant. The woman readily admitted her guilt, explaining that she had taken the food because her children were starving.

"Let her be executed,'' Dom Manuel said harshly. "Subject her to the Slow Death.'' Tired of passing sentences, he rose abruptly and left the hall, stomping off to his own apartment. There he gave vent to his rage, smashing a vase, then applying a riding crop to the servant who heard the crash and hurried into the room.

Dom Manuel paced furiously, the riding crop still gripped tightly in his hand. He would learn all he could about Soong Lai-tse lu's marriage, and swore he would obtain vengeance for the insult inflicted on him. God help the woman and her husband if either ever fell into his hands.

*   *   *

Bradford Walker had prepared his special report with infinite care, filling it with statistics it would be impossible for anyone to verify. Now, he knew, was the time for him to strike. Now, before Jonathan Rakehell returned from the Orient, was the time for him to make the bold move that, if it succeeded, would restore him to his former eminence as the second in command of the American end of the Rakehell and Boynton business. No law dictated that only Rakehells and Boyntons could reach the top; he was married to a Rakehell, and that was quite good enough.

His manner confident, he walked down the corridor in the headquarters building to the office of his father-in-law.

"Come in, Brad," Jeremiah Rakehell said quietly. "You said you wanted some time with me this morning."

"Yes, sir." Brad sat opposite the older man's large desk. "I wonder if you read my report advocating a sharp increase in the building program of brigs and schooners."

"I've read it several times, and I believe I've absorbed all of your arguments. You claim that the clippers Jonathan has been building ultimately will cause us to lose business."

"There can be no doubt of it, sir." Walker was firm, yet his manner was ingratiating. "I'll grant you that the speed clippers can achieve is spectacular, and that, given proper weather conditions, they sometimes can make two voyages to every one that an ordinary windjammer makes. But remember that a clipper can carry only one-third to one-half of the cargo that we can pack into our larger brigs and schooners. Our tonnage is certain to slip."

"So far," Jeremiah replied mildly, "our tonnage has been increasing steadily, ever since we began adding clippers to the fleet. And our overall profits are rising rapidly because we make so much on the clippers we sell to other merchants and trading companies."

The interview wasn't going as Walker had hoped it would, and he frowned, a grating note creeping into his voice as he said, "The brigs and schooners are still the backbone of our business!"

"I have no complaints about them."

"Some of them are more than twenty years old. We must

177

start replacing them before they become outmoded. I'm convinced this is essential!''

Jeremiah leaned back in his chair and removed his spectacles. "You're quite right to defend your division, Brad. But Alan Boynton and I must look at the overall scene. We've been expanding rapidly, but our shipbuilding facilities—both here and in England—are necessarily limited. And we earn more by selling a spanking new clipper to the customers clamoring for them than we can make on a dozen voyages of an ordinary windjammer.''

"The statistics in my report—''

"Ah, yes. The figures. I'm a trifle leery of them. If you can authenticate them by means of official U.S. Government statistics or the Association of International Merchants in New York, it would be very helpful." Jeremiah suffered no illusions regarding the character of his son-in-law. Walker had tried to sabotage the maiden voyage of *Flying Dragon*, Jonathan's first clipper, and since that time had lost no opportunity to denigrate his brother-in-law, whose success obviously nettled him.

For Judith's sake Jeremiah had kept his own counsel, and he never lost sight of the fact that this man was the father of his two oldest grandchildren. Walker was ambitious, which was all to the good, but he was ruthless and unscrupulous. There would be no problem if he were content to operate his own profitable division and stop trying to compete with the far more talented and energetic Jonathan, who already had earned a full partnership in the firm.

"I'd like to initiate a new building program at once, sir, and I already have the designs for two large brigs." Walker continued to press.

"I can't make an immediate judgment," Jeremiah said. "And in all fairness to Jonathan, I think he deserves the right to defend his clippers. I suggest we wait a few weeks. He should return from the Far East shortly, and as soon as he recovers his land legs, I'll ask him to submit a report on the future of clippers, as he sees it. Then I'll present both reports to the combined Anglo-American boards of directors for consideration.''

A deep-rooted rage leaped to life within Bradford Walker. Jonathan, even when absent, had defeated him again!

He forced himself to agree cordially with his father-in-law's decision and retreated rapidly to his own office. There he discovered that his fury was so great his hands were shaking, so he opened a locked cabinet and took a large swallow from a bottle of French cognac he kept there. The fiery liquor burned as it went down, and he was able to recover sufficient aplomb to function with seeming normality. Unable to concentrate on work, he clamped on his beaver hat and, his mood ugly, left the office for the day. His coach and driver awaited him, and he slammed the carriage door behind him. Unlike Jeremiah and Jonathan, he regarded it as beneath his dignity to walk to and from work.

When he reached the pleasant house on Pequot Avenue that Jeremiah had built as a wedding gift to Judy and him, he went straight to his small library, and there helped himself to a liberal quantity of cognac from a decanter. His anger seethed more coldly as the liquor burned.

Judith had heard him arrive and came in search of him. "You're a little early tonight," she said.

"Yes, thanks to your father. He and his beloved Jonathan make me sick!" He raised his glass again.

Judith had never heard him speak so bitterly about her family, whom she continued to love with the loyalty that all Rakehells felt for each other. "What is it, Brad?"

"He refuses to accept my recommendations for increasing the windjammer fleet. He won't do a thing until Jonathan comes home."

"That seems reasonable to me," she said.

Walker drained his glass, then splashed more cognac into it. "What in hell do you know about it?" he demanded savagely.

Taken aback, Judith could only reply, "Not very much, but I've never had cause to question my father's judgment, which has given us a comfortable living."

"Damn all you Rakehells!" Walker roared, his control slipping. "My God, I can count the victories I've won against you on the fingers on one hand!" Suddenly he laughed, and the rasping sound filled the library. "But there's one time I took care of Jonathan! His damned Puritan conscience will eat into him for the rest of his life!"

She couldn't imagine what he was talking about. "I'm afraid I don't understand."

179

Walker stared at her. She so closely resembled her father and brother that he felt an overwhelming desire to punish her, to inflict a deep and abiding hurt. "Don't you?" he demanded mockingly. "Let's find out if you have a good memory. A few weeks before Jonathan's wife died, you told me he had come to you in confidence and confessed he was in love with some Chinese girl—"

Judith's gasp interrupted him. "Oh, you didn't, Brad! You couldn't go to Louise and repeat what Jonnie said to me!"

"Couldn't I?" He laughed again. "It's what I did, though. And a week later Louise was dead!" He peered at her stricken face. "Now we'll see how that sits on your Rakehell conscience. Maybe you had a hand in killing Louise!"

Judith shuddered, then drew herself up to her full height. "Bradford, this is so—so despicable that I can never forgive you for it!"

Her contempt enraged Walker beyond all reason. He was sick and tired of being judged by members of her superior clan, who looked down their noses at him as though he was some inferior being. Unable to curb his fury, he lunged at his wife, then struck her with full force on the cheekbone.

She staggered backward, but even in this moment of crisis she did not cry out for fear that the children would come running to her and would witness the ugly scene.

"To hell with you—and all Rakehells!" Walker cried, and raced out of the house.

Judith stood unmoving, one hand on her bruised face, and heard the door slam behind him. For better or worse—and lately things had only been worse—this was the end of their marriage of thirteen years. For the past few months she had been tolerating his increasing unpleasantness, but the knowledge that he had violated her confidence was too much for her. And the fact that he had dared to strike her was a blow to her pride which she would never overcome.

Walker, meanwhile, hurried aimlessly through the streets, and a considerable time passed before he discovered that night had fallen. Somehow his footsteps had brought him to the Rakehell and Boynton shipyard. The cognac still burned in him, but he forced himself to concentrate. He knew his wife well enough to realize she would not forgive him, now or ever for resorting to physical violence. Previously he had been reduced to a position of secondary importance here, but that was mild when he thought of what awaited him. The moment Judith reported to her father, he would be discharged.

Very well. He would act first. Knowing what had to be done, what his self-preservation demanded, he went straight to the headquarters building, which was dark. As he fumbled for his key to the front door, the night watchman appeared.

"Evenin', Mr. Walker."

"Oh, hello, Jerry. Do me a favor, will you? I've got to go over some papers, and I can't find my key."

"Glad to oblige, sir." The watchman unlocked the door, then handed him a small, burning oil lamp. "You'll need this, Mr. Walker. Just leave it outside the door here when you leave. I'll get me another from the shed."

Walker mumbled his thanks, took the lamp, and mounted the stairs two at a time, going directly to his father-in-law's empty office. In a corner stood a large safe, and unless the combination had been changed recently, he would be in luck. Jeremiah Rakehell kept large sums of cash on hand to pay for cargoes. In addition to the elder Rakehell, only his absent son and his son-in-law knew the combination, so there would be no doubt of the thief's identity, but that couldn't be helped.

"No matter how much is in there," Walker said aloud as he dropped to one knee before the safe and placed the lamp nearby so he could read the numbers on the dial, "they owe me all of it. And plenty more, after all I've done to make this company successful. And have them give me the backs of their hands in return."

He twisted the dial one way, then the other, his heart hammering, and twice he had to stop in order to wipe cold sweat from his hands. One by one he heard the tumblers fall into place, and he uttered a muted, triumphant cry when he was able to pull the door open.

The cash rested in a tin strongbox, as usual, and Walker's hands trembled as he counted slightly more than fifty thousand dollars in bills of large denominations. He had come across a small fortune, and his luck was good.

Stuffing the money feverishly into his pockets, he remembered to close and lock the safe behind him so the watchman would not notice anything amiss when he made his rounds. Hurrying down the corridor to his own office for the last time,

Walker took another long pull at the cognac bottle. Deciding to take the bottle with him, he looked at the papers piled on his desk, and in a final gesture of contempt swept them onto the floor.

He knew of only one place, located in downtown New London, where he could buy a horse at this time of evening, so he took a shortcut through the plant. A half-moon had risen, and as he passed the docks where the new ships underwent their final stages of construction, he caught sight of an unfinished clipper. She had been moved to the berth for the stepping of her masts, which had not yet been raised.

God, how he hated clippers, the symbol of the man who built them!

The sleek, handsome ship was a magnet, and clutching the bottle of cognac in one hand and the lamp in the other, Walker moved closer to it. He halted beside a barrel filled with carpenters' wood shavings that the cleaning help had gathered but had not yet removed.

Suddenly a thought struck him with blinding force.

His rage gave him increased physical strength, and somehow he managed to push and haul the barrel across a short gangplank onto the clipper. He was sweating profusely by the time he managed to drag it to a place amidships. Then he returned for his bottle and lamp. Taking a last nip of cognac, he poured the rest into the wood shavings.

Laughing maniacally, he extended the burning wick, then hurled the oil lamp into the barrel with all of his remaining strength.

Retreating rapidly to the shore end of the wharf, Walker stood still and watched the barrel of shavings catch fire and burn. Flames leaped into the air, eating more slowly through the bottom of the barrel, but within a short time a stack of wood against which he had placed the barrel caught on fire. Soon the flames spread to the deck itself.

Walker watched the clipper burn, his fists clenched, and the glare of the fire lighted his white-splotched, red face, still contorted by his hatred.

Not until he heard the repeated sounding of a gong by one of the watchmen did he brush off his clothes, then silently vanish into the night.

It was mid-morning when Judith Walker appeared in the entrance to her father's office, a still-steaming pot in one hand. "I heard you were up all night, Papa," she said, "so I thought you could use some coffee."

"That's very thoughtful of you," a weary Jeremiah Rakehell said. "You'll find cups on the shelf yonder. Join me." He watched her as she wiped two cups with her scarf, then filled them with coffee.

"How bad was the damage, Papa?"

"The new clipper in the number seven berth burned to the waterline. I'm still waiting for a final report, but she was so badly scorched and gutted that I suspect there's little can be salvaged. But I'm not complaining. We worked right through the night and stopped the fire from spreading. The damage could have been far worse."

"Do you have any idea how the fire started, Papa?"

"None. To our knowledge there were no intruders on the property last night. One of the watchmen saw Brad, here at the office, and I'm hoping he can tell me if he spotted anything out of the ordinary, but I haven't seen him as yet this morning."

"You won't see him, Papa," Judith replied quietly. "Brad left the house in a rage before supper. After drinking rather heavily. And he didn't come back home last night."

Jeremiah stared at his daughter and became aware of the black and blue welt on her cheekbone that the rice powder she had applied to it could not conceal.

Aware of her father's close scrutiny, she raised a hand to her face, then forced herself to sip her coffee calmly. "Yes, Papa. Brad struck me."

"Good Lord!" His eyes became glacial.

Judith told him in detail about the quarrel, explaining that Jonathan had told her in confidence about his love for Lai-tse lu, that she had shared the account with her husband, and that he had confessed last night, boasting that he had told Louise. "So you see, she may have had a reason for killing herself. If she jumped to her death, it was because she cared more for Jonnie than anyone realized. She may have been in despair because she found out he loved someone else."

Her father took a swallow of his coffee and was silent for a time. "We'll never know, of course. But it doesn't surprise me that Brad went to her." He told his daughter about her husband's attempt to sabotage Jonathan's first clipper in order to demonstrate that this new type of ship was a failure.

"I wish you had told me earlier, Papa."

"I didn't think you were ready for the news at the time. You wouldn't have believed me, and I would have created a rift between us. I didn't tell Jonathan, either, because I expected that he and Brad would be obliged to work together for the rest of their lives." Jeremiah sighed. "Hindsight is wonderful, but let's have no regrets."

She nodded, and it was her turn to fall silent. "Papa," she said at last, "I'm sure Brad set that clipper on fire. You can't imagine how much he hated Jonnie's ships. Every time a clipper was mentioned he'd get a wild expression in his eyes."

"Do you suppose that's why Brad came back to the yard last night?" He sounded puzzled.

"That could have been one of the reasons, Papa," Judith said slowly.

They exchanged a long, unblinking look. Then Jeremiah wearily heaved himself to his feet and crossed the office to his safe. Dropping to one knee, he twisted the dials, then opened the door. Saying nothing, he rose to his feet and showed his daughter the empty strongbox.

"That's what I thought the moment you mentioned he had come back here last night. I'm afraid I know the way his mind functions. How much did he steal, Papa?"

Jeremiah did not reply immediately. He placed the box back in the safe, closed it, and returned to his desk, where he consulted a file. "Fifty-two thousand dollars in cash," he said at last.

Judith covered her face with her hands.

Jeremiah went to her and placed a hand on her shoulder. "Now, now," he said gently. "I haven't seen you weep in a quarter of a century. We can tolerate the loss, you know. There are a number of ships due home this week or next, two from the Caribbean and two from the Mediterranean Sea. Their profits will compensate us for the loss—and more."

She forced her hands to her sides.

Her father was relieved that she was dry-eyed. "Good girl," he said softly. "You're a true Rakehell."

Judith raised her voice for the first time. "You'll report this to the police, of course."

Returning to his own chair, he shook his head vigorously.

"Why not, Papa?"

"Because of Brad and Judy. Their schoolmates will torment them if their father is publicly branded as a thief. The shame would leave permanent marks on them."

"They—they'll have to know sometime."

"Later. When they're older they'll be better able to understand why their father vanished and never came back. And you can be quite sure that with this theft hanging over him, he won't return."

"Are you saying you intend to let him go unpunished?"

"It's a small price to pay, Judith. Bradford Walker has developed into a greedy criminal. We're well rid of him."

Judith straightened slowly, squaring her shoulders. She raised her head and her eyes cleared. Her father's gesture helped her to rise from the depths of her own misery. "You're right, Papa," she said firmly. "Good riddance to him."

Book
III

I

Jonathan insisted the voyage was routine, but Lai-tse lu, who had sailed only once on a clipper when she went with Jonathan to Bangkok, found it wildly exciting. To be sure, she needed time to adjust, and fell ill the first time the clipper encountered heavy seas. Soon thereafter, however, she gained her equilibrium, or, in the words of the crew, she "got her sea legs."

Thereafter she spent long hours on deck every day, relishing the sight of the great ship cutting through the seemingly endless ocean, enjoying the sharp, fresh smell of the salt air. Jonathan delighted in teaching her the principles of navigation, and with his help she studied the stars. Long before the voyage came to an end, she was drawing charts of her own each day at noon to show the precise path they had taken.

Sarah Applegate, completely at home from the moment she set foot on board the vessel, astonished the officers and seamen by knowing precisely what was expected of them in every kind of weather. "Ma'am," a grinning Homer Ellison told her at dinner one day, "it wouldn't surprise me in the least if you could stand a watch—and handle the ship creditably."

"I should hope I could, young man," Sarah replied tartly. "I was reared on my father's ship, and for the years I was married to the late Mr. Applegate, may the Lord bless him, I went to sea with him more times than I care to recall."

"Have you ever gone aloft, ma'am?" he asked.

Jonathan and Lai-tse lu could not curb their laughter.

Sarah looked at each of them in turn, glaring at them. "I take it I'm being ridiculed. Well, then. In my younger days I was as much at home in the rigging as the most experienced able seaman, and I'm ready to prove my abilities here and now.''

"That won't be necessary, Missy Sarah," Jonathan said quickly.

"It sure won't, ma'am," the alarmed Homer added. "We'll take your word for it, every last man on board.''

Lai-tse lu was enchanted when they put into the Sandwich Islands for several days. But Sarah was outraged because the young women wore no breastbands. "Now I know why Mr Applegate would never bring me here," she said. "The lack of decency is shocking!"

At Valparaiso Jonathan insisted that both women remain on board. Chile's principal port was a rough town, the new government was finding it difficult to establish its authority, and a girl as attractive as Lai-tse lu could have created a riot. Missy Sarah grumbled, but Lai-tse lu accepted her husband's word without dispute.

Her presence on board was a good omen, Jonathan said repeatedly, and although superstitious seamen believed women passengers meant trouble, they were forced to agree with him when the clipper reached Cape Horn. The weather was as mild and pleasant as it had been violent on the outward voyage, and Jonathan sailed serenely through the Straits of Magellan, with Lai-tse lu and Sarah marveling at the rugged scenery from a vantage point near the prow.

Another call was made at Rio de Janeiro, South America's largest and most prosperous community, and as Jonathan was in no rush, he granted the crew three days of shore leave, one watch at a time. The food was superb and the warm weather reminded Lai-tse lu of Canton, but not until they resumed their voyage did she reveal to her husband that she had not been enchanted by the town.

"Every time I heard someone speaking English to me with a Portuguese accent," she said, "I was reminded of that dreadful Marquês de Braga.''

"Put him out of your mind forever," Jonathan told her "He can never harm you.''

The clipper passed slowly but surely through the Doldrums, and subsequently, while cruising past the Windward Islands in the Caribbean, they encountered another Rakehell and Boynton clipper sailing in the same direction. Jonathan immediately invited her master on board for dinner.

So it was Captain Kenneth Adams who had the pleasure of bringing Jonathan up to date on all that had happened in the more than six months he had been away from home. Adams revealed the surprising news that Charles Boynton had married Ruth Barker and that they had gone off to England, taking Julian with them for a visit. Adams also mentioned, hesitantly, that Bradford Walker had left the company and that his present whereabouts were unknown.

Jonathan refrained from pressing a Rakehell and Boynton employee for more information on what was obviously a delicate subject. Something extraordinary had happened, but he would learn the details from his father and Judith in due time.

The marriage of Charles and Ruth pleased him. "I'm really astonished," he told Lai-tse lu. "But I'm delighted for both of them, even though I never would have guessed they'd be right together."

"Why shouldn't they be?"

"Well, they're so different. But don't let me influence your thinking. Make your own judgments when you meet Ruth. At the very least I'm grateful to be relieved of a problem."

She raised a thin eyebrow.

"As I told you, I brought Ruth and David into our house so she could take care of Julian and run the house for Papa. When we get home Julian will become your responsibility, and I daresay Missy Sarah will take charge of the household. I can't imagine her not doing it. Now that Ruth is married, I won't have to ask her to step down from her position of principal housekeeper."

His wife smiled. "You had a romantic interest in her when you were younger?"

"Oh, no," he assured her. "Ruth and I have been good friends for the better part of our lives, but we never had any deep interest in each other."

"I just hope your friends—and most of all, your family—will accept me," she said nervously.

Jonathan kissed her. "They'll love you as much as I do," he said.

She giggled. "I'll be satisfied if they love me a trifle less than that."

On the one hundred and eighteenth day of a leisurely voyage the great clipper rounded Montauk Point and entered Long Island Sound. As they passed Fisher's Island, which Jonathan explained to his wife was a part of New York State rather than Connecticut, he fired his signal guns. A short time later the Rakehell and Boynton complex came into view, and he saw his father standing alone in the crowd that was gathering on the shore.

Jeremiah Rakehell raised his hat and smiled broadly when he saw the lovely Chinese girl standing beside his son.

"He looks very austere and dignified," Lai-tse lu said, "but he has a very warm smile."

Jeremiah demonstrated that the warmth of his smile was genuine when Jonathan came ashore, escorting Lai-tse lu and Missy Sarah. Even before greeting his son, he kissed her on both cheeks and said, "Welcome to your new home and to my family."

She beamed at him, and their relationship was sealed.

Jonathan grasped his father's hand and was on the verge of presenting Sarah Applegate when the woman came forward herself.

"Your hair is gray and you have wrinkles in your face, Jeremiah," she said, "but I swear to goodness, I'd have known you anywhere!"

"Well, you've put on a few pounds, Sarah," he replied, "but that's an improvement. You always were too skinny."

Jonathan stared at them. He was a bit surprised at their informality and forthrightness. "I realize you two knew each other at one time, but I didn't think you knew each other quite so well," he said, a smile coming to his lips.

"I don't know of any law that makes it needful for parents to tell their children everything about their past."

"I was reared in Mystic, a few miles up the coast," Sarah said with a chuckle. "We went on the same picnics and clambakes. I was going with the late Mr. Applegate, bless him, when he worked as a mate for the old Rakehell Company. Jessica came to those parties, too, you'll remember, Jeremiah. It was before she married Alan Boynton. And when Mr. Applegate won his master's ticket, his very first ship was a Rakehell schooner. That was before he struck out for himself."

"When the news that he went down with his ship filtered

back here, Sarah," Jeremiah said, "everybody assumed you were on board. I didn't learn otherwise until Jonathan told me you'd reared Lai-tse lu."

Jeremiah offered Sarah Applegate his arm, and the older couple walked ahead to the waiting carriage, deep in conversation. Lai-tse lu, as surprised as her husband to see the familiarity between these two, joined in her husband's delighted laughter.

When they reached the imposing but dignified Rakehell house, Jonathan showed his bride the suite they would occupy, and Sarah protested loudly to Jeremiah that her quarters were too grand for her. "I've never in my life had a private sitting room and a dressing room. What on earth will I do in them?"

"I reckon you'll learn to cope," Jeremiah replied, a twinkle in his eyes.

The clothing boxes arrived, and while the ladies unpacked, father and son retired to the library to bring each other up to date on personal and business matters.

"She's lovely, exquisite," were the first words Jeremiah Rakehell said to his son. "You're lucky to have found such a wonderful bride."

"I'm the luckiest man on earth," Jonathan said, beaming. Then he added with a sly smile, "Perhaps you're in luck, too, Papa. Sarah Applegate and you seem to have a lot in common."

"Now, I'll have none of that, Jonnie," Jeremiah said, his expression austere. But in a moment he relaxed, and both men broke into laughter.

"I'll write Charles and Ruth at once," Jeremiah said, still smiling. "They'll bring Julian home as soon as they hear you've arrived, and David will come with them, of course. Julian is fine. He's in perfect health, and he's already learning to read and write. I'll show you all of Ruth's letters."

"I was surprised by her marriage to Charles, Papa. I never thought of them as—well, compatible."

"I couldn't have imagined it, either, but they appear to have adjusted well. Jessica and Alan are very fond of Ruth, and I gather that Elizabeth and Wu-ling are inseparable. So much so that Elizabeth may be making the voyage with them."

Jonathan nodded, then asked quietly, "Has Uncle Alan accepted David?"

"He didn't for a time, but suddenly Alan changed. No

one knows why, and no one cares. He takes David to the office on Saturdays and has even taken him to his club for a meal!"

Jonathan laughed. "If David is anything like Julian, he probably solved the problem himself."

His father smiled, then sobered. "I could temporize by bringing you up to date on business, but there's something we'll have to face sooner or later." He plunged into a full account of the violent departure of Bradford Walker.

Jonathan listened in silence, pale beneath his tan. "I had a notion," he said, "that Louise guessed I was in love with Lai-tse lu. Now there's no question she knew."

Jeremiah reached out and gripped his upper arm. "Don't torment yourself, son. We'll never know whether her death was accidental or deliberate. That's a secret she took to the grave with her, and you can't ruin your own life. You have a lovely bride, a son, and the business, and all of them need your time and attention."

"They'll have my complete dedication, Papa," Jonathan replied firmly. "Louise and I never loved each other, and my conscience is clear."

"Does Lai-tse lu know the story of Louise?"

"Of course. I keep no secrets from her."

"Well, if you don't mind a word of advice, Jonnie, let her become adjusted to a new land, a new way of life, and a different culture before you tell her about Brad's two-faced perfidy."

"I had already made up my mind to do precisely that," Jonathan said.

They were deep in a discussion of business affairs when Lai-tse lu and Sarah joined them after making a tour of the house.

"I am so pleased," Lai-tse lu said. "This is so much like my father's house."

"I can't imagine anything less like it," Jonathan said.

"Neither can I," the confused Sarah said.

"You will know what I mean." Lai-tse lu appealed to her new father-in-law. "Like my father, you are a man of great wealth and position. You have a very large, very comfortable house. But you do not show off your wealth. This is a private home, not a palace."

"Daughter," a beaming Jeremiah told her, "I've never been paid a higher compliment!"

Judith and her children arrived for supper a short time later, and the children were shy in the presence of the strikingly beautiful Chinese woman. But Lai-tse lu quickly won their confidence by asking them about their school work, their hobbies, and their interests in sports. She won them completely when she promised to go fishing with them, saying it was a sport she loved.

She had never mentioned fishing to Jonathan, and he had no idea whether she was speaking the truth or was being inventive for the sake of putting the children at ease. There was so much about his bride that he still had to learn.

Judith's quick smile and wink told him she approved of his new wife.

Before they went to supper Jonathan presented the members of his family with gifts which Kai had purchased on his behalf because of his inability to move freely around Canton. There was a handsome jade bracelet for Judith, a statuette of a warrior for young Brad and one of a dancer for Judy, and he gave his father a curved sword with a jeweled hilt for his collection.

Lai-tse lu had a surprise in store, too. Taking an object from the silk container she carried suspended from one shoulder, she turned to her new father-in-law. "I bring you the greetings of Soong Chao," she said. "He asked me to tell you that he has come to know and appreciate you because he knows Jonathan. He said also to tell you what you already know, that the child is the reflection of the father. In the Middle Kingdom here is an old saying. When one looks into a reflecting pool, one sees the faces of one's children there. Therefore, my father has concluded that you are a fine and honorable person, and he sends you a token of his respect and admiration."

Surprised and somewhat overwhelmed, Jeremiah studied the gift, an exquisite, carved ball of ivory, with a second ball within it and a third sphere, still smaller, inside the second. As he examined the spheres, it suddenly became clear to him that the gift had been made for him alone. At the core was a tiny but perfectly reproduced clipper ship. The gift was a miracle of craftsmanship.

"In your hand," Lai-tse lu said, "you hold three worlds. The world of the East, the world of the Americas, and the world of Europe. It is your clipper ships that bring these worlds together and make them one."

Jeremiah was deeply touched. "The clippers are Jonathan's, not mine," he said, "but I am pleased and flattered to accept this lovely gift in the spirit your father showed in sending it to me. I shall write to him at once."

A short time later they adjourned to the dining room for a celebratory supper, an old-fashioned New England clambake. They started the meal with steamer clams, which they dipped in melted sweet butter, and the dish was followed by a rich clam chowder. Then came the main course: lobsters, corn on the cob, and potatoes that had been steamed in seaweed, and Lai-tse lu was ecstatic.

Sarah was even more emphatic. "Now I know I've come home!" she exclaimed.

The adults ate so much that only Judy and Brad were able to eat the hot apple pie with vanilla ice ceam that comprised the dessert.

That night, when Lai-tse lu and Jonathan retired to their own suite, the girl clung to her husband. "I was afraid I would feel very strange in this place so far from the Middle Kingdom," she said. "But I know already that this is my home."

The *Green Frog* reached New London from England late one morning, and before she docked Jonathan hastily sent a carriage for his wife so she could stand beside him as the passengers came ashore.

Charles Boynton was in the lead, with Julian perched on one shoulder and David on the other. He placed the children on the ground, and even before greeting Jonathan, he hugged Lai-tse lu. "Cousin," he said, "I've waited a long time to speak to you as a member of the family."

"It is so good to see you again, Charles," she replied with sincerity. "Oh, how David has grown since I last saw him." Picking him up and kissing him, she addressed him in Mandarin. "How do you fare, small one?"

To her delight he replied in the same language, which he was learning from Wu-ling. "Very well, thank you," he said a bit awkwardly.

Julian swarmed all over Jonathan, who held him high in the air.

Ruth Boynton followed her husband and hated herself when she felt her heart pounding as Jonathan kissed her cheek. It was absurd that—even now—he could still cause her to become flustered.

Jonathan introduced Ruth to his bride.

The two young women took each other's measure in a brief moment that seemed to last for a long time. Their backgrounds were literally a world apart, but each recognized the integrity and honor of the other, and with one accord they embraced.

Jonathan placed Julian on the ground, and Lai-tse lu bent down, extending her arms to him. "You don't know how happy I am to see you, Julian," she said.

The little boy stared at her for a moment, then clutched Ruth and buried his face in her skirt "Mama," he said distinctly.

Jonathan felt a surge of anger. "Where are your manners, young man?" he demanded sharply.

Ruth was embarrassed as she addressed herself exclusively to Lai-tse lu. "I'm so sorry. He rarely behaves this way. I think he's being shy."

"He will overcome it." Lai-tse lu spoke with greater confidence than she felt and managed to conceal her hurt. She had not expected Jonathan's son to reject her, and she was bewildered.

The last to come ashore were Elizabeth Boynton and Wu-ling, wearing identical dresses with full skirts. Their long hair streamed down their backs, the blond and the blue-black in sharp contrast, and both of these half-women, half-children knew they made a startling pair. Each wore a faint touch of color on her lips, with a hint of shadow on her eyelids, the only cosmetics that Ruth had permitted them.

Wu-ling made a deep curtsy to Jonathan and Lai-tse lu, addressing them in Cantonese. "It is a privilege to see you again, honored sir and madam," she said.

Lai-tse lu instantly drew her to her feet and kissed her. "You have matured so much that I'm not sure I would have known you," she said, deliberately replying in English.

Jonathan was still upset by his son's behavior, so he com-

pensated by being overly boisterous as he embraced Elizabeth.
"My little cousin is almost a grown woman now," he said.
"Lai-tse lu, let me present the family beauty to you."

Elizabeth flushed, but her manner changed as she turned
to the woman who had destroyed her adolescent dreams by
marrying Jonathan. Her manner suddenly haughty, patrician,
she nodded coldly to the bride.

The gesture was so unexpected that Lai-tse lu was stunned.

Ruth and Charles exchanged a quick glance. It was all
well and good for Elizabeth to indulge in romantic, girlish
daydreams, but she was going too far, and her rudeness was
inexcusable. They would speak to her later, in private.

The party was so large that several carriages were required
to take them to the Rakehell mansion. Jonathan had planned
accordingly, and saw to it that he, Lai-tse lu, and Julian rode
only with each other, the little boy seated between the two
adults.

"I understand you're learning to read, Julian," his father
said.

"I'll show you, Papa!" Julian exclaimed.

"May I be there, too?" Lai-tse lu asked in a quiet voice.

The child looked at her, hostility in his eyes, then purposely turned his back to her and did not reply.

Jonathan clenched his teeth. "It seems to me," he said,
"that a boy I know has been spared the touch of a razor strap
on his hind quarters for too long."

Lai-tse lu shook her head vigorously. "That would only
cause deeper resentments," she said. "I shall find another way
myself."

"But I refuse to tolerate—"

"No, Jonathan." She was firm. "This is my problem,
and you must allow me to handle it myself, in my own way."

"You're welcome to use my strap," he said as Julian,
aware they were talking about him but not understanding everything they were saying, looked up at his father.

"I don't believe in such treatment," Lai-tse lu said. "I
will find some other approach." In spite of her confident air
she had no idea what she might do to win the affection of this
small boy who, for whatever his infantile reasons, disliked her
so intensely.

The other carriages had preceded them, and when they

reached the house they found Elizabeth waiting for them. Ruth and Charles had already expressed their opinions of her conduct in no uncertain terms, and she stood now, her head held high, her cheeks flaming. "I must apologize to you," she said stiffly to Lai-tse lu. "My rudeness to you—and I really was rude—was unintentional."

Jeremiah's arrival from his office spared them the need of a further exchange.

Sarah Applegate had already taken the role of principal housekeeper, and she coped coolly and efficiently with the arrival of so many guests. David and Julian were permitted to eat dinner with the adults, and both looked dubiously at the main course, codfish cakes.

"Eat it, children," Sarah said. "It's one of my favorites."

Jeremiah made no comment but barely touched the food on his plate.

After the meal ended, Sarah sought Jonathan for a private word. "Is Jeremiah ill? He ate almost nothing."

"That's because codfish cakes are one of his pet abominations."

"I see." Sarah vowed that she would never serve the dish again. Soong Chao had always eaten anything she had chosen to place before him, but Jeremiah Rakehell was stubborn as well as strong, and she reflected that even though he was missing a splendid dish, he had a right to be served meals he enjoyed under his own roof.

The three men went off to the shipyard for a long conference, and Ruth, taking care to make certain Lai-tse lu accompanied her, took the two little boys to the nursery for their naps. "I—I honestly don't know what's come over Julian," she said as the two young women retired to Lai-tse lu's sitting room to become better acquainted. "It's natural that he should be shy with you, but I've never known him to be so contrary."

"In my country," Lai-tse lu replied with a forced smile, "there is an old legend. The goddess of earth saw three of her children at play, and became very angry when they would not tell her what they were whispering to each other. She commanded them to tell her but discovered they could not because they had already forgotten. But the goddess did not realize this and punished each of them. By now they were so badly frightened they did not know what to say. She would have punished them again, but the god of lightning and thunder was present, and persuaded her to do nothing more to them. Then he took pity on her and told her that it is not possible for any adult to enter the mind of a child. The penalty of growing up—and all children wish to be adults—is that one loses one's ability to think and feel as a child."

"How wise." Ruth was impressed and had to admit to herself—somewhat grudgingly—that she could understand why Jonathan had fallen in love with this girl. Her physical beauty was flawless, she had a great strength of character, and her mind was agile, her thinking sound. "What will you do now?"

"Jonathan wishes to spank him, but that will only make the problem worse," Lai-tse lu said. "My mind is blank, so I shall need to rely on my instincts."

In addition to her other qualities, Ruth reflected, she was a woman of courage. Suspecting that she herself still would have preferred Jonathan to Charles, perhaps because old patterns were hard to break, she had to admit that Jonathan truly had found a wife worthy of him.

That evening, before the adults gathered in the parlor for glasses of sack, Ruth and Lai-tse lu went to the nursery so they could be present while the two little boys ate their supper.

Julian ate heartily but continued to ignore this strange woman who, he had been told, had become his new stepmother.

"I've made it a practice to tell them a bedtime story before they go to sleep," Ruth said.

Lai-tse lu saw a possible glimmer of light at the far end of a long, dark tunnel. "May I tell them the story tonight?"

"Of course." Ruth had no idea of what she had in mind but had the good sense to absent herself from the scene. "I'll go downstairs," she said, and withdrew quickly.

Uncertain of how to proceed, Lai-tse lu nevertheless followed her instinct. Taking David onto her lap, she paid no attention to Julian. "What would you like to hear?" she asked. "A Chinese story, an American story, or an English story?" She knew no American or English tales and would need to rely on her imagination.

David came to her rescue. "Chinese!" he said enthusiastically.

Julian did not speak.

"Shall I tell it in Mandarin or English?" Lai-tse lu went on.

"Mandarin!" David cried.

Julian addressed her for the first time. "I don't know Mandarin," he said sullenly.

"The day will come when you will speak a perfect Mandarin, Julian," Lai-tse lu said sweetly. "But this story is for you as well as for David, so I shall tell it in English."

David made himself more comfortable on her lap.

"Once there was a fierce dragon who breathed smoke and fire," she said. "He lived deep in a forest. Two boys—I think their names were David and Julian—decided to visit the dragon."

David giggled. Julian leaned closer in spite of himself.

"The old man who lived in a hut on the edge of the forest told the boys not to seek the dragon because he would destroy them with fire. But do you think they were afraid?"

Unable to help himself, Julian was the first to reply. "No!" he shouted.

David echoed him. "No!"

"You're right. Away they went into the forest. They looked and looked and looked, but they could not find the dragon. Then they lost their way, and they became very hungry. They came to a wao-tsing bush. The fruit of the wao-tsing bush is delicious, but it must be cooked before it can be eaten. When it is raw it is very bitter. Well, the boys could not cook it, so they were still very hungry as they fell asleep in the forest."

The door opened quietly behind the trio. Jonathan entered, interested in knowing how his wife and son were faring.

"What do you think happened next?" Lai-tse lu asked.

"The dragon came!" Julian shouted.

"That's exactly what happened. He breathed smoke and fire, and the two boys woke up. They were very frightened, but they didn't want the dragon to know it. So they stood up and they said, 'We would like to be your friends, Mr. Dragon. But if you don't want to be a friend, we will fight you.' "

Julian was impressed. "Those boys were very brave."

"Very brave," David repeated.

Jonathan, standing silently by the door, grinned.

"That's exactly what the dragon thought," Lai-tse lu said, "so he decided to be their friend. When they told him they were hungry, he was sad. He asked them why they didn't eat the fruit of the wao-tsing bush. They told him that people could not eat it raw. So—would you like to guess what he did?"

"I know, I know!" Julian shrieked. "He blew fire on the fruit of the bush—whatever the name is."

"How bright of you to figure that out all by yourself, Julian," his new stepmother told him.

"The wao-tsing bush," David said, seeing an opportunity to shine.

Jonathan withdrew as silently as he had come in. He should have known better than to worry, he reflected. His wife was capable of handling any situation.

Lai-tse lu ended the story by saying that the boys and the dragon remained good friends forever and played together often. "Now," she announced, "it's time for bed," and tucked them in.

David raised his arms to her. She bent down and kissed him, then turned to look at Julian. He was already lying down, wanting to be kissed, too, but too proud to ask, he looked up in silent appeal.

Lai-tse lu bent over him and pressed her lips against his face. His small arms curled around her neck, and he clung to her.

"I love you very much," she whispered, and left the nursery quickly.

Noting the sparkle in her eyes when she came into the parlor, Jonathan knew that all was well, but she made no comment. Plainly she regarded her relations with Julian as strictly their own affair.

When they went to the supper table, Sarah compensated for the error she had made at noon by serving one of Jeremiah's favorite dishes, corned beef with boiled cabbage and potatoes. He beamed at her.

Lai-tse lu contributed little to the conversation, preferring to listen, observe, and judge these family members for herself.

Most of the talking was done by Elizabeth and Wu-ling, and only when Jeremiah or Sarah spoke did they fall momentarily silent.

Watching and listening to these high-spirited young girls,

Lail-tse lu realized that Elizabeth was directing most of her comments to Jonathan, who was unaware of the attention she paid him.

Late in the meal, when Jonathan and Charles fell into a spirited discussion of the booming market for new clipper ships, Lai-tse lu saw Elizabeth steal a glance at Jonathan. In her eyes was the adoration of a puppy for its master.

So that was it! Now she could understand why Elizabeth had been rude to her and continued to feel uncomfortable in her presence. Not a blood relation, the young girl imagined herself in love with Jonathan! Smiling inwardly, Lai-tse lu concluded that it would be far easier to clear the air with Elizabeth than it had been to establish a rapport with Julian.

Her opportunity came sooner than she had anticipated. The business conversation of the men became so intense that Sarah ordered a bottle of port brought to them and suggested that the ladies retire to the parlor. There Wu-ling expressed a desire to learn how to sew the complicated buttonholes on a cheongsam. Sarah showed her with a needle, thread, and piece of cloth, and Ruth watched the demonstration, occasionally interrupting with questions.

Lai-tse lu noted that Elizabeth, who sat beside her on a sofa, was bored. Here was an opportunity for a private chat.

"You are fifteen?"

Elizabeth nodded stiffly.

"What a wonderful age!"

"You think so?" Elizabeth could not hide her belligerence.

"I didn't at the time, of course," Lai-tse lu said with a smile, "but now that I'm almost ten years older, I see life in a far different way. One's imagination is so flexible in the early teens. One can be an empress. Or the heroine in a great opera. Or the bride of a great warlord."

Elizabeth glanced at her obliquely. Charles and Ruth had sworn they would mention her long-standing infatuation with Jonathan to no one. It was impossible for his wife to guess her feelings, so it was probable she was speaking in general terms. The young girl nodded again.

The innumerable stories of Chinese mythology could be applied to many situations. "Let me tell you an ancient tale that will explain what I mean. The daughter of a warlord grieved because her father died when she was very young. But a few years later her mother found the favor of the emperor and was made his empress. The daughter fell in love with her stepfather, or so she thought."

Elizabeth smiled nervously. This story was cutting close to the bone.

"Naturally," Lai-tse lu went on, "the emperor had no knowledge of the girl's feelings and regarded her only as his daughter. The girl grieved terribly. She could not eat or sleep, and her condition became so pitiful that the principal gods of the Upper Kingdom took pity on her and asked if they could help. She told them she wanted to be the emperor's wife. The gods told her she could achieve her goal only if she killed her mother, but even then she would fail, because the emperor would be compelled to execute her."

Elizabeth could feel her face burning.

"Naturally," Lai-tse lu continued calmly, "the girl had not thought in such realistic terms, and swore she meant her mother no harm. She was so honest and sincere that the gods granted her a boon. 'Dream your many dreams,' they told her, 'and one day they will come true.' And that is what happened. She still dreamed, and when she became a woman the gods sent her a husband in answer to that dream, and they lived in contentment together for the rest of their days." She paused, then added, "It is a simple fable, but there is much truth in it Do as I did, and dream the dreams that bring you happiness."

"It's a very interesting story," Elizabeth said, and pondered It was absurd to hate this exquisitely beautiful, highly intelligent young woman for having become the object of Jonathan's love. Any man who failed to fall in love with her would be stupid. Certainly she herself was no match for Lai-tse lu, and her common sense told her to do what her parents, Charles, and Ruth had been preaching. She would put Jonathan out of her mind and heart, and would concentrate her dreams elsewhere At least she would try.

"I like you," she said suddenly. "Very much. You're so much prettier and wiser than I am that you had every right to take offense when I was rude to you this morning. Instead you're going out of your way to be nice to me, a little nobody who happens to be vaguely related to you by marriage."

Hereafter, Lai-tse lu reflected, this lovelorn adolescent

would no longer regard her as a "rival," and they would be able to establish a friendship on a firm foundation. Impulsively she reached out and patted the younger girl's hand. "I wish you the joy in life that the gods have granted me. May your dreams be realized."

Her generosity made it impossible for Elizabeth to continue to yearn for Jonathan. Somehow, she told herself, she had to find the strength to forget him.

Jonathan and Charles stood at the windows of the former's office, looking out at the four new clippers that were in various stages of construction.

"How soon will you be able to send the Fat Dutchman another wonder ship?" Charles asked.

"If you think it's important enough, he can have the first of them," Jonathan said. "I was intending to add it to our own fleet, but we can afford to wait an additional few weeks."

"When you look at our profits on the cargo of black pepper he sent us," Charles said, "I don't believe we have any choice. Molinda, the slave girl who appears to have become the Fat Dutchman's office manager, has written to me that when I next come to Djakarta I can have all the pepper I want. So we'll flood the Dutchman with our clippers. In addition to the one you'll send for his fleet, I'll go there with two of our own, after I stop in England for a few months and attend to business matters. Once in the East, I'll send a ship directly to England from Djakarta, and then I'll go on to Whampoa for some additional cargo. The demand for Chinese jasmine tea and embroidered silks is enormous."

"You might be wise not to call at Whampoa," Jonathan said.

"You were there just recently, old boy."

"I'm an American, Charles, and you're a British subject. It's the British who are creating all the trouble. Because of that damned smuggling of opium into China."

"I know," Charles said with a sigh.

"Lin Tse-hsü, the new viceroy, has a genius for rubbing the fur of Westerners the wrong way. And now that Sir William Alexander is being retired, there's no telling what Captain Elliot will do. Do you know Captain Elliot?" Jonathan asked.

"Not well. He has no friends. I know him just well enough

to call him the most bigoted, hard-shelled, arrogant snob in all of Great Britain. The worst possible choice for a position that requires tact, delicacy, and a genius for compromise.''

"All the more reason for you to avoid Whampoa. Let the American master and crew of the new clipper sail to Whampoa. If they can get in. Conditions were bad enough when I was there, and I'm dead certain that some stupid incident will spark a war between China and Britain."

"Are you saying that trade between China and the West will have to be suspended?"

"I hope not. My father-in-law and I have arranged to use the Fat Dutchman's facilities in Djakarta as a two-way clearing center. We'll carry our cargoes to Djakarta, and Chao's junks will do the same. We'll give the Dutchman a fee for transference and handling. Of course, if the Royal Navy should blockade Canton, it will be a different state of affairs."

"That can't be allowed to happen," Jonathan said.

"If Queen Victoria had a voice of her own in the matter, I'm quite sure there would be no war. She's been developing a great interest in China. But her ministers and Parliament can't see beyond the fat, immediate opium profits dangling within reach." Charles paused, then looked at his cousin. "What will you do—personally, I mean—if a war breaks out?"

"That will depend on the circumstances. If I could, I'd bring Chao over here until peace is restored, but he won't budge. Lai-tse lu will stay right here, naturally. I wouldn't permit her to go back there. As for me," Jonathan added with a tight smile, "I'll have to make a decision at the appropriate time. But it wouldn't surprise me if you and I should find ourselves on opposite sides, Charles."

"Never," the younger man replied. "Rakehell and Boynton's British and American branches might seek different goals for a time, but I can't imagine any circumstance, including a war, that would pit you and me against each other."

Bradford Walker had been in hiding for many weeks, but the passage of time felt like years. He had fled to Boston after stealing money from Jeremiah's safe and setting fire to Jonathan's new clipper, carrying no belongings other than his fat purse and the clothes he was wearing. He took a room in a small residential hotel off Tremont Street, a safe distance from the waterfront area where he was acquainted with so many people. He purchased a portion of a new wardrobe, but he continued to live in terror.

Each day he scanned the newspapers, but read not one word abut his embezzlement of funds or his criminal act of arson. The absence of a story was not particularly significant, at least in his thinking. All it meant, he believed, was that Jeremiah Rakehell had asked the police to conduct a quiet manhunt, without publicity.

Walker felt certain his father-in-law intended to have him arrested, returned to New London, and hauled into court to face trial. The mere fact that he had struck Judith was enough to guarantee him the lifelong enmity of the Rakehells he loathed. But in spite of his apprehensions he felt no remorse for what he had done. By rights the money should have been his because he had been underpaid for many years. Jonathan, who had cut him out of the line of succession at the company, deserved to lose a ship. As for Judith, she had needed the lesson of a punch to put her in her place.

Little by little Walker changed his appearance. He bought a pair of spectacles, used lemon juice to turn his thinning, sandy hair a paler color, and then grew a short beard. When others at the hotel began to stare at him, wondering about his transformation, he knew it was time to move on. So he went by stagecoach to Philadelphia, and his fear became a living thing when the heavy coach changed horses at New London.

Still haunted when he reached Philadelphia, he remained there only a short time, then went to New York. He took a room at a fashionable hotel on Fourteenth Street, as far uptown as possible from the waterfront area. His new sense of freedom made it possible for him to complete the purchase of a new wardrobe in relative leisure and to begin planning how he would lead his new life.

Then, unexpectedly one day, he saw—or thought he saw— Jeremiah Rakehell emerging from a restaurant on Eighth Street, and a fresh sense of panic assailed him. One fact emerged clearly from the chaos that cluttered his mind. There was no way he would continue to live safely in the United States. He had spent only a very small portion of the money he had stolen and still had enough to invest in enterprises elsewhere that would earn him a comfortable living.

Walker scanned the newspapers avidly, but their accounts of the arrivals and departures of ships was woefully incomplete, and he realized it would be necessary for him to pay a personal visit to the waterfront, where he was acquainted with scores of people. It was even possible that a Rakehell and Boynton ship, perhaps one of his own brigs or schooners, might be in port.

The relentless pressure of the knowledge that he had no real alternative forced him to overcome his qualms, and he made his plans with great care. That night he lingered over a late dinner at a tavern on South Street, and then he walked briskly toward the wharves, where thirty or forty ships flying the flags of many nations were docked. As he had anticipated, the streets were virtually deserted as he moved farther into the district. He took care to avoid the taverns and bordellos, where seamen were congregating, and he looked forward to a leisurely stroll along the wharves, where he could see for himself what ships were in port and could make whatever accommodations suited his fancy.

There was no sound on the street but the clicking of his heels and the tapping of his sword cane. Suddenly two youths emerged from an alleyway, both of them carrying heavy clubs. "You, there, stop!" one of them called.

"Just give us your money peacefullike and you won't get hurt," the other declared.

In spite of his various weaknesses and vices, Walker was no physical coward. He was in his early forties, about twice the age of the robbers, but he refused to let that deter him. He was carrying the better part of his cache, having stashed the rest in his hotel room, and he had no intention of losing it to a pair of petty thieves.

"Quit stalling or you'll get a bash over the head," the smaller of the pair snarled. "Hand over your purse."

Walker's reply was immediate and emphatic. He kicked the smaller youth hard in the groin, at the same time wrenching the covering from his sword cane. Then, turning to his other astonished attacker, he drove the double-edged blade deep into the youth's stomach.

The thief doubled over and dropped on the cobblestones, dead before he sprawled on the ground.

His companion hobbled off, anxious to put as much distance as he could between himself and the madman.

Walker recognized the gravity of the situation. The youth he had kicked had vanished, and he was alone in the street with the body of the thief he had just killed. No windows were opened, no lamps or candles were lighted, and as nearly as he could determine, no one in the neighborhood was aware of what had happened.

It would be sensible to report the incident to the police as soon as he could, but Walker had no intention of calling himself to the attention of the constabulary. It was likely they had a notice on hand, requesting them to place him under arrest and return him in chains to New London.

So he knew what had to be done. With meticulous care he wiped the blood from his sword, using the dead youth's shirt for the purpose. Then he returned the sword to the cane and resumed his walk, refusing to give in to the temptation to run and thereby call attention to himself. In a few moments he turned the corner and was safe. No passerby would connect the distinguished gentleman in the handsome suit, beaver hat, and polished boots, who carried a gold-headed walking stick, with the stabbing of local riffraff.

Arriving at the waterfront itself, Walker slowed his pace. A Norwegian brig caught his attention, but the stench emanating from it told him it was used as a fishing vessel. He automatically ruled out all American ships, regarding it as likely that officers and crew as well might know him. Perhaps some had been in his employ over the years. He hesitated when he saw a British schooner, its name telling him it was in the transatlantic trade, and he walked past a clipper, totally ignoring it.

Finally he came to a halt at the berth of a schooner flying the ensign of the Netherlands. There was activity on the deck, and the ship's company, he noted, were short, wiry, brown-skinned men. He walked down the wharf and called.

The seamen paid no attention to him, so he raised his voice a second time, then a third.

Eventually a bearded man in shirtsleeves, wearing a hat decorated with tarnished braid, emerged from a hold and looked hard at the stranger. "What you want?"

"May I have a moment of your time, sir?" It was difficult

for Walker to speak respectfully, but he managed the feat.

The ship's captain hesitated, then waved him on board. There was no gangplank, but Walker jumped gracefully from the wharf to the deck, a distance of about three or four feet. "I see this schooner is called the *Wadden Zee*, so I assume you're Dutch."

The captain nodded.

"You appear to be preparing to sail," Walker said. "May I ask your destination and route?"

"We go by way of Cape of Good Hope to Manila, Whampoa, and then home to Djakarta. Why you ask?"

The Far East was the most unlikely part of the earth where the police would search for him, Walker thought, and it would be impossible to extradite him. By going to Whampoa, which he knew about through correspondence with various factors, he would be beyond the reach of the Rakehells. "Assuming you have the facilities, sir, would you be interested in transporting a passenger to China?"

An avaricious gleam appeared in the dour captain's eyes. "*Ja*," he said. "I have cabin for passenger. I show you."

Walker accompanied him and was shown a tiny cubbyhole that contained a bunk, a small chest of drawers, and a single, straight-backed chair bolted to the bulkhead. He estimated there would barely be enough room in it for his clothing boxes. But comfort was secondary to his need to travel as far as possible from the United States. "I'll take it," he said.

"This cabin cost you one hundred dollars cash. Pay in advance."

The price was high, but there was no choice, and Walker took the money from his purse.

The captain grinned, showing two rows of yellow teeth when he saw the bulging purse. "Food extra," he announced. "Fifty dollars more."

Bradford Walker well realized he was being cheated, but without a word of protest he handed the man an additional fifty dollars.

"I sail tomorrow morning. Eight o'clock."

"Never fear, sir. I shall be here well in advance of your sailing time." This voyage to a distant, unknown land was far preferable to the prospect of spending many years in a Connecticut prison.

II

When Charles Boynton returned to England with his family, he was dismayed to discover that the London newspapers were bristling with accounts of the beginning of hostilities between Great Britain and China. Some of the papers had even begun calling it "the opium war," and more and more Britons agreed it had to be fought. Their country would no longer be "insulted" by the imperial viceroy in Canton.

A few days later Charles read that the Royal Navy squadron stationed off Whampoa was being augmented by two more ships of the line, three frigates, and an unspecified number of sloops of war and bomb ketches, all of them currently stationed in India. The squadron's expansion was transforming it into a full-fledged fleet.

Desperately hoping he could do something to stave off a tragic, unnecessary conflict, Charles wrote a letter to the prime minister, asking for an appointment. In the communication he stressed his own experience in the Orient. He did not have long to wait. A messenger brought him a note requesting him to appear early the following morning at Whitehall.

He arrived promptly at the cavernous complex of government buildings, and went directly to the prime minister's suite. Within moments he was ushered into the inner sanctum.

William Lamb, the second Viscount Melbourne, was a wealthy aristocrat who had spent the better part of his adult life in politics and was serving as prime minister for the second time. Acting as the young Queen Victoria's tutor in state affairs, he was said to have won her confidence because of his patience, humor, and tact. Others who dealt with him found it difficult to believe that he possessed any of these qualities. His Whig majority in Parliament was supported by so many rank-and-file Tories that the opposition to his policies was feeble, and he was high-handed in his dealings with his peers, his subordinates, and outsiders.

His smile was frosty, his manner imperious as he greeted Charles. "I found a place for you in my schedule, Mr. Boynton, because you said your mission was urgent," he said, wasting no time on polite small talk.

"It is, milord." Charles was equally blunt. "I've come to discuss the threatening situation in the Orient with you."

"Ah." Melbourne leaned back in his padded leather chair and, pressing his fingertips together, seemed to anticipate that his visitor would offer his services in the war with China.

Charles surprised him. "Milord," he said, "we'll be making a terrible mistake if we take the Chinese to war."

Lord Melbourne frowned. "You're the second person today to give me such a warning. Only this morning I received a letter from Sir William Alexander, written shortly before he sailed to India on furlough before coming home. He also urged me to keep the peace."

Charles was somewhat encouraged. Sir William, after all, held the rank of a rear admiral in the Royal Navy and had been stationed at Whampoa for many years.

"What are your arguments, Mr. Boynton?"

"The potentials of our trade with China are unlimited, even though we're permitted to use only one port, Canton. There is a tremendous market in China for our manufactured goods, just as the demand here for her tea, silks, and porcelain is almost unlimited. It's dreadful to think of that trade being disrupted because of our insistence on buying opium in India and smuggling it into China."

"We do not smuggle it, sir. The Chinese themselves do that!" the prime minister said curtly.

"We bring it to the Pearl River delta, milord, and I happen to know that quantities of it are hidden frequently in British-owned warehouses. Please keep in mind that an imperial edict prohibits the importation of opium into China."

"We have no such laws, Mr. Boynton. And I beg to remind you that the East India Company and other concerns are earning staggering sums of money in the opium trade.

Surely we cannot be blamed if the people of China have a craving for the filthy stuff.''

"There are people in every country on earth who will form an addiction to opium if given the opportunity," Charles said earnestly. "The habit is not a weakness only of the Chinese. There would be thousands upon thousands of addicts in the British Isles if opium were brought here."

"I find that hard to believe," Lord Melbourne said stiffly. "But that is beyond the point. The Chinese authorities in Canton have arrested British subjects, imprisoning them, and threatening to execute them. And that is something Her Majesty's Government does not tolerate."

The prime minister was as short-sighted as most Englishmen on the issue, and Charles sighed. "I'll grant you that Lin Tse-hsü is tactless and overly aggressive in his dealings with foreigners, milord. But his emperor has demanded that the opium traffic be halted. If you put yourself in his position—"

"No, thank you," the prime minister interrupted, his voice dry. "I am charged with the responsibility for the lives and property of Her Majesty's subjects, and that is quite enough to keep me fully occupied."

Charles tried to marshal additional arguments, but Lord Melbourne silenced him with a wave. "You waste my time and your own energies, Mr. Boynton. The matter has been settled. I'll tell you in confidence what you will read in the press in coming weeks. The Cabinet has made a determination, and the queen will sign an order giving Captain Charles Elliot the right to determine whether we can reach a peaceful settlement with the Chinese or must continue to use force. He is at Whampoa now, awaiting reinforcements. Not even your clippers can travel rapidly enough for him to obtain the Cabinet' approval to act in specific situations, so we are giving him free hand to deal with any crisis that may arise as he sees fit."

A despairing Charles took his leave. He thought of making a personal appeal to the queen but rejected the idea as rapidly as it occurred to him. Real power was vested in the prime minister, and Victoria, regardless of her personal sympathy for the Chinese, would sign any document that Lord Melbourne presented to her.

The worst of the situation was that Charles Elliot was cut from the same bolt of cloth as Lin Tse-hsü. Totally lacking in diplomacy, arrogant and stubborn, he was blind to everything but what he regarded as his own nation's best interests. He and Lin, between them, were certain to create havoc.

Going on to his office, Charles wrote a long, gloomy letter to Jonathan, in which he inserted several newspaper clippings about the enlargement of the Royal Navy forces at Whampoa. He carried the letter himself to the master of a clipper sailing that same day for New London. He found it difficult to concentrate on the papers that crossed his desk for the rest of the day, and his mind was seething when he went home.

At dinner he told his family the gist of his talk with the prime minister.

"This is more or less what I've expected," Sir Alan said. "We may find it necessary to curtail our trade at Whampoa for a time and temporarily expand our relations with Djakarta and Manila."

Jessica and Ruth appeared resigned to the situation, and a deeply concerned Wu-ling sat in silence, her eyes downcast.

"I am weighing the possibility of sending you back to the Rakehells for the duration of the war," Charles told her.

The young girl was stunned, and the others at the table were shocked.

"If you send Wu-ling to America," Elizabeth declared, "I'm going with her."

"Why should it be necessary?" Jessica asked quietly.

"Wu-ling is the only full-blooded Chinese in England," her son replied. "When the war starts in earnest, feelings here may run high, and I don't want Wu-ling to risk being attacked by a mob."

"That couldn't happen," Sir Alan said flatly.

"I'm new to this country myself," Ruth said. "But I see many Indians, Africans, and West Indians in town. People of every race and color."

"Londoners may have their faults," Jessica declared, "but I cannot imagine them assaulting a defenseless girl who has done nothing to cause ill will."

Wu-ling settled the matter. "I will not leave unless David is sent with me," she said quietly. "Only I can teach him the Cantonese dialect and the Mandarin that I myself am learning. Only I can tell him about life in the land of his mother's

214

ancestors, which is his heritage. You wish to keep David here, is that true?"

Admiring the girl's courage and determination, Ruth said, "Of course."

"Then I shall stay, too," Wu-ling said.

Julian ate breakfast and dinner regularly with the family and quickly became Lai-tse lu's shadow, following her everywhere and making a fuss when she occasionally failed to take him with her on an errand. He doted on her, calling her "Mama," and only on Saturdays, when he accompanied his father to the yard and spent several hours on board one or another Rakehell and Boynton ship, where Oliver and other boatswains attempted to explain to him the rudiments of seamanship, did he willingly part with her.

Not only was Lai-tse lu's conquest complete, but her courage was responsible for a significant change in the boy's life. He had seen almost nothing of his maternal grandparents since the death of Louise, and Lai-tse lu was shocked when she learned that Dr. and Mrs. Martin Graves never invited the child to their home, which stood across the street from the Rakehell house.

"It is the duty of children to respect their ancestors," she said, "but it is also the duty of adults to earn the respect of their descendants."

Telling her intentions to no one, she took Julian across the street the following day and tapped at the front door. The housemaids happened to be occupied elsewhere, so Naomi Graves came to the door herself.

"I am Jonathan's wife," Lai-tse lu said without preamble. "And this, as you surely know, is your grandson. No matter what feelings may separate you from Jonathan and his father, it is wrong that Julian should be deprived of your love and counsel."

"Come in, please," the flustered Naomi replied.

Julian, who had been carefully primed, said, "Hello, Grandma."

The gray-haired woman dropped to her knees and kissed him, tears in her eyes.

Dr. Graves was seeing no patient at the moment, so his wife summoned him. He accepted an introduction to the new

Mrs. Jonathan Rakehell awkwardly, and as soon as he seated himself, Julian climbed onto his lap. "I see you in your yard or on the beach many times, Grandpa Graves," the small boy said.

The gray-haired man cleared his throat. "I've seen you, too, Julian. If the truth be known, I often watch you at play."

"It is not easy for those who have suffered a great hurt to put that hurt out of their hearts, and I do not ask it of you," Lai-tse lu said. "But whatever your quarrel with Jonathan and his father may be, do not let it harm your relations with this child."

"Oddly enough, we have no real quarrel with either Jonathan or Jeremiah," Dr. Graves said.

"That's quite true," his wife added. "When Louise died so suddenly, we couldn't understand why she had been unhappy—or if she had been unhappy. In our grief we foolishly blamed the Rakehells, and by the time we recovered from the shock and could think logically again, the damage had been done."

"We should have known better," her husband said, "but our pride stood in the way."

"There is no damage when false pride is banished," Lai-tse lu declared solemnly. "In my land there is a myth about an emperor who was so proud that he ate all of his meals alone and would not speak to the members of his family. So the gods of the Upper Kingdom punished him by killing all of his wives, his concubines, and his children, one by one. When all were dead the emperor realized his error, but it was too late, and when he died of a broken heart, there was no one to mourn for him. If you wish," she added hastily, hoping she hadn't gone too far, "I will leave Julian here to visit with you for a time."

"Please don't leave," Dr. Graves said, waving her back to her seat as she started to rise.

"Will you have coffee or tea?" Naomi asked.

A smile lighted Lai-tse lu's face. "I am learning much that is American, but coffee is so bitter that I still drink only tea."

Naomi hurried off to the kitchen herself.

Dr. Graves showed Julian his collection of toy soldiers, and when the child became absorbed, he said, "You're a rather unusual young lady. I can't blame Jonathan for having the good sense to marry you."

Before she left, Lai-tse lu extended a dinner invitation for the following Sunday, which was promptly accepted.

Jeremiah was as delighted as he was astonished when he heard the news. "Lai-tse lu," he said, "you're remarkable. I had reconciled myself to the fact that Martin and Naomi would never speak to us again."

The Sunday dinner washed away the last, lingering hostilities on both sides, and the two families restored friendly relations. Although the intimacy they once had enjoyed was lacking, Julian was free to wander back and forth between the two houses, and Lai-tse lu always was welcome under the Graves roof.

At her insistence there was another notable development. She and Jonathan were remarried, quietly, in an Anglican ceremony at the Church of St. James, with only members of the family in attendance. "I am trying to learn more about your God," she told her husband. "Besides, it is right that we should be united in your church, as we were in my temple."

Thereafter Jonathan was not surprised by anything she did, and one evening, when he came home from the yard, he grinned broadly when he found Lai-tse lu and Julian being industriously busy in the second-floor sitting room. Books, clippings from magazines, and newspaper articles were piled on a table, and while Lai-tse lu wrote a letter in Chinese, Julian was painstakingly trying to form Chinese characters on another sheet of paper, copying them from a book that was open beside him. "What's all this?" he asked.

"I am writing to the Princess An Mien," Lai-tse lu said, "and tomorrow, when a clipper sails for Whampoa, I hope you will give the captain a package to deliver to my father. It will contain a long letter to him, as well as all this." She indicated the books and clippings.

Jonathan picked up two books at random. "A history of the steamboat and a technical book on the building of steamboats." He started to rummage on the table. "An article by a professor at Harvard Medical School on how to prevent epidemics."

"And that stack," his wife said, "contains many samples

217

of the types of printing used in American publications. Printing may have been invented in the Middle Kingdom, but my people have fallen far behind the West in the art of printing."

He began to understand. "Why steamboats?"

"They would be far more useful than barges on the Yangtse and other great rivers of the Middle Kingdom. As for the prevention of epidemics, I know nothing about the ideas of the teacher at Harvard, but they are worth an experiment. Many Chinese die each year of epidemic illnesses."

Jonathan nodded. "But why have you chosen the princess?"

"She will show all of these papers to the emperor and will persuade him to do something with suggestions she likes. I have become an American, but I cannot neglect my duty to the land of my birth."

"So you've elected yourself as the Tao Kuang's eyes and ears here." He chuckled.

"Do not laugh," she said with dignity. "The Middle Kingdom is sealed from the outer world, and other nations surpass her in many realms. The least I can do is help her become more modern." She turned to Julian, who was holding up his sheet of paper and tugging at the skirt of her cheongsam. "That is much better, Julian," she said. "Try again, but make your strokes bolder and stronger. Like this." She dipped a tiny brush in a jar of ink and illustrated what she meant.

"I'll see you downstairs," a smiling Jonathan said.

"Wait! Will there also be space on the clipper that sails tomorrow for two cartons I am sending to Kai?"

"How large are the cartons?"

"About five feet long, five feet deep, and four feet wide." Lai-tse lu hesitated for a moment. "They are rather heavy."

"No matter. I'm sure space can be found." Jonathan left the room without asking the contents of the cases. It was good enough that his energetic, ever-thoughtful wife was doing her utmost to improve the well-being of citizens of the isolated, heavily populated Middle Kingdom.

At supper that night the young couple were amused by the bickering between Jeremiah and Sarah, which seemed to grow more intense each day. The dispute began quietly when Jeremiah remarked, "I don't see a crock of butter on the table. I need some for my string beans and cauliflower."

"I deliberately asked the maid not to bring it out of the larder," Sarah replied quietly.

He raised an eyebrow. "Why not? You know I like it."

"Too much butter isn't good for you, Jeremiah. You use it on everything."

"Butter is a wholesome, natural product," he replied irritably. "What medical school did you attend, Mrs. Applegate?"

"None, Mr. Rakehell!" she retorted. "But I've watched you eating bacon with buttered toast every morning, potatoes at dinner, and more potatoes at supper, along with apple or peach pie. You're putting on too much weight. Your only exercise is your walk to and from the shipyard."

Jeremiah became indignant. "I am not fat!" He paused, thought for a moment, and then added more calmly, "At least, for a man of my age."

Sarah turned to Jonathan who was having difficulty keeping a straight face. "You've spent a great deal of time in China. Have you ever seen a fat Chinese?"

He shook his head.

"And you, Lai-tse lu?"

"Rarely."

Sarah looked across the table in triumph. "I read—just today—that the average age limit of American men who live in cities and towns is fifty."

"Then I should have died nine years ago," Jeremiah grumbled.

Sarah paid no attention to him. "Lai-tse lu, what was the figure the Princess An Mien told you was the average age limit of men in the Middle Kingdom?"

The young woman didn't want to be caught in the middle but had to reply truthfully. "Seventy-one, Missy Sarah."

"How were those statistics obtained?" her father-in-law demanded, challenging her.

Jonathan came to his wife's rescue. "The Chinese may be backward in many ways, Papa, but for more than two thousand years the rulers of various dynasties have seen to it that remarkably accurate census figures are taken. They do it once every hundred years."

Jeremiah began to eat his beans without butter. "I'll probably starve to death."

"I doubt it," Sarah said cheerfully.

"Well, if I don't, it won't be your fault!"

Jonathan hastily changed the subject.

Later, in the privacy of their own suite, Lai-tse lu said, "As much as I hate to suggest this, I wonder if we should find some other place for Missy Sarah to live."

"Certainly not! She's part of the family, and I wouldn't hear of it!"

"She and your father quarrel so often these days that I become upset."

Jonathan laughed. "They enjoy it. Each day they act more and more like two people who have been married for many years."

"It may be that they do." Lai-tse lu became thoughtful. "Are you suggesting—"

"I suggest nothing, dear one. I merely observe and remark accordingly. I see my father only through the eyes of a son, not a contemporary who knew him before I was born."

She smiled wistfully. "Missy Sarah has been a widow for many years, and Papa Rakehell has been a widower even longer. Wouldn't it be wonderful if—"

"Don't interfere and don't be a matchmaker!" Jonathan wondered why every happily married woman became evangelistic.

"I wouldn't dream of it, dear," she replied sweetly.

The following morning, after father and son went off to the shipyard, Lai-tse lu left Julian in Missy Sarah's capable care and went off in the carriage on business of her own, which she did not explain to her old governess, in whom she ordinarily confided.

Although New London had a population of more than ten thousand and was one of Connecticut's larger communities, its atmosphere was that of a small town, where everyone seemingly knew everyone else's business.

So it was not surprising, in mid-morning, that Jonathan's chief clerk came to him, the man's manner hesitant. "May I have a private word with you, Mr. Rakehell?"

"Sure. Close the door and sit down, Talbot."

"I don't want to push my big nose into places it don't belong," the clerk said. "But I just went to the post office to send off bank checks to our New York State and Massachusetts suppliers. And I happened to walk back to the yard by way of

Bank Street. Not that I'd stop in one of the sailors' taverns there, Mr. Rakehell.''

"It wouldn't bother me if you did.'' Jonathan was busy and wished the man would make his point.

"Anyways, I happened to look in the window of the Grog House, and I saw Mrs. Rakehell sitting with that fellow, Fletcher. Carl Fletcher. You probably know all about it, so I apologize for taking up your time.'' Talbot rose hastily and bolted from the office.

Jonathan was more upset than he cared to admit, even to himself. The middle-aged but handsomely dressed Carl Fletcher was a shadowy figure who apparently earned his living by obtaining difficult-to-obtain merchandise for shipping companies. Rakehell and Boynton dealt with him occasionally, and most recently had purchased from him some hard-to-find Spanish red copper to sheath a new ship's hull. Fletcher rarely failed to produce for his customers, and he charged fees commensurate with the rarity of the merchandise he bought and sold, but he was tight-lipped about his sources of various goods. Most of the owners of yards and ships seemed to regard him as somewhat disreputable, particularly because he went out of town every weekend and nothing was known about his private life.

Why Lai-tse lu should be having a private meeting with such a man, especially in a saloon frequented by seamen, was beyond her husband's comprehension. He trusted her implicitly, to be sure, but surely she knew that she was more conspicuous by far than anyone else in the entire state.

Shortly before noon a second surprise was in store when Lai-tse lu paid a visit to her husband's office. It was only the second time she had seen it, and the clerks gaped at her as she walked through the outer offices.

"What's wrong?'' Jonathan demanded as she entered his private office.

"Nothing, I assure you, my dearest,'' she replied, and it was plain she was in a happy frame of mind. "I've just delivered the crates for Kai to the clipper that's sailing for Whampoa today, so I thought I would walk home with you and Papa Rakehell for dinner.''

"*You* delivered the crates?'' he asked incredulously.

"Well, I didn't do it myself, of course. They were far too heavy and bulky. But I rode to the yard on the freight wagon

221

that brought them and made sure they were given to the captain of the clipper."

Jonathan had never known her to be so glib, and he jumped to the conclusion that her seemingly innocent posture was feigned.

"Why do you stare at me?" she asked.

"I find it very odd that my wife should ride on the buckboard of a freight wagon. Just as I find it even stranger that she should have held a meeting in a sailors' tavern with Carl Fletcher."

Lai-tse lu sighed as she sat opposite him. "I didn't want you to become involved, but I should have known you'd find out."

"So far," he said, "I've found out nothing."

"One day, some time ago, I heard you and Papa Rakehell talking about this Fletcher person. I—I wanted to buy some merchandise from him, and because he has no office, I've had to hold my meetings with him in the Grog House. It's truly quaint, and was filled with seamen. They stared at me, but not one forgot his place. I suspect they guessed I'm married to you."

"I daresay," he replied dryly. "What was the merchandise?"

Lai-tse lu remained evasive. "I paid him just this morning. That's why I was meeting him today." She paused and saw that her husband was still looking hard at her, waiting for her reply to his question. Well, there was no escape.

"When you were in Canton," she said, "you may have learned that Kai is a prominent member of a secret society, a patriotic society. He and Lo Fang are the leaders of the Canton branch."

"The Society of Oxen," he said as the mystery deepened. "They've been very helpful to me on occasion."

Lai-tse lu braced herself. "As you have seen yourself, the weapons of the British are far superior to those of the Middle Kingdom's soldiers. The British officers carry accurate pistols. Their troops use the best muskets on earth. But the old matchlocks that are issued to my emperor's men are old and rusty and clumsy. One English soldier could defeat many Chinese."

Jonathan had an inkling now of where she was leading. "It is true," he said, "that the man who uses a ku ming, no

222

matter how skilled he might be, cannot fight someone who can kill him with a musket at a distance of hundreds of feet.''

She nodded, and there was a hint of defiance in her voice as she said, ''I have sent the most modern muskets and pistols to the Society of Oxen in the cases addressed to Kai.'' Hesitating, she added, ''I have not wanted you to become involved in something that is not your problem. I have not thought it right for an American to be placed in the middle of a quarrel between the Chinese and the British. That is why I deliberately did not tell you of the weapons I was sending to Kai and Lo Fang.''

''I understand.''

''What is more,'' she added proudly, ''I have used my own money for the purpose, some of the money my father gave me before I left Canton.''

Jonathan replied very carefully. ''I am grateful for your discretion. But let me make it plain that my wife's causes are my causes. From now on there will be a much larger space that is available on all of our clippers when they sail to Whampoa. I will arrange myself to buy the arms. There is no need for you to deal with Fletcher, and we will use my money for their purchase because my money is also my wife's money.''

Lai-tse lu felt infinitely relieved and told herself she should have known he would feel as he did.

In the weeks that followed, the newspapers of the United States were filled with accounts about the mounting crisis in the Far East, and many editors speculated at some length, wondering whether America would be dragged into the situation. Then, unexpectedly, Jonathan was summoned to Washington City to confer with the President. He wasted no time traveling to Baltimore on one of his clippers and then going on to the nation's capital on horseback. Only five days after he received the communication, he presented himself at the President's Mansion, which more and more people were now calling the White House because it had been repainted after the War of 1812 to hide the ugly marks left on the outer walls when a British expeditionary force had tried to burn down the building.

President Martin Van Buren, known as the ''Little Magician'' because of his reputed cunning and skill as a politician, was serving the final year in his first term as Chief Executive. Aware that the acquisition of the Oregon territory would make the United States a Pacific Ocean power, Van Buren wasted no time finding out what he could about the situation in the Orient. "I'm grateful for your cooperation, Mr. Rakehell," he said after Jonathan had been ushered into the simply furnished room first used by Andrew Jackson. "I was told that you know more about China than any other man in the country, and I need your advice."

"I'm no political expert, Mr. President," Jonathan replied, "but I'll gladly do what I can."

"Is it true that the basic dispute between the British and the Chinese is the smuggling of opium?"

"In a sense it is, sir. The emperor is trying hard to prevent the entry of opium into his country. But the British East India Company and a number of smaller traders are making such enormous profits they ignore the ban. They feel they're free to do as they please because there's nothing in British law that prevents them from buying opium in India and then selling it for a huge profit to Chinese smugglers who pay them in silver."

"Incredible."

"Perhaps, but we aren't blameless, Mr. President. The United States has no laws on opium, either, so a number of our shippers buy the drug in the Dutch West Indies and elsewhere, and they follow the lead of the British."

Martin Van Buren frowned. "I see. That explains it. We're hardly on the best of terms with Great Britain. They dispute our claim to the Oregon country, even though we're establishing settlements there, and they're supporting the Mexicans in their border dispute with Texas, although we've made it quite plain to them that the Republic of Texas is populated almost exclusively by Americans and that one of these years in the near future we hope to bring her into our fold. Be that as it may, Lord Melbourne is asking for our active support in his quarrel with the Emperor of China."

"There's one other aspect to be considered, Mr. President," Jonathan said. "Behind the opium trade is the British desire—which American merchants certainly share—to expand trade with China. As you no doubt know, only the port of Canton is open to us. China is still virtually a closed country and has only a tiny trickle of trade with the outside world, the better part of it concentrated in the hands of my father-in-law. No foreign ship is allowed to put into any port other than Canton. I'm certain the British hope to use the opium issue as a wedge to force China to open other ports to trade, a move that would benefit our merchants. Including my own company,'' he added candidly.

"Then you recommend that we take sides with the British in this dispute?'' the President asked.

"I do not, sir!'' was the immediate, firm reply. "The opium trade is a degradation and a disgrace! In my opinion, only a nation that lacks a conscience would use force of arms to compel a backward country to open her doors to us. And to be blunt, Mr. President, Rakehell and Boynton will refuse to cooperate with any such national policy.''

"It is not our policy to go to war with the Chinese on this issue, Mr. Rakehell,'' Van Buren said. "I have the unanimous support of my Cabinet, as well as congressional leaders of both the Democratic and Whig parties. I wanted to speak with you to assure myself that we're not taking the wrong stand.''

Jonathan smiled faintly. "I would even go so far, sir, as to recommend that we take a stand on the side of the Chinese. My wife is a friend of the emperor's influential sister, and I'm sure we'd win the appreciation and friendship of the emperor himself. It might be a sound policy move as well as an ethical gesture because we well might secure special trade concessions.''

The President shook his head. "It wouldn't work, Mr. Rakehell. Our relations with the British would become even more strained if we took the side of a nation they now regard as their potential enemy. As things now stand we'll be fortunate if we avoid another war with them. And our people know so little about China, there would be no public support for a position in which we back the emperor. I'm afraid that if a war breaks out we'll be required in our national interest to adopt a strictly neutral position.''

Jonathan was disappointed but realized that President Van Buren was right. His choices were limited.

Soon after Jonathan's return home from Washington City, he received Charles Boynton's letter telling in detail about his conference with Lord Melbourne. "I believe there is no possibility that this dispute with China will come to an early end," Charles wrote. "The British are already sending an expedition to the north, and Lin Tse-hsü has no intention of giving in."

This opinion was corroborated by another letter, written some weeks earlier, by Soong Chao to his daughter and son-in-law. "I did not think that conditions could become even worse than they were when you left Canton," he wrote. "But they have continued to deteriorate. There is talk that Captain Elliot will attack Canton sooner or later, and there have already been bloody skirmishes at the factories."

That evening, at supper, Lai-tse lu openly voiced her concern. "How I wish we could persuade my father to leave China until this crisis has been settled!"

"I quite agree with you," Missy Sarah said. "I'm terribly worried about him, too. But his loyalty to the Tao Kuang Emperor is so great that even though he knows a war will solve nothing, there's only a slim possibility he might leave."

"What creates that possibility?" Jeremiah asked.

"Chao has a great regard for Jonathan," she replied, "and just might listen to him."

"Jonathan can be very persuasive," Lai-tse lu said, "but America is so far from Canton that my father still might be unwilling to come here. I do think, though, that he might consent to go to Djakarta and stay for a time with the Fat Dutchman, who is his principal trading partner."

Jonathan looked hard at his father. Jeremiah knew what was in his mind, and nodded.

"It seems to me I have no alternative," Jonathan said. "I'll sail to Whampoa as soon as I can." He smiled at his wife. "And rest assured my cargo will include a far larger supply of arms for the Society of Oxen. Perhaps Kai and Lo Fang can help me persuade him it is in his best interest to leave China while there is fighting."

"I hope so," she said, pleased by the increase in the arms shipment.

"On my way," he continued, thinking aloud, "I'll pay a visit to the Fat Dutchman in Djakarta, bringing him a gift I've long wanted to give him. Chao might be more easily persuaded if I carry with me a personal invitation written to him by the Dutchman."

"Oh, yes!" Lai-tse lu exclaimed. "That might be a big help!"

So Jonathan immediately began to make intensive preparations for another voyage to the East on board the clipper named for his wife. His officers, boatswain, and most members of the crew who had sailed with him previously were available, and he signed all of them.

In the meantime Lai-tse lu, to her own surprise, felt ill. Thinking her worry for her father's safety was responsible, she paid no attention to the ailment, but it became worse, and Missy Sarah urged her to pay a professional visit to Dr. Graves. So she went to him for an examination, her instinct prompting her to make no mention of it to her husband.

Martin Graves gave her a thorough examination and then told her, "You're going to have a baby."

"How wonderful!"

The physician frowned. "I hope it will be wonderful. But I believe in being honest with patients, and I'll be as candid with you as I would have been with my own daughter. According to my diagnosis, you are suffering from a disease of the tissues about which very little is known, and there's a possibility you may have serious complications during your pregnancy if you aren't careful. I'll want you to spend the last six to eight weeks of your confinement in bed, and I urge you to stay there for that time. I'll give you a special diet when the time draws near."

"I can't possibly go to bed for that long," Lai-tse lu replied. "I've got to look after Julian!"

"Mrs. Applegate will take charge, and my wife will help. Your situation is serious, and if you don't do what you're told you may lose your own life as well as the baby's."

"I see." She had not dreamed her medical condition might be serious.

"I can't stress this any stronger. If you're fortunate enough to remain unscathed after you've had this child, you're not to have another. Under any circumstances. Medical science has been making great progress in this century, and the day undoubtedly will come when a case like yours will cause no problems. But that time hasn't come yet. There's a strong possibility you may be in delicate health for the rest of your days after you bring your baby into the world."

A sober Lai-tse lu went home, and after suggesting a game to Julian that would keep the child occupied, she repeated the physician's words to Missy Sarah.

The older woman did not hide her concern. "Dr. Graves has earned the reputation of being the best in these parts. So we'll follow his instructions to the letter."

"I intend to, Missy Sarah. I promise you I won't behave foolishly."

"Also, I'm going to have a chat with him myself."

"What about?"

"I prefer Western medicine to that of China, but I've seen doctors in the Middle Kingdom perform remarkable deeds, especially with some of their herb prescriptions. I took the precaution of bringing a number of jars of medicinal herbs back here with me, and I want to see if Dr. Graves agrees with me that regular dosages of those given to pregnant women can do you no harm."

"I'll do whatever you and Dr. Graves think is best," Lai-tse lu said. "I have too many obligations to Julian—and now to my own baby, too—to take any unnecessary risks."

"Thank goodness for that. Jonathan will be pleased when he learns you're being so cooperative."

"He is not to know," Lai-tse lu said quietly. "I forbid you to say one word about all this to him."

The older woman was startled. "Land sakes! You can't keep all this secret from him!"

"But that's precisely what I'm going to do. You know how close we are. If Jonathan hears I'm pregnant and there's something of a risk involved, he won't sail back to the Middle Kingdom. He'll insist on staying right here, with me, and by the time he sails, hostilities may have started in Canton."

"You couldn't blame him for that!"

"Of course not," Lai-tse lu said. "But it is urgent that he tries to persuade my father to leave the Middle Kingdom until peace is restored. If he listens to anyone, it will be Jonathan."

"I'm afraid that's true. Chao is not only a patriot who strongly believes in doing one's duty, but he's also uncommonly stubborn."

"The life of my father is worth the small deception that will not harm anyone. When Jonathan comes back and hears

228

my reasons, regardless of whether the baby has been born yet, I know he'll forgive me."

Sarah sighed. "My own conscience will bother me something fierce, but I guess that can't be helped. You have the right to make this decision, not I, so I'm forced to accept whatever you think is best."

"There's something more," Lai-tse lu admitted. "Just last night Jonathan told me that half of his entire cargo will be made up of arms for the Society of Oxen. Without his active help, now, hundreds of Chinese will be fighting the British with weapons that belong in museums."

"You've trapped me," her former governess said. "You've put a gag in my mouth and tied my hands behind my back. But I'll never forgive myself if something terrible happens while Jonathan is away."

"It won't," Lai-tse lu assured her. "I've been learning as I've studied the religions of the West that your God is merciful and compassionate. I'm very certain He will allow no harm to come to me or my baby. After all, Missy Sarah, He knows my motives are pure."

Julian was content to remain at home with the stepmother he had come to adore, and Jonathan was relieved. Thanks to Lai-tse lu, potential problems shrank and vanished instead of developing. Plans for the voyage to the East progressed rapidly.

In one respect, however, Jonathan was thwarted. He was unable to obtain his usual cargo of looms on such short notice, so, after storing the cases of arms for the Society of Oxen at the rear of his holds, he filled the remaining space with Western medicines the Chinese would need once the cannon mounted by the warships of the British fleet crashed into China. At best he would show a small profit, but he didn't care. He owed it to the company stockholders not to lose money, so he would be satisfied to break even.

Lai-tse lu went to the markets herself to buy the fruits, vegetables, and such delicacies as jars of jams and preserves intended for her husband's private use on his voyage. Always cheerful in his presence, she took care not to mention anything that Dr. Graves had told her. And Missy Sarah, to her credit, exerted enough self-discipline to keep her own counsel, too

Lai-tse lu did unbend, however, to the extent that she wrote a letter to her father, telling him she was pregnant and urging him to come to America so he could see his grandchild. That bait, she thought as she carefully sealed the letter, was certain to bolster her husband's arguments. Not until he had departed did it occur to her that her father well might mention her condition to his son-in-law. Her oversight could not be helped now, and she had to rely on Jonathan's love for her to cushion him.

The sailing was scheduled for the afternoon tide. Jonathan spent the morning at his office, as usual, and the only indication that this was other than an ordinary day was the elaborate dinner served at noon. Then the family accompanied the departing ship's master to the wharf where the *Lai-tse lu* was tied. Jonathan took care not to call his wife's attention to the four nine-pounder cannon, hidden beneath canvas on deck, that he had obtained to augment the clipper's armaments. These heavy guns might make the vessel a trifle more sluggish, but that could not be helped. He had to be prepared for any emergency that might arise off the coast of Cathay.

Rakehell farewells never were perfunctory. Everyone in the family had too great a respect for the sea, for the power of the elements, and Jonathan, bidding farewell to his father, handed him his new last will and testament. In it he had taken the precaution of specifying that, if he died or was lost at sea, Lai-tse lu would become Julian's official guardian until the boy reached his majority.

"Tell Chao I'll cook him his favorite Cantonese duck with lobster sauce if he'll come back here with you," Missy Sarah said.

Julian hugged his father. "When I'm older, I'll sail with you," he said. "I'll be first mate."

"You will once you've earned the place," Jonathan replied. "You'll start as a cabin boy, and then you'll serve as an apprentice during the summers and school holidays. That's the Rakehell way." As the little boy listened intently to the words of his father, Jonathan continued to explain. "That's how I started, son. You have to learn the sea and how to sail in any weather. Gain an understanding of men by becoming a man, and ultimately you'll be fit to command others."

The little boy nodded solemnly, not understanding every word but realizing his father was explaining to him something very important.

Jonathan and Lai-tse lu embraced for a long time. "I'll do everything in my power, short of kidnapping your father, to bring him back here with me," he said.

"I know." Lai-tse lu clung to him.

"Take care of yourself," he said. "I've asked Missy Sarah and Papa to crack down if you try to do too much."

She wondered if he had guessed she was going to have a baby.

Their kiss was long and bittersweet. When they drew apart, Lai-tse lu whispered. "May God sail with you." This was her way of telling him she had adopted his faith.

Jonathan was piped aboard the clipper, and moments later she slid out of her berth, gathering speed in the estuary as she sailed out into the blue-green water of the sea.

The Tao Kuang Emperor was far too sensible to listen to the confidential reports of his military advisers in the presence of his entire court. The nobles, members of his personal staff, and eunuchs would be certain to discuss whatever they heard, and even the more intelligent of his concubines would whisper to each other, perhaps in the presence of servants.

So he abruptly ended the audience, adjourning to the small Chrysanthemum Room built by his grandfather. The walls and ceiling were made of yellow marble and were carved in such a way that the occupants of the room felt as though they were inside an opening chrysanthemum. Here the emperor sat on a chair of carved stone that resembled the open jaws of a dragon, and on which cushions of embroidered silk had been piled for his comfort. Below him sat the two generals in command of the imperial army, the two admirals who commanded the imperial navy, the grossly overweight principal eunuch, and the imperial chamberlain. The chamberlain, Tung-So, had served the emperor's father in a similar capacity and enjoyed a unique position of trust in the imperial household.

Only he knew that the large, triple-paneled screen of thick silk at the far end of the chamber had not been placed there for purposes of decoration. Behind it, comfortable on a large, three-legged hassock, was the Princess An Mien. The officials would have been shocked had a mere woman been invited to attend the meeting, so the emperor, who had wanted her present, had solved the problem by the simple expedient of concealing her behind the screen.

Tung-So opened the meeting by reading a report from Lin Tse-hsü, the Imperial Viceroy of Kwangtung Province. Bristling and aggressive, Lin wrote that he had rejected all demands made on him by Captain Charles Elliot, the official representative of the British Crown. He was preparing for new hostilities in the near future, he said, and he requested any additional aid the Celestial Emperor might care to give him.

The admirals were overjoyed. "Hundreds of war junks are now stationed all the way from the South China Sea to the Yangtze," the junior admiral declared. "At my direction, all are already filled with barrels of gunpowder."

The senior admiral, who had not gone to sea in forty years and had never seen a modern warship, chuckled and rubbed his hands together. "The moment the British attack," he declared, "fuses will be lighted and the junks will be set adrift in such a way that they will collide with the ships of the Fan Kuei. The waters of our port cities and rivers will be choked with the bodies of Fan Kuei, and we will be forced to dredge our channels in order to remove their sunken ships."

The chamberlain requested the opinions of the army commanders.

The junior general was cautious. "We have stone forts stationed on the heights that command the approach by either sea or land to our port cities. There we have more cannon than there are gulls in the harbor, with five thousand troops stationed in each fort. Perhaps we should minimize the risks to our glorious soldiers still more by doubling their numbers."

The senior general demurred. "Each of the forts was designed to hold no more than one thousand men. Five thousand must make living conditions intolerable, and if there were ten thousand, each fort would be so crowded it would be impossible to fire the cannon. A total of five thousand is sufficient, in my opinion."

The Tao Kuang Emperor asked a sensible question. "How many men are on board the warships of the Fan Kuei? We have been told no numbers."

The senior admiral consulted a sheet of parchment. "No

232

one knows for certain, Divine Son of a Divine Son," he replied. "Lin says the British have three thousand, but the admiral in command of the junks insists there are at least five hundred less."

The principal eunuch spoke loftily. "Three thousand at best," he declared in a high-pitched singsong. "But our forces number at least twenty-five thousand."

The senior general quietly reproved him. "You forget the garrisons in the cities themselves. Our soldiers and sailors number in the hundreds of thousands."

"Then the Fan Kuei will be crushed," the principal eunuch said. "For generations to come they will suffer from the humiliation of their defeat."

The Celestial Emperor looked slowly around the table. "Are the rest of you in agreement with that determination?" he asked.

The representatives of the navy needed only to exchange a quick glance. "Indeed we are, Lord of the Universe," the senior admiral said confidently. "The British will learn a lesson they will never forget."

The army representatives conferred in an undertone, and then the senior general said, "Great Master of the Middle Kingdom, it is true the arms of the enemy are modern and that they are skilled in firing these weapons. It is also true, from all that our spies who watch them night and day have observed, that they are very disciplined and are loyal to their own queen. But they are stationed many thousands of miles from their homeland, and they will become panicky when our soldiers and sailors assault them."

"After we win the glorious victory that is assuredly ours," the principal eunuch said, "we should insist that the queen of the Fan Kuei come to Peking and abase herself at the feet of the Divine Ruler of All Men!"

The Tao Kuang turned to the imperial chamberlain. "You have not spoken, aged one," he said.

The old man had retained his position longer than any predecessor by carefully refraining from giving counsel for which he subsequently could be blamed. "It is not my place," he said humbly, "to give advice to the One Who Dwells Above the Clouds. I await the inspiration that his fellow gods will reveal to the Divine Master."

His colleagues looked at him contemptuously. In certain situations they, too, were experts in the art of sidestepping responsibility, but in this problem they could afford to be bold because the forces of the Fan Kuei certainly would be shattered.

The Tao Kuang Emperor had heard enough, and knew how to get rid of them with dispatch. "We shall remain behind and seek the counsel of our fellow gods," he said, and waved them out of the room.

One by one they kowtowed, then backed out of the chamber.

After the door closed behind them, the Princess An Mien emerged. "The next time you want me to eavesdrop," she said, "the least you can do is provide me with enough cushions. The space back there was so cramped I couldn't lower my legs to the floor."

By way of apology her brother offered her candied kumquats from a porcelain bowl so thin that the light shone through it. She selected one, ate it with relish, and then dropped into a chair near his. "What interminable bores."

"I know, but they've risen through the ranks, all of them, and I'd upset tradition if I replaced them without due cause." The Ruler of Humankind peered at her. "Well?"

"You may have due cause to have them decapitated sooner than you think. All but Tung-So, the wily old rascal."

The Tao Kuang Emperor was surprised. "You do not agree that we shall win a glorious victory."

"We'll be fortunate if we avoid a terrible, humiliating defeat. Lin Tse-hsü is a competent administrator, but he isn't qualified to make judgments in a confrontation with a powerful foreign nation. I've seen the British warships, remember. I've seen their marines at target practice!"

The Celestial Emperor looked aggrieved. "But surely a paltry three thousand could not win even a minor battle against our hundreds of thousands!"

He was trying her patience, and An Mien became annoyed. "You are too trusting for your own good, Kuang," she said with asperity. "Haven't you learned yet that the military statistics you're given are rarely accurate? I am neither a general nor an admiral, but I trust the gods have endowed me with a little common sense. I sailed past the ships of the British fleet, and each of the largest must have a complement of about two thousand men. So I would guess their entire present force must add up to a minimum of ten to twelve thousand.''

He shifted uneasily. "Even if you're right, as you so often are, the odds in our favor are still overwhelming.''

The princess ignored his comment. "What is more,'' she went on, "I didn't hear anyone at your meeting just now as much as mention that thousands of British troops have been sent from India to supplement their naval forces.'' She paused, then tried another tack. "Do you remember what our grandfather told us so often when we were very small? There are many ways to defeat one's enemies. Send troops into battle only when you are certain they will win. He who sits on the Chrysanthemum Throne cannot afford to make major errors.''

The Tao Kuang Emperor swallowed his pride. "What would you have me do?'' he asked, spreading his hands in a gesture of helplessness.

"The Middle Kingdom has remained isolated from the rest of the world for thousands of years,'' she replied. "But that day is coming to an end. The clipper ship brings the Fan Kuei to our gates swiftly. Their cannon are so powerful they can pierce our thickest walls. So make a virtue of necessity. Open the doors wider to the foreigners. Let them send their ships to a number of our ports, and encourage their trade with us. Just as they have much to learn from us, we can improve our own society by learning from them. The looms that the husband of Soong Lai-tse lu brought to the Middle Kingdom make a better cloth than our own looms spin. Their physicians have found many ways to heal the sick, but we are ignorant of those ways. If they make better arms, we can learn to make them. If their scholars have discovered many secrets of the natural world, we can use those secrets for the benefit of our people.''

The emperor was shocked. "But the ways of the Fan Kuei may corrupt us!''

"We already know we are the largest, most heavily populated nation in the world,'' An Mien replied. "What have we to fear? Does the desire for drink that curses Shaong Wei abate while we hold him as a prisoner in Nanking? No. Only a strong wife who can guide him will help him. It is the same with us. If we remain isolated, our position will only worsen. If we try to keep our doors bolted, the foreigners will force

235

them open and will take unfair advantage of us. I say our defeat is inevitable, so we should act accordingly. If we deal wisely with the Fan Kuei, we can improve the lot of our people."

"Then still more opium will enter the Middle Kingdom." He was stiff-faced.

"We could offer a compromise to the British and other nations. We might offer to open our doors to their trade if they will abandon the opium traffic. I believe they would agree, that they would be eager to strike such a bargain with us. Even if the experiment failed, we have nothing to lose. And instead of suffering a defeat, you will save face because you have made them the offer."

The Tao Kuang Emperor weighed her advice in silence, then sighed as he said, "I am willing to admit you may be right in all you say, my sister, but you know that not one of my ministers would agree with you. The admirals and generals would protest violently. The corps of eunuchs would seek ways to undermine my decisions."

"But your subjects would be spared the misery of a war we cannot win. In time the people would recognize your wisdom and would hail you for it."

His face reflected his agony, but he shook his head. "For more than three thousand years the Middle Kingdom has been closed to foreigners. I cannot change the policies of my ancestors, policies in which our whole civilization is rooted. We will fight the Fan Kuei in our own way, with our own weapons. If it is the will of the gods that our ways be changed, that will be determined on the field of battle. I must persist in following the only path I know."

III

The *Lai-tse lu* tied up at one of the Fat Dutchman's wharves, and the efficient Djakarta constabulary promptly threw a protective cordon around the ship. The Dutch customs officials were surprised to learn that no cargo would be unloaded, but they sealed the holds, and Jonathan knew his vessel and its contents would be safe. So he gave his officers and crew a welcome shore leave of forty-eight hours, then rented a carriage and driver to take him to the estate of the Fat Dutchman.

Two of the wiry, brown-skinned security guards recognized him immediately, grinning when they saw that he carried in his belt throwing knives similar to their own, and they waved him toward the garden.

There everything was unchanged, reminding him of his first visit. Chattering parrots sat on perches, orchids bloomed, and gardenia bushes gleaming with white flowers filled the air with their fragrance. Semiclad slave girls lounged or sat in small groups, making idle conversation, and the Fat Dutchman, the master of all he surveyed, sat in his thronelike wicker chair, with Molinda seated beside him as he read a document.

A grin split the Fat Dutchman's broad face, and he heaved himself to his feet, extending his thick hand. "Rakehell! What a grand surprise, heh-heh!"

"I've stopped off for a brief visit with you on my way to Canton," Jonathan told him as they shook hands and he bowed to Molinda.

"This calls for a celebration!" The Fat Dutchman sent one of the girls for a bottle of chilled French champagne, while another brought a wicker chair for the guest.

After they exchanged amenities, Jonathan handed his host a small package. "It's a gift," he said. "I think you'll enjoy it."

The Fat Dutchman's eyes gleamed, and he tore off the wrapping with the eagerness of a small child. Opening the box, he saw a silver watch with two faces.

"Until recently," Jonathan told him, "the best watches were made only in Switzerland. But our New England watch-making industry is performing wonders, and this sample is extraordinary. One of these faces is set for your time here, and the other for New England time." He took a small silver key, inserted it into the side of the watch, and wound it.

The watch chimed, its tinkling sound like that of tiny, musical bells.

"It chimes every quarter hour," Jonathan said, "and as you'll soon learn, the on-the-hour chimes are longer and more elaborate than the others."

The Fat Dutchman was enchanted. Fondling the watch, he showed it to Molinda while continuing to hold it himself, and when he spoke to his visitor, his normally husky voice dropped lower. "I have done many favors for others in my lifetime," he said, "but only rarely does someone bring me a gift, and I've never had one the equal of this. Thank you, my friend. Heh-heh. I shall treasure it."

The champagne arrived, and Jonathan was quick to note that Molinda was given a glass. Obviously she enjoyed a special status.

"What cargo have you brought me?" the Fat Dutchman asked as he sipped his wine.

"None," Jonathan told him. "Your customs people have sealed my hold—at my request. May I speak freely?" He glanced at the girl.

"I keep no secrets from Molinda," the Fat Dutchman said.

"I'm carrying arms and medicines to my father-in-law in Canton," Jonathan said. "Has the war started there?"

"Not yet, but the situation grows more delicate every day. In the north, the British blockaded the Yangtze River and went up to the Peiho, one hundred miles from Peking. The emperor was so angry that he dismissed Lin Tse-hsü, sent him into exile, and appointed a new man to negotiate with the

British. A lot of good that did. Heh-heh. Negotiations broke down, the British are back in Whampoa, and their guns are aimed at Canton."

"And no one knows when the British will lunge," Molinda said, joining in the conversation for the first time. "The present situation is so precarious that it cannot possibly go on much longer."

Jonathan was surprised by her familiarity with the problem.

"Soong Chao," she went on, "has already sent most of his junks to us for safekeeping. We sail them, and we save half of the owner's share of the profits for him. He does almost no business out of Canton these days. So don't be surprised if he can provide you with little or no cargo for your return voyage."

"I've been afraid of that," Jonathan said. "If he has no cargo for me, I'll return here for it. What can you give me?"

"Anything you want, heh-heh," the Fat Dutchman replied.

Molinda was more specific. "I can obtain as much black pepper as you wish."

Jonathan noted instantly that she had said that she herself could obtain it. Her authority was growing. "Thanks," he said, "but Charles has a far bigger market for it in England. Hold it until he comes here."

"Will he come soon?" There was a note of eagerness in the girl's voice.

"If he holds to his schedule, he should be here in the next half-year."

Molinda's eyes were bright, but she returned promptly to the business at hand. "You have had a growing market in America for batik cloth."

"I'll be happy to fill my hold with batik."

"I shall make the arrangements," she said.

The Fat Dutchman beamed at his efficient protégée. "How I shall miss you when you leave," he said, then turned to the guest. "Would you object if Molinda dines with us? She eats most meals with me these days."

"I'd be delighted," Jonathan replied graciously, telling himself she well might add her voice to his when he asked if Soong Chao could find temporary refuge in Djakarta.

Misinterpreting the American's response, the Fat Dutch-

239

man jumped to the conclusion that Molinda had made another conquest. Every man who came to the estate on business wanted her, but her favors were saved for a select few. And here was a way to repay Jonathan for the gift of the unusual pocket watch.

When they went to the dining room, they were served the great meal of the Netherlands East Indies, *rijsttafel*, which the Dutch had adapted from the native cuisine. It consisted of literally scores of dishes, including meats, vegetables, and fish, prepared in ways that were alien to the Western palate. A guest was expected to taste everything, then ask for larger portions of what he liked. Some dishes were bland, but the majority were heavily spiced, and it was necessary to drink quantities of Dutch beer with the food.

Jonathan's tastes were simple, but he had learned to like *rijsttafel* on his previous visits to Djakarta. The Fat Dutchman was a lively conversationalist, and Molinda, who was surprisingly well informed on many subjects, contributed her fair share to the stimulating table talk. Jonathan enjoyed himself, and not until they were served a variety of candied, preserved, and boiled fruits at the end of the dinner did he bring up the subject that preyed on his mind.

"I do have an ulterior motive for coming here," he said.

"Ah." The Fat Dutchman folded his hands across his paunch.

"I am going to Canton in the hope of persuading my father-in-law to accompany me to the United States for the duration of the war."

Molinda rose effortlessly, crossed the room, and returned with a decanter of French cognac and two bell-shaped glasses.

"It is my further hope," Jonathan continued, declining the brandy, "that you would give him refuge here if he refuses to travel so far from his home."

The Fat Dutchman selected a dark cheroot from a box and lighted it from a taper that the girl held for him. "My dear Rakehell, you do surprise me, heh-heh," he said in an aggrieved tone. "You must think me lacking in hospitality. Molinda, how many times have you extended an invitation to Soong Chao to join us here?"

"I have written him three separate letters," she replied as she sat again.

"And I also wrote him in my own semilegible hand,

240

heh-heh. He has declined all our offers. Courteously but firmly." The Fat Dutchman went through the ritual of sniffing his cognac, inhaling deeply, then taking a sip and drawing on his cheroot. "I think you've set a difficult task for yourself. The Chinese upper classes lack the resiliency of the Westerner. I assure you that if the British fleet threatened to bombard Djakarta, I would sail without delay for Rotterdam, even though I haven't visited Holland for more than forty years. Heh-heh."

"I have seen British ships of the line and frigates when they have paid courtesy calls at Djakarta," Molinda said, "and their cannon are even more ferocious than those of the Dutch. If they attack Canton in earnest, little will be left of the city. Soong Chao already knows what is in store because his ships have come here laden with the stores he normally keeps in his warehouses."

"He is a man of great courage, and I think it unlikely that he will leave his home, heh-heh. But he knows I would be honored if he chose to make his temporary home with us."

Jonathan tried to thank him.

"Nonsense, my dear Rakehell, heh-heh. Soong and I were doing business together long before either of us knew of your existence." The Fat Dutchman splashed more cognac into his glass, then gripped the arms of his chair and managed to struggle to his feet. "Molinda will show you to your quarters," he said, picking up his glass and cheroot. Surprisingly light on his feet, he went to the door, then paused for a moment. "Molinda, you will entertain our guest for the night in your own incomparable way." He disappeared.

Jonathan was embarrassed. "I hope you aren't taking his suggestion literally."

"It is a command," the girl replied quietly.

He didn't want to hurt her feelings, but he had no intention of making love to her. "You are very beautiful, but so is my wife, whom I love."

"If I do not obey my master," Molinda said, "he will have me beaten with a whip of rawhide, and he might punish me still more by rescinding a promise that means more to me than life itself."

"You leave me little choice," Jonathan said with a sigh.

The girl turned and led him to a spacious chamber on the second floor, her hips swaying as she walked.

The chamber was huge, fitted with jalousies instead of glass windows, and was dominated by a mammoth four-poster bed protected by mesh mosquito netting. On a table stood a huge bowl of fresh fruit, a bottle of wine, and two glasses.

Molinda closed and bolted the door, then started to remove her breastband.

"Wait!" an alarmed Jonathan told her. "What happens on the near side of the door is only your business and mine. We'll talk for a time before we put out the lamps, if you wish, and then we'll sleep. But that's all we'll do." He tried to hide his uneasiness by removing the cork from the bottle of wine.

"You do not find me desirable?" Molinda asked.

"Of course I do," he said gruffly. "Any man in his right mind would want you. But my marriage is precious to me, and I prefer not to risk harming it by finding pleasure for a night with someone else."

"You are very unusual, Jonathan," she replied, wonder and a hint of amused respect in her tone. "Most of the men to whom my master has given me are married, too, but that has not prevented them from taking me."

"I'm curious," he said, pouring two glasses of wine and shifting the conversational emphasis. "How does it happen that you can read, write, speak several languages, and know so much about the Fat Dutchman's business? You appear to be in charge."

She sketched her background for him as they sat opposite each other in two wicker chairs. "Little by little I have relieved my master of responsibilities," she concluded. "Now he searches actively for others to take my place when I leave."

"You're going away?"

Her long, blue-black hair, reminiscent of Lai-tse lu's, swayed gently as she nodded. "May I confide in you?"

"I'd be flattered."

"When Charles Boynton comes to Djakarta," she said, "my master will give me to him for all time."

Jonathan was stunned. "Charles also is married," he said. She shrugged. "That does not matter."

He didn't know how Charles would respond, but he could well imagine Ruth's emphatically negative reaction. "Charles is my best friend as well as my business partner and my cousin," he said. "I hate to disappoint you, but I'm afraid there's no way—under the rules of Western society—that he could take you back to England with him."

"Oh, I don't ask that of him. I shall request only that he take me away from Java. I know he hates slavery, so it is my hope that he will set me free."

"Of course he will," Jonathan said. "If that's what you want, perhaps I could persuade the Fat Dutchman to let you come with me. Although Canton isn't the safest place in the world these days."

"My master would not agree," Molinda said flatly. "I worked for a long time in subtle ways to persuade him I love Charles. So he will give me to Charles in return for my loyalty and hard work."

"I see." What Jonathan also saw was that this exceptionally attractive girl had a clever mind. He hoped he'd have a chance to write to Charles to explain what was in store for him, but he also realized that by the time a letter arrived in England, Charles would probably be on his way to Djakarta, according to his plans.

"You will not tell my master what I have said to you?" she asked, rising and refilling their wine glasses.

"You have my word." Her plan was so audacious that he could scarcely accept it. "How will you survive if and when Charles takes you elsewhere?"

"I hope the war will end quickly," she said. "Then I will go to China. The British will force her to increase her trade with the West, and there will be great need for one who has learned much about the business conducted by merchant ships."

She was shrewd as well as clever, Jonathan reflected.

The girl showed him a ruby solitaire she was wearing, and lightly touched one of her long, ruby earrings. "My master has given me many expensive jewels," she said. "If I must, I will sell them so I may live until I find the position that suits me."

A thought struck him with great force. "Perhaps, after the war ends, you might want to consider the possibility of representing Rakehell and Boynton at the port of Canton."

"I would be honored," Molinda replied quickly. "And you will not be sorry you have hired a mere woman rather than a man."

"I'm sure of it," he said, and grinned at her.

"We will speak more about this in the morning," she

said. "But now we must extinguish the lamps. My master can see the reflection of their light from his quarters, and he will think it odd if we delay too long in making the room dark."

Jonathan realized she was right, but his embarrassment returned with a rush. Before he could protest, however, the girl snuffed out the lamps. "Now we will sleep," she said calmly.

He undressed in the dark, then raised the mosquito netting and climbed into the bed, staying close to the edge.

Molinda entered the bed from the opposite side. "I will not be offended if you change your mind and wish to make love to me," she said softly. "Then I could show you how grateful I am that you will take me into your employ."

Jonathan fought temptation and won the battle. "That won't be necessary, and I won't change my mind."

She sighed gently but obviously took him at his word because only a short time passed before her steady, even breathing told him she had fallen asleep.

A long time passed before he, too, dropped off, and his last conscious thought was the fervent hope that his impulsive offer of a responsible post to this ravishing beauty would not create more problems than it solved.

Shaong Wei, tall and broad-shouldered, strolled out to the balcony that encircled his suite on the top floor of the old imperial castle in Nanking. Then he increased his pace, his stride that of a natural athlete, because he badly needed the exercise. The view was spectacular, but the young nobleman had become so accustomed to it that he stared with unseeing eyes.

On three sides the bustling city, once the national capital but now reduced to a more modest role as the capital of Kiangsu Province, was surrounded by a magnificent wall that soared seventy feet from the ground. On the fourth side was the Great Bend of the mighty Yangtze River, a natural port with water deep enough to accommodate the many seagoing junks that were crowded into the harbor. Even when the British had blockaded the river some months earlier, the lowliest commoner was free to sail wherever he pleased in those junks or in the tiny sampans that carried food and water to the larger vessels. But Shaong Wei, the direct descendant of Manchu emperors, could not leave this hated place.

By looking down to his left he could see the broad avenue lined with plane trees and the gigantic figures of men and mythological animals that led to the tomb of the first emperor of the Ming Dynasty. And off to his right was the only edifice in Nanking that stood higher than the castle and was the only place that still captured his interest. Known as the Porcelain Tower because its outer walls were made of pure porcelain bricks, it rose two hundred and sixty-eight feet from the ground. It had been built more than four hundred years earlier by one of the Ming emperors in honor of his virtuous mother, and Shaong Wei thought, as he often did, that he was glad his cousin had not elected to incarcerate him there.

A bell tolled in the pagoda at the top of the Porcelain Tower, and as the last sounds died away, there was a discreet tap at the outer door of the suite. "You may enter, Doctor," Shaong Wei called in his deep baritone voice, knowing that the imperial physician who was the head of his household staff—his principal jailer—was punctual to the minute.

The short, bespectacled physician joined him on the outdoor walk, his silk robe rustling. "Too much fresh air will give Your Worthiness an ailment of the lungs."

"Too little fresh air increases my craving for drink," Shaong Wei replied bluntly.

The imperial physician hastily changed the subject. "Your Worthiness enjoys good health?"

"Why shouldn't I?" the young nobleman replied irritably. "I eat ample quantities of good food prepared by a splendid cook. I get more sleep than I need. I walk so much I wear out my shoes. And I am bored to distraction!"

"Do you require more reading matter?"

"Not until I finish wading through that history of the Ming Dynasty. By the time I've finished the various books you bring me, I'll know more about the accursed emperors of the accursed Middle Kingdom than anyone else in the land."

Even though they were alone, with no one to overhear their conversation, the physician glanced uneasily over his shoulder. "Your Worthiness should not speak of emperors with disrespect."

"If Tao Kuang doesn't release me soon, I shall do worse than that!"

The physician removed his spectacles, breathed on them,

and cleaned them on his robe. "Several young concubines sent here from Peking arrived today," he said. "I prescribe one of them for your pleasure this evening. Or would you prefer two?"

"Neither," Shaong Wei replied, his natural dignity seemingly making him still taller. "I am as tired of meaningless lovemaking as I am sick of every other aspect of my confinement here. Was my letter to the Tao Kuang Emperor delivered to him?"

"I swear to you it was placed in the imperial hands by the messenger who took it to him."

"Then why hasn't he replied?"

"As I have told you so often in recent days, Your Worthiness, the Celestial Emperor spends every waking moment thinking about the war with Great Britain."

The emperor's young cousin became contemptuous. "If he didn't think so much, and took action instead, the war would be over much more quickly."

"That may be so, but it is not my place to advise the emperor how to spend his time."

A faint smile touched the corners of the handsome young man's mouth. "You're right, Doctor, and I offer you my apologies. Was the oral message for the Princess An Mien, which you committed to memory, sent to her?"

"It was, Your Worthiness, and a reply came by a messenger who sailed here from Tientsin with the new concubines, who are a gift to you from Her Sublime Highness."

"Send her my thanks," Shaong Wei said dryly. "What word does the messenger bring?"

"The Princess An Mien informs you that when the distractions caused by the war come to an end, she will resume her search for the appropriate wife for Your Worthiness. When that wife is found, Your Worthiness will be released and may live wherever he pleases in the Middle Kingdom."

The young nobleman clenched his fists. "Doesn't An Mien realize I'm cured? Doesn't the emperor know I no longer have the desire to drink?"

"It appears they do not." The physician was sympathetic. "I have sent my own opinions and those of my colleagues to the Forbidden City, but the Celestial Emperor seems not to have accepted them."

"And why do they insist on finding me a wife? Why am I not free to marry someone of my own choice?"

The physician cleared his throat nervously. "It was the Princess An Mien who first suggested that the right wife could be a great help to Your Worthiness. And I must inform you, with all due candor and respect, that my colleagues and I were forced to agree with her. She is a wise woman, perhaps the wisest in the land, and she understands that your drinking was caused by the curse of boredom. She believes—and we agree—that a marriage to the right wife can bring Your Worthiness contentment and enable you to lead a life that is both useful and fulfilling."

Shaong Wei stopped pacing, walked abruptly into his comfortably furnished sitting room, and sank onto the cushions of a three-legged stool of stone lions' feet. Covering his face with his hands, he muttered. "May the spirits of the emperors who are my gods and my ancestors have pity on me. First I must wait until the Celestial Emperor destroys the soldiers and sailors of the British Fan Kuei. Then I must wait while An Mien resumes her search for the woman she will compel me to marry. Then they will find some other excuse, and I will remain in this crumbling ruin of a castle until I rot!"

Jonathan and his mates quickly became aware of the changed atmosphere as the clipper sailed up the delta of the Pearl River toward Whampoa. "This is strange," Homer Ellison said. "There are no commercial junks anywhere, and the fishing sampans have vanished, too."

Elijah Wilbor pointed toward a small island off the port bow. "But there are several war junks."

Jonathan nodded. "Ready for action, by the looks of them," he said, noting the presence of Chinese seamen in dusty yellow uniforms of padded cotton on the decks of the vessels. "The all-seeing eyes on their hulls have been repainted recently, so it's plain they're prepared for battle."

None of the trio smiled because, directly ahead as they drew nearer to Whampoa, stood the warships of the powerful British fleet.

"They're ready, too," Homer said somberly. "You'll notice there are ships of the line, frigates ahead of them, and

247

sloops of war. Either this is a gigantic bluff, or the Royal Navy really intends to bombard Canton.''

Soldiers filled the old stone forts that guarded the entrance to the harbor, and men in yellow were crowded around each of the ancient cannon that were now pointed at the British warships.

''Just look at all the cannon the *Nemesis* is carrying!'' Elijah exclaimed.

''I expect Captain Elliot is prepared to use them,'' Jonathan replied. ''I don't mind telling you I'd feel better if Sir William Alexander still had the command and were here in the *Invincible*.''

''Will you pay your respects to Captain Elliot, sir?'' Homer wanted to know.

''I think not,'' Jonathan said thoughtfully. ''A call may be customary, but not even the British can force an American merchantman to halt for an inspection. The War of 1812 ended that practice. We're vulnerable because of our cargo, so we'll sail direct to a berth at Soong Chao's wharves.''

As they passed within hailing distance of the *Nemesis*, the trio could see a half-dozen officers studying them and the clipper through telescoping enlargement glasses.

What stunned them was the appearance of the harbor itself, which looked deserted. In normal times, the harbor traffic was as thick as a city street's. Today the *Lai-tse lu* had the harbor to herself. The Chinese customs building was deserted, and there were no signs of activity in front of the factories.

As the clipper maneuvered in the direction of Soong Chao's complex, a number of dockhands came out of one of the buildings and ran toward the wharf. It was impossible to determine whether they were friendly or hostile.

They were followed by a familiar, burly figure clad in black, walking at a more stately pace, and Jonathan was relieved. The presence of Kai was an assurance that the dockhands would not resort to violence against the clipper.

Ordering lines thrown to the men on shore, Jonathan instructed Homer to allow no one to board the ship without permission, and then, in his eagerness, he leaped onto the wharf while the vessel was still being warped.

''You have come at the worst of times,'' Kai said, greeting him somberly. "There is no way that hostilities can be prevented for more than another day or two."

"Then this may be the best of times," Jonathan replied. "I'm carrying a cargo of medicines and arms for the Society of Oxen."

The giant's eyes gleamed. "The cargo will be removed after nightfall, and in the meantime my men will see to it that no one approaches the ship. Soong awaits you at his house, and I will take you to him. The warehouses have been vacated, and he no longer comes here."

"What do you mean?"

"The few Fan Kuei who have not sought refuge at Macao and have remained here hate him more than all other Chinese. They might kidnap him and hold him for ransom, or they might even kill him."

The deterioration of the port was even more severe than Jonathan had imagined possible. Before he could reply, he saw a Royal Navy gig being rowed ashore from the *Nemesis,* a fair-skinned man sitting amidships.

"That is Captain Elliot." Kai spoke the name as though it were a curse.

The official representative of the British Crown, in charge of all operations, Captain Elliot landed at the opposite side of the same wharf where the *Lai-tse lu* had made her berth. Without glancing at the clipper, he walked toward Jonathan briskly. "Mr. Rakehell, I presume," he said.

"Your servant, Captain."

"You've chosen an inopportune moment for a landing here, sir," Elliot said. "I understand you're related to the most prominent of the Chinese merchants here, so I can appreciate your position. But all merchant shipping has vacated the port—on my personal order. And I cannot permit you to remain here. It would cause too many international complications if a Royal Navy fleet reduced an American clipper to matchsticks. And naturally, you wouldn't want your ship destroyed, either."

"Are relations with the Chinese that bad, Captain Elliot?"

The square-faced Englishman became grim. "Indeed they are. We are prepared to attack Canton if the Chinese are unwilling to negotiate a peaceful settlement. But instead of coming to terms, they make warlike preparations and continue with

249

their acts of barbarity. Just the other day several of my seamen were captured, and I'm told they're being held in cages in a public square. I have given the Chinese authorities forty-eight hours to return them to me unharmed and to apologize appropriately. If they fail to obey me—and there has been no sign that they intend to do so—I shall be compelled to initiate hostilities here.''

He looked and sounded adamant, and Jonathan realized that, at least in his eyes, the Chinese were forcing him to do battle at Canton.

Several men emerged from some of the factories and drew nearer, wanting to see and hear the confrontation between Captain Elliot and the Yankee who was daring to defy the might of the Royal Navy.

Jonathan immediately recognized Owen Bruce but gave no sign that he knew the Scotsman.

''I came ashore myself, Mr. Rakehell,'' Elliot continued, ''because I want it clearly understood that I shall accept no responsibility for the loss of American lives and property. These gentlemen will be evacuated tomorrow, and I urge you to take your ship elsewhere by that time. At most you have forty-eight hours to leave this port. And please keep in mind, sir, that I am warning you, not threatening you.''

''You make your position plain, Captain Elliot, and I am grateful to you for your warning.''

Elliot bowed slightly, then walked off with long strides to his waiting gig.

Jonathan, with Kai beside him, had to make his way through the small crowd from the English, Danish, and Swedish factories. As nearly as he could determine, all of the Americans stationed here had already departed.

Owen Bruce blocked his path. ''Rakehell,'' he said loudly, ''you're a damned traitor to your race! Just because you're married to a Chink woman gives you no right to dock here in this hour of crisis.''

Jonathan's temper exploded, and he reached for his sword. Bruce did the same, but Kai intervened swiftly, coming between them, and his huge hand clamped Jonathan's hand in a viselike grip, preventing him from drawing his blade.

Two of the Swedes stepped in, too, and restrained Bruce.

Jonathan recovered his equilibrium, realizing he had to

250

attend to matters far more important than fighting a duel with the vicious Scotsman who had goaded him deliberately. "You and I have a final score to settle, Bruce," he said, "but it will have to wait until a more suitable time."

He and Kai made their way to a deserted warehouse, and there Jonathan translated what Captain Elliot had told him.

"The Chinese are as stubborn as the English," the giant declared. "There will be a battle. And you must go to the house of Soong as you left it, disguised as one of my men. No Fan Kuei could stay alive in Canton for more than a few moments."

They returned to the clipper, where Jonathan told Homer Ellison about the crisis deadline and explained that he himself would go to the house of his father-in-law. "If I can't persuade him to sail with us," he added, "I'll do what I can to evacuate some of the family heirlooms. I realize I'm taking something of a risk by going into the city, and if I haven't returned before Captain Elliot's deadline, leave port before you're caught in the bombardment."

"Shall I sail to Macao and wait for you there, sir?"

"Under no circumstances!" Jonathan replied firmly. "The Marquês de Braga might seize the ship and throw the whole company into a prison from which there's no escape. You'll find a marvelous, natural harbor on the mainland side of Hong Kong Island, which is uninhabited. I suggest you find an anchorage there, as I suspect a number of other merchantmen must be doing. Wait there for me. For a reasonable period of time."

"How long is reasonable, Captain Rakehell?"

Jonathan shrugged. "You'll have to use your own judgment. If I have severe problems, you'll return to Djakarta without me, pick up a cargo of batik cloth from the Fat Dutchman, and sail for home."

"I don't like this situation worth a damn, sir," a worried Homer said.

"Neither do I," Jonathan said, "but it can't be helped. My family duty must take precedence over my personal safety. I hope we'll meet again tomorrow."

He went back to the warehouse, where he changed into the black shirt, boots, and loose-fitting shirt that Kai had brought for him when word had been received that the clipper was moving up the delta. Then he donned a peaked, black coolie hat, and a dozen members of the Society of Oxen came in from the alleyway. Two of them carried his own clothes and weapons, which were hidden in bundles, and Kai handed the American a ku ming.

"I've never used a weapon like this," Jonathan protested. "I'm not even sure I can hold it properly,"

"You will carry it," Kai said. "No one in Canton would dream that a Fan Kuei is armed with a ku ming."

A large sentry detail was posted at the Petition Gate, but the members of the Society of Oxen were waved through, and Kai set a rapid pace. Jonathan, who marched in the center of the formation, was surprised to see that, in spite of the great danger that threatened the city, the people of Canton were taking no special precautions. The streets were crowded, as usual, women were cooking meals and washing clothes, and the only sign of impending trouble were the lines that waited outside the huts of soothsayers to have their fortunes told.

When they came to the huge square in front of the Temple of Heaven, Jonathan was shocked to see the captured British seamen in cages of bamboo, so cramped they could not stand, mounted on poles high above the ground. Occasionally a passerby prodded them with a sharp stick or threw stones at them, but most people went about their business calmly, paying no attention to the unfortunate prisoners.

At last the procession reached the Soong estate, and Jonathan was reunited with Chao. "I thank God I have arrived in time, my father," he said as they embraced.

"You look well." Chao's calm was astonishing. "I trust Lai-tse lu and Missy Sarah also are well?"

"They're fine, but they're very worried about you. I bring you letters from them."

"I will read them at the dinner table. Come."

He led the way to the dining pavilion, and as he read the letters the customary, elaborate meal was served. Nothing in this tranquil, well-ordered atmosphere even suggested that war might break out at any hour.

Holding Lai-tse lu's letter in one hand, Chao smiled at his son-in-law. "I congratulate you on the coming birth of your son or daughter. If the gods will it, I will live to see my grandchild."

Jonathan was stunned but realized instantly why his wife had kept her secret from him. Not even for her father's sake would he have left home had he known. Certainly he forgave the deception, and perhaps he could put the news to good use. Recovering as best he could from his surprise, he said earnestly, "If the weather is favorable, you and I could be present when the child is born. I have come to Canton to take you back to America with me, my father."

Soong Chao shook his head, his manner still imperturbable. "My place is here," he said. "I could have accepted the Fat Dutchman's offer to visit him in Djakarta, but I cannot leave the land of my birth when she is threatened by foreigners."

Jonathan knew he would not change his mind, but the attempt had to be made, and he argued long and vigorously.

Chao could not be moved.

"Surely you realize that the imperial forces will be defeated by the British. It would take a miracle to win them a victory."

Chao's jaw jutted forward and his lips compressed into a thin line. "I refuse to concede defeat before a battle begins. There have been many miracles in the long history of the Middle Kingdom, my son, and no man can fathom the secrets that are locked in the minds of our gods."

Jonathan realized that, for the moment, he had to give up. He would renew his pleas after a respite. "My ship is available for any heirlooms and other belongings you may wish to send to Lai-tse lu for safekeeping." There was no need to mention the possibility that looting could become widespread if chaos developed in the city.

Chao brightened, interrupting his meal to send for Kai and give the majordomo detailed instructions regarding precious objects of jade and ivory, gold and silver.

"The property will be crated and taken to the ship tonight," Kai said, and hurried away.

Soong Chao peppered his son-in-law with questions about the life Lai-tse lu was leading in New England, and Jonathan replied in detail, curbing his own mounting impatience, but at last he had an opportunity to ask a question of his own. "Is it possible that the authorities in Canton would receive me? Perhaps I could persuade them to compromise with the British."

The older man shook his head. "The hatred of the Chinese for all Fan Kuei is so great that if they knew you were here, they would order your immediate execution, even though you are my son-in-law.''

''But surely they know from the earlier skirmishes that their troops and old junks can't withstand an attack by a modern British force!''

''No, my son. The authorities have convinced themselves they will win a glorious victory and will expel all Fan Kuei from the Middle Kingdom for all time. They are so intoxicated by their own optimism that they will listen to no one.''

Jonathan remained silent for a moment. ''What do you expect to accomplish by staying in Canton?''

''When we finish our meal,'' Chao said, ''I will see to it that Kai and his men take my caskets of silver to your ship. You and my daughter may not need that money, and if you do not, keep it for my grandchild.''

''Fair enough, but you haven't answered me.''

''In Canton,'' Chao said, speaking with dignity, ''I own five large warehouses. They are filled with tea, silks, and porcelains. There was no space for them on the junks I sent to Djakarta. If I desert my country in her hour of need, I could not expect my watchmen to remain at the warehouses and guard my property.''

''Open the doors of the warehouses and let the people take what they please,'' Jonathan said forcibly. ''My family is anything but poor, and the silver in the chests you're sending to America will be there for you to use.''

''You do not understand,'' his father-in-law replied. ''For many generations the people of Canton have looked up to the family of Soong. For longer than the oldest inhabitant can remember, we have been leaders of the community. Viceroys have sought our assistance and counsel. The gates of the Forbidden City have opened to us, and emperors have taken our advice. For generations no family has stood higher in the regard of those who dwell in this province. No family other than that of the emperors themselves has been more honored throughout the Middle Kingdom. What will people think if Soong Chao deserts them? They will know their cause is hopeless. They will throw down their weapons and surrender to the Fan Kuei.''

''I see.''

"You do not, my son." Chao reproved him gently. "In the Middle Kingdom we do not think in terms of months and years. We think in centuries, in thousands of years. This war, whatever its outcome, will pass. This nation and her people will endure. If I run away, saving my own life when others will die, the name of Soong will be reviled. My daughter never again would be welcome in her homeland. People would spit upon her children. Your children. The honor of our family means more than the future of one man whose usefulness is drawing to an end. Whether I survive or die has already been determined by the gods. It is my duty to stay here so the honor of our name will not be tarnished."

Jonathan knew there was no way he could counter his father-in-law's argument.

"Stay tonight under my roof," Chao told him. "Return to your clipper ship in the morning and take my treasures, along with my love, to Lai-tse lu in America."

Jonathan awoke with a start and sat bolt upright in bed when, shortly after daybreak, Kai entered his pavilion. "What's wrong?" he demanded when he saw the majordomo's face.

"Your clipper has just sailed out of the port at my urgent request," Kai replied. "Soong Chao's art treasures and money chests are stored safely in her hold. I told your first mate it was your order that he should sail without delay to Djakarta for the cargo that awaits him there."

Realizing that he himself was being left stranded in Canton, Jonathan was confused and indignant. "Why?" he demanded.

Kai's expression remained grave. "Even as we were loading the last of the chests onto the ship, I received a message from a brother in the Society of Oxen. The British sailors who were our prisoners were executed during the night. Their heads have been sent to Captain Elliot."

"Good Lord! The British can't tolerate that challenge." Jonathan reached for his clothes.

"You will not wear a suit of the Fan Kuei," Kai told him. "You will be safe only in the dress of the Society of Oxen."

Jonathan knew he was right and began to dress accordingly.

255

"No one knows when it may be possible to smuggle you out of the Middle Kingdom," Kai said.

The implications of that statement did not sink in until later. A sound like the deep roll of thunder boomed across Canton and echoed through the hills.

Jonathan and Kai raced to the open, and from the crest of the high hill they could see in the distance flashes of light emanating from the harbor, quickly followed by the booming of cannon. Captain Elliot had received the heads of the executed British seamen, and a bombardment of the harbor complex had started.

The silent pair were joined by Soong Chao. He did not speak for a time, and then he shook his head. "Both sides commit crimes against all mankind," he murmured at last. "I know the gods must be weeping." In the distance the steady roar of the cannon underscored his words.

Royal Navy gunners were precise, and the crews of the warships demonstrated their marksmanship without delay. Their first targets were the three stone forts that guarded the harbor, and the concentrated fire of the ships of the line and the frigates was concentrated on them. Stones crumbled, and walls that had stood for two thousand years vanished in clouds of dust.

The Chinese who manned the forts tried in vain to retaliate. Some of their ancient cannon could not be fired, and two blew up, inflicting as much damage as the fire of the enemy.

Kai brought a portable telescope to the garden, and Jonathan was able to watch the progress of the one-sided battle. The bombardment of the forts lasted for no more than a half-hour, and by that time they were reduced to rubble, with the surviving soldiers fleeing into Canton. The first phase of the battle ended in a complete victory for the attackers.

While the British gunners were raising their sights, the Chinese launched their counterattack, sending scores of burning war junks in the direction of the warships. The tide was right for the purpose, and flames reached toward the sky from the decks of the brightly painted wooden vessels.

Kai was briefly encouraged, but Jonathan knew better and was not surprised when the British used a simple method of self-protection. Seamen armed with long poles lined the decks and were able to push away the flaming junks. Most drifted all the way into the harbor, and when the gunpowder on board exploded, many junks were destroyed but the British fleet remained undamaged. Jonathan realized that the Chinese were doing the work of the British for them.

The cannon began to roar again. The Royal Navy ships were using two kinds of ammunition, old-fashioned iron spheres that had been heated and that caused fires when they landed on wooden objects, and the more modern shells, filled with explosives that burst and created havoc wherever they landed.

"Canton will be destroyed!" Kai exclaimed.

Jonathan knew that if the city itself were attacked, the Chinese literally would have no way to fight back. The few antiquated cannon that stood inside the ruins of the Petition Gate were useless, and the fire of the ancient matchlocks the soldiers carried were incapable of reaching the decks.

By now the long rows of factories, shops, customs offices, and other buildings of the Western compound had been evacuated. Inside the city of Canton, a thin trickle of men, women, and children, fearing a British invasion of the city itself, took their most precious possessions and began to head for the hills beyond the inner city walls.

Suddenly Jonathan realized that his father-in-law was no longer standing beside him. "Where is Soong Chao?" he asked, raising his voice to make himself heard above the roar of the cannon.

"Stay here!" Kai commanded, and raced out of the estate grounds, a number of black-clad men materializing out of nowhere and following him.

Jonathan's heart was heavy as he resumed his watch. He was astonished when he saw through the enlarging glass a number of British troop transports sail slowly past the factories and begin to unload at the wharves. As he watched the smartly uniformed troops coming ashore, he realized that the transports had been anchored in some of the many hidden coves that were to be found in the delta of the Pearl River.

Boats were lowered from the larger warships, and Royal Marines headed for shore, too. Captain Elliot was coordinating the actions of the Royal Navy and Army units brilliantly, Jonathan had to admit.

Fires were spreading through the slum areas along the wharves, where most huts were made of wood, and elsewhere the small houses of concrete and stone were crushed by the falling shells. In Canton itself, more and more refugees were heading for the hills, fearful that the Fan Kuei would take the city and slaughter the inhabitants.

He was interrupted by the Soong cook, who came to him with a large bowl of rice, with bits of meat and shrimp in it, and a steaming mug of tea. "It is with sorrow that I offer the husband of Lai-tse lu this simple food," the man said. "But I am alone in the kitchen, and now I must go to join my own family. We are leaving the city."

Jonathan thanked him, then looked at the bowl of rice and mug of tea. He was sickened by the carnage below and had no appetite, but he knew he would be wise to eat. There was no way of guessing when another meal would be available, and he forced down the food.

The cannon boomed again, and hordes of Chinese soldiers appeared to halt the British troops, but the officers had never before fought any foe other than river pirates, and the aged matchlocks of their men were woefully inferior to the muskets of the British.

The invaders continued to land on shore, and although the Chinese bravely held their own lines for a time, they gave in to panic when the Marines systematically used their bayonets. A few spears were thrown, and some of the defenders courageously used ku ming, but they could not halt the landing of their disciplined foes. Here and there breaks appeared in the lines of the Chinese, and all at once it seemed as though entire regiments of the yellow-clad troops began to retreat in wild disorder.

The panic spread swiftly, and civilians by the thousands joined in the stampede to the open countryside beyond the range of the powerful enemy. It appeared that an undefended Canton would fall into the hands of the British.

Late that same morning, Kai and his men reappeared in the garden. In his arms the majordomo carried the bloody, lifeless body of Soong Chao.

"I found him near his warehouses," Kai said huskily. "He was attempting to prevent some British soldiers from entering the buildings. An enemy cannonball struck him, and he died swiftly, never knowing what happened to him."

Jonathan blinked away tears of sorrow and rage, and saw

that, although his father-in-law's eyeglasses had been shattered, his face in death was serene. He had done his duty to the end.

At Kai's order several of his men began to dig a shallow grave.

With difficulty Jonathan removed a jade signet ring from Soong Chao's hand and slipped it onto his own finger. He had no idea when or how he would be able to return to America, but he would give the ring to Chao's as yet unborn grandchild.

The body was deposited in the grave, and Jonathan spoke the words of the Twenty-third Psalm, his voice cracking as he said, "The Lord is my shepherd, I shall not want . . ."

Kai tapped him on the shoulder. "Lo Fang and our men await us outside the estate," he said. "And we have received word that the assault on Canton is over. The Chinese have paid the price of ultimate disgrace and have agreed to pay the British six million dollars to spare Canton from destruction."

"The cowards!" Jonathan was outraged by the realization his beloved father-in-law had died in vain. "Surely the Chinese government had the sense to know the British were bluffing. It was simple enough for them to shell the port of Canton, but they'd need fifteen thousand men to take Canton itself, and the Lord in His wisdom only knows how many to hold and pacify a city of this size."

Kai shrugged. "This day will not be forgotten. But I fear there will be new attacks. Canton was not the real target of the British. The attack on the port, which has won them a fortune of six million dollars, is only the beginning. We expect confirmation soon." Kai did not offer an explanation.

The ranks of the refugees pouring through the streets in the direction of the gates that led to the open countryside of Kwangtung Province had swollen to the proportions of a mighty torrent. Grim-faced men, weary, frightened women, and weeping, bewildered children were trudging in an unending stream. For them, the British threat to their city was not over, despite the settlement, and they wanted to be as far away from Canton as possible.

The Soong estate was deserted now. Jonathan turned for a last glimpse of his father-in-law's grave and the buildings he had come to know so well. Soon looters would appear, the flowers in the formal gardens would be trampled, and everything of value, from furniture to bric-a-brac, would vanish. An era had come to an end, and Jonathan was relieved that Lai-tse lu was not here to see the demolition of her home.

After the dismissal of Lin Tse-hsü, Lo Fang was still retained as majordomo in the imperial viceroy's palace, serving the new ministers the emperor had appointed. Now, however, Lo Fang's activities were entirely for the Society of Oxen, and he stood at the entrance to the estate, two of Jonathan's American pistols in his black belt, an American rifle clutched in one huge hand. Behind him, dimly seen in the deepening twilight, were a large number of men, similarly clad in black.

Jonathan and the former viceroy's majordomo silently gripped hands in a Western-style greeting, and then, with Kai beside them, they joined the refugees. When they came to the wall, which loomed forty feet above them, they ascended it by means of a ramp and, instead of leaving the city, climbed to the top.

The guns of the warships were silent now, but the steady crackle of musket fire could be heard as the British troops continued to wipe out the last pockets of resistance.

Suddenly a man in black, obviously exhausted, came to the leaders of the Oxen and said, "There is much news. Our eyes and ears in Hong Kong report that a British general named Pottinger has been sent to replace Captain Elliot, whose countrymen are displeased with his handling of the war. The British will send a fleet north to Kuan-choy. Only the harbor forts defend the port, and when they are destroyed by the British warships the enemy will occupy all of the city."

So Kai had been right, Jonathan thought. The British had not finished at Canton. They were bringing in General Pottinger and were now preparing for an all-out offensive.

He knew very little about Kuan-choy other than that it was walled and was a busy port, with a population of perhaps a quarter of a million, which made it small by Chinese standards. He knew, too, that Soong Chao had maintained a residence and a warehouse there, but he himself had never visited Kuan-choy because it was a "closed" port, which foreigners were forbidden to visit. Obviously the British intended to capture it for that very reason; they wanted to control all the Chinese ports, and they would not cease with their hostilities until China was completely in their hands. By taking Kuan-choy, the British were in a position to continue on north, perhaps to take the Imperial City itself!

"We will leave at once for Kuan-choy," Lo Fang declared.

A long march lay ahead. Kuan-choy was located almost three hundred miles to the northeast on the China coast, so the journey would take two weeks, at least. But the security the British felt in believing they could make easy conquest of the city soon would prove an illusion. The Oxen would see to that.

"We have long prepared for this day," Kai said calmly. "Now our work will begin."

"What work?" Jonathan asked.

"We will not allow the Fan Kuei to occupy our city in peace," Kai told him. "We will steal down from the hills at night and attack them, first striking an outpost in one sector, then in another. We will kill them one by one and two by two. We will strike terror into their hearts, until they know that no Englishman is safe in Kuan-choy."

"But you will be safe, son-in-law of Soong Chao," Lo Fang said. "Your weapons make it possible for us to fight the English as equals, and we are grateful for your help. So you will be escorted to Soong's country estate, which is a two-day march from the city of Kuan-choy, and there you will stay."

"The wives of our band will cook your meals for you," Kai added. "Perhaps your stay will be long. You will need to remain until the merchant ships of the Americans return to Whampoa or we can find some way to smuggle you out of the Middle Kingdom."

Jonathan absorbed their plans for him in silence. He could still see the broken body of Soong Chao, who had died defending his homeland, and he thought of Lai-tse lu, then of their unborn child whose heritage would be Chinese as well as American. He was mindful of the fact that he had close relatives and business associates who were British, and that, in addition, Charles Boynton was his best friend. But his loyalty to his wife was more important than anything else on earth. Certainly he could not hide in safety while her homeland was invaded and occupied, when others risked their lives in a fight for her freedom.

"Thank you for your offer," he said succinctly, "but I cannot accept it. I will join you in your war against the British."

*   *   *

The black-clad men of the Society of Oxen, more than one thousand strong, were taking their ease on the sheltered hillside, eating rice their women had cooked for them and drinking water from a clear stream, their arms close at hand. There was no shortage of food, landlords and peasants alike eagerly contributing to this band that was making life miserable for the British force that occupied Kuan-choy.

The small group crouching in a circle at the crest of the hill could see the British troops on patrol at the top of the city's wall. As had been predicted, the British had taken Kuan-choy quickly, and now the patrol troops marched swiftly, paced incessantly, determined to keep their conquest for themselves.

For the moment, the men of the Society of Oxen were paying scant attention to the enemy. Lo Fang, Kai, and three other leaders were listening intently to the American who had taken a place in their high command.

"Last night's raids were fairly successful," Jonathan told them, "but we needlessly lost two men. If we employ the tactics I've devised, we should reduce our losses appreciably."

"Show us again the marking that the British officers wear on their shoulders," Lo Fang said.

Jonathan picked up a sharp-pointed stick and scratched rough sketches in the black earth. "These are the insignia of the subalterns. These are worn by captains. We will find few of higher rank at the outposts, but these are the insignia of the majors, the lieutenant colonels, and the colonels."

The Chinese studied the sketches in silence, memorizing them.

"Make certain that every man in the band understands our tactics," he continued. "The British soldier fights with courage, but he is efficient only when he is told what to do. It is no accident that the Americans have beaten them in two wars."

"It is no accident, either," Kai said, "that your unit has enjoyed greater success in our raids than any other."

"That's my point," Jonathan said. "Every member of the band should seek the British officers first. Kill the officers, and their men become sheep. With no one to give them orders, they become confused and helpless."

"And that is why you have been able to demolish four enemy outposts in the past week?" Lo Fang asked.

"It is very simple," Jonathan replied firmly. "Kill or wound the captains and subalterns. Their men will still be courageous, but they won't know how to return our fire at night when there is no one to give them orders."

"We will use your tactics," Lo Fang said, and the Chinese went off to instruct their men.

Jonathan remained alone at the crest of the hill, and never had he felt so isolated. He was the only white man in the Kwangtung countryside, perhaps in all of the Middle Kingdom other than Kuan-choy. The troops of his cousin, his aunt, and his uncle had become his enemies. And for as far into the murky future as he could see, his situation would not change.

Members of the Society of Oxen disguised as peasants brought small quantities of produce to Kuan-choy every day, freely passing the British sentry lines, and when they returned to their headquarters they brought up-to-date news. The Royal Navy fleet had already left Kuan-choy, and when last seen had been moving north. It was obvious that, having captured Kuan-choy, General Pottinger intended to attack other major seaports. No coastal city in the entire Middle Kingdom was safe.

The espionage agents had obtained an accurate count of the garrison the British had left behind to hold Kuan-choy. It seemed absurd that a paltry force of twenty-five hundred men could occupy a city of a quarter of a million, but the British were well organized, the people suffering from confusion and fear. Long accustomed to blind obedience to the will of the imperial viceroy and his subordinates, the citizens now accepted without question the directives of the British brigadier in command of the occupying garrison.

Many of the refugees who had fled to the hills during the naval bombardment of Kuan-choy had returned to their homes. Activity in the city was still far from normal, but the brigadier had organized large work companies to clear up the rubble after the assault and build new dwellings. This activity kept men busy and out of trouble. Enough food flowed in from the countryside to prevent starvation, and although people were surly, they did what they were told.

All the same, Jonathan knew the brigadier and members of his staff had to be uneasy. The Society of Oxen attacked the sentry outposts regularly, sometimes striking three or four in a single night, sometimes granting a respite for a night or two in order to catch the British off guard. Certainly the troops of the garrison had to be frightened, knowing they were under extreme pressure when they had to keep a large population under control.

Now, Jonathan thought grimly, the raiders would become even more successful. It might take time before the British realized that their junior officers were the guerrillas' primary targets, but when they began to understand the situation, the captains and lieutenants would become increasingly nervous. He did not envy them.

Exercising rigid self-discipline, he did not allow himself to think of Lai-tse lu or Julian or his father, or his business responsibilities. And he tried hard not to dwell on the approaching birth of his new son or daughter. The present had to keep him occupied, and he concentrated as best he could on his immediate tasks, an image of the broken body of Soong Chao the ever-present reality that whetted his appetite for vengeance.

Watching the pacing British sentries a few moments longer, he turned and made his way down the hill to his own elite unit of fifty. Someone handed him a bowl of rice, and he was pleasantly surprised to see that it contained bits of meat and vegetables. He ate silently with his chopsticks, making plans for the next guerrilla attack.

After he finished his meal, he motioned his men closer, and his smile was hard. "Tonight," he said, "we will conduct a different kind of raid. Only today I have learned that the British Fan Kuei have moved their headquarters to a building on the square opposite the Temple of the Moon. It is an office once occupied by the imperial tax collector."

The men nodded. All of them knew the place.

"Wang will act as our guide, as always," Jonathan said, turning for a moment to a slender man who had the ability to move like a wraith through Kuan-choy after dark. "I will take ten others."

A sinewy former dock worker looked at him in awe. "You will attack the headquarters of the Fan Kuei?"

"I will. Who wishes to come with me?"

Every member of the unit raised his hand.

Jonathan made his selections with care, choosing those who were the most fearless, who had demonstrated their ability to move swiftly and kill silently.

The others were disappointed.

"Your turns will come," Jonathan told them. "There are many British who will still be alive tomorrow."

The men of the Society of Oxen laughed, delighted to be serving under the command of this extraordinary Fan Kuei who had become their brother, this determined leader whose skill in throwing the knives of Java was greater than their own talents.

Jonathan drilled those who would accompany him in the identification of British insignia.

Then the fifty-year-old Wang, formerly the head stable keeper for the imperial viceroy, took charge. "At the rear of the office of the tax collector," he said, "there is a garden. Strong vines have eaten into the stone walls and can support the weight of men. We will climb those vines to the second floor. I will lead you to the suite of rooms that were the offices of the imperial tax collector himself. In that suite is a kitchen and dining room."

"If we are fortunate," Jonathan added, "we will find the British commander and some of his high-ranking officers enjoying a meal. Englishmen of their class usually dine at the eighth hour after noon, so that is when we will strike. And that is why we will make our raid much earlier than has been our practice."

His men understood and were pleased. What made their leader superior to all others in the Society of Oxen was his intimate knowledge of the habits and customs of the Fan Kuei.

The heat of the day abated somewhat at sunset, when a cool breeze blew down toward Kuan-choy from the hills. Jonathan looked at his pocket watch, saw that he had only an hour left, and put his unit into motion. They made their way boldly toward the wall from their redoubt, exercising caution only when they came close enough to the wall to be seen by the British on sentry duty above them.

Wang led them unerringly to a tunnel in the thick wall that long had been used by smugglers. The stones that concealed the entrance were removed, then replaced by the last man in the line, and the little band crept silently to the inner side, where two of the men gently removed the stones, then carefully put them back in place again after the others had moved into the city.

As Jonathan and his subordinates well knew, they were as safe as they would have been in the open countryside. Relatively few residents of the city were abroad during these times of British occupation, but passersby glanced at the men in black walking quietly through the narrow streets, then looked away hastily, their faces impassive. Every man and woman in the city knew the uniform of the Society of Oxen, and it was easy enough to guess why members of the patriotic group had appeared. But no power on earth would impel a resident of Kuan-choy, no matter what his class, to reveal the presence of the band to the enemy.

The Temple of the Moon itself was being used as a British barracks, a desecration that enraged the people, and Jonathan had to resist the temptation to change his plans and conduct a lightning assault on the troops at rest there. He adhered to his original plan, however, following Wang into the garden behind the three-story stone building that had been the imperial tax collector's office.

The vines that had imbedded themselves in the concrete were somewhat slippery but firm, and Jonathan managed to climb swiftly, directly below the guide, with the rest of the band following.

When they clustered on the second floor, the American drew one of his thin, supple-bladed Javanese knives from his belt, and his men followed his example, clutching their own Chinese knives. Everyone knew that pistols were to be utilized only in the event that a dire emergency developed.

Wang crept down on the board, tile-floored corridor, the others followed silently in single file, hugging the wall.

Somewhere ahead they could hear voices and the clatter of dishes. Jonathan sniffed the scent of beef roasting and knew his hunch had been right. At least some members of the occupation force's high command were at dinner.

Halting abruptly, Wang raised a warning hand. A moment later a British orderly carrying a tray on which three bowls of soup rested, came out of the door of what was obviously a kitchen and started toward a closed door.

Wang raised his knife, but Jonathan tapped him on the shoulder and shook his head. He sought bigger game than an orderly.

The leader's signal caused the members of the band to

freeze. Although they could hear voices through the open door, he was choosing to delay the assault.

The orderly emerged, carrying his empty tray, and an expression of terror came into his eyes when he saw the men in black.

It was unnecessary for Jonathan to give an order. Before the orderly could cry out, two of the men in black sprang forward. One quickly looped a length of multistranded silk cord over the Englishman's head, tightened it around his throat, and strangled him. The other, meantime, clamped a hand over his mouth and caught hold of the tray before it fell. The unfortunate orderly slumped to the floor, and his body was left outside the entrance.

Jonathan took the lead down a short entrance hall and saw three officers dining at a small table. All wore the gold shoulder tabs of the general staff; one, facing the door, was a colonel, and opposite him were two majors, all of them eating soup while deep in conversation.

"The bloody wogs need to be put in their place, sir," one of the majors said. "But the brigade and a handful of marines can't do it alone. Do you know when the fleet will return?"

"The brigadier has asked for help, but General Pottinger hasn't replied yet. We—" The colonel broke off sharply when he saw the figures in the corridor, and he started to rise.

Before he could stand erect, one of Jonathan's knives flashed through the air, penetrating his tunic just over the heart. He collapsed without a word, blood staining his uniform.

The other officers jumped to their feet, simultaneously reaching for the pistols they carried in their holsters. Before either could fire, however, the Chinese overwhelmed them. One was stabbed to death, and the other's throat was slashed.

Jonathan retrieved his throwing knife, and signaled his men to be on their way. One of them, grinning wickedly, seized an unopened bottle of wine from the table and took it with him.

Jonathan brought up the rear on the swift, silent retreat, as befitted the commander of the expedition.

Wang led the party back to the tunnel in the base of the city wall, and a short time after they had started, the members of the expedition safely reached their hiding place in the hills.

The operation had been flawless, and three high-ranking members of the British brigadier's staff were dead, as was the poor orderly who had appeared at the wrong moment.

Jonathan reported to Lo Fang, whose eyes gleamed. Now the Fan Kuei who had dared to bombard and capture Kuan-choy knew that not even their leaders would be spared the vengeance of the nation they were supposedly conquering.

The Marquês de Braga, sanctimoniously declaring his neutrality because the British would not pay the bribe he demanded, refused to allow the Royal Navy to use Macao as a headquarters, so a staging area was utilized at the harbor adjacent to uninhabited Hong Kong Island. There the fleet was joined by two more ships of the line, along with a dozen smaller vessels. They were followed by transports carrying fifteen thousand troops, including artillery and sappers.

General Pottinger grudgingly allowed one thousand infantrymen to be sent to augment the hard-pressed garrison at Kuan-choy. The rest joined the main expedition in the north and participated in the capture of two more cities, Chinhai and Ningpo. In both ports the defenders fought bravely but ineffectively against disciplined seamen and troops armed with modern weapons.

But Pottinger was discovering that the conquest of seaports did not give him control of the Chinese interior. An attempt had already been made by his predecessor, Charles Elliot, to send a squadron of gunboats up the Pearl River past Canton, and for two days this expedition met no opposition. Then, on the second night, when the warships lay at anchor, members of the Society of Oxen had struck, the band's ranks swollen by volunteers who included humiliated imperial troops, townsmen who had lost their homes, and angry peasants who, never having seen foreigners, hated them passionately.

The expedition had been forced to halt, then fight its way inch by inch back to Canton. When the gunboats' cannon were fired, the Chinese had vanished. But mysterious logjams, sunken sampans, other obstacles in the river had had to be overcome, and whenever the boats were forced to halt, the Chinese had reappeared in vast numbers, firing weapons that ranged from modern muskets and ancient matchlocks to spears and arrows. The officers and seamen of the Royal Navy, true to their tradition, had fought courageously, but there had been no respite for ten days. Ultimately they had reached the haven of Canton, their gunboats battered, their ranks decimated.

Undeterred by the lesson the Chinese had taught his predecessor, Pottinger continued to sail northward, writing dispatches to London saying he intended to capture Nanking next, then march overland to Peking.

But the leaders of the guerrilla force that had inflicted heavy punishment on the British in Kuan-choy were encouraged. "This war is like others we have fought over thousands of years," Lo Fang said to Jonathan, whose men now hailed him affectionately as the "Chinese Fan Kuei."

"It is true," the American replied, "that China is so vast that she absorbs her conquerors. But this war is different. The British are so stubborn they won't admit defeat, ever."

"Then they must be taught anew," Lo Fang replied.

So it was agreed that Jonathan's unit would conduct another daring raid into the heart of Kuan-choy, with the headquarters of the newly arrived regiment as its target. The British were occupying a former garrison of the imperial army inside the city walls, and because the attackers had to infiltrate farther into the city, they would be taking a greater risk. So Jonathan decided to take twenty-five of his men with him.

The operation began auspiciously. Even though the sentries on the Kuan-choy wall had been doubled, the raiders crept unseen through the tunnel into the city, then made their way to the far side of town, always using narrow lanes and alleyways as they avoided the main thoroughfares where they might encounter British patrols.

They reached the garrison without incident, and there they managed to dispose of two officers, a major and a captain, in the manner they had made customary. As they started their withdrawal, however, their luck changed.

Through sheer happenstance, a full platoon of Royal Infantry was returning to the garrison from patrol duty, and the senior lieutenant in command, an alert officer who won a promotion because of his subsequent conduct, caught sight of the intruders who were sneaking out of the building and ordered them to halt.

Jonathan knew his band of twenty-five was no match for seventy-five British troops armed with muskets and bayonets, and told his men to run and scatter. Each man knew he would have to make his own way back to the hills.

As always, the leader brought up the rear, protecting the retreat.

"You, there! Halt!" the lieutenant shouted.

Afraid he had tarried too long, Jonathan began to run.

"Fire! Open fire!" the lieutenant ordered.

One bullet caught Jonathan in the leg, felling him, and at almost the same instant, another dug into his shoulder. Then, as he collapsed, a third entered his side, and he lost consciousness before he hit the ground.

Three of his men turned back in an attempt to save him but were shot to death before they could reach his side. The rest continued to flee and, following their strict instructions, scattered.

The British knew that a chase through the narrow, winding streets of Kuan-choy would be dangerous as well as futile, and made no attempt to pursue them. The lieutenant and his sergeant came forward and peered down at the still, black-clad figure lying in a pool of his own blood. "He's still alive," the sergeant said.

"I hope the rotter lives long enough for the colonel to question him." The lieutenant nudged the injured man with his foot, then stared at him in astonishment. "Good Lord! He's white!"

Agents arrived every few hours, day and night, at the Society of Oxen redoubt, bringing the latest word from the city. The British brigadier and colonel had conferred, and the wounded, unconscious "Chinese Fan Kuei" had been moved to the Soong Chao warehouse on the waterfront that was still intact and was being used by the invaders as a base hospital.

There a team of three surgeons had operated, removing all three bullets from the body of the patient. Jonathan was still alive but had not regained consciousness. Because of his precarious condition he was not taken to the jail but was kept in a private cubicle at the hospital, with guards stationed inside and outside the room. A hospital orderly also was in constant attendance, under orders to report to the brigadier instantly when and if the prisoner regained consciousness. The high command was anxious to interrogate him.

"If our friend was strong and in good health," Lo Fang said, "the British could question him until they lost their voices, but he would tell them nothing. But when he is weak and near death, no one knows what they might induce him to say."

Kai nodded, his expression grim. "We must rescue our friend," he said.

"We shall." Lo Fang studied his thick, scarred knuckles in the light of their small campfire. "We are in his debt after all he has done for us."

"He is the husband of Lai-tse lu," Kai replied, "so it is my place to lead the rescue team."

"No, it is my right as the head of the Society of Oxen."

Kai shook his head. "I know that warehouse well. I made many trips there with Soong Chao. I will lead."

"Both of us will go," Lo Fang declared.

"That would be wrong. If the British kill both of us, who will lead the Society? You must stay, Lo Fang, and I will go. This very night."

"Very well, but treat our brother with great care. His condition is fragile, and he might die."

"I will do for him what I know he would do for me," Kai said with dignity.

The rescue operation, mounted with great speed, was unique. More than two hundred men would participate, making it the first major expedition ever to infiltrate the city. Four separate groups were formed, and Kai gave explicit instructions to each of them. Then he led them through the tunnel, and once they reached the inside of the wall they parted, with each group taking a different route to the Kuan-choy waterfront.

Less than an hour later, in mid-evening, a fire of unknown origin broke out in a waterfront building not far from the warehouse that was being used as a hospital. The blaze grew rapidly, and virtually the entire battalion on harbor duty formed a bucket brigade in an attempt to quench the flames.

As soon as buckets of water were being passed from the harbor to those nearest the flames, a number of men dressed in black made their way through the corridors of the hospital, heading without delay to the room where the unconscious prisoner lay on his pallet. Wasting no time, three of the intruders swiftly and silently cut the throats of the guards stationed outside the room. They were joined by three others, and the raiding party entered the room where Jonathan lay, each man knowing his target in advance. The orderly suffered a merciful death, a knife driven into his heart. The two guards were garroted.

The men in the raiding party put together a simple but strong litter, each of them having carried a separate part. Jonathan was lifted onto it gently, and with Kai in the lead, the party left the hospital before anyone in authority knew the prisoner was missing.

Only one urgent task remained, and the group of men that had not yet seen action played its role brilliantly. A company of British infantry was stationed near the ruins of a stone fort, the only route open to the litter bearers. Suddenly a shower of arrows was fired with great force by pai pu wang, crossbows based on a model more than two thousand years old, each of them capable of firing four arrows simultaneously. The soldiers were formed in a hollow square, and each of the four lines was attacked at the same moment, killing a few and wounding many. The attack was as silent as it was unexpected.

The captain in command of the company rallied his men but did not know where to search for the enemy. The arrows had been fired simultaneously from four different directions, and there were so many arrows littering the ground inside the square that the captain thought he had been assaulted by hundreds. He had no way of knowing that a mere fifty could create that impression by using the pai pu wang.

Soldiers ran in all directions, peering into the night and firing their muskets blindly. The captain managed to restore order, but by then the members of the Society of Oxen had vanished. The pai pu wang had proved so effective that Lo Fang subsequently put scores of men to work fashioning more of them, and the multiple crossbow bedeviled the British for the remainder of the war.

At the height of the enemy confusion Kai led the litter bearers past the position of the British company. Running silently, the group raced through alleyways and narrow, twisting streets. Many of the citizens had learned through word of mouth about the exploits of the legendary Fan Kuei who had become a leader of the Society of Oxen, only to be wounded and captured by the British. They knew he had to be the occupant of the litter, and they stared at him before averting their faces. By morning all of Kuan-choy—with the exception of the British—would know that Kai and a team of Oxen had rescued one of their own.

What no one knew was whether Jonathan would live or die. After Kai reached the safety of the redoubt, he and Lo Fang bent over their brother, peering at him anxiously. His breathing was shallow, his skin was very pale, and occasionally his eyelids fluttered but did not open.

"There are no physicians in our camp," Lo Fang said. "Perhaps we should send into the city for someone."

Kai frowned. "I think it unwise," he said. "The physicians of knowledge and stature fled when the British took over. Those who remained are the physicians of the poor, who use primitive means, and they would be of no help to our brother." He was silent for a moment, then said, "I wonder if we might capture a physician in the camp of the British and bring him here."

"That also would be unwise. He would know this is the prisoner who was spirited out of Kuan-choy and that he is important to us. So the British physician would allow him to die, but always could claim he had done his best."

Kai nodded. "You are right." He had the litter moved to a crude, lean-to shelter, then filled a tiny brass jar with incense and, lighting it, placed it a few inches from the unconscious man's head.

That act, as everyone present well knew, would ward off evil spirits. Now it was up to the gods to determine whether the Chinese Fan Kuei lived or joined his ancestors.

Book
IV

I

The foreigners in Macao, including the factors from Canton who had moved there for the duration of the war, comprised a small, tightly knit community. Everyone knew everyone else, and they were bound together by self-interest, all of them knowing that a decisive British victory would result in vastly increased trade with China. So considerable curiosity was expressed when a dapper man in his early forties came ashore from a nondescript Dutch schooner, took quarters for himself at the Prince Henry, the colony's most exclusive hostelry, and reappeared a short time later in the hotel's tavern after changing his clothes.

Conscious of the impression he was creating, Bradford Walker walked with a swagger as he went to the long mahogany bar, his gold-headed sword cane held jauntily under one arm, and ordered a drink.

It was no accident that he stood near Owen Bruce. A dozen other men were drinking at the bar, but Walker chose his place deliberately after surveying the scene. The Scotsman also was carefully and expensively dressed, and the refugee from the United States was making his initial moves with cunning and caution.

Inevitably they began to chat, with Bruce as eager as anyone else to learn what he could about this stranger. They exchanged names, chatted about the progress of the war, and talked about the potentials of increased trade.

"You seem to know the shipping business," Bruce said.

"I should," Walker admitted. "I've been in it all my life.

I spent many years as the second in command at Rakehell and Boynton in New England.''

Bruce instantly stiffened. It was apparent at a glance that the Scotsman had no love for the firm, and Walker knew he was on safe ground. "I left them because I couldn't tolerate their ways.''

Bruce relaxed slightly. "They say Jonathan Rakehell is dead. He was in Canton when the fighting started there, and no one has heard a word from or about him since.''

"I'll drink to that!'' Walker lifted his glass.

Bruce clinked glasses with him, and they smiled at each other. They had found an enemy in common, and the ice was broken.

Ultimately, as they talked, Walker admitted he was seeking business opportunities and was prepared to make a substantial investment in the right enterprise.

The Scotsman suggested they move to a nearby table for dinner, and after they ordered their meal, Bruce spoke in earnest. "You well may be the very man we're seeking for a new enterprise,'' he said. "If you're willing, I'll arrange a meeting with the Marquês de Braga, the Portuguese Governor-General. He can't tolerate the Rakehells, either, for personal reasons of his own. He won't discuss them, but it's common knowledge he was going to marry a very attractive Chinese girl, the daughter of the late Soong Chao, but Jonathan Rakehell showed up and whisked her away.''

"I've spent many months in the East, searching for the right opportunities,'' Walker replied. "I'm open to any reasonable offer.''

"Let me sketch our plan for you. I'm returning to the port of Canton when the war's over and trading resumes. We're anticipating that it will be far easier to import opium into China after the emperor has been beaten to his knees. And I'm sure you realize there's more of a profit to be earned in opium than in any other trade.''

"So I've heard.'' Bradford Walker moistened his lips.

"Dom Manuel is a very rich man, but he has no objection to becoming richer. And he isn't cursed with the conscience that afflicts so many of the English and Americans.'' Bruce lowered his voice. "We're planning a simple operation. Ships carrying cargoes of opium will put in to Macao. The governor-general won't interfere when the cargo is transferred to a fleet of junks. The Portuguese government could lose this colony if it openly opposed Chinese policy, you understand, but no opium will actually be landed here. It will be transferred by the junks to my warehouse at Canton. Dom Manuel and I have been troubled because we've been searching without success for a third partner in the operation. A man who knows shipping and can make the arrangements on a steady, ongoing basis for the opium to be brought here from India, Ceylon, the highlands of Indochina—wherever it is grown.''

"I'm interested," Walker said flatly. "This is just what I've wanted. And while we're waiting for the war to end, Macao should be the perfect place for me to become acquainted with shippers. So much of the operation will depend on dealing with reliable people we can trust.''

Owen Bruce was elated, and the following morning he arranged for an audience that day with the Marquês de Braga. They met in the afternoon in the governor-general's office.

Somewhat to Walker's surprise, Dom Manuel questioned him at length about his relations with the Rakehells. He replied candidly, saying he had been married for many years to Judith Rakehell but had left because the rapid rise of Jonathan had destroyed his chance of becoming the next head of the American branch of the company.

"Now that he is dead," the governor-general asked, "would you return to the company?''

"Never, Your Excellency!" Walker did not mention that he had stolen money from Jeremiah and had broken irrevocably with Judith.

Dom Manuel's nod indicated that the reply satisfied him, and he leaned back in his chair. "Perhaps, after the war, Soong Lai-tse lu will return to Canton," he said, ruminating aloud. Suddenly he struck the arm of his chair. "I would have her brought here, no matter what the cost, and after I was finished with her, I would send her to a bordello for the rest of her days.''

His vehemence surprised Walker. Here was a man who hated the Rakehells with a loathing equal to his own.

The Marquês de Braga's mood changed again, and he peered intently at his visitor. "You are capable of taking charge of the shipping portion of our new venture?''

"I'm sure of it, Your Excellency."

Dom Manuel turned to Bruce. "You have told him why I am strictly a silent partner, that my name is never to be mentioned in connection with the enterprise?"

Owen Bruce became apologetic. "I've had no opportunity to go into detail with Mr. Walker, Your Excellency."

"It is a vital consideration, gentlemen! My position here makes it essential that no one ever learn that I am the senior partner. I would not hesitate to execute any man who revealed that secret!"

Walker saw that he meant what he said. "You can rely on my discretion, sir," he said.

"Very well." The marquês's eyes narrowed. "You are willing to invest your own funds in this business?"

"I am!" Walker replied loudly.

"And would you be willing to invest as much as twenty-five thousand American dollars?"

"Gladly," Walker said, hiding his relief. Had a considerably larger sum been requested, he would not have been able to meet the obligation.

"Then it is done." The marquês offered a clammy hand. "We shall prosper together, gentlemen. Be prepared to begin the operation as soon as the port of Canton is again opened to the trade of the West. The craving of the ignorant Chinese for opium will bring great wealth to all of us."

The *Lai-tse lu* reached New London safely after her long voyage from Djakarta, docking on a Sunday morning when the Rakehell family was attending church. A guard was established to protect the great clipper until her cargo could be unloaded the following day, the weary crew departed for their homes, and Homer Ellison went at once to the Rakehell mansion, arriving as the family returned from worship services.

The acting captain would have preferred to break his news to Jeremiah in private, but Lai-tse lu, immediately concerned by her husband's absence, had no intention of leaving the room. Uncertain how to break his news, Homer began by explaining that hostilities had broken out while he had been tied up at the wharf in the port of Canton and he had been ordered to set sail after taking aboard the Soong heirlooms and chests of silver.

Judith Walker and her children arrived just as he was launching into his recital, and he found it somewhat easier to go on. He and Judith had been schoolmates as children, and the atmosphere seemed less depressing with her present.

"I stayed for two weeks in Djakarta," he said. "I could have come home after a few days there. But the Fat Dutchman has his own sources of information, so I waited until I could bring some confirmed news. Ma'am," he said, bowing to Lai-tse lu, "it grieves me to tell you that your father was killed in the British bombardment."

The young woman's expression did not change as he told her the details of her father's death and burial.

"You are certain that Jonathan prayed over his grave?" she asked.

"The Fat Dutchman was very positive on that point, ma'am. And he'd have no reason to lie."

"What has become of my husband since that day?"

Homer shrugged. "He disappeared, ma'am. There were vague rumors that a white man was fighting on the side of guerrillas from a secret Chinese society, but not even the Fat Dutchman could confirm who the man was or where the fighting occurred."

Lai-tse lu nodded, then rose and went to Sarah Applegate, who was weeping silently. "You grieve for my father?"

The older woman could only nod.

"Do not." Lai-tse lu spoke firmly but gently. "When we sailed to America, he sensed—as I did—that we would not meet again in this world." She was dry-eyed, remarkably self-contained.

"What made you feel that way?" Jeremiah asked.

"I cannot explain. Only one who has lived long in the East might understand."

"That's true," Sarah said, managing to control her tears. "There are subtleties in the relationships of the people of Cathay that are lacking here. I've seen it demonstrated many times. If Lai-tse lu says she and Chao sensed they were parting for the last time on earth, she means it."

"My heart and mind also tell me Jonathan is alive," Lai-tse lu declared. "If he had died also, I would have had dreams or seen bad omens. But there have been none. I knew he would come to me in Canton. In the same way I know he

— 281 —

will return to me here." She turned to her father-in-law, her eyes wide. "Believe me, Papa Rakehell. I know you will worry about Jonnie. So will I. But until he comes to me in a dream to tell me he no longer resides in the land of the living, I know that you and I—all of us—will see him again. Let no one tell Julian his father has vanished," she added, looking around the room. "I don't want him needlessly disturbed."

They indicated they would do as she requested, but no one, not even Missy Sarah, could accept the situation with the calm Lai-tse lu displayed. Homer, who remained for dinner, noted that Jeremiah Rakehell ate very little, and the others were upset, too.

After dinner Lai-tse lu withdrew quietly to pray for her father, and Homer walked Judith to her nearby house. "I'll never understand the people of the East," he said.

"Nor will I. If I had heard my father had been killed, I'd be crushed. But I could see in Lai-tse lu's eyes that she felt calm and at peace."

"I reckon. I was so uncomfortable I couldn't really look at her. All I know is that it was easier for me because you were there, Judy."

She accepted the compliment gravely, then asked, "Do you agree my brother is still alive, Homer?"

"If those rumors were true and if he *was* fighting against the British, it isn't very likely. I saw the Royal Navy fleet. As I was leaving Whampoa, I watched the British troop transports moving up the delta. I'd hate to oppose them with the feeble defenses the Chinese were mustering."

She knew he was telling her, indirectly, that Jonathan's chances of survival were remote, and she was grateful for his discretion. "I saw you having a few words with my father before we left, Homer. How long will you be in port?"

"Just long enough to prepare for a voyage to England. Mr. Rakehell wants me to break the news to the Boyntons." He sighed. "But I guess anything will be easier than what's in store for me tomorrow. By early afternoon we'll have the Soong heirlooms and silver unloaded, and I'm going to deliver them personally to Jonnie's wife."

"Come to dinner first, and if you like, I'll go with you when you see Lai-tse lu."

Homer smiled for the first time that day. "There's nothing I'd like better," he said gratefully.

Lai-tse lu showed no emotion when the cases containing her father's most precious belongings arrived the next afternoon. But she spent a long time unpacking the statuettes and other art objects, staring for a long time at each of them, then explaining its history and significance to Julian, who sat quietly beside her.

She completed only a portion of the task before supper, then postponed the rest until the following day, when the little boy again would be present. "My heritage now is his heritage, just as it will be the heritage of my child who will be born soon," she said to Jeremiah and Missy Sarah. "It is important that Julian learn the meaning of each piece, just as I learned them when I was small. It is what my father would have wanted, and it is what Jonathan wishes."

Neither Jonathan's father nor her own longtime governess knew how she could speak so positively about Jonathan's current wishes, but they thought it unwise to press her too closely. If she was able to console herself over his disappearance by imagining that she was communicating with him in some mysterious way, they didn't want to disillusion her. Both were convinced that Jonathan, like Soong Chao, was dead.

"But if it comforts her to think she sees him in dreams and gets advice from him," Sarah said, "it would be cruel to force her to face reality."

"It's a nightmare for me," Jeremiah said, "so I see why she shrinks from the truth."

"You need some sleep—and some food in you," Sarah told him. "Come to the kitchen right now, and let me see what's in the larder."

"I'm not hungry," he protested.

"Jeremiah Rakehell, you've got to take care of yourself! Knowing the way you feel, you're going to stay in harness now for years longer than you'd planned. Until Julian is old enough to take charge of the business. And that means you've got to take care of yourself."

He sighed and followed her into the kitchen.

"Here," Sarah said, "I baked these myself."

"Molasses cookies?"

283

She nodded. She had made them because she knew they were his favorites, and she had wanted to find some way to arouse his appetite. Handing him the platter, she poured him a large glass of milk.

That night Jeremiah slept for the first time since he had learned that his son had vanished in Canton.

The next day Lai-tse lu unexpectedly went into labor nearly a month before her baby was expected. Dr. Graves was summoned, and for the next twenty-four hours he did not leave her side. Her delivery was difficult, exhausting her, and the physician needed all of the skill he had acquired in a lifetime of medical practice to save both mother and infant. Two midwives also were in attendance, and at last the trial came to an end when Lai-tse lu gave birth to a beautiful baby girl.

Missy Sarah knew at once that this was no ordinary infant. Endowed with exquisite features—the most striking of which were her large, shining eyes—the baby already bore an almost uncanny resemblance to both her parents.

Lai-tse lu lay with her eyes closed, and suddenly she spoke in a clear voice. "Yes, my darling! Yes! I understand, and I know what is to be done!"

Martin Graves and Sarah Applegate exchanged uneasy glances.

Lai-tse lu opened her eyes, took her daughter into her arms, and looked at her intently. "It is the wish of your father that you be called Jade, little one," she said. Then, still holding the sleeping infant, she dozed off, too.

Dr. Graves washed in a tub of clean water, then took his time rolling down his sleeves.

"Is she—out of her mind?" Sarah asked him in a whisper.

He shook his head. "Young mothers often think they're in communication with their husbands during and after childbirth. That's a fairly common phenomenon. That's not my worry."

"What is?"

"With Jonathan lost and possibly dead, do I assume correctly that you have more influence over Lai-tse lu than anyone, Mrs. Applegate?"

"I—I hope so, Doctor." Sarah was jarred by his solemnity.

"As I intend to tell her myself tomorrow, when she's in better condition to absorb what I say to her, she's been very fortunate. Twice during this travail she came close to death. Her health will be delicate for the rest of her days, requiring unusual care, and she must never again have another child. She'll recover sufficiently to lead a normal life—normal enough. But she won't ever enjoy truly robust health. So you'll have to convince her, Mrs. Applegate, not to tire herself and not to expend her energies recklessly. She's lucky to be here still."

Jeremiah Rakehell gave Homer Ellison permanent command of the *Lai-tse lu*. Elijah Wilbor was promoted to first mate, a new second mate joined the well-rested crew, and the ship was sent off to England. She carried a full cargo, even though the principal purpose of her voyage was that of enabling her master to break the unhappy news about Jonathan to the Boyntons. Not even in times of great distress did Rakehells allow themselves to forget business.

Homer reached London in eighteen days without extending himself, so swift was the clipper, and steeling himself for the ordeal that awaited him, surprised the Boyntons at the breakfast table.

Ruth knew immediately that he was the bearer of bad news and clenched her fists beneath the table. Sir Alan motioned the captain to take a seat, and Homer told his story somewhat more smoothly than he had done in the Rakehell house. He then gave them the letters which the Rakehell family had sent with him, announcing the birth of the daughter of Jonathan and Lai-tse lu.

Jessica Rakehell Boynton dabbed at her eyes with a lace handkerchief, then sat very straight and glared, daring anyone to claim that she had displayed a moment of weakness. Elizabeth turned the color of her white dress and, almost unnoticed, rose quickly from the table and raced off to her own room. Wu-ling followed in the hope that she could console her stricken friend.

But Ruth knew she would not succeed. Like Elizabeth, she felt as though something within her had died. Now she knew the truth about herself, and it overwhelmed her. She and Charles had established frictionless routines, and their marriage was more successful than most. She was a devoted mother to David, she had become a flawless hostess, and without a slip, she had made the transition from an American carpenter's daughter and a merchant marine officer's widow to the wife of a prominent English shipping magnate. She couldn't complain about her sex life with Charles, and knew he was satisfied, too, because her passions were a match for his. All the same, she had never stopped loving Jonathan Rakehell. Now she truly would have to put him out of her heart and mind for all time.

Sir Alan sat silent for a few moments. It distressed him to think that, if the rumors Homer Ellison had heard were true, his nephew was fighting against the country of his British relatives. Nevertheless, Jonathan was very dear to him, and he asked quietly, "Do you believe there's any possibility my nephew may still be alive, Captain Ellison?"

Homer's shrug indicated his feelings far more than his feeble words. "Mrs. Rakehell insists he is, Sir Alan."

"So do I!" Charles said sharply, speaking for the first time. "Jonathan is indestructible! The Royal Navy couldn't sink him, and the Royal Army couldn't kill him. What's more, I intend to prove it! Father, Sir Robert Tasker, the permanent undersecretary for foreign affairs, is your good friend. Mother, I'll be obliged if you'll invite him and Lady Tasker to dine with us."

Jessica heard the ring in her son's voice. "What do you have in mind, Charles?"

"I want him to grant me a permit the navy will honor—to land at Whampoa. As you know, I had planned some time ago to sail two clippers to the East, until this damned war broke out. But now I intend to go, even if mine is the first civilian ship to put into China in months!"

"What if Sir Robert refuses the request?" Jessica asked calmly.

"He can't refuse! It's only a matter of time until trading resumes, anyway. We've been winning so many battles the emperor will be forced to capitulate. But even if he does refuse, I'll go to the East regardless. I'll wait at Djakarta if I must. One way or another, I'm going to find Jonnie!"

A flicker of hope flared within Ruth, and she heard herself say, "Good for you, Charles!"

Sir Alan raised an eyebrow. "You've been in the East fairly recently, Captain Ellison. Do you think Charles would be dashing off on a wild goose chase?"

286

Homer had no desire to be trapped between a father and son who rarely agreed. "Well, Sir Alan," he said carefully, "I do know that the Fat Dutchman's general manager, a young woman named Molinda, told me herself that she's filling one entire warehouse with black peppercorns for Charles."

"You see?" Charles laughed. "At the very worst my voyage will earn us an enormous profit—even with the war going on. Perhaps we can work out an arrangement with Uncle Jeremiah so Homer can sail me there. The *Lai-tse lu* carries more cargo than any of our other clippers."

Ruth was absorbed in her own thoughts. Find Jonathan, she thought fiercely, whatever may have happened to him, and bring him home safely. When she could, later in the day, she would tell Elizabeth about the plan so the suffering girl could enjoy the respite afforded by a spark of hope.

Jessica Boynton placed no faith in her son's scheme, but she nevertheless extended a dinner invitation to Sir Robert and Lady Tasker. A few evenings later the permanent undersecretary of the foreign office came with his wife to the house in Belgravia. The war in China was mentioned infrequently during the meal.

When the ladies retired to the drawing room, the men remaining at the table to drink port and smoke cheroots, Charles girded for action.

"Sir Robert," he asked bluntly, "when do you expect our war with the Chinese will end?"

The gray-haired diplomat rarely was subjected to such refreshing candor, and smiled. "I'm surprised, actually, that it has gone on this long. Sir Henry Pottinger tells us in every dispatch that he expects an unconditional surrender. But the Chinese are stubborn brutes. In the end they'll pay dearly for what they're costing the Royal Treasury."

Sir Alan gripped the stem of his glass, his interest that of a businessman. Charles had an emotional stake in the war, however, and looked anxiously at the official who supervised the day-to-day activities of the Foreign Ministry.

"At the very least," Sir Robert said, "we shall insist that we be granted free trade rights in a minimum of five ports. We'll also help ourselves to some territory in each of them, establish our own concession there, and place these areas under British rule. So the Chinese won't be able to interfere with us again. The French, by the way, are planning to follow our example, and I'm quite certain that other nations also will be demanding trade rights. Naturally."

"Naturally," Charles echoed dryly.

"You know the East," Sir Robert said to him. "What's your opinion of a spot called Hong Kong, where our navy has been setting up a base?"

"As you undoubtedly know, Sir Robert," Charles replied, "the entire area, both on the island and the mainland opposite it, is virtually uninhabited. There's a tiny village called Kowloon on the mainland side where a few fishermen live with their families."

"To be sure, but what are the shipping potentials?"

"The harbor is completely protected from the elements, the waters are deep and tranquil, and from my own observations when I've gone ashore on the island, there are ample supplies of timber and stone for building purposes. The drinking water is pure, too, so I imagine the Chinese will build a seaport of some consequence there when they recognize the potential of the area."

"That potential has already been recognized by Henry Pottinger. We shall demand the cession of the island and a portion of the mainland as one of our basic terms for a settlement with the emperor."

Charles was shocked. "With all due respect to the prime minister and the Cabinet, Sir Robert, the emperor will refuse to cede such choice territory. The war will go on and on, even if it lasts one hundred years. The Chinese are a passive people and have been accustomed to autocratic rule for thousands of years. But they're patriots who truly love their country, and any emperor who gave away Hong Kong would be deposed—overnight."

"That's almost precisely what Pottinger has been telling us." Sir Robert chuckled indulgently. "So we've been considering a way to allow the emperor to save face, which appears to be an important consideration in the East. We shall lease Hong Kong, its outer islands, and a generous slice of the mainland, paying a nominal fee for the—ah—privilege."

"Ingenious," an admiring Sir Alan said.

Charles made an effort to conceal his indignation. China,

the helpless giant, would be robbed and humiliated by her conqueror. Knowing that nothing he said would influence Great Britain's policy, he concentrated on his own mission. "Peace treaties are never arranged overnight," he said. "Is there any chance that Whampoa will be reopened to merchant traffic while Sir Henry haggles with the representatives of the emperor?"

"Ah, you're like so so many other ship owners, Charles," Sir Robert said slyly. "You find it difficult to wait before dipping your fingers into that delicious China pudding again."

Charles had no intention of revealing his real motive for wanting to go to China. "Quite so," he said. "As it happens, I'm sailing to the East very soon to obtain pepper from my private source, and I've been hoping I might visit Whampoa, too."

"I know of no reason you shouldn't. Even with the war still going on, civilian ships drop anchor there—at some risk, to be sure. But I see no harm in telling Rakehell and Boynton what you, the East India Company, and others will be learning officially in the next few days. The prime minister has decided to teach an object lesson to the Chinese emperor in order to spur him into negotiating a peace treaty. Admiral Pottinger soon will receive orders instructing him to seize two crucial cities on the Yangtze River: Shanghai and Chinkiang. Nanking and Peking themselves will then be in direct line of attack, and if that doesn't force the Chinese to negotiate, nothing will, I can assure you. Whampoa will be reopened—as well as other key ports up and down the coast—and the warehouse owners and the international shipping companies will be invited to return. Within a very few months—as soon as Pottinger receives his instructions and carries them out—Whampoa will be thriving again."

"But what if there isn't a peace treaty?" Charles could not help asking.

Sir Robert was enjoying himself. "Without a peace treaty, Her Majesty's Government, based on the might of her fleets and her regiments, will take Peking and annex the entire country!"

Charles averted his face as he crushed the butt of his cheroot in an ashtray. Thanks to Britain's arrogance, the Chinese would hate foreigners more than ever, and the end of the current war would be a mere pause in hostilities rather than a fundamental solution of a pressing problem.

He knew that, peace-treaty or not, China would be in turmoil when he arrived there, her people restless and sullen after being subjected to insults by their conquerors. This would make his self-appointed task of finding Jonathan even more urgent. First he would need to locate Kai, and in order to achieve that end it would be necessary to win the confidence of any members of the Society of Oxen he could locate. He had his work cut out for him.

The Tao Kuang Emperor slowly opened the sliding door of the private pavilion, walking with a heavy tread to a three-legged, cushioned stool. The chilled, sweetened tea his sister had prepared for him was tasteless, and he was so weary he had to exert himself in order to haul off his pearl-studded headgear.

The Princess An Mien well understood his discouragement. "The fate of China is sealed?" she asked.

He sighed and shook his head helplessly. "The British have occupied six crucial cities. They are on the Yangtze. They are slowly battering down our gates. Peking will be next!"

An Mien pondered, then suggested gently, "Perhaps the time has come for you to appoint a commission to make peace with General Pottinger."

"I cannot!" The Celestial Emperor sounded tortured.

"British cannon and British muskets continue to kill innocent people in city after city," his sister declared. "We know that it is not possible for us to win this war. Perhaps the terms will be more lenient if we surrender now."

He shook his head. "Those who live far from the coast and have not felt the bite of enemy guns are defiant. In Honan and Shansi Provinces there have been riots in the past week, with millions of people shouting their defiance of the invaders. In the city of Hankow a Spanish missionary was mistaken for an Englishman and was torn apart. His head rots on a pike above the city walls, and the governor does not dare to remove it."

She stared at him. "Are you saying the suffering must go on still longer?"

Her brother shrugged hopelessly. "I cannot halt the war until those who live in the interior realize that we are certain to lose. I am encouraged only by the knowledge that the farther north the British armada sails the more troubles they encounter. So many of their soldiers and sailors have fallen ill that they have been forced to halt their expedition and rest. So it may be that time is on our side after all."

"True enough if you think in terms of tens of years," An Mien replied. "But in a few months, after the enemy sick have recovered, the bombardment of our ports will start again, and you will be compelled to grant all that they demand."

"I know," the Tao Kuang Emperor said, "but I have no choice. It was our great-grandfather who said that the greatest virtue of our land is the patience of our people. They must show infinite patience in the months ahead, and I must set the example for them."

She felt a great rush of sympathy, but there was nothing she could do for him. He was trapped in a maze from which there was no escape, like the maze of high hedges built in the imperial park adjacent to the Summer Palace. The Middle Kingdom could not win the war, but until the people faced that reality it would go on or they would revolt. For thousands of years the emperors had been regarded by their subjects as divine, but the armed might of Great Britain was destroying that myth.

Jonathan opened his eyes, blinked repeatedly, and realized he was propped up in a huge, divanlike bed, with his head resting against a mound of silk cushions. He felt certain he was dreaming when he saw that an attractive, broad-faced young woman was feeding him broth. "Where am I and who are you?" he asked feebly.

The girl stared at him and continued to spoon broth into his mouth. It occurred to him that she was Chinese, so he repeated his questions in the Cantonese dialect. To his surprise she placed the bowl of soup and spoon on a tray, then raced from the room.

Looking around, he found the chamber totally unfamiliar.

The ceilings were high, the walls were decorated with panels depicting dragons and a variety of other creatures from Chinese mythology, and he caught a glimpse of broad, rolling hills through the open windows. Beside him, on a lacquered table, were bowls containing various herbs and powders. He saw on his finger the jade signet ring of his father-in-law, and his mind grew clearer.

While he was assimilating the fundamentals, Kai came into the room, the broad-faced girl behind him. Stopping short, the burly Chinese peered hard at his friend, saw that his eyes were clear, and grinned broadly.

"I have burned joss sticks in the temple behind this pavilion for many days," he said, "and my prayers have been answered. Your mind has returned to your body."

"Have I been ill?"

"You have hovered at the door of death for a long time," Kai replied. "After we spirited you out of Kuan-choy, we brought you here, to your estate, and Heng-ho has been caring for you."

The girl smiled shyly.

All at once Jonathan remembered the musket fire of the British infantrymen.

"You suffered three serious wounds," Kai told him. "You were the prisoner of the Fan Kuei, and we knew they would kill you after they questioned you about the work of the Society of Oxen. So we waited until their surgeons removed the bullets from your body. Then," he added casually, "we took you from them."

Jonathan managed to smile and wanted to hear the whole story of his rescue, but Heng-ho had other thoughts. "The Chinese Fan Kuei needs more food, rest, and less talk," she said firmly, and placed the soup on a small charcoal brazier to reheat.

If Jonathan hadn't been so weak he would have laughed aloud when he saw the fearless Kai obey her instantly and sidle toward the door.

"It is not true," Kai said mischievously, "that Lo Fang and I are the principal leaders of the Oxen. We obey Heng-ho in all things. And you will be wise if you do as she orders, too. Mean spirits invade her when she is crossed." He left quickly, before the girl could reply.

Heng-ho brought the soup to the bedside and quietly began to feed the patient again.

"You have been looking after me?" Jonathan asked.

She nodded, indicating a pallet at the far side of the spacious chamber. "I have slept there," she said.

"Have I been unconscious all this time?"

"Oh, no. You have spoken often in Mandarin and the tongue of the Fan Kuei, but I did not understand your words. For many days you thought I was your wife."

He was silent, hoping Lai-tse lu was well, wondering if their child had yet been born. "Is the war ended?"

The girl's dark eyes flashed. "We still fight, but the war goes badly for us. When Lo Fang returns in a few days, he will tell you what is happening."

"Where is this place? Kai said it was my estate, but I own no property in the Middle Kingdom."

"This was a country house of Soong Chao. It was inherited by his daughter, so it is your property. You are now my master." She was matter-of-fact.

"I'm no one's master," he replied. "You have lived here?"

"I was born in this place. When Lai-tse lu and I were small, we played together when she came here with her father for a visit. Now she lives in a far place, and it is my responsibility to take care of you."

Jonathan was tiring rapidly and hoped there were no hidden meanings in her bland comment.

Heng-ho insisted that he drink a mixture of bitter herbs and water, and he soon dropped off to sleep.

Thereafter, he found the girl at his side whenever he awakened, and she left no doubt that she was in charge. Little by little she added solid foods to his diet, and she displayed no embarrassment when she decided to bathe him. He tried to protest, but she paid no attention. Her brisk, common sense approach permitted no arguments.

Kai had been teasing her when he had called her methods authoritarian, but there was more than a grain of truth in what he had said. She tolerated no disputes in the sickroom, and Kai hastened to obey her commands. Little by little the realization dawned on Jonathan that Kai was in love with her, but Heng-ho seemed to take him for granted and devote all of her thought and energy to her patient, her manner proprietary.

About a week after Jonathan regained consciousness, Lo Fang came to the estate in the Kwangtung hills, and before departing with Kai on a mission that neither explained, he brought the American up to date on the progress of the war.

Jonathan was told that the British, having been slowed by sickness and bad weather, had now begun to step up their campaign and had taken port cities along the Yangtze. He was appalled to learn, also, that the opium trade was already flourishing again.

China would lose the war, Jonathan knew, and would be forced to accept any terms that her conquerors imposed on her. He brooded, sharing the despair of the courageous men who had been his comrades in arms, and that night he had no appetite for the meal Heng-ho prepared for him.

She responded in typical, brusque fashion. "If you do not eat," she told him, "I will not allow Lo Fang and Kai to visit you again for many days."

He forced himself to eat.

A few days later the American's slow convalescence was interrupted by a commotion somewhere on the property. Men shouted, dogs barked, and Heng-ho went off to discover the cause of the disturbance.

She returned with surprising news. "A Fan Kuei has learned of your presence here and wishes to speak with you," she said. "If you do not want to have words with him, the men will drive him away with their sticks."

"I want very much to see him," Jonathan said hastily.

He was astonished when a white man wearing a clerical collar beneath a dusty cloak came into the sickroom.

"I am Jean-Pierre LaRoche," he said, speaking English with a heavy French accent. "Forgive this intrusion, but I have been hearing tales throughout the countryside about a Chinese Fan Kuei who fought with the guerrillas, and I had to see for myself if the rumors were true."

"They are," Jonathan replied, "but I'm amazed to see you here, Father. I had no idea there was another of our race in the interior." He motioned the visitor to a chair.

Heng-ho, unable to understand what was being said, hovered suspiciously inside the sliding door.

The priest realized at once that she was upset, and promptly switched to the Cantonese dialect. "A war does not interrupt

God's work," he said. "I've spent the past two years traveling through several provinces."

"You've had permission?"

"I have that of the Lord, so I have asked none of temporal authorities. St. Paul went on his missions without obtaining permits from the Romans."

"You're a brave man, Father."

Father LaRoche shrugged. "I must do what my conscience dictates, my son."

"Are you making many converts?"

The gray-haired priest shook his head. "The people of China cling to their own faiths, which is only natural in a time of trouble. They accept the gifts I give them, but they reject the doctrine I preach." Unaccountably he brightened. "But I'm not really discouraged. I am plowing the ground, and others who will come after me will plant the seeds. The work of the Lord is never done in vain. Now tell me about yourself, my son."

Jonathan briefly related his own story.

"There have been many reports that a white guerrilla leader was stolen from the British after they wounded and captured him, but people here have such fanciful imaginations that I refused to believe them. You're recovering now?"

"Slowly, Father. Far too slowly."

"I've had to learn something about medicine as I preach the Gospel, so perhaps you'll allow me to examine you."

"By all means," Jonathan said.

As the priest pulled down the coverlet, Heng-ho sprang forward, brandishing a huge, curved sword, but Father LaRoche did not flinch. "I mean him no harm, my daughter," he said.

Jonathan was more emphatic. "No, Heng-ho. He is my friend!"

The girl desisted but stood nearby, still holding the sword, as the priest conducted a thorough examination, then concentrated on the most serious of the patient's wounds, which he probed gently.

Jonathan couldn't help wincing, and Heng-ho took a single step forward, her eyes glittering menacingly. Jonathan waved her away.

"It's small wonder you're showing only slight improvement. This wound is festering."

"Heng-ho packs it with herbs every day."

Father LaRoche sighed. "It should be cauterized. But the wound runs deep, and the pain will be intense." He hesitated. "If there's a supply of opium on hand, I can give you some to lessen the pain."

"You'll find none here, Father. My comrades are devoted to the principle of ridding China of the drug."

"I see. Then you'll be wise to clamp your teeth on a block of wood so you don't scream. I've had to perform a similar operation many times in my travels here, and the pain is excruciating."

"Do what you must, Father."

The priest turned to Heng-ho and told her what he wanted. She made no move to fetch the wood, however, until Jonathan gave her an order.

"Our worst enemies here are ignorance and superstition," Father LaRoche said, reverting to English when the girl went off. "China is a land of contrasts. No people are more civilized than the upper classes, who have inherited the wisdom and tastes of their ancestors, and none are more miserable than the poor."

"Then you approve of the way Britain—and now France, too—are forcing China to open her doors?"

"I do not," the priest replied emphatically. "I do not subscribe to what some of my colleagues say: 'Only Christ can save China from opium, but only war can open China to Christ.' Change can come only when the people themselves demand it. People must truly want to learn to read and write. The people must respond of their own will."

Heng-ho returned with a chunk of wood approximately two inches thick, which she had crudely smoothed herself. The priest displayed infinite patience as he explained to the girl what he intended to do and why, but she remained dubious.

"If I cry out, pay no attention," Jonathan told her, then enlarged on his theme in terms she would comprehend. "My friend will burn away the evil spirits that inhabit my body. Then I will become strong again."

At last she understood, and her hostility lessened.

Father LaRoche moved the charcoal brazier closer to the bed, took a knife from his belt, and placed it on the grill directly above the red coals. Some minutes passed before the blade began to glow.

"Get ready," Father LaRoche said. "This will not be easy for you."

Jonathan placed the block of wood between his teeth and braced himself. The priest murmured a prayer, placed a cloth around the hilt, and held the flat of the knife against the open wound.

Although Jonathan thought he was prepared, the agony was the worst he had ever known. A blinding, searing pain encompassed his whole being, and sweat drenched him. But he made no sound, afraid that Heng-ho would turn on his benefactor.

The stench of burning flesh filled the room. Jonathan felt the world around him darkening, and he believed he was going to faint. But then the operation came to an end, and Father LaRoche cleaned the knife by placing it above the coals again.

Jonathan continued to writhe, but little by little the pain began to subside. Heng-ho wiped his eyes and face with a damp, cool cloth.

"This should rid you of the infection, my son, but I'm afraid you'll be scarred for the rest of your days. You've shown great courage."

"So have you, Father," Jonathan muttered.

His discomfort remained great, and Father LaRoche decided to stay the night.

When morning came, Jonathan's body was still tender and sore, but he felt better than he had since first awakening in the country house.

A cheerful Father LaRoche appeared to bid him farewell. "You don't know how badly you've spoiled me," he said. "I slept in a real bed, and I've just eaten a delicious meal that the household staff cooked for me. I won't forget my experience here."

"And I won't forget you, Father. You've saved my life."

"No, my son." The priest reproved him quietly. "Only God can give and take life. If I have been an instrument of His will, I am satisfied."

"There must be some way I can show you my appreciation, Father," Jonathan said. "I have no funds, but you're welcome to stay here and make this place your headquarters."

"Thank you, but I would become too indolent and would be tempted to abandon my work for a time. Remember me in your prayers, my son, just as I shall include you in mine. And may your cause prosper." Father LaRoche gave him his blessing and slipped out of the room.

Jonathan never saw him or heard from him again and never learned his fate.

Only two days later, shortly before sundown, Father LaRoche arrived in a small, inland town during a driving rainstorm and took refuge in the local, pagodalike temple used by both Buddhists and Taoists. The downpour continued through the night, and he was so weary that he slept until daybreak, long after the storm had subsided.

The villagers were unaware of his vocation and would not have cared had they known. It was enough for them that a Fan Kuei had appeared out of nowhere and had desecrated their temple by sleeping in it. The word spread, and by daybreak the villagers had been joined by forty to fifty peasants from the neighborhood, most armed with ancient battle-axes, spears, and knives.

When the priest emerged into the open, he was attacked at once by a howling mob. He lived for only a few moments before he was hacked to pieces.

No one in the mob understood his final words, spoken in his own tongue: "Forgive them, Lord, for they know not what they do."

Later his battered head was mounted on a pike and was displayed at the crest of the highest hill in the neighborhood.

When Lo Fang and Kai returned to the Soong estate for an overnight stay before resuming their incessant guerrilla warfare, they were surprised and pleased to see the American in a chair near the windows. His color was improving, and his listlessness had vanished.

As time went on, Jonathan became aware of subtle changes in Heng-ho's attitude toward him. She continued to wear the black shirts and trousers of Kwangtung peasant women, but it seemed to him that her trousers were becoming tighter, and he knew his imagination wasn't playing tricks on him when she left the top buttons of her shirt open.

He had to admit she was attractive in a robust, earthy way, but he had no interest in her. Besides, Kai had made it clear on his last visit that he was drawn to the girl, and Jonathan believed they would be good for each other. Both were blunt realists, sharing a common background, and both were ardent patriots devoted to the cause of Chinese freedom.

But Heng-ho had thoughts of her own. She first manifested them by protesting, although in vain, when he informed her he was sufficiently recovered to bathe himself.

A few days later, when she brought him his noon meal, she seated herself opposite him and watched him carefully, her eyes speculative. Her steady scrutiny made Jonathan uncomfortable.

All at once Heng-ho smiled. "Soon," she said, "you will be strong enough so we can make love. I have been waiting a long time for that day."

II

The *Lai-tse lu* arrived in Djakarta after a voyage from London by way of the Cape of Good Hope after one hundred and nine days. She dropped anchor in the harbor, all of the Fat Dutchman's wharves being occupied by other vessels in what was the greatest influx of shipping ever known there. Sentries came on board to guard her cargo, and Captain Ellison granted his crew a well-deserved shore leave, one watch at a time.

Meantime Charles Boynton hurried to the estate of the Fat Dutchman, who was delighted to see him. "I win a wager with Molinda, heh-heh," he said. "With your nose for commerce, I knew you'd be coming to the East now that the war is almost over."

"I knew the British had taken many key cities, but I didn't know the Chinese were already capitulating," Charles replied as they sat together in the familiar garden.

"It seems that way. The ships of every maritime power are racing here, hoping to cash in as soon as trade is resumed," the Fat Dutchman said. "That's why the harbor is so crowded."

"My situation is different. I've brought you a cargo and will take as much pepper back to England as you can give me, but I'm not intending to go to Whampoa for trading purposes."

The Fat Dutchman nodded, and his almost perennial smile faded. "You'll search for Jonathan Rakehell, no doubt."

"Precisely. Have you had any news of him?"

"Not a word. My sources there are reliable and accurate, but they haven't picked up even a whisper about him, heh-heh.

Ordinarily I'd regard that as good news, as an indication he's still alive. But the chaos in China has been so frightful that no one knows what may have happened to him."

Charles was disappointed, having hoped the Fat Dutchman would be able to provide him with concrete news.

"Some months ago there was a rumor to the effect that the British wounded and captured a white man fighting with the Chinese guerrillas—"

"That must have been Jonnie!"

"Perhaps." As always, the Fat Dutchman was cautious. "I'm told the British never learned his identity because the guerrillas rescued him while he was unconscious, mind you, and he disappeared. In fact, General Pottinger was so embarrassed by the incident that I'm told he gave orders to deny it ever took place. Heh-heh."

They were interrupted by the approach of Molinda, who had heard of Charles's arrival and had hurriedly changed her clothes. She was attired in a snug-fitting, ankle-length wrapped skirt of white silk with a matching breastband, and had rouged her nipples so they were half-visible beneath the thin cloth. A white orchid accented her glossy hair, heavy gold earrings fell to her graceful shoulders, and bracelets of heavy gold jangled on one arm. Artfully applied cosmetics emphasized her large, glowing eyes, her full, almost pouting lips, and the fine, symmetrical bone structure of her face. She moved slowly, confident of her feminine appeal, her hips swaying.

Charles sucked in his breath. He well recalled the affair he had enjoyed with her before his marriage, but she was even more beautiful and seductive than he had remembered.

The Fat Dutchman smiled knowingly, his eyes almost closed, and took little part in the conversation that followed.

Molinda discussed the situation in Whampoa and Canton with the authority of one familiar with every detail. "Only a few of the factories at Canton had been damaged, and they were repaired. Captain Elliot, before he was sent back to England, had been meticulous in the restoration of property. The factories that belonged to Soong Chao now go to his daughter. That means Rakehell and Boynton will own and operate the largest complex of warehouses in the port."

Charles admired her acumen as much as he was attracted

301

by her lush beauty. "I assume that's what Lai-tse lu and Jonathan will want, but we can't make use of the factories until trade is officially resumed."

The girl nodded crisply.

"I suppose the opium trade is still rampant?" Charles inquired.

"Unfortunately, yes," she replied. "There is no one to halt it. With legitimate trade at a standstill, merchants are resorting more than ever to selling opium. In the last five days, eight ships carrying cargoes of opium put in to Hong Kong. Those are the latest figures I've received."

"Is anyone in charge of the administration of Canton, Molinda?"

"Pottinger is busy in the north, and as you probably know, Lin Tse-hsü was recalled to Peking and was put into exile. No, little is being done to govern Canton. Crime was rampant there for several months, but we hear several of the secret societies have taken charge, and until a peace treaty is arranged, they're the real rulers of the city."

Charles was encouraged. The rise of the secret societies made it fairly likely that he would be able to get in touch with Lo Fang and Kai, assuming they were still alive.

"No one knows just when the emperor will surrender," Molinda continued. "There are rumors spread almost daily, but Tao Kuang has kept his plans well hidden so far."

The announcement by one of the slave girls that dinner was ready did not halt the flow of conversation. The table was loaded with *rijsttafel* dishes, and the chef, at Molinda's request, also had prepared whole chickens stuffed with pepper dressing and baked in clay, which she remembered that Charles had enjoyed on his last visit. The Fat Dutchman made certain their champagne glasses were kept filled but interjected only an occasional comment as they chatted.

When the meal drew to an end and Charles was served a superb French cognac, his host suddenly heaved himself to his feet. "I shall miss you," he told Molinda cryptically, then bade the guest good night, saying they would meet again at breakfast.

Molinda did not offer to explain the remark and instead deliberately drew her chair closer to Charles. He became uncomfortable and felt he had to be fair to her. "Since we last met," he said, "I've been married."

The girl's smile was unwavering. "So Jonathan told me when he came here." She placed her hand on his arm, then slid it up to his neck in a slow caress.

He needed no further invitation. His conscience untroubled by his infidelity to Ruth, he took Molinda to the guest suite that had been provided for him, and there they made love passionately and repeatedly. He had not remembered that she knew so many ways to arouse a man, and her sexual appetite seemed insatiable. Ultimately they dropped off to sleep, then made love again at daybreak.

Molinda retired to her own quarters for a time, and when they met again at the breakfast table, her manner was crisp as she presented him with the documents that verified the legitimacy of the shipload of black peppercorns that would be loaded in the hold of the clipper.

The Fat Dutchman had already eaten, having arisen early, but he joined them for a cup of strong Javanese coffee before going to the garden for a meeting with a trader from Siam. As he got to his feet, he glanced at Molinda, his expression quizzical, and asked, "Does he know? Heh-heh." Chuckling quietly, he waddled out of the dining room.

Molinda shook her head when he asked his question, then gazed innocently at the gardenia bush ablaze with white flowers. Charles looked at her over the rim of his coffee cup. "What is it I'm to know but haven't yet been told?"

The girl braced herself. The success or failure of the plan on which her future depended, the scheme she had developed with such care, depended on his reaction to her news. Prompted by her instinct to abandon the subtleties she had intended to employ, she took a blunt, candid approach.

"The Dutchman," she said, "has agreed—at my request—to make you a special gift. From this time onward I belong to you."

Charles's blood ran cold. "My God!" he murmured, then recovered enough to say, "I don't believe in slavery."

A dimple appeared in Molinda's cheek when she smiled. "I'm well aware of it," she replied calmly.

"What's more," he went on, becoming emphatic, "there

303

is no way I could take you back to London with me. You're too beautiful, too exotic. My wife would leave me, my family would disown me, and my reputation would be ruined for all time. I couldn't live down the scandal."

"That's what I thought you'd say." The girl's smile vanished. "I have no wish to embarrass you, Charles. And I don't want to take your wife's place in your life. Nor have I any desire to become your permanent concubine. I've had enough of that existence right here, thank you."

He looked at her in confusion.

"As you well know," she said earnestly, "I have been attending to many aspects of the Dutchman's business affairs. I have proved that I am competent in the handling of shipping deals."

He nodded, the realization dawning that she was engaging in some sort of shrewd maneuver.

"But I have gone as high as I can here. As long as I remain in this house, I am a concubine. I can be given to visitors for their pleasure, or beaten if I disobey my master. More than all else in the world, I want my freedom. As a woman, as a human being. I make love with you because I wish to do so, not because I must. I want that same privilege always, in my dealings with all men." She drew a deep breath, and her eyes looked fathomless. "I hope you will forgive me, but I am using you. Take me away from Djakarta and grant me my freedom. That is all I ask of you."

He felt a great rush of sympathy for her. "Of course I'll take you, and naturally I'll grant you freedom. You're free as of this moment. But what will you do?"

"I think I have greater knowledge of shipping and more wisdom than many of the men with whom I have been transacting business. It is my great desire to become active in trade myself. I do not yet know where, or how I shall do it, but I have faith in my future. And I have been saving the gifts of jewelry I have received from the Dutchman and others, so I can sell what I must in order to live until I make a firm footing in commerce for myself."

Admiring her courage and ambition, Charles also was keenly aware of his own obligation to her. He could not abandon her. Not in a world where few women were active in business, not in a world where her beauty would create countless problems for her.

"I feel responsible for you," he said. "I cannot take you to Bangkok or Bombay—or some such place—and then bid you farewell without knowing what will become of you. I agree with what you want, and I admire you for it. But you know little of the outside world. You have been kidnapped and sold into slavery because of your beauty, and the same could happen to you again. Or you could suffer an even worse fate. All this is so new to me that I can't yet advise you. But I have no intention of abandoning you. You will stay with me, here in the East, until we can find a secure place for you. Together."

Sudden tears smudged the kohl that rimmed her eyes. "I have tricked you," she said, "and I do not deserve such kindness."

Charles was embarrassed. "Nonsense," he said brusquely. "You took the only path open to you. And I certainly can't blame you for that."

She placed her hand over his. "I shall be grateful to you always," she told him. "Someday, in some way we do not yet know, I shall have the opportunity to prove to you that I do not speak empty words."

"We won't worry about that now," he said. "You'll need new clothes to wear on board ship and in ports we may visit. You can't appear anywhere outside this property dressed as you are. So have a more modest wardrobe made, and I'll pay for it."

"Thank you, but I prefer to—"

"That's the least I can do for you," he said, interrupting. "I'll be spending about a week here, so the seamstress will need to work quickly and diligently."

Molinda bowed her head in appreciative submission.

"I can't promise we'll solve your problem overnight. In fact, I must attend to more urgent business first, so I'll have to take you with me to Whampoa where I can begin my search for Jonathan Rakehell without delay."

"I will be honored to accompany you," Molinda said, lifting her head. "Perhaps I can be of assistance to you. I am in Jonathan's debt, and it would give me great pleasure to help in locating him."

305

*   *   *

Jonathan set a rigorous program of physical rehabilitation for himself and followed it faithfully. Every morning he spent an hour or two wielding a heavy ku ming in order to strengthen the muscles in his arms and shoulders. He practiced throwing his Javanese knives, and after eating a light meal at noon, he went for long walks in the hills that surrounded the Soong country estate, always taking care to return before sundown. Bandits infested the countryside after dark, Heng-ho warned him, so he knew it wouldn't be safe to wander alone at night.

Kai returned to the estate whenever he could for a visit, and Jonathan took advantage of his presence by engaging in friendly bouts of wrestling and the martial arts with him. The American's strength was returning, and his sense of restlessness increased.

One afternoon, after a particularly exhausting match with Kai, the two friends sat together in the garden, and for the first time Jonathan spoke of the future. "Soon," he said, "I must return to Lai-tse lu."

Kai nodded his head emphatically. "Lo Fang and I agree. But there will be many difficulties. It was not my wish to tell you this until we found some way to smuggle you out of the Middle Kingdom," Kai said, "but the British have placed a price on the head of the Chinese Fan Kuei whom they captured and who was spirited from them."

Although Jonathan was upset, he grinned. "How high a price?"

"One thousand pounds sterling."

"Whew! That's a fortune!"

"They have no accurate description of you, so they search in the dark. If Lo Fang or I should be captured, we can pretend to be stupid peasants, and the British will be no wiser. But if you should fall into their hands again, they would know you instantly. The war is already lost and is almost over, but you are still in grave danger. We must find a way soon to help our brother."

Jonathan was troubled, but he spoke calmly. "Well, the sooner I'm away from here the better. Besides, it becomes more difficult each day to hold off Heng-ho. Some night when I am asleep I expect to wake up and find she has crawled into bed with me."

"I will speak with her," Kai said. "She believes she is

306

smitten with you. It may be that she is jealous of Lai-tse lu, as she was when they were children.''

"I'll appreciate anything you can do. She nursed me back to health, so I'm indebted to her, but her attentions are embarrassing.''

"It will be done.''

"That brings up another matter, Kai. There must be at least a dozen people who work and live here. But they haven't been paid a single yuan since Soong Chao died, and I'll have no access to wages for them until I return to New England. I hope you can make them understand.''

"It is you who do not understand,'' Kai said with a smile. "There is poverty everywhere in the Middle Kingdom, and the war makes conditions worse. Those who worked for Soong Chao have a roof over their heads. They grow the food they eat, and they have the tools they need. They will live here happily until you and Lai-tse lu again pay them wages.''

"I see.'' The poor of China were among the most impoverished people on earth, Jonathan reflected.

"Now I have news for you,'' Kai said. "I received word from one of our men in Canton, who went to the house of Soong Chao there. A very few objects of value have been stolen, but most remain, and no damage has been done.''

"How is that possible?''

"Everyone in the city had great respect for Soong, and now his memory is respected. You cannot live there now because of the price the British have placed on your head, but the day will come when you and Lai-tse lu will return and make your home there.''

For the present Jonathan could think only in terms of returning to the Rakehell home in New London.

Leaving him in the garden, Kai went in search of Heng-ho, finally finding her in the kitchen, where she was telling the cook what to prepare for the evening meal. At his request she accompanied him to a small, decorative pagoda that stood at the far end of the property, where no one would hear their conversation.

"The Chinese Fan Kuei was near death when we brought him here, but you have helped to make him healthy and strong again,'' Kai said. "Because of all you have done for him, you have won a place in his heart.''

The girl sat on a stone bench, her hands folded in her lap and her eyes glowing as she listened to him.

"But his heart no longer belongs to him. He gave it to Lai-tse lu. You have seen the jade Tree of Life that hangs from his neck. That was her gift to him."

"I should have taken it and smashed it when his mind and body were separated," the girl said vehemently. "Then the spell that binds him to her would have been destroyed."

Kai knew he had to deal with her on a level she was capable of comprehending. "The gods have performed many deeds that unite them," he said. "Not even the gods of lightning and thunder could tear them apart."

Heng-ho stared at the tile floor, then raised her head and looked at him. "The Chinese Fan Kuei has told you he will not lie with me?" she asked quietly.

"Those were his words. But you and I have slept together," Kai went on, "and we can do so again."

"All was changed when he who was ill came here."

"No, Heng-ho. It is true that once you were my concubine, but now I offer you much more. I will make you my wife and take care of you as long as we live."

Heng-ho rose slowly to her feet, her dignity natural and unconscious. "Kai is a man of honor and courage and strength," she said. "There was a time that Heng-ho would have been happy to become his wife. But that cannot be now. Those who have been permitted a glimpse of the Upper Kingdom cannot be satisfied with life on this earth." Turning slowly, she made her way back to the house.

Watching her as she walked, Kai knew she was suffering bitter disappointment, but she was young and resilient, and he told himself that in time her hurt would heal. Then she would accept his proposal, and together they would rear husky sons who would join the Society of Oxen and work for the welfare of the Middle Kingdom.

Late in the afternoon nine members of Kai's guerrilla band arrived at the estate prior to a mission that would take them elsewhere the following day. Three formerly had belonged to Jonathan's unit, and their reunion was so warm he decided to prolong it by eating the evening meal with them in the open. At his request the menu was changed, and they sat around a fire, eating lamb that had been rubbed with garlic and cooked in ginger.

Jonathan listened to story after story as the Oxen told him, with great glee, how they had outwitted the British on numerous occasions.

The laughter of the entire group died away when the cook, obviously disturbed, came to them hurriedly. "Heng-ho is gone!" the old woman exclaimed.

Kai was irritated. "If she isn't in her room, she is strolling in the gardens or resting in a pagoda somewhere on the property."

The cook shook her head. "The gardeners, the housemaids, and I have searched everywhere for her. All that she owns is still in her room except her cloak and the shoes one wears when one goes for long walks. So we know she is no longer here."

Kai immediately guessed that the girl had been more disturbed that afternoon than he had realized. "We'll find her," he said.

Jonathan insisted on taking part in the search, and the trio who had been under his command volunteered to accompany him, an offer he gladly accepted. He was already carrying his throwing knives in his belt, and when someone handed him a long, heavy ku ming, he was pleased that he had learned to use the cumbersome but deadly weapon.

He led one group, and Kai took charge of the other. They separated outside the estate wall, facing the rolling hills, agreeing that each unit would make a wide sweep. If one or the other found the young woman, a bonfire would be lighted.

Jonathan and his men spread out, just as they had done on so many of their missions, and began to climb the wooded heights. The American quickly discovered that his night vision was still good and that he could move swiftly and silently without tiring. Now he knew for certain that his health had been restored.

He had no idea why Heng-ho had foolishly left the estate after dark, but he wasn't particularly concerned. She had spent her entire life in the area, so she had to be thoroughly familiar with every hill, every rice paddy, every patch of woods.

As the night wore on and neither his unit nor Kai's discovered any trace of the girl, his worry mounted. Surely she was too sensible to have taken needless risks in a countryside where bandits roamed at will. But not until dawn came was he willing to admit defeat, and he reluctantly gave the order to close the gap that separated him and his followers from the other group.

Jonathan walked more rapidly, ignoring the aches in his calves, then increased his pace to a run when he saw Kai and his Oxen standing silently in a semicircle on a hillside directly ahead.

No one spoke or otherwise acknowledged the presence of the new arrivals, and Jonathan edged forward into the front rank, then stopped short.

Only a few feet away lay the motionless, battered body of Heng-ho, her sightless eyes fixed on the early morning sky. She had been violated, then stabbed and beaten to death, presumably so she could not identify her attackers.

Kai stood over her, his dark eyes burning, all expression drained from his face. Only at that moment did Jonathan realize how much his friend had loved the girl, how intensely he was suffering now.

Saying nothing, Kai tenderly wrapped Heng-ho in her own cloak, lifted her limp body into his arms, and his footsteps slow, carried her back to the Soong estate for honorable burial.

The bandits who had raped and killed her, Jonathan knew, would not be safe unless they fled from the area and never returned.

The officers and crew of the *Lai-tse lu* were startled when Molinda boarded the clipper with Charles Boynton and her clothing boxes were stored in his spacious cabin. But his private life was Charles's own business, and as the men knew, Captain Ellison disliked gossip, so they kept their own counsel. They noted, however, that the Fat Dutchman paid a rare visit to the docks just before the ship sailed, that the girl hugged and kissed him, and that Charles shook his hand with great cordiality. Even Homer, who had known the position she had occupied on the Dutchman's staff, was bewildered.

But Charles offered no explanations to anyone. Exercising an owner's prerogative, he ate his meals with Molinda in the privacy of his cabin, strolled frequently with her on deck, and one afternoon conducted her on an inspection of the clipper.

Although it was obvious she was not Occidental, she wore only sedate Western dress, and her attire was particularly demure when the ship sailed past Macao and entered the delta of the Pearl River. Few foreign ships were at anchor in Whampoa, and no dockhands came forward to help as Homer maneuvered his ship into a berth, but whatever damage had been done to the warehouses had been repaired, and scores of Chinese continued to go about their business along the waterfront and in their junks and sampans.

The most startling indication of the difference the war had made was the absence of any Western officers. No foreign trade was being conducted, though some French, Swedish, and Danish civilians still resided at the factories, and some of them loitered aimlessly near the waterfront.

As Charles and Molinda came ashore, a Frenchman called out in English, "Do you know that you've tied up at the vacant Soong wharves, sir?"

"Indeed I do. They've been inherited by members of my family."

His companion, another Frenchman, now spoke up. "Owen Bruce and his new partner were hoping to get these factories and wharves as soon as the peace treaty was signed."

"Whatever terms the British and Chinese agree upon," Charles said to the men, "these factories still belong to the Rakehell and Boynton Company. Now if you gentlemen will excuse me, I am going to inspect the warehouses," and Charles, accompanied by Molinda and Homer Ellison, went to the Soong complex.

Any merchandise that had been stored in the warehouses had long since vanished, and the offices had been stripped of their furniture. But Molinda took a keen interest in everything she saw, asking the approximate dimensions of storage space and studying the empty offices with care.

"This room," she said when they came to the largest, which had a corner view and looked out over the docks, "had to be Soong Chao's office."

"It was," Charles told her.

A tiny smile appeared at the corners of her mouth and in her eyes.

Homer was surprised to discover that, although Molinda was voluminously clad from head to toe, wore a large hat, and used no makeup on her face, she nevertheless had a magnetic quality.

"So Bruce has a new partner," Charles mused as they resumed their inspection. "Whoever he is, the man must be a rotter."

He had no way of guessing that Bradford Walker had seen the familiar, handsome clipper entering the harbor and was taking care to remain out of sight in Bruce's old warehouse. Under no circumstances did he want to be recognized by any Rakehell or Boynton, or an employee who might reveal his present whereabouts.

So he stayed in the small, cramped office he had been given, and he was not surprised when Bruce joined him, obviously in a foul mood.

"I've just come from the waterfront. Wouldn't you know, that damned Charles Boynton has put into port and is already inspecting Soong's property."

"Too bad," Walker said. "If he hadn't showed up, we could have put those warehouses to good use."

"I'm not ready to give up quite yet," Bruce replied with a cold smile. "Young Rakehell is probably dead, and young Boynton is too grand a man to spend his life mildewing on the waterfront of a Chinese port. We'll see who takes charge for the company, and then we'll decide our next move. Come along, and we'll have a bracer of gin at the tavern."

Afraid he might be recognized by members of the *Lai-tse lu*'s crew, Walker demurred. "Not today, thanks," he said. "I'm still not accustomed to the heat at this season here, and I—I have a headache. I think I'll go to my own quarters and stay there."

Meanwhile, after Charles and Molinda completed their inspection of the Soong property, they returned to the ship. Half of the crew had been granted shore leave, but Homer Ellison was keeping watch for him. "Charles," he said, "a coolie who refused to identify himself came on board without an invitation, looking for you. He flashed an ugly knife when I ordered him ashore, so I thought it best not to make an issue of the matter."

"Where is he now?"

"In your cabin."

"Come with me, and we'll see what this is all about," Charles replied.

An abnormally tall, husky coolie in faded, padded cotton was sitting in the cabin and rose to his feet as Charles came in. "I greet the father of David and hope he is well," the man said, speaking in the Cantonese dialect.

The startled Charles peered at him, realized he had shaved off his mustache, and at the same moment recognized him. "Lo Fang!"

"It is best to mention no names. There are those who would pay a price for my head." Lo Fang grinned at him. "Word was brought to me that this great clipper ship, which even the most uneducated of my associates recognize, was coming into port, so I dressed in one of my convenient disguises and came to meet you."

"You don't know how pleased I am to see you!" Charles exclaimed.

"It is not difficult for me to guess. You seek one whose name also will not be mentioned aloud," Lo Fang said.

Homer Ellison, unable to understand a word, looked helplessly from one to the other.

"I may have word about Jonnie," Charles told the captain in an undertone.

Homer grinned and remained silent.

"It is good that you have come to claim the warehouses of Lai-tse lu's father," Lo Fang said. "He who is closer to her than anyone will be greatly relieved."

"Where is this person?" Charles demanded.

"At the appropriate time you will be taken to him," Lo Fang said. "There is much to be arranged."

"He's well and safe?"

"He was near death but has recovered." The head of the Society of Oxen became crisp. "You will sail tonight on the late tide. After dark a pilot will come on board. You will know him because he will identify himself with a token like this." A tiny, crudely carved pair of wooden oxen were displayed in his huge hand. "He will tell you where to sail. There are many islands off the coast of the Middle Kingdom that appear on no Fan Kuei charts. You will sail to one of them, and there this ship will lay concealed."

"The—the one I seek will meet me there?" Charles could scarcely believe his good fortune.

Lo Fang shook his head. "The British would kill him if they could. So you will be taken to him."

"I'm going, too," Molinda said.

The giant scowled at her. "The march will be long and hard. If we see patrols of Fan Kuei, there will be fighting, and men will die."

She appealed to Charles. "Take me, please. I want to go where you go. It would upset me too much to stay on board ship in a hidden harbor somewhere, not knowing what might happen next."

Charles turned back to Lo Fang and smiled wryly. "Lo Fang, this is Molinda. She is a very determined young woman and is accustomed to getting her way."

Lo Fang looked unhappy. "She will need a special disguise, but this, too, can be arranged. Now, for the rest of this day you will be very busy. Buy supplies of food and water, and let it be assumed that you sail for America. When the pilot comes to you, obey all of his instructions, even those that make no sense to you." Nodding curtly, he went ashore and soon was lost from sight in a crowd of Chinese boat people.

Charles explained the situation to Homer, but the master of the *Lai-tse lu* was apprehensive. "There are many pirates in this part of the world, and some of them have been known to play tricks on the unsuspecting. Can this man be trusted?"

Impulsively deciding to test Molinda's judgment, Charles looked at her. "What is your opinion?"

"He can be trusted," she said flatly.

"Indeed he can," Charles said with a grin. "It was he who united me with my son, and I know he's long held Lai-tse lu and Jonnie in high regard. We'll follow his instructions to the letter."

"Just don't forget," Molinda said, "that wherever you may go, you're taking me with you."

Oliver went ashore, going from tavern to bordello to tavern to round up the ship's company who had been given leave. Meanwhile Captain Ellison bought supplies of meat and fish, vegetables and fruit, then purchased enough kegs of water to see the clipper as far across the Pacific as the Sandwich Islands.

"I hate to spend all this money needlessly," he said, "but I reckon it can't be helped. Not if it will bring Jonnie back to us."

Charles decided it was necessary to tell the officers and boatswain the secret, and Oliver appointed himself to stand watch at the gangplank when night came.

The tide rose, but for an hour there was no sign of the pilot. Then a man in nondescript coolie's attire materialized on the wharf and showed Oliver the carved oxen he was carrying.

The man was conducted to the quarterdeck, where Homer and Charles awaited him. The clipper cast off and soon was threading her way down the delta. First mate Elijah Wilbor climbed to the masthead himself to make certain the ship was not being followed.

In the early hours of the morning the *Lai-tse lu* reached the open waters of the South China Sea, and the Society of Oxen pilot took command. The clipper headed north, and shortly before daybreak she tacked sharply, then sailed toward what appeared in the misty half-light to be a solid land mass.

"We'll founder on the offshore rocks," an alarmed Homer said.

Charles quickly translated his words. The Chinese pilot smiled but made no comment, and waited for a time longer before ordering sail reduced.

The clipper's speed was cut, and she seemed scarcely to be moving, but Homer was still apprehensive.

Charles grinned at him. "It appears to me there's a channel directly ahead," he said.

The ship's master peered through the fog, then exhaled slowly. Heavy foliage almost concealed a canallike opening between two islands. With Charles still translating the pilot's orders, the *Lai-tse lu* crawled into the deep-water channel, moved forward for several hundred yards, and then emerged into a placid lagoon, surrounded by high bluffs that concealed it on the side that faced the sea and sheltered it on the shore of the mainland. It would have been difficult to imagine a more secure hiding place for a large vessel with tall masts.

An anchor was dropped, bow and stern, and the pilot

announced he was hungry, indicating that his night's work had come to an end. Before going below for breakfast, however, he requested that a strong guard be posted and that any small boats approaching the clipper be ordered not to come near.

The rest of the day was anticlimactic. The crew slept, ate, and lolled on deck, with the pilot refusing to discuss what would happen next. When evening approached, however, his lethargy vanished. "The ship will remain at this anchorage until I return," he told Charles. "Perhaps she will stay here for many days, so the food that was purchased will not be wasted. Let none of the crew go ashore for any reason. Those who live nearby are not friendly to Fan Kuei, and anyone who sets foot on land, no matter what the reason, surely will die."

Charles translated for Homer, who looked dubious. "I don't like this arrangement," he said. "Do you suppose we can trust the fellow?"

"We have no choice," Charles told him.

The pilot handed the young Englishman a bundle he had brought on board with him. "Now you and the woman will wear these clothes. Let your Fan Kuei weapons be hidden beneath them, and bring with you the best of your own clothes. But do not make the package too large because a long journey lies ahead."

Charles and Molinda changed into the loose-fitting, pajamalike attire of Chinese peasants, and the girl giggled. Neither had any idea why they were being requested to bring items from their own wardrobes with them, and it was plain that the pilot had no intention of offering an explanation. Molinda solved the problem by taking one of her new Western dresses and a Javanese costume, while Charles hid his sword and a brace of pistols beneath his shapeless coolie coat.

The master's gig was lowered, and before Charles assisted the girl down the ladder to the boat, he shook Homer's hand. "I don't know when we'll meet again," he said.

"May Jonnie return with you," Homer replied.

Six seamen rowed the small party ashore under Oliver's supervision, and the pilot leaped onto a boulder, took the clothing bundle, and then bodily lifted Molinda ashore. Charles followed, and the gig started back toward the clipper.

The night was dark, with a hint of rain in the air, and the deep quiet made this alien soil menacing. Molinda shivered, and Charles comforted her by placing an arm around her shoulders.

"Now we will walk in single file, with the woman between us," the pilot said in a low tone. "Stay close behind me, and no matter what may occur, do not speak and do not fire a weapon of the Fan Kuei. Those who inhabit this region hate all outsiders and will kill you if they discover you are foreigners. If you grow too tired to walk," he added to Molinda, "touch my shoulder and I will halt for a few moments so you may rest. But remember we cannot tarry long in this area."

The girl looked as though she regretted the impulse that had caused her to insist on accompanying Charles.

Without further ado the pilot started forward through a patch of deep woods and seemed as much at home on land as he had been at sea. A steady drizzle fell, soaking the trio, but Charles realized that the rain was advantageous because their footsteps made no sound on the carpet of leaves, twigs, and pine needles underfoot.

The pilot maintained a steady pace, and the pair who accompanied him lost all count of time, having no idea how long they marched. Then, as they approached a clearing, he halted them by raising a hand.

The half-seen figures of two burly men, both armed with curved Chinese swords, narrow at the base, then flaring before coming to a hooked point, loomed ahead. The pilot went ahead to meet them. No words were exchanged, but Charles and Molinda heard the clinking of metal as the pilot handed them what appeared to be a small sack of coins. Apparently it was necessary to pay tribute of some sort in order to pass safely through this countryside.

The two men vanished, and the march was resumed. Again and again Molinda was tempted to tap the guide on the shoulder so they would halt briefly, but her pride was too great. Her own initiative was responsible for her presence on this journey, the prospect of being left behind having made her fearful, and she didn't want to be a hindrance.

In the early hours of the morning the sky cleared, stars appeared overhead, and occasionally, in the distance, Charles could see the dim outlines of a hut or a small pagoda. They were making their way along a narrow land, and on both sides were rice paddies, fields of growing green vegetables, and row after row of soybeans. In the Middle Kingdom no arable land was left untended.

Then they plunged into another wooded area, and when the light of the false dawn streaked the sky, the guide finally halted beside a small brook. Silently inviting the pair to drink, he handed each of them a chunk of a hard substance, indicating that they were to eat it.

So weary that her entire body ached, Molinda drank water from the brook, then bit off a small piece of the food. To her surprise it had a pleasant, bittersweet taste, and the realization dawned on her that she was eating meat and vegetables that had been dried in the sun and pressed into cake form. She was ravenous and consumed the entire chunk.

The march had come to a temporary end, and Molinda fell asleep in Charles's protective embrace. Soon he dozed, too, while the pilot sat cross-legged, keeping watch with a long knife gleaming in his belt.

The sun had risen when the pair awakened with a start. The pilot was nowhere to be seen, but they were astonished to discover they were surrounded by a half-dozen men in black boots, trousers, and shirts. Charles was taking no chances and reached for his pistols, but a member of the band reassured him by showing him a pair of tiny, carved oxen.

The men gave the couple more of the pressed food, and then the march was resumed. The pace was much slower than it had been during the long night, and the silent leader studied Molinda from time to time, then signaled for a halt when he decided she needed a rest. The members of the escort did not speak to the couple or to each other.

Charles's patience was limited, and at last he spoke to the leader in Cantonese. "How much longer will our journey continue and where are you taking us?" he demanded.

The expression in the man's eyes indicated that he understood, but he made no reply.

Throughout the day, when they came to open area, they could see women in black pajamas and broad-brimmed straw hats with pointed crowns working in rice paddies. Sometimes they passed men plowing fields behind teams of water buffalo, too, but none of the inhabitants even glanced in the direction of the travelers. It was almost as though they were invisible, Molinda thought.

By mid-afternoon the need for caution seemed to disappear, and the black-clad men exchanged occasional words with each other, although they did not speak to the foreigners. Late in the day a halt was called for the night, to the infinite relief of the tired girl. Firewood was gathered, and the men cooked lamb rubbed with garlic in a cauldron in which ginger, Chinese cabbage, snow peas, and water chestnuts also simmered. As they ate the delicious meal, the leader addressed Charles for the first time. "After we walk a few more hours tomorrow, our journey will end."

"That's good to hear. Where are we?"

"Kwangtung."

The province was enormous, so Charles had learned little. "Will we see the one we seek?"

The leader's eyes clouded, and he turned his back to the Fan Kuei.

That night Molinda and Charles enjoyed a longer sleep, but the march was resumed at dawn. Their clothes stained and dusty, their feet blistered, they were totally unprepared for what awaited them after they walked through a gate set in a high stone fence. Directly ahead stood a large pagodalike house, with several smaller outbuildings behind it, and coming toward them, clad in black like the escorts, was a smiling, tanned Jonathan Rakehell.

"Welcome to my wife's country house," he said. "Molinda, you're lovely even in those frightful clothes. Charles, you rascal, I was afraid we'd never meet again."

The reunion was joyous, and when Molinda was taken to a guest room to bathe and change, the cousins adjourned to a chamber lined with Chinese manuscripts, Charles postponing his own bath until he and Jonathan could exchange news.

For the first time Jonathan learned he was the father of a daughter named Jade.

"I haven't seen her," Charles said, "but your father and Missy Sarah write that she's beautiful."

"Lai-tse lu is well?"

"She had a difficult delivery, and Dr. Graves has told her to have no more children, but she seems to be recovering rapidly." That wasn't quite true, as Charles well knew. Lai-tse lu was still in a somewhat weakened condition.

In response to Jonathan's eager questions, Charles also

brought him up to date on the well-being of his own family and then learned for the first time how his cousin had been seriously wounded.

"Lo Fang and Kai smuggled me out of Kuan-choy, and now the Royal Navy has placed a price of one thousand pounds on my head. That's why you were brought here by such a roundabout route."

"My father and I have enough influence in London to have any charges against you canceled," Charles said. "You couldn't have done other than what you did under the circumstances. We may need some time, but I'm quite certain we'll succeed."

Jonathan thanked him and discussed the war and the current state of Rakehell and Boynton business affairs with him. Then, his eyes mischievous, the American said, "I trust you're enjoying your sojourn with Molinda."

An embarrassed Charles launched into an explanation of her presence with him.

Jonathan's whoop of laughter interrupted. "I know, ' he said. "Molinda told me her plan when I saw her in Djakarta, but I had no chance to warn you. I no sooner arrived in Canton than hostilities broke out."

"I'm not amused," Charles said. "I don't know what in the devil to do with her."

"I do," Jonathan said. "Kai has already told me that Soong's warehouses are intact, and his house in Canton also is available. When the war ends, it seems to me, we'll need to establish a permanent company headquarters in China. Molinda is exceptionally competent, and I suggest we give some thought to the possibility of placing her in charge."

"That would be a great responsibility for a woman."

"True, but I believe she'd live up to the obligations. There's no need to make a decision immediately, however. We have several weeks to consider the idea."

"We do?" Charles demanded.

Jonathan grinned at him. "When I first learned you had arrived in the *Lai-tse lu,* I was ready to sail for home with you. Without delay. There's nothing more I can do for China. But now a complication has developed, and as I can't leave you here, I'm afraid you and Molinda will have to come with me. We're leaving tomorrow for Peking."

Charles looked at him in surprise.

"Just yesterday, after I knew you were on your way here, I received a message from the Princess An Mien, the Tao Kuang's sister and Lai-tse lu's friend. She has asked me to pay her a visit, and a royal request is actually a command. I suspect she merely wants to thank me for whatever services I've rendered to China, but there's no way a journey to Peking can be avoided. Not if we want to do business in this country in the future."

"The imperial favor could be useful to us," Charles said thoughtfully.

"Kai is already rounding up horses for us." As a member of a secret society, Kai would have normally been forbidden to enter the Imperial City, but An Mien made it clear in her message that the Oxen members who had done so much for the Middle Kingdom were welcome, too.

"Will the clipper be safe in the lagoon where we anchored her?" Charles asked.

"If I didn't believe there's no safer berth for her in the Middle Kingdom, I'd have her moved," Jonathan said.

His experience with the guerrillas had changed him, Charles thought, as had his near-brush with death. He exuded a quiet confidence, knowing what he wanted and how to achieve his goals. At the same time he appeared more willing to take calculated risks. Certainly his wife and family would find him more mature when he returned to New London.

The sturdy Mongolian ponies plodded steadily, endlessly, toward the north, carrying Kai, his three foreign charges, and an escort of Society of Oxen members through hills and forests, plateaus, and huge valleys intersected by great rivers that flowed from west to east. The heavily armed men dissuaded bandits from attacking the party, and everywhere peasants tended to their own business when they recognized the black uniforms of the riders. Large cities and towns where people might cause unpleasantness for the Fan Kuei were avoided, and most nights the travelers slept in the open. Only infrequently did they halt at country inns where Molinda and the two men could enjoy the luxury of taking hot baths.

In spite of their unimpeded progress, the journey lasted for weeks. Jonathan and Charles took advantage of the long hours of travel by discussing every aspect of the Rakehell and

Boynton business with Molinda. The girl listened intently, learning rapidly, and often interrupted with questions that demonstrated her firm grasp of details. The cousins became increasingly convinced that she would be the right person to manage their Chinese headquarters, and Jonathan began to discuss with Kai various ways the young woman could be protected from predators.

The imperial seal affixed to the letter from the Princess An Mien provided the party with the only transit pass needed when yellow-clad troops were encountered on the road, and the officers in command of the units were unfailingly courteous. The capital of the world's largest, most heavily populated nation was approached from the west, and when the bulky, protective shield known as the Great Wall was sighted in the distance, the travelers knew their journey at last was coming to an end.

Peking had spilled far beyond its original borders and was several times the size of Canton. Never had Jonathan seen so many people as on the busy, crowded streets, and even Molinda, accustomed to the crowds of Djakarta, was awed. Virtually none of the residents had ever seen Fan Kuei, but the men of the Society of Oxen formed a tight cordon around the visitors, keeping the hostile at a distance.

Troops stationed at the high, forbidding walls of the Imperial City studied An Mien's imperial seal at length to assure themselves it was genuine, and as a precaution several hundred soldiers surrounded the party, conducting the travelers through the streets lined on both sides with government office buildings of gray stone.

After a time they came to the still higher walls of the Forbidden City, where the Tao Kuang Emperor, his family and concubines, his ministers of state and other high-ranking officials of his administration lived and worked.

Pagodas and palaces with walls of marble, onyx, and other valuable stones were everywhere, as were huge, seemingly endless gardens and temples. Kai explained that many of the palaces were uninhabited, and that in them were exhibited the priceless treasures that had been gifts to the nation's rulers for thousands of years.

The journey came to an abrupt end at a gracious, three-story building of gleaming white stone, which was graced by a pagodalike roof. Behind it stood a high, walled garden. Here the visitors would eat, sleep, and take their ease until such time as Jonathan was admitted to the august presence of the Princess An Mien. Although the American did not know it, Lai-tse lu had used these same quarters when she had been summoned by the emperor's sister.

The hour was growing late, but a full staff was in attendance, and the newcomers were served a sumptuous meal. Then baths were prepared for them in sunken pools, and their travel-stained clothes were removed for cleaning.

Jonathan, clad in a robe of featherweight silk, looked around his spacious bedchamber before he drifted off to sleep, his only thought the wish that his wife could be present to share the luxurious surroundings with him.

Charles and Molinda had been assigned adjoining chambers and could not resist the temptation to open the sliding door between their rooms and spend the night together.

Jonathan and Charles met for breakfast and, with nothing better to occupy them, adjourned to the formal garden after they finished their meal. They had no idea when Jonathan would be called to his audience with An Mien, although Kai had intimated that the princess was considerate and would give him an opportunity to recover from the rigors of the journey before she summoned him.

While the cousins chatted, Molinda came into the garden, and both men stared at her. She had changed into a breastband and wrapped skirt, used cosmetics artfully, and was wearing Javanese jewelry, with a delicate yellow flower in her hair. She had found it necessary for her peace of mind, she told them, to look like herself after spending so many weeks disguised as a peasant woman.

The morning passed lazily, and after a noon meal of tiny dumplings and other miniature dishes, Jonathan discovered the library. Here were volumes hand inscribed on parchment, many of them hundreds of years old, and he studied them at length, more familiar with the spoken Mandarin than with written Chinese characters. He became absorbed in trying to translate a volume of Taoist philosophy and did not even hear someone else come into the room.

A gentle cough startled him, and he looked up to see a wizened, white-haired woman who wore a sash of yellow silk that marked her as a member of the imperial entourage. She beckoned silently.

Jonathan followed her, and she led him into the open and across the garden, heading toward what appeared to be a solid wall of yellow brick. Then some of the bricks parted as a secret door set in the wall opened, and Jonathan could feel but not see the presence of hidden guards.

The door closed behind him, and the old woman led him through another garden to the entrance of a small, austere pagoda. She waved him in, then vanished.

He stepped over the threshold and saw a handsome, dark-haired woman in her thirties who was wearing a floor-length cheongsam, her only jewelry a huge, brilliant emerald and diamond ring. ''We have long waited to greet the Chinese Fan Kuei, the husband of our beloved Lai-tse lu,'' she said in a mellow voice.

Jonathan realized he was in the presence of An Mien and that he must be in a special room where audiences with foreigners were permitted. His principles would not permit him to kowtow before the princess, but he bowed to her from the waist.

''Sit beside me,'' she said, and arranged a large silken cushion for him on the stone bench with dragon's-claw feet.

He smiled, and oddly, he felt at home with her.

''My couriers have learned from your escorts of the birth of your daughter,'' An Mien said. ''I congratulate you. She binds you more closely to the Middle Kingdom, although it would seem you have needed no such ties.''

''The land of my wife's birth and heritage is my land, also,'' Jonathan replied.

''You have fought valiantly in our losing battle against the British.''

''I have tried to avenge the blood shed by Soong Chao for his country.''

As he spoke, a sliding door opened silently, and a man in faded, scuffed slippers and a scholar's gown of black silk came into the pagoda. He wore an embroidered, cloth-of-gold stole across his shoulders, on his head was a close-fitting cap studded with hundreds of pearls, and he bore a strong resemblance to An Mien, yet looked insignificant beside her. Not looking at the visitor, he seated himself on a cushioned, three-legged stool.

All at once Jonathan realized he was in the presence of the Lord of Ten Thousand Gods, the Divine Descendant of the Creators of the Universe, the sole ruler of the Middle Kingdom. Aware of his own shabby Society of Oxen black raiment, which had been cleaned while he had slept, he started to rise.

But the princess placed a detaining hand on his arm. "You and I are still alone in this pagoda," she said distinctly. "If you think you have seen another person enter, you are mistaken."

Jonathan understood at once. The rigid requirements of Chinese protocol would have made it mandatory for him to kowtow had the Celestial Emperor elected to make his presence official. By pretending he was not present, which was his prerogative, he could participate in an informal discussion to whatever extent he pleased.

The Tao Kuang Emperor was impatient. "I've heard second and third hand about the exploits of the Chinese Fan Kuei against the British invaders. I should like to hear his accounts in his own words."

Jonathan told several stories about his guerrilla encounters with the British at Kuan-choy, taking care to address his remarks exclusively to An Mien and trying not to see the emperor nodding and smiling.

"Give him the document," the Tao Kuang Emperor told his sister when the recital was done.

She handed the visitor a handsome, hand-inscribed parchment bearing the imperial seal. "In view of your services, Rakehell Jonathan, it has pleased our brother to prepare this official document. All that belonged to Soong Chao passes to your wife and to you, and after you to your children and their children's children, no matter what their sex "

"Tell him also about the additional property," the Celestial Emperor muttered.

"Oh, yes. It has also pleased my august brother to make you a gift of an imperial castle in Kwangtung. It, too, will belong to you and those of your blood who come after you, for all time."

"I'll be very much obliged," Jonathan said to the princess, "if you will express my eternal gratitude and that of Lai-tse lu to the Celestial Emperor."

Tao Kuang grinned and nodded, and then his manner

changed. Too agitated to use his sister as a go-between, he said to Jonathan, "The enemy has made a final demand upon us. Have you heard the details of our disgrace?"

Uncertain whether he could reply directly, Jonathan confined himself to a shake of his head.

"The enemy arrived so unexpectedly at Nanking," Tao Kuang said indignantly, "that we had to remove our cousin, Shaong Wei, and bring him here so he would not fall into the hands of the British."

The observation was irrelevant to the main issue, and An Mien intervened crisply. "Three imperial commissioners were appointed to deal with the British, but there have been no real negotiations. The enemy gave our commissioners an ultimatum. They demand that five ports be opened to their trade. Canton, of course. Also Amoy, Foochow, Ningpo, and Shanghai. In each of these cities land will be taken by the British, and will be under the exclusive rule of an official they call a consul. As if this were not bad enough, they insist we cede to them the island of Hong Kong and the territory opposite it on the mainland."

The Divine Ruler of Mankind lowered his head and stared with unseeing eyes at the floor tiles. "If we refuse, the British will attack Nanking, march to Peking, and destroy the Forbidden City with their cannon. If that should happen, the entire Middle Kingdom would collapse. We must accept the enemy's terms because it is our duty to maintain our dynasty, our laws, our customs—our very civilization itself."

"What of the opium trade?" Jonathan forgot to address the emperor through his sister.

"There is no mention of opium in the terms that have been presented to us," Tao Kuang replied, and seemed near tears.

Jonathan sought for an appropriate reply. "It is true that the demands of the enemy are outrageous," he said, "and that other Western nations surely will follow the lead of the British. Many in the West will want trade with China and will wish to establish consulates here. But that is not altogether bad, harmful, or cause of shame."

"How so?" the emperor demanded.

Jonathan sensed that the princess was sympathetic to what he wanted to say, so he addressed his next remarks to her.

"Once the Middle Kingdom had the greatest, most advanced civilization in the world," he said, hoping he would not unduly offend his imperial host while saying what he believed necessary. "But she has remained isolated behind her high walls and has stagnated, just as a rice paddy grows stagnant and the food it grows turns to rot when no rain falls. The younger, more vigorous nations of the West have far surpassed the Middle Kingdom in their knowledge of science and medicine, in the making of arms and ships, in the looming of cloth and ways to grow more food for the hungry. The heart of the Middle Kingdom is sound and her soul is strong, so she will survive the disgrace being imposed on her. Yet she will be forced, in spite of herself, to learn and adopt methods that will make her people healthier and more prosperous, that will banish disease, increase their food supplies, and become better able to defend themselves. Surely the day will come, although perhaps not in my lifetime or that of the Tao Kuang Emperor, when the Middle Kingdom will assume her rightful place as one of the great rulers of this earth."

The Princess An Mien sighed gently. "The Chinese Fan Kuei says the same words that I have repeated to my brother many times. He who sees us humiliated in defeat does not see with the eyes of an emperor, who must look far into the future."

"That's easy enough for you to say," her brother told her bitterly. "You won't be known as the one who lost this war."

"In the centuries to come, thanks to the changes and improvements that will be made here," Jonathan said boldly, "the Tao Kuang Emperor will be hailed as a great, far-seeing victor."

An Mien was grateful for his support. "You are wise beyond your years, Rakehell Jonathan," she said. "And now there is another matter we wish to discuss with you. Who is the foreign girl of great beauty who has come to the Forbidden City with you? She does not resemble Lai-tse lu, but in her own way her beauty is as great."

Surprised by her interest in Molinda, whom she apparently had learned about from her couriers, Jonathan quickly sketched the girl's background.

"Perhaps you would sell her to us," An Mien suggested.

"She is a free woman, so she cannot be bought or sold," he replied firmly. "Besides, a position of importance awaits

327

her." He went on to explain that he and Charles intended to offer her the managership of their Canton office and warehouse complex.

Sister and brother exchanged a long, significant look.

"She has a sound mind of her own?" the princess asked.

"I believe she knows more about the shipping business than any Fan Kuei in Whampoa!"

The emperor's eyes gleamed. "Wise as well as lovely," he muttered. "A rare combination."

Jonathan was afraid he would offer her a place among his concubines, which it would be impossible to refuse without offending him.

"Would this woman be able to do her work for you if she were married?" An Mien asked, reading his mind and speaking quickly to ease his fears.

"I don't see why she couldn't," Jonathan said, trying to conceal his astonishment. "But I know of no one who wants her as a wife." He wondered if the princess knew about Molinda's relationship with Charles and that he was not in a position to marry her.

"We do," the princess said, "if her virtues are equal to your praise of her."

The Celestial Emperor rubbed his hands together and laughed. "We shall soon find out."

An Mien explained to the American that they long had been searching for a wife for their cousin, Shaong Wei, and required someone who had a strong character as well as wisdom and beauty.

"I can't speak for Molinda," Jonathan said. "I honestly don't know how she might react. But I think I know her well enough to predict that she's eager to prove she can be successful in a man's world."

An Mien's eyes brightened. "That is the quality I most admire in her. Perhaps you will tell her of our talk so she will not be too surprised when I speak with her myself."

"Of course, ma'am."

The emperor rose abruptly, plodded to the sliding door, and vanished, and his sister paid no attention to his departure. "For a special reason, we shall meet again before you leave the Forbidden City, Rakehell Jonathan." He bowed, backed to the entrance, and there found his escort waiting to take him back to the guest house.

The emperor, Jonathan thought, in spite of his vast wealth and the absolute power he exercised, was a lonely man. Only by resorting to a clumsy subterfuge was it possible for him to enjoy even brief periods of normal relations with other people. It was small wonder that he knew so little about the world beyond the confines of his own realm.

Charles and Molinda were sitting together in the garden, both of them curious about his audience. Jonathan had no opportunity to speak privately with his cousin, so he went at once to the heart of the matter that concerned the girl.

"Molinda," he said, "I'm sure you know that Charles and I have been thinking for many days of offering you a position as the director of the Rakehell and Boynton interests in China. You would use the warehouses and offices in Canton that my wife has inherited from her father, and you could make your home in the house of Soong Chao."

"There is nothing more in all the world that I wish," she replied fervently.

"The reason I mention it now, instead of first making a final appraisal with Charles, is because a new element has been added." Jonathan told her in detail about the search the emperor and his sister had conducted in an attempt to find a wife for their cousin. "They think you might be the right woman for him," he went on, and repeated the conversation in the pagoda.

Molinda seemed to withdraw into a shell. Her eyes became veiled, her face showed no expression, and she sat very still.

Charles was astonished. "Are members of the imperial family allowed to marry commoners? And foreigners, at that?"

"Shaong Wei would retain his place as a mandarin, as I understand Chinese law," Jonathan said, "and his wife would automatically take his status. But he would be accorded no honors, and his children automatically would lose their rights to the imperial succession."

Molinda was looking off into space and gave no sign that she had heard him. Charles and Jonathan sympathized with her, realizing how severely she had been jolted.

What neither knew, however, was that her mind was clear, that she was sorting the thoughts racing through it. Not only was she being offered a business opportunity for which she had yearned, but there was a chance she might also achieve wealth and social standing beyond her dreams.

III

Molinda retired to her room in the guest house and remained isolated there for the rest of the day and night. Jonathan had a tray of food taken to her that evening, but she ate very little.

Neither Charles nor Jonathan could guess what was going through her mind, but they could not help speculating on the influence her marriage might have on their own business. "I should think," the young Englishman said, "that we'd rather quickly gain a bigger share of the China trade."

"Maybe, maybe not." Jonathan was more cautious. "You have a different tradition in England. Royalty make private investments. But it would be beneath the emperor and members of his family to engage in commerce because the ruler's status is regarded as divine."

"All the same, the association couldn't hurt us."

"Hardly. As the wife of the emperor's cousin, Molinda would outrank everyone in Kwangtung Province socially, even the imperial viceroy. I can see the distinct possibility that Chinese merchants might want to curry favor with her by offering her their best merchandise."

Charles grinned. "Well, I can think of at least a half-dozen companies that would wish themselves in our shoes."

"Not until I'm removed from the proscribed list. I'm afraid the Royal Navy may crack down completely on Rakehell and Boynton because of my guerrilla activities."

"The Admiralty doesn't have that much power. Besides, you misinterpret the British character, Jonnie. Once I've made it clear in the right places that you were fighting to avenge the death of your father-in-law, you'll be hailed in London as a hero." Charles's smile faded. "All that worries me is getting you out of China. With peace talks under way in Nanking, the better part of the British fleet will return to the Gulf of Canton— and the new anchorages at Hong Kong. Which will make it all that much more difficult for us to sneak out to sea in a ship as easily recognized as your clipper."

Before Jonathan could reply, Molinda came into the room, and both men wondered if it was a coincidence that she was wearing a skirt and breastband of yellow silk, with a cluster of miniature chrysanthemums in her hair. Surely she knew that yellow was the imperial color. Where she obtained this costume was also a mystery, but Jonathan and Charles well knew about Molinda's ingenuity and suspected she obtained it from one of the imperial servants.

Molinda gave them no clue of her thinking and instead peppered them with questions about the company's trade in the Orient. Replying in detail, the cousins realized that her grasp of their business affairs in the area was even greater than they had known.

"I have been wondering about the seagoing junks that Soong Chao sent to the Dutchman in Djakarta for safekeeping. When they're returned, after the peace treaty is signed, will they be placed in my charge?"

"I had almost forgotten the existence of the junks." Jonathan was a trifle sheepish. "Their voyages, between Chinese cities and to foreign ports like Bangkok and Manila, made up the better part of my father-in-law's business. If you could revive all that trade, it would be a magnificent achievement."

"It will not be as difficult as you may believe," she said, eager to meet the challenge.

The cousins exchanged a quick glance, and Charles said, "We'll give you a free hand, but you'll need to hire competent assistants if you're going to operate on that large a scale."

"What limits will you impose?" she demanded.

"None," Jonathan replied promptly. "In fact, if you're going to take on that heavy a burden, we'll need to work out some sort of profit-sharing agreement with you."

"I'll be satisfied with ten percent of the profits," she said, looking and sounding demure. "After all, you own the ships and the warehouses."

Her proposal was so fair they agreed to it without further

discussion Many details remained to be settled, but they were interrupted by an official in a yellow robe, who indicated that Molinda's presence was requested elsewhere.

"Perhaps I should change into something more suitable," she said.

"You are wanted now," the official replied, and led her off through the garden.

For years thereafter Jonathan and Charles wondered if she had purposely worn an imperial version of her own native attire On occasion, one or the other asked her outright if what she had done had been deliberate, but a small, slightly evasive smile was her only reply.

Certainly her manner was confident as she was taken to the pagoda where the Princess An Mien awaited her. She knew she was endowed with a rare beauty, and regardless of the outcome of the audience, her business future was assured. The years she had spent as a slave had sharpened her instinct, and she needed no prompting as she sank cross-legged to the tiles and gracefully touched her forehead to the floor.

An Mien had never seen a more attractive kowtow and was enchanted. She waved the visitor to a cushioned stool, then questioned her at length about her background. Molinda replied candidly, making no attempt to hide the less savory portions of her past

"And now you will work for Rakehell Jonathan in Canton," the princess said when she completed her recital.

"He will pay me, but I shall work for myself," Molinda said. "Someday I shall be the full partner of Jonathan and Charles."

An Mien made it plain that she approved but asked quietly, "Is there no place in your busy life for a husband?"

"That depends on the man," the girl said.

"I'll be as honest as you've been." The princess described her cousin's past addiction to liquor and her own conviction that a marriage to the right wife could make his cure permanent.

"Would I be blamed if he took to drink again?"

"No!" An Mien was equally blunt. "What's more, I give you my own word that, if you wished, the marriage would be annulled. So the risks you would take would be small, and the advantages of a marriage into my family—"

"Are obvious, Your Imperial Highness," Molinda said, interrupting softly. "Since yesterday, when Jonathan told me what you had in mind, I have thought of little else."

"Ah, then you agree to the marriage?"

"No, Your Imperial Highness."

An Mien was stunned.

"Surely," Molinda said, "no one could expect Shaong Wei or me to accept a marriage without first coming to know each other. What if one of us feels revulsion at first sight? What if he feels I am being substituted for the prison in which he was kept?"

An expression of grudging admiration crept into the princess's eyes. "You are truly wise and strong," she said. "I have spoken with many young women, and all would have married our cousin sight unseen." She laughed, then patted the girl's arm. "And you have courage! I like that! No one ever defies me here. Shaong Wei is already waiting to meet you, expecting that arrangements will be completed. How surprised he will be! I will send him to you at once!" She jumped to her feet and hurried off through the sliding door.

Molinda had not realized that the position she had taken would create such a strong impression on the princess. Sitting again on the cushioned stool, the girl folded her hands in her lap. She would satisfy her curiosity and would try to be open-minded. But the exciting business venture with Jonathan and Charles took precedence over everything else.

Suddenly a voice sounded behind her in a deep baritone. "You are Molinda?"

She had expected him to enter through the sliding door, but instead she saw a tall, broad-shouldered man with a chiseled face standing at the entrance to the pagoda. She felt her heart pounding as she replied, "You must be Shaong Wei." She curtsied but did not kowtow, making it plain that she would acknowledge no man as her superior.

He recognized the significance of her gesture and silently applauded it as he bowed to her. He hadn't believed she could be so independent, just as he had been skeptical of her ravishing beauty. He had been wrong on both counts. "I suggest a stroll in the garden," he said.

She detected a note of urgency in his voice, so she shrugged, then preceded him into the open.

"I hope it isn't too cool for you out here."

"Not at all."

"Good. Because the very walls in the Forbidden City have ears, and I dislike having every word we say to each other repeated to my cousins."

It had not occurred to Molinda that there might be eavesdroppers in the pagoda, and she laughed.

Shaong Wei chuckled, too, and the ice was broken. "This is very awkward, isn't it?"

"Embarrassing," she said. "I've been told all about you, and I'm sure you know my whole life story, too."

He nodded. "I feel like a champion racing stallion being paraded in front of a prized bred mare." He led her to a stone bench near a miniature waterfall and spread a large square of silk for her so she would not soil her skirt. "I suppose we ought to start by asking personal questions. You'll want to know why I almost drank myself to death."

His candor startled her. "If—if you want to talk about it."

"You have the right to know. You can't imagine how boring life can be for a member of the imperial family. One has no responsibilities. One has no duties other than to eat endless meals with relatives and gossip. Which concubine slept with the emperor last night. Which minister of state is being discharged because his last kowtow was slovenly. I would have enjoyed the life of a scholar, having studied the works of the Taoist philosophers and Confucius. But that would have been beneath the Manchu dignity. I developed a new type of printing press, but the eunuchs found my laboratory, and everything in it was destroyed. Instead I was given another concubine. I am making no excuses, but I hope you understand what I am trying to say."

Molinda found herself deeply touched. "I do understand. And I'm sorry."

Her unexpected sympathy disturbed Shaong Wei. "Tell me about this commercial enterprise you are entering," he said gruffly.

She told him about her arrangement with Jonathan and Charles, her enthusiasm surging as she talked.

"You have a right to be excited," he said. "I didn't

believe I would see the Middle Kingdom trading openly and freely with the outside world in my lifetime." He hesitated. "I would like to be of assistance to you."

"I'd welcome your help, your advice, and your judgment," she told him.

"That solves a great problem for me," Shaong Wei said. "If I had nothing to keep me occupied, I would want to drink again. But there will be much for me to learn before I can be of real help to you."

Molinda began to entertain the hope that their marriage might succeed. "Kai, who was the majordomo for Soong Chao, knows much about the business. I think he will agree to serve as my majordomo. That is important. He is a leader of a secret society—the Oxen—and I would ask him to hire the servants who would work for us."

Shaong Wei studied her with deepening respect. Finally he broke out into a broad grin.

Returning his smile, Molinda realized she hadn't expected him to be either personable or ruggedly handsome, but he was endowed with both qualities.

"It wouldn't be right to enter into a marriage in my wife's debt," he said. "How could I repay you?"

"Very simply," she replied. "In Bali, where I was born and reared, every husband has one wife, every wife has one husband. I am not lacking in vanity, and I would not be happy if you took additional wives."

"You have good cause for your vanity, and I assure you that one wife will be sufficient for me."

Molinda knew from his expression that he wanted her and that she would be receptive to his desire, but she still had point to make. "I was forced for too long to live as a concubine. My shame would overwhelm me if my husband needed concubines."

"I have known only concubines in my lifetime," Shaong Wei said gravely. "Until today I was afraid of marriage. I resented the idea, even though I have been weary of concubines. But you are even lovelier than I was told. With you as my wife, it would be easy to shun all other women."

Molinda heard the ring of sincerity in his voice. "Thank you."

"Marriage to me will not be easy, you know," he said earnestly. "I am a Manchu, so I am sometimes headstrong, and I know that on occasion I become arrogant."

"Well," she said, "I have a vile temper when I am crossed. I have been known to scream and curse, and in Djakarta I became so angry one day that I broke my favorite possession, a handsome porcelain jar "

"Perhaps we should have a special room in our house," Shaong Wei said with mock solemnity. "It should contain no furniture and no bric-a-brac We would use it only when we quarrel."

"That's a good idea, but I'd like to amend it." Molinda became bolder. "There should be one piece of furniture in the room—a bed."

He grinned, then sobered. "It was Confucius who first wrote that a husband and wife can solve all of their differences in bed. But I don't think he made the discovery himself He must have learned it from his wife." He took her hand and held it firmly.

"When is it planned that we be married?"

"I suppose An Mien has made all of the plans. She will tell the Tao Kuang Emperor, and he, in turn, will tell us "

"Must we have a large wedding?"

"I would like nothing better than to be married in private I've been the disgrace of my family for years, and I know what they would be whispering behind my back."

"Well, I know no one in Peking other than Jonathan and Charles. As one who had to live for too long as a concubine, I feel that a large and gaudy wedding would be a mockery "

He thought for a moment, and then his eyes sparkled "In the Forbidden City there are at least fifty temples. Perhaps one hundred. At any hour of the day or night one can find a priest at prayer. And being a Manchu does have advantages. Members of the imperial family do not need witnesses when they marry."

Molinda caught her breath. "That would be perfect!"

"Then we shall have it that way!" He stood, lifted her to her feet, and they walked together through the garden, their hands entwined

The Princess An Mien watched them from a nearby tower window. Guessing their intent when she saw them enter a

336

small temple at the far end of the garden, she smiled quietly. The couple had chosen wisely, on their own initiative, with no outside pressures, no hints or nudges from anyone, and as a consequence their future appeared even brighter than she had dared to hope.

Tao Kuang would be furious, of course, because he thoroughly enjoyed presiding at family weddings, which was one of the traditional prerogatives of his exalted rank. But it would not be too difficult to convince him that Shaong Wei and Molinda had been sensible, that an extravagant wedding would have been in poor taste at a time when Great Britain was forcing the Middle Kingdom to accept a peace treaty that the entire nation would regard as degrading.

At least she had done her share, An Mien reflected. The success or failure of the marriage would be the responsibility of Shaong Wei and his exotic, surprisingly intelligent bride.

Molinda did not return to the guest house after her audience with the princess, and not until that evening were Jonathan and Charles informed that she was now married. "I wish her every happiness," Jonathan said. "She deserves it."

Charles was relieved because he was no longer responsible for her. "I just hope her husband doesn't interfere with her work for us," he said. "We couldn't have found a better representative in Canton anywhere, and it will do us no harm to have someone who knows the Fat Dutchman's methods handling the better portion of our trade with him."

The next morning, after breakfast, they discussed the future with Kai. "Molinda knows much about trade and shipping," Jonathan said, "but she is still a foreigner in this land, so she will need guidance. And I doubt if there will be much her new husband can do for her. As a member of the imperial family, he is totally ignorant of all business matters."

Kai nodded calmly. "It is your wish that I work with them, as I worked with Soong Chao."

"There's nothing we'd like better," Jonathan told him.

"It will not be easy for me to take orders from a woman," the burly majordomo declared. "And a cousin of the Celestial Emperor could cause many problems if he decided to take charge. But for the sake of Lai-tse lu—and for your sake—I will do it. You are my only family."

The cousins were grateful to him.

"First," he said, "a way must be found for Jonathan to leave the Middle Kingdom in safety. More and more British warships will be gathering in the South China Sea, and if they see your clipper ship under sail, they will do their best to capture or kill you."

"We'll have to take our chances." Jonathan was confident that, given a good start, he could outsail any ship in the Royal Navy.

Kai shook his head. "No," he said. "Another way must be found." He refused to explain his cryptic remark.

In spite of the luxury of their surroundings, time passed slowly for Jonathan and Charles. They had little to occupy their time, and because they were foreigners, they were not permitted to visit the Great Wall or see any of Peking's other sights. After another forty-eight hours, Charles became impatient. "How much longer must we remain here? You know more about Chinese protocol than I do, but I don't see why you couldn't send word to the emperor that we're anxious to take our leave."

"That would be considered an insult to his hospitality," Jonathan said. "I'm sure An Mien has valid reasons of her own for this delay."

His guess proved accurate. The following morning he was summoned to the pagoda on the far side of the garden wall and found the princess waiting for him.

"I know how eager you must be to rejoin your wife and family," she said, "but it was necessary to make special arrangements before you could leave. Actually you will save much time."

Jonathan smiled in gratitude and waited for an explanation.

"The British have been notified by our representatives at the conference in Nanking," she said, "that our cousin, Shaong Wei, will soon travel to Canton with his bride in an imperial junk. The British Navy will respect the dragon banner that the junk will fly, and she will not be boarded. You also will be on board, and will be transported safely to your clipper's hiding place."

The plan was as clever as it was simple, and Jonathan laughed in admiration. Instead of making another long overland march, he could sail to his immediate destination in a relatively few days.

The sliding door opened, and the Tao Kuang Emperor, looking weary and grim, came into the pagoda. The American knew better than to look at him or otherwise acknowledge his presence.

"Have you told him?" The emperor's manner was brusque as he addressed his sister.

"Certainly not!" An Mien retorted. "You know I never interfere with your prerogatives."

The slightly built man nodded absently, and instead of sitting unobtrusively, as he had done in the past, he walked directly to the visitor and stood in front of him. The startled Jonathan rose to his feet, uncertain of what was expected of him.

The emperor hauled off his jewel-studded headgear. "At a moment such as this I must dispense with subterfuge," he said. "I do not speak to you as the Divine Ruler of Rulers. It is Tao Kuang, a man ignorant of the world beyond the borders of his own realm, who addresses the good friend of his nation."

The relieved Jonathan wanted to extend his hand but remembered in time that no man was permitted to touch the person of the emperor.

"You are truly my friend and the friend of my people," the Tao Kuang Emperor declared. "So I can tell you in confidence what I cannot reveal even to my ministers of state. If I had known the British possessed such powerful weapons and ships, I would not have gone to war with them. I have been humiliated because of my ignorance, and it is a lesson I do not intend to learn a second time. It is my duty to lead the Middle Kingdom into the modern world."

"I'm sure you won't regret it, sir," the impressed Jonathan replied.

"For all time I—and those who come after me—will regret that our centuries of innocence have come to an end. But I know now that the nation that fails to advance will perish. The Middle Kingdom has more people, more land, and more resources than any other nation on earth. The people must be educated and the resources must be marshaled so we can take our proper place among the great."

An Mien long had preached the need for modernization to

her brother and was pleased by his new sense of determination.

"Soon the ships of many nations will come to our ports, but most will be greedy men I cannot trust. I know of only one in whom I have unlimited faith. The son-in-law of Soong Chao, the husband of Lai-tse lu, who has shed his blood in an attempt to drive the invader from our shores."

Jonathan recognized the effort that this proud monarch's confession required and was touched by it.

"You go now to your own land, but you leave the bride of Shaong Wei to act in your place. And it is my deep hope that you will return often to the Middle Kingdom and that your children will follow you here."

"I shall return often," Jonathan said solemnly, "and I will teach my children to love this land as Lai-tse lu and I love it."

"We will bind our friendship with an exchange of gifts, a custom as old as the Middle Kingdom itself." Tao Kuang reached into a pocket of his robe and drew out a tiny sack of yellow silk, which he dropped into the visitor's hand.

Jonathan bowed, opened the bag, and blinked at the object he held in his hand. It was a black pearl, gleaming and flawless, its sheen exquisite, its size that of a bird's egg.

"You will give the pearl to Lai-tse lu," An Mien said, "with the love of the Tao Kuang Emperor and his sister."

Still numb, Jonathan could only shake his head. "I'm more grateful than I can tell you," he said, "but I cannot accept a gift of such priceless value. You said we would exchange gifts, but there is nothing I can give you that would equal the worth of this pearl."

Tao Kuang chuckled. "Place the pearl in your pocket and take care not to lose it. Lai-tse lu will wear it with great enjoyment."

Jonathan didn't want to be rude but felt he had no choice. "I don't know how many of my finest clipper ships I would have to sell in order to equal the price of this pearl."

The Tao Kuang's expression became grave. "Pearls and diamonds and gold are mere objects. The palaces of the Forbidden City overflow with my treasures, but they could not prevent the British from inflicting a shameful defeat on us. I ask of you a prize far greater than the worth of this pearl." He paused, then said slowly, "I ask you for that which is worth more than all else in the world. I ask you for knowledge.''

Those in the West who regarded the emperor as a backward man were badly mistaken, Jonathan thought.

"Send me books that will tell us how we can best use our water power and our coal. Send me the plans that will make it possible for us to build factories like those in your world. Send us models of the boats that are propelled by steam and would be useful on our rivers. Send me plows that will make it possible for our farmers to obtain a better yield from our ancient soil. Send me modern cannon and other weapons so we may copy them and be better able to protect ourselves from predators in the years ahead. Send me medicines and instruments used by your physicians to heal the sick Send me books—and more books—and more books. Ask your government for the right to send our brightest young scholars to your universities so they may learn the ways that will enable us to leap forward through the ages into the modern world. Do these things, and your gift will be worth more than all the treasures that are stored in my palaces!''

"I'll do all you ask, sir, to the best of my ability " Jonathan's voice was husky.

"You are indeed my friend." The Tao Kuang Emperor turned away abruptly and went off through the sliding door that led to his private quarters.

"It was Lai-tse lu who first whetted our appetites for the learning of the West by sending us books and other publications," An Mien said. "It is good to know that her husband will join in this enterprise. The Middle Kingdom will be in your debt until the end of time."

"I'm honored by the obligation you have given me," Jonathan replied.

Her mood changed, and she smiled. "See to it that you reach America safely."

"I'll do my best."

"And tell Lai-tse lu how much I look forward to my next meeting with her—and with your children." The princess rose, inclined her head slightly, and followed her brother through the sliding door.

Jonathan's mind whirled as the escort took him back to the guest house.

Charles listened openmouthed to his cousin's account of

the audience. "This pearl is priceless," he said, "but the emperor is right. You'll be doing far more for China by helping her enter the modern world. And," he added with a broad grin, "Rakehell and Boynton won't suffer. We've already won more favors than the Royal Navy and Army could wrench from the Chinese in a hundred years!"

Their talk was interrupted by Kai, who informed them they would leave Peking at once. They quickly packed their few belongings, and the black-clad guards of the Society of Oxen surrounded them as they walked through the Forbidden City, the outer Imperial City, and the sprawling community beyond the high walls.

When they reached the open countryside, they found one thousand yellow-clad horsemen awaiting them, and they were given mounts of their own. Then another large party of cavalrymen approached, and in the center of the formation, riding in a gold-encrusted chariot, were Shaong Wei, who held the reins, and a cheongsam-clad Molinda, who waved animatedly. There was no opportunity for conversation because neither the chariot nor the horsemen halted, and the group provided for the protection of the two Fan Kuei fell in behind them.

They rode all day, halting before sundown in a dusty, open field. Then tents made of double layers of silk were erected, one for the imperial kinsman and his bride, the other for the two foreigners. Cooks set up portable charcoal braziers, and the elaborate meal they prepared was an indication of the luxurious life the girl would lead.

Jonathan was favorably impressed by Shaong Wei's diffidence and his determination to make useful contributions to his wife's vocation. At first Charles was embarrassed by the presence of the husband of the young woman who had been his mistress, but it soon became obvious that Molinda and Shaong Wei had a deep respect for each other, so he was able to join in the conversation without feeling inhibited.

That night the cousins slept on thick mattresses covered with silken cushions, and early the next morning orderlies assigned to attend to their comforts brought them steaming basins of water for washing and shaving. "Molinda shouldn't find it too difficult to become accustomed to an imperial existence," Charles said with a chuckle.

Again they rode for the better part of the day, arriving

before sundown at the port of the town of Tientsin. Looking at the ancient fort that guarded the waterfront, Jonathan was bemused by the stone dragons, leopards, and lions that studded the outer walls. These creatures, along with the huge stone head of a tortoise, the symbol of immortality, had been erected to protect the defenders from their enemies. But they would have been no more effective in battle than the rusted cannon, some of them one thousand years old, that jutted out toward the sea. Had the British elected to attack Tientsin, their guns would have reduced the old fort to rubble

Tiny sampans awaited the travelers, including the Society of Oxen guards, and they were rowed out to the waiting imperial junk. Jonathan and Charles were fascinated by the single oar, wider than the little sampan itself, that the boat's rower manipulated at the end of a long pole held in place at the stern by a device somewhat similar to an oarlock. The man appeared to exert little effort, but the craft darted swiftly across the placid waters of the harbor.

The imperial junk, with its abnormally high poop and square bows, rode at anchor, its lugsails furled, and the master, in a gold-trimmed uniform of yellow, greeted his passengers as they came on board. Two very large cabins were located side by side at the stern, and the two Westerners, accustomed to the cramped quarters of their own ships, looked around their cabin in astonishment. The bulkheads were finished with wallpaper of silk damask, and scrolls of thick, embroidered silk could be lowered over the square windows to keep out daylight. The furniture included two full-sized divans, a table with dragon feet, and several comfortable three-legged stools. Fresh flowers rested in vases of priceless porcelain, and Charles whistled softly when he found a charcoal brazier that could be used to heat the cabin in cold weather.

"Build a cabin like this for me in my next clipper, Jonnie," he said, "and I'll never come ashore."

The cousins went to the deck to watch the sailing, and found the crew of thirty divided into three units, each commanded by a junior officer. No orders, as such, were given. The captain began to chant, the junior officers picked up the refrain, and the sails, made of matting stiffened with horizontal battens, were raised simultaneously on the two masts. Then the anchor was weighed, and at the same time three seamen who required no instructions lowered a very large, clumsy-looking rudder by spinning a large wooden wheel.

"Amazing," Charles said as the sails picked up the wind and the junk began to move briskly out of the harbor. "She must have a deadweight of close to four thousand tons, but her bottom is flat and she has no keel. I'm surprised her master can sail her."

"Don't let her appearance fool you," Jonathan told him. "The Chinese and Javanese have been using junks for hundreds of years. They're as seaworthy as any schooner, and they ride out storms in comfort. I made two voyages on junks during the year I worked with Soong Chao, and after I rid myself of my prejudices, I was impressed. They go everywhere in these waters, from the Philippine Islands to the Netherlands East Indies to India, and they carry enormous cargoes. They have only two drawbacks. They can't be maneuvered quickly to take advantage of shifting winds, and they're even slower than our brigs of the last century."

"Well, Jonnie, if our civilization was as old as that of the Chinese, perhaps we wouldn't be in such a hurry, either."

They remained on deck, watching the master, ruddermen, and sailing crew, until a servant summoned them to a cabin amidships. There they joined Molinda and Shaong Wei for a sumptuous repast that included lobster and shrimp, mussels and crabmeat, as well as chicken, beef, and pork dishes. As they ate heartily with their chopsticks, Shaong Wei asked if anyone knew why Chinese food always was cut into small pieces.

"I've always assumed it's made bite-sized for the sake of convenience," Jonathan said.

"That is an extra benefit. Ever since the times of the ancients there has been a shortage of firewood and other fuel in most parts of the Middle Kingdom. It was discovered, thousands of years ago, that food cooks more quickly when it is cut into small pieces, so less fuel is consumed."

"You know so much about so many things," Molinda said admiringly.

Her bridegroom shrugged. "Reading was a way of saving my sanity for many years. Now I hope I can use some of my accumulated knowledge."

"I'm sure there will be endless opportunities," Jonathan

assured him, and he was certain that Shaong Wei would be a valuable asset to Rakehell and Boynton.

Occasionally, in the days that followed, British warships were sighted as the junk headed southward down the China coast. At Kai's insistence the American and the Englishman went below until the Royal Navy vessels vanished over the horizon. "The glasses their officers use are very powerful," he said, "and even though we fly the dragon pennant of the Celestial Emperor, I am sure they would not hesitate to halt us and search us if their glasses revealed two Fan Kuei on board."

There were no other restrictions on their activities. At meals, in response to Molinda's request, they told Shaong Wei at length and in depth about the various operations of Rakehell and Boynton. Charles felt challenged by the junk and spent long hours with the ship's master, learning how to sail the vessel. Jonathan practiced each day with his Javanese throwing knives and, feeling the need for more violent physical exercise, engaged in bouts of wrestling and other martial arts with Kai.

The crew was delighted and most happily placed wagers on Kai, certain he would defeat the Fan Kuei. But they soon learned, to their chagrin, that the two contestants were more or less equal. Neither was able to achieve a decided advantage.

One afternoon, as the pair was finishing a wrestling match on a padded mat that had been spread on the sunny deck, Shaong Wei and Molinda came into the open, and the bridegroom watched the match closely.

"Kai," he said after they were done, "if you aren't too tired, try me." Not waiting for a reply, he stripped off his shirt.

A lifetime of obedience to the decrees of the Celestial Emperor caused Kai to hesitate.

Shaong Wei knew what was going through his mind and deliberately taunted him. "Are you afraid of me?"

"I fear no man," Kai replied.

They began to circle each other warily, the muscles in their arms, shoulders, and backs rippling.

The crew who were not otherwise occupied gathered to watch the emperor's cousin in personal combat. They well knew they were seeing a legend in the making.

Jonathan pulled on his shirt, standing beside Molinda,

and reflected that although Shaong Wei was young and husky, his courage was greater than his judgment.

The contestants came together at the center of the mat, then crashed to the deck, each trying to obtain a grip that would enable him to press his opponent's nose against the mat for no less than a slow count of five.

Molinda obviously disliked violence but couldn't help watching the man she had so unexpectedly come to care for, the back of one hand pressed against her mouth.

Jonathan had to revise his estimate. Shaong Wei was quicker, stronger, and more experienced than he had thought and was holding his own.

Sweat poured off the bodies of both contestants as they struggled. Twice Kai was on the verge of achieving victory, but the first time his opponent cleverly slid out of his grasp, and the second time, in an impressive exhibition, Shaong Wei used brute force to escape.

All at once Kai collapsed onto the mat.

The young nobleman was furious. "May the fires of dragons consume your children before they are born!" he shouted. "You deliberately allowed me to win!"

Kai's shrug was polite, indicating his belief that he had been given no real choice.

"Have you ever known a god to sweat?" Shaong Wei demanded angrily. "I am no god. I am a man!" Not waiting for a reply, he grappled again with the husky majordomo.

This time both men tried in earnest, thrashing wildly, then using cunning rather than strength to win the day.

"Why don't you go below?" Jonathan asked Molinda, who looked as though she might faint. Unable to speak, she could only shake her head.

Neither contestant could gain the upper hand, and the match might have gone on indefinitely if a strong offshore wind had not caused the junk to pitch and roll.

Jonathan was afraid the unpredictable turbulence could cause serious injury, so he intervened, clapping both men on the shoulders. "The match is a draw!" he announced firmly. "The way this ship is bobbing, one of you may break an arm or a leg!"

The contestants reluctantly drew apart, and when they grinned at each other with mutual respect, Jonathan was reminded of the fight he had once had with Lo Fang, which had caused him and the viceroy's majordomo to become friends.

"You're the best I've ever fought," Shaong Wei said.

"You may be as good a fighter as Jonathan," Kai replied.

"We'll finish this tomorrow, and the winner will meet him the next day."

Kai eagerly agreed, as did Jonathan.

"No," Molinda said sharply. "I forbid it!"

The men stared at her for a moment, then began to laugh.

"In this matter you have no choice," her husband told her, his voice gentle but firm. "The challenges have been issued and accepted."

Not until she thought about the problem at length did Molinda realize that Shaong Wei was right. He was winning acceptance as an equal in a man's world because of his masculinity, and his blood relationship with the Celestial Emperor was irrelevant. She had no right to interfere and knew she should be grateful for the niche he was carving for himself.

She absented herself from the subsequent matches, in which all three contestants suffered bruises and enjoyed themselves. Perhaps, as Charles later remarked, it was just as well that there was no single winner. "All I know is that I'd hate to face any one of you in a real fight. As for you, Molinda, with your husband and Kai to protect you, no harm will ever come to you!"

On three different evenings the junk slipped into small ports for supplies of fresh meats and vegetables, with the two white men prudently remaining out of sight. The ship's master was unwilling to predict the overall length of the voyage because, as Shaong Wei explained, he was afraid he would lose face if a storm blew up or a British warship caused an unexpected delay.

This was just one minor example, Jonathan reflected, of why bringing China into the modern world would be even more difficult than he had anticipated. An entire nation's way of thinking had to be changed.

Before dinner on the eleventh day of the voyage, Kai came to the two Fan Kuei. "We will go ashore tomorrow before dawn," he said. "Bid farewell tonight to Shaong Wei and his wife and do not worry about them. I will join them in Canton as soon as I have seen you safely on your voyage to

America, and until then they will be under the constant protection of the Oxen."

Jonathan broke the news to Molinda and her husband at dinner. "As soon as I reach New England," he said, "I'll start sending packages and crates to the Princess An Mien. There will be packages for her on every ship we send to the Orient, and their contents will be more valuable than any cargo. Make certain they reach her in the Forbidden City."

Molinda assured him that every precaution would be taken, and showed great delicacy by not asking the contents of the packages.

"How will you avoid the ships of the British when you put out to sea?" Shaong Wei wanted to know

Jonathan shrugged. "We'll need to learn where the Royal Navy fleet is patrolling. Then we'll find some way to evade them."

"I've been thinking of confronting Pottinger when he returns to Hong Kong," Charles said. "They had no right to put you on a proscribed list."

"Right or wrong, I'm on it," Jonathan replied with grim humor. "I suggest, urgently, that you save your arguments until you're back in London."

They lingered for a long time at the dinner table, and Molinda's parting words were succinct. "You will never be sorry you have given me the responsibility of directing your operations in the East," she said. "And I promise you, too, that you will not be sorry I have married Shaong Wei. No others, not even the great East India Companies of Great Britain and the Netherlands, will know the success and prestige that Rakehell and Boynton will enjoy."

Jonathan and Charles slept for only a few hours. Then they arose, dressed in black, and after checking their weapons, went to the deck. There Kai and the guards of the Oxen, all similarly clad, awaited them. The night was dark, with thick clouds hiding the moon and stars. A fine rain was falling, the water was tranquil, and the usual fog that rolled in every morning and evening made it difficult to see more than a short distance.

But the cousins realized instantly that the imperial junk had reduced her speed considerably, and Jonathan peered through the gloom, then said, "We're only a few hundred yards off shore."

Kai was astonished. "How do you know this when you cannot see that far?"

"Spend enough time at sea," the American told him, "and you learn to smell land."

No one knew when a British warship might loom up unexpectedly, so there was little further conversation. Ultimately the junk's master lighted an oil lantern, attached it to a pole, and held it over his head for a few moments.

All at once a tiny, answering gleam flickered about two hundred yards to the right and perhaps one hundred feet ahead of the vessel.

The navigation of the Chinese captain has been remarkable, Jonathan reflected.

The junk's anchor was lowered silently, the chains having been passed over heavy matting to achieve that end. Kai moved to the starboard rail, and the cousins followed him.

Jonathan was the first to see activity in the water, and a moment later Charles glanced at him and nodded. Together they watched a small fleet of sampans being poled quietly toward the junk.

As the lead boat drew nearer, a rope ladder was lowered over the side, and Kai's gesture indicated that Jonathan was to have the honor of being the first to leave.

The American descended hand over hand, and as he dropped into the sampan, a smiling Lo Fang stood beside him. Two of the Oxen came down the ladder, and the little boat headed toward the evergreens and bamboo thickets on shore. Others were picked up, a few at a time, the boats returning to the junk in a steady procession until the entire party had been removed.

Total silence was maintained until the junk weighed anchor and slipped off into the fog. Jonathan and Charles stood on the shore and noted that the sampans were vanishing, one by one, after discharging the last of their passengers. It was impossible to guess where they were headed, but Jonathan knew they would be concealed in places where they would not be seen by British warships on patrol when the weather cleared.

Lo Fang led the party a short distance inland, where a charcoal fire glowed in a pit that had been dug in a clearing.

Here the arriving travelers were given a breakfast of rice, pork, and mung bean cakes, served with large mugs of steaming, fragrant tea. Jonathan discovered he was ravenous, and he enjoyed the meal immensely.

Lo Fang and Kai ate apart from the others, conferring in voices so low that it was impossible to hear anything they said to each other. Lo Fang did most of the talking, Kai interrupting from time to time with questions. Apparently he liked what he heard because both men were smiling when they rejoined the group. Kai gestured that the march was to resume.

They made their way quietly through thick foliage, and it was plain to Jonathan that no path existed in this underbrush. Occasionally Lo Fang, who was in the lead, slashed at a bush that contained brambles. Then, suddenly the leader of the Oxen halted, and his curved sword flashed in the half-light as he struck hard at a thick vine hanging from an overhead branch.

Jonathan was astonished when the "vine" dropped to the ground, writhing convulsively. Lo Fang had decapitated a silvery green snake six to eight feet long, its diameter the size of a man's wrist.

Paying no further attention to the serpent he had rendered harmless, Lo Fang coolly continued his advance.

The fog continued to dissipate as the morning grew brighter, then began to burn away when the sun rose. Jonathan could not recall when the mistlike rain had stopped falling.

His sense of direction came to his rescue, and he realized the landing had been made at the northern end of the twin islands that concealed the bay in which the *Lai-tse lu* was hidden. Apparently his precious clipper ship was still safe.

Bamboo thickets were everywhere now, but Lo Fang took care not to cut any of them down, obviously wanting to preserve the natural wilderness of this harbor.

At last the evergreens, oaks, and bamboo thinned, and Jonathan followed Lo Fang to the edge of a cliff. In the early morning light he saw his clipper lying at anchor in the calm waters of the harbor, her masts stripped. He had never seen such a welcome sight.

Then he blinked in amazement, looked again, and couldn't believe what he saw. Beyond the *Lai-tse lu* swarms of black-clad men were working on the deck of a second clipper that was her precise duplicate! Some were sawing wood, others sewing canvas, and still more were busy painting.

Charles came up beside his cousin, and he gaped, too. "Good Lord!" he said in awe. "There must be a thousand men there. And unless I've suddenly gone mad, they're building a precise replica of the finest clipper ship on earth."

Jonathan's bewilderment grew as he watched the hundreds of black-clad figures at work. Then he turned to Lo Fang.

The leader of the Society of Oxen was enjoying himself, as was Kai. Grinning broadly but offering no explanation, Lo Fang beckoned, then led the party down a narrow path that led to the base of the cliff.

There the gig from the *Lai-tse lu* was waiting, and an overjoyed Oliver greeted the man responsible for his own rise in the world. "Mr. Rakehell," he said, "I never thought I'd see you again in this world!"

Jonathan and Charles were rowed to the clipper, where Homer Ellison and his officers awaited them. The normally restrained Homer gave in to his emotions, and his voice was husky as he said, "The Almighty has watched over you, Jonnie," and the usually undemonstrative crew, who clustered behind him, broke into spontaneous applause.

Their cheers were still ringing in Jonathan's ears as he led the way to the far rail and pointed toward the small army of Chinese workers who were building the clipper's exact duplicate. "What in the name of all that's holy is going on yonder?" he demanded.

Homer laughed, as did the ship's mates. "Blamed if we know, Jonnie. Lo Fang has refused to explain. All I can tell you is that they started construction only four days ago, laying a keel on the mainland. I've never in all my born days seen anything like it. One crew of workers starts at dawn and goes until dusk, and then hundreds more take their place and work all night."

Jonathan peered more intently at the other ship. "Is their construction work sound?"

"I haven't been allowed to board her," Homer replied, "but I've had almost nothing to do in all the time we've been in this concealed harbor, so I've been watching them pretty carefully. I wouldn't swear the ship would hang together and stay in one piece during a bad blow, but I reckon she could sail a reasonable distance in fair weather."

Jonathan restrained his curiosity, knowing Lo Fang and Kai would reveal the mystery to him at the appropriate time His long stay in China had changed him for the better, he realized, and he no longer suffered from the lack of patience that sometimes had handicapped him.

Homer insisted on vacating the master's cabin for him, and Charles moved into one of the passenger cabins. On this extraordinary clipper, the quarters were ample. That noon, at dinner, Jonathan ate his first Western-cooked meal in many months, and although the fare was plain, he relished it.

"The Chinese have kept us well supplied with meat, vegetables, and fruit," Homer said. "They've always seemed to know when we've started to run low And just yesterday they began to bring us provisions for a voyage Salt fish, smoked meat, and the like, along with barrels of that tomato sauce they use."

"That sounds to me as though they're expecting us to put out to sea soon," Charles said

"Seems like it," Homer said with a shrug.

Lo Fang and Kai did not interrupt Jonathan's reunion with his close associates until mid-morning of the next day, when hundreds of workers stepped the duplicate clipper's distinctive masts, raising and making them secure in an amazingly short time. "Perhaps," Lo Fang said as he boarded the clipper, "you would like to visit the new *Lai-tse lu* now."

Jonathan, Charles, and Homer eagerly went with him in the sampan that crossed the harbor quickly, and when they inspected the new vessel, they discovered at once that although she bore a remarkable surface resemblance to the original clipper, her interior was unfinished. There were no cabins or cuddy, no crew quarters, and in her rough-hewn hold were heavy rocks that provided ballast.

Kai, who had been supervising the workers' efforts, joined the group on deck as they completed their tour. "What do you think of her?" he asked.

Jonathan hesitated for a moment. "I don't want to hurt your feelings," he said. "But I'd sail in her as far as Formosa, maybe as far as Djakarta, only if I knew the sea would be calm and the winds fair. She looks like my ship, but I'm afraid she'd come apart at the seams in a storm.''

"What is important," Lo Fang said, "is that she resembles your clipper in every outer detail. Do you see any differences?''

"None," Jonathan replied "The resemblance is almost miraculous.''

The two Chinese were satisfied, and Lo Fang suggested they go ashore for a private talk. He and Kai rowed the sampan themselves and led the three Westerners to a fire at the base of the mainland cliff, where tea brewed day and night in large kettles for the workers' consumption.

"We have worried that the British might capture you," Lo Fang said "They could identify your ship at once, and they would know she has not sailed back to America already, as they were led to believe So a special plan was made. In the weeks of your journey to Peking and your return to this place, a close watch has been kept on the English sloops that patrol the coast ''

"They are swift, and their guns are powerful," Kai added, "but our weapons are more powerful.''

"At this time of the year," Lo Fang said, "a thick mist creeps in from the sea at dawn and at sundown. Only moments before the fog rolls in, a British sloop passes no more than a mile from the channel that leads to the sea. On the day after tomorrow, those who sail in the sloop will see a great clipper ship, and that could only be the *Lai-tse lu*, making her way out to sea. They will give chase, of course ''

All at once Jonathan understood "Now I see! While they chase the phantom clipper, we'll leave via the channel, take a different course, and be on our way home!''

The two leaders of the Society of Oxen exchanged proud glances and nodded.

"The scheme is fairly sound," Charles said, "but there is one flaw in it. If the sloop overtakes the duplicate ship, her commander will learn, even in a fog, that he's been fooled deliberately. He might suspect what's happened, and if he fires his signal guns, the sea soon would be filled with other patrol ships.''

"That will not happen," Kai said, "for reasons you will

be told before you sail. Be prepared to begin your voyage on the day after tomorrow at sundown.''

Jonathan knew they had to be satisfied, and he agreed at once. ''If it weren't for you two,'' he said, ''I'd have died long ago. I have faith in your judgment and plans.''

More provisions reached the clipper that same afternoon, and her crew, bored after weeks of doing nothing, went to work in earnest to prepare for the long-delayed voyage. The cargo of precious pepper, safe in casks sealed with heavy wax, had shifted somewhat and had to be removed, then stored again. Barnacles were scraped from the hull, the mates and sailmaker carefully inspected the sails, and paint supplied by the Chinese was used to change her color from a gleaming white to a dull gray. Now she would blend with the fog and would be far more difficult to see.

As the time for departure drew near, the decoy clipper was hauled through the channel by hundreds of workers lining both banks, and then the *Lai-tse lu*, her masts still bare, was dragged into a position astern of her.

Lo Fang and Kai came on board for a final farewell. ''My brothers,'' Jonathan told them, ''you will be ever-present in my mind. Lo Fang, I pray that living conditions in the Middle Kingdom soon will improve. Kai, we will correspond often you see to the needs of Molinda and Shaong Wei.''

They exchanged bows, then shook hands in the Western manner, and Kai lingered behind for a moment before going ashore. ''Until the end of your days, Rakehell Jonathan,'' he said, ''you will belong to the Society of Oxen, as will the son who comes after you.'' He handed his friend a small object, then hurried ashore.

Jonathan looked hard at the pair of tiny, carved wooden oxen that nestled in the palm of his hand. As long as he lived, they would be a symbol to him of man's unquenchable yearning for personal liberty.

The sails on the decoy clipper were hoisted, and the group on the quarterdeck of the *Lai-tse lu* watched in wonder as score of barrels of gunpowder were placed on the replica' deck, with a long fuse that extended from the rail to the midst of the barrels. Then a small boat was hoisted to the deck, the clipper's sails were unfurled, and she was hauled to the channel entrance, with the *Lai-tse lu* moving up

"I wouldn't believe it if I weren't seeing it happen myself," Jonathan said.

"Incredible," Charles murmured. "They're leaving only four men on board. They'll put out to sea, light the fuse, and escape in the boat while the decoy is blown to kingdom come."

"They're the most ingenious people on earth," Jonathan said. "Now you know why I'm convinced that no nation on earth will ever conquer China."

Oliver reported that the watch were at their stations. Jonathan assumed command of his ship, with Charles and Homer acting as his mates. The permanent mates took command of gun crews fore and aft; if the ruse failed they were prepared, if necessary, to fight for their freedom.

The decoy ship moved gracefully out to sea, her sails filling as she headed toward the southeast through the calm, open water.

"We'll set a course to the northeast," Jonathan said.

The decoy passed from sight behind the screen of high trees that sheltered the channel.

No more than a quarter of an hour later the fog came in from the sea, growing thicker by the minute. By now, if all had gone according to plan, the decoy had been sighted by the British sloop of war on patrol nearby and was being chased.

"Loose and make all plain sail!" Jonathan ordered. "Haul aft the sheets! Away aloft! Man tops'l sheets! Haul taut!"

The great clipper nosed out of the channel, picked up the wind, and her speed increasing swiftly, sailed toward the northeast.

"Let fall tops'ls and courses!" Jonathan commanded. "Sheet home!"

The yards were braced, and the course was set.

The fog was so thick now that the tense group on the quarterdeck could no longer see the moonsails and skysails high above them. There was no conversation, no sound but the creaking of the clipper, the lapping of water against her hull as she cut her way through the sea.

Another quarter of an hour passed, then yet another, and suddenly the silence was broken by a reverberating roar that sounded like the firing of a salvo. Moments later a dull red glow appeared far to the south, cutting through the fog.

Everyone on board the clipper knew that the decoy had

served her purpose. The hard labor that had gone into her construction had not been in vain, and she was burning fiercely, destroyed by the discharge of the powder on her deck.

Jonathan felt confident that the four men of her phantom crew had slipped away in their boat and were safe.

Night came, the heavy mist began to dissipate, and gradually the sky filled with stars. The lookout in the masthead reported there was no sign of another ship anywhere. The ruse had succeeded, and the great clipper was safely on her way home.

Book
V

I

The group that stood on shore eagerly searched the deck of the incoming clipper ship, looking for the faces of loved ones, and suddenly Julian Rakehell shouted exuberantly. "I see Papa!" he screamed, jumping up and down. "There he is!"

Jonathan grinned broadly, waving his hat to his son, studying the tiny face of the little girl who stood silently, clutching her mother's hand, then settling on Lai-tse lu. Even at a distance she was lovely beyond compare, but something about her was different, and at last he realized she was wearing Western-style dress.

The great ship maneuvered into her berth, dockhands made her fast, and Jonathan leaped onto the wharf.

His feet pounding on the wooden planks, Julian raced forward. "Papa! Papa!"

Jonathan lifted him high into the air, hugged him, and looked at him hard. "Well, son," he said. "You've grown a lot. But I'd have known you anywhere."

His attention was distracted when he felt something tugging at his trousers, and looked down to see Jade, her eyes wide. "Papa," she said, imitating her brother

Her father was stunned by her rare beauty. She was the image of her mother, but in some inexplicable way she resembled the Rakehells, too. "I've missed you, daughter," he said, and kissed her gently.

Lai-tse lu stood alone now at the foot of the dock, her hands at her sides, her eyes luminous.

Jonathan started to walk toward her, then broke into a

run. She alone filled his mind and heart, and he didn't even know it when others took the children from him. He swept his wife into his arms, and when they kissed, the long, cruel months of their seemingly endless separation began to fade from their memories.

Then drawing apart slightly, each searched the face of the other.

"There is gray at your temples," Lai-tse lu murmured, "and there are lines in your face."

"You haven't changed in the least," he told her, but even as he spoke the words, he knew they were untrue. There were faint smudges beneath her eyes, and although her beauty was undimmed, she looked more ethereal, more fragile.

"You're well?" he demanded.

"Never happier or healthier than at this moment," she replied, and they kissed again.

Someone sniffed loudly.

Jonathan turned to see Sarah Applegate, who stood beside Jeremiah Rakehell, holding his arm. "Missy Sarah!" He enveloped her in a bear hug.

"Land sakes," she muttered.

Jonathan grasped his father's hand, and their grips were strong and firm. Both men were beaming, and tears of happiness formed in Jeremiah's eyes.

Judith Walker stood off to one side with her children, waiting to greet her brother after she expressed her pleasure at seeing Homer Ellison again.

An exuberant Charles hugged and kissed the ladies and children, and was delighted when little Jade said to him, "Papa."

"Young lady," Jonathan said, laughing, "I know how difficult it must be at your age, but you'll have to learn to keep your relatives straight!" With this, he squatted down and showed the little girl the jade signet ring on his finger. "This ring belonged to your grandfather, Jade. It will belong to you when you are older."

Before they left the dock, Jonathan arranged with his father to have the clipper's officers and men paid a special bonus, immediately and in cash. Each of the able seamen would receive one hundred dollars, Oliver and the senior crew members would receive double that amount, while the mates would be paid five hundred, and Homer would be the recipient of one thousand. "They've earned the extra pay—and more," he said.

"Besides," Charles added, "we can well afford the payments!" A fuller explanation had to wait until later.

Jonathan shared a carriage only with his wife and children. Julian chattered incessantly, demanding his father's attention, while Jade tried her whole vocabulary, consisting of a half-dozen words, and had to be praised for each of them. So there was no opportunity for husband and wife to exchange more than a few words before they reached the Rakehell house and adjourned temporarily to their own suite.

The first thing Jonathan saw was a lacquered Chinese chest of drawers, formerly one of his father-in-law's prized possessions, in a corner of the sitting room. On it stood a carved tortoise's head of jade, the symbol of immortality.

There was no time like the present to unburden himself, and Jonathan told the full story of Soong Chao's death and burial.

Lai-tse lu was dry-eyed and very still as she listened. "He did what was right for the Middle Kingdom and his honor," she murmured, unconsciously speaking in Mandarin. "His gods will reward him with eternal happiness."

"Kai will have a pagoda of marble erected over the place in the garden where he is buried," he said. "I made all of the arrangements with him."

She nodded, then said forcefully, "Now we will speak of the living."

Talking in snatches, they tried to bring each other up to date on all that had happened, an impossible task. Lai-tse lu laughed as she explained that she had decided to wear Western attire, even though she had once vowed she never would. "Your country is my country now," she told him, "as much as China is. Besides," she added with a hint of merriment in her eyes, "I think this dress becomes me."

"You look beautiful," Jonathan said, taking her in his arms. "More beautiful than ever—if that's possible." Then he reached into his pocket for the gift from the Tao Kuang Emperor and the Princess An Mien.

Lai-tse lu gasped as she looked at the huge black pearl in the palm of her hand. It seemed to glow from within, as though it had some mysterious illumination of its own. She was fascinated, but all at once she astonished her husband by shaking her head. "It is too much," she said. "It is not for me "

"It's worth a king's ransom," Jonathan told her

"True," Lai-tse lu replied gravely, "but you are not a king, and I am not a queen."

"We'll soon be as wealthy as many kings and queens. I'll save the story of our business expansion plans until dinner."

She nodded and made no further comment, slipping the pearl into its bag of yellow silk so she could show it to the rest of the family.

"Before we go downstairs, there's one more thing you should know," Jonathan said. "I regard myself only as the caretaker for your father's house in Canton, the country estate in Kwangtung, and his fleet of junks, which soon will grow much larger and more prosperous. I've had a great deal of time to think on board ship coming home. I've decided that Julian will inherit my American share of the business, and Jade will inherit the Chinese share. How does that strike you?"

"Money and possessions mean little to me. I have a husband and children whom I love. No woman could ask for more."

Jonathan kissed her, and when he looked closely at her, he felt vaguely troubled. "You're certain you're in good health?"

Lai-tse lu told him her labor had been long and hard and that she had been told to bring no more children into the world.

"Fair enough. We'll do nothing, ever, to place you in jeopardy. But there's something different about the way you look. I can't quite put my finger on it."

She shrugged and smiled. "Lately I've been a little tired at the end of a long day. That is what comes from spending so much time with two small, active children. But now that you're home I'll revive fast enough!" She linked her arm through his, and they left the suite.

The entire family was gathered in the parlor, and Jonathan was pleased that Homer Ellison had been asked to dinner, too. So many people were talking simultaneously that Jeremiah felt compelled to terminate the bedlam.

"At the table," he said, "we'll speak one at a time. Jonnie has more to tell than anyone else, so I suggest you start now, son, while I pour you a glass of sack."

Jonathan launched into an account of the Anglo-Chinese

war as he had seen it from Canton. For his wife's sake he did not repeat most of the details of her father's death and hurried on to an account of his own involvement in the guerrilla warfare waged by the Society of Oxen. Then he interrupted long enough to beckon to his son, and Julian came to him.

"This talisman means I am one of the Oxen. One day you will inherit it from me."

The little boy's eyes gleamed as he examined the carving.

"But you must earn your own membership," Jonathan said. "These oxen will gain you admission to the Society, but you'll be on your own."

"I have already told him much about the Society of Oxen," Lai-tse lu said, smiling proudly at her stepson. "And you may be sure that Julian always will do what is expected of him. He is a true Rakehell."

The boy hugged her before she waved him back to his seat.

Jonathan resumed his narrative, explaining that he had been wounded and captured by the British, that the bullets had been removed from his body by a British surgeon, and that almost immediately thereafter, he had been spirited out of Kuan-choy and taken to the Soong country estate to recuperate.

"I was nursed back to health by Heng-ho," he told his wife.

"I was fond of her when we were children. Has Kai married her?" she asked.

He shook his head but didn't mention the grisly death of the peasant girl, not wanting to burden Lai-tse lu with too much tragic news at one time.

Charles took up the story, saying he had acquired a cargo of exceptionally valuable black pepper from the Fat Dutchman before sailing on to Whampoa. Then, not looking at either Jonathan or Homer, he added that he had been fortunate enough to hire Molinda, who had acted as the general manager of the Dutchman's business.

Jonathan came to his cousin's rescue. "I had met Molinda and had thought of hiring her myself, but we had no real need for her services when I was in Djakarta. So you can imagine how delighted I was when she showed up with Charles at the Kwangtung estate."

Charles was relieved. His affair with Molinda was past history, and no one needed to know about it.

Dinner was served, and the children, who were behaving well, were allowed to come to the table, too. Julian sat next to Missy Sarah, who cut his meat for him, while Jade was ensconced in a high-chair adjacent to her mother's place.

Jonathan resumed his narrative, telling of their visit to Peking, his two meetings with An Mien and the Celestial Emperor, and of Molinda's marriage to Shaong Wei.

"She must be a very unusual woman if An Mien chose her for Shaong Wei." Lai-tse lu did not mention her own escape from marriage to the emperor's cousin.

"Both of them are unusual people," Jonathan said, "and Shaong Wei will be of great help to us in Canton." He concluded his story by telling of the decoy ship, then doubled back to his final meeting with the Tao Kuang Emperor and his sister. "We exchanged gifts of friendship," he said, "and I will send them information, tools, and knowledge accumulated in the West." He repeated the emperor's solemn words about his hopes for the modernization of China.

The others listened in silence. Lai-tse lu finally broke the spell by taking the black pearl from its case. "This is the gift of friendship that the Celestial Emperor gave to Jonathan," she said. "For me."

The pearl was passed around the table, and even Charles and Homer, who had seen it previously, were impressed anew.

"It must be unique in all the world," Jeremiah said.

Sarah Applegate agreed but had her own opinion. "I can't imagine where you could wear it, child," she said. "It would be so ostentatious."

"Just owning it would be a thrill," Judith Walker said, "but I'd be afraid even to look at it for fear of chipping it."

Lai-tse lu kept her own counsel and returned the pearl to her pocket without further comment.

"The outcome of our various adventures," Jonathan said, "is that we've acquired the trading and shipping business that belonged to Lai-tse lu's father, with a cousin-by-marriage of the emperor operating it for us."

"And thanks to the friendship of the emperor and his sister," Charles added, "we'll win more than a fair share of the new China trade that the peace treaty guarantees. Rakehell and Boynton will soon become one of the largest, most powerful—and wealthiest—trading companies in the world.''

Jonathan and Homer agreed, and the latter said, "The potential is dazzling.''

"So dazzling," Jeremiah said, "that Alan and I are being far outstripped by our sons. You'll see what I mean, Jonnie, when I show you and Charles the current ledgers tomorrow. Our profits have been increasing steadily, I'll grant you, but we have no exciting business news here or in England.''

He seemed to stress the word "business," and Jonathan was slightly perplexed.

"There's some personal news that may be of interest," Jeremiah continued. "Nothing was said previously because it wouldn't have been appropriate until Jonnie came home safely." He looked down to the far end of the table. "Shall you tell them or shall I?''

Sarah Applegate became somewhat flustered. "I'd rather you do it," she said.

Lai-tse lu and Judith exchanged a long, significant look. "We were right!" the former exclaimed, and began to giggle.

"Indeed we were," Judith said with a laugh. "We've been watching the developments together for months.''

Jeremiah reddened. "Mrs. Applegate," he said, "has done me the great honor of accepting my proposal of marriage.''

There was a moment's electric silence, which was broken by Julian's loud whoop of glee. "You mean Missy Sarah is going to be our new grandma!" he shouted.

"Grandma," Jade echoed, adding a new word to her vocabulary.

Chairs were pushed back, and dinner was interrupted as the whole party crowded around Sarah and Jeremiah, offering congratulations.

"Papa," Jonathan said, "I couldn't have done better for you if I'd selected her myself.''

Lai-tse lu laughed and wept simultaneously as she hugged and kissed the woman who had been her devoted governess. Charles raced off to the kitchen, returning with two bottles of champagne.

"Mind your manners, young man," Sarah said as Jonathan embraced her. "You know how I can't tolerate having a fuss made over me."

"A toast to the bride and groom," Judith said.

"You offer it, Jonnie," Charles said, going around the table to pour wine into the adults' glasses and, after glancing surreptitiously at Judith, giving token portions to her son and daughter.

Jonathan raised his glass, then waited until the babble subsided. "Missy Sarah, Papa," he said, "I wouldn't have believed that anything could have added to my joy today, but you've made this a perfect homecoming. I can wish you only the happiness that Lai-tse lu and I know."

The entire party drank. Putting down his glass, Jeremiah began to reply, but became unexpectedly tongue-tied. Sarah intervened swiftly and decisively. "We love all of you," she said.

Gradually the excitement subsided. In response to questions, the happy couple revealed they had made no specific wedding plans. "Our first concern," Sarah said, "was you. Now that you have been returned to us, we can make plans for the ceremony."

As the meal drew to a close, Charles became more somber. "Everyone is so happy today—and with good cause—that I hate to bring up another matter, but I feel it must be aired. We do have a problem that neither Jonnie nor I mentioned directly. In case you've wondered why we had to resort to a subterfuge when we left China, it is because Jonnie has been proscribed by the Royal Navy and Army. He is charged with having fought against them on the side of their enemies."

Lai-tse lu sucked in her breath.

Jonathan covered her hand with his. "It's one of those technicalities that sometimes crop up in a time of war."

"I intend to straighten out matters as soon as I get back to London," Charles said. "My father and I, between us, shouldn't find it too difficult to clear Jonnie's name."

"I haven't discussed this with you, Charles," Jonathan said, "but with our business about to expand, I wonder if it might be wise for me to come to England with you and volunteer to appear before a Royal commission of some sort. Once they understand I was carrying on business for my father-in-

366

law, who had been killed that same day by British cannon, I'm reasonably sure I'll be exonerated."

Lai-tse lu gave Charles no opportunity to reply. "We have been separated enough!" she said firmly. "We shall not be separated again!"

Everyone at the table stared at her.

"Charles," she said, "Wu-ling wrote to me that you took her and Elizabeth to tea at Windsor Castle. So it is obvious that you know Queen Victoria."

"Of course I do. She—"

"Good. Our entire family will sail to England," she said, her manner unyielding. "And you will present me to the queen."

"One doesn't simply barge in on the queen," Charles said. "Besides, since that visit, she has married Albert of Saxe-Coburg-Gotha, a German prince, and the last I knew she already had two children."

"She will see me as soon as I arrive," Lai-tse lu said, her delicate nostrils flaring slightly. "We will talk as woman to woman, and this nonsense about Jonathan being listed as an enemy will be ended at once!"

Charles appealed silently to his cousin for help.

"Victoria," Jonathan said, "is a constitutional monarch. That is, she reigns, but she doesn't rule. The Tao Kuang Emperor is an absolute monarch, so he is obeyed by all, on penalty of death. Victoria is required to take the advice of her ministers, and—"

"That does not matter," Lai-tse lu said, interrupting him. "I lost my father, and I almost lost my husband in this war that the British should not have started."

"I have no basic quarrel with the English," Jonathan said to her, trying to calm her. "Circumstances forced me to stand against them. They're an honorable, fair-minded people, and I'm sure my present situation can be resolved quietly, without fuss."

"Quite so," Charles added. "It is almost inconceivable to me that Jonathan would be imprisoned if he were to come to London with me. By all means, come with him, Lai-tse lu. The family will love having you, and I'm sure Julian and David will enjoy a grand reunion. But you don't understand our institutions if you think that Queen Victoria and Prince Albert will open the palace doors to you."

She refused to give ground. "Queen Victoria will see me," she declared. "We will speak together, and she will learn what is in my heart. She will understand, because she, too, is a woman." She looked around the table, her manner quietly defiant. "My mind is made up, and nothing will change it! I will sail to England with Jonathan, and we will take the children with us."

Charles was not yet ready to give up. "I just wish you'd tell me what makes you so certain the queen will grant you an audience. I can't perform miracles."

Lai-tse lu's faint smile was as enigmatic as it was beguiling. "I will do what is necessary," she replied. "Plans are already forming in my mind."

Jeremiah decided the time had come for him to intervene. "Homer, do you have quarters on your clipper for some additional passengers?"

"Sure, Mr. Rakehell," the master of the *Lai-tse lu* replied

"And how soon will you be ready for a voyage across the Atlantic?"

"I won't need more than a week."

"You shall have two weeks," Jeremiah said. "Sarah, I suggest we marry and go to London with the young people. Judith, we'll make this a real family get-together; we'd like you and the youngsters to come with us, too. We have a clipper sailing to England tomorrow, so I'll write to Alan Boynton, telling him and Jessica to expect the whole Rakehell clan."

Excitement welled up around the table again, and Jonathan smiled, appreciating his father's motives. Jeremiah had decided to make the voyage himself so he could supervise the efforts to restore his son's good name, and, if necessary, intervene in order to prevent his headstrong daughter-in-law from acting rashly.

Lai-tse lu and Jonathan were closer than they had ever been. Their lovemaking was more passionate and demanding, yet was more tender. They communicated freely, revealing their most intimate thoughts. Never before had Jonathan loved his wife so much. Her devotion to the children during his long absence had been inspiring, the marriage of Jeremiah and Sarah delighted both of them, and with her husband restored to her, Lai-tse lu's health appeared to improve.

Jonathan worked from early morning until evening to catch up on all that he had missed at the shipyard during his absence, and when he returned home at the end of each day, his wife's genuine joy warmed him. But there was one subject she refused to discuss with him. When he asked her about her intended visit to Queen Victoria, she merely smiled and immediately spoke of something else. And some of her activities bordered on the mysterious.

She took charge of packing their clothes and those of the children for their trip to England, and one evening, when Jonathan came home a few minutes early, he saw a man's mandarin robe of heavy silk, embroidered with cloth-of-gold dragons, along with a matching, square headgear, on top of a pile near a clothing box. He assumed these clothes had belonged to her father and had no idea why she might be taking them to London When he asked, however, she replied with a careless shrug

On the eve of the wedding of Jeremiah and Sarah, Jonathan entered his private suite to discover his wife carefully examining some of the family heirlooms she had inherited. In her slender hands she was holding an exquisite box of carved, black jade that was no more than six inches long, slightly less wide, and perhaps four inches deep.

He took the box from her, saw that it was lined in shimmering, pure white silk, and nodded approvingly "This will make a lovely wedding gift," he said.

Lai-tse lu shook her head. "Missy Sarah has always loved the ivory Buddha that sat in a niche behind my father's desk. I know she would appreciate it, and I believe Papa Rakehell will like it, too." She nodded toward a nearby table.

"That's even more impressive," he said, recognizing the Buddha.

Lai-tse lu took the box from him and made no comment about it. Jonathan told himself that he was just imagining she was being secretive.

The wedding of Sarah and Jeremiah was quiet, with only family members and a few of Jeremiah's old friends—including Dr. and Mrs. Graves—in attendance. While the ceremony was in progress, Sarah's personal belongings were moved into the suite that Jeremiah had occupied alone for more than a quarter of a century. At the insistence of the bride, who demanded that "no fuss" be made, Lai-tse lu and Judith planned a simple reception at the Rakehell house, and that evening the two young women, escorted by Jonathan and Charles, dined at a local New London inn in order to give the honeymooners a greater measure of privacy in the house.

The following day the clipper set sail for England, her cargo of black pepper still in her hold. Homer Ellison gallantly surrendered his master's cabin to Sarah and Jeremiah. Lai-tse lu and her husband occupied a small but comfortable passenger cabin, and Jonathan, like Charles, was placed in the unusual position of having no duties to occupy him at sea.

This respite gave Jonathan the opportunity to spend hours with his children each day. He watched Julian climbing in the rigging with the agility of a monkey, and when he tested the boy's ability to use a sextant, he was impressed. "Charles," he said to his cousin, "I swear that Julian knows more about the sea than we did at his age."

"He has the flair," Charles replied with a grin. "He's a true Rakehell."

Every day, weather permitting, Jonathan went to the ship's bow, holding Jade in his arms, and these were moments to be treasured. The little girl chortled when the ship lurched and rocked, clapped her small hands together when she looked up at the billowing sails, and, her expressive eyes becoming pensive, stared out across the endless expanse of blue-green water.

Occasionally Lai-tse lu accompanied her husband and daughter, but she refused most of Jonathan's invitations. She was uncomfortable because of her illness, but she offered Jonathan another explanation. "The children inherit their instinct for the sea from you," she said. "I'm fortunate that I don't become sick in rough weather, but I'm much more comfortable on land."

"I'd be surprised if Julian didn't love life at sea," Jonathan said. "After all, he's a boy. But Jade astonishes me. She's so very little, but when I'm holding her, I can feel the excitement in her body as she looks out at the water. I've yet to find anything on board that she dislikes."

"She is like Judith," Lai-tse lu said. "I am convinced

370

that Rakehell women, like Rakehell men, have sea water instead of blood in their veins."

Certainly it was true that Judith Walker was enjoying the voyage, and she seemed to come to life for the first time since she and her husband had separated. At Homer Ellison's invitation, she paid frequent visits to the quarterdeck when he took the watch, but she took care never to interfere, never to speak when he was busy.

When Homer's duties permitted, he frequently joined the adults of the family for dinner or supper, and the realization gradually dawned on Jonathan that it was mutual choice, not coincidence, that caused Homer to sit beside Judith.

In the privacy of their cabin, he asked Lai-tse lu, "Do you reckon Judith and Homer are getting sweet on each other?"

She had spent enough time in the United States to have become familiar with the American colloquialism. "I know Homer dined at the Walker house several times before he and Charles went to search for you," she said, choosing her words with care. "They have known each other for a great many years, and I would say they have mutual, adult interests."

He frowned. "It could be that Judith is still in love with Brad, although I hope not."

"I believe she has put him out of her mind for all time," Lai-tse lu said. "Judith and I saw each other every day while you were gone, often spending hours together, and I never once heard her mention her husband's name. Neither do her children. It is as though he never existed."

"Well, he does exist," Jonathan said. "Unfortunately. I'd hate to see her hurt again, and the same is true of Homer, who is a fine fellow. So—for both their sakes—I hope they won't develop too keen an interest in each other. As long as Brad Walker lives, Judith can't remarry."

"Don't worry too much. She is the most sensible woman I know, and he appears to be very realistic, too." Lai-tse lu smiled confidently. "I am certain they know what they are doing and what risks they may be taking."

"Which is more than I know when I wonder what lies ahead for us in England," Jonathan said.

"Trust me," she said, sliding her arms around his neck.

"I don't seem to have much of an alternative," he replied, and kissed her.

The better part of the voyage was uneventful, the clipper plowing through a few squalls but, in the main, enjoying calm seas, brisk winds, and fair skies. Homer made no attempt to set a speed record, but Land's End was sighted only nineteen days after he had sailed from New London.

That same afternoon Lai-tse lu led Jonathan and Charles to the aft deck and, swearing them to secrecy, revealed a portion of her plan to them.

Her husband immediately protested. "Not only would I feel like an idiot," he said, "but your whole scheme is foolish."

"Not so fast, Jonnie," Charles said thoughtfully. "Lai-tse lu's idea is based on sound principles. She has a much better chance of pulling off this venture than I was willing to concede."

Lai-tse lu rewarded him with a ravishing smile.

"Like it or not," Charles told his cousin, "I'm afraid you'll have to go along with her, as I will. There's everything to be gained and very little to lose."

A grumbling, reluctant Jonathan was forced to accept.

The clipper made her way up the English Channel, and when she slowed as she moved into the estuary of the Thames, where sea traffic was even heavier than on the lower reaches of Canton's Pearl River, Jonathan and Lai-tse lu vanished into their cabin and locked the door behind them. The pilot was taken on board, and a steam tug towed the clipper to her berth in the Rakehell and Boynton yard at Southwark, directly opposite London, only twenty-four hours after passing Land's End.

Sir Alan and Lady Boynton awaited the party on the dock, flanking Ruth and little David, while Elizabeth and Wu-ling stood apart, conversing in whispers, looking like women one moment and small children the next.

The party came ashore, with Charles holding the hand of Julian and Sarah carrying Jade. The newlyweds and the youngest of the Rakehells were the center of interest.

Charles greeted his wife, son, and mother with kisses, then startled his father when they clasped hands. "Where is the queen in residence?"

"How the devil should I know?" Sir Alan replied.

Jessica came to her son's rescue. "She and Prince Albert are at Whitehall until the weekend."

372

"Good!" Charles summoned a company courier, handed him a sealed note, and at the same time requested that a special, separate carriage be sent to the wharf without delay

His family was mystified, and it was Ruth who finally realized what was amiss. "Where are Jonathan and Lai-tse lu?"

"Uncle Jeremiah will fill in all of you," her husband replied. "As best he can. With luck they'll join you at the house in an hour or two, and so will I. I'm sorry to delay our reunion, my dear, but I'm afraid this is one time when duty must come first."

Elizabeth pouted when she learned she would not see Jonathan immediately.

Charles was both apologetic and visibly apprehensive as he kissed Ruth and David again, then started toward the foot of the wharf, where the special carriage he had ordered from the stable was already pulling to a halt

Everyone else clustered around Jeremiah, who tried to explain, in as few words as possible, the scheme on which his daughter-in-law and son were launched. He completed his recital when they reached their waiting coaches, where the party paused to be sorted out for the ride to the Boynton house in Belgravia.

Suddenly Jessica Boynton gasped, clutched her brother's arm, and looked in bewilderment at him, then at Sarah. "Do I see what I think I'm seeing, or am I hallucinating?"

"Your eyesight is good," a tight-lipped Sarah assured her.

The entire party stared in silence at a couple making their way from the end of the pier to the waiting carriage. Slightly in the lead was Lai-tse lu, and rarely, if ever, had she looked so breathtakingly beautiful. Her incomparable body was encased in a high-collared, snug-fitting cheongsam that fell to her ankles, and only the knee-high slits at the sides of her skirt made it possible for her to walk. Even so, she seemed to glide in her matching shoes of iridescent pale green silk. Over her gown she had thrown a cape of white silk, with a dragon emblazoned on the back.

No one else could have worn her gorgeous jewelry with such a flair. Earrings of jade and diamonds fell to her shoulders, on her right hand she wore a jade ring, surrounded by a circle of diamonds, and on her wrists were matching jade and diamond cuffs. Ruth and Elizabeth were quick to note that in her lustrous hair was a jade and diamond comb.

A step behind her, walking solemnly in a mandarin's robe of scarlet, embroidered with figures from Chinese mythology in cloth of gold, came a tall man, who wore a square, high-crowned, and brimless mandarin's hat.

"It's Jonnie," Ruth said in astonishment.

"What's that he's carrying?" Elizabeth asked.

Sarah Rakehell's tone indicated that she disapproved of the masquerade. "A container of special tea, known as the emperor's tea. I'm not fond of it myself, but Lai-tse lu says it's a fitting gift for Queen Victoria."

Sir Alan blinked rapidly and shook his head. "Charles is actually taking them to Whitehall for a royal audience? Good Lord!"

Thanks to the shrewdness of Lai-tse lu, possible obstacles to a meeting with Queen Victoria vanished swiftly. Charles Boynton's note to the queen was succinct, saying only that, in the wake of the recently signed Anglo-Chinese treaty, two special emissaries from the Celestial Emperor had just arrived in London and wanted to pay their respects to her before going to their lodgings.

"It would be discourteous to refuse, so I am certain she will receive us," Lai-tse lu said.

Her prediction was accurate, and Charles's sponsorship of the visitors added weight to the request. The officer of the guard stationed at the entrance to the palace grounds had already been notified and waved the carriage through, and the queen's chamberlain was waiting at the main entrance to escort the guests inside.

Whitehall was an old, drafty building that had been the principal London residence of Britain's monarchs for centuries, and it was in a state of genteel disrepair. Tapestries that lined the walls of the corridors were priceless, but paint was peeling from the walls themselves. Here and there tiles were missing from the floors, and there were obvious nicks in marble columns. But no attempt would be made to put the building in better condition because Prince Albert had decided it would be less expensive to move, as soon as an appropriate place was found, to a more modern mansion.

An apartment overlooking a garden at the rear of the second floor, once occupied by the notorious Nell Gwynne when she had been the mistress of Charles II, was being utilized by the royal couple, and the furnishings, completely lacking in ostentation, reflected their personal tastes. A cheerful coal fire burned in a sitting room hearth, an old rug that had been a gift of an Ottoman Emperor to William III late in the seventeenth century covered the better part of the floor, and on the walls stood portraits of the two children of Victoria and Albert, Princess Victoria and Prince Edward. The overstuffed, velvet-covered furniture, like the apartment itself, had seen service for a long time.

The queen, who had gained weight as well as a measure of maturity since Charles had last seen her, sat comfortably in a rocking chair, a light shawl thrown over the shoulders of her black silk dress. Her only jewels were her wedding ring and a cameo brooch at her throat. Albert, solemn in his cutaway coat, black cravat, and immaculate formal trousers, his boots gleaming, rose from his own chair as the visitors were ushered into the room.

"Your Majesty, Your Royal Highness," Charles said, "permit me to present the personal envoy of His Celestial Majesty, the Tao Kuang Emperor, the daughter of the late Soong Chao."

Lai-tse lu curtsied deeply. "I am deeply honored," she said.

The queen was startled. "You speak English?"

"Of course, Your Majesty," the young Chinese woman said with a smile. "I knew it well long before I became a citizen of the United States."

"Permit me also to present my cousin and business partner, Jonathan Rakehell, who is this lady's husband."

Jonathan bowed, then quickly removed his mandarin's robe and hat, revealing his own Western attire.

The queen smiled uncertainly.

Prince Albert frowned. "I assume there was a reason for this—ah—disguise?" He spoke with a faint German accent.

"Indeed, sir, as you will learn in due time," Lai-tse lu

replied, intervening before her husband could speak. "Mr. Rakehell has just returned from China, where he brought gifts from the Tao Kuang Emperor and his sister, my good friend, the Princess An Mien."

"It is my wife's wish that I offer you this tea, Your Majesty," Jonathan said.

Prince Albert took the container and handed it to the queen.

"It is known as the emperor's tea," Lai-tse lu said. "There is none like it in all the world."

"Is it brewed in the usual manner?" Victoria asked. "Good. We'll sample it at once, if you'll join us." She rang for a servant, then gave swift instructions.

The prince consort offered chairs to the guests, but Lai-tse lu continued to stand. "Now, ma'am," she said, "it is my privilege to offer you a gift fit only for a queen."

To the astonishment of Jonathan and Charles, she took a small casket of black jade from beneath her cloak and handed it to the queen. Even before it was opened, Jonathan knew what it contained.

Victoria raised the lid, then caught her breath as she gazed at a magnificent black pearl, its sheen unparalleled. When it picked up the light that slanted in through the windows it seemed to glow from within. An inch and a half in diameter, it formed a perfect, unblemished sphere.

The prince consort looked at the pearl over his wife's shoulder, and he, too, was stunned.

"There is an ancient legend that tells of the supposed origins of the pearl," Lai-tse lu said as she sat gracefully on a small couch beside her husband. "It is said that the Great Emperor of the Eastern Peak, who ruled the seas of the world and was the nephew of Yu-ti, the Supreme Emperor who created mankind, fell in love with a mortal woman, the young Empress Yang Chen, who was the sole ruler of the Middle Kingdom. He made this pearl for her, and she, in return, fell in love with him. But Yu-ti ruled that she could not take it with her into the Heavenly World of the Upper Kingdom, so she left it behind for her human descendants." She paused, smiled, and added, "I suppose the real truth is that some fisherman found the pearl and sold it to a representative of an emperor, who knew he was obtaining an object of priceless value. I happen to prefer the legend, which is charming. All I know for certain is that it has been in the possession of the emperors of the Middle Kingdom for three thousand years, perhaps longer. I recognized it at once when my husband brought it to me."

The queen was quick to notice the slip. "He—brought it—to you?"

"I did, ma'am," Jonathan said firmly, refusing to go along with his wife's deception. "The Tao Kuang Emperor and the Princess An Mien gave it to me as a gift for Lai-tse lu."

"It is the most glorious object I have ever seen in my life, but I cannot accept it," the queen said primly.

"The instant I saw it, ma'am, I knew it could belong only to you," Lai-tse lu said with deep sincerity. "You are the ruler of the greatest, most powerful nation on earth. I am the wife of a man who builds ships, sails them, and carries the cargoes of the nations in them. There is no place in my life for an object of this magnificence. We live simply and quietly. This pearl belongs in your collection of crown jewels, collected for almost one thousand years by the monarchs of England. In your possession it finds its rightful home."

Prince Albert cleared his throat, intending to protest, but Lai-tse lu continued to address herself exclusively to the queen. "I know the Tao Kuang Emperor and the Princess An Mien will approve of my giving you this gift. In their hearts, as in mine, is the hope that the people of this great land and those of the land of my birth will become true friends and will remain friends for all time."

The queen finally found her voice. "What makes you so certain they feel as you do?"

"They suffered great grief when your soldiers and sailors made war against the innocent people of the Middle Kingdom."

The queen glanced at her husband. "I'm afraid that unjust war will haunt our consciences for a very long time to come."

"I have known my own share of grief," Lai-tse lu continued earnestly. "My father was killed by cannon of the Royal Navy. My husband, who was visiting Canton on business when hostilities broke out there, fought on the side of the Chinese guerrillas to avenge my father's death and was severely wounded. Even now his name stands on a list of those proscribed by

Your Majesty's generals and admirals But, for the sake of your children and my children and the generations who will come after them, there must be an end to hate. I want this pearl to become a symbol of healing. My children are American, and their cousins are English. In my daughter's veins flows the blood of both East and West. Charles Boynton's son is part-English, part-Chinese. These innocent babies must be given the chance to become adults who are free of prejudices and stupid hatreds.''

Queen Victoria looked again at the glowing pearl, which seemed almost like a living thing in its nest of white silk. "You're making it impossible for me to refuse your gift."

Lai-tse lu smiled and shook her head "No one, not even a queen, can refuse that which has already been done freely, gladly, and willingly."

The queen returned her smile. "You have the tongue of an orator, Mrs. Rakehell."

"No, ma'am, I do not. I am eloquent only in behalf of that in which I believe."

"How could I repay you?"

"By using your influence to end the shameful traffic in opium that is destroying so many of our poor."

Charles, who had said virtually nothing, saw an opportunity and intervened swiftly. "Many of your subjects who know the East, ma'am, regard the sale of opium to the people of China as a disgrace. I'm one, and I assure you I don't stand alone. The companies that are earning huge profits in the drug trade are wealthy and powerful, and they'll fight hard to preserve their gains. But they're sensitive to public pressure, as is everyone else in our society. I happen to be familiar with your dislike of the opium traffic. If your views became more widely known, it seems to me, the newspapers would speak up with greater candor, and it wouldn't be long before voices were heard in the House of Commons condemning the trade, too."

Prince Albert nodded. "It will not be difficult to give our private opinions in this matter greater circulation."

They were interrupted by the arrival of the tea cart, and the queen herself poured. "How extraordinary," she said, looking at the contents of her cup. "This tea is so colorless it has the appearance of water." She sipped experimentally, then

378

hook her head and smiled. "But the aroma is rich, and the taste is marvelous."

Jonathan exchanged a quick glance with his cousin. "Charles and I will see to it, ma'am, that regular supplies of the emperor's tea are sent to you. But so little of it is grown that it won't be possible to satisfy a commercial demand for it."

"I am beholden to you, Mr. Rakehell," the queen said, and her eyes gleamed mischievously. "Let me assure you that it won't be necessary for you to wear a Chinese disguise during your stay here. I may not be able to intervene officially on your behalf, but my prime minister calls on me every morning, and he's learned to listen when I speak. You may take my word that your name will be removed from the proscribed list tomorrow!"

"I'm grateful to you, ma'am." Jonathan was relieved, knowing he could visit England on business in the future without fear of arrest.

"Not at all." The queen looked at her husband. "When do we go to Windsor for the weekend?"

The prince consort consulted a small leather-bound book that he removed from a waistcoat pocket. "At noon on Friday."

She nodded brightly, then turned to Lai-tse lu. "Join us for luncheon on Saturday with your husband, Mrs. Rakehell, and be sure you bring your children. Charles, we shall expect you, your wife, and your son, too. Let us put into practice the principle of bringing the West and East closer together. All of which, dear Mrs. Rakehell, is my way of saying that you've given me no choice. I am pleased to accept your gift of the black pearl, and it will occupy a special place in the crown jewels."

A short time later the visitors left Whitehall, and Jonathan took his wife's hand as they sat in the carriage. "You astonish me," he told her. "I had no idea you intended to give Queen Victoria the black pearl."

"You would have objected," Lai-tse lu replied demurely. "But I knew the instant I saw it that it should belong to her, not to me. And in matters such as this, a woman must obey her instinct."

The family gathered at the Boynton house in Belgravia

379

listened in stunned silence to the recital by Jonathan and Charles of the visit to Queen Victoria and Prince Albert.

Jeremiah Rakehell was the first to speak "Thanks to Lai-tse lu, we've established a solid relationship with the Emperor of China and the Queen of England!"

Sir Alan Boynton sent for champagne. "We've enjoyed a good living for years," he said. "Thanks to Jonnie's clippers and Charles's pepper deals we've expanded our interests. But now, with strong bases here, in America, and in China, we're in a position to challenge the world's leading international traders. There's no limit to what we can accomplish."

"In this room," Jeremiah added, "are the founders of a dynasty!"

They raised their glasses, then drank solemnly.

Ruth, who had spent no time alone with her husband, sat beside him on a small sofa and all at once felt him grow tense

"I have a proposal to make," he said. "If we're going to become a true dynasty, let's behave like one. I suggest we buy out the shares of all nonfamily stockholders and that we distribute them according to the percentages that each family member now holds. But that's just the beginning. I propose that we make a formal pledge, in writing, never to sell to anyone outside the family."

"I'll go a notch beyond that," Jonathan said. "I propose we make the inheritance of Rakehell and Boynton stock by our descendants contingent on their signing of a similar agreement and that this practice be followed for one generation after another"

Judith Walker agreed enthusiastically, and so did Jessica Boynton

Everyone looked at Sir Alan and Jeremiah, the two principal stockholders "I hesitate," the former said, "only because—by buying the shares of outside stockholders now— we'll be shy of cash that we'll badly need for immediate expansion purposes."

"I'm afraid I must agree," Jeremiah said

Charles was undaunted. "Father, Jeremiah," he said, "with all due respect, I think you've forgotten the cargo of pepper that we brought here just today on board the *Lai-tse lu*. The sale of that pepper will more than meet all of our cash needs "

"What's more," Jonathan added, "before I left China, I

told Molinda to open negotiations without delay with the Fat Dutchman for two more shiploads of pepper. I've already sent a clipper from New England for that purpose, and as quickly as Charles can go over the shipping schedules here, he'll free another for the same mission. Pepper, of course, is only a means to an end. We're now in a position to capture the better part of the American tea market, and we can begin to compete here as equals of the British East India Company. There's literally no limit to what we can achieve!"

Sir Alan raised his hands in a mock gesture of surrender. "Very well, lads, you have my vote."

"Mine, too," Jeremiah said with a grin.

The thought occurred to Ruth that her husband and Jonathan already were beginning to supplant their fathers as the active directors of the company. She reached for Charles's hand. He hesitated for a moment before he responded.

In that instant Ruth knew he had been unfaithful to her during their long separation. At the same time she realized that, even if she should obtain the proof that she was lacking right now, a direct confrontation would be dangerous. She had two choices: either she could put the matter out of her mind permanently, or she could risk the dissolution of her marriage.

Her real problem was a lack of courage. Through her marriage she had gained privileges and luxuries that she had been denied throughout all of her previous life, and now, it appeared, the family was about to become far wealthier and more powerful. Someday, when Sir Alan died, Charles would ascend to his baronetcy, and she would become Lady Boynton. She was unwilling to give up that future for the sake of her pride.

So she would say nothing, continue to bring up David, and would, to the best of her ability, swallow her resentment. She had no idea whether her intimacies with Charles would continue to give her the sense of gratification she had known in the past. For the present, however, that was the least of her worries, and she forced herself to concentrate on what was going on around her.

"As all of you know," Jonathan said, "my clipper flies a special pennant that I had made for her. The Tree of Life symbol comes from this pendant, which my wife gave me years ago." He reached beneath his shirt and revealed the jade talisman. "I proposed sometime ago that we adopt the Tree of Life for our entire fleet. It seemed appropriate to me, because the three branches represent the three bases of our business, the United States, Great Britain, and China. But now there is an even deeper significance. So much of what lies in store for Rakehell and Boynton is a direct outgrowth of my wife's activities and influence. By adopting the symbol of the Tree of Life, we honor her."

Sir Alan and Jeremiah immediately agreed that the pennants, which Jonathan had already commissioned, should be adopted as soon as they were ready by every ship in the fleet, and one by one the others chimed in, too.

Jonathan and Lai-tse lu looked at each other, shutting out the entire world. Ruth felt an ache at the back of her throat. She and Charles never had known such mutual devotion, and now it was forever beyond their grasp.

Elizabeth Boynton averted her gaze. She had learned the necessity of accepting Jonathan's marriage as a fact, but she could not bear to witness his deep, abiding love for someone else. Common sense told her that, as a girl on the threshold of womanhood, she should put her love for him out of her heart, but she was asking more of herself than she was capable of doing. She had loved him so long and so much that her affection had become an integral part of her being.

Certainly all the others at the family gathering rejoiced. Lai-tse lu's selflessness when she had given the black pearl to Queen Victoria had cemented the family's relations with the British crown, and no obstacle stood in the way of rapidly growing success.

Jeremiah offered a toast to his daughter-in-law

Lai-tse lu acknowledged the gesture with a graceful smile, then raised her own glass. "Let us drink to all the Rakehells and all the Boyntons," she said. "We are one and indivisible." She linked arms with Jonathan, then with Ruth, who had been seated on her other side. With one accord everyone present did the same, and as they sipped their wine the scene was engraved on the mind of every Rakehell and every Boynton. A close family alliance was already being transformed into a great dynasty.

Princess Victoria was just old enough to be tolerated by Julian and David, who included her in their game of follow-the-leader. As the eldest, Julian took the lead as he darted through the gardens on the grounds of Windsor Castle. "Do as I do!" he shouted again and again.

David Boynton displayed the first signs of the diplomacy that one day would bring him renown. "You can do it, Vicky," he said. "Take your time. Not so fast, Julian, be fair."

Prince Edward and Jade, making their way on unsteady feet near their parents, were still so young they paid scant attention to each other. Ultimately, the future Edward VII took sufficient note of his guest's presence by trying the experiment of pulling her hair. An indignant Jade promptly retaliated in kind, and both wept, which caused them to be removed by nursemaids and put to bed for naps.

Lai-tse lu and Ruth were quick to discover that Queen Victoria's principal interests were domestic. She took care to write a recipe for a Chinese soup that could be made with Western ingredients, and she was delighted when Ruth gave her the name and address of a London toymaker with whose product she was not familiar.

Prince Albert, whose knowledge of every phase of life in his wife's realm already was encyclopedic, discussed significant aspects of the coming boom in world trade with Jonathan and Charles. To their surprise, his grasp of the subject was as great as their own. "Your clipper ships serve a need for speed in the movement of certain cargoes, Mr. Rakehell, and I'm sure there will be a place for them over the next quarter of a century, but I can see other needs developing."

"So do I, sir," Jonathan said. "The volume of international sea trade is just starting to grow. The increasing industrialization of both this country and the United States will increase our mutual dependence, and in our own trade alone I expect transatlantic traffic to triple or quadruple in the next fifteen years."

"How will you handle that traffic?" Albert asked. "The standard windjammers aren't fast enough, and clippers don't carry enough."

"We've been so busy establishing our clippers that we've

had no chance as yet to look that far ahead, Your Highness," Charles said.

"But we shall," Jonathan added. "I'm not prepared to make any long-range predictions as yet. But I suspect that steamships, which are being used mostly for river and intercoastal trade both here and in America, will become more important "

"Are you saying steamships will become larger and more powerful?"

"That trend is inevitable, sir," Jonathan said. "I intend to anticipate the demand, and I just hope to find the time for small-scale experiments in the next few years."

After the luncheon, as the guests prepared to depart for London and the children were already being taken to the waiting Boynton carriage, Queen Victoria halted them. "One moment before you go. Mrs. Rakehell, there's no way I can ever show you my gratitude for the superb black pearl But there is something I can do. I have recently founded a new order of chivalry, the Queen's Own, to which I make my own appointments, without first referring them to my ministers for approval. I take great pleasure in making you a Companion of that order."

She draped a broad ribbon of scarlet watered silk over Lai-tse lu's head, and when it fell to her shoulders they saw, attached to it, a tiny replica of Victoria's personal seal

"There is no monetary value attached to the order," the queen said with a smile. "But it will be inherited by your daughter, never by your son, and by her daughter after her. A Companion of the Queen's Own is entitled to attend any royal audience merely by wearing her decoration."

"I shall wear it with great pride, ma'am, as a symbol of our friendship," Lai-tse lu said, and curtsied low

II

Thousands of Chinese laborers accepted the wages offered by the representatives of various British companies, and the Royal Crown Colony of Hong Kong was transformed, almost literally overnight, from a deserted semitropical forest wilderness into a booming town. Less than a month after it was founded, it already had more warehouses than the port of Canton, and soon houses of stone, barracks for a permanent military garrison, churches, and schools were constructed, too.

The growing settlement needed barbers and tailors, greengrocers and butchers and fishmongers, and large numbers of native Chinese set up their homes on the island, which was named for Queen Victoria. Few harbors anywhere had the potential of the deep-water bay that separated Victoria Island from the mainland, where the British also were expanding at the site of the fishing village known as Kowloon.

The British, Americans, and Europeans whose flags were flying once again at the factories soon realized their operations at Canton would be dwarfed by the new burst of activities that would be centered in Hong Kong. No one was more aware of the situation than Molinda, and when she learned that Sir Henry Pottinger was now governor-general there, she decided the time had come to pay a call on him. Hong Kong would be her first stop, she said, on a voyage that also would take her to Djakarta for a business visit to the Fat Dutchman.

Shaong Wei escorted his wife, sailing from Canton on board a Rakehell and Boynton junk, and Kai went with them as a matter of course. A last-minute addition to the party was Lo Fang, who indicated that he was seeking new employment.

"You won't go to work as the head of the household for the new imperial viceroy?" Molinda asked him.

He shook his head. "The court of a viceroy is too dull after the life I have led. Kai tells me you might find a place for me in your company."

Molinda needed no time to make up her mind. "You're hired," she said, "for the same pay that Kai receives. And if all goes as I hope it will, I have an important place in mind for you."

So all three of the husky, athletic men stood with the young woman at the rail of the junk as it sailed slowly into Hong Kong harbor. Kai and Lo Fang studied the sea traffic, noting the ships of various nationalities lying at anchor, but Shaong Wei's attention was drawn to the activity near the top of the small mountain that stood behind the Victoria Island waterfront.

"I will make a large wager," he said, "that the palace for the new British governor-general is being built up there."

"What makes you so certain, my dear?" Molinda smiled at him.

He chuckled. "Because royalty everywhere is the same, I have decided, and the man who represents the Queen of England will want the highest place in the colony for his home."

They went ashore in a sampan, with Molinda wearing a cheongsam, as she did regularly in Canton, in order not to call undue attention to herself. But her beauty was so great that scores of men stared at her as she stepped onto one of the new wooden docks, and it was inevitable that she should create a stir in a community where virtually no wives had yet joined their husbands and the only women were the occupants of several busy brothels.

Shaong Wei, Kai, and Lo Fang closed ranks around her, their hands on the hilts of their long, curved swords, and no man dared to speak to her.

They walked the short distance to the one-story stone building, soon to become a Royal Customs House, where Sir Henry Pottinger maintained his headquarters. The building consisted of only two rooms, a large outer chamber occupied by army and civilian clerks, and a simply furnished inner sanctum, where the man who had won the Anglo-Chinese war kept his modest office.

Well aware of Shaong Wei's standing as well as Molinda's position with Rakehell and Boynton, he received the couple immediately, while Kai and Lo Fang took up places just outside the entrance. "What brings you here?" he asked pleasantly.

"The same thing that has brought so many others in recent weeks," Molinda replied, choosing to address him in his own tongue. "I have decided to purchase some waterfront property in the name of my employers, but I understand I must first obtain an official permit from you."

"I see. You'll want to settle in Kowloon, I presume."

"We wish to settle on Victoria Island, Sir Henry," she replied firmly. "I'm sure I need not remind you that Rakehell and Boynton is half-owned by Englishmen and half by Americans." Shaong Wei, who had taught himself English, was smiling steadily.

Pottinger unfolded a map of the island, then scowled as he looked at it.

"You are afraid that all choice locations for warehouses and wharves on this side of the harbor have been either rented or sold," Molinda said.

"That's the way it looks," the Englishman replied.

"What you are really saying, Sir Henry, is that although the absent owners of my company may be English and American, the business here is being managed by a woman who is not a Caucasian and has the further handicap of being married to a Chinese."

Sir Henry Pottinger was not afraid to speak frankly. "I must admit, Mrs. Shaong," he said, "that many of my fellow countrymen suffer racial prejudices, and it is true they're trying to keep Victoria Island for whites."

"Their policy is certain to fail," Molinda said.

Shaong Wei's smile vanished. "You defeated us in war, General, but you have not won the peace. Your buildings are being constructed and maintained by Chinese. In the short time required for us to walk here, I noticed that Chinese also work on the docks already in operation. Chinese sell meat and fish and other food to your people, and serve also in their new homes."

Pottinger became uncomfortable under his steady scrutiny.

"As you undoubtedly know, I can make my voice heard

in the Forbidden City,'' Shaong Wei continued. ''There is no clause in the peace treaty signed by you and the representatives of the Tao Kuang Emperor that forces his subjects to work for the English. An imperial decree would send them back to their homes overnight. The building of your colony would not be completed if they withdrew. There would be no laborers to load and unload cargoes, none to transfer the goods of the West to smaller ships for transfer to the treaty ports. Your people would be forced to depend for the food on the supplies your own ships bring them, and they would be required to cook it themselves. The future of Hong Kong depends on the good will of the Celestial Emperor, and surely you are aware of that fact!''

Henry Pottinger bristled. ''Are you threatening me, sir?''

The unsmiling Shaong Wei remained bland. ''I would not be so rash as to threaten the conqueror of the Middle Kingdom. I merely support my wife's statement that any attempt to keep nonwhites from doing business or making their homes on Victoria Island is certain to fail.''

Pottinger knew he was already being subjected to mounting criticism in the House of Commons and in the English press for his high-handed treatment of the Chinese, and that, more recently, voices were being raised in favor of ending the opium trade. Certainly Shaong Wei was no ordinary Chinese, and as he and his shrewd wife well knew, they could cause endless problems for the Crown Colony that was struggling to establish itself.

''I'll gladly approve of the sale or lease to Rakehell and Boynton of a choice waterfront property no more than a stone's throw from this building,'' he said.

''And you'll also approve of the acquisition of property on the side of the mountain for the building of a home?''

''I will.'' Pottinger paused. ''But I can't guarantee you protection against attempts by vandals to destroy the buildings you'll put up here. The Royal Navy and Army forces stationed here are not a constabulary. As Hong Kong grows, it will undoubtedly be required to recruit its own security force.''

The interview was developing precisely as Molinda had hoped it would, and her husband was playing the role she had assigned him to perfection. The British had rejoiced because they had won the war, but now they were beginning to learn what the Portuguese at Macao had known for centuries: their presence on Chinese soil, their ability to live and work here depended on their willingness to cooperate with the authorities of the Middle Kingdom as well as their facility in winning and keeping the good will of the Chinese people. Far more was at stake in Hong Kong than the fate of a few warehouses on the waterfront at Canton.

"I am so happy," she said, "that you are willing to accommodate us. Rest assured, Sir Henry, that I shall write to the Tao Kuang Emperor and the Princess An Mien. You need not fear that the people of the Middle Kingdom will be ordered to absent themselves from this place."

"I'm glad we understand each other." Pottinger took several forms from a small pile on his desk and began to fill them in, then sign them. "Please keep in mind that there is literally nothing I can do to protect Rakehell and Boynton property here."

"We shall be pleased to provide our own protection." Molinda glanced at Lo Fang, whose bulk loomed outside the door of the cubicle. She knew of no man anywhere better suited to the task she intended to give him. Anyone who raised a hand against him would be inviting swift and terrible retaliation.

Djakarta was unchanged, Molinda thought, as she rode toward the Fat Dutchman's estate, seated between Shaong Wei and Kai in the carriage that her former master had sent for them. The jumble of Javanese huts with bamboo frames that were clustered along the waterfront suddenly gave way to straight rows of stone Dutch houses that made it seem as though Amsterdam or The Hague had been moved to a tropical setting. All at once they entered a broad, palm-lined avenue and beyond the next sweeping bend in the road lay the Fat Dutchman's domain.

Something perverse in Molinda's nature had compelled her to dress as she had when she lived here, but now she wondered if her breastband and skirt were appropriate, whether it had been a mistake to halt and pluck an orchid from a tree as a hair ornament. Certainly she would not be harmed or humiliated physically; her husband and Kai would see to that. What really bothered her, she realized, was her overwhelming desire to be accepted by the Dutchman as his equal. She had won the respect of the traders in Whampoa, and her future in Hong Kong appeared bright now that she had won her victory over Sir Henry Pottinger. But she would not be truly satisfied until the Dutchman recognized her as a commercial agent of stature.

The same guards, armed with Javanese throwing knives, who had prevented her and the other girls from leaving the estate, were still on duty now, grinning and waving to her, and the young women who clustered around her when she descended from the carriage were old friends whom she greeted with hugs. Now the real test awaited her.

Flanked by Shaong Wei and Kai, she walked slowly down the path to the garden, hearing the raucous, familiar cries of the parrots sitting on their perches. The Fat Dutchman was seated in his thronelike wicker chair, as always, his bald head glistening, perspiration oozing from his corpulent body and dampening his short-sleeved shirt. Beside him, armed with a large ledger, stood her successor as his principal assistant, a bespectacled, middle-aged Javanese man who looked cowed.

Molinda's heart hammered, and she had to remind herself that it no longer would be appropriate for her to make an obeisance to the man whose slave she had been.

The Fat Dutchman seemed to know what was going through her mind and made the reunion far easier for her. Grinning broadly, he heaved himself to his feet, advanced down the path to meet her partway, then embraced her lightly before shaking hands in the Western manner with Shaong Wei and Kai. Chairs were provided for the guests, and soon Molinda found herself seated at her host's right, a glass of papaya juice lightly flavored with Dutch gin in one hand.

His manner jovial, the Fat Dutchman elected to converse in the Cantonese dialect for Kai's sake, but Molinda knew him well enough to realize he was studying her intently as well as taking her husband's measure. She was proud of Shaong Wei, whose dignity beneath his host's scrutiny remained unruffled.

On the surface, at least, the amenities were observed. "Your career and marriage agree with you, Molinda, heh-heh," the Fat Dutchman said. "You've become lovelier than ever."

"That's because I have everything I've ever wanted,"

she replied, not mentioning that her happiness would not be complete until he acknowledged her as his peer.

He chatted about Jonathan Rakehell and Charles Boynton, and after ascertaining that a clipper would be sailing to England soon after her return to Canton, he said, "Would it be convenient to ask the master to carry a small gift I'm sending to Charles?"

"Of course," she said graciously.

The Fat Dutchman's chuckle erupted at length. "Heh-heh. Tell me what you think of him." His wave brought one of the slave girls to his chair, and he directed her to bring a young, multicolored parrot closer for their inspection. "He's an extraordinary bird, heh-heh, and I think Charles will enjoy his company." He directed the girl to feed the bird some seeds.

The parrot pecked at them, then began to speak in Dutch, letting loose with a string of curses that would have made a veteran seaman ill at ease.

Neither Shaong Wei nor Kai could understand a word, and looked blankly at the bird, but Molinda clapped her hands over her ears. "Not even the masters of the merchantmen that come here from Holland use such vile language!" she exclaimed.

"Heh-heh. I taught him myself, once I realized he had a real aptitude for curses."

"Sir Alan and Lady Boynton are staid people, from all I've heard about them, and Charles has a wife and son. This creature will upset them!"

"I know Charles's sense of humor, heh-heh. I shall send him a note telling him what to feed the parrot, whose name is Dieter." More chuckles rumbled to the surface.

Molinda thought it unlikely that the gift would be appreciated but did not want to argue. She had conceived a bold commercial plan, and she wanted the Fat Dutchman in the right frame of mind when she broached it.

They adjourned to the dining room for the customary *rijsttafel* that was served here, and Molinda found it a simple matter to eat lightly, sampling only a few of the innumerable dishes. Shaong Wei and Kai had hearty appetites but quickly learned there was no way they could keep up with their host, and the young Chinese aristocrat, ever-mindful of his drinking problem, refused the mugs of ale that were offered to him and instead drank fruit juice with his meal.

After the main courses were cleared away and slave girls brought a stunning variety of chocolate dishes and candied fruits to the table, Molinda steeled herself. The right time to discuss business matters had come. "I'd like to talk about pepper," she said.

The Fat Dutchman's smile remained jovial, but his eyes narrowed.

"Rakehell and Boynton would like to work out an arrangement for regular deliveries of peppercorns," she said. "You mentioned to Charles that you could obtain all he needed, so I'm eager to establish a delivery schedule."

"Heh-heh, when I made him the offer I wasn't thinking in terms of regular, frequent deliveries. I'm sure you recall that the officials sent here from Holland have very rigorous rules, heh-heh, and that I must circumvent the law every time I obtain a cargo of pepper."

"To be sure," Molinda said. "You'll remember that I took charge of paying the bribes to the officials who conveniently looked the other way. You were never involved personally."

"I couldn't afford to take the risks," the Fat Dutchman said. "I still can't, heh-heh."

She well knew that others on his staff attended to bribe payments now. "When you sell a cargo to Charles," she said, "your profits are doubled. I have no doubt that Dutch law still sets a strict limit on the prices you're permitted to charge merchants in Rotterdam."

"Naturally, heh-heh." He was wary.

"I am prepared," Molinda said, "to pay you fifty percent of the profits we earn in London, with only the shipping costs deducted."

His eyes had become slits. "How much pepper do you want?"

"As much as you can obtain for me," she said vigorously, "but I don't want to be greedy. A guarantee of two tons per month would be ample."

The Fat Dutchman's roar of laughter shook the walls. "Heh-heh. Two tons! Do you realize what you're asking?"

"Of course. The key to the deal, it seems to me, is that there is no need for the pepper to be shipped from Djakarta, where the Dutch count every corn. It could be loaded onto our junks at a dozen ports in Borneo or Sumatra or Timor—any one of a number of islands. I would take the responsibility for transferring it to one of our clippers at Hong Kong. The pepper itself is easy enough for you to obtain.''

''It's true that the Dutch authorities form the only bottleneck, heh-heh. But if I'm taking the risks, I should receive more than fifty percent of the profits.''

Here was the crux of the deal, and Molinda was prepared. ''If you wish,'' she said sweetly, ''I'll take the responsibility for paying the necessary bribes. Thanks to your training, I know which officials to approach and which to avoid. In that case, however, Rakehell and Boynton should keep more than fifty percent of the profits.''

A hint of grudging admiration crept into the Fat Dutchman's expression. ''Let me think about the matter,'' he said. ''I'll give you my decision tomorrow morning before you leave, heh-heh.'' He turned to Shaong Wei and added lightly, ''Your wife drives a hard bargain.''

Molinda spent the afternoon visiting with some of the girls who had been her friends, and felt desperately sorry for them. Since they lacked the intelligence and ingenuity to create truly free lives for themselves, the best they could look forward to when the Fat Dutchman had no more use for them was to become the mistress, concubine, or wife of some outsider. Her own good fortune was extraordinary, and she wondered if she were wrong to be driving too hard a bargain.

As she well knew, there was an element of bluff in her offer. Although she had suggested that Rakehell and Boynton pay the bribes, she realized that only a citizen of the Netherlands was permitted to purchase pepper from the growers in these islands. That policy, firmly established in Holland, was intended to keep the world supply limited. Experience had taught the Dutch that one-third of all pepper sold would fall into the hands of foreign merchants and dealers, but they continued to control the supply at the source and in that way could maintain artificially high prices for the spice throughout the world. More pepper rotted in the fields every year than the quantities that found their way into the markets.

The evening was pleasant, with *rijsttafel* served again, and the Fat Dutchman was a convivial, thoughtful host. He continued to treat Molinda with consideration, and nothing in his manner indicated that she had spent years as a member of his household.

At breakfast the following morning, however, his approach became brisk. "I have decided," he said, "to provide you with the two tons of pepper per month that you seek. I shall attend to the necessary dealings with officials. Sumatra is the best source of pepper, so your junks should sail to Palembang, arriving there at the beginning of each month, and pick up their cargoes at my warehouses there. Heh-heh, I'll expect a regular accounting from you, in the usual manner."

Molinda was thrilled: her bluff had succeeded, and she had obtained precisely the terms she had wanted.

The Fat Dutchman's final accolade completed her triumph. Leaning toward her, his pudgy hand patted her arm. "You're the best pupil I ever had, heh-heh, and it won't be long before everyone in the business realizes it."

She could have hoped for no greater compliment from him, and she was still glowing when she and her companions left Djakarta.

Returning to his dining room for another large mug of Javanese coffee after the departure of his guests, the Fat Dutchman laughed silently. His maneuver had been perfectly timed, perfectly executed. Having previously whetted Charles Boynton's appetite for pepper, he had known that Molinda would seek a regular supply from him, and having taught her all she knew about the business, he had correctly gauged the nature of the deal she had offered him. Aware of her craving for his approval, he had gratified that whim, too.

A slave girl he had purchased recently in Bali because she bore a strong physical resemblance to Molinda approached the table with a pot of steaming coffee, and he absently stroked her backside as she filled his cup. In another decade or two, after he retired, Molinda well might replace him as the shrewdest, most successful trader in the East. As long as he remained active, however, he had no need to fear competition from anyone.

In the meantime, he had made her happy at no expense to himself, and soon he would demand subtle repayment in return. As soon as the new Rakehell and Boynton facilities in Hong Kong were built, he would use their warehouses and wharves, making it unnecessary for him to construct his own. Life was sweet when one learned how to savor it to the full.

Bradford Walker and Owen Bruce sat on the terrace of the recently completed house on the heights of the peak, overlooking Hong Kong harbor, eating a peaceful breakfast of fish caught that very morning and bread baked at daybreak by their cook. Later the day would become hot, but a cool breeze was blowing across the water from the direction of the uninhabited outer islands, and the pair ate in a contented silence. The Chinese girls with whom they had spent the night had been paid and dismissed, and their serenity was undisturbed.

Their new wharf and warehouse, built with funds supplied by the Marquês de Braga—as this house also had been built—already were laying the foundation for a flourishing, legitimate business. Bruce remained in charge at Canton for the present, while Walker organized the business here, and in neither place was it necessary to conceal the opium that came from India. Ships bound for either Canton or Hong Kong first put into Macao, and there the drug supplies were unloaded before the vessels went on to their final destinations with merchandise that could be unloaded openly. The system was foolproof, and the overall profits were enormous, even though the Marquês de Braga demanded half of all they earned.

A manservant poured tea, and suddenly Bruce's good humor evaporated. "Damn you!" he shouted, slashing the man across the face with the edge of his hand, "never bring me lukewarm tea! I want my tea hot!"

The Chinese bowed and retreated, his resentment hidden behind an expressionless face.

Walker was accustomed to his partner's outbursts of temper and calmly buttered a chunk of bread.

"Force is the only language these heathen understand," Bruce muttered.

Walker was inclined to agree but he saw no need to dwell on the matter. "Look yonder," he said, using his bread as a pointer. "It appears we'll soon have a neighbor on the waterfront."

They gazed down at the harbor, and could make out scores of Chinese at work on the property adjoining their own. Some were painfully and slowly digging an excavation for a new

building, while others carried the heavy boulders they ha
unearthed to the waterfront, where they were smashed to mak
smaller stones for a new wharf.

Bruce regarded them in silence for a time. "Whoever ou
new neighbors may be, they aren't worried about expenses
There must be at least two hundred coolies at work."

"Only the East India Company can afford to hire tha
many," Walker replied. "But both of their warehouses are
done, and they're putting the finishing touches on their second
dock."

The manservant approached the table tentatively, his hand
trembling as he placed a pot of very hot tea in front of the
Scotsman.

Bruce tasted it, grunted in sour approval, and waved the
Chinese away. "We'll find out soon enough, and I can restrain
my curiosity until we go down there."

"I reckon every major shipping company in the world
will soon be clamoring for space here. In almost no time Hong
Kong will become one of the busiest ports on earth, and we'l
be among the first to be well-entrenched."

"If we maintain the present pace of our special Macao
traffic, we'll be able to retire in a few years. And by then our
facilities here should bring a fancy price."

"I'm not so certain I'll want to sell out my share." Walk
er dreamed of establishing his own shipping empire but was
telling no one his hopes and plans.

Bruce's tight smile was dour. "There's no way of esti-
mating how long our Macao operation will continue. Those
stories from London in the newspapers that came in by clipper
the other day are unsettling."

"You mean the rumors that Queen Victoria and Prince
Albert disapprove of the opium trade?" Walker laughed. "I
noticed that the queen wasn't quoted directly."

"She rarely is quoted. It isn't necessary. If she's spoken
harshly about the drug traffic, the climate in Great Britain wil
change overnight, and only renegades and pirates will carry
opium to China."

"Then we should double our trade without delay."

"That's up to you, Walker. Dom Manuel stores the merchandise, and I've been finding the buyers for it. We'll take all
the chests that the ships you find for us are willing to carry."

396

Walker bit back an angry retort. At no time did he enjoy the company of this surly Scotsman, but he wanted to avoid an open quarrel at least until he had recovered in full the cash he had invested in their joint operations. He ate the last of his bread and butter, gulped his tea, and stood. "Are you heading to the harbor?"

"No, I want to pack first. I'm sailing to Whampoa as soon as the schooner unloads the machines for the new British textile factory that will be built here. I want to supervise the loading of tea myself."

Bradford Walker shrugged, went into the house for his beaver hat and walking stick, then went to the side door, where his small open carriage and Chinese driver awaited him. Coolies already were at work widening the road that led to the top of the peak, he noted, and were filling in holes made by rains in the dirt road. Perhaps it wouldn't be too long before this place became habitable.

The truth of the matter, he thought as he was driven past dozens of buildings in the process of construction, was that he had no real affinity with the East. A man who had spent the better part of his life in New England found the heat ghastly, the Chinese and British foods barely edible, and the Orientals who worked for him a surly, stubborn, and unpleasant people. His only solace was his earnings from the opium trade, and he suspected—but so far could not prove—that both the Marquês de Braga and Owen Bruce were cheating him out of his fair share.

Instead of going directly to his new office or learning for himself whether the unloading of the schooner was almost done, Walker paused to watch the hundreds at work at the next-door property. They had broken ground only this morning, apparently at dawn, and were working harder than he had ever seen coolies labor. The extent of the excavation they had been digging for only a few hours indicated that the warehouse to be constructed on the site would be huge.

The giant in charge of the project was extraordinary. At no time did he raise his voice, and when groups lifting and moving boulders encountered difficulty, he pitched in beside them. His strength was so great that he looked as though he could lift a boulder unaided.

Walker moved closer to him. "Whose property is this?"

he asked. Then, not waiting for a reply, he simplified the question and shouted, "Who—own—this?"

Lo Fang knew what the man was screaming and could have replied in English, having learned the rudiments of the language from Jonathan. But he felt such a deep contempt for these arrogant foreigners who couldn't bother to learn the languages or customs of China but were so quick to exploit her people that he pretended he couldn't understand. Instead he shrugged and went on with his work.

Walker recognized the giant's rudeness but didn't know what to do about it, so he stomped off to his office. Not until he made certain that his own staff was functioning smoothly did he go to the office of Sir Henry Pottinger and inquire about the identity of his new neighbors.

He was in a foul mood when Owen Bruce finally joined him late in the morning. "You'll find this hard to believe," he said, "but the property next door is owned by Rakehell and Boynton."

"You joke!"

"It isn't a laughing matter to me," Walker said. "The last person on earth I want to see is Jonathan Rakehell."

"I wouldn't object to a final meeting with him," Bruce said grimly. "But who knows if and when he'll come back to the Orient? What bothers me is that his managing director is a woman from the Dutch East Indies and her husband is a Chinaman. Land on Victoria Island is supposed to be reserved for whites!"

"Rakehell and Boynton qualify. Technically, at least."

"You can do all of us a favor, yourself included," Bruce declared. "You know what needs to be done. I'm acquainted with a man who will attend to the job, and I'll send him here before I sail. Pay him whatever he asks, and take the money from general operating funds."

By mid-afternoon Walker's mood became frenzied. Bruce had already sailed off to Whampoa, no stranger had come to the warehouse, and the coolies at the adjacent property were making visible progress. The heat was so intense that Walker's head ached, so he walked out to the wharf, which stood in the shade. The breeze had died away, and several boats entering the harbor barely moved, their sails limp. At least the heat was bearable now.

"Mr. Walker?"

The deep voice sounded so close that Walker started. He had neither heard nor seen anyone approach. He turned and met the steady gaze of a man with sandy hair, pale green eyes, and several livid scars on his face, dressed in the rough attire of a merchant seaman.

"I'm Hazzard," the man said. "Owen Bruce said you have work for me." The man's accent sounded more American than English. "I earned a fair enough living as a freebooter in these waters until the Royal Navy became nasty. But I haven't gone hungry yet, and I don't come cheap. What do you want done?"

Bradford Walker drew a deep breath, then nodded in the direction of the Chinese at work on the adjacent property. "Some of the shippers and others who have been moving here had an understanding with Sir Henry Pottinger—informal, to be sure—that Victoria would be reserved exclusively for whites. The company moving in yonder is run by a Chinaman and a woman from the Dutch islands."

A slow, ugly smile spread across Hazzard's face. "Chink workers discourage fast," he said. "Break the leg of one and a hundred of them limp." He laughed harshly at his own joke.

"I'm sure you know what needs to be done and how to do it."

"No problem, Mr. Walker. But I'll want ten pounds sterling as an advance payment, and five pounds for each of the seven lads who'll be joining in the fun with me. Then, after the Chinks have cleared out for good, you'll make us a second, equal payment. I needn't tell you that the lads and I aren't fond of them who don't pay their debts promptly."

"You'll find me both prompt and appreciative," Walker assured him, sorry that Bruce had made him responsible for the unsavory aspects of the task. "Come along to my office in about two hours, after our staff has left for the day, and I'll give you your initial payment."

Hazzard nodded, turned, and stalked off.

He returned a little more than two hours later, appearing silently in Walker's tiny office.

The funds had already been removed from the strongbox, and Walker counted out the money slowly, placing each crisp five-pound note on his desk. "I'm sure you realize," he said, trying to gain the upper hand, "that I won't tolerate delays."

"You'll get action," Hazzard said as he scooped up the money and vanished into the dusk.

Too nervous to go back to the house on the side of the peak for supper, Walker thought of being driven to a new, rapidly growing district farther down the waterfront, which the Chinese coming to Hong Kong were calling Wanchai. There, so it was rumored, liquor and girls were readily available. The area needed constables, but none had yet been hired by the local administration whose formation was not yet completed. Walker had heard that order was maintained in Wanchai by secret Chinese societies, but he knew literally nothing about such organizations. Afraid he might be robbed, he decided boredom was the lesser evil to be endured.

As he walked to his waiting carriage, he saw that the workers next door were eating rice or noodles they were cooking in large cauldrons. Some already were stretched out on the ground and appeared to have fallen asleep.

The evening dragged. Walker drank a bottle of wine with his dinner, but it neither induced sleep nor enabled him to cast aside his apprehensions enough so he could read a book. He spent hours pacing the terrace, smoking a cheroot, then another, but he could see nothing at the waterfront below. The cooking fires of the Chinese workers long had been extinguished, and the only oil lamps and candles that had been lighted were burning in the windows of a recently completed hotel that was located several hundred yards from the construction site.

He did not fall asleep until the early hours of the morning, so he remained in bed later than was his custom. Then he dawdled over breakfast, afraid of what he would find when he went to his office.

The coolies were hard at work when he drove past the construction site, but he did catch a glimpse of the giant foreman in charge of the property standing in a small knot of men at the far end of the property, engaging in conversation with a young Royal Navy lieutenant in full uniform.

The Scottish foreman was waiting for Walker as he entered his office. "You've heard the news, sir?"

Shaking his head, Walker braced himself.

"Two of the Chinamen working on the excavation were murdered in the night. Decapitated, sir!"

"What a barbaric act. Who was responsible?" Walker's throat felt dry and it ached.

The foreman shrugged. "Mayhap they had a feud with some of their own. Some of our dock workers claim it was the Fan Kuei who don't want Chinamen on the island. But you know how them ignorant coolies lie and exaggerate, sir. So there's no telling who did it. The foreman complained so loud that the navy finally sent an officer to hear him out. But the navy has no men to investigate private killings and hires no constables. And there's nought Henry Pottinger can do. I suppose the Chinese will take their dead to the mainland for burial, Mr. Walker, and that'll be the end of the affair."

It was virtually impossible for Walker to concentrate on the documents that crossed his desk that day, and even the arrival of a brig that had stopped at Macao before sailing on to Hong Kong failed to cheer him. He was sure that Hazzard and his associates were responsible for the brutal murders of the two workers. He tried to tell himself their viciousness had been necessary, but the mere thought of decapitation made him wince.

By that afternoon, at least, the killings had not succeeded in driving off the Chinese workers. Their excavation was completed well before sundown, carts were bringing lumber and rocks for the construction of the Rakehell and Boynton warehouse, and the pilings for the wharf already were in place. If Hazzard was trying to create panic in the ranks of the coolies, which appeared to be his intention, he had not yet succeeded.

That evening Walker left his office earlier than usual and had himself driven without delay to the house on the side of the peak. He had no appetite for dinner but forced himself to eat, and later he refrained from going out to the terrace. Instead he locked himself into his bedchamber and spent a restless night.

The following morning a sense of dread filled him as he was driven to his warehouse. His feeling that a catastrophe had occurred was confirmed when he saw Sir Henry Pottinger, an aide-de-camp, and two junior officers, all in civilian clothes, awaiting him at the far end of the warehouse. His one thought, as he walked slowly toward the group, was that he would deny any involvement in new murders.

Suddenly Walker stopped short. Sprawled on the hardwood floor of the warehouse, their bodies in grotesque positions, were two men in their late twenties or early thirties, both of them white, both dressed in the rough, casual attire of merchant seamen. They had been garroted, and the multiple strands of silk that had been used to choke them still dangled from their necks. Apparently they had been tortured before being killed, because there was a livid burn mark in the center of each man's forehead.

Afraid he would become ill or faint, Walker reached for the support of the wall.

Sir Henry Pottinger came up beside him. "I'm sorry your day must have such a grisly start, Mr. Walker. Do you know either of these men?"

Walker forced himself to look at the faces of the strangled pair more carefully. "No, sir," he replied truthfully. "I've never set eyes on either of them!"

"Might you be able to explain why their bodies were found here, in your warehouse, this morning?"

"They—they were killed here, Sir Henry? My God!"

"I have no idea whether they were executed here or whether their bodies were dumped here after they were killed." Pottinger spoke dryly, with a hint of irony in his voice. "I am an army officer who has some knowledge of the politics of China. I am not a policeman, and I do not intend to become one. I was hoping you could shed some light on this mystery. None of your employees can provide us with as much as a clue."

"Neither can I, Sir Henry." There was no doubt in Walker's mind that the dead pair had been Hazzard's associates. Apparently the Chinese workers next door could play rough games, too. "This is dreadful, but I don't know these poor devils, and I can't imagine why their bodies were left here."

The expression in Pottinger's eyes indicated he did not believe a word, that he could easily guess why a partner of Owen Bruce might become involved with unsavory mercenaries when a property that would be managed by Orientals was being constructed nearby. The realities of the East had forced him to change his own thinking, and he was now trying to give others the benefit of his experience. "We've ruled out robbery as a motive. Each of these men was carrying a new five-pound note in his pocket," he said.

Walker could only nod.

"What I find unusual," the general continued, "is that such men should have more than a few coppers in their pockets. Unfortunately, Hong Kong is filled with adventurers who are encountering hard times now that the political situation in the area has settled down."

Again the American didn't know what to say.

"I'd like you to see something I regard as odd," Pottinger said. "Look closely at the marks on their foreheads."

Conquering his repugnance, Walker bent down to examine the bodies. "They look like brands," he said. "They appear to be animals of some sort."

"Oxen, as nearly as I can make out."

"Oxen," Walker agreed. "What does that mean?"

"I have no idea," Sir Henry replied. "But I do know that two more Chinese workers were decapitated last night. If you're connected in any way with this matter, Mr. Walker—and I assure you the Royal Army or Navy doesn't care, one way or the other—I urge you to call off your hirelings before this situation gets out of hand. When we first began construction work on Victoria Island, I tried to accommodate some of the shippers and traders who intended to settle here by reserving this portion of our territory exclusively for whites. But I realize now that it cannot be done. The success or failure of Hong Kong as a colony will depend on our willingness and ability to deal with the Chinese on equal terms. For every Briton, American, and European who comes here, there are one million Chinese out there." He waved toward the mainland. "We must cooperate with them, accept them, and deal fairly with them—or perish." Not waiting for a reply, he walked out of the warehouse, his juniors following him.

Walker had the task of getting rid of the bodies of Hazzard's men. "Dispose of them in some way," he told the foreman. "Hand them over to the clergy for burial."

The Scotsman looked aggrieved. "No missionaries have arrived here yet," he said.

Bradford Walker's nerves were raw, and his temper flared. "Then find some place to bury them," he said, "or have their bodies weighted and thrown overboard at sea!" Unable to contemplate spending the day at his desk, he stalked out, stood indecisively in the open, and finally walked down the waterfront to the new hotel, where a tavern had just been opened.

A glass of strong whiskey took the edge off his apprehensions but in no way improved his state of mind.

Someone sat heavily in a chair opposite him, and he was horrified when he saw Hazzard. The mercenary was unshaven, there were dark shadows beneath his eyes, and he looked gaunt.

"You shouldn't be seen with me here," Walker said sharply.

"To hell with that." Hazzard summoned the Chinese waiter and ordered whiskey for himself. "I need to have a few words with you, and you weren't in your office." He sat back in his chair, his eyes hard and brooding as he waited for his drink.

Walker could only hope they weren't seen by anyone who would be able to piece together the full story of his complicity in the violence of recent days.

Hazzard downed his drink in two gulps, then ordered another. "This assignment has been much harder to work out than I thought it would. Most Chinamen are cowards, as yellow as their skin, but these men at the construction site have backbones. What's more, they were lying in wait for us last night. We managed to get rid of a couple, but the rest refused to panic, and two of my lads were separated from the band. With results you already know."

"Is it necessary to discuss this with me?" Walker demanded. "I'd rather remain in the dark."

"Your convenience be damned," Hazzard said, his voice becoming metallic. "My lads are threatening to walk out on me, and my own enthusiasm for the job isn't what it was. These Chinese aren't like the sort we've known previously."

"Maybe it would be wise to drop the whole enterprise," Walker said as he remembered Sir Henry Pottinger's advice.

"It's too late for that. I've got to prove to these damn Chinamen—for my own satisfaction—that nobody pushes me around!" Hazzard grimaced. "I'll need the rest of our pay so my lads don't desert me, but that's only the beginning. We require a third payment—in advance."

"We agreed on a price," Walker told him, "and I expect you to fulfill your part of the bargain."

"Circumstances have changed the deal, and if you know what's good for you, you'll pay." Hazzard fingered the butt of the pistol that protruded from his belt, and smiled coldly.

Walker all too clearly recognized his vulnerability. This

was not a situation in which he could take a fellow business-man to task for failure to abide by the terms of a contract. "This is outrageous," he said, "but it appears I'm being compelled to accept your demands."

"That's the best way to keep your good health," Hazzard told him, and gulped his second drink. "Thanks for the whiskey," he added casually as he pushed back his chair. "I'll drop around later."

Walker wanted to stay at the tavern and drink himself unconscious. But he knew he would need his wits in what lay ahead, so he ordered some beef and bread, then drank a cup of tea before reluctantly returning to his new office. He was beginning to hate Hong Kong, where men took the law into their own hands and justice was unknown.

Somehow he managed to get through the rest of the day, handling routine matters and, ultimately, arranging to send the willing master of a nondescript brig to India for another shipload of opium. At last the end of the day came, and he was alone in the warehouse.

The coming of night frightened him, but Hazzard had not yet appeared. Soon the other offices and warehouses would be emptied until morning, and he could easily imagine the Chinese working on the Rakehell and Boynton construction site slipping into his office and dropping a noose around his neck. It was not his fault that the leader of the band of ruffians was tardy, so he locked his desk, then extinguished his oil lamp.

"Don't light a lamp or a candle," a voice told him in the darkness. "Just open your strongbox and give me the money."

Although he recognized Hazzard's rough voice, his flesh crawled as he hastened to obey the instructions. Fumbling with his keys in the dark, he found the one that opened the strongbox and raised the lid. His unwelcome visitor moved up close behind him and breathed down the back of his neck.

Trying to accustom himself to the gloom, Walker had to hold the money up to the half-light seeping through the windows in order to identify the denominations of the bills.

"All this cash going to waste," Hazzard said. "Maybe I'll help myself to a trifle extra." He dipped into the strongbox.

Walker had no idea how much the man was taking, and at the moment he didn't care. He was in a dangerous spot, and was afraid he might be killed if he protested too vehemently. Clenching his teeth, he said nothing.

"Much obliged. By tomorrow the Chinamen next door will be gone." Hazzard disappeared into the night.

His hands trembling, Walker made the strongbox secure. He would wait until morning before counting the money that remained and figuring how much the outlaw had stolen.

Then, only slightly relieved when he found his driver waiting for him, Walker ordered the man to take a wide detour around the construction site. The situation was rapidly developing into a nightmare.

That night was the worst he had yet endured. To the surprise of his cook, manservant, and the two housemaids, he appeared for breakfast soon after dawn, but was in such a sorry state that he could take only a few token bites of his meal. The sun was rising over the Chinese hills to the west of Hong Kong as he was driven to his warehouse. When he reached the place, he found that the coolies and a few of the white supervisors were just arriving for the day, the latter showing surprise that he was making such an early appearance.

He nodded to them curtly, then made his way through the cavernous building to his own tiny office. He opened the door, stood for a moment in stunned horror, and then heard a scream of terror and anguish rip from his throat.

In his chair sprawled the dead body of Hazzard, his face twisted in agony, a silken cord of several strands knotted around his thick throat. His shirt had been removed, and his torso, arms, and face were covered with ugly brand marks. Suddenly the whole room seemed to be filled with oxen.

Bradford Walker retched, backed out of the office as some of the supervisors and coolies hurried toward the room, and then fled to his carriage. The driver was nowhere to be seen.

His legs buckling, Walker somehow managed to scramble onto the buckboard. The horses responded slowly, and his fear forced him to glance in the direction of the construction site. The walls of the Rakehell and Boynton warehouse, at least twice the size of his own, were being erected, and the busy Chinese workers gave no indication they were aware of his existence.

The manservant failed to appear when Walker drove the carriage to the front door of the house on the side of the peak, and after hurrying from room to room, he was forced to conclude that all four of the household servants had vanished. He unharnessed the horses himself, took them to the stable, and then raced back to the house. His fear feeding on itself, he locked and bolted the front and back doors, then closed and locked all the windows, even though the sun was hot and there was almost no breeze.

Panting as he stumbled into the sitting room, Walker tore the stopper from the bottle of Portuguese brandy that the Marquês de Braga had given him, and not bothering to look for a glass, he poured the raw liquor down his throat.

Then he fell into a chair, his teeth chattering. As the brandy took effect, he became flushed, and perspiration suddenly soaked his clothes. It was difficult to think logically, but he knew he had to. Certainly it was no accident that all of the house servants had vanished, just as it could not be a coincidence that Hazzard's tortured body had been deposited in his own chair, in his own office.

Heaving himself to his feet, Walker fumbled in the drawer of a small table. There he found a pistol, made sure it was loaded, and returning to his chair, placed it on the table beside him.

His blood froze when he saw the door that led to the corridor creak open. Somehow an intruder had managed to enter the locked house, and although paralyzed by fear, Walker started to reach for his pistol.

"No touch!" The giant Chinese supervisor of the building project loomed in front of the terrified American, a miniature ku ming in one hand.

Walker saw the icy expression in the eyes of the Chinese, looked at the hooked blade of the knife held in the man's huge hand, and told himself he would surely die.

"Five Fan Kuei dead," Lo Fang said, his tone matter-of-fact. "Hazzard hate Chinese, now Hazzard dead."

Suddenly the wicked tip of the blade was pointed at the cowering man hunched in the chair. "Not know for sure if you pay Hazzard. If know for sure, then you die, too." Lo Fang paused for a long time before he added, "Other Fan Kuei run away. Now you go, too. Not come back Hong Kong."

To Walker's astonishment, the giant Chinese went to the door, bowed formally, and left as silently as he had come.

The renegade sat in his chair, unable to think, move, or feel. Gradually the realization dawned on him that he was still alive, that he had not been tortured or put to death, at least not yet. But he had been warned to leave, and he didn't need to be told a second time.

Jumping to his feet, he hurried to his bedchamber and in frantic haste began to throw his belongings into his clothing boxes. He had been given no deadline, but he had no intention of tempting fate. At least one or two junks sailed from Hong Kong to Whampoa on the afternoon tide every day, and no matter what he was forced to pay, he would leave this very day. He would change places with Owen Bruce, or at the very worst they would hire someone to take charge of the operations on Victoria Island. He was fortunate to be escaping with his life, and would take no needless risks.

Hitching up the horses again, he found the strength to pick up his leather boxes and throw them into the carriage. Assuming that Hazzard's tormented body had been removed from his office, he would stop there long enough to pick up his strongbox, and then he would arrange his passage to Canton.

As Walker drove down from the heights toward the waterfront, still terrified and shivering, the thought occurred to him that the Rakehells were responsible for his predicament. It was their warehouse and wharf whose construction he had tried to halt, and the curse of his association with them continued to follow him. Obviously the Chinese giant was in their employ, and although it was unlikely that he knew the identity and background of the refugee, he was behaving as Jeremiah and Jonathan would have wanted him to act.

"May God damn the souls of all Rakehells," Walker muttered, shaking his fist in impotent rage. "My feud with them isn't ended. Now I have a bigger score than ever to settle with them!"

III

During each day of his London sojourn, Jonathan spent several hours looking for information and data that would be useful to the Tao Kuang Emperor and the Princess An Mien. Usually accompanied by Lai-tse lu, he visited bookshops, searched periodicals, and even visited the headquarters of companies whose products would help speed the modernization of China.

One morning he found a lavishly illustrated volume on the latest developments in steam engines, and at the office of a concern that made agricultural equipment he obtained a brochure on the newest types of plows. Thanks to the Rakehell name, the managing director of a company that made steamboats gave him blueprints of the latest designs for vessels that sailed on lakes and rivers. He paid a long visit to the Boynton family physician, from whom he obtained data on the most recent methods of curing a variety of diseases; then he went to the proprietor of an apothecary shop for samples of medicines, and the pharmacist obligingly told him what ingredients went into the making of many medicines. It was from him that Jonathan learned opium had beneficial as well as harmful uses. Laudanum, commonly used in Western nations to kill pain, was made from an opium base.

Lai-tse lu dutifully translated articles and entire books into Chinese, but Jonathan accumulated them far more rapidly than she could translate them, so Wu-ling was pressed into service, too. Because of the education she had been acquiring, the young girl was a great help, but the task remained hopeless.

"In the long run," Jonathan said as he, Charles, and their

wives sat at breakfast together, "I'm convinced there's onl
one way to overcome the language barrier. The Tao Kuan
Emperor will have to send a number of young scholars t
England and the United States to learn English. It will tak
them several years to understand the language well enough t
translate it, and in the meantime I'm afraid there's a bottlenec
that will severely impede any efforts to introduce present-da
inventions and techniques into the Middle Kingdom."

Charles and Ruth agreed, and neither could think of hov
to solve the problem.

"I wonder," Lai-tse lu said, pondering aloud, "if Wu
ling might be interested in returning to the Middle Kingdon
for a few years as an interpreter."

"Maybe. She would live in the Forbidden City and woul
see the emperor and An Mien frequently," Jonathan said
"Millions of Chinese would envy her. Besides, she'd be fre
to return here or come to us in America as soon as the scholar
learn English sufficiently well to take over the work."

Lai-tse lu looked first at Ruth, then at Charles. "Woul
you release her for the purpose?"

Ruth smiled. "Wu-ling is free to do as she pleases and i
old enough to make up her own mind."

"I don't know what future she may have here or in the
United States," Charles added, "so I wouldn't know what t
advise her. But it's plain that she has the chance of becoming
person of great consequence and responsibility in China."

They lingered at the table, with Charles delaying his de
parture for his office, until Wu-ling and Elizabeth came down
stairs for breakfast. Then Jonathan carefully explained the sit
uation, with Lai-tse lu occasionally amplifying.

"Don't go," Elizabeth Boynton said to her friend. "We
have such wonderful times together!"

Wu-ling smiled a trifle wistfully, then shook her head.
"Charles took me from the gutter, and all of you have beer
wonderful to me. If it weren't for you, I might have starved tc
death long before now. At best I would be living in a Cantor
slum, unable to read or write, and would have no future."

"Don't desert me, Wu-ling," Elizabeth wailed.

"As Jonathan explained, it would be for no more than a
few years. What is more important, I am still a subject of the
Tao Kuang Emperor and owe my fealty to him and to our

410

people. I have lived here and in the United States, but I am not English and I am not American. I cannot forget my heritage and do not wish to forget it. A part of me always will belong to China.''

"I know," Lai-tse lu said softly. "I feel as you do.''

Wu-ling, her breakfast forgotten, turned to Elizabeth. "You take it for granted that you and your family know Queen Victoria, who makes you welcome as her guests. So you cannot imagine how a Chinese feels when offered a chance to meet and talk often with the Tao Kuang Emperor and his sister There are more people in the Middle Kingdom than there are grains of sand on a beach. Only a small handful of them will ever see the Celestial Emperor face to face, and of these, fewer still will ever speak a single word in his presence. I am being offered an opportunity so unusual that it overwhelms me!''

Elizabeth had to concede defeat. "I'll miss you," she said.

"I shall return here," Wu-ling said firmly. Then she asked Jonathan and Lai-tse lu, "Might it be arranged for Elizabeth to visit me in the Forbidden City?''

"You will be making a great sacrifice to work for your native country," Lai-tse lu replied, "so there is little doubt in my mind that the Princess An Mien will be pleased to grant you that small favor.''

Wu-ling was pleased, and Elizabeth's good humor was restored at once. "I'll be the only girl in all of Great Britain ever to see and talk with the emperor of China! Oh, I can hardly wait!''

Lai-tse lu said she would write a letter to the Princess An Mien and would send it, along with the books and other material being gathered in London, via the next Rakehell and Boynton clipper that would sail to the East.

So the problem appeared to be solved. For the years immediately ahead, a large share of responsibility for the gargantuan task of transforming China into a modern, nineteenth-century nation would rest on the slender shoulders of a girl in her teens.

Later, when Jonathan was alone with his wife, he said, "The agreement of Wu-ling to return to the Middle Kingdom clears the path for another plan I have in mind. For many weeks I've thought of finding a physician, someone who is competent, yet young enough to be filled with a spirit of adventure, who would be willing to spend several years at the imperial court, teaching Western medicine to the doctors of China.''

"What a wonderful idea!" Lai-tse lu said. "An Mien would approve instantly!"

"It crossed my mind that while in London we might want to go up to Edinburgh to meet some of the recent graduates there. For the right person, we'd pay expenses, provide free transportation, and take care of his salary for a period of three years, let's say. The problem, though, is that we know no one at Edinburgh.''

"Why don't we wait until we return home?" she asked. "Two of your Yale College classmates attended the school of medicine at Harvard and became physicians. Surely they would help you find a young physician who has acquired great knowledge and who would respond to the challenge.''

"That makes a great deal of sense," Jonathan said. "We don't want to be in so much of a rush that we select the wrong man. Your way is the right way.''

That morning Homer Ellison, who had gone back to the United States while the Rakehells sojourned in England, returned to London with a cargo and a sack of business mail for his employers that included several long reports from Molinda.

Jonathan and Charles devoured her communications and were delighted. "Her old relationship with the Fat Dutchman is paying dividends, Jonnie," the latter said. "Even though we'll be splitting the profits with him on pepper cargoes, we'll be making a great deal. What I like is that I'll be in a position now to offer contracts for future deliveries. This establishes us as major importers of pepper.''

"But that's just the beginning. Molinda has put us in business in Hong Kong. That's where the real future of the China trade lies. And she's shown real genius by hiring Lo Fang to work for us. I don't know of anyone, anywhere, I'd rather have on our payroll. Conditions in Hong Kong are primitive and will be for some time to come, but you can bet that Rakehell and Boynton will survive there!''

"He won't be buying and selling merchandise, will he?"

"Oh, no. He'll be in charge of the local staff, as Kai has been for so long in Canton. Molinda will handle the large accounts herself and will hire someone to look after the day-by-day business.''

"I'm still trying to tell myself that we're operating on three continents,'' Charles said with a grin. "Some days I find it hard to convince myself that we've already become a major force in the business.''

"Believe it,'' Jonathan replied, "because we have. My one regret is that we'll no longer be able to act as masters of our own ships. And we'll still have to find competent people to work with us in the offices. I don't feel much like a magnate myself, but like it or not, I've become one, and so have you.''

Late in the morning Homer Ellison made a full report to Jeremiah Rakehell, in his temporary office at the Boynton headquarters, and then had a talk with Jonathan about current problems.

"Jonnie,'' he said, "it seems to me we're being inefficient by keeping the clippers and the older cargo ships on separate schedules. That was fair enough when the clippers were still proving themselves, but there are more of them flying the Tree of Life pennant than there are brigs and schooners.''

"Can you be more specific, Homer?''

"You bet. The old windjammers still have a greater cargo capacity, but some of the clippers need more crews. In my opinion, an ablebodied seaman can move from one type of ship to the other without trouble. Give the windjammer officers occasional cruises on clippers so they can acclimate themselves to that way of sailing. Then we would be far more flexible, and could assign officers and men according to our greatest needs in any given period. Here. I've made a list of the ships currently in port in New London, those now at sea, and the backlog of merchandise awaiting shipment that's piling up in our warehouses. This second list will show you how we can reduce the pressure and increase our actual trade volume by making interchangeable assignments.''

Jonathan studied the statistics. "Good thinking, Homer. You've seen a major deficiency I hadn't noticed, and I'm beholden to you. Come join us for our noon meal at the Boynton house, and we can discuss all this in detail with my father after we've eaten.''

"Make it a supper invitation, and I'll accept with pleasure." Homer was embarrassed. "I sent Judith a note when we landed this morning, asking her to dine with me this afternoon, and the messenger brought back her acceptance."

Jonathan was startled.

"I know what you're thinking," Homer said defensively.

"My one thought is that I'm pleased you and Judith have struck up a friendship. Both of you are fine people, and I'm sure you can help each other."

The red-faced Homer rose slowly to his feet. "Thanks for your confidence, and I wish I had it in myself. The problem with our—ah—friendship is that we're walking blindfolded on the edge of a precipice, and our common sense keeps telling us to remove the blindfolds so we don't fall into empty space."

Less than two hours later, as Judith Walker and Homer sat in a quiet inn, sipping small glasses of unfermented cider as they awaited the Channel sole they had ordered, he repeated his conversation with her brother.

"I'm not ashamed of the way I feel," Homer said huskily. "We made the mistake of not recognizing each other's worth when we were youngsters, and we've paid for our ignorance. You know very well I'd ask you to marry me if you were free, Judy."

"I shouldn't listen to you," she said, but made no attempt to withdraw when he reached across the table and took her hand.

"I haven't said this to you before, and I ought not be saying it now. But you'd be deaf, dumb, and blind if you didn't know I love you, Judy."

There was a long silence, and then Judith said, "Unfortunately, my name is Walker, not Rakehell. Wandering somewhere on the face of the earth is my legal husband."

"He may be dead."

"I doubt it. He'd stay alive just to spite me." She paused, then asked in a voice that trembled slightly, "What shall we do, Homer?"

"Do? Continue to love each other. And hope for the best."

"You have patience and will power," she said. "You proved it when you gave up liquor. I'm not sure I have your courage."

"Lord help us, Judy, you're a Rakehell. That means you have a backbone of steel."

"Maybe I do. That's what Brad always told me, but he didn't mean it as a compliment. How awful to wish him dead! When we get home I'm going to see our family lawyer. There must be something he can do."

"If you don't hear from Walker or learn of his whereabouts in seven years, you can have him declared legally dead, Judy. But that's about all anyone can do."

"Seven years!" Judith was dismayed. "That means we—we have almost five years to wait, Homer!"

"We'll wait as long as is needful," he replied firmly. "Don't take me wrong. I want you. Bad. Right now. But I have too much respect for you to have an affair with you. I want you as my wife."

"I want you as my husband," she replied, and her voice became faint as she added, "But what if I'm not as strong as you? Suppose I—weaken?"

"You can't!" the alarmed Homer replied. "You mustn't! Your whole family would find out, and so would others. I won't have your good name dirtied! I'll try to be strong when you feel like giving in, and you do the same if and when I weaken."

She nodded but did not reply.

Their meal came, and not looking at each other, they ate their broiled sole, boiled potatoes, and Italian salad greens, tasting nothing.

Only when they had left the inn and were walking back to the house in Belgravia did Homer observe mildly, "We don't need to behave like characters in a tragedy. We should be thankful to the Almighty that, after all this time, we've found each other."

Judith sighed, then smiled up at him. "You're right, Homer," she said firmly and took his arm.

That evening, when Homer joined the Boynton and Rakehell families for one of Jessica's multicoursed meals, all of the adults noted silently that Judith Walker was radiant, that Homer Ellison's eyes sparkled, and that young Brad and Judy exchanged frequent significant glances.

Ruth Boynton was startled to discover that she was jealous, even though Judith and Homer faced a seemingly hopeless predicament. Her own situation, she reflected, was just as bad. She and Charles had made love a number of times since their reunion, but the incandescent excitement was missing, and so was the sense of deep physical gratification. So their intimacies became less frequent, and the strains on their marriage, although invisible, were increasing.

The situation might improve, Ruth thought, if Charles would stop pretending that nothing had changed and would bring his affair into the open. That way, perhaps, they could relegate it to the past and try to forget it. Ruth was tempted to bring up the subject herself, but she knew her husband well enough to realize he would deny having been even remotely interested in another woman. Then the barrier that separated them, instead of vanishing, would grow higher.

No, Ruth told herself, it wasn't Judith and Homer that she envied. It was Lai-tse lu. Adored by her husband, the most solid, honest, and charming man on earth, she felt the same way toward him. Just seeing them together made Ruth all the more miserable.

She discovered she actually felt relieved, at the end of the meal, when Jeremiah announced, "Homer tells me he'll be ready to start loading his cargo late tomorrow, so we'll be sailing for home in four days. Before we outstay our welcome."

Sir Alan protested, and so did Jessica.

"It will be a relief not to have us underfoot," Sarah said. "Besides, the menfolk have work to do." She looked hard at her husband.

Jeremiah well knew the significance of that look. Sarah had forced him to promise that he would delegate more responsibilities and work less hard in the future. "I've been widowed once," she had told him, "and I don't intend to go through all that again for a good many years! So you'll start taking life a mite easier, Jeremiah Rakehell."

The men remained behind at the table for port and cheroots when the ladies withdrew, and Jonathan got down to business as soon as his uncle had offered the customary toast to the health of Queen Victoria.

"Homer," he said, "I've shown your scheduling plans to Papa, and I thought Uncle Alan and Charles should see them, too."

"Most good ideas in business are so simple they cause others to wonder why they hadn't thought of them, Homer," Jeremiah said. "Your scheme is brilliant. I've figured we can increase our profits by a whopping seven percent annually at the American end alone, and the adoption of the system won't cost us a penny."

"I must congratulate you, Captain Ellison," Sir Alan said. "As soon as Charles and I analyzed your plan, we decided to follow the same procedure here."

"You've done great work, Homer," Charles told his former shipmate with a grin. "You've made a major contribution to the health of the company."

"Thank you, gentlemen." Not having expected such a strong response, Homer was overwhelmed by their unanimous praise.

"Putting the new system into operation does create one problem in our office," Jeremiah said. "My wife persuaded me to concentrate my own attention exclusively on finances, and this places the entire operations burden on Jonnie. He can't possibly handle it alone, not when he's continuing to build clippers, too, and is starting to think in terms of experimenting with transoceanic steamships. There have already been some transatlantic crossings, but I still don't think steamships are practical. However, I was mistaken about clippers, and I'm willing to concede I may be wrong again, although that's beside the point. Homer," he added abruptly, "how do you like your present post?"

"I enjoy it very much, Mr. Rakehell. A few years ago I wouldn't have thought it possible that I'd be in command of the largest clipper ship afloat."

"Might you be amenable to being beached—permanently?" Jeremiah wanted to know. "We'll need someone to take charge of this new operation and to help Jonnie discharge all of his other responsibilities."

"We agreed," Jonathan said, "that you're the right man for the post. I realize it's a wrench to give up a life at sea—I've had to face that myself. But we'd rather promote a captain than a businessman who has never held a sea command, and you're our natural choice."

Homer mulled the offer, then said, "I'm flattered, naturally, but I'd like to be blunt, if you won't be offended."

"Please speak freely," Jeremiah told him.

"If you're offering me this place on merit, if you think I'm really capable of discharging the responsibilities, I'll accept happily. But there's another element that comes into all this. I'm sure it's no secret to you, Mr. Rakehell—and I know it isn't to Jonnie—that Judith and I have an understanding. I'll grant you that we'll have to wait five years, more or less, before Bradford Walker can be declared legally dead and we can be married. But I wouldn't want the job given to me, Mr. Rakehell, because you want to make a place for someone who may become your son-in-law."

The Boyntons were somewhat embarrassed. Jonathan remained silent, knowing that only his father could reply.

"Thank you for your candor, Homer, and I'll be honest in return. Your relationship with my daughter, regardless of whether you marry someday, is irrelevant to this situation." Jeremiah spoke forcefully. "I've learned a lesson, and I'll never again promote a man because he's my son-in-law or future son-in-law. If you had no capability of becoming more than a first mate on a clipper, that's what you'd remain, and if Judith wanted to marry a ship's mate, that would be up to her and to you. I want you as a Rakehell and Boynton executive for only one reason. I believe you're the best man available, and believe—as Jonnie does—that you can perform accordingly."

"In that case, Mr. Rakehell," Homer said with a broad smile, "you've just hired a new front office man."

Homer was elated and knew Judith would share his joy. He had traveled far, rising higher than he had ever anticipated, and he felt confident that he was competent to discharge his new duties. But a disturbing thought crept into his mind. Had he continued to work as a ship's master, he would have spent the better part of his time at sea. Instead he would go to the New London shipyard every day, so it was inevitable that and Judy would spend most of their evenings and Sunday together. That continuing proximity would create temptations, and it would become far more difficult for them to keep their resolve and refrain from making love.

On the day before the clipper sailed to the United States, Lai-tse lu and Jonathan received a sudden, unexpected sum-

418

mons to Whitehall and were ushered promptly into Queen Victoria's sitting room.

They found the young monarch alone, Prince Albert having gone to one of the business-government conferences that he was attending with increasing frequency.

Queen Victoria made a point of serving the emperor's tea. "I very much wanted to see you again before you left our shores," she said. "When will you return?"

"If there isn't a business crisis of some sort, Your Majesty," Jonathan replied, "we should come back in another two years."

"You'll bring Mrs. Rakehell with you?"

"Of course, ma'am."

Victoria turned to Lai-tse lu. "Please remember that, as a Companion of the Queen's Own, you need no invitation to join me, wherever I may happen to be in residence."

"I look forward to our next meeting, Your Majesty," Lai-tse lu said.

"By any chance," the queen asked, "are you intending to visit China before then?"

"Yes, ma'am," Jonathan replied. "Some urgent matters will make it necessary for me to go to Canton and to your new colony of Hong Kong."

"Forgive my ignorance of Chinese geography, but will you be a great distance from Peking?"

"I plan to go to Peking to pay a visit to the Princess An Mien," Lai-tse lu said.

"Perfect!" The queen was delighted. "Will you also see the emperor?"

"One never knows, ma'am."

"No matter, really. I want your advice, and I want to ask a favor of you." The queen tugged at a bell rope, and two liveried servants came into the room carrying what looked like a large, rolled rug.

At her direction they unrolled it, and the visitors saw a very large tapestry. On it was a pastoral scene, showing ladies and gentlemen in medieval attire enjoying a picnic, with a castle looming in the background. Although the tapestry obviously was far from new, its colors were strong and pure, and its exquisite blues were extraordinary.

419

"By Chinese standards this work is anything but antique," Queen Victoria said. "In fact, it was made in Paris less than two hundred years ago by the Gobelins. It was commissioned by Louis XIV of France as a coronation gift for Charles II. I know little about the worth of most material things, but I'm assured by experts that no price can be placed on the tapestry. Do you regard it as a fitting gift to the Tao Kuang Emperor?"

Jonathan deferred to his wife.

"There are many tapestries in the Forbidden City, ma'am," Lai-tse lu said, "but none are equal to those produced by the great Gobelins of France. The Celestial Emperor knows a great deal about works of art, and he appreciates them, as does his sister. I'm certain this gift will have real meaning."

"I'm so glad I made the proper choice. I could send the gift through the Royal Navy's auspices, but I think it is only fitting, Mrs. Rakehell, if you will present it to the emperor and his sister on my behalf."

"I can think of no task I would enjoy more," Lai-tse lu replied.

"Then it's settled. I'm sure you will tell them how much the black pearl dazzled me, and I shall appreciate it if you'll tell me how they react to my gift."

"I shall write you, ma'am, as soon as I make the presentation," Lai-tse lu said.

Soon the audience came to an end, with the queen saying she would send the tapestry, under guard, to the Rakehell and Boynton shipyard the following morning. Jonathan promised he would supervise its storage for the voyage himself.

"It is strange," Lai-tse lu told her husband on the carriage ride back to the Boynton house. "I think of Victoria as a friend, not as a queen, just as I think of An Mien in the same way."

"That is because you're so extraordinary," he told her, taking her hand. "I'm grateful every day of my life for the miracle that brought us together."

The following morning the Boyntons went to the yard to bid farewell to the Rakehells and Wu-ling, who would sail to China after Jonathan and Lai-tse lu accumulated still more books and samples of manufactured goods to send to the Forbidden City. David was elated because he and Julian would be sailing, too, and were going to begin their sea training, and the two boys became boisterous and engaged in a wrestling bout on the pier, which made it necessary for Lai-tse lu and Ruth to separate them.

At last the moment of parting came. Elizabeth and Wu-ling, clinging to each other, burst into tears.

Jonathan made a clumsy attempt to console them. "When you next meet," he said, "you'll both be grown women." Putting an arm around Wu-ling's shoulders in order to lead her to the ship, he paused for a moment and kissed Elizabeth Boynton on the cheek.

He failed to note that she turned scarlet, then froze as she stared at him rather than at her friend.

The parrot arrived on a clipper that reached London a few days after the departure of the Rakehells, and the ship's master brought the bird and its perch to Charles's office. "The damned bird belongs to you, Mr. Boynton," he said, "and you're welcome to him!"

Charles was amused. "He's a handsome fellow. Reminds me of the Fat Dutchman's birds."

"All I know, sir, is that I kept him in my cabin, all the way from Cathay, and he never stopped talking, although I had no idea what he was saying. Mrs. Shaong asked me to bring him to you. She's written you a separate letter about him that she enclosed in her report."

The parrot glared and remained silent.

"Here's his food," the captain said, "and glad I am to be rid of him!"

Molinda's letter on the subject was brief:

Dieter is a gift to you from the Fat Dutchman. I tried to persuade him not to send the creature, but he insisted. His perch is to be kept in a warm place, away from draughts. He flies occasionally but always returns to his perch. I'm instructed to inform you that he will eat seeds of any kind. I will only add that I hope you and your family will appreciate the Dutchman's sense of humor.

Sir Alan looked dubiously at the bird on the carriage drive home that evening. "Colorful chap. I don't know what your mother and Ruth will think, but if he doesn't behave himself, I daresay we'll be trying a dish of parrot soup. Does he talk?"

"So Captain Myers told me, but so far he's been as silent as the tomb."

Lady Boynton and her daughter-in-law showed no enthusiasm for the parrot, although Elizabeth was intrigued.

"I've got to keep him," Charles said. "There's no one more important to us these days than the Dutchman, and he'd be insulted if we got rid of the bird."

"How would he know?" his practical mother asked.

"Well, I suppose I'll be obliged to tell him anecdotes about Dieter when I write to him, and I know too little about parrots to rely on my imagination. Also, he'll make a wonderful pet for David when he returns from his voyage."

Ruth relented a little. "We'll keep his perch in the dining room bay because more sun comes in through those windows than it does in any other room. Are you quite certain he speaks, Charles?"

"I only know what I'm told, Ruth."

The silent parrot suddenly became voluble, in Dutch. "Speak! Speak!" he said. "I hate the filthy intestines of you rotten scum." Dieter paused, then cursed the Boynton family at length.

Charles, the only member of the family who knew Dutch, had to fight for self-control to prevent himself from whooping with laughter.

"What did he say, Charles?" Ruth demanded.

"Nothing, to my knowledge. I believe he was just spouting bird gibberish of some sort."

Jessica saw her son swallowing his laughter. "I'm not certain I believe you, Charles," she said.

Ruth felt positive her husband was telling an untruth, for whatever his reason. For all she knew, however, the parrot was speaking in a Javanese dialect.

The parrot let loose with another string of curses so vile that Charles had to escape from the dining room before an explosion of laughter gave away the secret. Ruth and Lady Boynton followed him to the sitting room, exchanging quizzical glances.

The subject of the bird was dropped while the family exchanged glasses of sack before their dinner, but during the meal the parrot kept up a constant chatter, virtually all of it obscene.

"Isn't he wonderful, Father?" Charles asked, holding back a smile.

"Well, I wouldn't go quite that far," Sir Alan said, "but his nattering is unusual, and I don't find it offensive. I believe I'm willing to admit I like him, Charles."

"So do I," Charles replied, now breaking into a grin.

Dieter joined in the conversation by making scathing scatalogical references to Sir Alan's ancestry, and Ruth saw that her husband's whole body shook with suppressed laughter. Thereafter, throughout the meal, as the bird continued to chatter, Charles occasionally chuckled.

Elizabeth went off to a chaperoned party after the meal, and the adults returned to the sitting room. There Jessica knitted a new sweater for her grandson, Sir Alan and Ruth read, and Charles made a careful study of Molinda's report, occasionally scribbling comments and figures in the margin.

"We're doing even better everywhere in the East than I had hoped at this stage of our development there," he told his father, handing him the report. "Molinda is remarkable, worth her weight in gold to us."

"I'll take this upstairs with me," Sir Alan said with a yawn, "and read it in bed. Come along, Jessica."

After the older couple went off, Charles reached for a book, and for a long time there was no sound in the room but the hissing and occasional crackling of the coal fire in the grate.

Every night was like every other now, Ruth thought. When she and Charles spent an evening at home, they rarely communicated. Now she waited a little longer, then said, "There's something out of the ordinary about that parrot."

Charles did not look up from his reading. "You think so?"

"I know so!" she replied emphatically. "I have no idea what language he speaks, but I'm quite certain he says real words and that you understand them."

Taking his time, Charles looked at her over the top of his book, then said deliberately, "My dear, there are times when what you don't know won't hurt you."

Ruth felt rebuffed and made no reply. Charles returned to his reading.

Ruth sat for a time, no longer able to concentrate on her

423

own book. "I'm going to bed," she announced as she stood.

Charles's smile was vague. "I'm not sleepy," he said, "so I'll stay right here for a while longer. Good night, my dear."

"Good night." Perhaps her hurt was responsible, but the breach that separated them seemed to be widening rapidly.

Their situation did not improve in the weeks that followed. Charles was kept so busy at the yard that, at least two or three nights each week, he ate an evening meal of cold beef and bread at his desk and did not come home until midnight or later. Sometimes he could not escort his wife to dinner parties and other functions, so she accompanied various friends, and several astute hostesses began to plan accordingly, inviting an extra man to functions at which the Boyntons were expected to be present.

"We're searching for someone who can help Charles," Sir Alan said at dinner one night, "but it isn't easy to find the right man. Even after we've made our selection it will take months to break him in properly, so I'm afraid it will be some time before Charles can lead a fairly normal life again."

Jessica looked at her daughter-in-law sympathetically. "I hope you don't mind too much," she said.

"Oh, I'll manage, never fear." Ruth's reply was casual, almost too casual. "A price must be paid for success."

"True enough," her father-in-law declared, then leaned back in his chair. "We're growing so rapidly and becoming such a force in the Empire that it won't surprise me in the least if Charles is raised a notch or two in the peerage. Within the next ten years, I should think, after I've retired. I predict he'll be made a viscount, at the least. Your husband is well on the way to becoming one of the most influential men in England, Ruth—far more important than I've ever been."

Jessica smiled broadly.

Aware of their great pride in their son, Ruth could only reply, "He deserves recognition for his work." Privately, however, she would have been satisfied if Charles earned a fraction of his growing income and never received a title of his own. She wanted his love, not increased renown and wealth.

If Charles was conscious of a growing rift with his wife, nothing in his manner indicated it. On the contrary, he apologized every time his work delayed him at the office, and it did not appear to bother him that he and Ruth no longer made love. He was unfailingly courteous to her, and he tried, on Sundays and evenings when he did come home for dinner, to spend as much time as possible with his family.

At breakfast one morning Sir Alan followed his usual practice of opening his pocket watch, glancing at it, and then snapping it shut again. "Come along, son," he said. "Traffic may be heavy today, and we have an early meeting."

"One moment," Ruth interjected. "Charles, I do hope that this evening you can either clear your desk on time or leave the emergencies until tomorrow. I'll be appreciative if you can come home, and I'm quite certain your mother feels as I do."

"Indeed," Lady Boynton said.

Charles looked blankly at his wife, then at Jessica.

"We're giving a dinner party," Ruth explained patiently. "A rather important dinner party. Two Cabinet ministers and their wives will be here. So will the American, Dutch, and Spanish envoys. Lord and Lady Hale. The Earl and Countess of Warwick—"

"So they will, and thanks for reminding me," Charles said with a grin as he pushed back his chair.

"What Ruth is being too kind to mention," Jessica said, "is that the only bachelor is the Dutch minister, and if you aren't here we'll be forced to seat him beside her. He speaks such a frightful English it's almost impossible to understand a word he says, and you'll be guaranteeing your wife a miserable evening."

"I've been accumulating material for a long letter to Jonnie, but he'll have to wait an extra day." Charles kissed Ruth lightly and started toward the door. "I give you my solemn pledge I shall be home on time and save my wife the punishment of trying to decipher what old Willem van der Luen is trying to say."

He kept his word, actually returning home an hour earlier than expected. He bathed, shaved, and dressed quickly, then wandered from his dressing room to his wife's so he could ask her to knot his white evening tie for him.

Ruth sat at her dressing table, already dressed in a gown of pale gray silk, and was wearing the diamond earrings and bracelet Charles had given her on successive anniversaries.

425

Charles stopped short. "You're the best-looking woman in a city renowned for its beauties!" he said.

She felt herself redden beneath the cream she had applied to her face. The compliment was totally unexpected, and she murmured her thanks as she put the last combs in her upswept hair.

"I mean it," Charles said and advanced across the dressing room.

"Don't dare touch me until this rouge dries on my cheeks," she said in alarm.

He bent down and kissed her on the back of the neck. "I'm none too demonstrative," he said, "and lately I've had far too much on my mind, I know. So we've allowed too many cobwebs to gather. We need to have a talk that will sweep them away."

Ruth was relieved but frantic. This was the worst of all possible times for a discussion of their problems. "Your mother and I are meeting in the dining room in ten minutes to arrange the seating. That's one thing the butler can't do."

"Our chat can wait," he replied, and sauntered out, deciding he would ask Elizabeth to knot the bow in his white tie.

Not until he was gone did it occur to Ruth that she had wanted to ask him if they might move the parrot elsewhere for the evening. When she and Lady Boynton met in the dining room, however, they discussed the matter, then made up their own minds.

"Dieter has never left his perch in the presence of guests," Jessica said. "He's been well-trained by Charles's friend, I must admit."

"And he's being mercifully quiet," Ruth added as the bird glared at her. "He's colorful and unusual, so perhaps we'll let him stay." She began to concentrate on the task of where to seat each of the guests.

The dinner party was a success from the start. The staff functioned smoothly under the suave direction of the butler; the cook and her assistants worked hard preparing the dishes that Ruth and Jessica had planned with great care. The Boynton ladies were free to devote their complete attention to the guests.

Ruth enjoyed herself thoroughly in the drawing room as the company ate hot canapés and sipped glasses of sack. She put people at ease, made small talk, and moved from one group to another with the self-assurance of one who has been a hostess all of her life. Her metamorphosis, she well realized, was astonishing. She was the daughter of a New England carpenter, and when she had wanted a new dress she had saved for weeks in order to buy the material, then had made the dress herself. The clinging gown she was wearing tonight was symbolic of the changes in her life: it had been made for her by one of London's leading seamstresses, who was often called to Whitehall to fashion clothes for Queen Victoria.

The men paid considerable attention to the attractive young woman, and she flattered them subtly. But she devoted the better part of her attention to their wives, and consequently she was popular with them, too. As she took the arm of the United States minister for the walk down a flight of stairs to the dining room behind her mother-in-law and the senior Cabinet member, she could feel Charles's admiring look. Obviously he was proud of her, and she prayed that tonight they would, as he had put it, sweep away the cobwebs.

As Ruth took her place at the table she couldn't resist exchanging an amused glance with Jessica. They had given Willem van der Luen, the Dutch minister, a place between a lady who was slightly deaf and a noblewoman who was known for her incessant chatter and who never listened to anything that was said to her.

Course followed course, each accompanied by its own wine, and the party proceeded without a hitch. Conversation flowed and bubbled, and Charles told several hilarious stories about his experiences in the Orient. Gradually Jessica and Ruth were able to relax; the dinner party was an unqualified success.

Before the ladies withdrew at the end of the meal, more champagne was served, and Sir Alan rose, bowed to the American envoy, and toasted John Tyler, now President of the United States, who recently had married a lovely young lady from Virginia. Other toasts followed, and then the Dutch envoy, Willem van der Luen, struggled to his feet.

"I am much more at home in my own tongue," he said, speaking slowly, "so, with your permission, I will offer a toast to the American President and his bride in Dutch." He raised his glass and solemnly recited an old proverb.

The parrot, sitting on its perch behind the speaker, had remained silent throughout the meal. Now, however, Dieter

427

heard a familiar language and instantly came to life, accusing van der Luen of anatomical and character deficiencies. Even in a Rotterdam seaman's tavern the bird's description would have turned the air blue.

The startled envoy had just taken a mouthful from his glass. Stunned and unable to swallow, he spewed the champagne onto the table in a sudden shower.

Lady Boynton admirably demonstrated her poise by pretending that nothing out of the ordinary had taken place, and the guests were sufficiently sophisticated to follow her example.

Ruth noted that only the Dutch envoy and Charles, who was making a supreme effort to keep a straight face, had understood what the parrot had said. Charles avoided her gaze as she and her mother-in-law led the ladies from the dining room.

The men remained behind for their port and cheroots, and the parrot, having already expressed an emphatic opinion, did not misbehave again. The party proceeded smoothly, and even the more curious refrained from asking embarrassing questions. The gentlemen rejoined the ladies for a final hour of conversation, and when they departed Ruth realized that the Dutch minister was still shaken.

She waited until she and Charles retired to their own suite, and before he could disappear into his dressing room she demanded, "Well?"

He pretended he didn't know what she meant.

"It was obvious that Dieter speaks Dutch," she said.

"I don't think you want to know the details," Charles told her.

"I insist!"

He sighed, then began to translate the bird's outrageous curses.

Ruth clapped her hands over her ears. "Enough! Oh, poor Mr. van der Luen." All at once, in spite of herself, she began to laugh.

Charles roared, no longer able to control himself.

"We mustn't tell your mother," Ruth gasped between spasms of giggles. "She'd get rid of Dieter, and David wouldn't get to see him when he returns."

Holding his sides, Charles could only nod.

They laughed until they wept, and the ludicrous situation appeared to dissolve the invisible wall that had separated them. One or the other initiated a fresh outburst as they undressed, and it was only natural, when they climbed into bed, that they should start to make love.

The thought occurred to Ruth that she owed a debt of gratitude to the parrot.

As their passions became aroused, the absurd incident faded from their minds, and the breach that had kept them apart seemed to be healed. Both were fulfilled, and Charles soon drifted off to sleep.

Ruth remained wide awake, however, pervaded by an increasing sense of restlessness. Ultimately she climbed out of bed, donned a dressing robe, and wandered into the adjoining sitting room. For a long time she couldn't understand why she was upset. She and Charles had reestablished the healthy relationship they had enjoyed in the early days of their marriage. Perhaps she had only imagined he had been unfaithful to her.

All at once her perspective was restored and she felt cold as the truth dawned on her. She had given herself to Charles without restraint and consequently had been blind to a subtle but nevertheless marked change in his attitude toward her.

His lovemaking had been perfunctory. Her instinct told her, insistently, that although he had obtained satisfaction, she no longer held a special place in his affections. He would have enjoyed the experience as much with any attractive woman who had responded to him with such enthusiasm.

The worst of her new predicament was that it was impossible for her to prove that anything was amiss. She tried to tell herself she was being overly sensitive, that she was creating a problem where none existed. But deep within herself she knew better. His affair—and it no longer mattered to her who the other woman might have been—had coarsened him.

Perhaps she was expecting too much. Perhaps the mending process would take time and would require her to show patience and understanding. Well, she had nothing to lose by trying, but in the same breath she was convinced she had been cheapened. She had to give her marriage a chance, but she was afraid that the tear in the closely woven fabric could not be repaired.

Although David and Julian were still too young to serve as cabin boys, they were placed in Homer Ellison's charge for several hours each day on their voyage to the United States. Jonathan insisted they be shown no favors because they were the sons of principals in the company, and he took care not to interfere in the disciplines to which they were subjected.

It was far more difficult for Lai-tse lu to turn a deaf ear when she heard Oliver bellowing orders to the small boys. Wu-ling, who would stay with the Rakehells in New London until the Princess An Mien formally accepted her services as a translator, was even more sympathetic to the boys and remained in her cabin during the hours they received instruction.

Only Sarah Rakehell approved without reservation, telling Jeremiah, "The day will come when those two youngsters will need to know everything about the shipping business. Jonathan and Charles wouldn't be achieving all they're doing today if you and Alan hadn't given them the right training. It's good they're carrying on the family tradition so faithfully."

The voyage was quiet, with the clipper sailing at a somewhat slower pace because the customary west-to-east headwinds were encountered. Then, when the clipper was only three days out of New London, Jonathan was disturbed when Lai-tse lu remained in bed instead of dressing for breakfast. Never before had she failed to join him, and he asked, "What's wrong?"

"It's nothing," she said. "I just don't feel like getting up this morning, that's all."

He looked at her carefully, saw that her eyes were dull, and put a hand on her forehead. "You have no fever."

"I could have told you that." She made an attempt to smile. "Go have your breakfast. I may go to sleep again."

Jonathan went directly to the elder Rakehells' cabin. "Missy Sarah," he said, "something is the matter with Lai-tse lu, but she won't admit it to me."

Sarah went to the younger woman at once and remained with her for a quarter of an hour before joining the men. "She doesn't want you to worry, Jonnie," she said. "It appears she has a touch of the same ailment that caused her trouble when Jade was born."

Jonathan immediately went to the quarterdeck, where Captain Ellison had the watch. "Homer," he said, "crowd on as

430

much sail as the ship will tolerate. I want to get home as fast as possible."

Continuing to protest that her condition was not serious, Lai-tse lu nevertheless stayed in bed for the rest of the voyage. Thanks to the skill and dedication of Homer and his crew, the clipper reached her home port in two days rather than three.

Jonathan insisted on carrying his wife to their waiting carriage, and Dr. Graves hurried across the street as soon as they reached the Rakehell mansion. He subjected the patient to a thorough examination, then said to her, "I'm afraid it's as we anticipated when you had your baby."

Lai-tse lu nodded. "I knew from the moment the pain began that it was the same ailment."

"Then you realize," the physician said gently, "that I can do nothing to cure you. If you wish, though, I'll give you laudanum to ease the pain."

She shook her head. "The pain is much less today than it was in the beginning. Soon it will pass completely."

"Until it does, there's no need for you to suffer." Dr. Graves reached for his black leather bag of instruments and medicines.

"No!" Lai-tse was firm. "I hate opium so much that my conscience would not permit me to take even one dose of laudanum."

"I admire your courage," he said, then paused. "From the few words I had with Jonathan, I gather he knows virtually nothing about your illness."

"I've seen no need to cause him concern."

"He has a right to know, and he'll start asking questions as soon as he comes in here. Do you prefer that I tell him?"

"I'll do it," she said with a sigh.

Dr. Graves went to the door and called to her husband, who was waiting in the sitting room.

Lai-tse lu wasted no words. "I have known, since before Jade was born, that I have an ailment for which there is no cure," she said. "Occasionally it has caused me mild discomfort, but the attack on board ship was the first time I've felt truly ill."

Jonathan stared at her, then at the physician.

"It's true," Dr. Graves said. "She may not have any further spasms for years, or she could suffer another severe attack today or tomorrow. In cases like this, no physician can predict what will happen next."

Jonathan drew in his breath. "Is this disease fatal?"

"There are cases on record in which women have lived full, useful lives for fifty years after first contracting the disease. Others have been known to die within a very short time. I know of no rules to guide you."

Lai-tse lu reached for her husband's hand. "Ever since I first learned I had this ailment," she said, "I have tried to live each day for its own sake and not look too far into the future. If I am fortunate, I will live to see my grandchildren growing to manhood and womanhood. I cannot allow myself to brood. That would spoil however much may remain of my appointed time on this earth."

Jonathan admired her as much as he loved her. "You've marked the way," he said huskily, "and I'll do as you do."

Julian and Jade were badly upset by Lai-tse lu's illness, and David was almost as deeply affected. They felt infinite relief the following morning, when she appeared for breakfast. And when Jonathan came home at noon for dinner, her ailment went completely out of their minds.

All three children stared wide-eyed at the long-haired black dog he was leading on a leash, a frisky animal, less than a year old, whose mouth and tongue were as black as his coat.

"One of our clippers arrived this morning from Hong Kong and Whampoa," he said, "and on board was this chow-chow, a gift to the children from Kai."

"He belongs to us?" Julian shouted.

"Go slowly, boy," his father said. "You'll have to speak to him only in Cantonese, at least until you teach him English. That's the one language he knows."

"Does he have a name?" David wanted to know.

Lai-tse lu was reading the letter that Kai had sent with his gift. "Indeed he does, and Molinda not only translated it into English, but taught him to understand it. He is called Harmony," she said with a smile.

The dog heard his name and wagged his tail furiously.

Jonathan unfastened the leash, and the children approached the animal cautiously. "Harmony," Julian said, then spoke slowly in Cantonese. "Will you be our friend?"

"He is our friend," David declared, speaking in the same tongue.

Somehow Jade managed to say "friend" in Cantonese, too.

The ecstatic dog licked her face, and the little girl hugged him fiercely.

"Be gentle," Jonathan admonished.

The children were too excited to heed his warning, and soon all three were romping around the parlor with the happy, barking Harmony.

Sarah Rakehell became grim as she observed the bedlam. "We certainly don't need a dog in this house," she said.

The children halted and gaped at her. The dog stopped racing, too, and cocking his head to one side as he looked at her, he wagged his tail more tentatively.

"I will permit no running and rough games indoors," she said. "What's more, this animal will eat his meals in the kitchen. He will not be permitted to set foot in the dining room." For the dog's benefit she translated her words into Cantonese.

"Kai says in his letter that Harmony is housebroken, Missy Sarah," Lai-tse lu said.

"When I next see Kai, I intend to give him a piece of my mind!" she retorted.

Jonathan discreetly opened the French doors that led to the side yard, and within moments the children and Harmony were playing there.

Jeremiah expressed himself for the first time. "There's no dog more loyal and faithful than a chow, or so I've been told," he said mildly. "And I know of no gift that would give the children so much pleasure."

His wife replied with a loud sniff.

He grinned at her. "My dear," he said, "I hope you know the principal difference between you and that animal. In Harmony's case, I'm sure his bite is worse than his bark."

The convalescing Lai-tse lu and Jonathan averted their faces so Sarah Rakehell wouldn't see their broad smiles.

Jeremiah soon proved to be an accurate prophet. Harmony immediately became a member of the family, and no one spoiled him more assiduously than Sarah. Conveniently forgetting her own rules, she took the lead in surreptitiously feeding the animal tidbits from the kitchen.

Harmony quickly demonstrated that he had a mind of his own. Intelligent and responsive when addressed in Cantonese, he stubbornly refused to obey any orders given to him in English.

"It may be just as well," Lai-tse lu told Jonathan. "Now the children have a natural reason to speak Cantonese. Wu-ling and I will find it much easier to give them Chinese language lessons."

Guests who came to the house soon discovered it was unwise to approach any of the children until Julian or David assured Harmony that the outsider meant no harm. Until duly warned, the chow bristled, a menacing growl emanating from deep inside him when anyone came within arm's reach of a child.

The principal problem created by the arrival of Harmony was the nightly squabble between the children. "He's going to sleep with David and me in our room!" Julian declared.

"No!" Jade insisted. "Sleep with me!"

Harmony solved the matter in his own diplomatic way. Lai-tse lu left the door ajar between the two bedrooms, and the dog wandered back and forth at will, always managing to be close at hand as a child was dropping off to sleep in the evening or awakening in the morning.

As Lai-tse lu recovered her health, she resumed her task of obtaining printed matter and product samples for the Tao Kuang Emperor and the Princess An Mien. Jonathan wrote to his former classmates who had gone on to Harvard medical school, asking them to suggest names of young physicians who might be willing to spend several years in China. He was heartened by their promises to conduct a search on his behalf.

But he himself had little time for such a hunt. His wife's swift recovery from her illness enabled him to devote his full attention to the rapid expansion of Rakehell and Boynton shipping activities. For the first time since the company had been founded a century earlier, the yard couldn't produce new ships as swiftly as they were required, and it became necessary to purchase several schooners and brigs elsewhere.

"Our growth is almost too rapid," Jeremiah told his son at the office one morning. "What with buying the stock of outside shareholders and purchasing more standard ships for our increased trade, we've almost depleted our cash reserves.''

"Surely that's a temporary situation, Papa," Jonathan said. "The new schooners and brigs, like the clippers we're putting into service, should pay for themselves within a year to eighteen months.''

"I'm quite certain they will," Jeremiah said, "so I'm not too concerned, and neither is Alan. We're just being overly conservative. No doubt because we've kept such unnecessarily large cash reserves in the past, and we're creatures of habit.''

"If you and Uncle Alan are uncomfortable, Charles and I can cut back on our rate of expansion. We've been jumping in with both feet, so to speak, because the China market is opening wider and wider, and because the German states and the Ottoman Empire are broadening their international trade.''

"Do it your way," Jeremiah said. "You and Charles have earned the right to move in your own direction and at your own speed. The cash flow will increase as the new markets begin to pay off, and I can see no crisis ahead that would make it necessary for us to sell some of our new ships. Our reserves may be low, but we've been paying for our cargoes as we buy them, and we have no appreciable debts.''

"I'll grant you that we'll be able to afford few luxuries in the next year or so," Jonathan said, "but in addition to our trade growth we should see some first-rate results from Homer Ellison's new operations system, too. I'd lie awake all night if I thought I was placing my children's future in jeopardy, but I'm having no trouble sleeping.''

"You have my unqualified confidence," his father told him, and that ended their talk.

That same afternoon, when the men had returned to the yard after dinner, Sarah went marketing and Lai-tse lu busied herself with a translation into Chinese of articles in New York and Boston newspapers of a new surgical technique that was saving the arms or legs of people injured in accidents.

Wu-ling took Julian and David to the beach of the Rakehell house on the estuary of the Thames. The boys were accomplished swimmers, and as they raced each other, Harmony ran up and down on the beach, barking happily but taking care not to get wet. When Jade awakened from her nap, she joined them, but obeyed Wu-ling's injunction to paddle in water no higher than her waist. Harmony seemed to sense that the little girl couldn't yet swim: he stopped running, no longer barked, and with his ears erect and his curled tail wagging slowly, he stood on the beach watching every move that Jade made.

It was ironic that the unexpected incident should have been caused by one of the large, freight-carrying schooners that Jonathan had recently purchased. Making her first voyage under the Tree of Life pennant, the heavy vessel left her berth at the Rakehell and Boynton yard, more than a mile up the river, and gradually adding sail as she moved downstream began to move more and more rapidly.

Julian and David recognized the flag and stopped swimming long enough to wave madly, Jade imitating the boys. Someone on the quarterdeck waved in return without ever guessing the identity of the children.

A wave created in the wake of the heavy ship rolled across the placid water toward the shore. Julian and David saw it and were sufficiently experienced to plunge beneath it. But Jade, blissfully unaware of danger, continued to hold both arms over her head as she happily called to the men on board her father's ship.

The wave knocked her off her feet forcefully, and then, as it retreated, sucked her far out into the estuary. Wu-ling, who could not swim, ran to the water's edge and called frantically to the boys to help.

Julian and David rose to the surface, heard Wu-ling, and looked around in bewilderment. But Harmony was already in action. Instantly conquering his dislike for the water, the dog plunged in, then began to swim, his feet thrashing furiously as he headed for the child.

Wu-ling was close to hysteria as Jade vanished from sight and the boys, although they now understood what she meant, looked in vain for a glimpse of the little girl. But Harmony's instincts were true. Swimming rapidly, he reached Jade's side as she rose momentarily to the surface, her small arms and legs waving wildly. She had already swallowed some water and was in danger of inhaling still more as she sobbed.

The dog ducked beneath the surface and came up under the child, literally lifting her out of the water. Then, gently but firmly, he took her long hair in his mouth and, still managing to hold her head out of the water, started toward the shore.

By now the boys realized what was happening, and David started to swim toward the dog and the little girl. But Julian had better sense. "Stay clear, David!" he called. "Let Harmony do it!"

Harmony was doing all that the circumstances required, and continued to swim steadily. Soon Jade knew what was happening. Her frenzy subsided when she knew she was safe, and her small hands clutched the dog's long hair, making her even more secure.

The animal did not halt until he had dragged his burden high onto the beach. Jade had suffered no injury and hugged the dog fiercely.

Wu-ling swept the little girl into her arms, lavishly praising Harmony in a stream of Cantonese. Then the boys ran up beside her and did the same.

Lai-tse lu came to the door when she heard the commotion and was shocked when she learned what had happened. Cradling her daughter in her arms, she first assured herself that Jade was intact. Then she dropped to her knees and took the dog's head in both hands. "Harmony," she told him in Cantonese, "you are truly a member of our family."

Jonathan and his father praised the dog when they came home, Jeremiah by now having learned a few of the words that the dog understood. But it was Sarah who awarded Harmony the supreme accolade. That night she insisted that the dog's food dish be moved into the dining room, and after selecting and cooking the largest beefsteak in the larder for him, she cut the meat for him herself. "After all," she said, "that's the very least we can do for him. He deserves the best!"

Book
VI

I

Owen Bruce and Bradford Walker changed places, with the former taking charge of the growing complex in Hong Kong and the latter operating out of the factory at Canton. They met at the end of each month, and on these occasions it was necessary for Bruce to come to Whampoa. Walker had been so badly frightened in Hong Kong that nothing would induce him to return there, even for a visit of a day and a night.

The exchanges of information were necessary and useful, and one month both of the partners had more than usual to report. They sat together in the small parlor of Walker's quarters behind the factory, sipping glasses of Scotch whiskey and water, and even though the servants had been dismissed and no one was within earshot, Owen Bruce lowered his voice.

"I've just paid a visit to our friend and partner in Macao," he said, "and we're on the verge of making our biggest financial killing yet. And this time you'll play the key role."

Walker was enjoying himself now that he had switched with his partner, and he nodded comfortably. "I'm glad I've earned Dom Manuel's trust," he said.

Bruce's grin showed his tobacco-stained teeth. "Listen, Eddie, and you'll have reason to rejoice. I'm glad we changed places. Hong Kong is the perfect listening post for me. Recently I learned of a huge cache of opium—five tons of it—"

"Five tons!" Walker was stunned.

"Aye. The purest, finest quality, grown in the isle of Ceylon, off the coast of India, by a planter who knew what he was about. The British East India Company learned of the cache, as did others, but the two ships I sent to Ceylon arrived

there first,'' Bruce's grin broadened. ''The planter was relu
tant to sell to my people, but they had their own means
persuasion.'' He paused for an instant. ''You can be sure l
widow won't starve.''

Walker had to control a shudder.

''For the moment our ships are lying low in a lagoon
an uninhabited isle. They'll wait until the fuss and fury ov
the planter's death calms a bit, and then they'll take the car
to Macao. It will be landed there in the usual manner. Tha
when you'll take charge.''

''I will?'' Walker was surprised.

''Even more than ever, the Marquês de Braga does
want to be directly associated in any way with the cargo.
you'll hire a band of Chinese. They'll take it from the wa
house in Macao late one night. They'll load it onto junks th
will vanish in the Pearl River. You'll take the cargo asho
You'll be there to receive the opium and pay off your handle
and I'll join you there. So will the Chinese smugglers w
have been my clients for years. They'll pay us in hard cash
the best quality Chinese silver—for a cargo that's worth
fortune to us. I'll take my share and our partner's, which l
deliver to him in Macao, and you'll come back to Canton wi
more money than you've ever seen in your life.''

Walker nodded. ''The plan is good, but the one proble
as I see it, is where I'll find dependable men who will take l
cargo from the Macao warehouse to the rendezvous point
the Pearl River Delta.''

''I leave that matter entirely in your hands.'' Bruc
voice hardened. ''You'll be expected to make a positive co
tribution to this operation. Dom Manuel expects you to ea
the fortune that will be coming your way, and so do I.''

Bradford Walker gnawed on his lower lip.

Suddenly Bruce laughed, clapped him on the should
and poured more whiskey from a decanter into their glass
''Cheer up, laddie. The men you hire may suspect they
moving opium, but they won't know for certain that it isn't t
Besides, it's no problem to find willing hands in this heath
land. You can have fifty men, a hundred, or a thousand. Wh
ever you think you'll need. Drop a few yuan into a Chinama
hand, and he'll belong to you, body and soul. Never forg
these are the most corrupt people on earth.''

"I'll take your word for it," Walker said and became brighter. "I can find no holes in the scheme."

"That's because it's simple. That's why Dom Manuel and I are convinced that nothing can go wrong. That five tons of quality opium will buy whatever you want in this world, be an estate of your own, a beautiful woman, or a fat bank account."

Walker laughed aloud, rubbing his hands together. "I have a contribution of my own to make to our bank accounts," he said. "I haven't been idle since I've returned to Canton, and I've found a way to kill two birds with a single shot. You and the marquês and I share a strong dislike for the Rakehells—"

"What have they to do with our earnings?" a scowling Bruce interrupted.

"Hear me out. They've placed a woman who is Eurasian in charge of their entire Eastern operation. She's a beauty, far more fit to be a bedmate than a woman of business, and even though she's married to the emperor's cousin, I can only figure she must also be the mistress of Jonathan Rakehell or Charles Boynton."

"I still don't see the connection with us."

"Hear me out," Walker said. "I've been cultivating the lady, and I believe I've won her friendship. Now I'm ready to strike. I intend to ask her for the loan of a very large sum of money on behalf of our company and will offer her an attractive rate of interest."

Bruce stared at him incredulously. "You're proposing that we borrow money from Rakehell and Boynton?"

"Call it a loan. It will never be repaid. No one nation has jurisdiction over the port of Canton. They can't sue us, because there are no law courts here. They can whistle for their money."

The Scotsman was slightly mollified. "It seems to me a strange way to strike a blow at our enemies."

"Ah, that's just the beginning. Remember that I'm familiar with the Rakehell and Boynton operation. I've been astonished at the sums of money they've been pouring into their operations. New warehouses, more ships. You'd think they're made of money. But they're not. When we fail to repay the loan, and they find there's no action they can take against us, I'm hoping they'll be driven into bankruptcy."

"Ah. That would be pleasant." Bruce leaned back in h[is] chair and smiled.

Walker laughed again. "Best of all, we pick up the piece[s] when they founder. We have more than enough cash on han[d] to buy their warehouses, offices, ships, and merchandise [at] bargain prices. We'll quadruple our own operation at very litt[le] cost to ourselves, and at the same time we'll put our enemie[s] out of business!"

The Scotsman contemplated the plan in silence for a mo[o]ment, then raised his glass. "Walker," he said, "I salute yo[u] I'm stopping at Macao on my way back to Hong Kong, an[d] you can be sure that Dom Manuel will be very happy, too. B[ut] what makes you so sure you can persuade this woman to mak[e] you the loan?"

"Her lack of experience, combined with the flattery that [a] woman who fancies herself loves to hear. She won't be able [to] resist the deal that I'll offer her. I've been building up to th[e] situation for weeks, and I hope to make the final arrangeme[nt] at a meeting I'm holding with her tomorrow."

"If you succeed," Bruce said, "your scheme and th[e] profits we make on the new opium operation will give us a fre[e] hand. By taking over Rakehell and Boynton, we'll be in [a] position to challenge the British East India Company and b[e]come the largest shippers and traders in the Orient. I'll enjo[y] that. I won't even mind postponing my own retirement for [a] few years."

They drank until nightfall, when Bruce sailed off to Maca[o]. Bradford Walker had no appetite for food but realized [he] would need all the acumen and charm he could muster for h[is] meeting with Molinda the following day. So he dined at a ne[w] inn that had opened in the area after the signing of the pea[ce] treaty, then went to bed and slept soundly.

In the morning he dressed with great care and was unab[le] to concentrate on the routine paperwork that crossed his des[k]. It was a relief, shortly before his appointment, to saunter dov[n] the waterfront to the complex that had belonged to the la[te] Soong Chao. A clipper and two brigs, all flying the Tree [of] Life banners, were tied up at the Rakehell and Boynton wharve[s] as were several of their junks, and he marveled at the volum[e] of their trade. There was no doubt in his mind that their expa[n]sion was far too rapid. Now, if he could persuade the woma[n]

444

o make him the loan that would never be repaid, the empire hey were building on such a fragile foundation would topple.

Molinda, impeccably groomed and attired in one of the orm-fitting cheongsams she habitually wore in Canton, greeted ler visitor with a gracious smile. Knowing nothing of his background, unaware that he was Jonathan's brother-in-law, she had come to like this earnest American. He knew the shipping business, was never reluctant to share information with her, and had given her sound advice in recent months.

She ordered tea, a ritual that was scrupulously observed when doing business at Canton, and for some minutes they chatted about inconsequentials.

Then, easing into his subject, Walker said, "I'm amazed o see so many of your ships in port."

"Yes," she replied happily, "our program is developing ahead of schedule, thanks to the support I've received from our principal partners in America and England."

"You don't find that absentee owners create more problems than they solve?"

"They've created none."

"I wish I could say the same." His sigh was exaggerated. 'Our representative in Hong Kong, Owen Bruce, and I are just working partners in our company. In order to trade at Macao," he went on, telling the falsehood that had been deliberately concocted to justify their activities in the Portuguese colony, 'we had to give far too many shares to investors in Lisbon. They knew nothing about trade, nothing about shipping, and only a steady flow of profits will satisfy them."

Molinda nodded sympathetically. "It must be very difficult."

"It's worse than that. Strictly between us," he said, and lowered his voice, even though they were alone in her office, 'their greed, based on their ignorance, may force Bruce and me to sell all the stock in our warehouses for less than we paid or it."

"Oh, dear."

"Our absentee investors in Lisbon demanded every penny of profits due the first of this month. So we sent them the money, even though it left us temporarily short of cash. And now one of our principal suppliers in—ah—Ceylon—is unexpectedly demanding full payment for his products. We

hadn't anticipated paying him for another two months, by whic
time we'll be on our feet again. But he's had troubles of som
sort, and our reputations can be badly hurt if we don't pay hi
immediately."

The situation he described was common in the shippin
business, and Molinda had no reason to suspect he was lying t
her. "What a dreadful position to be in."

"We're afraid to approach the East India Company for
short-term loan because they're so ruthless we don't trust them
No matter that we're prepared to offer them a very attractiv
arrangement."

Molinda's business interest aroused her curiosity, as h
had hoped it would. "What sort of deal were you planning t
offer them?"

"We want to borrow sixty thousand pounds sterling fo
sixty days, and we would offer to pay fifteen thousand pound
interest."

"You want over a quarter of a million dollars for a ver
short period and would give them a profit of twenty-five per
cent?" Her eyes widened.

Walker nodded. "We'll have to look elsewhere, here an
in Hong Kong, although there aren't many companies wealth
enough to make us a loan that large."

Molinda's mind worked furiously, and she made som
rapid calculations as she stalled for time by pouring more tea
The profit he was offering was worth what the Rakehell an
Boynton operation in the Orient would earn over a period o
several months, and the opportunity was too good to be ig
nored. "I might be able to help you," she said casually.

"You?" Walker feigned astonishment.

"We've become so active in our trade with Manila
Formosa, Bangkok, and the Dutch Indies that we keep fairl
large sums of cash on hand here. Interest of twenty-five per
cent on a loan of sixty thousand pounds sterling is very temp
ing. But I must make it clear that I could grant no extensions
I'd need repayment in full in sixty days. I wouldn't mind if yo
needed a little longer to pay the interest."

Inwardly rejoicing, Walker playacted expertly. "I couldn
ask it of you," he said, shaking his head.

"It seems like a sound, clear-cut business arrangement t

ne," she replied crisply. "I assume that both you and Mr. Bruce would sign the loan agreement."

"Of course." He continued to demonstrate reluctance. "You're sure this won't inconvenience you?"

"Not at all," Molinda said, "provided you repay the principal on time."

"We'll pay promptly," Walker said. Not only was he helping himself to another substantial chunk of Jeremiah and Jonathan Rakehell's money, but he was virtually guaranteeing the collapse of their proud company.

The letter, written by the senior clerk on the White House staff, was succinct. President John Tyler invited Mr. Jonathan Rakehell to call on him at his earliest convenience to discuss a matter in the national interest. A postscript, which the President penned himself, added that he and his young bride, the former Julia Gardiner, would be pleased to welcome Mrs. Rakehell, too. Neither Jonathan nor his father could guess the reason for the summons.

They decided to travel by rail, and Lai-tse lu was thrilled about making a railroad trip to Washington City. She packed one of her more glamorous cheongsams for the occasion, and they traveled in a comfortable, private compartment. Lai-tse lu particularly enjoyed their brief stopovers in New York, Philadelphia, and Baltimore. "Living quietly as we do," she said, "I sometimes forget that America is a great, growing country. The cities are so busy they remind me of Canton and Peking."

Their suite at O'Neale's Hotel, which Jonathan had reserved by letter, was waiting for them on their arrival in Washington City. They reached the nation's capital in midafternoon, and Jonathan sent a brief note to the White House by messenger, saying he and his wife had arrived and that he awaited the President's pleasure. He expected an appointment to be made for the following day and was surprised when the messenger returned with a dinner invitation for that same evening, signed by Julia Tyler. Whatever business the President had in mind appeared to be urgent.

The Rakehells bathed hastily, and Lai-tse lu changed into her cheongsam of violet silk, with which she wore some of her

447

rare jade jewelry. Never, her husband assured her, had she looked lovelier.

The lean, energetic John Tyler and his lovely dark-haired bride surprised their guests by greeting them at the main entrance to the White House, the President displaying the innate courtesy of his native Virginia. As Jonathan well knew, he was determined to leave his mark on history. Martin Van Buren had not been reelected president in 1840, and Tyler had succeeded to the high office when his predecessor, William Henry Harrison, had died a month after being inaugurated. Tyler had no political constituency of his own, and his fellow Democrats had already nominated James K. Polk as their candidate in the coming election. But Tyler was in no way deterred by being confined to a single term, and continued to lead the country with vigorous skill and determination.

"I thought the ladies might enjoy a before-dinner chat, Mr. Rakehell," he said, "while we adjourn to my office for a discussion on the China trade."

"With all due respect, Mr. President," Jonathan said, "I'd like to suggest that Mrs. Rakehell sit in with us. I've acquired more than a passing interest in China, but her expertise is far greater than mine."

Julia Tyler smiled. "That's exactly what I told him."

The President grinned at her. "I stand corrected," he said amiably and offered Lai-tse lu his arm.

Although the United States was far smaller than the Middle Kingdom in both population and size, Lai-tse lu nevertheless was surprised by the unpretentiousness of the Chief Executive's office. John Tyler used the swivel chair that had been Andrew Jackson's, sitting behind a leather-tooled desk that Thomas Jefferson had brought with him from France. But a hooked farmer's rug covered a portion of the floor; the visitors' chairs were made of plain maple, and aside from a few personal mementos that sat on the desk, the only decorative notes in the room were the flags of the United States and Virginia behind the President's desk. There was no grandeur here, no hint of the rich panoply that was everywhere in the Forbidden City.

Jonathan was mildly surprised when they were joined by former Congressman Caleb Cushing of Massachusetts. In his early forties, with a reputation for "getting things done," Cushing

as a former Whig who had given Tyler his full support, and
s Jonathan well knew, the Whigs in the Senate had punished
im by refusing to confirm his appointment as Secretary of the
reasury. For the moment, his presence was unexplained.

"I asked you here, Mr. Rakehell," the President said,
because you know more about the China trade than any other
merican and because of your reputed connections with the
nperial family."

Jonathan smiled and shook his head. "Again I must defer
o my wife," he said. "She has long been close to the imperial
amily."

"Then I shall address my remarks to both of you," Tyler
aid. "I've been told repeatedly that the potential market for
ade with China is very large. Is that true?"

"It is far larger than anyone in the United States can
magine," Jonathan replied. "There's a crying need in China
or many of our products, and an unlimited market here for
heir tea, silks, and porcelains, among other goods."

"Thanks to the treaty that Great Britain forced on China
t the end of the Opium War, the British well may monopolize
e China trade," the President declared. "With the French,
e Portuguese, and a few others snipping away at smaller
hares. Am I correct?"

"Well, Mr. President," Jonathan said with a smile, "my
ompany is trying hard to restore a balance so we aren't
ompletely locked out."

"Are the Chinese receptive to us, do you think?" Cushing
ddressed the question to Lai-tse lu.

"There can be no doubt of it," she replied emphatically.
The Tao Kuang Emperor has friendly feelings toward this
ountry. His sister, the Princess An Mien, who is something of
e power behind the throne, has a lively interest in America,
articularly since my husband and I have sent her so many
ooks and magazines on American industry and science and
edicine. She leans very strongly toward this country."

The President hitched forward, resting his elbows on his
esk. "Do you believe China would be amenable to the mak-
ng of a treaty that would open her ports to our trade, as
ey've been opened to the British?"

"By all means," Lai-tse lu said, "provided the terms
ere fair."

449

"Can you be more specific?" Tyler wanted to know.

"Let me try," Jonathan said. "If her ports are opened us, we should open our ports to her. Even though she has ships that could sail this far. The principle of reciprocity is stake, and it's the sort of gesture the Chinese appreciate. If o citizens are given the right to visit China, we must open o gates to her people, and I believe many will want to con here."

"More than all else," Lai-tse lu added, "the United Stat should seek no territories from the Middle Kingdom. We shou not demand a Hong Kong. Or the right to establish an Amer can concession responsible only to the American governme in any Chinese seaport. Then there will be no resentmen against America, as there are resentments against the Britis An honest, open relationship will win the United States th friendship and respect of the rulers and people of the Midd Kingdom."

"Well said, Mrs. Rakehell," the President declared. "Ob viously you understand the principles on which this nation wa founded. Do you think Caleb Cushing would be received fa vorably if I appoint him as a special minister to negotiate treaty with the emperor?"

Lai-tse lu laughed. "The Tao Kuang Emperor has see my husband informally, but neither the emperor nor his an cestors have ever received any foreigners in a formal audi ence."

"We've been hoping he'd see me."

Her eyes sparkled mischievously. "Would you kowto before him, Mr. Cushing?"

"Well, no. Certainly not." The envoy-designate wa flustered.

"You begin to see the problem," Lai-tse lu said, an giggled.

"If the Tao Kuang Emperor should be favorably incline to the idea of expanded trade with the United States," Jonatha said, "he would appoint a commission to negotiate with M Cushing. And under no circumstances would those meeting be held in Peking. Mr. Cushing would be lucky if he wei allowed to penetrate as far as the Imperial City."

"I'm wondering how best to insure that the emperor wou be made receptive to the prospect of a treaty with us," th

President said. "Could you accomplish that task, Mr. Rakehell?"

"My wife could do it far better. I'd be glad to help her, naturally."

"Thank you." Tyler looked around the room. "How much advance notice would be necessary to give the emperor?"

Lai-tse lu thought for a moment. "If I write to An Mien at once and the letter is sent on a Rakehell ship that sails in a few days, we could follow within a few weeks. Mr. Cushing and any others you wish to send with him should be on board the ship. If the emperor agrees to hold the negotiations—and I can think of no reason he would refuse, although I'm certainly in no position to speak for him—he would expect them to begin at once."

"Will you make such a voyage, Mr. Rakehell?" Tyler asked. "We'll pay whatever fee you request."

"My conscience wouldn't allow me to charge the United States anything except the passage of Mr. Cushing and his assistants," Jonathan said. "We've been planning a voyage to China on company and personal business in any event, and we're obliged to deliver a gift from Queen Victoria to the emperor. All we need do is move the date forward."

"I'll make your appointment official at once, Caleb," the President said, "and you can work out the sailing details with Mr. Rakehell. Now, regarding this matter of a gift. What should the United States send to the emperor?"

"Nothing," Lai-tse lu said emphatically.

John Tyler stared at her. "But you said that Queen Victoria is sending—"

"Crowned heads of state may exchange gifts under special circumstances, and in this instance they are unusual." Few people would have dared to interrupt the President, but Lai-tse lu was impassioned. "The emperor would think you were trying to bribe him, and he would be greatly insulted. All the wealth in the world could not induce him to accept. If you wish to give him and the people of the Middle Kingdom a true gift, request the Congress to pass a law that forbids American citizens the right to engage in the opium trade."

The President was startled.

"You should have been a politician, Mrs. Rakehell," Cushing said with a chuckle.

Lai-tse lu looked at him indignantly. "I have seen people who have been destroyed by the drug. I have seen their suffering and that of their families. I speak as one who has regard for the dignity of human beings, not as a politician!"

John Tyler grinned. "I wish I could persuade you to become a member of our negotiating team, Mrs. Rakehell. Your suggestion is brilliant. I've had a natural abhorrence for the opium trade, but it never crossed my mind that this country could do anything about it. An American law might not accomplish much, but at least we'd be setting an example for other countries. I'll speak to the Democratic and Whig leaders of the Congress tomorrow, and I can imagine no reason they wouldn't see to it that a bill is passed. Probably by acclamation."

"In that case," Lai-tse lu said, "I can virtually promise you that the Tao Kuang Emperor will approve of a trade treaty with the United States."

"We can finish our talk at dinner," the President said, and stood. "We've kept my wife waiting long enough. And from the way she looked at your dress, Mrs. Rakehell, I'm certain she'd like to find out where she can have one made that's like it."

As marital tensions multiplied, Ruth Boynton discovered, they became increasingly difficult to discuss, and this, in turn, made the problems still worse. She and Charles, by unspoken consent, did not repeat their experiment of lovemaking, but they remained polite, even affectionate at times. Although David was still visiting in the United States, both were conscious of him and his welfare. Friends with whom the couple dined and occasionally attended the theater had no idea that anything might be amiss between them. Sir Alan, immersed in the struggle to raise cash for the expansion of the business, did not realize that his son and daughter-in-law were drifting in opposite directions. Lady Boynton had her suspicions but kept them to herself.

Ruth continued to hope the situation would cure itself. As nearly as she could glean, her husband had engaged in an affair while on his travels, but he did not appear to be pining for some woman who lived in a far place, so she had reason to

452

hope that his interest in the outsider, whoever she might be, would prove to be a passing fancy.

Then, suddenly, everything was changed. Charles stayed late at his office one night, as was his custom, then sent a message to the effect that he would not return for dinner. Ruth stayed up until midnight, and when she finally heard him stumble to the divan in his dressing room more than two hours later, she pretended to be asleep.

The next day was Sunday, and as Ruth dressed for breakfast and church, she heard him snoring gently and did not disturb him. She looked into his dressing room before going downstairs and saw his shirt on the floor at her feet, where he had thrown it. Picking it up automatically, intending to drop it into the laundry hamper, she caught her breath.

On the white linen collar was a long smear of lip rouge.

Charles stirred, saw his wife, and hoisting himself onto one elbow, looked first at her, then at the shirt. "You needn't lecture me," he said thickly. "I spent a couple of hours with a high-priced trollop, but that's no criminal offense. A man needs an occasional physical outlet as much as he needs food and drink." He fell back onto the pillow. "And sleep," he added before dropping off again.

She continued to stand for a long moment. Then she placed the shirt in the laundry hamper and went down to join Charles's parents for breakfast. Both before and after church her manner was so subdued that Jessica looked at her repeatedly. After they returned to the house in Belgravia, Sir Alan went off to his study, saying there were some financial statements he wanted to read before dinner, and the two women were alone in the family sitting room.

"You've known all morning that I'm upset," Ruth said.

Her mother-in-law nodded. "Yes, I've been well aware of it, dear, but I'm not prying."

The younger woman felt a desperate need to confide in her. "When Charles last went out to the Orient," she said, "he had an affair."

Jessica wasn't surprised. "He confessed it to you?"

"No, I've guessed, but I haven't discussed it with him. Since he's come home our lovemaking has dwindled, and the last time—several weeks ago—was a failure." Her insides churning, yet managing to maintain a calm facade, she told the story of what had happened earlier that morning.

"What are you going to do about it?" Jessica's bluntness was typical of the Rakehells.

"I—I don't know."

"I was asking, indirectly, whether you intend to leave him, dear."

"Oh, no," Ruth replied instantly. "David needs me. So does Charles, although he may not realize it."

"I'm very pleased and relieved that you know it. For David's sake. And for the sake of Charles's future, too, although he doesn't really deserve it." Jessica hesitated for a long moment, then said firmly, "Perhaps you can do better with David than I appear to have done with Charles. In the Boynton family, I'm afraid, it's like father, like son."

The surprised Ruth could only stare at her.

"A great many years ago—although in some ways it seems like yesterday," Jessica said, "I faced the same decision that you're making today. Alan had more than his fair share of courtesans, and I know of at least one so-called friend of mine with whom he had an affair. I've never mentioned a word of this to anyone. The Rakehells aren't like the Boyntons, and I see no need to upset my brother at this late date."

Ruth nodded but didn't know what to say.

"I decided, as you seem to have done, to make the best of my marriage. My pride was shattered, as yours must be—"

"Call it bent pretty badly out of shape," Ruth said with a rueful smile.

"I stayed on, being a stubborn Rakehell who was determined to make her marriage succeed. I knew—or at least I believed—that Alan's affairs meant nothing to him, that he really loved me. I don't want to influence you, but I think Charles is the same way, that he'd be lost if you left him."

"I hope you're right," Ruth said, "because I'm going to stay. I've been telling myself all morning that Charles's behavior is like David's when he sneaks out to the kitchen and helps himself to a cookie. It gives him such a feeling of accomplishment, especially if he thinks no one knows, and I have a notion that makes the taste of the cookies much sweeter."

"You're wiser than I was at your age."

"No, I'm not wise," Ruth said. "I'm stubborn, as you

454

were. And I'm selfish. I enjoy the luxuries that Boyntons can afford.''

"Of course you do. But that doesn't mean you've chosen an easy row to hoe. I've had the same experience, and if Charles continues to indulge in affairs, as I'm afraid he well might, there will be times when you'll be discouraged.''

"I have one advantage," Ruth said. "I've discovered a kindred spirit in my mother-in-law, so, if I may, I'll come to you whenever life becomes unbearable.''

"By all means, although I'm not sure I can offer you anything but a sympathetic ear. I might have a talk with Charles myself, of course.''

"I wish you wouldn't, Mother Boynton. Charles is still a little boy in many ways. He'd resent both of us, and he'd have that many more affairs, just to spite us.''

"You really do understand him.'' Jessica rose, went to her daughter-in-law, and kissed her. "For whatever this may be worth to you, I admire you.''

"Thanks to your example, I'll try to find the courage to see this thing through.''

Jessica smiled, then sobered. "As a mother who has observed her son fairly closely, I'm convinced Charles does love you.''

"I think so, too, or I wouldn't stay.''

"If he's like his father, and the resemblance appears to be close, he forgets his affairs as soon as he's had them. I'm frank to admit that I don't understand the souls of men. Some men. I'm certain my brother was faithful to his late, first wife, just as he's undoubtedly being faithful to Sarah. And as we've learned, Jonathan would have destroyed his own happiness rather than be unfaithful to Louise. The way he looks at Lai-tse lu, you know that no other woman exists for him.''

The very mention of Jonathan, combined with the thought of the life she might have led with him, sent a spasm of pain through Ruth. "As you've said, Mother Boynton, the Rakehells are different. Most men who can afford mistresses have them.''

Jessica sighed. "Whatever comfort this may be, if you can be patient long enough, Charles will outgrow his folly. As his father did. I won't pretend to you that Alan and I enjoy a perfect relationship, but we do get along well. Of all the couples I've ever known, only Jonathan and Lai-tse lu have achieved a perfect marriage."

Ruth replied with a sigh.

"I cannot tolerate morbidity." Jessica went to the bar and poured two glasses of sack. "We won't wait for the men to have a drink before dinner."

Charles came into the room as they were raising their glasses in a silent toast. "Celebrating, ladies?" His manner was defensive.

"If you must know," his mother replied tartly, "we're exchanging condolences."

Ruth looked up at Charles and having decided on a course of action, she forced herself to smile at him warmly. She knew he would interpret the gesture as a sign of forgiveness for his infidelity of the previous night, so she was not surprised when he gripped her shoulder, silently thanking her.

Not until Sir Alan joined them and, a few moments later, escorted Lady Jessica to the dining room, did Charles have an opportunity to speak privately to his wife. "Thank you," he said, "for putting up with a damned fool. I swear to you, the wench I had last night means nothing to me."

She inclined her head but preferred not to speak. Charles put an arm around her shoulders as they neared the dining room. "You're the only one who matters," he murmured.

Ruth knew he was telling the truth, but she realized at the same time that he would be unfaithful to her yet again when the occasion arose. Henceforth she would need to harden herself, learning to accept his way of life.

Molinda was in a turmoil. The day that Bradford Walker had agreed to repay the nearly three hundred thousand dollars of Rakehell and Boynton funds she had lent him came and went, but he failed to appear at her office. She saw no sign of him the following day, either, and curbing a sense of panic as she assured herself that all would be well, she asked Kai to find out what he could about the American's whereabouts.

The majordomo went off for several hours, first chatting with several of the Owen Bruce employees as they left the factory, then wandering around Canton in a seemingly aimless manner. That evening, after dinner, he came to the house that had been Soong Chao's home and made his report.

Molinda and Shaong Wei were drinking tea in the pavilion they used as a sitting room, and invited him to join them.

Kai scowled as he lowered himself onto a padded, three-legged stool. "I don't like the facts I have put together," he said. "Walker was at Canton yesterday and today, but he stayed in his living quarters. He kept the doors barred, and not even his servants were permitted to enter."

"Then he didn't forget he was scheduled to repay the debt yesterday." Molinda's concern deepened.

"So it appears," Kai said, shaking his head. "Perhaps you noticed that two junks were tied up today at the Bruce Wharf."

"I was vaguely aware of them," she said.

"They brought no cargo, and they sailed without cargo after sundown this evening. Walker was on board one of them."

Molinda was alarmed. "Then he's running away, you think, and has no intention of making the payment?"

"No," Kai said flatly. "The junks carried no food and water for a long voyage. It is odd. On board were many Cantonese men. Some have been suspected of opium smuggling in the past. Walker does not know this, but he and his junks are being followed. With your permission, I shall leave Canton myself tonight. I hope, when I return, that I will be in a position to give you much more information."

Molinda watched him as he walked quickly down the gravel path and was joined by several other black-clad figures. "He has offered little consolation that we will recover the money," she said. "I dread writing to Jonathan and Charles that I have been fooled and cheated."

"Don't lose confidence in Kai," Shaong Wei told her. "Before we were married and I moved to Canton, I believed what I had been taught all my life, that the Celestial Emperor is the sole ruler of the Middle Kingdom. Now I know better. It is the secret societies—like the Oxen—who intervene on behalf of justice when they find it necessary. Kai will accomplish what no imperial viceroy could do."

A day and a half later, shortly after the deeply worried Molinda reached her office, Kai returned.

"One mystery has been solved," he told her. "The Cantonese men hired by Walker took the two junks to a small island filled with trees in the delta of the Pearl River. There they dropped off Walker, then continued on their way to Macao, where they unloaded sealed cases of tea and placed them on the junks. They were instructed to then take the cargo back to the island where Walker and his partner, Bruce, awaited them. But my brothers in the Oxen and I asked ourselves why any merchant would bring tea to the Middle Kingdom when we already have more here than we can use. So the men hired by Walker were relieved of their burden.'' His strong features hardened. ''As my brothers and I suspected, the cargo consisted of opium. It was taken to a secret place, and the fires that consumed it are still smoldering. Walker and Bruce will never know what happened to the drugs they intended to smuggle into this country.''

''What you have done is good,'' Molinda said. ''I had no idea that Walker was that kind of a man, and now that I have learned better, it is too late. The funds on which I had hoped to earn such a large profit for Rakehell and Boynton will not be returned to me.''

''Don't despair,'' Kai replied. ''Only last night I learned that Walker and Bruce have a partner who is a man of great wealth—the governor-general of Macao. It is no accident that some of our brothers serve on his staff and know all that he does. He is very angry because the opium has vanished, and he has summoned Walker and Bruce. They will meet with him today. Then a chastened Walker will return to his warehouse, and you will demand payment from him. He wishes to maintain his pose as a respectable merchant, so he will find some way to obtain the money from his wealthy partner, the governor-general of Macao.''

Molinda could only hope that his predictions would prove accurate.

What neither she nor Kai knew was the extent of Dom Manuel Sebastian's anger. The disappearance of the cargo of valuable opium enraged him, and he worked himself into a cold fury while he awaited the arrival of Bradford Walker and Owen Bruce.

The badly shaken pair reached Macao in mid-morning on board one of their junks, and the Marquês de Braga granted them an immediate audience, receiving them in the private sitting room of his personal suite in his palace. Staff members

458

and servants were ordered to leave the quarters, and the doors were closed.

"Walker," Dom Manuel said in a voice he could scarcely control, "I hold you personally responsible for the disappearance of opium worth more than five hundred thousand of your American dollars."

"I told Your Excellency all that I know in the message I sent to you," Walker replied. "The men I hired reported to me that the sealed boxes were taken from them by force. The thieves were Chinese who were dressed in black, wore masks, and did not speak a single word. The men I hired were afraid for their lives because the thieves were heavily armed, and they saw no reason why they should die to protect what they believed to be cases of tea."

A heavily jeweled forefinger jabbed at him. "You lie!" the Marquês de Braga shouted.

Walker was stunned.

"You had your men take the opium to another hiding place. You intend to sell all of it yourself and keep the entire profit!"

Owen Bruce turned to the American, his own eyes suddenly glacial. "That possibility never occurred to me," he said. "You are stupid if you think you can cheat your partners!"

"I—I wouldn't try to cheat either of you," the horrified Walker cried. "I didn't!"

"If you're wise," the Marquês de Braga told him, "you'll reveal the location of the opium to me this instant. Then you'll turn it over to Bruce, so he can sell it through his customary sources."

"There's no way you can dispose of it yourself, Walker," Owen Bruce added. "All of the Chinese smugglers know each other well, and word would leak out in a day or two. There's no way you can pull off this scheme!"

"I swear to you there's no scheme," Walker cried. "You were right there with me, Bruce, when my men reported the cases had been taken from them! I've been honest and open with both of you in my dealings. In everything I've done. Didn't I give you fair shares of the money I obtained from Molinda, the woman who works for Rakehell and Boynton?"

Bruce was forced to concede the point and nodded, but

Dom Manuel was contemptuous. "My share was a paltry hundred thousand. We're dealing now with merchandise worth five times that amount!"

"I've told you the truth, so help me!" Bradford Walker was frantic.

The Marquês de Braga ignored the protest. "Bruce," he asked, "is it possible that this woman is Walker's accomplice? She might have connections he lacks that would enable her to sell the opium. I became suspicious when she granted him that loan. It occurred to me then that they might have worked out such a scheme to throw us off their trail in some larger enterprise."

"I think it unlikely," Bruce said. "The woman is very beautiful, as attractive in her own way as the daughter of Soong Chao, whom Rakehell married. But I've never heard her mentioned in connection with any shady dealings. Besides, she is married to the emperor's cousin."

"Shaong Wei lost his official status many years ago," Dom Manuel declared impatiently. "He may be related to the Tao Kuang Emperor, but he no longer has a place in the imperial hierarchy, much less a position at the imperial court in the Forbidden City."

Walker was searching wildly for a way to restore himself to the good graces of the Marquês de Braga. Well aware of Dom Manuel's penchant for lovely concubines, the American thought of a way to kill two birds with a single stone. "I can prove to you that the woman isn't associated with me in any underhanded scheme, Your Excellency!" he declared.

"How?" The governor-general's eyes were narrow slits.

"As Bruce has just said, she is very beautiful. I—I'll contrive to deliver her to you for your stable of concubines. She'll come to you naked. In a bamboo cage."

Dom Manuel was intrigued. "It would be amusing to have the woman delivered to me in such a manner, particularly if she is as lovely as both of you claim. Very well, Walker. Do as you have said, and I'll grant you a respite. But I still hold you responsible for the return of the stolen opium."

A respite was all Bradford Walker needed. He didn't know how to begin to search for the missing opium, but if he managed to bring Molinda to Macao as a concubine, he would have enough time to flee to some place beyond Dom Manuel's reach. Perhaps he would go to the Netherlands East Indies or to India. But he couldn't allow himself to think in such terms yet. He would have to move one careful step at a time.

"As for you, Bruce," the Marquês de Braga declared, "I urge you to work with him. If Walker fails to bring this woman to me, and fails to recover the opium, I will lose confidence in you and will terminate our business relations."

Owen Bruce was appalled. Without the active support of the governor-general of Macao, he would once again become a marginal operator, living precariously while he earned what he could through making deals that respectable merchants shunned.

Dom Manuel dismissed the pair with a contemptuous wave. "Don't keep me waiting too long, Walker," he said. "My patience is as limited as my arm of vengeance is long."

The pair bowed themselves out and did not speak until they had left the palace and were walking to the wharf where their junk was docked. Then Walker broke the silence. "I swear to you," he said, "that I didn't steal that opium. It would be insane to make an enemy of Dom Manuel."

"Indeed it would. If you tell me the truth—and may the Lord have mercy on you if you lie—the delivery of the wench will placate him for a time. Long enough, it may be, for me to trace the opium, if I can, through my own sources of information. But it will be touch and go at best."

It was only a faint consolation to know that Bruce also had a great deal to lose. But he was not suspected of theft, and hence his life was not endangered.

"Have you some foolproof scheme to spirit the wench out of Canton and bring her here?"

"Not yet," Walker said. "The last thing I expected was to be accused of taking the opium and hiding it somewhere. I—I made the offer out of desperation."

"Never mind now. I'll plan with you, and between us we'll make certain there can be no slips. Your skin and my livelihood depend on the delivery of the wench, as you promised."

A scant two days before Jonathan had scheduled his sailing for China, he received a letter from Molinda in which she told him about the loan to Bradford Walker. He read the communication as soon as it was delivered to him by the master of a clipper that had just arrived home, and then he went straight to his father's office down the corridor.

Jeremiah read the letter twice, then sighed. "So that's where the bad penny has turned up," he said.

"And in partnership with Owen Bruce," Jonathan added bitterly. "Not that I blame Molinda. She acted in good faith."

"This couldn't come at a worse time," his father said. "Alan and I will need to scrape up more than a quarter of a million dollars to keep our operation in the Orient afloat. Coming at a time when cash is already so scarce, this places us in a very delicate financial position. If we're forced to sell any of our major assets, Jonnie, we'll be crippled for years to come."

"I'm sailing first to Tientsin," Jonathan said grimly, "so Lai-tse lu and I can deliver Queen Victoria's gift to the emperor and, I hope, make the arrangements for the appointment of imperial negotiators to meet with Caleb Cushing. As soon as that's done, I'll go straight to Whampoa, as I had already planned. Brad Walker and Bruce will repay the loan, and Brad will also return the money he stole from us when he left New London—or I'll bring him home in chains to face charges of theft and embezzlement here."

"Nothing would give me greater pleasure than to see Brad in chains," Jeremiah said, "but that won't necessarily restore the money that's been taken from us. Money we desperately need to insure the survival of Rakehell and Boynton."

"I'll do my damndest," Jonathan said.

"I'm sure you will." Jeremiah ran a hand through his thinning hair and looked old and tired. "Do you want to break this news to Judith and to Homer Ellison?"

"I'll show the letter to Homer right now and then let him tell Judith. It will be a shock when she learns Brad is definitely alive—and still engaging in skulduggery at our expense. I believe Homer can cushion the blow for her better than either you or I could do."

Homer was stone-faced when he read the letter a short time later. "I'd like to carve his heart out with a butcher knife, Jonnie," he said.

"I'm not sure what I'll do when I confront him," Jonathan said. "But it won't be pleasant."

That evening Homer ate supper with Judith and her children, as he frequently did, but he said nothing until the youngsters weren't off to their rooms to do homework for school. Then he braced himself and told Judith the contents of Molinda's letter.

Judith became pale but showed the fortitude of a Rakehell in adversity and did not weep. "I wonder why it is," she said, "that so many good and kind and honorable people die in accidents, but the evil continue to flourish."

"Bradford Walker won't do much more flourishing after Jonnie gets hold of him," Homer said. "And when he's brought back here to face criminal charges, I see a way out of this dilemma for us. We'll have to wait until he's convicted, of course, and then I don't think there's any doubt that the law courts will grant you a divorce. I had a talk with a lawyer friend of mine since I learned the news today, and he told me there's a precedent. A few years ago the Connecticut Supreme Court granted a divorce to the wife of a convicted felon."

"Then there's really hope this nightmare will come to an end?"

"You just bet there is," he said, and embraced her "It will be up to Jonnie to haul Walker back here for a reckoning, and I can't think of a better man for the job. Then we'll do the rest, and you'll be free to marry me."

II

The junk flying Owen Bruce's distinguishing pennant tied up at his wharf at Canton early one morning, and Bradford Walker came ashore. Although his walk was jaunty and his manner self-assured, his insides were churning as he went straight to the Rakehell and Boynton headquarters. This was one occasion when his playacting had to be perfect.

Molinda was writing a business letter in Chinese, her hand deft as she formed the characters with a fine brush. She looked up when a clerk entered to tell her that Walker had come to see her, and she merely nodded, then continued to write as the visitor entered her private office.

"I owe you an apology," Walker said.

"More than an apology," Molinda replied, laying down the brush. "You owe me a very considerable sum of money."

Paying no heed to the cold reception, he continued to smile as he sat opposite her desk. "I'm afraid I've caused you some anxious moments for this past week, and I'm truly sorry. But I've needed to work out some details, and I'm pleased by the results, as I'm sure you'll be."

He was a trifle too glib, the young woman thought, and made no comment.

"I've not only obtained the funds to pay you in full, including the entire interest," he said, "but as a sign of my gratitude, I'm also giving you an additional twenty-five thousand dollars."

"That's a rather considerable expression of gratitude," she said dryly.

"It's the best way I know to show you that I hope to do

more business with you in the future. I have a business associate in Macao who is supplying the funds in full, and his only condition is that he be allowed to hand you the money himself.''

"You wish me to go to Macao to be paid. Is that correct?'' She was mildly surprised.

"My associate has heard of your skill and acumen in business, and this gives him an opportunity to meet you himself.''

The brief journey to Macao was well worth an additional payment of twenty-five thousand dollars. Molinda was relieved but still wary. "I daresay my husband and I could arrange a visit to Macao in the near future.''

"There's no need to make formal arrangements.'' Walker's whole scheme depended on his ability to persuade her to come with him to the Portuguese colony at once. "I have a junk waiting at the dock,'' he said. "Come with me now, and you'll be back in Canton this evening. With the money in hand.''

She hesitated, weighing the offer.

"My associate, whose identity will surprise you when he reveals it to you, is in a position to offer your company far more trade than all of your other clients put together,'' Walker went on, his manner now casual but cajoling.

Molinda had already learned from Kai that his associate was none other than the unsavory governor-general of Macao, who reputedly ruled the tiny but lucrative colony with an iron hand. She had no idea why the Marquês de Braga might want to meet her, nor could she gauge whether the offer of immediate repayment of the loan, including the interest and a bonus, was genuine. But she was afraid to take the risk of losing the entire sum, and there was only one way to find out.

Walker realized she was rising to the bait and held his breath.

"Very well,'' Molinda said, "I'll come with you.''

He exhaled slowly. "If we leave right now, before the traffic on the river becomes heavier, I'll have you back here in time for your regular closing hour.''

"It will only take a moment for me to finish this letter,'' she said.

He watched idly as she picked up the brush, dipped it in jar of ink, and resumed writing Chinese letters.

Walker had no way of knowing what she was actuall writing: *Kai—the man called Walker has promised payment i full, including interest and a bonus, if I will come with him t Macao for the money. He promises that I will return here b the end of the day. We sail on a Bruce junk. Molinda.*

"I am ready," she said, and picked up the laquered bo containing cosmetics and other belongings, which she wore o a thin chain suspended from her shoulder.

Walker exulted silently. The cage of bamboo, four fee high, four feet wide, and four feet deep, built to his specifica tions, complete with discreet opaque curtains that could b opened or closed, was awaiting its victim on the aft deck of th junk, covered by a tarpaulin. The young woman was as goo as imprisoned in it already, awaiting delivery to Dom Manuel

Molinda paused at the desk of the clerk who sat outsid her private office. "When Kai returns from the errand o which I sent him," she said, "please ask him to attend to th letter on my desk. I'll be back this evening."

She would never see Canton again, Walker told himsel as he moved up beside her for the short walk to the dock.

An hour later Kai came back to the office. The messag that the clerk passed on to him puzzled him, but he went to th inner room and picked up the letter. The note addressed to hin caught his eye at once because it was written in larger charac ters than the uncompleted business communication above it He glanced out of the window, and cursed when he saw tha there was now no ship docked at Bruce's wharf.

He raced to his own small office down the corridor an spoke urgently to the black-clad man who sat there. "Go a once to Shaong Wei. Tell him his wife is in grave danger. As him to join me at our wharf, where I must find the fastest o our ships to take us to her side. I will not wait for him if h hasn't joined me by the time I'm ready to sail."

The Society of Oxen member asked no questions. Boltin out of the warehouse, he started at a run toward the house tha lay at the far side of Canton.

Ordinarily a journey across Canton took at least a half hour, but the messenger reached his destination in less tha

466

twenty minutes. He found Shaong Wei sitting in the shade of a stately li-chi tree, reading a book of Taoist philosophy.

On his feet before the man could repeat all he had been told to say, Shaong Wei raced into the sleeping pavilion for a curved sword. "Lead the way," he said, and together he and the messenger ran through the crowded streets to the waterfront.

The sails were being raised on a small junk manned exclusively by black-clad men as a panting Shaong Wei leaped on board.

Kai supervised the sailing, instructing the master to ignore the courtesies customarily offered to other vessels and barges on the congested Pearl River. Then he handed the letter to Shaong Wei.

Knowing nothing about the seamier side of life to which ordinary mortals were exposed, Shaong Wei was perplexed. "I see nothing wrong," he said.

"Don't you?" Kai was finding it difficult to control his temper.

"My wife has been worried about the sums owed to her company. It appears that she is being paid in full today, which will make her happy."

"The offer of repayment is a trick. Walker works with the governor-general of Macao, who has more beautiful concubines in his palace than even the Celestial Emperor. Some he has bought. Others have been kidnapped or stolen from the homes of their families. If Molinda disappears into that palace, you will never see her again. Not even the Oxen could attack that palace without causing a war with Portugal, which is the close ally of the British. The Tao Kuang Emperor cannot run the risk of plunging the Middle Kingdom into another war with the British."

The reality of his wife's situation dawned on Shaong Wei. "We must overtake that junk," he said.

"We'll do our best," Kai told him, and moved to a place beside the ship's master.

On board the other junk, Molinda felt no sense of impending danger and gradually her misgivings subsided. Bradford Walker was exerting his utmost charm. He had a chair brought for her comfort on the deck, and his comments on the ships they saw on the crowded Pearl River estuary told her that whatever his faults, he was a man who was thoroughly familia with the shipping industry. Walker further demonstrated hi hospitality by inviting the young woman to join him in th cabin for what he called a light meal. Molinda was surprise when they were served one elaborate dish after another. Al ways careful of her weight, she ate only token portions.

Walker was too nervous to appreciate the meal. His pur pose in having it served had been that of passing the tim harmlessly without alarming the young woman, and the tacti succeeded. The last dishes were cleared away as they saile into the Macao harbor.

He glanced at his watch. "Ah," he said, "our timing i perfect. My associate is just finishing his daily visit with hi elephants and soon will be ready to receive you."

"His elephants?" Molinda was startled.

Walker shrugged. "I haven't seen them myself, but I'n told he recently bought a pair of Indian elephants that ha special training of some sort, and I've gathered he's fond o them." He summoned a crew member. "Go to the palace an inform His Excellency that I shall arrive shortly with our guest," he said, and the man disappeared.

Molinda smiled. "There is only one palace in Macao, an only one man here entitled to be called His Excellency. As thought, your business associate is the Marquês de Braga."

"You're very clever." The moment had come to tell he the fate that was in store for her. "But not quite as clever a you might think. I hope you'll enjoy the Marquês as much a I'm certain he'll enjoy you."

"I beg your pardon?" She was puzzled.

"I needed to buy time in my own dealings with him," Walker said, "and through you I can do it. I'm presenting yo to him as a gift."

All of Molinda's latent fears suddenly were confirmed She looked around, saw an oil lamp, and picked it up, intending to throw it at this vile man who stood opposite her in th cabin.

"Please don't behave foolishly," Walker said quietly "There are seven men on board this junk, and all of them wil obey my orders. If they must, they'll subdue and strip you. regret the need to use you, but you'll buy me the time I need

468

So put down the lamp, please, and be good enough to disrobe.''

She knew physical resistance would prove futile. Perhaps, if she could stall long enough, Kai might come to her rescue—provided he had read the message she had left for him and had decided to follow her here. If he had followed her example, however, and had trusted Walker's promises, she would have to abandon all hope.

"I salute your ingenuity," she said, "and I admit defeat. But why must we rush to the palace?"

Her meaning was plain, but Walker recognized her intent. She hoped to disarm him and perhaps even planned to kill him. Then she would find some way to escape, perhaps by exerting her wiles on the junk's impressionable master, who had stared at her hungrily when she had sat on deck.

Swallowing hard, he removed a pistol from his belt and, pointing it at her, shook his head. "I'll tolerate no tricks," he said.

Molinda realized that, in spite of the stand he was taking, he wanted her. So she continued to smile steadily at him as she slowly unfastened the hooks of her cheongsam.

Never had Walker seen a woman as entrancing as Molinda, and the trollops with whom he had satisfied himself over the months were nothing compared to her. Her rounded, firm body was alluring, and her limpid eyes were urging him to take her, telling him he could do with her as he pleased. Slowly his resolve weakened.

He stood with his back to the door, still gripping his pistol, as he watched her remove her clothes.

All at once the pistol was wrenched from his grasp, the arm of a man clad in black encircled his neck, and a pronged, double-pointed knife blade was held close to his throat.

"There has been a change in plans," Kai announced quietly.

Shaong Wei raced into the cabin, embraced his wife, and then shielded her as she dressed again.

"My brothers have taken temporary control of your junk, Walker, and will return it to Owen Bruce on your behalf. You will forgive us if we don't remain in Macao with you. The atmosphere here doesn't appeal to us. But you have an appointment here, and you shall keep it."

A few minutes later the junk moved away from the pier

and moved out of the harbor, passing close to the two Portu guese gunboats that guarded the entrance to the channel. The bored officer of the watch paid no attention to the vessel or the black-clad seamen on her deck.

Meanwhile, four hired bearers carried the cage, its cur tains drawn, up the hill to the palace. The few Europeans who saw them glanced briefly at the cage, then at the bearers, and went about their business. So much that was bizarre happened at the headquarters of the governor-general that they no longer bothered to gossip about him. The Chinese who passed the bearers took care to avert their faces. Those who lived in Macao, as most did, were not regarded as Portuguese subjects, but they had learned it was not healthy to inquire into the activities of the man who governed the island. His punish ments were cruel and swiftly administered, and the inhabitants of Macao took themselves elsewhere with great haste.

The bearers deposited the cage at the main gate, then hurried away before the sentinels could halt them. The officer of the day was summoned.

Adjusting his sash of office, the young lieutenant hurried to the gate, then brightened when he saw the cage. "His Excel lency has been expecting this—ah—package," he said, and assigned four of his men to take it to him.

Dom Manuel Sebastian was in high spirits as he returned to his personal suite from his daily visit to his new elephants. Both were almost white in color, exceptionally intelligent, and had been superbly trained. He had paid a fortune for them, but not for a moment did he regret having purchased them.

The cage was resting on the floor of his private sitting room, and the four soldiers who had brought it stood at rigid attention as the governor-general came in.

"What's this?" he demanded, and then remembered. "Nev er mind. You're dismissed."

The relieved infantrymen saluted and marched off.

For a long moment the Marquês de Braga stared at the curtains on the cage, rubbing his hands together and moistening his lips. Then he hurried to a bell rope and tugged it.

His personal manservant appeared and bowed.

"You are alone in the suite, Chang?" Dom Manuel demanded.

"Yes, Excellency."

"Very well. You may lay out my new dressing gown and slippers. Chop-chop! Then get out, and if you or any other staff members appear before I ring for you, I'll have you hanged."

Chang raced off to his master's bedchamber, placed the new dressing gown of embroidered silk on the bed, with a pair of slippers on the floor directly beneath it. Then he fled.

Dom Manuel locked the door, then thoughtfully took a riding crop from a wall peg. If the wench proved troublesome or reluctant, she would have to be taught her place. Stepping forward and grinning, the Marquês de Braga pulled aside the curtains. Then he could only gape.

On the floor of the cage, stark naked, with hands and feet tightly bound and a gag in his mouth, lay Bradford Walker.

Caleb Cushing was prone to seasickness, as was one of his associates, so Jonathan did not push his clipper to her limit, and the voyage to Cathay took three weeks longer than he had planned. In spite of his own anxiety to reach Canton as soon as possible in order to obtain repayment of the loan Molinda had made to Bradford Walker, Jonathan felt compelled to take the comfort of the diplomats into consideration.

Lai-tse lu was secretly relieved. Although she said nothing to her husband, she felt recurrent attacks of the condition that plagued her, but the pain was bearable.

Certainly the children enjoyed the voyage. Each day Julian and David received instructions in seamanship from the boatswain, and Jonathan, who had elected not to take command of the ship himself, spent long periods teaching the boys navigation. They took sightings, charted the clipper's progress, and under his tutelage, learned the principles of seamanship. He drilled them in how to handle the ship as the winds shifted, and they were quizzed frequently on the quarterdeck by Elijah Vilbor, who had been promoted to captain, having received his master's ticket.

Little Jade pouted for a time because she did not participate in the boys' lessons, but she spent long periods with her mother, conversing in private. At the little girl's insistence, Harmony had accompanied the family on the voyage, and Jade romped with the chow on deck. Crew members quickly learned was unwise to speak to the child until she had ordered the dog to sit quietly beside her. Harmony was fiercely protective and allowed no one to approach her without her specific approval.

At last, after spending about four months at sea, the lookout in the masthead caught sight of the stone fort that guarded the entrance to the harbor at Tientsin. The long journey was coming to an end. The Tree of Life pennant was sighted by the duty officer at the fort, and the imperial banner that flew from a flagstaff dipped in salute; the fort's cannon, which were so ancient they were unreliable, could not be fired.

The anchor was dropped in the harbor, the commandant of the fort came on board, and arrangements were made for a convoy to take the Rakehells to Peking. Caleb Cushing and his two associates would remain behind, as planned, until Jonathan and Lai-tse lu made the necessary arrangements with the Tao Kuang Emperor and the Princess An Mien for their reception. In the meantime, the diplomats were free to go ashore at Tientsin whenever they pleased but would continue to sleep on board the clipper.

A messenger was sent ahead to notify the Celestial Emperor that the Rakehell party had arrived and would be accompanied by Wu-ling, who was prepared to take up her post as an interpreter immediately. The girl, wildly excited, looked very grown up when she went ashore in one of the cheongsams that she and Lai-tse lu had made on the voyage. Jonathan was amused when he saw the young officers of their cavalry escort eyeing the girl surreptitiously. His wife had been right when she had told him that Wu-ling would be besieged by suitors when she reached the Forbidden City.

The escort was even stronger than it had been in the past because the garrison commander insisted on providing enough cavalrymen to guard Queen Victoria's gift and the many cases of books and manufactured goods that the Rakehells were bringing with them for the edification of the emperor and those members of his staff who would be charged with their use in propelling the Middle Kingdom into the modern world.

Horses were provided for the visitors, and the mares that Lai-tse lu and Wu-ling would ride were equipped with elaborate saddles on which padded, chairlike contraptions were mounted for their comfort. The three children rode Mongolian ponies, and Harmony happily trotted beside them, moving back and forth constantly from the place of one youngster to another. Julian and David practiced their Mandarin on the officers, and Jade imitated the boys. At no time did Harmony relax his vigil over the children, and permitted no one, including the commander of the convoy, to approach them without permission.

Wu-ling was awed when they reached Peking and rode past one high wall after another as they penetrated deeper and deeper into the heart of the capital, coming at last to the Forbidden City, where sumptuous quarters in a private building, complete with its own garden, had been provided. A full staff of servants was on hand to attend to the needs of the party.

Lai-tse lu bathed and changed into a cheongsam as soon as they arrived, not knowing when they might be summoned to the adjacent palace. Her foresight proved wise; she was just finishing using cosmetics in the large bedchamber that she and Jonathan shared when a messenger arrived with word that the Princess An Mien awaited the visitors.

A number of bearers followed the couple and the guide through a door set in the stone wall, and the party was conducted to a chamber in the main building of the Imperial Palace that neither Lai-tse lu nor Jonathan had ever before visited. The walls were made of thick, glistening marble, a heavy rug covered the better part of the floor, and the many pieces of furniture included divans, chairs, and three-legged stools. Various art objects, including rare pieces of carved jade, stood on tables. The thought occurred to Jonathan that an exception was being made in his behalf: no foreigner had ever visited the living quarters of the imperial family.

A door opened, and the Princess An Mien came into the room, quietly attired in a cheongsam of dark, embroidered silk. "Welcome to my house," she said, embracing Lai-tse lu and offering her hand to Jonathan in Western fashion.

She was followed by her brother, as always insignificant-looking in his ankle-length robe of black silk. Only his inevitable pearl cap indicated his exalted rank. It was obvious that he was highly pleased to see the visitors, but in spite of his broad grin of greeting it was essential that he remain "invisible," so he did not address them, instead seating himself quietly.

Jonathan wasted no time, and while the two women chatted animatedly, he went into the corridor, where the bearers waited with the various boxes of gifts. He had them brought

473

into the sitting room, and the Celestial Emperor so forgo[t] himself that he helped the American pry open the crates.

An Mien examined a new type of oil lamp critically, the[n] announced that she approved of it because it cast a brighte[r] light and apparently used less fuel than any lamp made in th[e] Middle Kingdom. While she continued to study the various objects of American manufacture, the Tao Kuang Emperor eagerl[y] leafed through various books, although he could not read [a] word of English.

At last the time came to open the box containing the tapestry that Queen Victoria had sent as a gift. Lai-tse lu explained its background, and the emperor peered over his sister's shoulder as Jonathan unrolled it.

"It is lovely," An Mien said.

The absolute ruler of the world's most populous nation frowned unhappily. "It is not seemly," he said, "that we should receive a gift from the ruler of the English when we have sent her nothing."

Jonathan deferred to his wife.

Lai-tse lu was embarrassed but knew she had to explain and, observing the demands of protocol, pretended that it was the princess who had made the remark. "Your Imperial Highness," she said, "I gave to Queen Victoria the overwhelming gift of the black pearl that you and the Celestial Emperor sent to me. I presented it to her in your names."

The Tao Kuang Emperor could not conceal his astonishment. "That pearl is worth an untold fortune."

Lai-tse lu inadvertently replied directly. "That is why it is worthy of a queen rather than a commoner," she said.

An Mien's quick smile indicated her approval as well as her understanding.

Her brother shook his head and sighed. "I have more wives and concubines than I care to count, so I should realize by now that I shall never understand the mind of a woman."

Jonathan discreetly changed the subject. "It was our intention," he said, "to bring with us a physician who could introduce the medical practices of the West to the Middle Kingdom. But a diplomatic mission took precedence, so I will be obliged to find the right physician after we return to America. The girl, Wu-ling, who has accompanied us, can act as his interpreter until such time as he learns Mandarin."

The emperor gave his sister no chance to speak. "We will see this girl subsequently. For now, let us hear about this diplomatic mission. You have already sent us a letter, but we would like to learn more."

Careful to speak only to An Mien, Jonathan explained that President Tyler had sent an emissary to obtain a treaty granting American merchant ships the right to engage in trade at the ports that had been opened to Britain.

Again the emperor gave his sister no chance to reply. "If I refuse," he said, "I suppose the Americans will send warships to bombard my cities and kill my subjects. I suppose they, too, will subject me to humiliation until I consent."

"Please tell His Imperial Majesty," Jonathan said firmly to An Mien, "that the United States, whose citizens believe that all men are created equal and who have no wish to humiliate any nation, wish to conduct fair negotiations. They will send no warships or troops to the Middle Kingdom. Clipper ships have made the world grow smaller, and soon ships propelled by steam—that will not depend on the vagaries of the winds—will shrink the world even more rapidly. My country believes that all nations should live in peace, prosperity, and friendship with each other. We believe that trade between nations brings friendship as well as prosperity to all, and that nations less advanced in the making of machinery have an opportunity to make more rapid progress. The United States seeks only that which is fair to all, and will neither use force nor the threat of force to attain these aims. The representatives of President Tyler, who even now wait at Tientsin, come with open hands and carry no concealed weapons."

The Celestial Emperor glanced at his sister, seeking her guidance.

"When I think of the many books of information and the samples of manufactured goods that Rakehell Jonathan and Laise lu have sent to us," she said, "I believe we would be foolish if we failed to take advantage of the opportunity to deal more often with Americans. The British and the Europeans seek benefits only for themselves. The Americans realize it is to their advantage to help us."

Her brother nodded gravely, then smiled broadly. "I wonder where it might be convenient to hold the talks between

these Americans and the negotiators whom I shall appoint th
very day.''

Jonathan dared to think in terms of the emergency th
was taking him to Whampoa. "I shall sail to Canton on pe
sonal business and to allow my wife and children to visit the tom
of her father.''

The Tao Kuang Emperor rubbed his hands together, ind
cating that he was pleased. "Splendid! Let the Americans b
housed in the palace of the imperial viceroy there, where the
will be treated with the dignity and consideration due the
master, the American President. I will instruct my envoys—o
pain of death if they fail—to negotiate a treaty that will benef
both nations!''

Jonathan was elated. Lai-tse lu was equally pleased, a
though she had expected no less. But there were other matter
to be settled. "Wu-ling, who has volunteered to serve as
translator, still awaits an interview.''

The emperor was restless. "Why don't you see the gi
and speak with her?" he asked his sister. "I've been holdin
audiences all day, and I need some fresh air to clear my head.''

An Mien knew his attention would wander if he stayed, s
she waved him away. He pulled himself to his feet and did n
look at either of the Rakehells again as he took his leave.

Had this been an official audience his own subjects woul
have been required to prostrate themselves on the floor whe
he departed, and foreigners would have been expected to d
the same. But the fiction that he had not been present wa
maintained to the end, and neither Lai-tse lu nor Jonathan too
the slightest notice as he eased himself out of the chamber.

Wu-ling was summoned, and while they awaited her ar
rival, Lai-tse lu answered the princess's many questions abou
her children and her life in America.

"I envy your happiness and freedom," An Mien said
"but you have deep smudges beneath your eyes. Are you ill?"

"It is nothing," Lai-tse lu said, speaking too quickly.

Her husband saw fit to correct her. "She suffers from
most unusual disease that our physicians cannot cure," Jonathan
said. "They cannot predict whether it will overcome her o
whether she will conquer it.''

"I will send the imperial physicians to you today," A

476

Mien said, "and they will examine you. Our medicine may not be as advanced as that of the West, but in some matters our physicians may have a greater knowledge."

Lai-tse lu tried to protest.

"I'm grateful to Your Highness," Jonathan interjected, cutting his wife short.

"They will come to the guest house within the hour," An Mien promised.

The door opened, and a shy Wu-ling came into the chamber.

"Your Imperial Highness," Lai-tse lu said, "permit me to present Wu-ling, formerly of Canton."

Aware she was in the presence of the emperor's sister, Wu-ling kowtowed.

"Stand up, child, and let me look at you," An Mien said, slipping easily into the Cantonese dialect. "I expect we'll see a great deal of each other while you translate many books, so please confine your kowtows to ceremonial occasions in the future."

The awed girl struggled to her feet.

An Mien inspected her critically. "Pretty," she said to Lai-tse lu. "Almost too pretty for her own good, and young enough to arouse the interest of every lecher at the imperial court. Very well, child, we shall take proper precautions accordingly. You shall have a sitting room and bedroom of your own here in my suite. I insist that you come to me with your personal problems, no matter how trivial they may appear to you to be, and I shall let it be known that I have placed you under my personal protection, which will keep the lechers at more than arm's length from you. You are voluntarily giving up a life of freedom in the West in order to serve your native land, so I'll never be able to do enough for you. Do you have any immediate wishes you would like fulfilled?"

Wu-ling drew a deep breath. "My grandmother was still alive in Canton when I went to the West, Your Imperial Highness, but I do not know if she is still living."

"Write her name and address for me. If she is alive, I will have her brought to you and you will be provided with funds that will make her comfortable for the rest of her days."

Tears came to the girl's eyes.

"We'll have none of that," the princess said. "Accustom yourself to life as a privileged member of the imperial household."

Wu-ling quickly blinked away her tears and, trying to become businesslike, began to discuss her duties.

Meanwhile the Tao Kuang Emperor wandered out into the open and strolled through the garden. He appeared deep in thought, and although many members of his staff sought decisions from him on various matters, none dared to disturb him. All too often dust storms from Mongolia turned the sky over Peking gray, but today a brilliant sun was shining, and the Celestial Emperor wandered aimlessly, enjoying its warmth.

The shouts of small children and the barking of a dog on the far side of the brick wall that separated his personal compound from the guest quarters attracted his attention, and giving in to impulse, he opened the heavy door and slipped unnoticed into the guest house garden.

Two boys, one white and the other Eurasian, and a smaller girl, also Eurasian, were playing a game of hide-and-seek, while a happily barking chow dog frolicked with them, more often than not revealing the whereabouts of the child who was hiding. Obviously these were the son and daughter of Rakehell Jonathan and the son of his partner and cousin. The emperor was astonished to hear them shouting in Mandarin, so he seated himself on a stone bench to watch and listen.

Gradually the children became aware of the proximity of the quiet, middle-aged gentleman. Stopping their play, they approached him tentatively.

He grinned and motioned them closer, and the dog began to growl.

Julian addressed the animal in Cantonese. "Behave yourself, Harmony!" he commanded, and the dog subsided. Approaching the man, the boy spoke to him in Mandarin. "Please excuse our dog, sir. He isn't really ill-mannered, but he considers it his duty to protect us from strangers."

"So he should." The Tao Kuang Emperor patted the stone bench, inviting the children to sit. "You speak Mandarin and Cantonese well."

"My father and mother believe it is proper to speak the language of the land one is visiting," Julian replied gravely.

478

"My father also believes it," David said. "Besides, this is my second homeland."

"Jade's, too," Julian said proudly, and the little girl mimicked her brother. "Jade, too," she said, kneeling on the bench beside the emperor.

"Ah," the sole ruler of the largest nation on earth said. "So you sometimes think of yourselves as being part-Chinese?"

"I am all English," David said, "and all Chinese, too."

"She's American and Chinese," Julian explained, gently placing his hand on his sister's shoulder to restrain her from climbing on the emperor.

"And you?" The emperor looked at the completely Caucasian Julian. "You didn't say what you are."

"Although it is true, sir, that I have no Chinese blood, I know much about the Middle Kingdom. I love the Middle Kingdom. I know about her history and her art and her people. I know about the lives of the emperors—"

"Do you know who the present emperor may be?"

"Of course, sir! The Celestial Tao Kuang Emperor." Julian was enjoying showing off.

"And what do you know about him?"

"Well, he is very powerful, of course, but he is also wise and kind, and my parents say that is more important. My father, who fought for him, says that more than anything in the world, the Tao Kuang Emperor works for the welfare and good of his people."

"So he does," the man murmured, and turned to the younger boy. "What do you think of this place?"

"It's just like a palace," David said.

"It *is* a palace, silly," Julian told him loftily.

"Well, it doesn't look like Queen Victoria's palace!" David retorted.

"Palace, palace," Jade called out in delight. She had managed to wiggle free from her brother and was sitting on the emperor's lap after all. Harmony circled the man, decided he liked him, and wagged his tail.

"Hat pretty," Jade said, pointing to the emperor's head.

The Tao Kuang Emperor removed the knitted symbol of his exalted rank, on which row after row of pearls concealed the material beneath them. Smiling broadly, he handed it to the little girl.

"Pretty!" she exclaimed, and began counting the pearls. "One, two, three—"

"You may keep the hat," the kindly gentleman told her.

Julian's breeding took over. "I can't let her take it," he told him. "Mama says it is wrong to accept a gift without giving a gift in return."

"Tell your mother that you have given me a great gift, a respite from cares. She will understand."

"Do you know my mama?"

"Yes, and your father, too. Boys, I also have small gifts for you." The Tao Kuang Emperor reached into a robe pocket and produced two pieces of carved ivory, each about the diameter and thickness of an American twenty-five-cent piece.

Julian became wildly excited, but still had the good manners to speak in Mandarin. "Look, David!" he shouted. "The Tree of Life!"

"Oho!" The emperor smiled broadly. "So you know the symbol?"

"The ships of our fathers' fleet fly flags with the Tree of Life on them," David said proudly.

"Then you must rejoice," the Celestial Emperor said, "because the Tree of Life will bring good fortune to you and to generations who will come after you." He frowned slightly when he heard a crashing of cymbals on the far side of the wall, indicating that an imperial audience was about to begin. Duty beckoned, so he sighed and stood up, patting each of the children on the head. Harmony trotted as far as the door set in the stone wall, and received an imperial pat, too. "I shall treasure my memory of this meeting," the Tao Kuang Emperor said, one hand on the latch. "I hope you will remember it, too." He disappeared through the open door, perhaps forgetting, perhaps not caring that he was bareheaded.

The children had no immediate opportunity to tell Lai-tse lu and Jonathan about their experience or show them the treasures they had been given. Three imperial physicians were waiting when the couple and Wu-ling returned from their audience, and Lai-tse lu was subjected to a thorough medical examination.

Then she and Jonathan joined the men of medicine in the sitting room of the guest house suite, and the white-haired enior physician addressed them. "We know that our methods nd techniques are far different from those of our colleagues in ae West," he said. "We realize we have much to learn from aem, and it is our fond hope that they can learn from us in eturn. One day we hope we can pool our knowledge. In this astance we are in agreement with them." He bowed to Lai-tse a.

She graciously inclined her head in return and was at eace within herself. A tense Jonathan envied her calm.

"With great regret," the senior imperial physician de-lared, "we concur in the diagnosis of our colleagues in the Vest. Rakehell Lai-tse lu suffers from a malady whose origin unknown and for which no cure has ever been discovered. Ve regard it as inevitable that you will suffer new attacks. One f them will take you out of this world into the land of your acestors."

"How much longer do you predict she will live, Doctor?" onathan asked hoarsely.

"We must tell the truth, not what you wish to hear," the nysician replied. "The disease is already far advanced. You aould rejoice each day she remains at your side, sir."

An oppressive feeling of dread filled Jonathan, but Lai-tse a was unmoved. She already knew what the physicians had ald her, and when the children raced into the room, all of them lking and shouting simultaneously, she laughed freely as she apped her hands over her ears.

"Gracious!" she said. "One at a time, if you please!"

The boys controlled themselves, but little Jade continued babble excitedly, describing the meeting with the kindly entleman as best she could, then showing her parents the earl-studded headgear.

Lai-tse lu and Jonathan exchanged startled glances.

David followed with an account, and Julian, by far the ost articulate of the trio, filled in details. Then he and David splayed their carved Tree of Life medallions.

"Do you know the identity of the man with whom you sited?" Lai-tse lu asked. "You had a private audience with e Tao Kuang Emperor."

The children gaped at her, and only the black chow, his il wagging, seemed unimpressed.

481

Jade, thinking her mother meant to take away the gift
clutched the pearl hat tightly. She relaxed her grip when sh
saw her mother smile.

"Our ivory pieces are more important than all the jewe
on Jade's hat," Julian said. "Jewels are nice, but the Tree
Life is more important because it flies on every ship in o
fleet!"

"All of your gifts are important because they were giv
to you by a great man," Lai-tse lu said, "a lonely man wh
devotes his whole life to the improvement of the welfare of h
people."

The children raced off with the dog to play in the garde
again. For the sake of the tearful Wu-ling, who would mov
into the inner palace the following day to begin her new lif
Jonathan made no mention of the physician's visit. He had n
opportunity to bring up the subject until that night, when the
retired early, prior to a return to Tientsin early the next day

Lai-tse lu tenderly placed a graceful hand over her hu
band's mouth. "We will not speak of this matter again," sh
said. "I knew when we sailed on this voyage that I would n
see Missy Sarah or your father again in this world. I will b
ready to go after I have paid my respects at the tomb of m
father. I would have preferred to be buried in New London, m
new home, but the God of the West and gods of the East hav
willed otherwise. So I will be content to rest in a grave besid
that of my father, and someday you will join me there."

So choked with emotion that he could not speak, Jonatha
embraced her.

"Do not grieve for me when I am no longer here, m
beloved," she said firmly. "You and I have known a love tha
few people on this earth ever have been granted. You hav
work to do, and you must guide our children so they wi
follow in your footsteps and mine. Rejoice forever in the lov
we have known."

"I'll try," he murmured, trying to match her courage.

"Someday you will marry again—"

"Never!"

"But you will," she said, "because you must. It is n
fitting that a man live alone, and the children will need the hel
and guidance and counsel of a woman. I shall not mind. I a
secure in the knowledge that the love we have shared is uniqu

482

and I know that my place in your heart is secure. Enjoy to the full the years that remain to you on this earth. And know, as I know, that the day will come when you and I will be reunited, whether in the heaven of the West or the afterworld of the Upper Kingdom. It does not really matter where we shall meet again, because our spirits surely will be reunited for all of eternity.''

That night their lovemaking was gentle but completely uninhibited, and never had they been so close.

The following morning they said good-bye to Wu-ling. The children clung to the girl who had acted so frequently as their nursemaid.

"You'll have more than enough translating to keep you busy," Jonathan told her. "Write to us when you can, and we'll write to you, too. And we'll see you whenever we visit the Middle Kingdom. Keep in mind that your real work will begin in earnest when I find the right physician to send here."

The farewell of Lai-tse lu and Wu-ling was silent, both knowing they would not meet again. They embraced, then turned away from each other without a word.

The return journey to Tientsin was uneventful, and Caleb Cushing was overwhelmed when Jonathan told him in detail about their visit with the Tao Kuang Emperor.

"You and your wife should be in the diplomatic corps," President Tyler's envoy said. "It sounds to me as though our negotiations with the Chinese who'll represent the emperor will be cut and dried."

"Well, they won't be all that simple," Jonathan told him. "Chinese enjoy bargaining for its own sake, but when they know you're fair they'll be equally fair in return. There's no doubt in my mind that you'll return home with a treaty that the Senate will be pleased to ratify by unanimous vote."

The great clipper sailed out of the Tientsin harbor on the final leg of her journey to Canton. Jonathan stole a glance at his wife as she stood beside him on the deck, and he marveled at her serenity.

The cell that Bradford Walker occupied in the dungeons beneath the palace of the governor-general of Macao was damp and infested by rats, but he was beyond caring. Still as naked as he had been when he had been so ignominiously delivered to

Dom Manuel Sebastian in the bamboo cage he had prepared for Molinda, he found that the heavy chains attached to his ankles and wrists made every movement an agony. He was served a bowl of rice and cups of plain water three times each day, but food and drink no longer mattered to him.

His one overwhelming dread was the ordeal to which he was subjected every afternoon before sundown. He was dragged from his cell, and the bayonets of Portuguese infantrymen prodded him as he was led, stumbling and almost fainting, to the governor-general's audience chamber. There the Marquês de Braga, surrounded by several concubines, awaited him and watched impassively as he was tied face down on a table.

The torture was merciless. Each day two jailers, one Portuguese and the other Chinese, took turns whipping the victim, and the more loudly he shrieked and screamed, begging for mercy, the harder they struck him.

Dom Manuel invariably fondled one of his concubines as he watched the spectacle, sometimes squeezing the girl's breasts so hard that she gasped. But no concubine dared to complain. When one of the torturers said that the prisoner soon would lose consciousness, the Marquês de Braga called a halt, then demanded in a loud voice, "Walker, where did you hide the stolen opium?"

The reply was the same each time. "I didn't steal it, and I don't know," the tormented man moaned.

Then the marquês nodded to the torturers, and they varied their treatment by beating Walker across the soles of his bare feet until he lost consciousness. He awakened sometime later in his cell, more dead than alive.

One day was so much like another that he lost all count of time and had no idea whether weeks or months had passed. He prayed for release, and death was more welcome than the interminable torment to which he was subjected.

Suddenly the ordeal came to an end when he was so weak he could scarcely move. His shackles were removed, and he was carried to the wing of the palace occupied by the concubines. To his astonishment the young women treated him with kindness. They bathed him, allowing him to soak for a long time in a tub of warm water. Then, after shaving off his beard, they anointed his back and the soles of his feet, which were

484

covered with lacerations and welts. And when they had made him comfortable they fed him a nourishing broth.

Only when night came was he given a forcible reminder that he was still a prisoner. A cuff of heavy metal was locked around his neck, and a chain attached to it was fastened to a heavy steel loop imbedded in the wall, making escape impossible.

Thereafter the young women, all of them attractive, continued to care for him and nurse him back to health. He was bathed every morning, healing ointments were applied to his wounds, and soon he was able to eat solid foods. The menu was varied and the food good, but the concubines allowed him to use no eating utensils himself, but insisted on continuing to feed him. Only the metal collar placed around his neck at nightfall was a reminder that a grim fate might be in store for him.

Apparently the girls regarded him as something of a plaything, and in some ways their treatment of him was odd. They shaved all the hair from his still naked body, shaped his fingernails and toenails, which had grown long in confinement, and amused themselves by painting them with shades of lacquer which they changed from day to day. They paid particular attention to his hair, which also had grown long, washing it and brushing it each day, sometimes experimenting by curling it and invariably anointing it with strong scents.

Ultimately Walker overcame his embarrassment over being seen in the nude by these amiable young women. His treatment was far better than the incarceration in a cell and the daily beatings he had been forced to endure. But he was frustrated by his inability to communicate with his gentle jailers. The majority were Chinese, two were Portuguese, and the others appeared to be representatives of other nations of the East, but he could not identify them. None spoke English, the only language he knew, and although he had picked up a smattering of Cantonese during his stay in China, his attempts to communicate in that language were met with stony silence.

The idea of making an ally of one of the girls occurred to him, but he soon had to abandon it. At no time was he ever alone with any one concubine; no fewer than three or four at any one time came into the room he occupied, and they invariably administered to him in groups.

Little by little he regained his strength, and one day the new routine changed abruptly. The girls, giggling and laughing, painted Walker's cheeks and lips with rouge, placed towering clogs on his feet, put a flower in his hair, and dressed him in a long gown of red net, then looped a leash of heavy leather around his neck. The girls surrounded him and, still giggling, led him from their quarters for the first time. He was conducted to an inner courtyard, where they left him standing alone.

A gate at the far end of the courtyard was opened, and a spasm of fear convulsed the painted, absurdly dressed man when the Marquês de Braga's two elephants were admitted to the enclosure. They lumbered toward him, stopped short, and appeared to be studying him. He knew nothing about elephants, but felt totally helpess as these huge beasts towered above him. Then the pure white male lifted his trunk and trumpeted loudly.

A trainer appeared instantly, calling to the animals, and the elephants obediently left the courtyard.

Within moments the concubines returned, and conducted the prisoner back to his quarters. There they stripped him and scrubbed the cosmetics from his face before feeding him his evening meal and placing the metal collar around his neck for the night. As they filed silently out of the chamber, one of the Portuguese concubines stayed behind for a moment, and Walker was stunned when she addressed him in English.

"Soon," she said, "you will be the bride of Siroso."

She was gone before he could ask any questions, and when he tried to question her in the days that followed, she looked at him blankly. He could only conclude that she had been taught the one sentence in English but was unable to converse in the language.

Puzzling over the strange experience and trying to find some pattern in the change in his treatment, he was able to reach no firm conclusion. Red, he knew, was the color worn by brides in the Middle Kingdom. But he had never heard of someone called Siroso. He could only guess that Dom Manuel intended to emasculate him, and the dread that filled him haunted him night and day.

Certainly he knew he was helpless, unable to avoid any punishment that the Marquês de Braga wished to inflict on him. He had not tried to cheat either Dom Manuel or Owen

486

Bruce, but they did not believe him and were free to do as they pleased with him. It was impossible to appeal for either justice or mercy, and there was no way he could avoid the fate that might be in store for him.

One day, about a week after he had been left with the elephants in the courtyard, he knew that a climax of some sort had come. The concubines bathed him in strongly scented water, then carefully shaved all of the new growth of hair from his body. Some painted his nails with a brilliant shade of red lacquer, while others encircled his eyes with kohl, smearing a black substance on his lashes and painting his lips and cheeks in the same shade of red as the nail lacquer.

Some giggling and some shrieking with laughter, they dressed him in a red net gown, so snug-fitting that it obviously had been made to his measurements. Only slits in the sides of the long skirt made it possible for him to move. They strapped red clogs on his feet, and for some reason the entire group concentrated on the arrangement of his hair, on which they first poured a scent so strong that the odor filled the room. They tried one style, then another before they could agree, and finally they pinned a cluster of bright red flowers to one side of the crown. After loading his fingers with rings of silver and gold and placing heavy bracelets on his wrists they led him to a mirror.

Walker winced as he looked at the caricature of himself.

By this time he had become so docile that his keepers had decided no leash was necessary, and when they beckoned, he accompanied them as they again conducted him to the courtyard. In the center of the open space several stakes had been driven into the ground, and the concubines led him to a place between the stakes. Then they lifted him into the air and spread-eagled him on the ground, tying leather thongs to his ankles and wrists and affixing the other ends to the stakes. He quickly discovered it was impossible for him to move even a fraction of an inch. One smoothed and adjusted his long skirt, while two others approached with a cube of heavy, hard wood, painted bright red. His head was lifted and placed on the top of the cube, about twelve inches from the ground.

Then the English-speaking Portuguese concubine stood in front of the prisoner, so he could see her. "It is fitting," she said, "that the bride of Siroso kowtow before the bridegroom."

The others walked behind her to the far side of the court-yard and entered the palace.

A few moments later a pair of French windows opened on the second floor, directly facing the yard. By craning his neck Bradford Walker could see Dom Manuel Sebastian, Marquês de Braga, governor-general of the Royal Portuguese colony of Macao, seated in a high-backed chair. The concubines surrounded him now, and although a few were still giggling, the majority had become solemn.

The miserable prisoner's instinct told him that at last he was about to learn the meaning of the bizarre charade to which he had been subjected.

The gate at the far end of the courtyard opened, and the white male elephant moved slowly into the enclosure.

The grating voice of Dom Manuel could be heard distinctly as he said, "Siroso, you may greet your bride."

The elephant trumpeted loudly and began to advance.

A growing sense of unreasoning fear enveloped Walker, and he strained in a fruitless attempt to free himself from his bonds.

The concubines fell silent. What they had regarded as an innocent game had come to an end, and one of them, sensing what was about to happen, began to weep.

The Marquês de Braga leaned forward in his chair so he could observe the spectacle more closely and, a faint smile on his lips, indiscriminately fondled the girls who were closest to him.

There was no sound but the thud of the elephant's heavy feet as he walked slowly across the courtyard. He halted direct-ly above the grotesque, spread-eagled figure, then trumpeted again.

"No, in God's name!" Walker shouted hoarsely.

Dom Manuel's voice was cold. "Siroso," he called, "you may claim your bride!"

The elephant placed a huge forefoot on the victim's head, then stood uncertainly for a moment until he smelled the pow-erful scent that had been poured so liberally on Walker's long hair. That smell was the final signal the beast awaited, and he began to press downward.

The pressure became intolerable, and Bradford Walker's

high-pitched scream of terror and agony echoed and reechoed across the courtyard. It was the last sound he ever made.

The elephant's forefoot crushed his skull as effectively as a man could have crushed a bird's egg beneath his heel.

It was not accidental that the victim's crimson blood precisely matched his bizarre costume and the red of the painted block of wood.

III

The disturbing letter from Molinda that told Charles Boynton about her unfortunate loan reached London one afternoon, and shortly thereafter Jonathan's longer, more detailed letter, written prior to his departure for the East, was in his cousin's hands. Badly upset by the news they contained, Charles took the two letters from his own office to that of his father, which was located on the top floor of the headquarters building that overlooked the shipyard and the Thames.

Sir Alan donned his glasses, read both communications slowly, then threw the letters onto the desk and sighed. "I knew it was a mistake to buy the shares of the outside stockholders," he said. "But what's done is done. The milk is already spilled."

"Is the financial crisis we face as severe as Jonnie indicates?"

"Easily as bad and perhaps worse. At least from this end. And it wouldn't surprise me if Jeremiah's monthly survey makes matters still worse. The loss of over a quarter of a million dollars in cash, with little hope of recovery, comes at a most inconvenient time. There are four clippers under construction in the United States, and we're building two schooners here. But we won't receive as much as a ha'penny for any of them until next year. And thanks to our continuing expansion, especially in the East, our operating expenses are very high."

"What can we do about it?" Charles demanded.

Sir Alan removed his glasses, dropped them onto the desk, and rubbed his eyes. "I've never seen the junks that operate out of Whampoa and Hong Kong under our flag. But, assuming they're in good shape, I suppose we could get a reasonably good price if we chose to dispose of them."

"Jonnie wouldn't stand for it. Those ships were part of the estate that Lai-tse lu inherited from her father, and Jonnie takes the attitude that we merely operate them on her behalf and for her heirs. He'd be horrified by the very idea of selling them to raise cash."

"One alternative," his father said mildly, "would be to dip into the opium market before it shuts down. The Americans are taking the lead in making the buying and selling of the drug illegal, and Queen Victoria and Prince Albert have made their feelings so plain that we won't be far behind. For the present, however, the trade is still legal, so we well might recoup quickly. Even Jeremiah could see the logic of entering the opium trade now."

"I'd rather that we go bankrupt," Charles replied, his voice harsh, "and I know for certain that Jonnie feels as I do. We'd resign from the company before we'd touch a cargo of opium!"

"You asked for suggestions, and I made one," Sir Alan said hastily. "I lost the opium battle a long time ago, and I'm not going to get into another fight."

Charles thanked him, then moved on to other possibilities. "I'm not certain the Fat Dutchman could sell us enough pepper in time to raise a large sum of cash fast enough," he said. "Molinda knows more about the pepper potentials than I do. Here, read Jonnie's last paragraph again. It makes great sense to me. He'll spend several months in the East, since he'll be expected to bring the official American treaty negotiators back to the United States. He thinks it would be wise if I meet him out there, and I believe he's right."

"How so?" Sir Alan raised a thick, gray eyebrow.

"You and Uncle Jeremiah are locked in, so to speak. The American and British operations are stable. Homer Ellison's new operating system will save money, but it won't earn enough additional capital. We could cut back here and in America, but that's a drastic step no one wants to take. There's no way to raise large sums of cash quickly in either country. The situation in the Orient is far more fluid. The Fat Dutchman's pepper could produce miracles for us if we could figure out some way to utilize it as a money-making weapon. There may be a market in products like rare silks from China. Or cargoes of the emperor's tea, if enough of it is available for immediate export.''

"You may be right," his father said thoughtfully.

"We have a clipper leaving for Cathay the day after tomorrow," Charles said. "I'll travel on board. Jonnie and I can survey the situation together, and since we know the markets and products of the East, I hope we can work out some way to solve our problems. I'll bring David back home with me."

"Will you take Ruth on the voyage?" Sir Alan asked quietly.

"Not on this trip. The primary scene of action has been shifting rapidly from Whampoa to Hong Kong, and the new colony is no place for a lady. It's still wild there, and it won't be safe until the government sends out a large constabulary force that can establish order. People of quality won't be able to take their wives and daughters to Hong Kong for at least another year, perhaps longer."

"I strongly suggest that you explain the situation to Ruth in detail," his father said. "I know she has been looking forward to making a visit to the East with you, particularly since Lai-tse lu has gone there with Jonathan. She may be bitterly disappointed."

"She'll understand that I have no choice," Charles said, an irritable note creeping into his voice. "I'm not going there for pleasure. My sole purpose is to help Rakehell and Boynton survive."

Later in the day, as Charles pondered his father's advice, he knew it was sound. So, when he returned to the house in Belgravia that evening, he made it his business to speak privately with his wife, explaining the company's predicament in detail then telling her why she could not yet take the risk of visiting Hong Kong.

She did not protest. "You mean I'd need to sleep on board ship to be safe?"

"Even a clipper isn't necessarily a safe place in the Hong Kong harbor as yet," he replied as they started downstairs. "Guards are posted day and night on board all ships to prevent thieves and pirates from climbing aboard. The American fron-

'tier country at its worst is mild compared to Hong Kong these days.''

Before dinner, when the Boyntons had gathered for glasses of sack, Charles told his plans to his mother and sister.

"May you prosper," Jessica said, raising her glass to him. "I'm sure we can rely on you and Jonnie to do whatever is needed."

"I'll do my best, Mother."

"And do keep a close watch on David during your return voyage," Ruth said. "I shudder whenever I think of him scampering in the rigging of a ship at sea."

"He's a Boynton, my dear, and that means he's a sailor," Charles said cheerfully.

Elizabeth, looking sophisticated in a gown of pale, clinging silk, sipped her drink in silence, then said, "When you see Jonathan, please give him my love."

Her brother grinned broadly.

"Lai-tse lu, too," she added hastily.

At dinner Charles explained that he would sail first to Canton for his meeting with Jonathan and thereafter would travel wherever they deemed necessary. "I haven't seen our new facilities in Hong Kong, and I'll want to register Rakehell and Boynton as a British company, so I daresay I'll spend quite a bit of time there. And I'm equally sure I'll go to Java for a discussion of the pepper situation with the Dutchman. Whether I visit still other places will depend on the plans that Jonnie and I make."

Ruth was very quiet during and after the meal, leading her husband to believe she felt slighted because he wasn't taking her with him on the voyage. So, when they retired to their own suite, he told her for a second time why he regarded Hong Kong as too dangerous for her.

"Oh, I understand your point, and I accept it," she replied.

"Something is bothering you."

Ruth took a deep breath. "If you must know, I wonder if you'll resume your affair with the woman you knew on your last voyage to the East, whoever she may be."

Charles was astonished. "You knew?"

"I guessed. But it wasn't difficult. Your attitude told me." She turned away from him.

493

He followed, placing a hand on her shoulder to detain her. "I'm sorry," he said. "My relations with her had no effect on my feelings for you and in no way detracted from them. But let me relieve your mind. In answer to your question, I won't have anything personal to do with her. She has been married since I was last in the East."

Ruth heard the ring of conviction in his voice and was satisfied.

Charles refrained from mentioning that, although Molinda was no longer available, he felt certain that he would be offered another of the Fat Dutchman's concubines during his visit to Djakarta.

Lai-tse lu stood on the deck of the clipper, drinking in the sights and smells and sounds of the world in which she had been reared. Then, when the great ship was eased into her berth at one of the old Soong Chao piers, she gathered the excited children and followed her husband ashore.

A grinning Kai awaited the party, and after embracing Jonathan, he bowed low to Lai-tse lu. Then, to the astonishment of the children, he lifted her high in the air and did an impromptu dance.

"Put me down this instant," she cried happily, while Harmony barked approvingly.

At last Kai placed her on the ground again and, turning to the youngsters, delighted them by picking up all three of them simultaneously and doing another dance.

Meanwhile Jonathan presented Molinda to his wife. The two young women, both lovely, both fiercely independent, struck an immediate rapport.

"Let me show you the changes we've made in the factory buildings and docks since you've last seen them," Molinda said. "Then, when you go to the house, I've arranged—naturally—for you and Jonathan to move into your old quarters."

"Thank you," Lai-tse lu said warmly. "I hope we aren't causing inconvenience for you and your husband."

"Shaong Wei and I are as pleased as we are honored to have you here."

"First," Jonathan said, "we must make arrangements to

494

have the American diplomats escorted to the palace of the imperial viceroy."

"The escort already awaits them," Molinda said with a smile, nodding in the direction of a company of yellow-clad infantrymen. "Their quarters have been prepared for them, and I have found an interpreter who will accompany them. Unfortunately he speaks only Cantonese and doesn't know a word of Mandarin, so I think it will be necessary to hold the treaty talks in Cantonese."

"That will be more than good enough," Jonathan said, and went off to see Caleb Cushing and his subordinates ashore. He explained the situation to Cushing, then added, "I'll keep in touch with you, and you can let me know if there's anything you want or need. If you want to find me, simply send a messenger to the old Soong Chao estate, which my wife and I inherited. It is no more than a ten-minute walk from the palace."

"I've already written once to President Tyler," Cushing said, "to tell him how much you and Mrs. Rakehell have done for us. By the time I'm finished singing your praises, Congress should award you a medal."

"The increase in trade with China that your treaty will make possible is the only reward I want," Jonathan told him with a grin. "And don't forget that we're always available to help you at any time."

After watching the diplomats start off into Canton with the escort, he rejoined Lai-tse lu and Molinda, who had found they truly were kindred spirits and were chatting happily.

As Molinda conducted them through the expanded warehouse facilities, she told them of her recent near-escape from tragedy in Macao, then added, "In my own land of Bali, the gods would say that he who tried to deliver me into the hands of evil was paid in full for his treachery. But his death was horrible." She described the execution of Bradford Walker, which now had become public knowledge.

Jonathan and Lai-tse lu halted and looked at each other "I hate any kind of torture," he said, "but I can't feel bad for Brad."

"Neither can I," his wife said, thinking of all that Judith Walker had suffered.

"Molinda," he demanded, "when is the next of our ships sailing to New England?"

"Early next week."

"Good," Jonathan said. "I'll give the master a letter to my sister and Homer Ellison."

"I'm sorry she was set free in such a dreadful way," Lai-tse lu said, "but Judith and Homer are free to marry now."

Unaware of what they were discussing, Molinda could think only of the loan that had not been repaid. "When we go to the house, Jonathan," she said, "I will show you the loan agreement. The signature of Walker was clear, but that of Owen Bruce was no more than a scribble. I didn't realize it at the time, but I'm not certain it can even be identified as his signature."

"That was deliberate, of course, and doesn't surprise me," he replied.

When they completed their tour, Lai-tse lu elected to walk to the house on the far side of Canton. She and Molinda took the lead and were followed by Jonathan and Kai, with the latter carrying Jade, at the little girl's specific request. Julian and David elected to accompany the men.

Because of the children, the party attracted considerable attention. Few Eurasians had ever been seen in the city, so Jade and David received more than a fair share of the stares of passersby. And there were many who gaped at Julian because he was the first white boy ever to have visited Canton.

A number of local children were playing in the great square in front of the Temple of Heaven, and when they saw Julian one boy of about his own age began to chant, "Fan Kuei!" His friends immediately picked up the refrain.

Julian promptly halted and doubled his fists. "You're very rude," he told them in Cantonese, and pointed at the boy who had created the confrontation. "Step forward, if you dare, and fight like a man."

David became equally belligerent. "I'll fight any two of you!" he shouted in Cantonese.

Jade refused to be left out. "I hit you, too!" she called in the native dialect.

Harmony sensed that trouble was brewing and growled.

Lai-tse lu and Molinda were upset, but a smiling Jonathan

496

cautioned them, "Let the boys handle this in their own way."
He halted, ordering the chow to remain close beside him.

A grinning Kai stopped, too, and kept a firm grip on little
Jade, who was trying to wriggle out of his grasp.

Julian and David advanced on the group together.

"They'll be hurt," Lai-tse lu said to her husband. "They're
outnumbered by six to two."

"Watch what happens and don't interfere," he replied
with a chuckle.

"We may be foreigners," Julian told the local boys, "but
we're not devils. My father fought in the war against the British
and was almost killed. Were any of your fathers killed for the
honor of the Middle Kingdom?"

The young Chinese were so astonished to hear these outsiders speaking in accentless Cantonese that they were dumb-
founded. Then the leader took a step forward and bowed.

"My grandmother told me a wonderful story about strangers who speak as we do," he said in awe. "I thought it was just
a myth, but she told the truth. Accept a thousand pardons for
insulting you."

Julian stopped short, thought for a moment, and then
returned the bow, with the younger David following his example.

The amused Jonathan and Kai knew there would be no
need for them to intervene.

"You will be our friends?" Julian asked.

"Of course," one of the Chinese youngsters said. "See if
you can beat me climbing to the top of that big tree!"

Julian looked eagerly at his father. "May I, Papa?"

"Go ahead," Jonathan said. "You, too, David. No, not
you, Jade. You haven't learned to climb trees yet."

Harmony stopped growling, and the boys began to scramble madly up the towering tree that stood at one side of the
great square. David, smaller and lacking his cousin's greater
strength, was in the midst of the pack. But the sure-footed,
agile Julian, accustomed to climbing in the rigging of a clipper, hauled himself upward hand over hand and took the lead.

Unable to watch, Lai-tse lu averted her gaze, but Molinda
was fascinated. Kai shouted in triumph when Julian was the
first to reach the top of the tree.

"He is truly your son, Jonathan," Molinda said admiringly.

"Julian, come down now. You, too, David," Jonathan called. "You'll have lots of time to play with your new friends."

They resumed their walk, and when they started up the hill to the old Soong estate, Lai-tse lu instinctively increased her pace. She halted for a long moment at the front gate, and Jonathan quietly moved up beside her and placed his arm around her shoulders.

With one motion they moved to the pagoda that had been erected over the grave of Soong Chao. They entered together, then prayed in silence, and the children, entering behind them, huddled together and watched.

Ultimately becoming aware of them, Jonathan said, "Jade, you never knew your grandfather, but always remember he was a wonderful man, a man who loved his family, his honor, and his country."

The wide-eyed child nodded solemnly.

"I think of him as my grandfather, too," Julian said firmly.

They went on to the pavilion that had been Lai-tse lu's, with the children installed in the adjoining pavilion. Jonathan accompanied Molinda to her office, where he met Shaong Wei who, as always, was reading a book of philosophy, and then Molinda showed him the loan agreement that had proved so costly for Rakehell and Boynton.

Shaong Wei scowled. "The good name of my wife has been at stake," he said, "so I have investigated this situation thoroughly, and all I can tell you is that Walker and Bruce knew what they were doing when they signed this agreement. The document was executed in neutral territory in Canton, where the laws of the Middle Kingdom do not apply. But there is also no foreign authority who has jurisdiction in the port complex—not the British, not the French, not the Americans. If the agreement had been executed in Hong Kong, it would have been possible to appeal to the British courts, even though no magistrates have been assigned to the colony as yet."

"What you're telling me," Jonathan said, "is that no nation has the authority to force Owen Bruce to repay this loan, even if we could prove that the scribbled signature is his."

Shaong Wei and his wife nodded grimly, and then Molinda

said, "When I first learned that Walker was dead, I hoped to obtain repayment from his estate. But he had no estate."

"We are forced to guess," Shaong Wei added, "that Bruce and the governor-general of Macao, who were his partners, simply pocketed the money he left behind."

Jonathan absorbed the information in silence, then said, "We seem to have no choice. We must take the law into our own hands if we hope to recover the funds that belong to us."

"I'm to blame for this predicament," Molinda said.

Jonathan shook his head. "You acted in good faith. You had no idea you were dealing with criminals who not only evaded the laws of every civilized country, but who seemed determined to destroy Rakehell and Boynton."

"After my own near-escape in Macao, I understand these men," Molinda said, "but now it is too late. Bruce owns a dock and a factory here and has more extensive holdings in Hong Kong, but no law anywhere in this part of the world can compel him to give his property as repayment of the debt."

Foremost in Jonathan's mind was Rakehell and Boynton's urgent, immediate need for money owed to them. "I'm afraid," he said slowly, "that I must take the law into my own hands."

"How?" Shaong Wei wanted to know.

"Bruce now lives in Hong Kong, and from what you told me earlier, Molinda, he rarely visits his complex here. Is that correct?"

The young woman swallowed hard and nodded.

"I have disliked Owen Bruce as long as he has hated me," Jonathan replied, "and my life would be far more peaceful if I never set eyes on him again. But I'm being compelled to go to Hong Kong, meet him face to face, and insist that he pay his just debts. I don't know whether I'll succeed, but I must make the attempt. Molinda, I'll be obliged if you'll assign one of the junks to take me to Hong Kong tomorrow morning."

"That is the very least I can do," she said.

"Take me with you," Shaong Wei declared. "I would like to stand beside you when you face Bruce."

His presence might contribute to the pressure being applied to the Scotsman, Jonathan thought, and gave his consent.

That evening neither Lai-tse lu nor Jonathan could enjoy the sumptuous meal that the servants prepared at Molinda's direction. As they sat in the familiar dining pavilion, their memories overwhelmed them, and both could feel the presence of Soong Chao and Missy Sarah. Jonathan began to wonder if he had been right to bring his wife back to the home in which she had lived for so many years.

The following morning he and Shaong Wei left early for the waterfront to board the junk that would take them to the new British colony, and early in the afternoon the junk tied up at the new Rakehell and Boynton wharf in Hong Kong. Lo Fang was on hand to meet them, and after bowing to Shaong Wei, the burly giant embraced Jonathan, his brother in the Society of Oxen.

After making a brief inspection of the new impressive facilities, Jonathan came to the point of his visit. "Owen Bruce owes the company a large sum of money taken from us by trickery," he said. "I want to see him."

"I will take you to him," Lo Fang said. "His complex is very near."

Flanked by Shaong Wei and Lo Fang, Jonathan walked to the adjoining property. He carried a sword and pistol as well as his Javanese throwing knives, and both of his companions were armed with curved Chinese swords. Uncertain whether they might meet a hostile reception, all three were prepared.

The majordomo in Bruce's warehouse office was not co-operative. "My master is not here," he said.

"Where is he?" Jonathan asked.

The man shrugged.

Lo Fang caught the majordomo by the collar. "You know me," he said, "so you realize it is not wise to try my patience. I saw Bruce on his wharf this morning. Where has he gone?"

Again the man shrugged.

Lo Fang's grip tightened. "Don't trifle with me," he said ominously.

The majordomo gasped. "Bruce was upset when he saw the Fan Kuei come ashore," he said, nodding in the direction of Jonathan. "So he went into the new town, and I do not believe he will return until the Fan Kuei has departed."

Releasing the man so suddenly that he staggered and fell, Lo Fang beckoned to his companions. "Come," he said, and led the way toward a proliferating jumble of stone and brick buildings constructed in the Western style, new Chinese pagodas, simple huts of clay, and houses, shops, and other native tructures that used frames of bamboo. "Hong Kong," he said, "is even more wild now than it was before the British came and started to build a town. But if Bruce is hiding from you, Jonathan, we will find him."

So many Chinese construction workers, longshoremen, and purveyors of food and other services had come to Victoria Island that the trio had to push through crowds almost as thick as those found in the more heavily populated portions of Canton, Peking, and other major cities. Occasionally the black-clad Lo Fang paused to confer in an undertone with someone similarly clad, and Jonathan knew he was making inquiries about Owen Bruce's whereabouts from fellow members of the Society of Oxen. Judging from Lo Fang's reaction, no one had seen him, and certainly he would have been conspicuous in a neighborhood where few whites were to be seen.

At last Lo Fang halted at the base of a narrow, winding lane, with rickety structures on both sides, that ascended toward the heights behind the town. "This is Cat Alley," he said. "Sometimes Bruce comes here to visit a prostitute whose shack stands near the top of the alley. We will question her." He started up the slope.

Jonathan and Shaong Wei walked side by side behind him, squeezing past open-fronted sheds where sellers of fruits and herbs, fish and meats, and inexpensive items of clothing displayed their wares on rickety tables in the open. The climb was steep, and although Jonathan was in sound physical condition, his calves soon ached. Some of the stand owners called to him, trying to interest him in their merchandise, but the majority guessed he hadn't come to Cat Alley to buy, and simply stared at him. Gradually the stalls gave way to the huts of newcomers to the rapidly growing colony.

Suddenly a whistling noise sounded in Jonathan's ear, and at almost the same instant Shaong Wei collapsed, blood pouring from an ugly knife wound in his throat.

Lo Fang saw what had happened and, without a word, raced off in the direction from which the knife had been thrown.

The startled Jonathan dropped to his knees beside the fallen man, but realized nothing could be done for him. Shaong Wei was already dead, his sightless eyes staring up at the blue, subtropical sky.

The knife that still protruded from his throat was a double-

bladed Chinese weapon with a bone handle, and there was n
doubt in Jonathan's mind that he himself had been the intende
victim.

No one came near him and the dead man, and the seller
of food and other merchandise farther down Cat Alley eithe
were ignorant of what had just happened or pretended not t
know.

After a long time, a quietly seething Lo Fang returned. ''
found no one,'' he said, pity in his eyes as he glanced a
Shaong Wei. ''I am sure this was done by Bruce or someon
hired by him. Our brothers will ask many questions before th
day ends.'' He scooped up the dead man's body as though i
were weightless and carried it down Cat Alley, his stride rapi
as he headed toward the waterfront. The stall owners looke
away as he passed them.

A silent Jonathan walked beside his friend, unable t
concentrate on his own narrow escape and thinking only o
Molinda. ''We'll go to the British shore headquarters,'' h
said.

Lo Fang's shrug indicated his contempt for the British
''They will do nothing,'' he said, ''and you may be sure Bruc
has friends who will swear he was with them elsewhere.''

The sight of the murdered man created a commotion at th
British headquarters, where Jonathan learned that Sir Henr
Pottinger had left, having been reassigned to a post in Madras
A junior captain was in temporary command pending the arriv
al of the new governor-general and was indignant when h
emerged from his private office.

''This is not a morgue for dead Chinese,'' he said.

Jonathan stared at him coldly. ''Unfortunately,'' he replied
''the victim was a cousin of the Tao Kuang Emperor.''

''We can accept no responsibility for his death, sir,'' th
captain replied hastily. ''You'll find notices posted in prominent places throughout the town that, pending the establishment of a constabulary and the formation of law courts, those
who visit Hong Kong or intend to make their homes here com
at their own risk.''

It was too much to expect justice, and Jonathan turned
away abruptly, followed by Lo Fang. They took the body to
the junk, where it was wrapped in sheets, and then Lo Fang

502

disappeared. He didn't return until late in the evening, as Jonathan was preparing to sail back to Canton.

"I will wager my right hand Owen Bruce was responsible," the head of the Society of Oxen declared. "But he is very clever. Two Englishmen claim he spent the entire afternoon with them at a new club on the slope of the peak. Sooner or later the Oxen will learn the truth, and I will send word to you at once."

Molinda had not shed tears in many years, and she remained dry-eyed when Jonathan told her the shocking news of her husband's murder. "I am glad I was able to help him find happiness in his last years after he suffered for so long," she said. "He deserved a better fate."

Although she had not been in love with Shaong Wei, she had found a measure of contentment with him and was deeply saddened by his passing. At her request he was given temporary burial on the estate, and she sent word at once to the Forbidden City. *He earned the right to rest in a tomb beside those of his imperial ancestors,* she wrote to the Princess An Mien. *I hope you will see fit to grant him that honor.*

The captain and the colonel in command of the small permanent British garrison stationed at Hong Kong also sent letters of condolence and apology to the Celestial Emperor and his sister, promising to conduct investigations of their own in order to find and punish the killer. But Jonathan placed little faith in their efforts. "If anyone finds the murderer—and I believe it was Bruce—it will be the Oxen," he said to Lai-tse lu and to Molinda, who now wore white, the Chinese traditional mourning color. "Shaong Wei had no enemies, and I am convinced that knife was aimed at me."

Certainly he knew that Bruce had taken pains to avoid a confrontation with him, and the possibility of obtaining repayment of the money that Molinda had loaned to Bradford Walker became even more remote. Jonathan could only hope that Charles Boynton would arrive in Canton soon. Then they would conduct a joint review of their financial situation and seek means of improving it. And until they established new policies, he decided, Rakehell and Boynton would suspend credit arrangements and would insist on being paid in cash for all merchandise they sold in the Orient.

Meanwhile the official United States delegation continued to hammer out a treaty with the negotiators who represented the Tao Kuang Emperor. Jonathan paid frequent visits to the palace of the imperial viceroy, where he was kept up to date on the progress of the talks. "We move at a snail's pace," Caleb Cushing told him. "At every meeting we review what was accomplished the previous day. We waste an hour making small talk over tea. Finally we move forward another inch—no more—before we adjourn."

"That is the Chinese way," Jonathan told him. "Great patience is required in negotiations with them. But the treaty you're working out with them is fair to both sides, and I'm sure that when we sail for home you'll have an agreement that will win the enthusiastic approval of the president and the Congress."

One morning, after a visit with Cushing, he went on to Whampoa, where a Rakehell and Boynton clipper had just arrived from Batavia, and the ship's master handed him a brief letter from Charles, who wrote that he had reached Djakarta and was holding talks with the Fat Dutchman before joining his cousin in Canton.

Returning to the estate in mid-afternoon, Jonathan was surprised and dismayed to find that Lai-tse lu had spent the day in bed.

"I'm having another attack of my ailment," she told him, and it was obvious that she was in pain.

He immediately sent Kai to summon the best Chinese physicians available in the city. The majordomo returned with two doctors, both white-haired and highly respected.

A short time later, while they were seeing the patient, Molinda came home, accompanied by a young Danish physician who had landed in Whampoa that same day on board a schooner from Copenhagen. He, too, went to Lai-tse lu's pavilion, and Jonathan paced restlessly in the office pavilion, where Molinda tried to calm him.

"Between them," she said, "the physicians of East and West will find some way to help Lai-tse lu." Her voice lacked conviction.

At last the physicians emerged, and Jonathan went to them outside the pavilion where his wife rested.

"If you wish," the senior Chinese doctor said, "we could prescribe an herb tea for the lady, but it will do her no good. She is not the first to suffer this disease, and she will not be the last. Medicine has been practiced in the Middle Kingdom for thousands of years, but no cure has ever been found for the lady's condition."

The young Danish physician confirmed the prognosis. "I wish I could do something for her, Mr. Rakehell, but I know of no way to arrest her ailment. Her condition is grave, and all I can do is leave some laudanum with you to ease her pain when it becomes unbearable."

"Will she recover from this attack?" Jonathan asked hoarsely.

The Danish doctor's shrug was eloquent.

Kai insisted on taking a bowl of broth to Lai-tse lu, allowing no one else to wait on her, and after he left her pavilion, he went privately to Molinda. "Missy will die soon," he said morosely. "I saw death in her eyes."

That same afternoon the Princess An Mien reached Canton on board an imperial junk, and as soon as she took up residence in the viceroy's palace, she was escorted to the estate by an honor guard of troops. "My brother has granted your request," she told Molinda as she embraced the younger woman. "The remains of Shaong Wei will be removed to the Forbidden City, where he will join his ancestors."

Their travel plans had to be delayed, the grateful Molinda explained, because of Lai-tse lu's critical illness.

An Mien was stunned. "What may I do for her?" she demanded.

"I'm afraid there is nothing that anyone can do."

Jonathan, who had hurried to his wife's side after the physicians had departed, was unaware of the arrival of the princess as he took up his vigil at Lai-tse lu's bedside.

Refusing laudanum because it would make her drowsy, she managed a smile. "I wish to see Julian now," she said.

At Jonathan's request, Kai brought the solemn boy to the pavilion.

"Do all that your father commands you so you become

505

like him when you are a man," Lai-tse lu told him. "Help your father, Julian. He will need your help." She held out her arms to him.

Exercising a degree of will power he hadn't known he possessed, Julian did not weep until he had left the chamber.

The next to be summoned was David.

"You are English now," Lai-tse lu told him, "but never forget you are also Chinese. Never forget that the Middle Kingdom is your native land. Serve her as you serve Britain. Be true to your heritage."

Tears streamed down David's face as he raced out of the pavilion.

Lai-tse lu was weakening, but her voice was still firm. "Now I wish to see Jade," she said.

"I'm afraid the strain is too great for you," Jonathan protested.

She shook her head. "It is my privilege as well as my duty to say good-bye to my daughter."

Kai brought the wide-eyed little girl to the door, and Jonathan carried her to the bed, depositing her in her mother's arms.

"Remember me, Jade," Lai-tse lu said.

The child began to cry.

"Don't weep, darling. It will be very peaceful in the place where I am going. Love Papa, as I love him." Her breath was short, and she paused to regain what was left of her ebbing strength. "I will be with your grandfather. Papa will join us one day. Then, a long, long time from now, you and I will meet again. Remember what I have tried to teach you, and may God bless you."

Jade, soothed by her mother's voice, tried in vain to stifle a sob.

Lai-tse lu kissed her, and then Jonathan carried her back to the entrance, where Kai quietly took her and carried her away. Jonathan returned to the bed, sat, and tenderly held his wife's pain-racked body.

"That feels so good," she murmured. "Hold me close, my love."

He felt her breathing become more labored.

"We have known a love that so few have known," she whispered. "Oh, my love, my love."

Jonathan kissed her, and she died in his arms.

As she expired, the jade Tree of Life medallion that had become a part of him suddenly glowed with a fiery heat. In this moment of bleak sorrow he was only vaguely aware of the pain, but the next day, when he saw the blisters and burns on his chest, he recalled the experience. Neither then nor for the rest of his life could he explain the extraordinary phenomenon.

An Anglican clergyman from the new British concession in Canton performed the funeral service, and a large crowd was gathered outside the pagoda, listening through the opened sliding door. Kai stood in the front rank, flanked by the captains and crews of Rakehell and Boynton ships as well as of junks that had flown the flag of Soong Chao and had known Lai-tse lu since childhood. Dock workers were there, too, as were scores of plain people whom she had befriended through the years.

Only a few people were present inside the pagoda. Jonathan was alone, the whole world excluded from his consciousness. His great love was gone, and something within him had died, too, never to be revived. Molinda held the weeping Jade, and beside them was the Princess An Mien, dressed in the white she had worn to mourn Shaong Wei. Julian, his back rigid, remained close to his father on one side, and on the other was David, less successful than his cousin in his effort to appear manly, but nevertheless struggling.

The service came to an end, and those outside the pagoda stood aside to clear a path for the principal mourners.

Ultimately Molinda persuaded Jonathan to come to the dining pavilion, where the children were already eating. There the Princess An Mien greeted him.

"You do not weep alone," she told him. "The Middle Kingdom has suffered a great loss, too. Lai-tse lu brought our world and your world together, and now you must carry that burden. Please know, always, that you are one of us, that the Middle Kingdom is as much your land and home as it was her land and home."

An Mien's words comforted Jonathan, and he thought of them often in the dismal days that followed. Molinda went off to Peking with the princess for the entombment of Shaong Wei with his ancestors, so, for the present, Jonathan was alone with the children, Kai, and the servants. He took Jade, Julian, and David with him whenever he went to his complex of offices and warehouses and they even accompanied him on his visits to Caleb Cushing. It was almost impossible for him to believe that Lai-tse lu was no longer alive, and he made a supreme effort to come to grips with reality. But the only harsh reality he could accept was the tomb that had been erected over her grave in the pagoda.

He sent the clipper that bore his wife's name to Djakarta to bring Charles to Canton, and he wrote his father and Missy Sarah, telling them the tragic news. Only the knowledge that his sister and Homer Ellison were free to marry now gave him pleasure.

One morning, as he tried hard to concentrate on the ships' manifests piled on his desk, he was vaguely aware of Kai's voice through the open windows. The majordomo was giving Julian and David their daily lesson in the martial arts, and Jonathan had to smile when he thought that Jade insisted on receiving instruction, too.

Then small feet pounded on the floor of the corridor, and the children burst into the room.

"My father is here!" David shouted.

"The ship is coming into the harbor," Julian added.

Scooping up Jade and carrying her, Jonathan walked to the waterfront, with the boys racing ahead of him.

The *Lai-tse lu* was moving slowly toward the pier, and Jonathan looked hard at the graceful clipper. She was alive and vibrant, and all at once he knew that, through her, his wife's spirit still lived, too.

Although something would be missing from his own existence for the rest of his days on earth, he could not allow his grief to stand in the path of his duty. For the sake of Julian and Jade and Charles's son, he had to fight for the restoration of the health of the Rakehell and Boynton Company.

His own ancestors had known lean times often after they had founded their dynasty, and now his turn had come. His children's future would be bright only if he and Charles waged a successful campaign here and now.

The great clipper ship, her white sails sparkling in the sunlight, her copper gleaming, was a symbol not only of what he himself had accomplished, but of the vision of those who

ad come before him. At the same time it represented the
omorrows that awaited the two small boys and the little girl
who, for better or worse, would be the inheritors of the Rake-
ell dynasty.

Jonathan raised his head and became aware of the salt-
cented breeze that blew in from the South China Sea. All the
seas of the world were his, and would belong to his children,
oo, if he lived up to his own obligations here and now. Sitting
ade on his shoulder and holding her in place with one hand, he
emoved his hat with the other, saluting his arriving cousin, the
Lai-tse lu, and the precious heritage he would pass on to those
who would come after him.

INTRODUCING
THE RAKEHELL DYNASTY

BOOK ONE: THE BOOK OF JONATHAN RAKEHELL
by Michael William Scott (D95-201, $2.75)

The bold, sweeping, passionate story of a great New England shipping family caught up in the winds of change—and of the one man who would dare to sail his dream ship to the frightening, beautiful land of China. He was Jonathan Rakehell, and his destiny would change the course of history.

THE RAKEHELL DYNASTY—
THE GRAND SAGA OF THE GREAT CLIPPER SHIPS
AND OF THE MEN WHO BUILT THEM
TO CONQUER THE SEAS AND
CHALLENGE THE WORLD!

Jonathan Rakehell—who staked his reputation and his place in the family on the clipper's amazing speed.

Lai-Tse Lu—the beautiful, independent daughter of a Chinese merchant. She could not know that Jonathan's proud clipper ship carried a cargo of love and pain, joy and tragedy for her.

Louise Graves—Jonathan's wife-to-be, who waits at home in New London keeping a secret of her own.

Bradford Walker—Jonathan's scheming brother-in-law, who scoffs at the clipper and plots to replace Jonathan as heir to the Rakehell shipping line.

THE BEST OF BESTSELLERS
FROM WARNER BOOKS

THE KINGDOM
by Ronald S. Joseph   (85-699, $2.75)

Out of the rugged brasada, a powerful family carved THE KING-DOM. Joel Trevor was willing to fight Mexicans, carpetbaggers, raiders, even Nature itself to secure his ranch. Then he won the beautiful Spanish Sofia who joined her heart and her lands to his. When control passed to Joel's daughter Anne, she took trouble and tragedy with the same conquering spirit as her father. These were the founders—and their story blazes from the pages of THE KINGDOM, the first book of a giant trilogy.

THE POWER
by Ronald S. Joseph   (81-468, $2.50)

The children of Anne Trevor and Alex Cameron set out at the turn of the century to conquer the world in their own ways. Follow Dos, the reckless son, as he escalates youthful scrapes into crime. Travel with Maggie from boarding school to brother to Congress. Meet Trev and the baby daughter to whom all the kingdom, power and glory will belong.

THE GLORY
by Ronald S. Joseph   (85-469, $2.75)

Meet the inheritors: Allis Cameron, great-granddaughter of the pioneers who carved a kingdom in southern Texas. Go with her to Hollywood where her beauty conquers the screen and captures the heart of her leading man. Cammie: Allis's daughter, who comes of age and finds herself torn between a ruthless politician and a radical young Mexican. They were the Cameron women, heirs to a Texas fortune, rich, defiant, ripe for love.

WYNDWARD PASSION
by Norman Daniels   (82-669, $2.25)

At Wyndward plantation, the Turners grew tobacco and raised horses, but slaves were their most profitable product. Jonathan Turner mated bucks to wenches and produced prime black stock for sale. Between white and black, passions turn to lust. Between Fitzjohn and Nina, lust ripened into love, and the very foundations of the Turner empire shook in the fury of the WYNDWARD PASSION.

WYNDWARD FURY
by Norman Daniels   (92-991, $2.25)

Of the land and the slaves they owned, the Turner men gave no one else an inch. For the women they loved, they battled all rivals. Against those they hated, they schemed, raged and fought. But such passions sow anger and jealousy in others, and it was inevitable that the Turners should reap the bitter harvest of revenge.

IF YOU LIKE ROMANCE...
YOU'LL LOVE VALERIE SHERWOOD

THIS TOWERING PASSION
by Valerie Sherwood   (81-486, $2.50)

They called her "Angel" when she rode bareback into the midst of battle to find her lover. They called her "Mistress Daunt" when she lived with Geoffrey in Oxford, though she wore no ring on her finger. Wherever she traveled men called her Beauty. Her name was Lenore—and she answered only to "Love."

THESE GOLDEN PLEASURES
by Valerie Sherwood   (95-744, $2.75)

She was beautiful—and notorious and they called her "That Barrington Woman." But beneath the silks and the diamonds, within the supple body so many men had embraced, was the heart of a girl who yearned still for love. At fifteen she had learned her beauty was both a charm and a curse. It had sent her fleeing from Kansas, had been her downfall in Baltimore and Georgia, yet had kept her alive in the Klondike and the South Seas.

THIS LOVING TORMENT
by Valerie Sherwood   (95-745, $2.75)

Perhaps she was too *beautiful!* Perhaps the brawling colonies would have been safer for a plainer girl, one more demure and less accomplished in language and manner. But Charity Woodstock was gloriously beautiful with pale gold hair and topaz eyes —and she was headed for trouble. She was accused of witchcraft by the man who had attacked her. She was whisked from pirate ship to plantation. Beauty might have been her downfall, but Charity Woodstock had a reckless passion to live and would challenge this new world—and win.